Star Bird
ONEIDA'S FURY

Schultz, Robert, 1961-
Starbird; Oneida's Fury: A ScFi Novel/ by Robert Schultz –
1st edition
RJS Publishing

ISBN-13: 978-0-9960448-4-4
Titling & Cover by Anina Laird Swallow
Summary:

Gunnar Conrad and Audra Atlanta have a wonderful life together
with the Kalamar Flight Ministry. Gunnar, as the top ace fighter
pilot and Audra as lead sector traffic control officer. But
Gunnar's high risk profession has long troubled Audra. Her
hopes of getting him out of the cockpit are finally realized when
Gunnar's lifelong friend and wingman, Rick Niker, recommends
him for a command chair of one of Kalamar's new Assault
Corsairs, the Starbird.
Tough, compact and powerful, the Starbird is a radical new
breakthrough in Corsair design. But even new technology has its
limits. So, when Gunnar and Rick are dispatched to rescue
several Kalamarion freighters caught in the expansive
gravitational fields of the class four Black Hole, the Oneida
Cauldron, they find themselves in a no win scenario. A
miscalculation in a theoretical escape maneuver sends their two
ships across time and space to another galaxy. Now they find
themselves in the middle of a conflict that has the potential to
destroy several galactic civilizations at once.
Enduring personal tragedy, Gunnar and Rick find new friends in
unlikely places as they are relentlessly pursued by the warring
factions of Hadrian for the vastly advanced technology that is,
the Starbird.

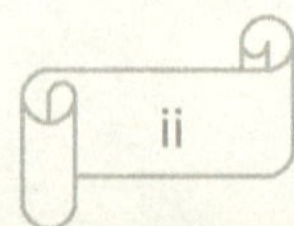

A Note from the Author

The making of this story began in the late 70's. As a young teen, I wanted so badly to be a part of the myriad of Science Fiction movies being produced. The only way I could make that happen was to write my own stories, with me in them. What adventures I would have! My imagination would simply swirl in those worlds I created. I used to tell my friends that I was born at the wrong time, on the wrong planet. I think most of them silently agreed, just not for the same reasons I was thinking.

The universe I've created is not a copy of someone else's ideas. While it's my hope you'll experience a familiar feel with Starbird, I'm confident you'll find it original, fun and engaging.

Our minds are such wonderful platforms for whatever we can conjure up. I love to tell people; "The adventure is only as good as your imagination." I think those are great words to live by when starting any adventure. It's my hope that you'll use your imagination to its fullest as you start on this adventure that is, Starbird.

In a galaxy beyond the boundaries of known space and time.

In a galaxy being pulled apart by conflict.

In a galaxy where the knowledge to command the elements is afforded to a select few.

Two friends fight to survive in the only home they have ever known, outer-space.

"You may be good at what you do, but we make you look good doing it." *Lieutenant Commander Audra Atlanta, First Officer, Constellation, SAC10*

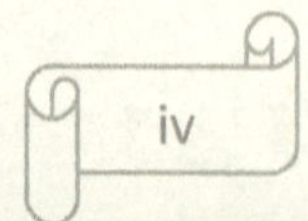

Dedicated to my son, David Robert.
Because he has a better imagination than I.

Crew assignments of a Starbird Assault Corsair:

Constellation SAC10

Commander- Colonel Gunnar Lee Conrad
First officer- Lieutenant Commander Audra Atlanta
Interceptor Pilot 1- Captain Dakota Abrams
Interceptor Pilot 2- Captain Logan Dalley
Chief Engineer- William "Billy" Moon
Engineer's Mate- Frank Cooper
Turret Gunner- First Lieutenant Hayden Hunter
Chief Medical Officer- Fuji Yamoto MD
Medical Assistant- Sindee Conner
Helm Pilot- First Lieutenant Lynette Starman
Navigator- First Lieutenant Nigel Kramer
Weapons Officer- Second Lieutenant Doran Cartwright
Com Officer- First Lieutenant Lana Nevall
Science Officer- Mr. Pippin Habba
Artificial Intelligence- Alex 7001

Athena SAC9

Commander- General Richard Alexander Niker
First Officer- Lieutenant Commander Jayda Niker
Interceptor Pilot 1- Captain Zek Korack
Interceptor Pilot 2- Captain Zak Korack
Chief Engineer- Clancy Warnick
Engineer's Mate- Thomas Mace
Turret Gunner- First Lieutenant Paul Nomad
Chief Medical Officer- Rhett Kelly
Medical Assistant- Danica Whales
Helm Pilot- Captain Lisa Dayton
Navigator- First Lieutenant Virgil Antilles
Weapons Officer- Second Lieutenant Gigi Tewa
Com Officer- First Lieutenant Laura Habba
Science Officer- Mr. Toby Mavis
Artificial Intelligence- CORA 500

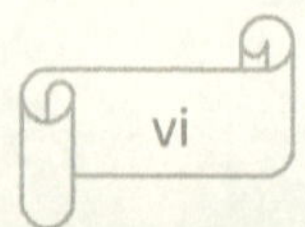

Carolon Command Staff

Base Commander- Colonel Casey Janae "CJ" Barker
Command Staff Personal Aide- Lieutenant Willis Ruston
Command Com Officer- Talia "Bubbles" Reese

Albion Battlecruiser Command Staff

Commander of Albion's Medium fleet- Queen-Captain Drax Blair
Commander of Albion Battlecruiser *Tarzana*- Dalton SoKnack
Albion Thane- Blinda Koss
Moylian Black Market Arms Dealer & Exotic Hunter- Seelix Monroe

Other key characters

Administrator of Cross- Diord Vandmire
Self-appointed Queen of Colonia- Stephanie Benetar, Duchess of Teleknee
Tomplie Pirate Commander- Lou Aura
Paternal Twins of Caidin Mantose- Taron and Tiana Mantose

Star Bird
ONEIDA'S FURY

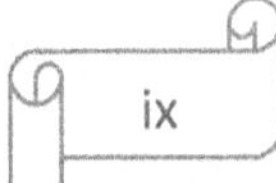

STARBIRD
Oneida's Fury

An Ace made Whole

1st Lieutenant Rick Niker rubbed two pass chips in his fingers as he leaned against the wall of the base billeting complex. He strained a little to look around the corner, but pulled back quickly. He was nearly struck by several officers moving quickly past him down the hall. He was trying not to be noticed by any lower ranking officers as he'd have to go to attention and salute. A couple of times he had to acknowledge a salute, but only halfheartedly waving his hand and continuing his vigil. His level of impatience was quickly rising until a familiar figure appeared from the locker room and started down the hall toward him.

"Have you zero concept of time?" Rick asked impatiently, glancing at his wrist display.

"If I'm going to go to this thing, I might as well be clean." 1st Lieutenant Gunnar Conrad spun around the corner next to his friend and out of the way of foot traffic.

"Doesn't take that long to scrape off dead skin cells."

"Does for me. My skin doesn't scrape so well, remember?"

Rick gave his friend a once over and nodded.

"Do we really need to wear uniforms for this? I thought we were on leave?" Gunnar complained.

Rick shoved a pass chip at Gunnar.

"Condition of the leave buddy. We're lucky we aren't back out on another deep space recon."

"Gardner wouldn't dare send us out on another one. Not after this last one to Kimi. If that wasn't full on Valkyrie territory, I don't what is."

"Well thank goodness the Thunder-Jug is as fast as it is."

"It has to be. They barely put any guns on it."

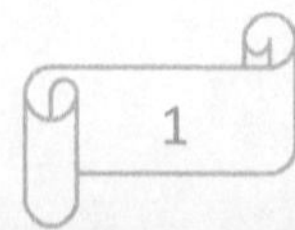

"Ok, enough with all this flying talk. Tonight, you and I are just going to find a couple of ladies and enjoy the evening."

"Ladies at a concert. Not sure I get how that's going to work. Have you been to one of these lately?" Gunnar shoved the pass chip into his front pocket and started down the hall, shoulder to shoulder with Rick.

"Why wouldn't there be ladies at a concert? Usually, the man to woman ratio at one of those is pretty lopsided in our favor."

"Yeah, but most of the females there are far younger than we are. We're old enough to be a father to most of them. Besides, aren't you seeing that princess girl? What's her name, Jayda?"

"Relax there, geezer boy," Rick slapped his friend on the back as they made their way out of the billeting complex and to a waiting transport.

"You're older than me," Gunnar said. "How am I the geezer here?"

"I'm sure there are some older women in anti-gravity chairs that will be there in the handicapped section. Plenty there to turn your fancy."

"So far, you're saying nothing to endear me to this idea of yours."

"Just quit worrying about. I've got it all planned out." Gunnar crowded into the shuttle and Rick squeezed in after him.

"Yeah... I have no doubt you do."

The shuttle quickly accelerated away, speeding off base and into the glistening metropolis of Geffen. Gunnar glanced at Rick, who was scanning the crowd pressed into the transport, most of them were flight officers. Gunnar looked around, taking note that he and Rick appeared to be the oldest in the crowd. He loved the fact that he and Rick could still out fly anyone in the flight ministry and as squadron commanders, they could teach the up and coming fighter pilots how to hone their skills to a razor's edge. He never considered it a competition, but he couldn't help but feel like the squadron under his command was just a little bit better than Rick's. But he had never said anything about it because it really wasn't in his nature. Quite often he and Rick would either join up or be paired up by Commodore Gardner for specialty missions requiring their combined talents. That's where Gunnar felt the most in "the zone", when he was flying wing for Rick or the roles were reversed. Together they seemed to be unstoppable.

Presently, the shuttle stopped and almost half the occupants piled out, nearly taking the two flight officers with them. They had to grip the safety handles as if being torn from a flag pole in the wind.

"Glad that crowd wasn't going to our stop," Gunnar spoke up, relaxing a little now that it wasn't quite so crowded. He wasn't sure he hadn't gotten groped during the mass exit.

"Yeah, I'm sure there won't be too many people where we're going," Rick replied, bracing himself as the transport began to accelerate again.

"Remind me again why we didn't just take a private shuttle craft?" Gunnar complained after several more stops.

"None available and the Major wouldn't authorize it. Said we needed to acquire a better understanding of the term 'appreciation'."

"I don't get it; we take on one of the biggest deep space probes in Valkyrie territory. Pull it off exactly as we had planned it and return home without a scratch on either ship and we're verbally thanked with a hand shake, a pat on the back and then a shut up and get the heck out of my face. We ought to be the two greatest war heroes in the system."

The transport suddenly slowed, ground to a halt and the doors popped open before it came to a complete stop. Rick motioned Gunnar to exit and the two stepped out into a sea of seething masses moving toward a large circular arena style building, covered with a multitude of lights and displays.

"Do you think you're a war hero?"

"No," Gunnar shrugged. "We were just doing what we do best, our jobs."

"Exactly." Rick put his arm around his friend's neck and squeezed him good. "Now come on. I was able to get us through a special entrance where we don't have to go with the flow here." Rick and Gunnar steered through the crowd to a less populated area and slipped through a much smaller door than what the crowds were moving through, then made their way to their seats in a large elevated box. Not exclusive and certainly not the only box within the arena, it had many seats in it and was slowly filling as other people made their way to their seats. As Gunnar went to sit down, he noticed the vacant seat on his right and the one on Rick's left. Good, he'd have a place to pull his uniform jacket off and relax. Depending on if the concert was any good, he might even be able to get some sleep. No one was silly enough to buy a single seat to a concert and come by themselves. Gunnar leaned forward and grabbed some of the snacks that had been laid out on the slender table attached the backs of the seats in front of them and picked up a drink a hostess had just set down. He noted other drinks being set down and he smiled. He didn't have to be a hero. This felt good enough. As he settled back and munched, he recognized several government officials stepping down the walkway and stop at their row looking around.

"What's this all about?" Gunnar whispered to Rick who was looking all around with a bewildered look.

"You got me, buddy. They look like royal secret service people, but what are they doing here? You didn't do anything stupid did you?"

"Me? Why would you think I would do something stupid? You're the one that knows the Princess."

"Indeed I do, but she would be in her own royal box, not here amongst the commoners."

Gunnar noticed a couple of shorter figures moving down the aisle through the wall of guards and coming to a halt at their level. He carefully put a hand to Rick's shoulder, who turned to see what had caught Gunnar's attention. Standing in front of him was a vision of beauty. She was short with long silky blonde hair, flowing like sheets of amber down past her shoulders to the small of her back, and a lightly freckled complexion with wonderful blue eyes. Princess Jayda Thron stood before them with her hands on her hips, a small purse that could hardly hold anything, dangling from her narrow shoulders.

"Hey mister," she smiled. "Buy a girl a drink?"

Rick smiled sheepishly and stood up, offering the Princess the seat next to him.

"Certainly, your Highness."

Gunnar noticed someone had stopped just behind one of the guards and clumsily got to his feet. Watching the royal guards carefully, he was a little worried he and Rick were going to get searched right in front of everyone.

The Princess went to sit down, but suddenly stopped and turned.

"Oh, I'm sorry. I'm here with a friend. Audra Atlanta, this is Rick Niker and Gunnar Conrad. Would you gentlemen mind if she joined us?" Standing there, with a pleasant grin, was a short attractive brunette, her hair sciffing just above her shoulders in pretty curls.

"Pleased to meet you," Rick greeted politely. There was no response from behind him. "There's a seat available on the other side of my friend here." Rick motioned to the empty seat next to Gunnar. "Is that ok, buddy?" Rick asked, looking at Gunnar. His friend's focus was on Audra, standing in the aisle between the security guards.

"Sure," Gunnar fumbled quietly, watching her beautiful brown eyes, accentuated by her long eyelashes. Audra smiled broadly, shuffled past the others and sat in the empty seat next to Gunnar. Rick passed Gunnar a secret fist bump behind their

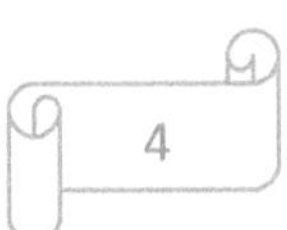

chairs. "What are the odds that the Princess would be here at this concert and in this box?" Gunnar mumbled to his friend as he shifted to get comfortable in his chair.

"Go figure."

"And what are the odds she would have a friend here with her and... Good heavens to existence, she's about as fine looking as they come?"

"Tough odds," Rick mumbled back. "Just be cool, ok? I'm working with royalty here and I can't have my wingman making an idiot of himself. It'll look bad."

"Pardon me, I'll do my best to stay out of your way." Gunnar felt a tug on his shoulder and turned to Audra.

"Would it be ok if I shared your convenience?"

Gunnar froze, looking at her, mesmerized.

"I'd be happy to pay for my share," she quickly added. "I have plenty of credits with me. I'm sorry for being so forward. It's just I haven't eaten since this morning."

"Why didn't you eat before you came?" Gunnar quickly pulled himself out of his idiot dive and motioned for her to help herself to what was available on the small table in front of them.

"I had time to rush home after work and get ready, then go through the goon squad's security check and then get here." Gunnar looked over at the security now taking up positions at the top and bottom of the stairs and in other locations around the box.

"I wonder why we're not getting frisked down?" Gunnar asked leaning over to his friend.

"Because you guys were already cleared," Princess Jayda piped up quietly before Rick could answer.

"Wait," Gunnar asked surprised. "Already cleared? How did they even know who we are?"

Rick started to slink down in his chair as an awkward silence began to develop. Princess Jayda paused for a moment, as if trying to make something up.

"Because you guys are in uniform and with the Royal Flight Ministry." Jayda only blinked calmly. "You don't need any more clearance than that."

"Oh, that makes sense." Gunnar leaned a little closer to Rick. "Thank goodness for the boys in uniform." Gunnar gave the security guards looking at him a smile and a nod, then turned back to Audra.

Rick let out a quiet sigh and sat back up straight in his chair, looking back at Princess Jayda. She only smiled quietly and took his hand.

"So where is it you work that you got off so late?" Gunnar asked settling back.

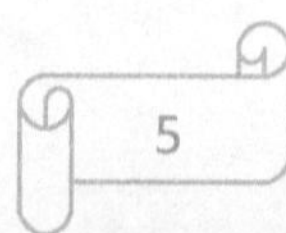

"I work in the traffic control center for the Royal Flight Ministry."

"Doing what?"

"I'm one of the long range traffic controllers."

"Really?" Gunnar grabbed his glass, not even realizing that he had become completely enamored with Audra. "I talk to those people almost every day. What are the odds that you would work there and that we would meet here?"

"Serious?" she asked trying to eat and speak without sounding like she was stuffing her face. "Where do you work?"

"Squadron leader for B flight. Royal Kalamarion Flight Ministry Delta Recon unit. I fly a lot of sorties with Lieutenant 'Dingle Fritz' over here," Gunnar said casually pointing over his shoulder at Rick.

"B flight," Audra repeated thinking as she took a sip of drink. "B flight." Audra took another bite. "You're the squadron that is usually hanging around out in the far side of Tundance."

"That's right," Gunnar said, starting to realize that he had heard Audra's voice before. "Bravo Sage one?"

"You're Bravo Sage one?" Audra nearly coughed.

"You're the voice!" Gunnar nearly jumped out of his seat. "I've been listening to you call in my traffic for nearly a year now and been telling my friend here," Gunnar slowed his speech and started to turn, "that I wanted to meet the girl behind the voice." Both Audra and Gunnar looked back at Rick and Princess Jayda, but found them preoccupied, kissing somewhat robustly.

"This explains a lot," Audra commented suspiciously, still eyeing Rick and Jayda.

"My, my," Gunnar said turning back to Audra. "Seems he's not too worried about me making him look like an idiot after all."

"You've done this before?"

"What, met strange women at concerts?"

"No, made him look like an idiot."

Oh, she's good, he thought grinning as she smiled and took a drink, glancing over at him as she did so. Rick and Gunnar had set each other up with different women over the years. Most of the time, they didn't work out so well. On occasion, the date would lead to another, but most of the time the dates were one and done. This was only the third time Rick had doubled with Gunnar when he had gone out with the Princess and the last couple of times had been complete disasters. One girl was so talkative and full of herself that Gunnar could barely get a word in edgewise. She was a good kisser, he had to give her that. One was so shy, he could scarcely get her to speak and the other was down on every subject he tried to talk about. He could tell right off the bat that Audra wasn't any of those things. He was

so hoping for that when he did eventually meet the woman behind the voice over his headphones. Regulations didn't permit casual conversation over military channels and for security reasons, he had been unable to find out any information on the mystery voice for security reasons.

Gunnar looked down into the arena at several technicians making final preparations for the start of the entertainment as a waitress sped quickly down the row setting more food on the tables in front of everyone. He noticed Audra glancing over at Rick and Princess Jayda and looked over at the two still lip locked.

"They, uhm, certainly like the taste of each other, don't they?"

"I never kiss on a first date," Audra whispered leaning forward next to Gunnar.

"Well to be fair to her highness and Lieutenant Snizzle-Fritz there, this isn't their first date. He's been trying to get something steady going with the Princess for some time, but it's been hit and miss. How long have you known the Princess and what did she have to do to get you here? Surely you knew this was a setup."

"Setup? Yes, I knew, but I'm so cooped up at work that I never have time to get out, so I try to take whatever I can get. Be nice to be independently wealthy so I didn't have to work. Then maybe I'd buy a nice quiet place a long way from here and just settle back, read some books and maybe raise some animals."

"Sounds like a nice idea for retirement. So how did the Princess get you here? Did she have her royal guards deliver the message that you're ordered to appear at such and such time or else?"

"No, nothing like that. The Princess," Audra stopped and looked over at the couple, then back at Gunnar. "She told me to just call her Jayda. She hates being called Princess."

"Why? She's a Royal Princess of Kalamar."

"That's true, but there are a bunch of them and she would just as soon be a regular person, no title, no royal anything."

"Hard life when you're a royal?"

"Very little. Anyway, even royals are required to serve in the military, though I understand most of them are given light duty rear-line positions where it's highly unlikely they would be put in harm's way. Jayda spent her time with the Flight Ministry, in the traffic/flight com control center. I was her trainer and co-controller. She still comes in a couple of times a week when she's not busy doing all the stuff a Princess has to do."

"Good friends then."

"Certainly. So when she announced that she wanted me to accompany her to a concert, of course I jumped. Even if you were going to be some *shlump*, as long as I could keep your hands off me, I could have some time to relax and enjoy an evening."

"Ha! And have you decided if I'm a, *shlump*?"

"Jury's still out on that one. I'll let you know." Audra took a bite of something without evening looking at Gunnar, who held a raised eyebrow at her comment. "Mmmm, this is so good. You be sure to let me pay for my part?"

"I'll let you pay for the whole thing if you'd like," he said watching her eat.

"That wouldn't be fair."

"Would be if you eat everything."

"Not going to happen."

"Why?"

"Because they'll keep bringing it to us as long as we keep eating."

Gunnar realized that she was right and could rack up a bill fairly quick. He put his hand down on hers, drawing her attention.

"Slow, down. Chew your food. Savor the flavors. That's real synthetic stuff you're scarfing down."

They both burst into muffled laughter, but it was loud enough to bring Rick and Jayda to attention.

"You two want to hold it down over there?" Rick said sitting back with his arm around Jayda.

"Yeah, Rick and I are trying to take care of *'bi'ness'*," Jayda chastised, good naturedly.

"Looks like you were plenty busy with your *'bi'ness'* without us bothering you," Audra giggled.

"So, Gunnar," Jayda said settling with a smile.

"So, Princess... uhm, Jayda," Gunnar responded quickly.

Jayda smiled broadly as she leaned forward.

"Rick tells me you're the Flight Ministry's best pilot. Is that true?"

"I do pretty good," Gunnar responded looking around at the still gathering crowd. Their box was nearly full now and the waitresses were bustling.

"Pretty good," Rick repeated seeing his friend switch into humility mode. "Audra, you're sitting next to the only Kalamarion pilot who has held current top Ace status in the entire Flight Ministry for the past year."

"I'm impressed," Audra said. Gunnar seemed a little uncomfortable as Rick tried to boast about his friend.

"Technically, we're not really at war and kills can't be counted for anything."

"So how do you get kills if we aren't at war?" Audra asked.

"No 'official kills' and even then, it's not something that we should be talking about. But I've been able to score the highest in the Ministry in all flight evaluations."

Rick rolled his eyes at his friend's modesty, pulled his arm out from around Jayda and leaned closer so Audra could hear better.

"This guy can fly anything without even looking at a manual. He teaches our instructors how to fly. In fact, they don't even bother with him anymore because they can't teach him anything."

"You can always learn something from anyone," Gunnar said trying to make sure Audra understood that he wasn't some high and mighty, overconfident, hotshot. Rick and Jayda laughed, but Audra remained silent, watching Gunnar. He seemed a little embarrassed by the good natured ribbing coming from his friend.

The lights in the arena dimmed and everyone finally sat back to watch the start of the entertainment. Audra and Gunnar continued to eat from the narrow table in front of them and as the evening progressed, they drew closer together. At one point, Gunnar shifted in his seat, folding his legs away from her and let his hand come to rest on the table in front of him as he watched the show. A moment later, he felt a warm hand slide under his as Audra leaned against him, resting her head on his shoulder. A completely new sensation fired through Gunnar's very being. He froze, afraid to move for fear of disturbing Audra. He didn't want her to withdraw her hand and sit upright. After a while, he was becoming uncomfortable with the position, but held out as long as he could, enjoying the contact. He finally had to move. Shifting the other way, he raised his arm and Audra naturally settled under it, sliding as close to him as she could get. This was even better! Gunnar could sit this way all night. Audra raised her outer hand and interlocked her fingers with his as she continued to watch the show, not even looking up at Gunnar to see what his comfort level was.

At intermission, everyone sat forward and refreshed themselves with drinks the waitress had provided and were enjoying casual conversation when Rick took notice of a uniformed officer working his way down the walkway above them. He observed the Royal guard stopping the officer and questioning him. As the officer was explaining himself, he pointed toward Rick and Gunnar.

This can't be good, Rick thought as he watched the guards and officer move toward them. He gave Gunnar a tap to the

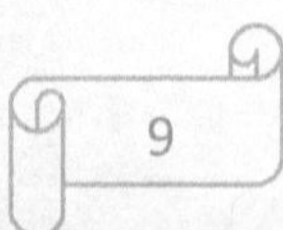

shoulder and turned his thumb toward the approaching men. Gunnar stared at the men as they made their way toward them, hoping it wasn't what it looked like.

"What's wrong?" Audra asked noticing Gunnar's attention had been drawn away.

"We've got company," he said.

Audra seemed to hide behind Gunnar, peering over his shoulder to see the approach of the men at their level.

"You two didn't wreck something and then leave the scene, did you?"

Gunnar and Audra looked at each other. Gunnar wasn't sure how serious she was about the question she had just asked.

"You're kidding, right?"

"Yes, of course," Audra responded with a big grin. "Mostly," she added after a long pause.

"Lieutenants Niker and Conrad?" The officer had an urgent tone in his voice.

"That's us," Rick said carefully.

"You need to come with me immediately."

"What's this all about?"

"You're being recalled."

"To what?" Gunnar jumped in.

"Gentlemen, please follow me and I can fill you in at a more appropriate location." The officer's demeanor was changing by the second.

Rick and Gunnar got to their feet and prepared to say good night to their dates, but the guard that had accompanied the Ministry officer leaned forward.

"Princess, your presence is required immediately in the Royal waiting room for a declaration announcement." The guard held his hand out to help the Princess to her feet, but Rick was already helping her up.

"What's going on?" Audra asked, gathering her things.

"Tell you when I know," Gunnar said helping her to her feet. Arm in arm, they followed the others from the box and the inner arena, weaving through several hallways and finally being ushered into a private room. As the doors closed behind them, Rick took note of several other high ranking government officials milling about next to their commanding officer and another gentleman he only barely recognized. Jayda broke from the rest of the group and stepped quickly to her father. After a short greeting, Jayda turned to her friends and presented her father to them. As they exchanged introductions, a large number of officers joined the group until the room was quite full. A buzz of excitement filled the room as male and female officers, spoke in lowered tones. Finally, one of the officers stepped to the front of the room and called for their attention.

"Ladies and gentlemen, I am Major Yom, Liaison officer for the Kalamar Flight Ministry. After a brief announcement from General Tings, I will answer all the questions you might have. All leave passes have been cancelled and you are ordered back to your duty stations immediately. Please allow the General to make this announcement and leave the questions to me. General Tings." Major Yom gestured to the General and stepped out of the way.

"Men and women of the KFM; A state of war has just been declared against Imperial Valkyrie." A rumble rolled through the crowd as the General continued. "Early this morning, the Valkyrie attacked and destroyed sixteen land based outposts in the Enda system. At the same time, they orchestrated ten other coordinated attacks on six base stations in the Manse cluster, destroying all six and engaging the third, eighth and ninth fleets. We sustained heavy losses to all three fleets. They also attacked and destroyed the fighter base over Munsee." General Tings glanced over at the royal entourage and continued. "We received the official declaration of war from Roland Wence of the Imperial Valkyrie High Command only an hour ago." General Tings appeared quite shaken by the grim news he was delivering. He paused a moment, looking as though he was finished, but then scanned the silent crowd with sad eyes. "I can only ask you to be strong and do your best. Major Yom..." The General slowly stepped out of the way and the Major quietly stepped back in front of everyone.

"Ladies and Gentlemen, it's my job to answer any questions you might have, but there is little to no time to do so," he said, looking at a time piece on his jacket sleeve. "You are to report immediately to your respective posts where you will be briefed on all the details that pertain to your duty assignments. For most of you, I hope this will be business as usual. For the rest of you, you'll be just fine." A hand went up in the crowd from an unknown officer and the Major acknowledged them.

"Who fired the first shot, Major?" Everyone knew of the tensions that had been ever rising between the Imperial Valkyrie and the Federal Republic of Kinder. Territorial disputes and power grabs had long been subversively percolating through political circles and diplomacy had run its final course. The Major looked over at General Tings and then at the Royals.

"Does it matter?" the Major answered quietly. "Some of you have a long way to travel. I suggest you all get moving. You are ordered not to speak about this to anyone. The public will find out in a declaration from the Royal Kalamarion family first thing in the morning. Dismissed."

Quiet disbelief rolled through the group as they made a hasty exit from the room to find their ways back to their assigned areas. After some discussion with the other Royals, Jayda broke from her family to say goodbye to her friends.

"Guess I don't get to walk you home and get a kiss at the door," Rick said taking her hands.

"I think you two have already had enough kissing for one night," Gunnar jabbed playfully, holding onto Audra. Rick smiled, watching Gunnar and Audra enjoy each other's touch. He gave Jayda a quick look. They winked at each other at the same time, silently heralding their success. As this kind of setup had been done before, they had become accustomed to what the norm was. This time it was very different and they had high hopes.

"Well, at least we got to it," Jayda teased, leaning back in Rick's arms.

"Got to it?" Audra repeated. "We'll show you 'got to it'." Audra pulled from Gunnar's arms, turned and abruptly threw her arms around him and planted her lips squarely on his. She being a short woman, nearly pulled him over in the maneuver, but it didn't take long for him to regain his balance and bring his arms around her to return the embrace. Rick and Jayda stood casually watching them kiss for some time, until Major Yom started looking in their direction from another group.

"Uhm, do you two need to get a room?" Jayda asked trying to bring them back to reality.

"What for, you two didn't seem to need one," Audra panted, coming up for air.

"We weren't standing in the middle of a hallway right after a declaration of war," Rick pointed out, trying not to laugh. "Come on buddy," Rick beckoned, glancing at the Major. He could see the Liaison officer was about to break from his group and come over. "We all really need to get back to our stations."

"I thought you didn't kiss on the first date?" Gunnar asked Audra as they reluctantly pulled apart, still holding hands.

"Well," she finally responded, remaining close to him, her forehead against his. "Since I seriously doubt this will be our last date, I think it's appropriate."

"I agree," Gunnar said quietly.

"We really need to get going," Rick urged, turning to Jayda and giving her a kiss goodbye.

"Bravo Sage One," Audra reaffirmed, reluctantly letting go of Gunnar and backing toward Jayda.

"I'll never forget the voice," Gunnar smiled watching her and the Princess turning in the other direction. "And now I have a face to go with it."

Rick herded his friend down the hall while Gunnar continually turned, watching Audra disappear around a corner at the other end of the hallway.

"Eyes forward, Bud," Rick said knowing he was about to get a reprimand. Gunnar hated that nickname.

"Call me that again and your head will roll," Gunnar commented quietly. He was still completely enamored with thoughts of Audra.

"Easy there, Pete," Rick defended. He was trying to divert his friend's attention back to what he did best, fly. He knew the best way to get him fired up was to call him by a name he hated the most, Bud. Gunnar's reaction wasn't at all what Rick had expected. It had him a little worried. Would this top fighter ace still be able to perform at peak being so emotionally twitter-pated? "The future is going to be quite entertaining, isn't it?"

Gunnar finally quit looking back, knowing she was gone from sight, but a vision of her was permanently imprinted in his mind, in his very soul.

"Only if I can spend all of it with her."

The Call of Duty

Twenty-five years later

Gunnar Lee Conrad stood with his arms folded looking out the glass wall of Republic Headquarters. At more than eighty-five stories up, the glass cross section he was standing in was only the halfway point. Looking up, he couldn't see the rest of the building as it was obscured in Kalamar's lower layers of clouds. Watching the sky traffic moving at a constant pace back and forth across his view, he turned his gaze down at the ground traffic. It was every bit as congested, if not more so. From this height, the people below were the size of tiny ants scurrying around the ground traffic. Looking up again, he searched the skies through a couple of scattered holes in the cloud layer of Kalamar's dense atmosphere. Larger objects in orbit could easily be seen without the need for vision enhancements. He knew Kalamar Command's main space station was right overhead, but he was more interested in seeing the orbiting shipyards.

He glanced down at the new silver Colonel clusters on his high cuffed collar and the sleeve cuffs of his new navy blue uniform. He loved the jacket. It felt good and he looked good in it. Even so, he still missed the familiar feel of his fighter pilot's flight jacket and the Major's bars on his shoulders. He missed his squadron most of all. He searched the skies for perhaps a glimpse of a T-6 Tempest or two buzzing high above the civilian traffic. But it was only a hope. He knew the chances of seeing the familiar shape of the fighter this close to the ground was highly unlikely.

"Come on buddy ol' pal," Rick Niker said, coming to a stop next to his longtime friend. "What's with the long face? We're moving up in the world. This is what we've been shooting for."

"I know, but it was something that didn't seem like it would ever happen. Now, here it is and all I want to do is turn around and get back to my squadron."

Rick smiled, understanding exactly what his best friend was feeling. Both had just been transferred from fighter squadron operations, having enjoyed long careers in the cockpit.

"Time to let the young bucks learn to be the hotshots now. We've got something new to figure out."

"Well, I wouldn't be doing this at all if anyone else but you had designed these new Starbird class Assault Corsairs."

"I did have some help."

"Sure, Billy Moon and Clancy Warnick, engineers of all things great and small helped you iron out most of the design criteria for these newfangled birds, and yes, even those silly 7000 series droids had a big hand in them."

"The 7000 series is the best AI to date."

"You're only saying that because you designed them too. Which, by the way, since you designed them, tell the whole class here why you didn't have one assigned to your ship."

"Already got my own?"

"CORA 500? I admit she's pretty smart, but as AIs go, she's kind of old."

"Boy, don't let her hear you say that."

"Hey, I know how you feel about CORA. Heck, it's like the two of you are married."

"Married? I think not. Maybe brother and sister, but not married. That would just be weird."

"I've heard of stranger things."

"Like what?"

"Like how you sweet talked a Royal Princess of Kalamar into marrying you."

"Nothing strange about that. Jayda has always said I've got the stuff."

"Yeah, there's stuff all right." Gunnar smirked looking up again.

"Jayda feels the same way about CORA as I do. She updates all of CORA's evolving parameters."

"CORA is old tech. You got her out of an old Recon Viper when you were a teenager."

"She's alien tech that's way ahead of our time. She can think just as fast as the 7000 series, and guess what? I out rank you and don't have to be bothered with a droid following me everywhere I go."

"Thanks for reminding me." Gunnar turned his lips down and kept his gaze outside, trying to see the sky.

"I could have all ten of the 7000 series droids assigned to the *Constellation* and you wouldn't have to worry about a human crew." Rick grinned broadly knowing of Gunnar's distaste for artificial intelligence.

"That's not even funny." Gunnar shot his friend a worried look. "The 01 unit, Alex, is going to be quite enough."

"You know I wouldn't do that to you...well, maybe..."

"Hardy, har, har." Gunnar turned his gaze back out the window and up. He still hoped to see their new charges housed in their orbiting shipyards. Rick turned with his friend, hoping to catch a glimpse as well. "Still," Gunnar started quietly. "I wouldn't have even dreamt that you could have pulled this off. The Starbird is the perfect blend of fighter, bomber and fleet ship. I can only hope Admiral Mandell has the smarts to assign them to the Fighter branch and not Fleet operations."

"The admiral is a smart guy, despite being a bit rigid. The purpose of the Starbird design was to fill multiple roles with any branch of the service. That's why he's got you and me commanding our own and other branches commanding their own, to see how they'll work in filling the roles."

"You really think these birds will be able to pull maneuvers like you and I use to do back in the day?"

"They'll maneuver just fine as long we remember what their limitations are. Speaking of, how is Audra settling in as your first officer?"

"Ok, I guess," Gunnar said with a heavy sigh. He turned around, leaning against the window. "I'm afraid she's way out of her element."

"I think in this situation, we're all going to have our struggles," Rick replied.

"Her more so. She knows her duties and can command. Fifteen years of approach control, ordering jugheads like you and me around, has earned her that. She just has zero combat experience."

"You should have told her more about what we did on missions."

"Phish! Did you ever tell Jayda?"

"Top secret, we weren't allowed." Rick glanced up at a display, checking the time. "Besides, she would have freaked out and I'd never hear the end of it."

"There ya go then," Gunnar said.

"Where are they anyway? We're due in briefing in two minutes."

Gunnar turned toward the briefing room, seeing several officers taking their seats inside. Rick looked up at the display again.

"It won't look very good if we stroll in late," Rick said looking around and spotting two figures moving quickly towards them.

"Where have you two been?" Gunnar asked nervously.

"And please don't tell us you were picking out different uniforms," Rick added.

Jayda Niker and Audra Atlanta separated and fell in line with their husbands as they started toward the briefing room together, big smiles drawn across their lips. Audra darted a glance up at Gunnar.

"Nothing?" Gunnar asked bewildered.

"You may be good at what you do, but we make you look good doing it," she snickered as they entered the room.

"Just what I need," Gunnar breathed. "Another me."

"Almost late, gentlemen," Admiral Mandell barked as the four found their seats and sat smartly down. "And ladies," he added.

"Not at all, sir," Rick responded confidently. "We're right on time." He glanced at the display behind the admiral. It had just changed. Admiral Mandell eyed General Niker and Colonel Conrad carefully, glancing up at the display behind the four officers. He smiled slightly, looking at their two first officers.

"We'll dispense with the minutes and meeting agenda and I'll get right down to business. Welcome to the great experiment," he said, touching a control on the table in front of him. "It's unfortunate it took so long to get this project off the ground. We might have been able to shorten the war had these Starbirds been available sooner." The admiral looked over at Rick and nodded. "Our thanks to General Niker and his team for providing so much design engineering that will make these birds a force to be reckoned with." A holographic image materialized over the table so everyone could see a map of the galaxy. "Now, if I can have your attention up here. This is Kalamar," he said, pointing to a large glowing ball suspended among many. "We're currently tracking Croft Heckla out here," he continued, pointing to another location in the hologram. "We're hopeful that he's on his way home after being chased out of the Caney system. No one is exactly sure what he's up to, but he's likely heading home to lick his wounds so he can come back another day. We all wish he'd get the hint and surrender his fleet so we can put an end to this madness once and for all."

"So why are we worried about him?" one of the other officers around the table inquired.

"Because even beaten, he's unpredictable and dangerous," the admiral answered quickly. "While we believe he has every intention to head back to the Titan system, we've noticed four of his destroyers are unaccounted for. Smaller ships can slip away and not be much of a threat, but several destroyers could pose a serious problem."

"Why not just give chase and finish him off then?" another officer inquired.

"Because we lack the manpower ourselves," the admiral answered, looking right at Audra and Jayda. "The collapse of the Imperial Empire has left both sides severely short of manpower and machines, hence the need to deploy these Starbirds immediately." The admiral gave Audra and Jayda another quick look, but tossed that same look at several other women in the

room as well. "Now, I'm going to make this quick and simple.
With the rest of our fleet spread out paper thin in other parts of
the galaxy, there is no way we can mount anything viable to
finish Croft off before he can reach his stronghold on Darion.
The best we can do is give him a show of force to help direct him
home. But it has to be quick. Therefore, all Starbird launch time
tables have been accelerated. I've already transmitted orders to
the orbiting shipyards to arm your ships with a full complement
of Pin Missiles and the new Mark Five Torpedoes."

"Accelerated launch schedule, sir?" One of the other officers
at the table was quick with the question everyone was thinking.
"We weren't scheduled to launch for another month. What are
we talking about for a timeline? A week, a couple of days?"

"The following will launch immediately," Admiral Mandell said
shutting off the holographic image and touching another control.
An audible ruckus rolled through the room as a display popped
up in front of each individual around the large elliptical table.
"Our flagship *Starbird, Hyperion, Sulairus, Tut,* and the *Sung.*
These five have already been fitted with Asium Crystal
Assemblies and are awaiting final loading of ordinance and
personnel. The *Lexington, Pandora* and *Avenger* will launch as
soon as their chamber assemblies can be installed and
calibrated. General Niker and Colonel Conrad, the *Athena* and
Constellation will be the last ones out. You two are to run
backup sweeps between Kalamar and Caney."

"Do you have an ETA on the Asium delivery?" Rick asked
noticing Gunnar's shoulders slump as he leaned back in his chair.
They had hoped to be the first out to engage Croft head on. Rick
especially wanted to show what a Starbird could do.

"We're having some logistical problems," Admiral Mandell
paused, noticing the look of disappointment on Gunnar and
Rick's faces. "They'll get there when they get there."

Several hands went up, including Audra's. The admiral zoned
in on the new first officer, anxious to see how she would perform
in her new role.

"But we'll see if we can hurry it along a little. Lieutenant
Commander Atlanta, you have a question."

Gunnar stiffened up in his chair and looked around the room
with muffled pride. He and Rick were the only two in the room
with wives as their first officers and he was supremely confident
in Audra's ability to engage anyone in this room at their level.

"Begging the admiral's pardon, but we weren't scheduled for
launch for another month. Sending any untested ship out,
capitol, fleet or assault, for active duty without a proper shake
down and subsequent break-in time, is asking for trouble. Not to

mention having green command crews. Simulators and manuals can only go so far."

Rick leaned forward and tried to motion to Gunnar, but found his friend already trying to veer off his first officer. Admiral Mandell stared blankly at the short brunette. Finally, one of the admiral's aides stood up and pressed a control on the desk console in front of him. Audra noticed the display in front of her change and studied it carefully.

"This list is all neat and fine, but I've already seen our command crew list," she responded just as upfront as before. "This still doesn't answer my question."

"Every commander in this room was handpicked for their assignments." Admiral Mandell kept his growing glare at Lieutenant Commander Atlanta. "It's incumbent on each commanding officer to choose from the best available personnel to make up their respective command crews. If the command personnel chosen can't handle the job assigned to them, then it is the responsibility of the ship's executive officer to advise the officer in command and together review the personnel choices and make whatever changes are necessary. Otherwise, perhaps a change in command is needed."

"I understand military procedure, sir," Audra countered undeterred. "But to give command crews only a couple of hours at best to acclimate, isn't what I would call…" Audra felt a firm hand squeezing her arm and glanced in Gunnar's direction, trying to pull her arm free. He shook his head slightly, passing her an angry look. She noticed Rick and Jayda giving her similar signals.

"Colonel Conrad? Does your first officer have anything further to add?" Admiral Mandell kept his glare on Audra, not noticing the quiet signal's the other three officers were trying to send her. Gunnar tightened his squeeze a little and addressed the admiral.

"No sir. I think we've got everything we need here."

"Good," he snapped back sharply, holding his glare on Audra. "Is there anything else anyone would like to bring to my attention?"

Gunnar released his grip on Audra, feeling her relax somewhat. He could sense that she still had a lot to say and was apt to do so, but was now compelled to remain quiet. Silence prevailed long enough in the room that the admiral and his aides finally got to their feet. Everyone came to attention as the admiral started for the door.

"You have your schedules, good luck." Before he got out the door, the admiral called out without looking back. "General

Niker and Colonel Conrad. I'll have a word with you outside, alone."

"We'll catch up with you at teleporter room five," Gunnar huffed, as he and Rick started after the admiral. Audra tried to respond as Gunnar and Rick quickly made their way to the door, but she could only read his angry look as he exited the room.

Gunnar and Rick came to a halt and saluted, standing at attention in front of the admiral. The three stood some distance away from the briefing room and the admiral's aides.

"At ease gentlemen. There'll be no yelling here. With the careers you two have shared together, you've already had your fair share."

"Yes, sir," they both responded relaxing a little.

Admiral Mandell looked at them for a long moment, then took a step closer, focusing on Gunnar.

"Colonel, you understand why you're here, why you were assigned this command?"

Gunnar shifted his eyes sideways, trying to get a little help from Rick.

"Because I'm the best, sir?"

"That's a cocky, arrogant statement. Sounds like a certain branch of this military I know. Go on, best what?"

"Best fighter pilot, sir."

"There it is! Exactly! No two ways around it. You can fly anything better than anyone else. You're the best, even better than the general here." The admiral motioned toward Rick, who smiled proudly. "As smart as he is and as long as he's been flying, you're still the better pilot. Seems like I read a report or listened to one where your fighter took a hit and had zero instruments for navigation or basic flight functions and somehow you still managed to make four kills, saving several of your squadron mates and then brought your bird back and landed it like it was some routine maneuver. Is that how you told it, General?"

Rick shuffled slightly and glanced in Gunnar's direction.

"Battle of Tarlow, sir. It was six kills after his T-6 took a direct hit from an Imperial Pan missile and several Photon blasts." Rick looked forward again noticing the admiral starting to smile.

"Six kills and a Pan missile," the admiral repeated. "Guess I'll have to reread that Tarlow report. And how did you survive that one?"

"The Tempest is a tough bird, sir," Gunnar started. "The cockpit is designed to keep the pilot alive even under the abuse we received that day. If a fighter is still flying and firing, it's still a fighter and able to engage."

"But you had no instruments to maneuver with." A big grin found a place on the admiral's face as he tried to imagine what Gunnar's landing must have been like.

"That's what the rest of my squadron mates are for."

"Commodore Gardner wasn't going to let me have either of you," Admiral Mandell said, shaking his head slightly. "He made a very compelling case to keep you right where you were, but in the end, he understood the dynamic we're all facing here. It's likely you'll both be back under his command again if this Starbird project pans out the way I think it will. Gunnar, your Dialabron physiology doesn't mix well with the requirements of any branch of the service, but somehow, you've managed to beat all the odds and for that, you have my awe inspired respect. It's another reason you're here. That and Rick here has nothing but unending praise for you. He's stuck his neck out quite a way to get you into this program." The admiral paused a moment, relaxing. "I haven't said anything to either of you about your choice of first officers for a couple of reasons, but I'm going to voice my concerns now because I want you to understand why I'm not screaming obscenities here. Couples in command positions together have been tried before with miserable results, so normally Kalamar Command doesn't allow them, but our loses at the end of this war have been catastrophic and good people are hard to find, so in this instance, we've given you both some rope. Jayda and Audra have good service records, perhaps a bit inexperienced, but I have no doubt you two will remedy that in short order. Rick," the admiral toned down to a personal level. "I suspect Jayda understands command protocols better because of her background as a Royal Princess of Kalamar."

"Former, Royal Princess, sir."

"How you talked her out of that is beyond me," the admiral chuckled shifting. "Gunnar, I know Audra is a capable officer, but an abbreviated briefing is not the time to ask questions time won't allow to answer. But more to the point, I never make any decision lightly, either well thought out or in hast and I will not have those decisions questioned in front of the entire Starbird fleet command, is that clear?"

"Yes, sir." Gunnar wanted to get answers to the questions Audra had tried to ask as they were still burning in his mind, but he knew better. Aggression was one of the side effects of his alien physiology and years as a squadron commander netted him the insight into when to ask a question and when to keep your mouth shut.

"Good, now how are you doing with your little medical problem?"

"Problem, sir?" Gunnar asked.

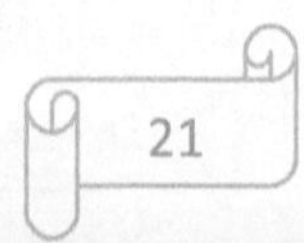

"Alleviate my worries about your dormant second heart. Does the flight surgeon still think your dormancy exit is beginning?"

"We visited with Flight surgeon Tanenberg right before the briefing," Gunnar started. "He's confident that under the proper medical supervision, I'll be able to remain fit for duty."

"And your aggression levels? Heard you've had some difficulties in the past." The admiral passed Rick a glance then focused back on Gunnar. "How are you handling that little gem?"

"Keeping a tight rein on it, sir."

"Feeling any of that now?" Admiral Mandell asked noticing a change in Gunnar's eye color.

"Yes, sir."

"Because I've reprimanded you about Audra?"

"As you've indicated, she's a bit inexperienced."

"You're doing pretty good at keeping that aggression penned up. Saving it for Croft I expect."

"Yes, sir."

"Never had a Dialabron under my command before. Having two hearts operating inside you at the same time ought to be quite the experience. I can't wait to see what you can do once you get through all this. You'll make sure you see your ship's doctor before you launch?"

"Yes, Admiral."

"Good enough." He shook both their hands and turned to leave, but stopped. "Gentlemen, in a fighter cockpit you have no one to order around and share your thoughts with but yourself. I'm sure you'll find Starbirds vastly different in that respect. You'll do well to learn to share your thoughts with your first officers." He paused, hoping to the see the depth of his council register. "Good luck."

Gunnar and Rick saluted and watched as the admiral stepped quickly down the hall with his aides in tow.

"You ok?" Rick asked as they turned in the other direction.

Gunnar rubbed his lower back a little.

"Been aching down where the other heart is all morning. No arm pain though, so I must be fine. Wished I knew when this thing was going to finally fire itself up."

"Should have started the dormancy exit years ago, why would you expect it to all of a sudden speed up?"

"It just picked a really stupid time to finally get to it."

"Can't argue with that. So how are you going to approach Audra?"

"Well," Gunnar took a deep breath as they turned a corner. "As soon as I can get my anger under control, I imagine I'll need to apologize for leaving bruises on her arm and then try to explain the need for restraint in a command briefing."

"I'd buy tickets to that conversation," Rick chuckled. "But I have a ship to get ready."

"You better have it ready," Gunnar said pointing toward one of the many teleporter rooms. "I'd hate to have to come alongside and pull your sorry behind out of a jam."

*　　*　　*　　*

Audra glanced over at Gunnar as they stepped onto the teleporter pad for transport up to the *Constellation* still moored in its orbiting shipyard. He had remained silent since he and Rick had returned from speaking with the admiral. She could see Gunnar was still angry. No doubt the admiral had chewed him out.

"I know you're angry, but you need to talk to me," she said as they finished materializing in their ship's small teleporter room. Gunnar only looked at her with a tolerant expression she knew all too well. "I only asked a question. You were thinking the same thing. Why is everyone so upset? Jayda wouldn't even talk to me afterwards. I just wished they could have given us a little more training is all," she complained. "With the armistice enforce now, I can't see the admiral's urgency to be blasting off so quickly after Croft."

"Clearly," Gunnar responded, trying to control his tone.

"Command crew orientation takes a minimum of two weeks," Audra reaffirmed. She had to step quickly to keep up as the two emerged from the teleporter room and into the hall in front of the engineering vestibule.

"I'm pretty sure the Admiral is aware of that," Gunnar commented through a tight jaw.

"Apparently not and his aides looked pretty clueless too."

"I can assure you that wasn't the case."

"Then why are we rushing around trying to get airborne before we're ready?"

"Because Admiral Mandell, the commander of the whole Starbird fleet, issued orders to haul our butts out of space dock as soon as we can and run sweeps in case Croft Hekla decides to do the unexpected, that's why." Gunnar's tone was sharpening.

"Croft Hekla is a power hungry nincompoop who needs his butt kicked into a Black Hole." Audra and Gunnar had to press themselves against the outer wall to make way for several techs moving bulky gear out one of the main boarding doors.

"Well, between you, me and this wall, it sounds like we're going to get a crack at him," Gunnar said. "I think the admiral was being purposely vague in that briefing. There's more to it than Croft is just heading home to lick his wounds. With Kalamar Command tracking him skirting this system, my bet is he'll make a right turn Clyde and head straight at us. Try and knock out as many of these Starbirds as he possibly can before we're operational."

"Our command personnel need way more time to learn our jobs and get to know this ship better."

"You'll get no argument from me," Gunnar jabbed. "But if I'm right, there's no time. And you can't go around facing up to an Admiral in a command briefing, trying to tell him what his job is."

"Somebody has to do it," Audra retorted. Any other superior officer and she might get a reprimand for speaking in such a manner.

"Well, it's not going to be my first officer." Gunnar turned and faced Audra. "Is that understood?"

"Just like that?" she asked indignantly.

"Do I need to make it an order?"

Audra went silent, looking up into Gunnar's firm glare. She could tell by the dark color of his normally light hazel eyes that he was still angry, but doing a remarkable job of holding it in check.

"You've got to learn when to speak and when to keep your mouth shut," Gunnar huffed, heading into the engine room.

"What about systems shakedowns? We've got a brand new bird. This is her maiden flight." Audra was puffing, trying to keep up.

"I think in this branch of the service; they're calling these ships."

"Whatever."

"Look, what more do you want? I don't like these orders any more than you do, and for the same reasons. You know me, I'm just as lazy as the next guy. I'd feel a whole lot more comfortable sitting in an easy chair sipping a drink watching the engineers test and calibrate everything to make sure it doesn't all blow up when we hit the start button. But sadly, those conditions don't exist right now."

"Enough Starbirds have already launched to handle this little skirmish with Croft. By the way, for the record, it took them three weeks to complete their shake downs, not two. And their command crews were already in place. Four Starbirds are more than enough to escort Croft to wherever he's trying to go. We should be standing down long enough to do this right, everything by the book."

"Can you remind me again why we're still talking about this? And where is Billy Moon?" He looked around the engine room for the chief engineer and started for the turret elevator.

"Shouldn't we at least call Command back and explain our situation to them?" Audra was having a hard time remaining in Gunnar's focus.

"Billy, where are you?" Gunnar called out, moving past the turret's inoperative seat cradle and to the elevator shaft ladder, Audra hot on his heels.

"Just give me the order and I'll call them myself." Audra looked up the elevator shaft as Gunnar grabbed at one of the rungs of the inner ladder, but then stopped and turned around.

"Commander Atlanta, this conversation ends now," Gunnar said sternly. "It's not that I don't agree with you, I do. But, orders are orders and that's the end of it. Now, you need to get up into both Interceptors and check on Captains Abram's and Dalley's progress. I'm going up to the turret to check on some stuff, find Billy Moon and maybe after that, I'll be able to calm myself down enough to go see Dr. Yamoto, as the Admiral ordered before we leave."

Audra's expression softened and she reached out and took Gunnar's hand, intertwining her fingers in his. Gunnar instantly relaxed and she watched his eyes quickly melt back to their hazel color.

"You don't need to climb into the turret to calm yourself down," she said quietly.

Gunnar froze, as if trying to decide whether to stay angry or not. Holding his breath, he quickly scanned the engine room then looked down into Audra's lovely brown eyes. He finally let his breath go and dropped his hand away from the ladder, slipping it around her waist.

"How is it modern medicine can't control my anger, but you seem to have no problem doing it?" He was trying to sound irritated, but he couldn't hold a stern look on her and smiled. Audra snuggled up into his arms and held him.

"Because I won't let it come between us, even if it's in your chemical makeup. There are some things stronger than what's pumping through those tough veins of yours."

Gunnar stroked her hair gently, listening to the ship wide com chatter and the noises that a ship makes all on its own. Noises from the top of the elevator shaft brought them back to their surroundings and they pulled apart.

"Meet me in Fuji's office when you're done in the Interceptors?"

"Do I get to do all the talking this time?" Audra asked.

"Don't you always?" he said letting her go and heading up the ladder.

Smiling, Audra shook her head and running both hands through her short brown hair, turned from the elevator shaft and moved toward one of the Interceptor access tubes, hoisted her small frame into the body cradle and activated it. With a sudden rush of acceleration, she was catapulted out through the massive wing of the Starbird and right into the cockpit of one of the integrated wing mounted Interceptors. A large, heavy fighter, its design was such that when integrated with its mother ship, it provided extensive firepower and enhanced maneuvering capabilities in atmospheric conditions.

Audra scanned the console in front of her carefully, letting her hands come to rest on the flight controls. Like Gunnar, she had flown fighters before, but never in combat. Fighter aces loved it and while she enjoyed the freedom of space flight in such craft, she much preferred other technical tasks not quite so prone to putting a person in harm's way. She wished Gunnar felt the same way, but alas...

Her attention was drawn away from the dark instruments in front of her to outside the cockpit windows. Through the surrounding structure of the orbiting shipyard, she could clearly see Kalamar below their orbit. The large red sun Sancho, and Kalamar's closely orbiting blue moon, Tundance, were rising above the planet's terminator. In the distance was another shipyard. She could just make out the shape of the *Constellation's* sister ship, the *Athena* moored within its frame. Several tiny one man tugs zipped across her view, moving back and forth between freight lockers and the ship. Looking forward, she could see several technicians in space suits working on the hull of the heart shaped bridge pod. Her heart nearly leapt from her chest when a face appeared right outside where she was sitting. Another technician was just finishing up his work on the hull around the Interceptor's docking socket. The tech smiled broadly and motioned an apology, then turned and jetted away from the ship, back toward the superstructure of the orbiting shipyard.

"Yeah, I hate it when they do that too."

Audra nearly jumped out of her seat again, startled by a voice from behind. She hadn't even noticed Captain Dakota Abrams working directly behind the pilot's seat in an access panel near the floor.

"Like what you just did was any better," Audra complained, putting her hand to her chest to try and calm her elevated heart rate.

"What?"

"Scared the bageebees out of me is what."

"Sorry 'bout that. The seat cradle is so quiet I almost didn't hear you come up." Captain Abrams had an amused tone in his voice as he closed the panel door he was working in. "So what's the latest word? We gonna get out of here, or are we stuck doing more drills?"

"The Colonel and I just teleported from the command briefing. The *Constellation* and the *Athena* will be the last two ships out of the yards. The other ships have orders to depart immediately. Our Asium crystal assemblies are scheduled to arrive within the hour and since we'll be the last group to get them installed, we leave last. That leaves us no time for any kind of orientation. Talk about on the job training."

"Sorry about that ma'am," Dakota offered. "They didn't exactly have a large pool to draw from. The war decimated all the fleet crews. It's been tough on every branch. Fighter squadrons are about the only groups left to draw on. Clearly the reason I'm here. I'd much rather be back at my T-38 squadron than sitting here playing second fiddle in a command crew, no offense."

"None taken." Audra turned in the pilot's seat and faced Dakota. "I realize the war is over and all branches of the service have taken a heavy toll, I'm just really worried about sending an inexperienced command crew out for police action and exploration with a green bridge crew. This isn't what I would consider intelligence at its finest."

"You'll get no argument from me, but it sounds to me like it can't be helped. Still, from what I've observed from my interaction with this bridge crew, the colonel couldn't have chosen any better. I didn't get here because I'm the general's cousin." He motioned he was ready to exit the craft. "Captain Dalley has already finished with the other Interceptor."

Audra touched a control and the cradle instantly plummeted her back to engineering. After she sent it back up, the cradle reappeared a moment later and Dakota climbed out.

"I'd love to actually fly that bird in some actual action instead of in its simulator or puttsing around in a trainer orbiting Kalamar."

"That's just the point. We don't know this ship well enough. We need time to get to know it. What it will and won't do."

"General Niker and Engineer Moon know these systems like the back of their hand," Dakota pointed out. "In fact, this ship and most its systems are General Niker's brain child."

"Let's not forget Billy and Clancy's contributions on this project and without the 7000 series, even the general would have had a struggle."

Dakota stopped next to the engineering consoles, looking at Audra. He came from the same mold as her husband and Dakota's cousin Rick, a fighter cockpit. It's what they knew and understood. Sometimes you just had to jump into things whether you were ready or not.

"I'd say that gives the *Athena* and the *Constellation* a distinctive edge over the other ships," Dakota finally blurted, trying to find the point to the conversation. "Is there anything else, ma'am?"

Audra scanned the look on Dakota's face and settled back with a sigh.

"Just wondering if I'm the only one that's concerned about all this."

"We're all right there rowing with you, Commander." Dakota stepped past her and disappeared up the other Interceptor shaft on the opposite side of the engine room, leaving Audra to wonder what was taking Gunnar so long in the turret.

Stepping up to the enormous engineering console, she let her eyes sweep across its smooth, glowing surface. She shifted her view past the vertical displays at the massive engine bulkheads. Normally, technology didn't get her giddy, but as she looked all around the room at the insides of this marvelous machine that was to be their new home, she could hardly contain her excitement. Even though this Assault Corsair was outsized by even the basic of capital ships, it had capabilities beyond that of its mammoth counterparts. Significantly smaller in size and crew compliment, it could go farther, faster and pack far more punch for its size than any other design comparable.

Audra stepped around the engineering console and approached the main engine bulkhead. It was a smooth mound of parts, pipes and hoses neatly combed and dressed tightly together. Folding her arms, she examined an empty enclosure built into the front of the engine bulkhead where the Asium containment chamber would be mounted. The heart and soul of the ship, the crystal assembly delivered exponential power utilizing a number of carefully sized crystals. As these crystals could be fickle and somewhat unstable if not kept precisely positioned away from each other, this enclosure kept them from moving while in service and buffered their exposure to the outside elements.

"Pretty cool, huh?" a gruff voice spoke quickly from behind. Audra turned to the tall chief engineer stepping up to the engineering console.

"Billy, weren't you up in the turret?" she asked, stepping around next to him. She watched his fingers working the dazzling displays in front of him.

"What for? I've got way too much to do down here. The chamber tech is on his way here right now with the Asium module and I still have the flux dampers to calibrate and the venting scrubbers to make sure are working before he plugs it in."

"Seems like a whole lot of work for something so simple to install."

"True that, but without all those complex components or the crystal chamber, we don't go much of anywhere for very long."

Audra looked past the engineer toward the turret elevator shaft.

"If you're looking for the Colonel, I saw him headed toward the medial bay. Said something about needing to meet the new Doc," Billy trailed off, becoming engrossed in getting his work completed.

"Thank you, Mr. Moon."

Audra turned to the engineering door, still looking all around at the vast array of machinery that made this class ship unique. She looked forward to getting to know it and learning how to use it. She just wished they had more time to do so before they left for their first deployment. Exiting engineering, she nearly ran into a small white airborne droid entering the engine room. Boxlike and only a couple of feet tall, these droids were the horsepower behind the design and integration of these Starbird Corsairs.

"Pardon me, ma'am," Alex said, trying to maneuver around her. Caught up in going the wrong direction at the same time, they shifted back and forth trying to get around the other only to remain in the other's way. Finally, Audra stopped and waited.

"Alex, pick a direction and I'll go the other way."

"Certainly, Commander, my apologies." The little droid maneuvered around her and into engineering, spinning its head to the rear as it went. "The Colonel is looking for you. I last detected him moving toward the medical bay only a couple of moments ago."

"Thank you, Alex."

Looking after the little droid as it disappeared behind the engine bulkheads, Audra lingered in the doorway for a moment. The machine's voice had an accent, no doubt a byproduct of its specific programmer. It also sounded irritated, Gunnar must not be far away. Having dealt with AI systems in her work environment as a long range traffic controller, Audra was still getting used to having one that could move about freely and think on its own. She had already witnessed Gunnar's interaction with Alex 7001 on several occasions and was painfully aware of his feelings toward the 7000 series. Gunnar hated them, but puzzling to Audra, she was never able to get it out of him why. Droids were some of the most useful tools she had ever worked with.

Audra's studies of the 7000 series indicated a whole new set of artificial intelligence parameters in their design protocols, ones that included self-learning and human emulation. Her observations of these new attributes appeared to be what frustrated Gunnar the most. Her husband was used to subordinate computer systems in a fighter cockpit environment that did exactly what they were programmed to do without trying to second guess the pilot. She could see how having an AI wandering all over a ship, interacting as one of the crew, would create a peculiar situation for command officers not used to such interaction.

Audra stepped toward the medical door, watching crew personnel ahead of her bustle in and out of the bridge. For the most part, the ship was self-sufficient now. They just needed the Asium crystal assemblies and they would be out of here. As Audra entered sickbay, she found Gunnar sitting at the doctor's desk. The medical officer was pressing a hypo to his shoulder and hovering around his medium build with some sort of probe. Fuji Yamoto's demeanor wasn't too reassuring.

"Colonel, I don't know what to do with you." Dr. Yamoto sounded quite exasperated. "I have no expertise with your kind."

Leaning around the Doctor, Gunnar pulled his tinted glasses from his face.

"Hear that? I have a kind."

"You're definitely kind of something," Audra jested. "Remember, it's my turn to do all the talking this time? What's the problem, Fuji?"

The medical officer scanned Gunnar for a moment longer, then studied the readouts on her probe.

"There is definitely a heart problem here," she stated slowly. "In fact, based on my preliminary findings, any episode would be easy to predict. How in the world were you able to clear your medical and what doctor released you for flight duty for as long as you've been in a cockpit?"

Gunnar winked at Audra, but offered no explanations, smiling broadly while running his fingers through his sandy blonde hair.

"If you'll indulge us for a couple of minutes," Audra offered, quietly motioning for her husband to move to an examination table.

Gunnar stepped over to one of the beds and lay back, the medical monitor over the head of the bed instantly activating. Fuji and Audra watched carefully as the many life readings stabilized, with the exception of those associated with heart rate and blood pressure.

"Look at this," Fuji said, pointing at the information. "His heart is under a lot of strain here. He should be blowing a vein just anytime with readings like this."

"Are your Arterial scanners operational in here?" Audra asked.

"Yeah," Fuji responded, grabbing a small glass plate device and touching it in several places. "Just got this thing working this morning. Nurse Conner and I took turns scanning each other."

A thin mechanical arm swung out from the wall and waved over the entire length of Gunnar's body, a tiny pinprick of light emitting from the end. A holographic image of the interior of his anatomy appeared directly above him, along with much of the information displayed on the medical monitor.

"I guess I should have asked what race you are," Fuji trumbled off carefully while studying his interior more closely. "Cause you aren't human."

"Nope, I'm not," he agreed.

"My apologies, Colonel. I haven't had time to go through anyone's medical files yet. I'm still trying to figure out what I still need in here. Some of this stuff I've never seen before." Fuji and Audra scanned the room, Fuji passing a glance at Audra. "I only got about two weeks of command training and twenty minutes notice of my deployment onboard."

"You're rowing with the rest of us," Audra commented, curling her expression to disdain as this all sound too familiar.

"So, I'm a little bit at a disadvantage here," Fuji started, studying his interior. "I see a lot of familiar human stuff in here, but there's some extra pieces parts. And why are you wearing those glasses? You should have had your eyes corrected at the DNA level while you were still in the womb. You were conceived and grown in the womb, right?"" Fuji was being purposely basic in this instance. She was sure these officers, whom she had only met early this morning, had little expertise with detailed medical terminology. She paused a moment, looking at the information flashing in the image. "His blood composition and bone scans are off the chart though. What planet do you hail from, Colonel?"

"Commenor," Gunnar responded.

"He's a Dialabron," Audra added instantly.

"I'm sorry." Nothing registered for Fuji. "I'm still on a pretty steep learning curve here. I'm aware of Commenor's existence and the Dialabron race, but that's about as far as it goes."

"Yeah, there aren't too many of us in the service," Gunnar informed the medical officer.

Audra smiled at the puzzled look Fuji had just developed. Gunnar and Audra had been through this conversation many times in the past and had it rehearsed.

"Commenor is a primitive planet by Kalamar standards," Audra began. "Not exactly sure why they were included in the Republic Federation. You won't find any fleet ships hanging around there, no armies per se. There are several cultures living there, Knockian, Palitarion, Dyclotarion, Dialabron, just to name a few. Each is unique in how they've evolved in the planet's dense atmosphere and heavy gravity. In the case of Dialabrons, an odd mutation thought to be linked to a certain kind of gamma radiation from Commenor's sun, is to blame for some born with a couple of extra organs. Because the organs are genetically dependent on each other, neither can be removed without killing the subject. There is no medication or procedure that can fix this condition either. Most don't live to see the age they are eligible to enter the service, not that Kalamar Command would let them. If they do survive their extra organ functions, they usually can't pass the physical. The Colonel here somehow got through as a late bloomer. On Commenor, they're called *Shunts*."

"I don't understand how you got past the command officer's examination," Fuji said, turning the image of his interior with her touch control. "I understand a fleet chair is far more restricting than fighter command."

"I received a special waiver through General Niker. As long as I don't exhibit any symptoms that could be a detriment to duty, I'm good to go."

"Well that sort of puts me in a bit of a quandary," Fuji murmured. "If you're having heart problems now, I can't clear you for duty. I have to report this and let Kalamar Command decide what they're going to do." Fuji continued to look all around his anatomy. "Why can't I find it?" she asked, becoming a little frustrated. *How hard can it be?*

"You're looking in the wrong place," Gunnar grinned. "It's back here," he pointed up into the hologram at another lump in the image.

"Well, of all the backward..." she mumbled, turning the image upside down and in the other direction. "Seems like an odd place to put another heart."

"I doubt he had an option," Audra chuckled.

"Well, regardless of where it is, the fact it's causing problems is enough for me to have to recommend he be relieved."

"Yea, not going to happen, Doc," Gunnar stated, becoming cold. "General Niker will never allow it."

"Even Rick has to follow command regulations, Gunnar," Audra pointed out. "Is there anything in the regs that would allow for his condition if it were deemed temporary and controllable?"

"Good thinking," Gunnar agreed. "Do you have any Furlitron onboard?"

"I've never heard of the stuff. Is that supposed to speed up your processes or stunt them? What?"

"It calms the astiatic nerves surrounding the dormant heart. It won't stunt the awakening process, but will mask its outward effects on my system."

Dr. Yamoto thought a moment as she turned off the holographic scanner and Gunnar sat back up.

"Where's our first deployment?"

"You don't have any onboard, do you?" Audra asked, reading Fuji's expression.

"Like I would keep something like that?" Fuji pointed out. "Remember the whole, I haven't even had time to read any crew medical histories yet? This entire deployment was super rushed."

"Colonel Conrad and Commander Atlanta, to the bridge," a voice fired from the com panel on the doctor's desk. Fuji let out a big sigh, watching Gunnar get to his feet.

"Any way we get can our hands on this Furlitron?"

"I think we're all in luck," Audra announced as they headed for the door. "First assignment takes us close to Commenor, the only place we can get it."

"Have you got anything else that you think might help until we get there?" Gunnar asked as the door hissed open.

"Maybe," Fuji called after them. "I'll see what I can conjure from my magic hat." Then the two officers were gone, leaving the ship's doctor to try and figure out how she was going to deal with the situation.

"She's a little off the wall," Gunnar commented as he and Audra started up the hall toward the bridge door.

"Have you taken the time to look her profile over?"

"She definitely has a profile." A stupid grin slithered across Gunnar's lips and he abruptly got an elbow to the ribs. "Hey, what was that for?"

"Keep your eyes where they belong."

"What?"

"Need another elbow?"

"No, I'm good. Yes, I have looked at all the command personnel profiles. First officer, medical officer, two Interceptor pilots and the chief engineer. Have I missed anyone?"

"Don't need any more than that to command a Starbird." Audra was about to bring something else up, but a warning indicator began to flash on the wall ahead of them.

"Red alert, red alert. Battle stations, battle stations." The voice rang out through the entire ship with accompanying alarms. Both officers quickened their pace toward the bridge.

"How do you have a battle station alert in a shipyard?" Audra asked glancing at Gunnar. He remained silent, focused as the voice over the ship's alert com rang out again.

"Colonel Conrad and Commander Atlanta, to the bridge."

The bridge door instantly snapped open when they reached it. Being met with a barrage of noise and bustle, Audra came alive as Gunnar stepped past a noisy communications console to Science Officer Pip Habba working his scanning equipment.

"Colonel on the bridge," Audra announced, heading directly forward to helm and navigation. "I need status reports now." Not being tall made Audra somewhat unassuming, but as the first officer she could certainly make her presence known. She turned back to the engineering consoles opposite the communication and science stations.

"What's this all about, Pip?" Gunnar looked up at the information displayed on the many screens in front of him. There was a lot of communications noise issuing from the station next to them and Gunnar passed a glance back at the com officer, Lieutenant Lana Nevall. She instantly read the look the Colonel had just shot her, dousing the noise coming from her sound system and pulling her headsets back up into place.

"*Starbird*, *Hyperion* and *Sulairus* report being attacked by several Imperial fighter groups in the Nantse system."

"Probably part of Croft Hekla's rogue fleet, ain't that just the neatest thing," Gunnar responded. "Any casualties?" He looked over his shoulder at Lana, who instantly noticed the attention was on her.

"No, sir. They report making quick work of the attack with minimal to no damage."

"So why are we at battle ready, sitting without a crystal assembly?"

"Approach control reports Imperial bombers with heavy fighter escort have dropped out of light speed on the other side of Tundance, inbound. Estimate two minutes to contact."

"Ah-ha, there's Croft's right turn Clyde. The other attack in the Nantse system was just a diversion," Gunnar fathomed, turning to Audra as she stepped across the bridge.

"All ship stations at battle ready," Audra reported. "Engineering reports Asium crystal chamber installed and operational. Your orders?"

"Has Kalamar Command given us any direction here?"

"Nothing, sir," came the calm reply from the com officer.

"Anything from the *Athena*?"

"They're asking the same questions."

Gunnar fidgeted nervously, fighting his natural inclination to act first and ask questions later. Fighter pilot mentality would have him already holding the turbo thruster control down on launch. He had no doubt Captains Abrams and Dalley were acting in a similar fashion. As the *Constellation* was still sitting in its shipyard, the Interceptors could not launch, but it was a good bet their engines were up and ready.

"We hold our position until ordered out and given clearance from the yard master," Gunnar finally said.

Watching Gunnar closely, Audra noted the restraint holding him down. In his younger years, he would have claimed communications problems and launched anyway.

Gunnar sat back in his chair and pushed his knuckles against his teeth. Looking back over at the information on the displays above the science station, he watched the scanners tracking the incoming Imperial ships. He knew their tactics would make him and Rick easy targets. He looked out ahead of them. Not far away was a second orbiting shipyard structure, the *Athena* nestled within its superstructure, waiting.

"Get me the *Athena*. I want to talk to General Niker," he ordered, throwing a glance at Lana then turning forward to the weapons officer. "Charge the secondary gun pods and standby. Helm, maneuvering thrusters at station keeping."

"Sir?" Lieutenant Lynette Starman at the helm inquired, giving him an odd look.

"We're still clamped," Audra pointed out. "They haven't even taken the moorings loose yet."

"General Niker, sir," Lana announced.

Gunnar touched the com control on his armrest.

"What do you think, buddy?"

"I think someone at command has fallen asleep at the wheel," Rick called back from the hidden speaker. "I'm still waiting for my Asium crystal assembly to be installed. I'm bug mash here!"

Gunnar instantly motioned to Lana.

"Call the yard master, we have to launch now!" Gunnar knew his friend couldn't even get his Interceptors out.

"We have incoming torpedoes, bearing two seven three mark four zero five," Pip reported, responding to the proximity alarms.

Audra turned to the images displayed over Pip's head, then to the weapons officer.

"Weapons, can you get any kind of a target lock?

"Not on all of them, Commander."

"Turret, what about you?" she inquired, calling back to Lieutenant Hunter in the turret.

"I have a whole bunch of shipyard in my gun sights," the turret gunner responded from his perch at the top aft of the ship. A moment later, the bridge door popped open and Alex 7001 flew in.

"Alex, can you override the docking clamps from the yard moorings?" Audra asked, watching the torpedo returns streaking toward them.

"Highly irregular, Commander. Such actions are an unsafe breach in launching protocols."

"Torpedoes in fifteen seconds," Pip called out, keeping his eyes glued to the returns.

"Alex! Do it now!" Audra barked, becoming frantic.

The little white droid chirped loudly as it scanned the readings Audra and Gunnar were looking at, then swooped forward next to helm control.

"We're loose!" Lynette grabbed the throttles.

"Go! Go! Go," Gunnar ordered, activating his safety locks. A padded clamp popped out of his seat on both sides and pressed firmly down over his thighs. The crew did likewise as Lynette gave the powerful Corsair throttle and guided the ship straight out of the skeletal construction of the shipyard. Several escape pods blasted away from the shipyard at the same moment the Corsair throttled away.

Gunnar watched horrified as a volley of torpedoes pummeled the shipyard the *Athena* was moored in. The *Constellation* shook from the concussion of their own exploding shipyard as it too took numerous direct hits. Framework and debris expanded past them as they exited. Both Interceptors ejected from the rear wings of the ship and throttled away to intercept the incoming bombers and associated fighter escorts.

"Helm, get us down to the *Athena* now!" Gunnar ordered, watching several more torpedoes strike the *Athena's* already mangled yard structure, sending it tumbling out of orbit and toward the surface of Kalamar.

"Weapons, do we have full power to the shields?" Gunnar asked Doran Cartwright.

"All systems at your command, Colonel," the weapons officer responded after a quick check of his instruments.

"Helm, can you follow the *Athena's* path well enough to give the weapons officer room to work?" Gunnar asked.

Lynette looked over at Doran, wondering what the Colonel was thinking.

"Aye, sir," she responded a little uncertain. As the debris started to clear, they could see the *Athena* trapped in the tangled wreckage of its shipyard as it tumbled toward the surface of Kalamar. It would only be a matter of minutes before the tangled mess started bouncing along the outer atmosphere. Without a controlled reentry, the twist of metal and debris would superheat and break apart, taking the *Athena* with it.

"Com, do you still have the General?"

"On the line, sir."

"Rick, are you still in one piece?" Static crackled back at Gunnar.

"Yeah, we're fine. Still trying to get our engines online. We've got our shields up, but we're pinned in this pretzel mess and she's going down fast. What do you have in mind?"

"Gonna see how good my helm and weapons officers are today," Gunnar answered with a confident grin. "Have you out of there in two shakes of a Tiffen's ear."

"Don't be late." Rick sounded a little worried.

"Getting a little tired of always having to save your sorry butt."

"My what?"

Audra was a little more than worried, recalling several close calls and near scrapes these two had together. A normal decaying orbit could take days or weeks before the atmosphere was reached. This shipyard was doing more than decaying. Its trajectory had been so severely altered that the crumpled mess was diving toward the surface of Kalamar.

Several explosions buffeted the *Constellation* as it raced to catch the falling yard structure, Imperial fighters streaking past the front of the ship. With smaller craft moving all around them, the weapons officer had plenty of targets.

"More torpedoes incoming," Pip announced.

"Weapons, ignore the fighters," Audra ordered from her locked position. "Work with helm to start cutting the *Athena* loose with the cutting beam." A moment later, another Imperial fighter erupted into a ball of expanding metal and a second followed suit as one of the *Constellation's* Interceptors swooped in, letting its powerful guns light it up.

"Just like surgery," Gunnar instructed, as Lynette pulled the ship within targeting range of the falling mass. "Just don't be cutting through any vital parts inside."

"Turret," Audra called over the com. "Ignore the fighters. Let the Interceptors handle them. Can you get a target lock on the incoming torpedoes?"

"Now that I'm not looking at a wall of metal. Keep me on the zero mark three zero axis plane or at least keep the torpedoes behind us and I think I can make it happen, Commander."

Doran focused on the targeting sites in front of him, gently working the powerful cutting beam, slicing away at the crumpled structure surrounding the entombed *Athena*.

"Can you get me any closer?" Doran asked carefully.

"You want me to land on it?" Lynette came back casually.

"Only if you have money for the parking meter. Move a little further forward so I can cut that beam out of the way."

"How about trying for the top piece up front. Keep the beam cutting straight ahead and I'll guide us all the way around it, then the top will lift right off?"

"Ah! Good plan. Great minds think alike."

Lynette carefully guided her ship in as close as she dared and positioned the *Constellation* toward what was left of the rear opening of the yard structure. When ready, she motioned for Doran to begin. The thin, blue cutting beam started slicing through the yard structure like it was tissue paper. The Starbird pilot carefully eased the ship back, letting it glide gracefully around to the other side with the beam cutting, holding a stationary line the entire time.

"Torpedoes closing," Pip called out. "Impact in 20 seconds."

"Rick, you still with me?" Gunnar leaned to his com panel.

"My compliments to your surgeons back there. I can see sky, I mean stars, I mean..."

Gunnar noticed they were tumbling right along with the *Athena* and her tangled mass of yard structure. He watched with profound satisfaction as the pieces being cut away, separated and tumbled off behind the falling mass.

"We're starting to hit the outer atmosphere," Audra exclaimed, watching the ship's surface temperature readings.

Gunnar could see the front edge of the structure starting to glow as it superheated.

"Have you got any maneuvering thrusters at all?"

"Hold the clamps in place and try to drive this wreckage out?"

"At least until I can cut the rest of you loose."

"Turret, how are you doing back there?" Audra called back to Hayden in the turret.

"Swing me back around to the rear and I think I can keep those torpedoes from reaching us, Commander."

"Helm," Audra called, seeing Gunnar nod his head. "Get in behind him as fast as you can."

"You mean like this?" the Starbird pilot smirked, correcting her ship's tumble and quickly maneuvering around behind the *Athena*.

"You know, General, you could try blasting some of that crap away from the front end there," Gunnar suggested casually. "You do still have weapons, right?"

"Don't you think I already tried? What are you doing?"

"Trying to keep you from getting your numb-chucks blown off." Gunnar looked over at the tracking screen, watching some of the incoming torpedoes disappear. Several torpedoes exploded close enough their concussion caused the ship to quake gently. He could hear the distinctive muffled thumping sound of the twin photon cannons of the turret hard at it.

"I'm not going to be able to get them all," Hayden grunted.

"Rick, it's now or never." Gunnar leaned forward, watching more debris swing away in the intense heat of the atmospheric friction.

"Hull temperature heading into the caution zone," Audra announced, watching their readouts.

"Gonna miss four of them," Hayden remarked casually. "Weapons, coming up on your left. Helm, roll it right and they'll miss us!"

The *Constellation* shuddered with the nearby explosions from behind as Lynette tipped the ship on its side, allowing the remaining torpedoes to pass directly beneath them on their left. Doran struggled to track them as the corona flaring was scrambling all of the ships instruments. The ship bucked violently as the first torpedo was destroyed and shuddered again as a second disintegrated directly in front of them. Doran managed to get another shot off at the last two torpedoes, one erupting into a ball of flame. The final torpedo slammed into the melting pile encasing the *Athena*.

"Peel off! Peel off!" Audra called out, watching huge sections of debris flying directly back at them. Lynette gently tapped a control on her vast touch panel and pulled the *Constellation* away from the snarling ball of fire, keeping it in view. Now fully in the upper atmosphere, the surrounding sky became bright and blue.

Gunnar watched carefully, listening to the static crackling from his armrest com panel. The ball of fire began streaking a brilliant contrail behind it as gravity pulled it down through the super-high, scattered clouds of Kalamar. A moment before it disappeared into obscurity, Gunnar thought he could see a form emerging from the burning mass.

"Pip?" Gunnar edged at the science officer.

"A few shorts, sir," Pip responded, carefully working with his instruments. "The corona flaring has caused a scramble here."

"I've still got a primary object on my tracking screens," Doran reported.

"Helm, switch to infrared on the glass," Audra ordered. The outside windshield tinting changed color and the clouds outside instantly disappeared from view.

"There he is!" Gunnar exclaimed relieved. He slapped the sides of his chair, watching the *Athena* still plummeting. "Com, do you still have the General?"

"I have to reboot everything as well, sir. Give me a moment." Seconds later, Lana's communications console came alive with a flurry of noise and information streaking across her displays. "Kalamar Command has ordered the *Constellation* and the *Athena* to engage the Imperial bombers attacking the other shipyards."

"Now they start talking."

"Sir?" Lana turned to Gunnar.

"Colonel," Audra interjected. "We have to comply or risk losing more shipyards."

"As soon as the *Athena* is alongside this ship," Gunnar maintained. "Helm, get us closer. Weapons, standby your tractor hawser."

Audra rolled her eyes closed. This was reckless, plain and simple. With the other ships already deployed elsewhere, the *Constellation* was the only sure bet to stop Croft Hekla's Imperial ships attacking in orbit.

"The *Athena's* in range, sir," Doran announced, looking back for further instructions.

Gunnar unclamped from his chair and stepped forward between helm and weapons.

"Grab them mid-ship with the towing hawser. Helm, as soon as the weapons officer has ahold of them I want you to pass right over them and turn back for space."

Audra was out of her chair in an instant, as the rest of the bridge crew looked wide eyed at the Colonel.

"That maneuver will likely snap us both in half." Audra stopped behind Gunnar. "Even if he was under power it will probably pull something off. The tow hawser wasn't designed for that much stress."

"Alex?" Gunnar turned to the floating droid that had remained silent up till now.

"Theoretically, it is possible, but your margin for error is quite thin. It is not advisable."

"Helm, get us in there now," Gunnar ordered, passing a glance back at Audra. She shook her head angrily and stepped back to the engineering station to safety lock herself back into her seat.

"General Niker on the line, Colonel," Lana announced as Gunnar clamped himself back into his chair.

"Got those engines up yet?" Gunnar asked, touching the comlink panel.

"Almost there," Rick responded sounding frazzled. "I hate days like this."

"Don't worry," Gunnar assured him. "I won't tell anyone I'm about to pull your sorry butt out of a sling, yet again."

"Tractor hawser swing?"

"Yeah, we're needed up top. Hekla is messing with the other yards."

"I should be online by the time we're pointing up again."

"Make it quick, gonna grab you in two shakes."

Audra was furious, as this all sounded familiar. She had overheard Gunnar and Rick on many occasions boasting about the many dumb, reckless stunts they had done. Stunts even ace pilots would be leery of attempting under controlled conditions. There was hardly anything controlled about these conditions. What's more, they had been ordered to protect the shipyards. How was that going to happen falling from the sky? Gunnar turned to the weapons officer and nodded.

"You're running out of room fast, Lieutenant. Helm, you're gonna need all the power this bird can deliver. Just make your maneuvers back up as fluid as you can. Apply your power in the same fashion." Gunnar looked over at a fuming Audra. He was regretting not letting her in on some of his and Rick's past exploits, but at the time, it seemed the better part of valor to keep those things to himself.

"Can you at least get your anti-grav online?" Gunnar asked, turning back to his comlink with Rick.

"The yard structure sort of did some damage here. We're hanging onto the furniture with our fingernails right now."

"Here goes buddy," Gunnar announced, watching Doran activate the tractor hawser.

"I've got them," the weapons officer grunted. He motioned to Lynette to begin her pull out and then braced for what was sure to be a wild ride. "I'll adjust the length as you adjust your arc and power curve."

"Ground is coming up hard and fast, sir," Pip reported.

Gunnar tensed up a little as the tumbling *Athena* disappeared beneath them and Lynette continued to apply back pressure to her controls, holding a smooth, even arc to power increase ratio. There came a noticeable shudder to the ship, followed by an enormous jolt, activating several different alarms all around the bridge. Knowing Commander Atlanta was addressing those issues at engineering, Lynette and Doran focused on their assigned task. The bridge view outside jumped violently and suddenly yawed heavily, then it was as if they had been cut loose from an invisible trap trying to pull them down. A moment later, the *Athena* streaked ahead of their view, climbing fast, her Interceptors launching and throttling hard to engage an Imperial enemy that was sure to detect them as they powered back into orbit.

A collective sigh of relief wisped from the entire bridge crew of the *Constellation.* Lynette leaned back and passed a one handed knuckle bump behind the navigator to the weapons officer. Months of training had paid off here, but perhaps more importantly, it was their ability to work as an integrated team that enabled them to achieve such fluid results.

"All in a day's work," Lynette chuckled with glee.

"It's how we roll," Doran boasted.

"Well, that's gratitude for ya. No goodbye or so much as a thank you very much?" Gunnar relaxed a bit, leaning toward his comlink panel again.

"I feel certain you'll never let me forget about it," Rick responded. "I'll take the first yard we find not falling and you sweep around on the outside for the next one. That should give Hekla's boys something more to think about."

As the ride had now stabilized, Gunnar noticed Audra standing next to him and touched the control on his chair to mute his link with Rick. He looked up at her, knowing he had some explaining to do. Her expression indicated a controlled desire to put a stun gun to his neck, but only out of love would it be set to low.

"What about the shipyard wreckage, Colonel?" Audra inquired sternly. "There were a lot of good men and women manning it. We don't know if they all got to an escape pod, not to mention where did all that mess end up when it impacted? Shouldn't we be finding out, render whatever assistance we can?"

"Kalamar command gave us orders to protect the orbiting shipyards. Our job is out here in orbit," Gunnar responded carefully, trying to focus on the forming battle. "Command's job is down there on the ground. We're not doing anyone any good buzzing around over a big hole in the ground."

Audra's indignation cooled as she thought things through. Of course Gunnar was right. She knew he wasn't trying to sound callous about what had happened. As a fighter pilot and squadron leader you have to learn to focus on the job and not on the death surrounding you. To do so would be a death sentence for any warrior, ground based or in flight.

Audra turned back to her station at engineering. She sort of already knew where they needed to be and why, she was just looking for a better reason to be angry with him. Saving the *Athena* was the right thing to do, but in her mind, the method was reckless and dangerous. Gunnar had treated it like another one of his and Rick's careless stunts, like it was some sort of a game. It seemed to her they had little to no respect for life and the dangers associated with doing the crazy things they did. Even though she had come to terms with it while he and Rick had been fighter pilots, now it was different. In the cockpit, there is only you and you are in charge of just you. Yes, there are external consequences, but ultimately, it's just you. Being a little lucky and a lot reckless makes a good combination for a fighter pilot. But this ship was not a fighter and the bridge was not a cockpit. There wasn't just one person here. There was a crew of 15 individuals that a ship commander was responsible for and that responsibility had to be taken seriously.

As the ship rose from the atmosphere and began zeroing in on the closest Imperial ship to engage, Audra quietly summoned Alex 7001.

"Alex, when this battle is all said and done, can you help me run a ship wide diagnostic? Right down to the Asium assemblies, the arrays and the substructure?"

"Certainly, Commander. Are you looking for anything specific that might help narrow the diagnostic parameters?" The droid gently landed on the top of the engineering console, extending a tiny appendage into a small socket and began to make a purring sound.

"I just want to make sure we didn't do any damage on that last little maneuver."

"This ship was designed to take such stresses, Commander. The Colonel's methods may have been a little unorthodox and a bit brash, but they did produce the intended results. If he had not acted in such a manner, the *Athena* may well have crashed with the yard."

"I understand, but humor me all the same," Audra said, quietly watching a fray of fighters and bombers swarming in a chaotic tangle all around them.

*   *   *   *

The attack over Kalamar didn't last long. Croft's Imperial ships were no match for the might of the two Starbird class Corsairs. After several hours of lengthy ship scans and onboard diagnostics, the *Constellation* was ordered to proceed at light speed factor four to its first assignment. The *Athena* however, would have to wait a day or so as it had been ordered back for repairs to damage sustained during their escape from their falling shipyard.

A quick briefing in the command ready room, revealed their first assignment would take them to the Oneida Caldron, a class four Black hole. Kalamar Command had received several automated distress beacons from four Kendalon freighters carrying Starbird spare parts. Naturally, Command was anxious to make sure these freighters were secured. Once information and assignments had been given, the *Constellation's* command crew was dismissed, but Colonel Conrad and Commander Atlanta remained behind at the request of the ship's doctor, Fuji Yamoto. The doctor was going over Gunnar's medical records and had been doing some deeper research on the Dialabrons of Commenor. Her research had confirmed most of the grim facts that had already been made manifest about this odd, elusive race.

"It's rough trying to figure you out, Colonel," Fuji said, pulling out a small display from her bag.

"Meaning?" Audra asked, trying to follow.

"I'm a complicated man," Gunnar poked.

"There just isn't a whole lot of credible information published about your race, Colonel," Fuji continued.

"Yes, my kind don't like people snooping around our world," Gunnar responded. "We're sort of funny that way."

"Kalamar Command is fortunate to have Gunnar at all as few Dialabrons with mutations live through their metamorphosis."

Audra reached for Gunnar's hand and squeezed it gently. Fuji looked up from her display, looking at their hands and then at them, then back at their hands. Open affection in a command was a bit unusual.

"Uhm, yeah, and that sort of makes it difficult to get any information on you. That and your planet's government won't allow anyone from Royal Command to render any help to do anything about it. I did find out why you wear those glasses. You don't need them on Commenor, do you?"

Gunnar smiled and shook his head slightly.

"No, the atmospheric pressures there are far different than they are off world, does something to the eye and science just can't fix it. Implants aren't an option as nothing can be fitted to the design of my eye. At least no one has come up with one yet. No demand. The tint is to keep certain light wavelengths down as it causes some discomfort. They've never been a problem."

Fuji was busy taking notations for further study.

"Well, everything else I was able to find is stuff you've already told me. Mutations producing multiple organs in random children, with the second organ remaining dormant until around twenty years. The dormancy exit is exceptionally demanding on the Dialabron physiology. Most don't make it through. Skin tissue similar to human, muscle fiber and bone structures are a complete mystery, as is your blood work. You've got a real cocktail there. Can't get anything definitive from Commenor, but the scans I've run on you are almost off the chart. Your muscle fiber is vastly different than human and your bone structure is quite impressive. We'll just say you've never broken any bones. If you had the circulatory intensity, you could lift ten times what any human could. Run faster, longer and further. You certainly have the respiratory ability for it. The only thing holding you back is a single heart can't keep up. If you make it through this, which because of your age and Dialabron history, I'm extremely worried about, you'll do things we humans can only dream about."

"Sort of makes you want to be the one holding my hand, doesn't it?" Gunnar smiled, squeezing Audra's hand.

"I don't think you fully grasp the gravity of your situation, Colonel." Fuji became serious and a little irritated at how lightly Gunnar seemed to be treating this issue. "You should have had your dormancy exit fifteen to twenty years ago. Your age makes your chances of making it through alive, far less than someone who was supposed to go through this as a youth in the first place."

Gunnar sobered up a little trying not to dismiss Fuji's concerns. Still, he acted far less concerned than someone facing certain death ought to. Perhaps it was the fighter pilot mentality in him. Of course, Audra had been worried about this for a long time and certainly she was even more so now.

"I've searched through all my stores," Fuji continued. "Seems like there ought to be something that would work to hold your symptoms down until we can get our hands on some Furlitron, but what I have isn't going to do much. Be like putting a bandage on a compound fracture. How fast can we get to Commenor?"

"Is this an emergency?" Audra asked.

"In my opinion, yes."

"It's on our way to the Maylar system in the Topaz quadrant," Gunnar pointed out.

"It has to be a declared emergency for the record if we're to divert from a distress call and possible rescue," Audra informed them.

"If I'm to keep the Colonel upright and in the command chair, I am declaring this an emergency." Fuji got to her feet, grabbed her bag and started for the door. "You'll let your first officer and I know where we're supposed to find this Furlitron by the time we get there?"

"Uhm, yeah, 'bout that," Gunnar said, stopping her at the door. "No one has clearance from my government to land on the planet, except me."

"Sort of funny that way, huh? Can someone at least accompany you down?" Fuji asked. "I'd feel a whole lot better if one of us could tag along."

Gunnar shook his head slowly, thinking hard. Fuji turned a frustrated look. She had been naively led to believe things worked like a rigid mechanism in the military and the government. Nothing was following a set pattern or an established protocol here. By all rights, she should be insisting this ship redock and Gunnar be relieved of command, but she had her own career to consider. How would it look if her first assignment on one of the finest ships conceived, she had it run aground by removing its commander?

"I'll be in sickbay trying to concoct something to keep you going until we get there. In the meantime, please try to take it easy and get plenty of rest. Commander Atlanta, you'll help see to that?"

Audra nodded, folding her arms. The two command officers watched after the doctor as she disappeared out into the hallway. Gunnar stood up to leave, but Audra stopped him and he melted back to a chair next to her.

"Gunnar, I want to apologize…"

"Wait," he interrupted quietly. "I know what you're going to say, but I'd like to go first. Then we'll see if that changes what you have to apologize for."

Audra held her breath for an instant, not sure what she was supposed to do. Gunnar wasn't too big on apologies. She usually had to back him into a corner and spell it out.

"Ok," Audra hedged cautiously, searching his eyes.

"I truly appreciate how badly you wanted me to take this command, and don't get me wrong, I really want to be here."

"Oh boy…here it comes."

"No, before you get all tuned up, hear me out," Gunnar reassured her, taking both her hands. Audra drew in a careful breath and held it.

"I'm just trying to say you need to give me a little time to adjust here. You know I'm a fighter pilot, born and bred. It's what I do better than anything else, even after all this time. But I realize I'm getting older and while I still believe I can kick any of these younger hotshots into the next system without even turning on a targeting computer, I have to step aside and let others have a turn at it. This is a new chapter for me, for us and I really want to make it work. I think I can be just as good at being a ship's commander as I am a fighter pilot, I just need a little bit of time." Gunnar paused a moment, squeezing her hands gently. "And I'm going to need a lot of help from my first officer."

Audra thought she detected a little mist forming in the corner of his eyes, but his tinted glasses hid them well enough that she wasn't sure. She had been worried about him trying to make the transition from the cockpit to the command chair.

"As your executive officer," Audra started carefully. "It's my duty to assist you in every aspect of the operations of this ship. You've got to get your head out of the cockpit and keep it out. I'm sorry I questioned your maneuvers to save Rick and the *Athena*, but knowing what you're going to do before you do it would be helpful to me and give the crew confidence in us as a team."

"I should have told you more about some of the things Rick and I did together a long time ago, but I felt like..."

"I know," Audra cut in. "You were just considering me. I would have worried myself to death if you told me all the things you two did together."

"You have no idea."

"But I suspect even you and Rick thought those maneuvers were risky when you did them. This ship is not a fighter and you have others to think about now."

"I understand all that, and I will try to do better. I'm asking for your patience to help nurse-maid me through these difficulties."

Audra leaned forward and kissed him, Gunnar gladly returning the embrace.

"Commander Atlanta, to the bridge," Lana came over the ship wide com system. Audra reluctantly pulled back, resting her forehead on Gunnar's.

"I think I'm going to need a little patience here too."

Gunnar smiled, snaking his fingers through her dark brown hair.

"Come on, Commander, be tough for the crew."

"Pulling rank, are we?"

"Gotta keep this ship running."

"And while I'm checking on our freighters and exactly where they are, you will be doing what?"

"As little as possible."

"Doesn't exactly seem fair."

"I'm back in engineering with Mr. Moon and Cooper. Shake down inspections. Want to trade?"

"Uh, no. I think I'll pass." Audra got up and headed for the door. "Have fun, sweetheart," she said, trailing off toward the bridge.

Gunnar chuckled softly, understanding they were at a bit of a disadvantage here, as couples in command situations rarely worked out well. But he and Audra had already discussed this and were resolved to work together. He feared he would be the weak link, as she seemed to always have everything together.

My Happy Birthday

The planet Commenor sat at the outer most orbit in a tiny cluster of planets called the Mila system. Its sun, a blue giant star, made travel beyond Commenor to the inner planets impossible, as the sun's radiation emissions were too high. The solar storms the blue giant induced were so intense, the atmospheres of the inner planets had been torn away eons ago. Even the largest of fleet ships would be mortally wounded should one wander too close to the no man's zone a short distance outside the Orbit of Commenor.

After some lengthy discussions with the Commenor government, the *Constellation* was allowed to approach and establish a low level orbit around the oddly white shaded sphere. Gunnar and Audra tried repeatedly to negotiate at least two command personnel being allowed to teleport to the surface, but they were emphatically refused. Gunnar was the only one allowed to teleport down to his hometown, Dante. It appeared that even he was under some suspicion. Why would he need a body chemical that was supposed to be used for the youth of the planet undergoing a dormancy exit?

Materializing in the town center, Gunnar admired the smooth concrete sidewalk utilizing a crushed glass material that sparkled in the blue midday sunlight. He remembered standing here next to the town center fountain as a youth. The pavement, even the traffic signs and lights on the corners of the intersection were the same. While no mechanized vehicles were present, their existence was evident in the well-worn streets. He noticed a small shuttle craft passing overhead making a horrible noise. It sounded more like it utilized a rocket propelled engine rather than the usual Parch drive found in most shuttle craft.

Presently, a rumbling vehicle glided up next to him and four uniformed guards piled out, each bearing a weapon strapped to their forearm and helmets with dark shields pulled down in front of their faces. One motioned toward the open vehicle door, and Gunnar cautiously climbed in. Once situated inside, he sat directly across from a large bald gentleman about his same age. As the vehicle began to move, Gunnar pulled his service cap from his head and gestured to the man, who was holding a small scanning device out toward him.

"You look pretty silly in that colorful bath robe," Gunnar said.

"As you look rather ridiculous in that fancy service jacket and cap," the man responded. Satisfied with the results of the scan, he shut the device off. Gunnar looked at the emblem above the shiny black brim of his service cap.

"I gots to look good for the natives. I don't wear the hat much, only for formal ceremonies and special circumstances like this. The jacket ain't so bad. I kind of like it."

"Likewise for the robes," the man responded, trying to get untangled from them. "Easier to go to the bathroom."

"It's good to see you, Joanus. How are you?" Gunnar asked, chuckling.

"It's been a long time, Gunnar. I am well, but I never expected to ever see you again my good friend. Not in this life anyway. If your dormancy exit didn't get you, certainly your crazy piloting would have."

"You made it through your exit."

"I was lucky," Joanus replied smiling. "Sometimes I wished I hadn't. It can really do something to the brain. I liked the way I was before I had two stomachs. I understand your mutation gives you two hearts?"

"Yes, aren't I the lucky one?"

"How has it been for you off world, being Dialabron?" Jonas inquired.

"Thankfully, with exception of a few close people, no one has known."

"Still sealed to Audra?"

"Stronger than ever. Why would you doubt?"

"Your mentality puts you at odds with success as a couple."

"Well, she's a good woman and thankfully very even tempered when it comes to our differences in physiology."

Joanus let a hearty laugh go, glancing out at the empty city streets as their vehicle moved rapidly along.

"And children?"

"In the military? No, besides, our DNA don't mix. What's with all the negotiating tangle going on here? I understand we don't let everyone in all at once, but what you guys put us through just for some medication is a little overboard, isn't it?"

"We're under siege by Terrellian pirates."

"The Terrellians?" Gunnar repeated surprised. "We didn't see anything in orbit when we got here. Besides, you guys know how to deal with pirates."

"Not these. Their operatives have infiltrated our society here in this specific region. Have been for quite some time. We didn't even realize it until it was too late."

"Too late? What are you talking about? Too late?"

"I'm afraid I can't go into any more detail here as you don't have the proper clearance."

Gunnar fingered the Kalamarion emblem on his cap and the Colonel clusters on his sleeve cuffs. He knew Joanus could see the clusters on his high fold collar. How much more clearance did he require?

"Let's just say that Furlitron has become a scarce commodity anywhere on Commenor now."

"So why didn't you just hand me a bottle and send me on my way, or better yet, just give us the location and we could have teleported it up?" Gunnar noted their surroundings were changing to parts of Dante he didn't remember.

"Because the Terrellians are on the watch for it. No doubt we are being observed and pursued for its location. We have a safe facility where we can make the transfer and you can then return to your ship from the square."

"Since when did Furlitron become such a precious commodity? It's only practical use is aiding the DE of cultures on this planet."

"The Terrellians have found other unintended side effects when used on other races on other planets and the demand for it is so high they are willing to do whatever they have to, to get it."

"I had no idea," Gunnar wondered. "So how much is this going to cost me?"

"There is no cost to you. You're a Dialabron. Commenor is your home."

"Well, space is my home now."

"In any case, it would be wrong not to give it to you if it can save your life."

Presently, their vehicle was swallowed into the darkness of a narrow underground tunnel. Snaking downward, they slowed, following the lit passage into a small underground compound. As the vehicle came to a stop near a set of stone steps, the occupants were hustled out and up a dark cramped stairwell. Gunnar was starting to wonder why they had gone to all the trouble of taking him so far underground, only to bring him back to the surface. Had official sources of governmental control been so severely breached that Joanus had to resort to underground guerilla tactics to deliver the lifesaving Furlitron?

After several twists and turns, the dark narrow stairwell opened into a more finished, open underground complex bustling with people. Gunnar looked around constantly, trying to figure out what this place was and what all these people were doing here. After weaving through a labyrinth of hallways, Joanus stopped the group in front of a set of glass doors and pushed his hand onto a sensor pad. Once the doors started to open, he motioned the guards off and they melted into the crowd as Gunnar and Joanus stepped inside. He looked back outside at the doorway security system. High Tec for what he remembered when he lived here. Still, everything around him in the room seemed to be a long way behind what he was used to, living on other planets.

Stepping forward, they came to an outer desk checkpoint, where they were body scanned and hand checked for weapons. Gunnar had to remove his jacket and pull off his boots to be sure he was clean. The only thing he had brought with him was his pocket communicator.

"What's this all about, Joanus?" Gunnar asked, his irritation building. He felt a dull pain shoot down his left arm toward his hand as he pulled his boots back on.

"More precautions. My sincerest apologies my friend."

Joanus turned to a large door and had his hand scanned again, but this time he was required to speak his name and submit to a retinal scan. Once recognition was achieved, the thick door swung slowly open and the two entered another hallway lined with more doors. After passing a number of them, they stopped at one and knocked.

Gunnar felt all turned around. *This is like a maximum security unground complex and now they're knocking on doors to get in? Shouldn't whoever was on the other side be pounding on the doors to get out?* Joanus was about to knock again, when the door finally came open.

They were greeted by a nice looking young man in his early thirties, long blonde hair but well kept. He appeared genuinely glad to see them and immediately welcomed them inside. Motioning for them to sit down, he then turned to an adjoining room.

"Hey sis, we've got company. It's Joanus."

"It's about time," a voice grumbled from around the corner. "We've been locked up in here for weeks and I've just about had my fill of social..." A woman the same age as the young man emerged from around the corner and stopped short when she saw Gunnar pop to his feet. Joanus also came to his feet as the woman stumbled forward a bit. Much shorter than their two visitors, she was curvy with lovely brown hair curling down around her shoulders.

"Colonel Conrad," Joanus said, gesturing to the woman and young man. "May I introduce Tiana Mantose and her twin brother, Taron."

Taron greeted the Colonel, all the while, Gunnar noticing Tiana staring at him as she finally approached him with her hand held out. He carefully took it and gently kissed it.

"Pleased to meet you," he said looking back up at her. He took special notice of the glowing stones hanging from their necks and passed a glance over at Joanus for some kind of an explanation. As they all took a seat, Gunnar felt another angry twinge in his lower back. He understood his symptoms as he rubbed his aching left arm, but was in hopes Joanus would produce the Furlitron and he could just take a dose right away. These twins must be the guardians of Commenor's Furlitron stores.

"I am so sorry for your confinement," Joanus finally said leaning forward. "It's the only way to ensure your safety."

"Yes, we know all about that," Taron said, sitting forward as well. "What we want to know is what you're doing about it?"

Gunnar felt sweat starting to creep down his back while trying to remain patient with the conversation.

"We have your exit ready," Joanus replied. "If you and your sister will make yourself ready, you can leave immediately."

"It's about time. Where are we being taken this time?"

"Kalamar," Joanus responded. The big man carefully hedged a look over at Gunnar, who blinked largely, finding it difficult to follow anything being said as the pain in his lower back increased to almost intolerable levels.

"Joanus," Gunnar puffed. "I think I need to be in your infirmary, now." Gunnar wobbled sideways, then slumped forward into Tiana's arms.

Joanus cursed silently, helping Tiana lay him back on the couch, then pulled a communicator from his robes while Tiana cradled Gunnar's head in her lap. Presently, a small army of medical technicians were coming through the door.

"Furlitron," Joanus barked. "He needs Furlitron now. He has two hearts!"

"He's too old," a Tec objected.

"He's a *Shunt*, like me. Give it to him now!"

The head Med-Tec didn't hesitate, pulling a small hypo cartridge from a box, loading it into a pistol-like instrument and pressing it to the side of Gunnar's neck. The other Med-Tecs continued to work with several different probes watching for signs of improvement. Tiana carefully stroked his hair as the head Med-Tec removed Gunnar's glasses and looked into his eyes with yet another probe.

"I think he's gonna be all right," the Med-Tec announced with his eyes still glued to his instruments. "When did you find out he was going through his dormancy exit?"

"It's what he came here for," Joanus answered, motioning for Taron to gather their belongings.

"What's he doing in here then? He should be in the infirmary." The Med-Tec sounded angry, pulling his instruments out of the way as Gunnar began to blink his eyes, looking around.

"Oh crap," Gunnar grumbled, looking up into Tiana's admiring eyes.

"You passed out," she smiled. "They gave you some Furlitron. How are you feeling?"

"Like I've just flown through a concussion blast."

"Just lay still for a couple of minutes, Colonel," the Med-Tec cautioned him. "You let this one go a little too long, so it's going to take you longer than normal to recover. How long have you been going through these episodes?"

"Couple of weeks," Gunnar replied. "But none of them have ever been this bad. A little discomfort in the lower back and an ache down the left arm. I just sit or lay down for a couple of minutes and I'm good."

"I'll feel a whole lot better once we get him down to the infirmary and give him a thorough looking over."

"There isn't time," Joanus objected. "He needs to get back to his ship as soon as possible. He's on an emergency rescue assignment."

"Colonel, do you have a store of Furlitron aboard ship?" The Med-Tec was far more concerned with his patient than his assignment.

"No," Gunnar responded rising from Tiana's lap. "That would be why I've come." He looked at Joanus, bewildered.

"Let's get you down to the infirmary," the Med-Tec ordered, gathering up his equipment. Taron reappeared with a couple of small bags draped over both shoulders.

"There is no time for a visit to the infirmary," Joanus objected. "There are better med facilities onboard his ship. Let's get him the Furlitron he needs and get him back to his ship right away."

The Med-Tec opened his mouth to object, but stopped, reading the firm look on Joanus's face. He looked back down at Gunnar, who was looking better all the time.

"Colonel?"

"Yeah, I think I'm fine," Gunnar nodded, moving to get up. Tiana was quick to help him as everyone made their way out into the hallway.

As the group carefully made their way back through the complex and out into the main hallways, an uneasy feeling began to claw into Gunnar's mind. They had just picked up two extra people from a near maximum security facility where the Furlitron was supposedly housed and were now back in the minimum security area. As they turned into a large medical complex, Gunnar stepped a little closer to Joanus.

"Thought we weren't going to the infirmary?"

"Medical stores," Joanus responded. The Med-Tec disappeared through a set of doors, reappearing moments later with a large bottle of pastel blue colored liquid.

"Does your ship's medical officer know the proper dosage?"

"I think she can manage." Gunnar was glad to have the bottle in his hands and anxious to get back to his ship. He turned back to his friend.

"Thanks for all your help, Joanus. Can you get me back up to where I can get back to my ship?"

"Can't you teleport from here?"

The uneasy feeling in Gunnar's head now escalated into confusion and suspicion.

"Yes, I can...but I thought you said I had to do it at Dante's square? That was one of the conditions of my landing. Joanus, what's going on here? You don't look very good."

Joanus fidgeted nervously, finally pulling Gunnar away from the others.

"You need to get out of here now my friend." Joanus was near to panic, looking all around the room. "The Terrellians have breached this facility's security systems. No doubt there are operatives closing in on our position as we speak. You need to get back to your ship as soon as possible. Please take these two with you." Joanus motioned for Tiana and Taron to come closer. "Colonel Conrad will take you from here and get you to Kalamar where you'll be safe."

"Wait a second," Gunnar objected as Tiana and Taron stepped a little closer to him. "No one said anything about me taking on passengers. Joanus, who are these people? What's this all about?"

Joanus opened his mouth to speak, but was drowned out by an ear splitting shriek followed instantly by a skull cracking explosion that threw them against a far wall, structure wreckage and debris spilling on top of them. Everything went black as a secondary explosion followed.

Gunnar groaned and rolled over beneath a pile of rubble, his ears ringing savagely. He felt a hand holding onto his and could make out Tiana in the darkness next to him. Her backpack over her head had probably saved her life.

"Are you ok?" Gunnar grunted, listening to their surroundings for a secondary attack.

Tiana gulped a couple of times, then nodded.

"Yes, I think so. What happened?"

"I think the Terrellians are trying to get at Dante's store of Furlitron. Do you know where your brother is?"

"No idea. I can't move. My other arm is pinned and something is lying across the back of my legs…"

Gunnar suddenly put a finger to her lips. He could hear movement where the outer door used to be. Straining, he carefully looked out over the debris at several figures moving through the dimness. He could make out some type of tracking instruments and a weapon in their hands. As they moved closer, Gunnar formed what he thought was a wondrous plan. He was about to execute what was sure to be a big surprise for the Terrellians, but a tremendous hail of blaster and projectile gun fire erupted, keeping him pinned down as brilliant flashes of light and smoke filled the room. Now he counted himself fortunate they were still mostly buried beneath the rubble. Something fell through an opening in the debris covering him. He looked down next to his leg. Several glowing lights on the tiny round orb were blinking faster and faster. He reached down and pulled it close to his face.

"Not good!" he yelped, tossing the object back out as hard as his confinement would allow. A moment later, a brilliant flash and another explosion tore through the shambles of the room, then things became eerily quiet. Gunnar carefully poked his head back up and looked around. There was enough light streaming from the hallways to see there was no one standing. A body lay motionless right in front of him. He pulled a rifle from the lifeless form and checked the projectile weapon. His attention was drawn to what was left of the wall that had separated them from the Furlitron stores. The wall was mostly gone, but the rows of shelves filled with Furlitron bottles were still intact. Sitting up in the rubble, Gunnar looked around, carefully pointing his weapon at the bodies around them. None of this made any sense. Why would pirates be tossing grenades into a room they were trying to loot? Yes, the Furlitron canisters were tough, but why take the chance of damaging something valuable enough to risk heavy losses?

Pulling himself out of the debris, Gunnar set the rifle down between his legs and tried to lift the broken wall pieces off Tiana as she struggled to pull herself free. No sooner did she wiggle loose than she grabbed the rifle and started pumping shots between Gunnar's legs. Nearly dropping the wall pieces back on her, Gunnar turned in time to see two bodies fall in a heap behind him. He turned back to Tiana and helped her to her feet, taking the rifle from her and scanning the room again. Tiana carefully groped in the dim light for her brother, finally seeing him pop his head up and look around.

"Nice party," Taron coughed. "Mr. Joanus is lying on me. I can't move." He tried to push him off, but Joanus was a large man. Taron pushed away some of the debris and tried to worm free.

"Is he still alive?" Gunnar asked, looking both directions down the shattered hallway.

"I can't tell. I think he is."

"Let's get him out of there," Gunnar said, moving back to help Tiana free her brother from the rubble. "We need to get as far away from here as possible. If there are more pirates, and there usually are, they'll be coming here, I think." Gunnar scanned the destroyed room, trying to make sense of what was happening. "By the way," he said without looking up. "Thanks for taking those guys out. You're very good with a rifle. Where'd you learn to use one like that?"

"Boarding school," Tiana answered.

After some grunting and pulling, they had Joanus out in the hall and leaning against a wall. Moments later, several guard personnel appeared at the end of one of the hall, their weapons raised and coming at the four, shouting at the top of their lungs for them to disarm and get down on the ground. Complying quickly with the demands, the three dropped to their knees with their hands behind their heads. Before a thorough search could commence, the hallway erupted into hail of gunfire, projectiles filling the hall from the other end. Gunnar motioned for Tiana and Taron to move along the floor in the opposite direction. Passing guards dropping to the floor, Gunnar glanced back as more pirates advanced on their position. Some were kneeling and firing, others advancing toward the broken Furlitron room. To Gunnar's surprise, they didn't give the medical stores any notice, but kept advancing on them.

Grabbing a rifle, Gunnar returned fire as they continued to back up along the floor toward a corner. He looked back at Joanus, still lying unconscious against the wall as their assailants completely ignored him and the storeroom. Gunnar reached for his communicator that had suddenly come alive as Taron helped pull Tiana around a corner.

"Are you about done down there, Colonel?" Audra's voice sounded elevated.

"Yeah, you could say that. They always throw me a big party whenever I come home. Sounds like you're having one of your own," Gunnar responded, popping off a couple of blind shots around the corner. He could hear warning alarms sounding off in the background of the transmission as he pulled himself around to the relative safety of the corner next to Tiana and Taron.

"Didn't want you having all the fun," Audra replied. "Four Terrellian gunships and they don't seem to be too afraid of what we can do to them."

"You gonna be able to take care of it, Commander?"

"Sure, but any chance you could wrap it up down there any time soon?"

"I think I can arrange that. Are you good to teleport me out of here?" Gunnar peered around the corner again. The pirates had completely ignored the store room and were totally focused on him now. What did he do? He had nothing and no one knew he was coming except for Joanus. They must be after his ship. It was the only explanation.

"Say the word."

Gunnar emptied his projectile magazine in the pirate's direction then dropped the rifle and got to his feet. He took a step into the middle of the safe hallway just as a hail of gunfire slammed against the corner where he had been sitting.

"Colonel," Tiana called, holding tightly to her brother. "It's us they're after," she admitted. "Please, I'm begging you. Take us with you or we're dead."

Gunnar covered his head as a spray of debris from a nearby wall strike peppered him. He looked down at the Mantose twins, then back around the corner at the advancing pirates. Ok, so this made a little more sense, but now was not the time for explanations.

"Three to teleport," he called over the noise, pulling Tiana to her feet. Taron was right with her as Gunnar hastily maneuvered them into position.

"Three?" Audra repeated. "Why am I not surprised?"

"Just get us out of here!"

Moments later, the hallway began to crackle and pop, the figures of the three sparkling out of existence.

Gunnar didn't even finish materializing when the ship shuddered violently. He glanced at the engineering tech as he steadied himself while helping Tiana and Taron from the teleporter transmission pads.

"Get Doctor Yamoto in here to check these two out on the double. You two stay put." Gunnar bolted from the room, dashing down the hall toward the bridge.

"When did these guys show up?" he asked, hurrying through the bridge door. Audra was out of his chair in an instant.

"Shortly after you teleported to Dante. Abrams and Dalley are handling the gunships well enough and Hayden is giving them something to think about if they get too close. That's not what's disconcerting."

"Torpedoes!" Pip announced.

"Nuts! From where?" Gunnar asked, scanning the displays in front of the science officer.

"They brought a couple of Delta class destroyers, converging from the poles." Audra informed him while looking at the tracking returns. "What did you do to piss them off so much?"

"Don't know what you mean. I'm the nicest guy you'd ever want to meet."

Gunnar could barely figure this whole mess out. The Terrellians weren't after the Furlitron at all, nor were they after him or his ship. Joanus had tricked him into taking the Mantose twins, but what did the Terrellians want with twins?

A long series of blasts shook the ship, followed by a big quake that knocked everyone off balance. Instantly, a burly long craft bolted past the bridge and ahead of them followed closely by one of the Interceptors. The Terrellian gunships and the Interceptors were evenly matched in firepower, but the Interceptor had the edge in maneuverability and shield power. Captain Dalley continued to pound the gunship's rear deflector shield as the Terrellian ship weaved madly, trying to escape its pursuer.

"We ready to leave?" Gunnar watched the tracking returns on the inbound torpedoes.

"Not a good idea to jump to light speed with torpedoes tailing you," Audra said.

"Then let's take care of that problem." Gunnar turned forward and was about to call out orders, but caught himself. He turned back to Audra and folded his arms.

"Commander Atlanta has the con."

Audra hesitated a bit, knowing what Gunnar had in mind. This would be her first time ordering combat tactics on larger hostile ships. Gunnar could read her hesitation and popped a confident grin.

"Remember me telling you about the mission Rick and I flew over Tallus Nine?"

Audra nodded nervously.

"Use your imagination."

"Torpedoes inbound, contact in twenty seconds," Pip announced excitedly. The *Constellation's* shields could handle a hit or two from Terrellian torpedoes, more than that and things could get complicated. Audra cracked a grin and turned forward.

"Helm, come about at thirty-two mark nine zero point one five, one quarter sub-light. Weapons, quad spread on the pulsar cannons." Audra touched a com control on the armrest of the command chair. "Turret, target any homing targets that get through our pulsar patterns. Weapons, standby to fire four Pin missiles each as we pass between them, aim for their launchers."

Gunnar raised an eyebrow moving to the engineer's chair. *Bold move to take on two destroyers at once. Exactly what I would have done.*

"Deploy the chaff pods," she barked, carefully melting into the command chair. The ship jolted several times and another gunship streaked ahead of them followed closely by an Interceptor. Doran directed his guns at the fleeing gunship as well, careful to avoid hitting the Interceptor.

"Gonna need some help back here," Hayden called from the turret.

"Weapons," Audra spoke up.

The weapons officer activated several automated guns located on the aft section of the ship. Lynette eyed her controls carefully, looking out at the two cigar shaped ships converging on them. She had timed it so they would pass between the destroyers just as they would turn to engage the Starbird head on.

"Two gonna get through," Doran announced.

Lynette glanced at her displays, twisting the control yoke, tilting the ship slightly. The *Constellation* shuddered again as a couple of torpedoes bounced along the underside of the ship's shields on one side. Once ahead of them, the deadly tracking torpedoes split and made a wide arc away from the Starbird in opposite directions, trying to reacquire their target. Lynette took note of the torpedoes as they streaked away.

Gunnar kept a close eye on the shield generators as they started taking hits from the destroyers, who were making their turns to come into close quarters. The shield arrays were quite effective at absorbing light blasts, but direct projectile strikes presented different challenges. He struggled to remain quiet as the two enemy ships finished their turns, moving to pass the Starbird on either side and rake them with their powerful Snuff cannons and missiles. The ship began to buffet as the Terrellians opened up with all weapons.

"Weapons, pin missiles," Audra barked as they approached.

Doran casually touched a control and a blast of pencil thin flashes streaked from either side of the bridge pod almost instantly piercing through the destroyer's shield defenses and slamming into their armed torpedo launching ports. With active torpedoes ready to launch, the ensuing explosions produced brilliant balls of primary and secondary blast flashes obscuring the dimming bridge windows.

Gunnar nervously twiddled his fingers, watching everything play out.

"Torpedoes," he mumbled. "Finish them, use those MKVs."

"Three quarters sub-light," Audra ordered. "Helm, pull us up and out."

Audra and Gunnar glanced up at the aft viewer at the same time, watching two objects on either side of the Terrellian ships streak right at them. Torpedoes intended for the Starbird, slammed into the outside of the two destroyers. No sooner did Lynette pull back on her controls and move the throttles ahead, than the *Constellation* was rocked by a violent concussion. Gunnar looked again as the explosion flares faded. Both destroyers had been nearly broken in two. Twice the size of the Starbird, they would be lucky if they survived to maintain any kind of an orbit and if they did, it was doubtful they could ever maneuver away from Commenor to try and get home. No, these two ships were doomed, the *Constellation* barely receiving a scratch.

As Lynette guided her ship out into open space, she took note of their Interceptors finishing off the remaining gunships and turning to follow. She relaxed a bit, preparing to take up their previous course into the Maylar quadrant. Doran leaned back, reaching behind the navigator to give Lynette another knuckle bump.

"Nice work," Audra announced, getting to her feet and taking a couple of steps forward. "Call the Interceptors back and let's get going. Helm, as soon as they're secure aboard, take us to light speed." She passed a glance back at the rear viewer with profound satisfaction. Smiling, she felt proud of her victory, but then thoughts of those crews and what fate awaited them, quickly sobered her.

"Don't dwell on it," Gunnar said quietly from behind. "This is what war is all about and that could have easily been us back there and we would have to deal with the situation, except they probably would have finished us off." He put his hand on her shoulder. Audra instantly reacted, putting her hand on his. Of course he was right again and she understood it, but she had never experienced battle on this scale before. "Congratulations, Commander. Well done. I might have done things a tiny bit different, thought it through a little better."

"Oh really? You? Think something through?" Audra grinned broadly, dropping her hands to her hips. "So would you like to let me in on what created all this ruckus to begin with?"

"Sure, as soon as I know myself. I suspect our answers are down in sickbay going through decon. Probably be a couple of hours before they're finished getting checked out." Gunnar turned and sat down. "In the meantime, I need to know how much damage you did to my ship. Can you have it to me before we jump to light speed?"

"I think I can handle that, sir," Audra said, turning for the engineering station.

"Navigator, estimated time to the Oneida Caldron once we get under way?"

"Approximately twelve hours, sir."

"Impressive machine," Gunnar muttered, sitting back to relax.

*   *   *   *

The commanding officer's quarters were quiet and dark. The desk comlink lights silently winked amid the bedroom light filtering through the dark Lexan doors into the front living room. Sitting on the bed, Gunnar and Audra were playing a card game. It was a game of speed to discard all your cards in a pile before your opponent could. So far, the point spread in this particular game was running even, but Audra was discarding cards at an alarming rate giving Gunnar cause to fumble constantly through his deck.

"Come on mamma!" He barked like a well-seasoned gambler. "Daddy needs a new pair of shoes!"

Audra kept on, Gunnar continuing to fidget.

"Come on sweetheart, put something down I can use".

"I do and you might win," she countered, dropping more cards without looking up.

"Isn't that the whole idea of the game? Ah-Ha! I see, you're holding back," he accused her.

A smile melted into Audra's expression.

"You know once I get started, I'll go out before you do," Gunnar said.

Audra's smile turned to a grin.

"That medicine you've been taking hasn't been messing up your brain after all."

"Oh man!" he blurted dismayed.

Audra continued to slap down more cards until he finally caught an opening.

"Ha!" he yelped. He moved to discard his final card, when Audra threw her last one. She looked slowly up at him with a big cheesy grin. "OOOHHH," he hissed narrowing his eyes. "There is great evil behind those lovely brown eyes." He held his card over the pile, then finally dropped it. "And I love every bit of you."

Audra let out a surprised yelp as Gunnar lunged onto her, slathering her with affection, which she gladly returned. Finally, after a lengthy game of wrestling on the bed, they both fell into one another's arms.

"Have you ever been around someone and had the distinct feeling that you could have had a life with them?" Audra puffed, settling down from their tussle.

Gunnar picked up his shaded glasses from the bed stand and put them on.

"Yea, sure, when I'm with you." He silently congratulated himself for having the right answer.

"No I mean with someone else, besides me." She snuggled in next to him.

"Now what's brought this on?"

"Just answer the question."

Gunnar thought a moment after looking long into her soft brown eyes.

"Ok, yes I have, but only on a couple of occasions," he admitted.

"Who?"

"Who? That's not generally something you want to discuss with your wife. Have you ever felt that way about anyone else besides me?"

"Come on," she nudged. "I asked first. It's not like it's gonna happen, it's just one of those feelings you get when you're around a certain person."

Gunnar looked up at the stars through the overhead window.

"Ok, Melinda Martin on Challis Nine, and..." he hesitated.

"Are you even being serious? Really? She's not even your type!"

"Oh, I have a type now?" Gunnar chuckled softly. "First I have a kind and now I have a type. Just for that, I'm not giving you the other one."

"Come on, who?" she asked, after a long moment of silence. He looked over at her, then back up and out at the star field.

"Lynette Starman."

"Our own Lieutenant Starman? The one at the helm right now? She's kind of young. Don't you feel a little creepy about that? I figured it would have been Fuji for sure."

"I like her hair. She has that cute sausage curl thing happening on top of her head."

Audra just stared at Gunnar.

"You're serious. Does she know about this?"

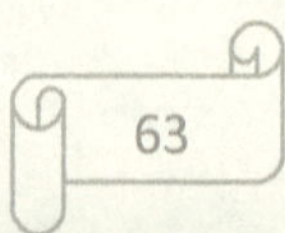

"Oh yea, I wrote her a love note," he teased good-naturedly. "Fuji goes without saying for every man on this ship, but somehow I don't think marriage is what they have in mind when they think of her," Gunnar stated coolly, "Now, how about you, missy?"

"Starman…" she repeated softly. "Never would have figured that one."

"Oh come on. It's not that bizarre. So let's hear your weirdness."

"Well, let's see. There's Rick's cousin, Dakota, oh, and Captain Dalley, and what about those Korack boys on the *Athena*? I always like going after them flyboys. So cute in their little flight jackets."

"At least you've got some good taste."

"Married you didn't I?"

"Say, what's with this strange line of questioning anyway?"

Audra shook her head slightly as she too gazed out at the stars.

"Nothing really. Just a strange feeling you get every so often."

The two lay quiet for several moments.

"Happy birthday," Audra smiled looking over at him.

"Some birthday," Gunnar responded sitting up after a moment of silence. "Attacked first thing this morning before we even launched. Saved Rick's bacon, then got bobbed again for our two new passengers in the back and now we're blasting toward the Oneida to haul someone's careless backside out of a mess. What more could a guy ask for on his birthday?"

"Love me?" Audra asked, sitting up as well.

"You know I do," he answered, helping her clean up the cards.

"A girl likes to hear it said to her you know. Now kiss me you fool." She jumped across the bed, spilling the cards and landing a big kiss on him. The two held one another for several more moments, and then continued to clean up.

"Ok, now I've got one for you," he said, handing her a stack of cards.

"Fire away."

"If I finally bought the big one, for one reason or another, would you marry again?"

"Boy, that's a loaded one." Her tone was solemn as she put the cards away. "That's a doozy," she admitted. "I don't even want to think about that one."

"Oh, come on." He walked around the bed to her side.

"Would you want me to? I am still youngish, lots of life left in me." Audra smiled broadly, popping her eyebrows in a teasing look.

"Well," he fidgeted nervously. "Yea, to the right guy, I guess."

"The right guy?" she repeated smiling sarcastically. The expression on Gunnar's face changed.

"Well, yeah, the right guy."

"The right guy."

"Well, I wouldn't want you to go out and marry just any schmuck that should happen to fly by and wink ya know."

"Well that's a relief." Audra's expression turned somber, leaving him to wonder if she wasn't tearing up or something. He didn't want to retract the question as he thought it only fair he get an answer.

"Gunnar," she finally stuttered. "I - I'm not prepared to answer that."

Gunnar picked up his uniform jacket and shoved an arm down a sleeve.

"Was it unfair of me to ask?"

Audra stepped over to a window.

"No, not unfair, not at all. Just…," she hesitated, looking for the right words. "It's just that it's taken me a long time to get used to being married in the military. Can't tell you how grateful I am Kalamar Command offered you this command. A bit unorthodox as you and Rick were commissioned through a different branch of the service. Even though the war is over, the thought of you still flying fighters right now, scares the life outa me. I guess I'm getting older, right? I know that's what you and your friends love the most, but I thought I'd lost you for sure the last time you and Rick were assigned sorties in Imperial territory. When you didn't come back and didn't come and didn't come… The worry and the wait were almost more than I could stand. Now the war is over and I've gotten you safely out from behind the stick and into a command chair, and I want to keep you there until we retire."

Audra felt warm arms slide around her waist and she turned around, putting her arms around his neck.

"You are mine," she spoke softly, "and I am yours, and together we are one. I love you more than anything, I always will." She kissed him with all the emotion she was feeling. Gunnar too, felt the electricity of the moment and returned her embrace with the same intensity. Finally, he looked down into her big brown eyes. Even after the many years they had been mated, he still got excited holding her.

"You are truly amazing," he spoke softly.

"It's true," Audra smiled, as the comlink sounded. Gunnar reluctantly broke from the embrace, turned and activated the communicator.

"Conrad here."

"Sensors are picking up some early data returns, sir. It could be our freighters," came the cool announcement from the communications officer.

"I'll be right in." Gunnar turned back to his wife, who was now busily engaged in making herself presentable as the executive officer. "Guess it's time to start pulling rank again."

"Sometimes," Audra started, heading through the sliding Lexan doors with Gunnar at her side, "I really hate being first officer or in the military for that matter."

Exiting their quarters, they turned up the hall toward the bridge.

"Rather be on Commenor with two kids in a big house, waiting for my shore leave?" They slowed on approach to the bridge door and Audra stopped, letting out a sigh.

"Just wished we had more time."

They looked at each other, and then both straightened up to enter.

"Hey," Gunnar whispered, looking over at her again.

She looked back up at his smiling face. She thought she detected a wink from behind his tinted glasses.

"Always," he choked out barely audible, and then activated the door.

"Status," Audra ordered, directing her attention at Captain Dakota Abrams.

"All ship's functions normal. Light speed cruise at factor four. ETA to Caldron zone, one hour, forty minutes. She drives like a dream, Ma'am." The Captain vacated the command chair and stepped to the back of the bridge.

Instead of taking his seat, Gunnar veered to the science officer's station and looked down at one of the many large panels angled along the entire console system of the bridge. The science officer looked up from his scanners.

"Calling it a zone now, are we? "Gunnar finally spoke up. "Report."

"Getting some wild fluctuations on both Dyno-scanners. I've got a couple of the freighters, I think. I'm only getting partial echoes though, nothing determinate." Pip carefully made a couple of calculations and checked the screens in front of him again.

"What a surprise. What can you determine?" Gunnar glanced over at several other monitors at the science station. "Tell me why I'm here."

Pip swiveled his chair to face his commander.

"At first it looked like they had broken up or experienced some kind of catastrophic explosion. But the closer we get, the ships appear to be phasing. The energy fluxes are registering off all my scales, in both directions."

"Phasing? Come on, let's see how well you know your black hole theory, and use simple terms. No fair trying to BS me with techno-babble."

Pip returned his attention to the information in front of him.

"Well," the science officer continued, adjusting several controls to the side of his monitors, "Normally, black holes remain constant in what they're doing by our space-time standards. You know, the whole, pull everything around it into its density's center, leaving next to nothing around its space fabric. Get too close and you start phasing your own space-time fabric." Pip paused a moment looking at his readings again.

"So, phasing freighter returns?"

"Like I said, indeterminate. At this distance, even debris is hard to identify."

Gunnar looked out at the stars while twiddling his thumbs behind his back. Checking the ship's chronometer, he turned to the command chair as Audra stepped next to him.

"We should be able to at least hear their beacons, even if they got caught in a fabric bend," Audra pointed out in a low-keyed voice.

Gunnar looked back over at the science station, then across at Captain Abrams at the engineering station.

"Sure don't like the sound of it," he said quietly. "Kendalons know better than to get close to the Oneida. Even at that, their ships have more than enough horse power to run through the middle of a fabric bend. Just hit the Light speed throttle and get the heck out of there."

Gunnar scanned the entire bridge crew, watching as they performed their assigned duties. Audra took notice and leaned a little closer.

"Everything all right?"

"How is it they all look a little young."

"You picked them all out and you're just noticing this? Besides, at our age, everyone looks a little young." The comlink on the armrest sounded off and Audra poked her finger at the control. "This is Atlanta."

"Is the Colonel available?" the ship's nurse inquired. "We've finished our examinations on the Mantose twins and have assigned them crew quarters 14B. They're asking for him, well one of them is anyway."

Audra's eyes swung up to Gunnar. His expression indicated he didn't want to be bothered with this.

"He'll be right down," Audra responded, touching the control again.

"I wish I could dump those two off somewhere." He gave out a heavy sigh. "The last thing we need right now is them getting in the way. I've got a bad feeling about all of that business."

"Nothing is going to feel right until they're somewhere else, and until we're finished out here, we're stuck with them," Audra said.

"Doesn't mean I have to like it," he said, rubbing his left arm.

"Want me to come along?"

"No. Need my best officer here in case there's more fighting to be done. You have the con."

He turned for the bridge exit. Audra looked after him a little concerned. He looked as though he might be favoring his arm, a sign of another pulmonary episode, but as he approached the door, he dropped his hand.

*   *   *   *

Walking toward the crew's quarters, Gunnar pulled at his left arm again, feeling a sudden spike of pain streak through his shoulder and down his back. Changing course toward sickbay, he veered to the wall with an expression of pain rippling across his face.

"Oh come on," he complained, pain shooting up into his chest. "You pick the stupidest times for this," he panted, trying to rub the discomfort out of his lower back. Seeing he wasn't going to make it to Fuji's office, he struggled to reach a wall comlink. "Sick bay," he gasped. An eternity of silence crawled slowly by before the familiar voice of the ship's chief medical officer came on.

"Yes, Colonel, what is it?"

Gunnar struggled to remain on his feet as the pain spiked.

"Need a little help here, Yamoto," he gasped, his legs giving way. "Alfa hall." He barely heard the medical officer acknowledge as he slid down the wall, finally plopping to the floor. The pain in his back felt like something was trying to escape. Drifting in and out of consciousness, he saw his demise in his mind. He was in the cockpit of a fighter, going down in a flaming blaze of glory into the bridge or the main thruster pods of an Imperial capital ship. No, he was sitting in the hallway of his own ship, clutching his chest and back. He was probably drooling down the front of his uniform. Just so long as no one saw him this way. Regaining some sense of reality, he cracked an eye trying to make sure he was alone, but noticed a form moving quickly toward him from the medical doors.

It took Fuji only a few moments to reach him, and in an instant had an injection hypo to his shoulder. As the pain began to ease somewhat, Gunnar grabbed at the hall rail and slowly pulled himself back to his feet.

"Take it easy, sir," Fuji instructed, helping him.

"We've got to stop meeting like this, Yamoto." He wrung out a smile. "The crew will start to talk. How many more of these stupid injections is it gonna take?"

Fuji focused on replacing the empty hypo into a small black pouch on her hip.

"You tell me, mutations in a Dialabron are difficult to guestimate." She held an analyzer up to Gunnar's chest and studied the readouts. "I'd love to give you your own med-hypo so I didn't have to come running every time you start to have an episode, but they don't make a personal transfer streamer that will penetrate your skin. It'll be a moot point as soon as your second heart comes out of dormancy. I don't suppose I can talk you into another examination. At least more rest?"

"I'm already resting more than my job is supposed to allow." The look Gunnar was giving her told Fuji exactly how far she was going to get with her suggestions.

"Ok, Colonel. Please try not to overdo it."

Gunnar gave the gorgeous medical officer a quick side glance, and then gingerly started down the hall again. Stopping at one of the many doors, he pulled a small gadget from his belt and pressed it to a metallic pad next to the door. As he pressed a series of colored buttons on the box, the door suddenly popped open. Stepping inside, he looked at his two unlikely passengers. Taron was playing some kind of a game on a small handheld device, while Tiana was creating music from a set of tiny holographic generators stuck on her fingertips. Gunnar took a couple of steps into the room to find a seat.

"So, would either of you like to explain to me why I have you here?" He took special note of the glowing stones on chains around their necks. They were rather large to be just ornamental necklaces and males generally didn't adorn themselves with such things. Bracelets and necklaces were for the females. The only time he had ever seen men wearing such jewelry was when he encountered pirates. Such things were too cumbersome and certainly not allowed in the military. He wore a wedding ring and that was it.

"Protection," Taron finally blurted out. "We've been in protective custody for the past four months, bounced around from one maximum security facility to another. Joanus promised to get us to Kalamar, but the Terrellians had blockaded Commenor and he didn't have anything that could breach their blockade or outrun them."

"Ok, let's pull back a little further. Why were you in protective custody? What did you two do?" he asked looking over at Tiana.

"We haven't done anything. Our father is Caidin Mantose," Tiana replied.

Gunnar sat patiently waiting for someone to continue. It seemed to him they thought he already knew who Caidin was. The blank look on his face told the twins otherwise.

"Mantose surgical instruments?" Taron probed, trying to help Gunnar with recognition. "Toberrian synthetic parts growth systems? The Thulport holographic analyzer?"

Gunnar was having a hard time recognizing any of this as he usually had little to do with anything medical related because of his own physiology.

"These are all medical related items. Were your parents medical people?"

Exasperated, Tiana drew in a deep breath, but a glance and raised finger from Taron kept her quiet.

"Our father was one of the wealthiest commodities brokers for interstellar medical supplies in the Topaz. He had a hand in these tool's development, marketing and distribution. Your ship has the latest version of the Thulport holographic imaging system. Your doctor used it on both of us when we were being checked out."

"Ok," Gunnar responded, feeling reprimanded. "Do I owe a bill on it or something? What's that got to do with you two in protective custody? Dad should be able to afford his own security to take care of business."

"They're both gone," Taron came back. His voice wasn't combative, though the look on Tiana's face would indicate if it were her speaking, it certainly would be.

"We lost our mother when we were born. Our father was gone a lot, but remarried and our stepmother raised us. She was nice enough until the contents of our father's will were revealed."

"You'd be surprised what greed will do to a person," Tiana piped, becoming angry about what their stepmother had turned into.

"Surely your father didn't cut her out of the will?" Gunnar sat up. He hated drama of this sort. *Why can't people just be civil and happy with what they have?*

"Not entirely," Taron responded. "The Mantose fortune is quite substantial, but not in monetary assets, though if you were to sell it all off, you'd still end up with a sizable amount. It's the holdings in all the different companies. Each company holds several patents that produce vast royalties. That's where the fortune is produced. Our stepmother holds the controlling interest in everything right now. It's part of the will decree."

"Then your father is dead?"

"Missing," Tiana corrected him. "He was lost in a meteor shower in the Mira system about twenty-five years ago."

"That's practically on top of where we're going," Gunnar noted. "But I gotta tell ya, if it's been that long since he's been seen, it's a pretty good bet he's dead. The Mira system lies in the Oota asteroid belt's path. Conditions there can be unpredictably wicked. That belt is constantly moving and throwing junk all over the place. Nothing stands still there."

"No, he's missing," Tiana reaffirmed, refusing to believe her father was gone. The expression she held told Gunnar that trying to explain sense to her was pointless.

"No one has ever found any evidence of wreckage, nothing," Taron confirmed Tiana's attitude about their father.

"So what now, your stepmother decided she wants it all?"

"We've both lived privileged lives, thanks to a mandated stipend provided from a trust created by our father in the event of his demise."

"He's not dead," Tiana grumbled.

"Tiana," Taron scolded his older sister.

"When we were either married or reached our thirtieth birthday, we inherit the entire Mantose fortune. But if something were to happen to us, our stepmother gets it all."

"So are you telling me she hired the Terrellians to take you out before your birthday?"

"Can you think of any better assassins than the Terrellians? I can't understand what she's complaining about. The stipend our father set up for her in any event was twice what we were getting."

"That must be a pretty sizable price she offered them to take you out for them to try and take on a Kalamarion ship." Gunnar cracked a smile. "Bit off way more than they could chew attacking a Starbird."

"We escaped to Commenor where Joanus offered to help keep us safe, but when Nora hired the Terrellians..."

"There was no way he could protect you for an extended period of time."

"Hence tricking you into the Dante facility and getting us out. He made arrangements with your Kalamar high command to come and get us, but it was taking too long and..."

"I just happened by for some medicine," Gunnar finished putting everything together. He was a little put out that he hadn't been apprised of the situation before hand by Kalamar Command, it was his home planet after all.

Now, his only wish was to avoid trouble for himself and his ship and that meant getting these two into protective custody elsewhere as soon as possible. He looked at them for a moment, then down at the floor, letting out a soft sigh. Tiana could sense his uneasiness and cleared her throat. Gunnar looked back up.

"Well, now what am I supposed to do? Can't take you back to Commenor, not until my assignment out here is finished anyway. Besides, if I know the Terrellians, they'll be back. Can't teleport you down to any planets due to an acute lack of planets in the general vicinity. Besides, my teleporter is offline thanks to your Terrellian friends."

"I guess you're stuck with us for a while." Tiana smiled at him, changing her demeanor. "We've been held up in that secure room for quite some time. It would sure be nice to get out, even for a little while. Care to show me, I mean, us around your ship?" she asked smiling.

Gunnar stared at them, trying to figure out why he felt so uncomfortable about having them onboard. Audra had just decimated two Terrellian destroyers and it wasn't like these two were going to break something. Still, he couldn't shake his uneasiness.

"I'm afraid you'll need to remain in here for a while yet," he finally said shaking his head. "I can't afford you getting in the way right now. Once our assignment is completed out here, you'll be free to move around the ship, as long as you don't get in the way. A Starbird isn't a particularly big ship, so the grand tour takes all of about ten minutes. I'll have someone look in on you every so often until Kalamar Command and I can figure out what to do with you. In the meantime, you should be quite comfortable in here. You're welcome to use the Hallavertor. Do you need someone to show you how this thing works?"

Taron rolled his eyes and stepped to the Hallavertor control on the wall, touched the screen and pointed at the manufacturer's logo on the startup screen. *Mantose Holographic industries.*

"I think we can figure it out."

Gunnar gave the logo a double take and looked at the twins who were eyeing him impatiently. Standing up and starting for the door, his curiosity about the strange glowing stones about their necks held him back. He turned back around and came face to face with Tiana. A lump caught in his throat, as she appeared to soften from her stern demeanor.

"I do hope you'll be able to take a little time out of your busy schedule to look in on us," Tiana said.

Gunnar stuttered for a moment, trying to change the subject.

"So, what's with the rocks you've got chained around your necks there? Never seen the likes of those things anywhere, not on Commenor anyway. Looks like some kind of servo stone or something. It's not one of those mood rocks is it?"

"It's a Chyropaz." She looked down at the glowing stone resting at the top of her cleavage. "Surely you've heard of them before?"

Shaking his head, Gunnar didn't mind looking a little closer.

"Well," she started, reading his expression and arching her back a little. "They act as a guide by showing images of what has or can happen. Here," she held the stone out for Gunnar to have a closer look. "See if you can see anything."

Gunnar gave Tiana an uneasy look and glanced nervously over at Taron, then looked closely at the stone. Surprised, he could actually see images materializing. Together, they watched for several seconds. Stunned, Gunnar suddenly backed away.

"If you need anything, just let the medical people know." He turned for the door and locked it as he left.

"Just what are you trying to do, sis?" he asked furious. "Get us set adrift in a life pod or teleported onto an asteroid?" It was going to be hard enough to convince this officer they shouldn't just be shot off into space, and Tiana's behavior wasn't helping their cause.

"Just trying to show him what our father's stones do."

"By sticking your boobs in his face?"

"I wasn't sticking my boobs in his face, just...helping him get a better look... at the stone."

"Right, that's what you were doing. Glad you cleared that all up. I was confused. So what was it all about? What did he see?"

Tiana turned spellbound by the scene she and Colonel Conrad had witnessed in the Chyropaz.

"We were kissing at a wedding."

The Caldron Zone

Audra vacated the command chair as Gunnar entered the bridge.

"Twins. Why do I get stuck with all the hard luck cases?" He mumbled in dismay.

"What are you talking about? It's the first time you've ever been saddled with extra cargo. Besides, what's so strange about twins? We have three sets between this ship and Rick's."

"Navigator," Gunnar directed his attention forward. "How much longer until we cut back to sub light?"

"Thirty-three minutes, sir," Nigel responded.

"What do you think we'll find?" Audra asked.

"I'm afraid they went and got themselves caught in the Oneida somehow," Gunnar said.

"In which case, they could be in a time dilation or maybe not even there anymore," Audra said grimly.

Gunnar shook his head slightly.

"I know Manx; he's scared of his own shadow. He would never even come within a parsec of a fabric bend if he didn't have to and Constance, well we both know she is one of the best freighter commanders the Kendalons have. She'd never lead her group anywhere close to a hole and if they did, she's more than capable of getting herself back out. They all know how dangerous the Oneida can be. They must have had a good reason for being in that area. What did you say they were carrying, spare parts?"

"Starbird spare parts to be exact. We didn't get a complete manifest, but I suspect they're full of Massey FTL engine assemblies, Fulton sub-light drives, Asium chambers and Interceptors."

"No wonder command wanted us to check this out. It's always good to have spare parts in stock when you need them."

Gunnar clinched his fist and carefully bumped the armrest of his chair. He went to raise his fist again, but a gentle hand on his shoulder melted him. He glanced back and had to smile. Audra's brown eyes always seemed to melt his tensions.

"How do you do that?"

Audra grinned.

"Do what?"

"Calm me so easily."

"As one?" she offered, lowering her eyes.

Gunnar noticed Pip look up from his scanning instruments.

"What is it Pip?" he asked, moving from his chair. Pip remained silent, staring at the screens in front of him, giving cause for his commander to become impatient.

"Pip?"

"I've recalibrated three times, but my readings are unchanged. I'm picking up all four freighters now, but their positions make absolutely no sense." The science officer kept his eyes glued to his scanning equipment. "They're still phasing too much to get a good lock on them."

Gunnar looked out into the star field ahead of them. Rubbing his chin, he detected Lana tipping her head and pressing on her ear piece a little harder.

"Com, you have something?"

"I'm hearing something on the emergency channels, sounds like an SOS. The automated beacons are loud and clear, though their telemetry is all mixed up, but I'm just making out a faint voice signal." Lieutenant Nevall adjusted her gains. "Sounds like it could be Captain Fowler."

"I've received the ident codes for one, but..." Pip hesitated.

"Which one?" Audra inquired stepping closer for a better look.

"Ident codes are the *Stark's,* but..."

"That's Constance's ship," Gunnar stated. "Do you have the other three?"

The science officer developed a perplexed look and started scratching the back of his neck. Working his equipment as if he were one with it, his expression deepened.

"I can't get anything determinant until we secure from Light speed. There's too much garbage coming at us."

"Garbage? Explain."

"In simple terms, Black holes not only suck a bunch of stuff in, they also release a bunch of stuff. Space distortion and extraneous fabric matter that we haven't even been able to analyze, let alone know how it all works. I believe it's these factors that are preventing our equipment from getting a good lock on the other freighters."

"So what can you see?" Audra asked leaning closer. Pip touched several other points on the screen in front of him.

"The *Stark* is here," he pointed to a symbol on the screen. "But the other ships seem to be phasing in and out at different positions around the Oneida." Pip shrugged, gesturing at his console. "I'll keep scanning, but until I can get closer and cut through the fabric ripples, I can't give you anything further."

Gunnar slowly stepped back over to the command chair.

"Yea," he mumbled, "You do that."

An instant later, the helmsman turned to her commander.

"Sir, our speed is increasing."

"That's to be expected. Best slow us down," Gunnar ordered, turning for the helm to watch Lieutenant Starman work.

"Slowing engines to light speed cruise factor one," Lynette announced, while studying several readouts. "Estimate new arrival time, a hasty minute and a half."

"It could be even faster," Gunnar said, looking at several displays above the science station. "Stay on your toes, helm. Commander Atlanta, take us to yellow alert."

No alarms sounded, but several warning lights began to flash all around the bridge. For several stretching moments, the crew kept their eyes glued to the instruments in front of them, until Lieutenant Starman took hold of the ship's manual controls.

"Ladies and gentlemen, we have arrived at the Oneida Caldron. Cutting back to sub-light."

As the FTL engines were shut down, the braking thrusters fired and the stars outside streaked to a crawl. Things appeared normal enough ahead of them until a blinding shower of light streaked past the front of the ship. Everyone onboard shielded their eyes until the auto dimmers in the glass could compensate.

"What do you make of that?" Gunnar asked, stepping forward.

"Pretty lights," Audra responded in a sarcastic tone, blinking her eyes.

The science officer looked up and out at some debris floating by.

"Instruments still fluctuating. Be a couple of minutes before I can get anything readable. We're in the Caldron zone, on our lower port side."

"Should I turn into it?" Lynette asked, setting her controls.

"Affirmative," Gunnar nodded. "Be prepared to use reverse thrusters to hold her in place. Bring the sensor array tie-ins to the spectrum analyzers online. It'll make for a nice light show. See if you can get a bead on where the Oota asteroid ring is. It should be somewhere close, following the spin of the accretion."

"To the port, moving in our direction," Pip announced.

"Did we come out of light speed too close?" Audra inquired.

"No," Gunnar answered.

"Still trying to scan." Pip sounded a little frustrated. "I don't get much practice with Black Holes. It's like looking at a mirror ball except when something floats by in close proximity. I've had to recalibrate the prox alarms twice to keep them from going off with false readings."

"I've got a feeling we're going to need those," Audra mumbled closely.

"You'll get no argument here," Gunnar whispered back.

"I should have fabric bend information for you momentarily," Pip reported calmly.

As the ship pivoted and the windows dimmed, there was an audible gasp as the swirling accretion disk of the Oneida Caldron filled their vision. Huge chunks of asteroids, comets and other debris were visible in the disk of the celestial hole in time and space. At its edges, visible space was either reflected back or distorted and warped around the center of nothing but a black reflective sphere.

"Can you overlay the projected fabric bends?"

"Certainly," the science officer acknowledged. "This will shift and warble a bit, but I think you'll get a pretty good idea of where it is."

"Can you get a composition of the accretion disk?" Audra inquired.

"It will take some doing, but if we can get closer, I think I can coax these instruments into telling us what's in there."

"Looks like mostly hot gas," Gunnar said.

"Could be where we'll find wreckage," Audra pointed out.

Gunnar turned and studied the tidal wave of information blitzing across the science station, then stepped forward.

"Com, are you still getting the *Stark*?"

The communications officer appeared to ignore Gunnar as she worked with her instruments, listening and adjusting.

"Just bits and pieces, sir. Something about time dilation and trying to escape an orbit."

"Helm, take us in a little closer and hold her just outside those fabric bends. We don't want to get caught up in any of the cosmic winds that gas is producing. And keep an eye on your chronometers for gravitational time dilation."

"What do you think?" Gunnar asked Pip and Audra.

The Starbird science officer only sucked in a large breath of air and held it. He too was a bit taken back by the galactic death trap in space.

"It would appear the *Stark* and her sister ships have gotten caught in the Oneida's accretion disk somehow. The Oneida Caldron is the third largest class four Black hole in the Della Montrose galaxy," he replied, arms folded. "It has taken countless ships since its discovery and continues to create navigational havoc as its vast gravitational fields continually modulate, shifting its fabric bends in completely unpredictable directions. Add to that the Oota asteroid ring spinning aimlessly through its accretion ring in unpredictable directions and you have all the makings of something quite dangerous."

"The *Stark* and the other freighters?" Gunnar asked.

"I've got them all now, but in really weird places."

"Show me."

"You'd think they'd all be bunched together here, but they're spread out across the Oneida's axis." Pip adjusted several of his controls, looking back at Audra who leaned in a little closer.

"You don't think the fabric bends are messing up our view?" she asked.

"It is entirely possible," Pip replied. "But we've got the latest and greatest onboard and the engineers have worked most of the bugs out of this scanning equipment. Of course nothing is infallible against something like this."

Gunnar studied the images in front of them closer, then turned to communications.

"Com, have you been able to get through to the *Stark*?"

"Been trying, sir. They're trying to communicate, but their transmissions are very garbled. I can't tell if they can hear me or not."

"If they're in a time dilation, it might be next to impossible to talk to them," Audra interjected. "What we're seeing may have already happened a long time ago. Combine that with the fabric bends the Oneida is producing and who knows what we're looking at."

"Can we move through those bends without adverse effects to the ship?" Gunnar asked, glancing outside.

"Yes, but I suspect none of this crew have ever operated under such conditions. It will certainly be a new kind of drug."

"Have you ever been in one?" Gunnar asked.

"No, sir."

Gunnar straightened up, turning to Audra.

"Rick and I have been through one and I think Billy has."

"When was that?" Audra asked half surprised, half not. Gunnar felt a little burble of guilt.

"I thought you said you'd read all our mission reports?"

"Must have missed that one," Audra responded letting him off the hook.

"Helm, take us in a little closer."

"Into the fabric bends, sir?" the pilot inquired.

"Yes, drive her just inside the perimeter. All of you need to keep your focus. No doubt we'll experience some odd sensations in here."

As Lynette turned to carry out her orders, Dakota stepped into the bridge, followed by Alex 7001 floating close behind.

Both human and machine headed directly toward the engineering consoles.

"Oh look, the Calvary has arrived," Gunnar snarked under his breathe. The little droid had an amazing ability to hear even the quietest of sounds.

"Colonel, I go where I am needed," the droid responded, its accent sounding irritated.

The logic processors of the droid were keenly aware of its commander's feelings and ignored the uselessness of the comment when its sensors picked up the image of the Oneida. Emitting several electronic tones, Alex 7001 peeled off from Captain Abrams and hovered over Pip, an obvious annoyance to the science officer.

"The vicinity of the Oneida Black hole isn't the safest place to linger, Colonel."

"Have you been talking with Felix 7000 again?" Gunnar asked, looking up at a display.

Alex 7001 kept his sensors on the Black hole.

"Might I suggest backing the ship away, Colonel?" The droid floated around the science station for a look at more information.

"Alex, this is a rescue mission. Don't worry I've done this before. Everything is under control." Gunnar didn't want to get into an argument with the artificial intelligence right now, not in front of the crew. If he had to have one of these onboard, he wished it wasn't mobile and had an easily accessed *OFF* switch.

Gunnar opened his mouth to further defend his actions, but the prox alarms came alive at the same moment the ship lunged violently to one side, throwing everyone from their seats. Toppling over next to the communications console, Gunnar's ears rang with the sound of a barrage of alarms. Unaffected by the ship's unrest, Alex 7001 spun his head assembly in his commander's direction.

"Under control huh?" the little droid teased.

Gunnar gave the Alex a mean look as he struggled to his feet.

"Talk to me, Pip!"

"Multiple torpedoes incoming from astern!"

"Where are the prox alarms?" Audra demanded. "Why didn't they go off sooner?"

"Recalibrated, remember? Battle stations! Shields," Gunnar called as Audra reached for the ship wide alarm. "Launch the Interceptors and have the turret light those torpedoes up." Dakota was already gone, bolting from the bridge as the ship was knocked about by multiple strikes.

"Helm," Gunnar called. "Set two seven one and bring her about ninety degrees to the starboard, axis one twenty, one quarter sub-light."

"You can't bank that hard this close to a fabric bend," Audra objected, noticing an odd ripple of distortion wave through her vision. "The gravity flux will tear the ship apart!"

"Those torpedoes will cut us in half if we don't move. Helm, get us out of here," Gunnar ordered, watching the inbound objects materialize directly in front of them. "This is a really bad place to be," he mumbled.

A torpedo exploding close by buffeted the ship, causing it to tilt hard to one side. Audra and Gunnar noticed several other hull strikes that sounded quite different to that of the torpedoes.

"I think some of those torpedoes were duds," Audra commented, looking up as if to see where the odd noises were coming from. Her bewilderment broadened as several more, odd sounding hull strikes, shook them. "That can't be good."

"I think something else is hitting us," Gunnar responded scanning Pip's displays.

"You would be correct, sir," the science officer confirmed. "We're passing along the edge of the Oota asteroid belt swinging this direction from the Mira system."

Audra moved next to Gunnar and held on to the command chair as the ship pitched again. The gravitational pull on the ship's hull nearly overrode the *Constellation's* anti-grav system as Lieutenant Starman banked the Starbird hard to the right and away from the Oneida. Scanning her instruments for the source of the warning indicators flashing on her displays, she noticed something streak past directly in front of them.

"Right on top of us," the weapons officer announced, firing the ship's guns at the inbound targets.

The Starbird pilot adjusted her controls and banked the ship hard to the left, then let it roll over on its back as she maneuvered the ship between two torpedoes and directly under a third.

"They'll circle around." Lynette glanced at her glass displays. "I need a couple of moments to setup for light speed operations," she called to the navigation officer.

"Where are they coming from?" Audra inquired turning to Pip.

"Sensors picking up four Imperial destroyers coming at us at flank speed."

"Wonder where they came from?" Audra asked.

"Give you three guesses and the first two don't count," Gunnar fumed.

"Croft's missing destroyers," Audra gritted as the ship shuddered again. "So, we get our chance after all." Gunnar passed her a sarcastic glance, then turned forward to watch the weapons officer.

Doran continued firing, but his targeting system was becoming overwhelmed with inbound ordinance.

"Nothing like getting rocks thrown at you too! Need a little help here, turret," Doran complained into his headset pickup.

"This is what we live for," the turret gunner replied, ignoring the smaller space rocks of the Oota in favor of the more volatile nature of the torpedoes. Even with shields, multiple strikes from exploding ordinance posed a significant problem.

With impact strikes continuing to rattle the ship, Lieutenant Starman was finding it difficult to avoid collisions, even when she throttled back. The gunners had their hands full as asteroids strikes continued to pound them.

"Helm! I would love to see any place other than where we are!" Gunnar's concern elevated as several more alarms went off.

"With this many torpedoes coming at us all at once, I'm sure they've used up their entire inventory," Audra pointed out.

"Don't you even bet on it," Gunnar huffed, knowing their tactics. "If they can't get at us with torpedoes, they'll start spitting missiles and if that doesn't do the job, they'll lob mines at us."

"Mines?" Audra asked as the ship shuddered again. "What good will those do?"

"High velocity mines. They're not as fast as the torpedoes, but they don't have to be. They track better and can be programmed to evade incoming fire. It can also be programmed to detonate if something gets too close to it. They fill them with a lot of nasty junk that sprays all over the place when it explodes."

"Several of the shield emitters have sustained significant damage," Alex 7001 announced from the engineering console. "We're losing shield integrity on the starboard side."

Pip studied the readouts in front of him, finally looking up.

"Another fabric bend coming right at us from the left, sir," he reported as they took another hard hit. "This will severely strain those shield emitters."

"Helm!"

"Doing the best I can, sir," Lynette said, banking the ship hard to avoid another torpedo. Two large v-winged fighters crossed paths directly in front of the ship, guns blazing. A myriad of circling enemy ordinance crisscrossed ahead of the ships and exploded as the Interceptors ran an effective interference against their tracking systems. Starman rolled the ship on to her side, then swung back level again, allowing another torpedo to pass just beneath. Lieutenant Cartwright targeted the torpedo as it began to arc back around at them.

"Two more! Roll her right and I'll split them right down the middle," the weapons officer called out, activating his weapons. "Hayden, you still with me?"

While the bombardment from multiple destroyers had the crew's attention, Gunnar recognized an odd distortion ripple through his vision.

"Starboard shield strength down to twelve percent," Alex said, adjusting the shield array circuits. "A couple more hits on those arrays and it will be gone."

Lieutenant Starman scanned a salvo of torpedoes arcing back at them, noting the two Interceptor fighters firing as they gave chase. Jockeying her throttles, she steered to avoid as many as possible and took note of a series of brilliant flashes ahead of them.

"Uhm," she edged nervously. "Those aren't what I think they are, are they?" She studied her readouts and waited for Pip to confirm her suspicions.

"They've fired their missiles," Gunnar said backing up to his chair. "And probably launched a bunch of high velocity proximity mines."

"I can confirm nearly four dozen missiles and at least a half dozen slower moving objects. Probably your mines," Pip confirmed.

"Four dozen," Audra repeated, a look of fear streaking across her face. "There's no way..."

"Stow it," Gunnar cut sharply. "Weapons officer, full weapons spread auto-pulsed in two second increments at my command. Have Lieutenant Hunter deal with the rest of those torpedoes." Gunnar turned to the communications station. "Com, I need to talk to Captain Abrams."

"He's already on the line, sir," the com officer responded instantly.

"Dakota?"

"I see them, sir, already going for it."

"Ignore the missiles. Six proximity mines coming in behind them. Get too close and they'll go off. We'll take on the missiles. It'll take you a while, but you have to get to those mines before they get to us."

"All textbook training for us, sir. Just tear out of there at light speed and we'll catch up."

"No good," Gunnar responded grimly. "Fabric bends preventing that kind of navigation. We have to clear all this before we can shift to light speed and I don't want to leave those freighters to Croft. Just keep those mines away from us and we'll take care of the rest." Gunnar deactivated the com and turned, Audra right there in his face.

"You just killed those two pilots. There's no way they'll be able to get to all of those without getting too close."

"Their job is to protect this ship at all costs," Gunnar fired back. "Sometimes you do the impossible in order to save lives."

"Whose lives?"

"Ours...Helm, steer to port and run along just inside these bends. Croft's destroyers don't dare come in this close. All this distortion should really mess with the tracking telemetry of their torpedoes and missiles. Navigation, have those light speed calculations ready for helm when we get clear of this mess. I want to be out of here as soon as it's safe to do so."

Audra turned to the myriad of flashing objects displayed at the science station. With torpedoes still chasing them and a wall of inbound missiles, it appeared a hopeless gesture to send Interceptors after the deadly proximity mines hurtling at them. With her limited combat experience, she could only reason and hope, this is what the Interceptor was designed for.

Lieutenant Starman dodged two more torpedoes and throttled up to try and outrun the rest. She eyed the shield information to her left. They had been lucky so far playing dodge with the torpedoes as they were a sluggish weapon that didn't maneuver well. The missiles were a different story. They traveled at a significantly faster speed and while they couldn't navigate well in close quarters, they didn't have to. They were well aimed and made most of their tracking corrections long before they reached their intended target. A hit from a missile wasn't as bad as one from a torpedo, but having a wall coming at you, more than one was bound to find its target through the shield energy. Gunnar gave the incoming targets on Pip's monitors a quick glance, then looked ahead.

"Weapons ready... Now, Lieutenant Cartwright." Gunnar dropped back into his chair, watching the darkness ahead of them fill with brilliant streaks of light as the weapons officer began firing, the patterns auto-pulsing.

"Try to boost the power to the forward shield arrays," Gunnar ordered, Audra instantly moving to the engineering consoles with Alex 7001 hovering close.

"We have a lot of our own ordinance, sir," Audra pointed out. "It would be nice not to have so much of it onboard if we were to take a good hit." Audra sat down and started working with the shield controls.

"Yeah, I was getting to that," Gunnar responded tensely.

"Weapons, send our friends out there half of our pin missile inventory. Everybody gets an equal share. Target their shield arrays. You'll find them directly under their engine exhaust ports on their port side aft."

It took the weapons officer only a moment to make the adjustments and let the ship's deadly weapons go. A brilliant flare on both sides of the bridge pod indicated the missiles were away.

The space some distance ahead of them suddenly began to erupt with quick, brilliant explosions growing closer with each flash.

"Helm, begin an eight-point roll and accelerate to full sub-light."

Lynette instantly tapped several points on the glass in front of her and moved her controls like it was all a part of an elaborate dance. She glanced at her tracking screens, then passed a look over at Doran's screens as she performed her maneuvers. She could see the missiles still coming at them, arcing in a big curve. So far they were tracking accurately. At least they weren't getting slammed by asteroid chunks from the Oota anymore.

Doran watched his readouts carefully, noting the forming of an impossible situation. There were still six torpedoes tracking them and a wall of missiles coming at them from the starboard side, arcing along their flight path just outside the accretion ring of the Oneida. Following them were a half dozen prox mines that would track the nearest target and explode once they got close enough. Additionally, there were fabric bends from the Oneida playing havoc with the navigational controls, not to mention their eyesight.

"Keep your roll as precise and continuous as you can," Gunnar coached the Starbird pilot.

"Any time to explain why I'm doing this?" Lynette asked carefully.

"You're harder to hit rolling like this, less of a target."

Lynette followed his logic and nodded. She could see his thinking were they in a fighter, but the *Constellation* was significantly larger. They were going to get hit no matter what maneuvers they were doing.

Doran checked his batteries and continued firing at the incoming missiles, but they were small enough that a target lock at this distance would be lucky at best. Never the less, he kept his weapons pulsing as ordered, firing his auxiliary guns at anything coming into range. Lynette looked overhead at the missile wall approaching from the starboard side in a wide arc.

"This is going to get a little rough," Gunnar cautioned.

As the ship rolled on its back, the rampart of missiles converged, many passing by, some bouncing across the hull and harmlessly away, others exploding as they struck the energy shields. But some found their target. The starboard side took the brunt, pitching and bucking up the aft section, spinning the ship out of control.

Lynette tried to compensate, but her controls were not responding well to her commands. Hayden barely blasted several missiles coming right at his turret, but could no longer hold a lock on any of the incoming torpedoes still dogging them. Two flew harmlessly by and detonated, intensifying the missiles explosions. One found its mark, exploding against the ship's wing, between his turret and the empty Interceptor wing mounts. The ship took several more direct hits to her underside and along her mid-section as warning indicators sounded off throughout the vessel.

"Hull breach at mid-section, starboard side," Alex 7001 announced, quieting the alarms. "Shield generators adjusting. Structural integrity holding."

Keeping her cool, Lynette adjusted the window controls to black out the spinning star field. Fighting a mixed bag of stabilization issues was a lot of work. Watching her instruments, she worked the maneuvering thrusters to correct the attitude axis. Once stabilized, she brought the *Constellation* out of the roll, and started working on correcting the other axis problems. Working to get her craft slowed down to a standard operational speed, she readjusted the windows and the stars reappeared with the Oneida and its accretion ring now on their left.

As everyone began to relax, they collectively noticed their vision starting to blur, straight lines bending all at once. Doran heard Hayden yelling something about a torpedo, but there was a sudden jolt from the rear and a blinding flash from overhead, then the ship was slammed to the left, tossing anyone not safety locked. Toppling forward, Gunnar slid up next to helm control.

"Now what?" he asked, getting back to his feet.

Lynette scanned her consoles. Nothing appeared to be solid any longer. Anything that was supposed to have straight lines was now bending and wobbling. Confused, she held her hands up in front of her, looking curiously at them. It was as if they were made of rubber. She wondered if her bones had somehow been removed. She looked around, noticing her bewilderment shared by the rest of the crew.

"I was hoping you could fill me in, Colonel," she grunted, trying to refocus on running diagnostics. Her voice now sounded hollow and distant. Gunnar steadied himself against the right helm console, turning to the science station. He was experiencing the same thing, but understood what was happening.

"Talk to me, Pip."

"We took a torpedo hit next to the main engine nacelle," Pip answered. "Fulton drive is offline. The hit has thrown us into the deep roll of a fabric bend, go figure."

"Not good!" Gunnar swung back to Lynette. "Helm, status?"

Trying hard to ignore the distortion in her vision and the weird sound to the crew's voices, the Starbird pilot touched several controls on the touch panel in front of her and worked the sub-light throttles. She froze, trying to sense the ship following her commands, but nothing was happening. The sub-light drive seemed to be completely dead. The ship trembled, veering toward the Oneida's accretion ring as Lynette turned to her commander.

"No response from the helm." She worked her maneuvering thruster controls, but found them nonresponsive as well. "No sub-light drive or maneuvering thrusters."

Gunnar reached over and worked the controls himself, nearly blinded by the flashing alarms on the helm display.

"Let's try some light speed. Factor one, go!"

"I can try," she said, working the light speed controls. Lieutenant Starman wasn't so sure about the order. FTL drive was the same as folding space in front of the ship and stretching it behind. Here, the space fabric was already bending in the form of a rolling tidal force. Trying to go to light speed in a fabric bend with gravity fluxing like this, could be catastrophic, but she had no alternatives to offer.

The ship instantly started to produce a washboard shuddering. A low whine screamed from somewhere inside the engine compartment as the FTL engines strained to pull against the gravitational flux exerted against the hull of the Starbird. The *Constellation* felt like she was going to move, the protesting scream growing louder, until a myriad of alarms started to blare from the engineering console. Lynette frantically worked with her fitting instruments until one of her own consoles started to act erratic, the display fizzling out and becoming nonresponsive to the touch. Deadly Scalder plasma appeared around her displays, crawling angrily around her controls on either side and sending violent energy fingers spiking through her hands and arms. When it finally ended, Lynette let out a shrill yelp and slumped forward.

"Take the helm," Gunnar motioned to Audra as he pulled the unconscious pilot out of the way. "Com, get Yamoto in here on the double," he called back to the communications officer. Gunnar looked the unconscious Starbird pilot over as Alex 7001 scanned the engineering readouts. "Can you get us moving?"

Gunnar asked, the ship starting to spin again and seep toward the Oneida's accretion ring.

"Highly unlikely, sir," Alex 7001 commented, landing next to Colonel Conrad. "FTL drive power couplings have burnt out, creating a Hap void and crashing our Navi-computers. A Hap void is like being nowhere in space. We can't drive in any direction without the help of something external and right now, the Oneida is the strongest thing externally driving us."

"What's creating the Hap void?" Audra asked turning her chair as Fuji came running in. "The maneuvering thrusters are back online and it looks like the lower end of the sub-light drive might be functional, but nothing works."

"The FTL drive is creating the Hap void," the droid informed them as it became airborne.

"You said it's offline."

"I said the power couplings were burnt out. The FTL drive unit is still online and generating a light speed signature, locking out the sub-light drive. Without the coupling engaged, the Hap void around the ship is stuck in place and the fail safes won't release until it receives the required telemetry from the couplings. The sub-light drive won't reengage unless the FTL drive is shut down. You can't run both at the same time."

Gunnar gnawed on his knuckles, thinking of what might come next.

"She's going into dorma-shock, Colonel," Fuji announced looking up. "We're spread kind of thin back there, can you help me get her to sick bay?"

"We'll have to make this real quick. Commander Atlanta has the con." He scooped up the pilot and carried her out, followed closely by the ship's doctor.

*   *   *   *

Entering the main hall, the damage to the ship's mid-section became apparent. Hallway lighting was wrecked with only a few still operating, some only sporadically. Ceiling and wall debris littered the hall, making walking difficult as Gunnar struggled with the unconscious Starbird pilot. As they stumbled past several crew's quarters with their doors blown out, he could see mostly blackness, but one of them, he thought he caught sight of the star field outside. Approaching the door to the Mantose twin's quarters, he watched Fuji's assistant struggling in the doorway with Taron. He was clearly in pain and barely able to stand, even with the nurse's help. Fuji stepped quickly to help Sindee and as Gunnar went by the open door, he glanced through. The entire room was a twisting spin of stars and the

Oneida. Finally making it to sick bay, they had to force their way through the jammed turbo door. Feeling a twinge of pain from his chest, the Starbird commander set Lynette on one of the four tables in sickbay. A moment later, the engineer's first mate stumbled inside holding his arm to his side and limping. After helping a grimacing Frank to a table, Gunnar turned to the medical officer's desk and the com panel.

"Bridge, how are we holding out?"

"Ok for now," Audra answered cautiously. "Those missiles you sent into the shield arrays of Croft's destroyers seemed to have done the trick. Two of them are moving off, but the other two are holding their position. Should I send them a couple of these new MKV torpedoes?"

"No, I want them to stew a little about what they think they're up against."

"They appear to be a little hesitant to approach us."

"Wouldn't you be? We just took out their shield arrays and their tech doesn't play well with this kind of spacial distortion."

"Neither does ours," Audra said.

"They think we're not going anywhere quick, so they'll take their time. Any luck with sending out a distress call?"

"Com got one off before her systems went down. Hopefully we'll be rebooted and reconfigured shortly."

"Any word from Dakota?"

"Nothing, but Pip observed several large energy releases right before we had our bout with the missiles. He couldn't get anything determinant because of the fabric bends we're in and his instruments went offline shortly after that, but he's guessing they were mines exploding."

"Just two?"

"Just two," Audra repeated. "But Hayden is reporting two more explosions in different locations behind us just now. Could be our boys are still at it."

"Sounds like it." Gunnar recalled doing similar things when he and Rick were flying together. High velocity mines were tricky monsters, a bit fickle. Get too close and they blow up, releasing immense hull damaging shock waves and debris. But you had to get close enough to one to target it, and that usually meant you were within its explosion envelope and damage path.

"Have you received any kind of a ship's damage assessment yet?"

"Only preliminary, we're still trying to get all the systems back up and running. I'm trying to stabilize the ship with maneuvering thrusters, but it's slow going. I've got Alex doing a ship wide scan with his own sensors. He'll be all over the ship before he can get that completed."

"Not that there is anything we can do about it. Do we know where the freighters are?"

"Pip had them pinpointed on the other side of the Oneida before we were attacked. They're certainly safe where they are for the time being."

"And what about us? You said you're using maneuvering thrusters to regain control?"

"Yes," Audra reaffirmed. "But it will take some time. The ship is spinning across both axis's and drifting right into the Oneida's accretion ring."

"Fabric bends get a lot worse in there," Gunnar warned.

"Yes, sir," Audra agreed. "We really need to get those power couplings back online. I've checked with Billy in engineering and he's working on it, but he's short Frank."

"Yeah, he just showed up here in sick bay."

"Looks like the sensors are almost back online. I'll contact you again when I have more details."

"Stay on it. I'll be back up in a few minutes." Without another word, he shut off the comlink and clutching his arm, turned for the door.

"Colonel," Fuji looked up from her patients. "Are you all right? Maybe you should have another Furlitron booster."

Gunnar only shook his head, turning back for the door.

"I'll be ok."

He looked at the empty fourth table and then scanned the room. The nurse had pulled Taron from their quarters, but where was Tiana? Trying to ignore the stabbing in his lower back, Gunnar headed through the open sickbay door and back toward the bridge.

Stopping at the open door of room 14B, Gunnar stepped cautiously inside. He surveyed what was left of the room. With the exception of a slight rumble from the ship's hull, it was completely silent. A slight tingle slithered down his back as he looked nervously at where the opposite wall should be. It was completely gone. There were parts of the wall still hanging from the ceiling and some jagged edges close to the inner walls, but that was it! He carefully stepped over to the large opening. The ship's shields had sealed the breach, but it was still a little unnerving to be standing right next to it and looking out at a spinning star field. Rushes of random light flashed constantly past the opening, with visions of the accretion ring and the Oneida coming into view. Looking back, toward the rear of the ship, he could clearly make out the aft wingtip.

Vertigo

Audra sat back mesmerized, silently gazing at the Oneida Caldron on a display in front of her. It had taken her and Alex several attempts to get the helm control system to reboot and come back online. The ship's autopilot computers were working on correcting the ship's spin and drift with the maneuvering thrusters, but it was a slow process. She was suddenly brought back to attention by a voice in her headset.

"Commander Atlanta, you there?" Fuji asked softly.

The first officer found it almost impossible to keep her eyes away from the hypnotic celestial caldron.

"My body is anyway. That Black hole out there has my mind. It may have us all if we don't pull out of this pretty quick. Where's the Colonel?"

"He didn't make it back up to the bridge?" Fuji sounded worried. "I just wanted to check on him, I think he was working on another episode."

Audra glanced all around the bridge. Maybe Gunnar slipped back in without her knowing it. She sat forward and started working with some of the controls to her right.

"Doesn't sound right to me," Audra finally responded. She tapped several spots on the touch screens in front of her. "I've got his transponder mid ship, room 14B. That's the Mantose quarters."

"I've got one of them down here, but Sindee said she couldn't find the other one in their room. That whole section was part of the hull breach. Maybe the other one got sucked out?"

"Technically, they would have gotten blown out."

"Whatever."

"Can you meet me there right away?"

"On my way."

Audra pulled headset off as the rear helm console disappeared beneath the left allowing her to exit. Ensign Kramer immediately took over as Audra strode to the bridge door.

"Commander," Lana stopped the first officer. "Response from the *Athena*. General Niker is at maximum light speed and estimates arrival in about an hour."

The first officer turned and looked back out at the star field, then over at one of the displays on the science officer's station. Pip was still working to get his systems back up and running.

"Understood, keep me informed. Pip, you have the con," Audra said, leaving the bridge.

*   *   *   *

Fuji was already waiting at the open door leaning against the wall. A younger, slender woman, she wasn't much taller than Audra. She had much lighter colored hair and more of it, curling down around her shoulders. Audra peered cautiously inside and started in, but then hesitated, noticing Fuji wasn't moving to follow. Normally, medical personnel would be pushing to get right where the problem was.

"We're going in," Audra announced, motioning at the doorway. Fuji didn't move.

"Doctor?"

"Yeah, 'bout that," Fuji edged, nervously glancing inside. It was then Audra perceived the fear in the doctor's eyes. "I have a little trouble with open space."

"You're kidding," Audra twisted her lips dismayed. "And you're on a Starbird..."

"This is my first deployment. Gotta start somewhere."

"Didn't you take zero G training?" Audra was a little irritated.

"Well, yeah, I did, but the body just didn't seem to want to adjust and the trainer took pity on me."

Audra sized up the medical officer. She could have a field day with this. And the doctor wanted to have Gunnar removed for being unfit for duty? More than likely her instructor was after something entirely different than just passing her through the required zero gravity training.

"Great," Audra grumbled. She grabbed the reluctant medical officer by the arm and pulled her through the open door, into almost pitch black. "You've got a couple of patients in here that require your help and training or no, you're going to help me get them out."

Audra cautiously stepped to one side, allowing Fuji to hug the other side of the door frame. She tried the lights and several bars instantly popped and crackled, their circuits burning up. It was going to take their eyes some time to adjust to the available light. The room was a disaster. Only after they had both entered the room, did Audra realize just how bad the conditions were. The further in they stepped, the more frightened Fuji became, realizing the entire outer wall was completely gone and it was just a black rolling star field.

"Holy smokes!" Fuji backed up a little bit, fearing she might fall out. She had no idea how things worked on a Starbird, or any space vehicle for that matter. Being her first deployment in space, she never actually had to deal with situations like this.

"Why don't I just wait outside… I mean out in the hall?"

Audra reached back and grabbed the ship's doctor by the front of her uniform, pulling her close.

"You're sort of harshing my buzz here," the first officer complained. "You'll get used to it, eventually."

"I doubt it," Fuji grumbled, holding onto the first officer.

"Gunnar, where are you?" Audra was more than a little worried as Fuji pulled her pocket scanner and turned it on. Grabbing the communicator from her belt, Audra raised it to her mouth as she scanned the room for her husband. "Alex, can you bring up all the ship's exterior running lights?"

"Are you working on something I should know about, Commander?" the droid's voice responded instantly over the com device.

"I'm working a rescue in the mid-section hull breach area and I need some exterior light."

An instant later, several exterior lights flashed on. Adjusting her communicator, she raised it to her mouth again.

"Is that all there is, Alex?"

"That's all that's working, Commander. I can provide you with more if you require, but it will take me a few moments to reach your location as I'm on the port side aft, inspecting the outer hull and injecting Nano-mech as per your orders."

"You're outside the ship?" Audra gazed out at the swirling star field. Even with her zero gravity training, she couldn't help but be a little nervous. Thinking of being on the outside of the hull right now even set her off a little. She could feel the nerves in her toes and fingers tingling with just the thought of it.

"Do you require my help, Commander Atlanta?" the droid asked.

"If you have a moment and can manage it," Audra responded, taking a deep breath and refocusing.

"It will take me a couple of minutes," the droid replied.

"How come we're not just floating away?" Fuji asked, looking at the edge of the floor that dropped away into outer space. "Better yet, flung out screaming hysterically?"

"Because you're still within the ship's anti-grav envelope. It keeps all things right in your world."

"My world is certainly not right, there's no wall. How come we're able to breath? How come we're not dead right now?"

Audra reached down and picked something up, tossing it out into space. As the object reached where the wall should be, it dropped to the floor like it had struck something unseen.

"The ship's shields automatically sealed the breach," Audra explained. Looking around, she spotted someone lying against a partially broken wall.

Gunnar groaned as Audra and Fuji knelt down next to him, turning him over. They tried to help the Starbird commander up as he opened his eyes, but the pain he was experiencing was excruciating, so they set him back down against the wall. He let out a heavy sigh while Fuji held her scanner to his chest, Audra taking her mate's hand.

"You know, you have a communicator," Audra chastened him, holding the device to his face. "You've about given Fuji and I heart failure."

"You're talking to me about heart failure? I feel terrible," he moaned, astonished at the amount of pain he was enduring.

"I'm certain you do," Audra responded as Fuji injected something into his shoulder.

"Furlitron and a de-nueralizer," Fuji responded to an unasked question. She glanced at Audra, not realizing she had completely forgotten her fear of being in the wrecked room. "In most people, it instantly blocks the pain receptors of the core. Not sure it will do him any good, but I'd like to think I tried something."

"Happy birthday to me." Gunnar winced again as the two women lifted him to his feet and toward the door.

"It's your birthday, Colonel? Where's the cake?"

"He doesn't like to share," Audra remarked smiling.

"You need to get Tiana... she's between the two rooms." Gunnar tried to stand and point behind him.

"Come on," the medical officer ordered. "Let's get him down to sickbay."

Gunnar squirmed painfully as the two helped him into the ship's medical facility. As he lay back, a life monitor above the medical bed came on while the ship's medical officer ordered another hypo of Furlitron. Working her instruments, Fuji turned on the holographic imager, scanning his entire body and displaying his internal workings directly above him. The electronic cross-hairs jumped on the monitor above his bed, measuring heart action and eight other vital body functions. The information being displayed gave Fuji cause to give the display a queer look. At first, she thought it might be malfunctioning. The heart beat indicators were acting quite erratic. Another Furlitron hypo was quickly put to his arm and the fluid pumping into his veins, but much to Fuji's dismay, it had little effect on the heart activity.

"Dang it..." Fuji cursed beneath her breath as she reached up and adjusted the touch control directly on the monitor. "Ah, here we are, no wonder," she discovered, seeing the readouts stabilizing. "Get a load of that." Delighted, she turned to Audra. "If I'm reading this right, his other heart is functioning."

"Does this mean the dormancy exit is complete?" Audra studied the medical information carefully.

"Certainly it does, if we can just get him to rest for more than a couple of minutes. It's a huge strain on the primary heart adjusting to the pulmonary episodes produced by the secondary one coming out of shunt. I'm going to give him a mild sedative and hopefully relax him enough that he can power nap for a half hour or so. Unfortunately, medications of any kind will have a tough time having much of an effect on his system. This should give the rest of his system some time to adjust to what twin hearts will do for him."

A myriad of questions ran through Audra's head now, but she noticed Taron on the next table and remembered his sister was still missing.

"Fuji, we need to go back and find Tiana.

"I'm not sure how she could even still be in there let alone still be alive." The ship's doctor looked back at Taron, but realized Audra was right. If there was even a slim chance the other twin was still alive, they needed to make sure, so she turned and followed the executive officer back down to the room.

*   *   *   *

Stepping back through the door of 14B, Audra spoke into her communicator.

"Alex, you still with me?"

"I have remained in the same position, Commander," the droid responded, appearing seconds later at the edge of the torn hull. "Looks like this section could use a couple of bricks of Nano-mech." Bright, penetrating lights were protruding from his head and torso assembly.

"Can you run a scan of the room? Is there anyone else in here?"

Alex floated effortlessly around the hull breach, his internal scanners looking all around.

"Thermal scans showing a signature to your right, just inside the next room."

"Could it be one of the crew?" Audra inquired, stepping over the debris to the right wall. The closer you got to the hull breach, the more the walls were torn up, but she still couldn't detect anything. Fuji held firmly to the back of Audra's uniform as they moved closer to the edge.

"All the crew are accounted for and I'm not picking up any transponder signals. Even if they were dead, the transponder would still be operational."

"He's right," Fuji whispered. "I have to deactivate those when I pronounce a time of death." Though there was plenty of light now, Fuji stumbled, nearly knocking Audra into the wall, toward what was perceived as nothing but an open abyss. Audra's heart was racing now. While she knew the shields would have kept her within the confines of the ship's atmosphere, the shield barrier was invisible so being so close to the edge of something like this still played on the mind.

"You're right on top of the heat signature now," Alex announced. He couldn't see into the next room, as its wall was still mostly intact, only a small corner of it had been pulled away.

Both women hugged the wall, Audra kneeling to look under it. She heard a groan at the same moment she touched what felt like an arm.

"I think I found her," Audra grunted, trying to find something recognizable. "Miss Mantose, can you hear me?" There was no movement at first, but once Audra found a hand, she felt it moving to grab hold. "Can you go around to the other room?" Audra asked, directing her attention at Fuji.

"Did you see that door? It will take Billy an hour to get it open."

"Well, how in the world did she get in there?" Audra tugged on Tiana's arm, trying to move her.

"Just be glad she is," Fuji looked up at the missing wall. "It's a wonder neither of them got sucked out or torn apart when the pressure popped. It must have been a nightmare in here until the shields came online."

"Yeah, that would have been a very long half second." Audra finally dropped to her stomach, straining to see under the broken wall. "Alex, can you move over here a little closer?"

The intensity of the droid's lights focused in on the location Audra was working and craning to see under the wall, she caught sight of Tiana's eyes on the other side.

"Can you hear me? Are you all right?" Audra lay silent for a moment, listening to the injured Mantose sibling trying to speak. It was breathy and labored.

"I'm stuck. I can't move my feet."

Audra looked back up at Fuji.

"Can you look around the edge of the wall and see what the problem is?"

Fuji's face went a little pale and trying to overcome her fear, she carefully got down on her hands and knees, crawling past Audra to the edge of the wall and floor. With the ship still tumbling and drifting toward the accretion ring of the Oneida, she felt like she was going to fly right off into space. It so unnerved her to be this close to the edge of a spinning *nothing,* she couldn't control her fear and had to back away from the edge, retreating behind Audra. Exasperated, Audra got back to her knees and turned to the ship's doctor.

"What are you doing? Come on!"

Fuji folded her arms like she was cold, shaking her head, looking at the edge of the wall.

"Nope, I'm sorry, it ain't gonna happen. I can't, you check."

Audra read the look of panic on the MD's face. She wanted to grab her by the lapels and give her a good head butt, but decided she wasn't going to get anywhere with her.

"Oh for the love of Pete," she muttered, motioning for Fuji to trade positions. Being close to the edge unnerved her too, but she had more training with this kind of environment and was able to overcome the feeling of floating away.

"Alex, can you slide further forward and point your lights back a little?"

The lights from the droid outside were moving before Audra even finished her sentence.

"Gotta tell ya, when Gunnar and I signed on for this commission, I never thought I'd be hanging my rear end out the side of a ship," Audra grunted, reaching for Tiana's feet. Fumbling around behind the wall, she felt the boots of the Mantose girl and tried pulling on them. She tugged and twisted, but they were stuck fast. Audra finally pulled her arm back out and pressed her face to the opening between the broken wall and the outside. She could clearly see her boots, the soles hanging out over the edge of the broken floor.

"If I may offer additional information, Commander," Alex said. "My scans show her boots are frozen in the ship's shield energy."

"Rubbish," Audra cursed, reaching back in, trying to free the boots. "How does someone get their feet stuck in a deflector shield?"

"How's that?" Fuji asked.

"Her feet are hanging out in the shield's energy field. The soles of her boots are stuck, and there is no way to release them without turning off the shields."

"Uhm, that would be bad for all of us," Fuji responded, checking Tiana's vital signs as best she could. The Mantose twin

was in shock, but unless they could get to her, there was no way
for them to ascertain her condition any further.

"Most humans cannot survive open space for long," Alex said.
"If the extreme cold didn't flash freeze you, your lungs could
burst if you didn't take a proper breath before being exposed to
the vacuum of space. Then there are the cosmic radiation bursts
out here and debris clouds that would blast your skin and muscle
tissue right off your bones."

"Alex!" Audra hushed the droid.

"I think I could have gone my entire career without hearing
that," Fuji stated wide eyed.

"How's she doing?" Audra asked.

"Hard to tell for sure. We need to get her out of there first."

"Do you think we can pull her back under the wall if I can get
her loose?"

"You get her loose and we'll make it happen. What do you
have in mind?"

"Fashion of the day, her boots have buckles all the way up
the side. If I can get them undone, she can just slip out," Audra
grunted reaching for the buckles. "Oh, and these are really
pretty ones too. You've seen them haven't you? I wonder where
she got them?" It didn't take long for her to have one boot
undone, feeling Tiana trying to squirm her foot out.

"Have you been to the Foot Armor at the Gateway tower in
Geffen on Kalamar?" Fuji asked. "I'm sure I've seen those boots
there. It would appear our patient likes what you're doing back
there," Fuji strained to get her head down close enough to hear
Tiana's whispered voice.

Audra felt a foot slip from the boot, and reaching for the
second, started undoing the buckles. As the last clasp opened
up, she could feel the other foot drawing out the top. Fuji
carefully instructed the injured woman how they were going to
try to pull her back into the room. After positioning themselves
to make the operation more like a conveyer belt extraction, Fuji
worked to get Tiana's head and body positioned to maneuver
beneath the jagged edges of the wall while Audra carefully pulled
her through. It took several minutes and painful moments for
Tiana, but the two women finally pulled her out from under the
wall and helped her to her feet.

"Thanks, Alex," Audra said turning to the droid on the
outside. "You were a big help."

"Always glad to be useful, Commander."

*   *   *   *

Gunnar felt like he had been asleep for hours. Opening his eyes, he had to blink several times to clear the blur from his vision. Sitting stiffly up, he looked around the room. He had a searing headache and while it was quiet in sick bay, there was an awful high pitched tone piercing through his head. The life monitor behind him caught his eye and he turned around to look at the information on his vital signs. As he did so, he noticed Taron's sleeping figure on the bed to his right. Standing carefully on uncertain legs, he leaned on his own bed and glanced to his left. It was occupied by the motionless Starbird pilot. Making his way around to Lieutenant Starman, Gunnar studied the life monitor over her bed. Everything looked fine, just a little low. She had medical gauntlets on her hands and forearms. Her skin was slightly pale in color and for a moment, he could detect no breathing, but as he bent closer, he could hear a steady, shallow suspire. As he straightened up again, he felt a hand touch his arm.

"Colonel," Lynette's hoarse voice whispered from the bed. "What happened, what's going on?"

Gunnar looked back down at Lynette and leaned a little closer.

"Take it easy, Lieutenant, need your rest. You've had a busy day. Yulan poisoning can take quite a lot out of you. That was a pretty good jolt you took."

"Sir, what about the Oneida?" Lynette mustered from the bed.

"We've gotten ourselves stuck in a Hap, so the hole is pulling on us. The *Athena* ought to be pulling alongside just anytime to pull our sorry butts out, and I want you at the helm when we do it, so get your rest." He smiled and patted her hand.

Gunnar turned around as Fuji and Audra struggled in holding up a nearly unconscious Tiana. He stepped over to help them get her onto one of the other medical beds as Sindee activating the life monitor. While the nurse started the automated medical assistant for the preliminary inspections on Tiana, the ship's doctor pulled a little probe from her hip pouch and stepped over to the ship's commander. She held it to his chest, then moved it to his lower back. Gunnar smiled at Audra, who returned a look of relief.

"Well doc, do you still want to recommend I be relieved of command?" He could see the frown on the doctor's face and realized he was probably in a little trouble.

"If you'll lie back down, I'll try to find out," she gruffed.

Gunnar only shrugged, lying back on the bed. The display above his head instantly popped back on, its electronic cross hairs jumping up into the normal areas. Fuji studied the readouts carefully, a frown of disdain still deeply engraved on her face.

"It would appear that we're done with the Furlitron injections, Colonel," Fuji announced, letting the frown melt away. "Both your tickers are running normally now. Well, as normal as a person with two hearts can be," she said, passing Audra an amused glance.

"Am I good to return to duty?"

Fuji hesitated. She would love to run more tests on him, maybe learn a little more about the anatomy of a Dialabron, but she understood the current situation facing the ship and decided her curiosity could wait.

"Yes, Colonel. I'm glad I didn't start filling out that relief of command paper work." She held him to the bed with a firm hand and looked him straight in the eye. "But if you have any problems and I mean ANY, you let me know immediately. Conventional medicine doesn't cover much on Dialabrons and this ship needs its commander."

"Got it," Gunnar agreed readily, coming up from the bed. He passed Audra a quick wink and started for the door.

Fuji turned to Audra as Gunnar left the room, heading forward.

"You might find a behavioral change in him now that he has two hearts to contend with. Besides what we've already discussed with his physical strength, other changes will likely manifest themselves over time, as new synapsis in his metabolism form. It could create some severe emotional swings. Not necessarily toward depression, could be quicker to anger. Aggression could be his worst enemy. The challenge will be recognition and doing something about it before it becomes a problem." Fuji turned as Taron began to stir.

"Challenge will be putting it mildly," Audra agreed, nodding and leaving for the bridge.

Rescue

Ensign Kramer vacated the helm chair and reported to his own station, allowing Audra to take the helm. The guidance control computers had just finished bringing the *Constellation* out of its tumble, signaled a stable orientation to the Oneida. Gunnar leaned down a little closer to the communications console in front of Lana talking to General Niker as the *Athena* was just coming out of light speed near their position.

"Yeah, look who's all busted up and needs my help now." Rick enjoyed a good needling, especially when it was directed at Gunnar. A little payback was always a sweet savor.

"Thanks for scaring off those two destroyers," Gunnar breathed a sigh of relief.

"Can't leave you alone for two minutes."

"Where are they now?"

"Hiding with their buddies to the side of the Oneida. My bet is they're trying to decide if they want to take on two Starbirds. Caught you off guard, didn't they?"

"Came out of nowhere."

"Got yourself into a pretty good fix down there."

"I think you're enjoying this far too much."

"Oh, no I'm not."

"We're losing ground faster than I'm comfortable with." Gunnar tried to smile, but was too worried about their situation. "I want to try and stay clear of the accretion disk but I've got nothing over here. Can't do anything unless we can get the FTL drive power couplings back online. This Hap void has us dead in space."

"How's your anti-grav taking to the Oneida's gravity well?"

"The Hap is masking the gravity flux of the fabric bends, so there isn't much of a drag on those systems. But I'd sure feel a whole lot better if I were moving in the opposite direction of that sink hole.

"I feel certain," Rick responded. "You know it looks more like a mirror ball to me. Kind of pretty when you're not about to get pulled apart and crushed. From our vantage point out here, you look like you're sitting close to the edge of the gravitational time dilation field. All sorts of bends rolling through there. It's tough to tell, as there is so much reflecting distortion. You go in much further and you'll think we're taking forever to get to you. My pilot thinks if we edge in from behind, we ought to be able to get you out using our aft tractor hawser. We'll get you far enough away you can make repairs, take care of your friends out there and then see about getting you back to the Kalamar shipyards. Happy birthday ol' man."

"Thanks, now where's my cake?" Gunnar rubbed the back of his neck. "Important safety tip; don't get too close to the Oneida. We took substantial damage from Croft's torpedo and missile attack. Your cousin and his wingman are still out there somewhere dealing with some HV mines. We think they've destroyed as many as four, but we're still trying to get our sensors back online and can't see a thing."

"Yeah, Toby has them. I'm sending Zek and Zak out to help. We'll leave them to do their business so we can do ours."

"You missed a wonderful meteor shower from the Oota belt as well."

"Yeah, we can see that too. I think you ordered all these conditions. There's no way they could all just happen on their own like this. What else is busted up?"

"Got a sizable hull breach on the starboard side mid-section. Crew quarters there had some serious remodeling done. We've got Nano-mech working all over the ship, but that stuff is stretched pretty thin."

"Oh goody," Rick complained. "And we're adding to the list."

"Yes, nice birthday present," Gunnar chimed back sarcastic.

"Did you lose anyone?"

"No, Cooper broke his arm and Starman got buzzed up with Yulan poisoning. Yamoto got Frank taken care of right away and Starman will be just fine. The Mantose twins got the worst of it. They were in one of the crew's quarters that had its wall torn off. I sure wish they weren't here.

"Mantose twins? "The" Mantose twins? Where did you pick them up?"

"Commenor."

"Oh, there's a story here I'm sure I can't wait to hear."

"I don't suppose I could pawn them off on you?"

"Funny man. Not a good idea. Trying to use something like a teleporter out here while you're wallowing around in a fabric bend with low power wouldn't mix well. A teleporter is a little temperamental as it is."

"Lovely."

"Better stand by, we've got a visual on you now, be behind you in two shakes of a Fornax's brain."

"Conrad out." Gunnar turned to his chair at the same time Alex 7001 floated in.

"Colonel, Mr. Moon and I have repaired the power couplings."

Overjoyed, the Starbird commander nearly jumped up and grabbed the little white droid.

"We may not need the *Athena* after all." He stepped anxiously forward to where Audra sat waiting at helm control. "Let's get out of here." Excited at first, a spark of doubt crept to mind when Alex 7001 joined him forward. "You're sure about this Alex?" Gunnar asked nervously.

"Quite sure, Colonel." The little droid sounded insulted.

"Should I inform the General first?" Lana asked turning to her console.

"Never mind. He'll love the surprise."

"Should I just take her to light speed?" Audra asked, pausing.

"Not in these fabric bends. We could get flung off to who knows where."

"Prudent thinking, Colonel," Alex commented. "It would be wise to wait until we have completely cleared the Oneida's influence."

"Ok, helm," Gunnar said, looking out at the Oneida mirror ball. "Bring the sub-light drive back online and let's get the Hap out of here."

Responding to the command, Audra touched the helm controls, concentrating on the displays directly in front of her, bringing the power couplings online and watching the representation of the Hap void disappear from around the ship. Bringing the sub-light drive system online, she reached for the controls that would activate forward motion. Anticipating acceleration, she prepared to manually guide the ship in a different direction, but nothing happened. The ship continued to drift. Heads turned to the engineering section of the bridge as the console began to blink with warning lights and alarms.

Outside, the star field began to twist to one side again, as a vicious booming sound tore at the *Constellation* from somewhere deep in the aft section. Seeping rapidly toward the Oneida's accretion disk, the crew switched on their safety locks. Audra grabbed at the maneuvering thruster controls, trying to keep the ship from rolling over as the stricken craft tilted sharply on her side.

"Dang it! All my hard work and now this," she complained.

Unaffected by the listing, Alex floated over the fitting engineering console and shut down the emergency alarm, the bridge becoming quiet again. Gunnar had to grab hold of the underside of the helm console as the *Constellation* capsized onto her back. Hanging from the floor now, he looked over at Audra, as the coms came alive with the sounds of Billy Moon yelling something about power routing in the engine room.

"Can someone explain to me why the anti-grav isn't doing its thing?"

"Looks like it's doing its thing to me," Audra commented, passing Gunnar a look. If their circumstances weren't so dire, this situation would seem quite comical.

"The anti-grav compensators have received a massive energy flux from the sub-light coupling." Alex 7001 turned himself upside down as he approached Audra and Gunnar. "With the fabric bend warping space at our location, it will take a couple of moments for the regulator systems to stabilize."

"At your earliest convenience," Gunnar grunted, looking back at Audra. "Could you please try to lose the anti-grav or get us back to a more comfortable orientation?"

Gunnar was trying to remain calm, as getting hysterical about any of this wasn't going to do any good. He was experiencing some mildly intense sensations of anger that were quickly spiking.

After some fighting from an upside down position, Audra coaxed the ship slowly back upright again and those that hadn't been able to get locked into their seats, picked themselves up and moved back to their stations.

"What happened?" Gunnar asked, getting up.

Audra scanned her controls for the requested information.

"We're out of the Hap void, but there's no sub-light coil ignition and there is barely any operational control of the maneuvering thrusters. A whole lot of drifting is going to be happening if we don't correct this problem now. This put us into the accretion disk. I might be able to keep us in a flat orientation to it, but that's about it."

"I think we're in trouble," Gunnar grumbled, swirling in Alex 7001's direction. "Alex…" his voice rising in frustration. "You said you fixed the power couplings."

"I did, Colonel," the droid commented, scanning the consoles in front of him for information. "The sub-light fail safes have engaged. Diagnosing the problem now."

"In the meantime, let's see if we can go directly to light speed."

"You said that was a bad idea," Audra countered.

"An idea that is not only bad, but unavailable," Alex voiced.

"The sub-light drive is in fail safe, the FTL drive is still there. What's unavailable?"

"The Para-light system is the final propulsion stage for the FTL drive. It's coupled directly to the sub-light fail safes. With the fail safes engaged, the Para light system is locked out."

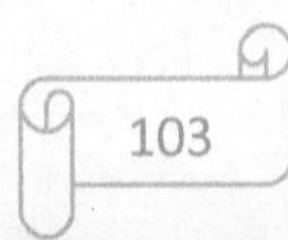

"We're in trouble," Gunnar reaffirmed his first inclination. "This has been the worst birthday of my life."

*   *   *   *

Rick turned forward in his chair at the summons of his pilot.

"Something's going down out there, sir," Captain Lisa Dayton announced.

Rick stood up, watching the *Constellation* slowly roll over and dip into the accretion disk. Assessing the situation, he ran his fingers straight back through his brown hair and turned his attention to his com officer.

"Now what's he doing? Get the *Constellation* back on the horn. Helm, head straight for them!" He turned his attention to the ship's onboard AI. "CORA, we need those numbers! They're in a time dilation now and I'm sure they're wondering what's taking us so long to get to them. Weapons officer, be ready to grab them with your tractor once they're in range." Stepping over to the science officer, he scanned the readouts in front of him. "Toby?"

"Scanning, sir. The Hap void is gone, but it appears their sub-light drive train is inoperative. They have limited maneuvering thrusters and now their ignition coils are starting to overload. If we don't move fast, they'll flatten and be pulled apart, then there won't be much to grab."

"Helm, move it!" Rick barked. "You'll have to download from CORA as we go." Rick turned to his command chair at the summons of his communications officer.

"Colonel Conrad on com two, sir. Be advised of the latency in his response time. They're close enough to the event horizon now, it's affecting the transmission."

Rick touched the button on the armrest of his chair.

"Gunnar, why are you practicing acrobatics now?"

Static snarled back at him while several tense moments passing anxiously. Warbled and muffled sounding, Gunnar's voice crackled back over the transmission.

"My know-it-all AI droid that you assigned to my ship said he fixed the FTL drive, but the tin can failed to give the Para light system a good going over. Everything is in fail safe mode now. I'm gonna lose my ignition coils here pretty quick if something doesn't change. Stupid 7000 series, I thought they were supposed to know everything about these ships?"

"Calm yourself. We'll maneuver in from behind," Rick said anxiously. "It will feel like about three hours to you, but we'll have ahold of you in about three minutes."

"And what am I supposed to do for three hours?" Gunnar responded, the com fading out with a rasp of static.

"Transmission lost, sir," the communications officer announced, searching for the problem.

"Never mind," Rick said, sitting back down. "Steady as she goes helm."

The turbo door behind him snapped open and his first officer, Jayda Niker stepped in. Standing next to her husband at the command chair, she could barely discern the outline of the crippled *Constellation* through the mirk of the accretion debris.

*   *   *   *

"Com, where are you with getting the *Athena* back on the line?"

"Doing the best I can, sir," the com officer answered without turning. Lana touched her console in multiple locations, reconfiguring her instruments to get ship to ship communications back online. She was resorting to an unconventional configuration with equipment that was never designed to do what she was attempting.

Gunnar was tired, they all were. The gravitational time dilation slowed everything down, even dragging on the physiology of the human machine. Somehow they would have to rest easy as it would take some time for Rick to reach them. As the hours drug slowly by, the crew remained silent, performing what tasks they could. The ship continued to rumble and shudder from occasional debris strikes in the accretion disk and the gravity stress of the Oneida drawing them closer to its event horizon.

Finally, Gunnar's attention was drawn to the overhead window, detecting movement directly above. He stood up, watching as the belly of the *Athena* glided silently ahead of them. While they were still in a lot of trouble here, now there was hope. Gunnar glanced back down at a flashing light on the armrest of his chair.

"General Niker on the line, sir," Lana informed him.

"If you had gone in any further, you would have thought I was taking days to reach you."

"You have no idea how glad I am to see you in front of me," Gunnar sighed, still worried. "I imagine Command is going to be thrilled with our communications blackout. We're losing all kinds of time in here."

"We're going to lose a butt load more time hanging around in here as it is, but I think we're ready, buddy ol' pal. Bit of a

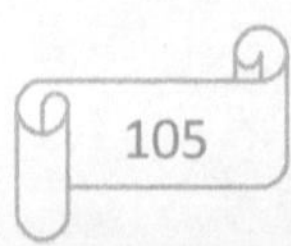

change in plans though. You've altered your orientation from what we had previously calculated for, so instead of backing you out, we're going to try pulling. Makes for a little more strain on us, but what can ya do? Seems like I'm always having to save your sorry butt from something."

"My sorry...."

"Hang onto your hats. Have you out of there in two shakes of a Thornax's tail."

"Just do whatever it takes," Gunnar nodded, sinking back to his seat and snapping his safety locks into place. He watched as the *Athena* maneuvered into position ahead of them.

"Here it goes kids," Rick announced. A positioning light came on at the rear of the *Athena*, activating the tractor connection to the hull of the *Constellation*.

Gunnar felt his crippled ship quake as the powerful tractor hawser grabbed them. A spark of hope materialized, listening to Pip announce movement out of the accretion disk and away from the bending effects of the Oneida. Out here, time dilation wasn't going to be a problem. If they could just get far enough away to maintain their distance with what they had operating, they could make the needed repairs and send for help. Even after several minutes of travel, he found himself breathing nervously, having an awful feeling that even though they were moving, it wouldn't be for long. Still, he hoped he was wrong.

A sickening feeling blanketed the entire bridge crew as alarms started going off. First at weapons control, followed almost instantly at the science station.

"Prox alarms are picking up inbound ordinance!" Pip shouted.

The *Athena* started firing from her forward guns and aft turret at the same time Lieutenant Cartwright activated his guns at an unseen, inbound target.

"Let me guess, they've launched more missiles," Gunnar complained from his chair. "How come we didn't see them coming this time?"

"No, sir, not missiles, they've launched five more HV mines, all coming in at different trajectories."

"Tactical," Gunnar snapped.

"Not available, sir," Pip responded grimly.

Alex 7001 floated in a moment later, gliding directly over to the engineering station. With the heavy strain on their already overloaded ignition coils and their diminished power reserves, this couldn't have come at a worse time. Feeling helpless, Gunnar reached for one of the flashing com buttons and activated it. He didn't even get a word out before the response.

"I see them," Rick responded from the hidden speaker. "Hard to get an exact fix on them for a target lock. This is really good!" Rick's voice was usually quite cool when stress was high, but this time something else was there.

The other com channels suddenly came alive with chatter from all four Interceptor pilots. Lana moved to shut the channels off, but Gunnar stopped her.

"No, leave it on."

"Logan, sweep past the first one and see if you can draw it off," Dakota ordered. "Zek, Zak, you two see if you can lead off the other one and we'll either lead them into the Oneida or back toward Croft's destroyers."

"They're too far away, Captain," one of the Korack pilots answered.

"Is there any way to see what's going on out there?" Gunnar asked, frustrated. He stood up in hopes of seeing something outside. Pip worked furiously to figure out something, finally calling to Gunnar.

"Sir, I've patched into the *Athena's* sensors and tactical systems. We're seeing exactly what they're seeing now."

Gunnar studied the readouts carefully, a grim look etching into his expression. He turned to Audra who was looking to him for some kind of hope, but she saw only fear streaking across his face. With two slow moving ships, they were easy targets. There would be no way for the Interceptors to draw all of them off without one getting through and if they got close enough to them to shoot, they would be close enough for the mine to go off.

Dakota made several checks of his scanners as he pushed his throttles a little harder toward the incoming target. A quick calculation confirmed that even if they were able to get all the others, a fifth would still have time to reach the *Athena* and the *Constellation* before they could draw it off or destroy it. He blinked several times. Even at this distance he was feeling the effects of the fabric bends the Oneida was rolling out. A thought popped into his head as he made a wide arc around the trajectory of one of the inbound mines. Working as fast as conditions would allow, he started working with his onboard computer while still maneuvering into position to intercept. A sudden flash of light filled his cockpit and an instant latter, Zak Korack was yelling from the com system.

"Step up to the bar boys, I'm buying the first round. Smoke one mine!"

"Track to one five seven one," Dakota called out. There was a second flash that filled the cockpit, followed moments later by a concussion wave that rocked the fighter.

"Second round is on me," Logan celebrated.

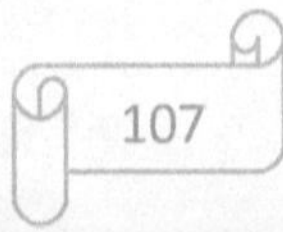

"Do we even have alcohol aboard ship?" Zek asked, holding his firing buttons down.

"How you doing out there brotha?" Zak inquired of his twin.

"This one is a little tough to deal with."

"It's moving slower than the others, what's the deal?"

"They've programmed this one to zig-zag and from this distance it makes it a little harder to hit it without getting too close."

"Can you hack its guidance system?" Dakota asked, still working his computer.

"Uhm, no, sir, not really. Sort of fell asleep during that training seminar."

"Leave it. Go help Zak and Logan with the other two," Dakota ordered. As the other fighters narrowed in on one of the inbound targets, he turned his ship hard and headed toward the slower moving mine.

"These two are going to be really close, stay on your toes. Hurry up and get up here Zek," his brother called.

"Dak, are you sure you can stop that last one all by yourself?" Zak asked.

"You're kidding," Logan answered back. "It's Dak. I think he can handle it."

"Hey guys?" Zek cut in. "I think I've got this one to follow me. What am I supposed to do with it?"

"Lead it back to where it came from."

"That won't do any good. Its inertial program is set for the Starbird's signature."

"Yeah, but it might buy us some time to take care of the other ones. Just don't outrun it."

"So you want me to play capon with a mine?"

"Just keep it busy long enough for us to take care of these other two."

"So capon..."

"Give the boy a yellow sticker."

"I think I have a splendid idea."

"Yeah, sure, you're a hero." His twin brother didn't sound very convinced. "Just take care of it and then come back and tell us all about it."

Zek was already making a wide bank away from everyone else. Zak took note of his direction on his scanner and after a moment, a grin formed up across his lips.

Another blast of light flashed closer to the two Starbirds moving away from the Oneida's accretion ring. It was like viewing a sporting event from another planet, all you could do was sit and watch nervously as the players worked the playing field. Both Corsairs fired in the same direction at the inbound targets streaking toward them.

"This one's going to be close," Logan announced. He banked hard and held his firing controls down in a steady pattern.

"I'm trying to figure out how we haven't hit this dumb thing," Zak responded, still firing.

"Maybe it's not as dumb as we think it is. Come on!" Logan was near frantic as he watched the target streak across the imaginary lines defining it within range of its target. "Finish it!" *How were they not hitting it?* There was fire coming from both Starbirds and two of the fighters. It was unclear as to whether it was finally struck or it reached its preprogrammed detonation point, but the resulting explosion nearly blinded those trying to track it.

The concussion began its grim work of destruction, violently buffeting both Interceptors as they tried to bank away from the ensuing shock waves and damaging debris cloud expanding from the detonation zone. Many of the onboard systems of the big fighters either went offline or were scrambled with the accompanying spacial interference. All but Captain Abrams and Zek had gotten too close on this one.

Dakota banked his fighter sharply, turning parallel of the *Athena* and *Constellation*. Checking his scanners and still furiously working his computer, he passed a momentary glance out as the shock wave and associated debris struck both Starbirds. Horrified, he watched helpless as both ships were nearly rolled over by the concussion turbulence washing over them. Momentarily blinded, he could only look back down at what he was doing and steer for his objective.

The *Athena* took the brunt of the blast. Captain Dayton tried to turn directly into the shock wave to bring the forward shields to bear against the ring of rolling debris that would no doubt be hurtling at them. The *Athena's* hull glowed where she was taking hits, much of the shrapnel piercing right through the shields and into her composite structure. Several secondary explosions tore at her skin as most of her shielding failed, tearing at her bridge pod and the aft engine compartment.

The *Constellation* received nearly the same carnage. Still held close to the *Athena* by their tractor hawsers, the concussion's spacial turbulence twisted the inoperable Starbird so far forward, it nearly struck the aft section of the *Athena*. It was only by some miracle that Audra was able to keep a collision from occurring. Several more slabs of outer composite skin peeled away from the stricken *Constellation* as both ships rolled together, back toward the Oneida. The occupants of both ships thought the light show outside was the other ship exploding under the damage caused by the impacts, but as suddenly as it had started, it was over. Even so, they continued to roll back in the direction of the black hole's accretion disk.

Most primary power sources went offline, including all engine functions, navigation and weapons, with only emergency power keeping emergency shields and life support operational. The last mine would surely finish them off and their burnt out hulks would drift into the Oneida's accretion ring, being slowly pulverized and swallowed by the event horizon.

"Whatever you have in mind, you better do it now," Logan called to Dakota as his com system came back on line.

"Need you guys to form up on me. I think I've got this."

"Got what?" Zek called, bringing his fighter alongside Logan, as they swept parallel to Captain Abrams.

"And what did you do with your little follower?" Logan asked checking his scanner.

"I'm sorry, was I supposed to bring it back with me? Dang it! It had a run in with some rocks in the Oota belt. I'm not even sure I can find any of the pieces."

"Where's Zak?" Dakota inquired.

"Check right," the other pilot called. Dakota glanced to his right noticing another fighter sweeping alongside his own.

"Good, the gangs all here. Inverted box on my axis and just do what I do."

"Are you nuts?" Logan protested as the other two formed up on both sides of his fighter.

"We need a bigger footprint, Logan," Dakota came back quietly. "Today is the day to be a hero. I have a present for our Imperial buddies over there."

Logan maneuvered his ship into position, inverted directly above Dakota and the Korack twins. A moment later, his comlink came alive.

"Captain Abrams, Dakota, get your guys out of here! Get clear of this mess! We're done for!"

"My coms are damaged. I can't make out what you're saying."

"Did you hear anything?" Logan finally called out.

"I'm serious Abrams! You guys can't do any more good out there. Use your FTLs and get out of here!"

"My com arrays have been damaged, your transmission is garbled," the Interceptor pilot remained resolute in his stubbornness. "Can you repeat your last message, sir?" Dakota looked out at Zek and Zak, then up at Logan.

"Let's give this present a little better heading, shall we?"

"You hacked its inertial program."

"Shut down its proximity sensors and we'll give it a better target when we get close enough. We'll give Croft's boys a little present, shall we?"

"I like giving presents like this."

"Me too."

The formation streaked in a wide arc away from the two stricken Starbirds, heading directly toward Croft's Imperial destroyers.

*   *   *   *

Onboard the *Athena*, Rick turned to Toby Mavis, still breathing a little heavy with the excitement of the wild ride they had just endured. His science officer's eyes were glued to the instruments in front of him as main power came back up and his systems rebooted.

"Toby, how bad is it?"

"The good news is, well, there is no good news. We're still in a monster fabric bend, the deepest I've ever seen."

"What about the *Constellation*? Is there anything left of her?"

"Sensors are offline, so I can't tell. Visual scanning isn't showing any pieces of her out there."

Rick's heart sank, thinking of his friend and his crew.

"Sir," the weapons officer spoke up, checking his controls. "Our tractor is still active. I think we still have them."

"Helm, level us out! Jayda, I need to know how bad we're hurt." Both pilot and first officer were already at work, anticipating the commands. "Lieutenant Habba, as soon as your systems are back online, open a channel to the *Constellation* and get the Interceptors on the line." Rick stepped up next to the weapons officer with hopeful excitement, looking at his readouts.

"Conrad here." Static popped through the transmission. "We're still in one piece here, thanks to you guys."

The entire bridge of the *Athena* erupted in cheers and high fives at the sound of Colonel Conrad's relieved voice.

"Bunch of idiots anyway and that goes double for those four nut jobs outside."

"All in a day's work," Captain Abrams responded casually. He grinned broadly as he swung his big fighter in a circle around the two stabilizing Corsairs.

"Your coms seem to be working just fine now," Gunnar shot back, never happier to hear the voices of his fighter pilots.

"Yeah, funniest thing. Must have been all the electromagnetic, astro-static, magna flux, hyper terminal, space waves or something."

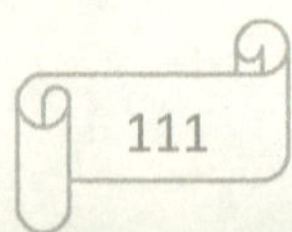

"Yeah, must have been whatever that BS was you just made up. Now, if you could please follow orders. Stay in close to us. I don't want you getting lost in a time dilation if something else happens."

"That won't be a problem since that blast damaged our FTL drive inducers."

"Just stick close. We may be bringing you back onboard real fast. For now, keep an eye on those destroyers." Gunnar was relieved that Captain Abrams hadn't followed orders. Both ships and crew had made it through alive, something that could be directly attributed to the skill and bravery of the Interceptor pilots and his best friend's tenacious nature.

"Alex, we need a ship wide systems analysis ASAP," Audra ordered, working with the helm controls.

"I think we're still in one piece here," Rick announced, a shower of static blasting the com line. As several long moments passed, Gunnar could hear Rick barking out orders to his crew through a constant flow of static. "Navi-computers are down and my TICs are damaged. Skinned up my hull good too. I've got no MFC systems now and our FTL drive train is completely out. My Fulton drive is offline so we're on maneuvering thrusters only now. Looks like I'm going to get to use up all my Nano-mech too. Got any extra?"

"Sorry buddy. We're all tapped out over here. What about your Asium crystals, what condition are they in?"

"It appears they're fine for now. What we really need is to get back up and running. Give me a call when you have a better idea of what you can get working."

You want to do what?

The *Constellation* and the *Athena* now maintained a stable orbit around the Oneida just inside the outer edge of the accretion disk. Clinging to each other by their mooring tractors, they maintained a safe distance from the Oneida's event horizon. Being tied together had bought them time to make hasty repairs, restoring control and partial power to their sub-light drives and maneuvering thrusters. Still, they were far enough inside the accretion disk that neither ship had the thrusting power available to break free of the gravitational pull. It would require their FTL engines that were currently inoperative. Messages had been sent out on distress beacons, their emergency hyper channels and all available subspace frequencies. But being in a time dilation, they had calculated that by the time it reached someone and there was a response, if there was a response, the Oneida's event horizon would have them.

Both crews found it tiring to physically move as the gravitational pull had the ship's anti-grav systems so loaded down that it couldn't compensate, making the gravity in the ships several times more than the human body was accustomed to. The deep fabric bends they were riding in and out of continuously warped their vision in differing angles and directions, making focusing on their work difficult. Though the channels were static obscured and constantly modulating their voices like breathing inert gases, a constant line for communication remained open between the two ships. Alex 7001 and CORA 500 were tied together by separate data channels, running complex formulas for the potential maneuvers facing them. With the exception of the Interceptor pilots, command staff had been ordered to their respective ready rooms. Gunnar and his staff studied the calculations and conversed with Rick and his staff through a static obscured display.

"We've run all of the Asium power data through Alex 7001," Gunnar informed the group grimly. "Using what conventional propulsion methods we have operational, he calculates the odds of successfully breaking free of the Oneida's gravity field about... Well, there are no odds of breaking free. It can't be done. Right now we're both sort of stuck in here without light speed, a basic requirement for breaking away."

"Even if we could get out, what about Croft's destroyers waiting for us out there?" Jayda asked.

"We have to consider the amount of time we've been sitting here in a gravitational time dilation," Rick explained. "For us we've been here a couple of hours, for those destroyers and our home worlds, exponential time has elapsed. No doubt we're now facing the same challenges the *Stark* and the other freighters faced."

"We noticed the *Stark* accelerate around the far side of the Oneida and disappear shortly after we were caught here in the ring," Pip said.

"So it appears they might have figured out a way to beat it, or escape," Audra suggested.

"Maybe," Rick agreed. "But if their FTL drives were damaged as ours are and they aren't here anymore, there are only two possibilities. They either fixed their FTLs and drove out on their own, in which their time dilation would be certainly aged way out there, or the unthinkable, the event horizon got them."

"None of our telemetry logs showed them breaking apart at the event horizon," Toby stated.

"But those logs can't really be trusted, can they?" Jayda asked.

"No, not really. The time dilation and fabric bends distort everything," Rick shook his head slowly.

"Last reliable information on them was their peculiar positioning all around the Oneida's accretion ring and their acceleration," Pip offered.

"We can still see some of those destroyers out there," Jayda said pointing at one of the portal windows in the ready room.

"Because of the time dilation, we disappeared from their view shortly after we got caught in here. And for every minute we spend in here, depending on how close or far away from the event horizon we are, translates into a huge shift in time for the rest of reality on the outside. Our time to them, sped up. Their time to us, has slowed down. That's why they're still visible."

A muffled murmur rolled through the group assembled on both ships.

"Any chance of getting the Interceptor's FTLs operational?" Jayda asked. "Load everyone on them, abandon ship and get out."

"They do have big cockpits, but you couldn't get everyone in them, so who are you going to leave behind? Besides, like you said, their FTL drives are busted," Gunnar explained.

"Then what would be the point of breaking loose anyway?" Fuji asked trying to follow the science. "If you're not sending out for help, then why try to break out in the first place? Why not just turn into the event horizon?"

"So you want to get flattened and pulled apart at the subatomic level?" Billy asked a little irritated. Rick jumped in before words could heat up.

"No, I'm suggesting something else entirely. The Oneida has robbed us of time and the longer we stay, the more time gets sucked away from what was once our reality."

"I hate Black holes," Fuji mumbled.

"So here's something to consider," Rick continued. "Let's rob the Oneida back, take back that time we're losing. Gunnar, you pulled us out of a jam on Kalamar by grabbing us with your tractor hawser and sling-shotting us back into the air so I could get my engines online and have the speed and height to keep from hitting the ground."

"Yeah, I was a real hero that day."

"Why not do that here?"

"You're talking about slinging us out of orbit?"

"Yes and no. Just slinging you won't get either one of us very far at all. Even in my condition, I can't get out. We need more than just speed. I have partial sub-light power, but not enough to generate the speed to get out. So why not use orbital gravity to produce the speed required to break free?"

"Because, you said it yourself, neither ship has enough sub-light power and there is no way to get my crew over to your ship and abandon mine."

"We don't have to abandon your ship. We need to take it with us."

"Ok, this sounds crazy enough to work. Let's hear your master plan, Skip Bo."

"We start out together. Since the *Athena* is faster, I'll orbit around the Oneida picking up as much speed as I can until I catch up to you."

"Won't you time dilate if we break contact?" Audra asked.

"Not if we maintain exactly the same distance from the event horizon the entire time," Rick reassured everyone. "As I catch up and pass by we grab each other with our tractor hawsers. This will create a sling shot effect and increase our speed. We then alter course to travel as close to the edge of the event horizon as we can without flattening. This will multiply our speed to the lower end of the light speed threshold."

"Enough speed to break out of the accretion disk and away from the Oneida and its influence, then what?" Gunnar was right with Rick in his thinking.

"We recreate your Hap void as we're reaching top speed away from the Oneida."

"Uhm... won't that...?"

"Creates a time winding worm hole that'll shoot us back in time. About ten minutes of travel, then fire the breaking thrusters to slow us back to sub-light and...dun, dun, dun. We set course back to the Kalamar shipyards."

"Why so long in the worm hole?"

"Well, the Oneida is quite large and can basically do whatever it wants with time and space. We are significantly smaller and have to work a little harder at it."

Except for the background static in the com transmission, the room remained silent, everyone thinking about how and if this could work. Looks were exchanged around the room, each person hoping someone would speak up and point out some flaw in the plan. There was sound logic at play here, but it was still just theory. While not necessarily reckless, it was somewhat outlandish and certainly brash, something Audra was growing accustomed to. Gunnar drew in a deep breath and looked over at her, then up at Alex 7001.

"No doubt you're still running calculations, Alex, what do you think?"

"Certainly unconventional, Colonel, but the General's plan is sound."

"There is no room for error with this maneuver," CORA interceded. "While there is some adjusting that can be accomplished *on the fly*, so to speak, much of it will require precise control."

"Vary any from the assigned orbital path and you'll be in a different time dilation," Alex cut in. "Fail to make the proper adjustments to the tractor hawsers as you connect and it will over-sling you into the event horizon and the singularity. Get too close to the event horizon and the tidal forces will pull both ships apart. Create the hap voids too late and the time winding worm hole will not form. The projected density parameters of the worm hole will stress our hulls at their max test strength. If our guidance systems vary out of allowable tolerances, structural damage will occur that could be catastrophic. Finally, the braking thrusters would have to be timed to bring both ships out of the worm hole at exactly the same moment. Then you have to figure out where it is you sent yourself. You could be halfway across the universe, so to speak."

"Can our limited guidance systems navigate under the parameters you're proposing?" Audra asked. She had been carefully running as many contingencies through her head as she could think of.

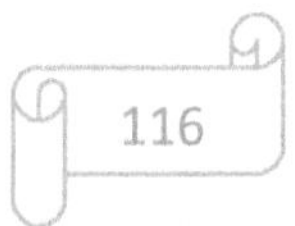

"CORA and Alex can run all the guidance systems and make all the inflight adjustments," Rick informed them.

"As long as they can maintain a link, right?" Audra was looking for something absolute.

"Yeah..." Rick slurred his answer. There was a lot riding on everything going off without a hitch and in their condition, those odds weren't good. He gave his friends another not so reassuring head nod.

"We'd better get to work then," Gunnar finally said, resolutely. He could see the whole thing in his head, just like he knew Rick could see it. He did wish they had a little more to go on, some kind of an absolute that would be a better guarantee of success. But, this was something every commander would face at one time or another during their career, he just wished it wasn't his career.

The looks around the room were equally depressed thinking of the enormity of everything that had to happen just right. Gunnar gave Audra a long look, then one by one passed glances at everyone else in the room, then looked at Rick and Jayda.

"I like this plan! I'm excited to be a part of it! It's full of simple mathematics and it's easy to understand. I think we should go for it!"

Audra gave Gunnar a look, then turned to the viewer. She was going to ask if they all felt comfortable with the plan, but then realized there really wasn't a better alternative. The longer they sat here, the more time they would have to overcome and the closer they would be drawn to the event horizon.

"Are there any objections?" she asked.

"I object," Billy Moon piped up, looking around. "I'm getting the distinct impression here that everyone thinks this plan is crazy and there's no way it's going to work. You all think we should be able to just drive back out the same way we came in. Well guess what folks? The Oneida doesn't work that way." The engineer paused a moment to see if anyone was going to own up to their feelings vocally. "If you're still looking for something a little easier, then please, let's step down the hall to the teleporter room and we'll teleport you out into space right now, cause that's the alternative. I think we can agree we're all scared to death. As chief engineer of this ship, I certainly have my concerns, especially considering our conditions, but I have to tell ya, I've known these two meat-hooks since they were squadron Captains using Stumpers and T-6s to knock heads with Croft Hekla's Tau and Mu clones. And even though they've torn up more ships than I care to mention here, they've never failed to bring themselves, their ships or their groups home. Granted, some of them have been in cargo containers and body cases, but

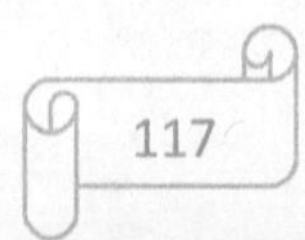

they've always brought them home and while this plan is way out there, given what these two can accomplish together, gives me every reason to believe that this will work."

"Engineer Moon is correct," Jayda agreed, trying to help rally the crew. "We all need to get behind this and focus like it's just another one of our duties and let the mission go off without a hitch."

Audra could see the crew settling in and becoming a little more optimistic with what lay ahead of them, so she stood up.

"Let's get our punch lists setup and get to it, dismissed," Audra ordered.

As the rest of the staff scurried out of the ready room, Gunnar and Audra turned back to Rick and Jayda.

"We have most of the more complex calculations almost complete now," Rick said, glancing at some information flashing across a display close to him. "I've had CORA running the calculations on this since we arrived. It's the kind of thing you hope you never have to use but are glad when you have it."

"Nice of you to anticipate the outcome of this conversation," Gunnar commented good-naturedly.

"Be on time to staff meeting next time," Rick countered trying to grin.

"How much time until we can proceed?" Audra inquired.

"At this point, we take all the time we need," Gunnar popped, trying to be funny.

"You want to sit here in orbit around that thing and just stare at it? Barring any major problems, we should be ready in a couple of hours." Rick looked over at a readout next to him on the desk.

"Ok, we're on it. Better bring the Interceptors back now." Gunnar let out a big sigh as the transmission ended. Stepping into the hall toward the bridge, they were joined by Lieutenant Starman, carefully walking up the hall. Gunnar smiled slightly, watching her make her way to the bridge door. "How are you feeling, Lieutenant?"

"Fine, sir," she responded, looking a little bedraggled but fit. "Dr. Yamoto gave me an accelerator. I just can't sit by and watch all this happen without me. Permission to resume my duty status?" She looked determined to get back to her station.

"If the good doctor released you for duty, then that's good enough for me," he said stepping through the bridge door behind the others. "Glad to have you back at the helm. Commander Atlanta will help bring you up to speed on what we're doing." Gunnar turned to Alex 7001 sitting locked to the floor near an access panel by the engineering consoles.

"Sure you can hack this one?" Gunnar asked, angry they were even in this situation to begin with.

"I have already apologized for the condition of the Para light system, Colonel," Alex answered in his defense.

"Gunnar," Audra interjected, before an argument with a machine could commence. "Remember, it's only a machine and it's been doing the work of five people. The last thing it needs right now is attitude from you, he's got enough to deal with."

"Hate it when you're right," Gunnar admitted with a smirk. He stepped over to his chair and sat down. "Good luck, Alex," he said with a little effort.

"I'll do my best, sir," the droid replied.

"What we all need to be doing," Gunnar mumbled.

What time is it?

Soon enough and not long enough, the *Athena* set out in a precise orbit around the Oneida with the slower moving *Constellation* following suit, each ship keeping to the exacting requirements of distance from the event horizon. As the *Athena* became but a tiny ripple in the superheated gases of the accretion ring, Gunnar ordered the *Constellation* to its fastest speed possible. Relying solely on the ship's AI assisted guidance systems, the *Constellation* held a precise course around the Oneida as it reached its full velocity. Lynette and Nigel watched with eyes transfixed on the dazzling light show of the gases boiling outside as the ship raced through the accretion ring. The speed at which they were traveling created a violent nose wake against the superheated gases, causing suspended particles to glow in a rainbow of crimson on dark saturated colors.

Gunnar looked over at Audra, then down at Alex 7001. The droid looked peaceful enough, no smoke coming from its head or torso, that was a good sign.

"Is your gear up and running enough you'll be able to see the *Athena* coming from behind?" Gunnar asked, turning to Pip. He found the science officer's gaze turned up at the glowing gases just outside.

Pip moved like he was going to look at his instruments, but the light show outside held his eyes. He finally broke from the trance and turned to his displays.

"Not from far away, but in plenty of time to give the guidance systems enough time to make calculations and any corrections."

"Do you have everything you need, Billy?" Audra called into her headset pickup. She too was having difficulty focusing on anything but the light show outside.

"Some engineers, a couple of Interceptor pilots, a turret gunner and a gimpy ship. What more could a guy want?" Audra passed Gunnar a quick reassuring glance and turned back to her displays.

"Are we going to be able to see a little better once we get away from the accretion disc?" Gunnar asked.

"Once we start pulling away and pick up more speed, we should be able to see everything that's happening," Pip said.

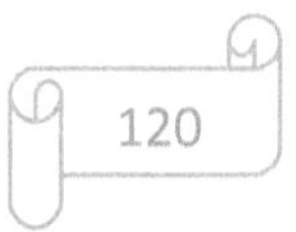

"I'm a little concerned about maintaining contact with the *Athena* when we enter the winder. Transmissions don't do so well in worm holes."

"Com?" Gunnar turned.

"I'll try to work something out, sir," Lana reassured him.

Pip continued to call out their increasing speed and position relative to their starting point. Additionally, he was calling out the calculated position of the *Athena* traveling at a faster speed. Occasionally, they felt a strike from a chunk of space debris to their shields, but it was harmlessly deflected away.

"Is there any way to see if the *Athena* is behind us yet?" Gunnar asked becoming impatient.

"Not in these conditions," Pip responded. "Every signal being sent out right now is either pulled away into the Oneida or sent back so distorted, it's unreadable. I can see primary targets directly in front of us and behind, but that's it."

"Can you tell how many orbits we've made?"

"Three so far. We should be seeing or hearing from the *Athena* momentarily." Pip paused at the same time Doran Cartwright at weapons turned in his chair.

"I have a primary target approaching from astern."

"Confirmed," Pip agreed. "It's big enough and the calculated rendezvous point is correct, should be them. I'll know in a moment." As he worked with his instruments, Gunnar noticed the dimensional display light up and an image materializing.

"General Niker on the line," Lana announced as a light on Gunnar's armrest lit up.

"Ready to stare into the jaws of hell and spit in its eye, buddy?"

"The sooner the better. Just hope there isn't a headwind," Gunnar called back. "Plan still holding?"

"Unless you've broken something else while I was gone," Rick commented as Gunnar watched the representation of the *Athena* form up on the dimensional scanner.

"I think I'm done for one day."

"You in position?"

"Just getting ready to execute our final maneuvers." Gunnar shifted his eyes to Lynette, who turned back to her controls.

"His positioning looks perfect," Pip reported, bringing up the visual of the *Athena's* quick approach from astern.

Lynette gently rolled the *Constellation* one hundred and eighty degrees. Now inverted in relation to the other, the *Athena* and *Constellation* activated their tractor hawsers as they came within targeting distance of each other. As the tractors were locked and adjusted, the *Athena* and *Constellation* flew keel to keel, both ships increasing their speed as they completed their slingshot maneuver.

"How does it look?" Gunnar asked looking over at Audra as she scanned all the readouts in front of her.

"Nothing alarming, always a good sign," she reported not even looking back at him. Gunnar turned forward to weapons and helm. Both Lynette and Doran nodded with thumbs up. He finally turned back to Pip.

"Everything looks good."

"Rick, we're ready to go."

"Righto sports fans. CORA and Alex, transferring all guidance system control directly over to you. Next interface will be after we clear the ring on the other side."

There came a noticeable shift in the direction of the gas flow outside and after several moments, the gases disappeared. Both ships emerged from the accretion disk, headed for a theoretical point near the edge of the event horizon. As the ships veered toward the outer edge of blackness, their speed doubled as the gravitational forces acted exponentially on them, drawing them faster and faster along their preprogrammed trajectory.

Audra sat back uncomfortably. There was nothing more anyone could do at this point, as it was all up to math and both ship's ability to deal with the stress loads facing them. She glanced at the pilot and navigator, holding a white knuckled grip on their chairs as they watched the Oneida, elongating and magnifying light from the stars in front of them as they rocketed closer to the event horizon. Audra became aware that she too was grasping her armrests a little tighter than normal. She looked down at her instruments while Pip called out their trajectory, then looked back out at the hugely magnified vision in front of them as both ships executed their turn around the Oneida.

Audra felt like she was in a steep, high G turn or climb in a standard atmosphere. She found herself slinking lower in her seat as if an invisible weight were bearing down on her. She turned to Doran at weapons, slumped sideways in his seat unconscious. She pulled her headset from one ear and tried to look back the other direction at Pip Habba, darkness starting to shroud her sight as she raised her hand into what was left of her vision. Every line began to bend and blur to her left. She could hear Pip's slurred speech, still trying to call out their position, as the ships moved past the apex of the Oneida and the outer areas of the event horizon. They were traveling faster than the speed of light now. Above them, nothing but black as both ships angled their bank around their orbital paths. Here, there were only theories, but now those theories were being chiseled into facts.

A violent vibration rippled through the ship as Audra dropped what was left of her vision to the displays in front of her. She could hear Alex 7001 at her feet, letting out fast bursts of chirping sounds. Her mind began to flatten, unable to recognize the information in front of her. All their hopes hinged on Alex and CORA operating both ship's guidance systems flawlessly. Now the differences in a miscalculation or a burp in the binary stream feeding the guidance systems, could spell disaster. Both ships could break apart or veer into the Oneida and be pulled apart by the enormous gravitational tidal forces pulling at anything that got too close. Audra let her eyelids droop, as the blackness clouding her vision seemed to fill all of it, her eyes becoming itchy and tired. She could still feel the ship vibrating and a soft moaning sound in the back ground as gravity pulled harder at them, her head tilting to the left.

Eternal silence slipped by before Pip began calling out their position again, announcing that they were starting their level out and veering back away from the event horizon, their speed holding steady. Audra tried to sit back up, opening her eyes again and looking at the information on her displays. Blackness still clouding her vision, she was able to recognize the *Constellation's* orientation displays showing level flight in relation to the Oneida. She could see stars beyond the accretion disk as it rapidly disappeared beneath the nose of the ship. As her sight cleared, the crushing weight of gravity began to lift and her ears popped, clear sounds finally coming back to her.

Pip announced another speed increase as the vibration in the ship settled and Lynette came back to full awareness. She nudged Nigel good as she pulled herself all the way back upright in her chair. They were now approaching the predetermined max speed for the creation of the Hap void and the time winding worm hole. All stations were reporting in, Pip still calling out their increase in speed.

"Can you show the whole class how you created that Hap void you had going on earlier?" Rick mussed over the com.

"Very funny," Gunnar responded. "Just don't run into me when we separate."

"Oh, not much chance of that. Here's hoping it works."

"Tractor hawsers have separated," Doran reported turning to his commander.

"Helm, ready to maneuver ahead," Gunnar called out. "Audra, standby to work your magic on Pip's signal."

"Hap void in five, four, three, two, one, execute." Pip monitored the guidance systems as the FTL controls were activated. There came a sudden swirl of the light outside, surrounding the entire ship, forming a tunnel of sorts. While Pip announced the Hap forming and the chronometers rolling backward, a noticeable vibration began to build as they traveled through a winding shaft of time and space. Gunnar looked up at the displayed images above Pip, seeing the *Athena* directly behind them and feeling the vibration increase.

"This should be a slickery ride, talk to me people," Gunnar commanded, looking around for answers.

"I'm getting a nasty yaw developing across all axes," Lieutenant Starman called back.

"Confirmed," Audra agreed checking her instruments. "FTL coupler resonance is starting to destabilize. Huge energy spikes are modulating back down the power heliax."

"Can the guidance system remain viable? Do we need to drop the Hap and let her coast?"

"Compensating for the flux. Billy thinks we can hold out to the end of the run if we can stabilize the yaw."

"Helm."

"I'll do my best, sir," the pilot responded without looking up. She worked for several moments trying to regain control. "Inertial stabilizers aren't responding to commands, or at least they aren't having any effect."

Alex 7001 began chirping louder as the ship's yaw increased. Gunnar held tight to his chair as the yaw continued to pitch. He touched his comlink button as guidance alarms started sounding.

"Rick? I've got a slight inconvenience here." He tried to sound casual, watching Audra and Alex for a sign of how bad the problem was.

"Probably the same excitement I've got going on, I'd wager," came the garbled reply. "I'm having Toby run a diagnostic sequence on the trouble."

"I concur. Sure wish we had full power to the Fulton drive."

Gunnar wondered how much more of this his ship could take. There appeared to be nothing Lynette or Alex could do to hold the ship on an even keel. Moments later, he could hear another alarm come alive on Audra's comlink panel.

"Engineering, Commander," came the garbled call from Billy. "I need more help down here."

"Where's the other four you have down there?" Audra complained.

"They've got their hands full with other things keeping this ship in one piece," Billy responded sternly. "I need somebody down here that knows something about the Asium core. It's got to be you, Alex, or the Colonel."

Gunnar passed a glance at Alex 7001. The droid knew everything there was to know about this ship, especially the Asium core, the heart of the ship's power. But he was obviously occupied. That left himself or Audra. Command protocols were clear.

"See what you can do," Gunnar motioned to Audra who was already making her way from the bridge.

"Atlanta is on her way," Gunnar called back.

Lieutenant Starman tried to adjust her controls to neutral, but that only worsened the ship's attitude. Several minutes crawled painfully by as Gunnar waited for some sign of stability. Another alarm sounded off and a flurry of information flashed across the many screens at the engineering station. Responding to the alarms, Pip popped his safety locks and dashing across the bridge, nearly tripping over Alex 7001 still locked to the floor next to the engineer's seat. He scanned the information displayed in front of him as the com system came alive again.

"Colonel?" Something different was riding in Billy's voice this time. "Commander Atlanta is going to need someone else down here to help keep this core stabilized. The energy fluctuations building on the Asium inverter have become erratic."

Gunnar glanced down at Alex again. The guidance systems were having enough problems without taking a chance of interrupting the droid's link with CORA 500.

"I'll go," Pip volunteered.

"How much Asium core training have you had?"

Pip hesitated, lowering his eyes.

"Sorry, sir. Introductory only."

Gunnar unlocked his seat locks.

"I'll be right down." He turned for the door, looking back at the science officer. "Pip, you have bridge experience, so you have the con. Keep her going all the way to the end of the run if you can."

Under normal operating conditions, the ship's anti-grav system allowed the crew to walk freely about the ship. However, the stresses being exerted on the ship's hull from the worm hole interfered with this systems ability to function properly. Walking was a practice in drunkenness.

Stepping deliberately, Gunnar was half way down the hall when there came a noticeable tremble streaking throughout the entire ship. He stopped, grabbed ahold of the railing and waited a moment. Moving again toward the first set of doors at the end of the hall, he saw a wave of distortion pulse from the bulkhead in front of him. At the same instant, there came a low frequency rumble rolling through the ship. Before Gunnar could reach the mid-ship turbo door, it slid open and an angry cloud of white smoke belched into the mid compartment after two staggering engineers.

"What happened? Where are the others? Where's Audra?" Panicked, Gunnar stopped where Billy was trying to recover against the wall. Coughing, the engineer reached for the emergency air control.

"Crystal number five cracked and ruptured the Asium containment chamber. The pilots are in their cockpits. The other two went up the turret shaft." Billy continued to hack and wipe his eyes as the door behind him closed. It took only a moment for the air to clear. "Commander Atlanta was right behind me."

Gunnar's face went pale, his mind ajar with thoughts of Audra. Pivoting on one foot, he reactivated the door but was instantly met with another angry white cloud of hot billowing smoke. Catching his shoulder trying to get through before the doors had fully opened, he careened toward engineering, dodging pieces of metal and splintering composite from the ceiling and walls. All he could think of was Audra.

Where is she?

Struggling through the rushing smoke, he nearly crashed into the engine room door. As it opened, he was met with more eye burning smoke, and a searing wave of heat rolling around him. Gunnar hit the air control on the wall, instantly pulling back the toxic cloud. Brilliant flares from the engine room nearly blinded him, then came an ear cracking boom. Through it all, Gunnar watched a short figure struggling toward the door.

"Get out of there!" he hollered over the noise of the air control. The engine room rumbled, merging with another sound. There came the distinct sick groaning noise of metal twisting against itself and composite material cracking. Shards of debris launched from the ceiling and popped from buckling walls. The engine room doorway began to warp as Gunnar stepped out of Audra's way as she stumbled through the open door. She let out a frightful scream as the ceiling above her dropped, burying her beneath a mound of debris. Gunnar stood frozen, watching dumfounded for a moment, until it registered what had happened and he charged the pile of rubble. Billy and Frank moved to try and help, but Gunnar started tossing debris and steel panels like sheets of paper. It took him only a few moments to clear everything away. Positioning himself over Audra, he held his arms against the distorting walls, as she pulled herself along the floor and clear of the damaged doorway. Once she was clear, Gunnar picked up a broken wall beam, effortlessly wedging it between the walls to keep them from collapsing any further.

Audra groaned as he scooped her up and stepped toward sickbay, amid the sounds of creaking and moaning structure. She cracked her eyes, wincing in agony. It didn't take a doctor to tell this was serious.

"Had to stabilize crystal number five. I guess...I didn't move fast enough, sir." Gasping painfully, she looked into her husband's frightened eyes. She had never seen him like this before. "Gunnar, I don't..."

"No dying on me, Commander, that's an order," he said, kicking at the sickbay door. It still wouldn't open automatically and he had his hands full. Moments later, one of the doors slowly and stiffly pulled aside with the aid of Sindee and Fuji. The ship's doctor carefully ushered them through the shambles of sickbay to one of the beds, clearing it of debris. Gunnar practically had to be pushed back to allow Fuji to work, while Sindee attended to the Mantose twins on the other beds. As the ship's doctor worked, Colonel Conrad stepped over to the medical officer's desk and pressed her comlink.

"Bridge," he spoke, regaining his composure a little. Static crackled back at him as the walls around them quietly moaned and bits of ceiling material continued to pepper the occupants. Gunnar stepped back over to his wife's side as the doctor worked a scanning probe all around Audra's broken body.

"Yamoto," Gunnar fidgeted impatiently as the lights flickered several times.

Fuji wiped her forehead, glancing over at Sindee attending the other patients. Focusing back on Audra and the scanner flashing technical data, Fuji could hear queer moaning noises coming from one of the sickbay walls. Several alarms flashed across the overhead monitor and the desk comlink. Gunnar pushed closer, trying to attend to Audra.

"Colonel." Fuji cringed as something struck her on the back. "I appreciate your concern for Audra, but if you don't attend to your ship, what I do here isn't gonna matter."

Gunnar looked over at the door that was starting to buckle, then back at his mate. He didn't want to leave her, but if he didn't, things would certainly get worse.

"Gunnar, please!" Fuji pleaded, trying to shield Audra from bits of debris.

Almost panicked with indecision, Gunnar scanned the room, a frightened look rippling across his face. He would not leave Audra. Feeling a warm hand touch his clinched fists, he leaned down to his wife and clasped her hand in his.

"Go," she wheezed.

"I won't leave you," he replied, calming down.

"You must...save the ship," she uttered.

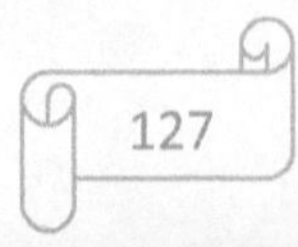

Gunnar looked up at Fuji.

"I'll take care of her, Colonel," Fuji said. "Now go," the doctor urged.

"Go," Audra repeated painfully. "Save the ship."

Finally, he turned, uncertain at first, then moving to the door, forcing it open further, and stepping out to help the engineers. Fuji looked down at Audra, who had put her hand on the doctor's arm.

"Fuji," she said in pain. "Neutranize my Nociceptors."

The doctor looked at the first officer horrified.

"I do that and you wouldn't last very long. I've got to keep you in full awareness to repair the damage to your-..."

"Don't throw effort after foolishness. You've got the makings of a great M.D." Audra gritted her teeth. "Don't waste your efforts on something that has no hope of success."

Fuji opened her mouth to protest, but Audra stopped her again.

"I have something difficult to do," she said, welling up with emotion, "and I can't do it in this condition."

"I will not condemn you," Fuji objected.

"That sentence has already been passed," Audra reaffirmed.

Fuji searched Audra's eyes for another reason not to do what she was asking. She glanced up at the life monitors and thought a moment. This went against everything she had been taught about life and medicine. She looked back down at Audra, pain rippling across her face and tears filling her eyes.

"Sindee," Fuji said, dodging a piece of ceiling, "prepare a Nitrozene hypo."

*   *   *   *

Hallway bulkheads continued to moan as Gunnar and the two engineers worked. Thus far there had been no outer hull breaches, but at the rate internal frame supports were twisting, a structural failure wasn't far away.

"What do you need?" Gunnar hollered over the noise of the air control systems.

Billy shielded his eyes from the arc flares coming from the Asium containment chamber as he tried to read the information on a handheld scanner. The heat issuing from the engine room was becoming uncomfortable.

"We need to get the fire control system working first. The Asium venting system is directing the plasma radiation out the exhaust ports, but the corona flares are super heating the air."

"So why isn't it working?"

"The fire control system won't engage unless the engine room doors seal. This section of the ship is twisting, preventing the doors from sealing."

"How can we stop the twisting?"

"Drop out of the wormhole."

"Anyway to stabilize the ship's structure in the meantime?"

"The ship's hull is base-fabricated utilizing a honey comb poly carbon composite. Parts by themselves can be easily twisted, but put them all together in a certain manner and they become nearly impossible to break. The composite is able to bend within limits, sort of a way of absorbing shock and stress to the ship's construction, but the Asium blast exceeded those limits. The supporting structure for this entire section is located there at the engine room doorway. We've got to stabilize that support structure." Billy studied several readouts on a small wall panel next to the vestibule door.

"Where?" Gunnar asked, looking through the twisted hallway.

"The archway, sir. The Asium blast from engineering tore away some of the secondary support structure. But even if I could get to the door, all my tools are in the engine room. I can't get things straightened out enough to reinstall an emergency support without those tools."

"How long can you guys stand that kind of heat?"

"It'll be mighty warm." Billy checked the readings on the small wall display. "Maybe five minutes at the most."

"But you're still going to have to stop the corona flares from the Asium chamber whether the doors seal or not," Gunnar pointed out squinting.

"Get these doors closed and evacuate the atmosphere, then we can stabilize the ship's hull integrity. Dakota or Logan can put on a G-suit and make repairs to the chamber from the other side."

Billy reached into an access panel in the wall next to him as Alex 7001 glided up next to Gunnar.

"Ship's hull integrity at maximum stress. Estimate hull breach in three minutes."

"What are you doing down here?" Gunnar turned to the droid that was supposed to be guiding the ship. "Who's driving the guidance systems?"

"CORA 500 and I are still in control of the guidance telemetry, sir. How can I help?"

"Seal off this compartment," Gunnar ordered, turning to the engineers. "If I can straighten the archway, can you guys get a support in place?"

"You figure it out, sir and I'll lift it into place myself," Billy exclaimed, touching a control in the panel to seal the air lock.

"Not likely," Gunnar replied, wiping his eyes. He stepped over debris and wall supports toward the engineering door, lung choking smoke continuing to pour from the open engine room.

"What's he doing?" Frank asked, watching the Colonel make his way to the deformed archway.

"Wishful thinking, I think," Billy replied, watching Gunnar position himself in the archway. Planting both hands on one set of bulkheads and positioning his feet on the opposing structure, he began to exert pressure. The ship moaned and whined, seemingly unaffected by Gunnar's feeble attempts at whatever he was trying to do.

"Oh please," the assistant engineer hollered, "It would take ten men and a hydro lifter to force that support..."

Gunnar's face turned red, straining against the pressure he was exerting. He let out an energy swelling yell, straining against the bulkheads, and slowly, to the complete surprise of both human and droid, the archway began to inch back out, the moans from twisting honeycombed alloys and composites softening. Finally, Moon and Cooper scrambled over the debris to reach the archway. Gunnar now had his feet on one bulkhead and pushing with his back on the other, while the two engineers strained to lift the end of a main support to the wall. However, it was far too heavy, until a hand reached down and grabbed it from above, lifting the end from the floor.

"Get something under it!" Billy ordered, reading the terrible strain on Gunnar's face.

Cooper struggled with broken supports to hold the beam up as one end slid up the side of the wall.

"Get the end in place!" Gunnar grunted, great beads of sweat forming on his face and neck.

The two men strained, heaving the beam up into its original hole. Alex 7001 floated over beneath the heavy support, trying to help lift with his small anti-grav system. Slowly, the beam slipped up into place and while Gunnar shifted most of his focus to the opposite wall, Moon and Copper struggled with a smaller support to use as a temporary until the main support could be pressed back up into place.

"We're gonna need it pushed out a little further, Colonel," Billy panted, as the stifling heat sapped at their energy reserves.

As Gunnar exerted more pressure against the buckled bulkhead, the temporary slipped into place. The bulkheads continued to moan quietly, but everything appeared to be holding together. Making a quick survey of the buckled walls and the supporting beam on the floor, Gunnar reached up and with a hefty yank, pulled the wall covering from the interior and tossed it aside. He could actually see the ship's structure bulging and twisting. If he had any hope of getting the support back into place, it would have to be now while the ship's structure was distorted.

Stepping away from the walls, Gunnar reached for the other end of the main support which still lay at his feet. Starting to tire, he was spurred on by the still constant moans of the ship. As he began to lift, Alex 7001 floated past him, disappearing into the darkness and heat of the open engine room. Hefting the heavy beam higher, the end soon met with the twisting ship structure and it became necessary for Gunnar to position himself under it and push with his back. However, it became apparent it was going to take more than Gunnar had to give. Two hearts enabled him to do many things normal men could not do, but his energy burn was equal to his strength. The support felt stuck in one place and he was losing his grip, even as Alex 7001 rolled out of the shadows on his two tank-like motovacs, towing two pneumatic lifters.

"Calvary to the rescue," Gunnar puffed holding his position.

"Give me a hand with this," Billy barked to his assistant. Both men quickly went to work setting the lifters up on each side of Gunnar.

"Please boys," Gunnar gasped, "let's not dawdle... in our labors."

"Heavy huh," Billy grunted, working swiftly to position his lifter in the right place.

"I've 'bout run out of gas," Gunnar gasped.

Finally, both lifters were in place and the lifter rods applying pressure against the support. Slowly, the huge beam pushed toward its hole and finally, with a deafening boom, popped into place.

"Glad my fingers weren't back there," Billy commented, hitting the emergency door seal and activating the fire control system. Gunnar slowly sank to his knees, bringing both engineers instantly to his aid.

"You ok, sir?" Cooper asked, helping Billy set their commander against a rippled bulkhead. "You've done the work of fifty guys just now," he continued.

Gunnar looked weakly up at Alex 7001, who was now airborne again, working a megawatt composite welder on the main support joints.

"If he hadn't, we'd all be in real deep doodoo right now," Billy commented, sitting down next to his commander.

"I need bridge com, Billy," Gunnar slurred.

"Corridor and medical coms are out, sir. Only teleporter and crew's quarters coms are working in this section. Do we need to get you back to sickbay?"

Gunnar shook his head, struggling to get back up, letting out a long groan as he tried pushing himself back up the wall. Only when Billy got up and helped him stand was he able to make his way into the teleporter room. After sitting down in the controller chair and reassuring Billy he was all right, he turned to the comlink panel.

"Bridge," he spoke tiredly, activating the link. Static crackled back at him.

"Pip here, sir."

"Ship status please," Gunnar requested, resting his head on the console in front of him.

"Looks like Alex 7001 dropped us out of the worm hole just a moment ago. We're still moving quite fast, just under the light speed envelope. Main guidance system is only barely functioning, but helm reports she's able to maintain enough control that we aren't doing the tumble dance anymore. I'm letting the ship coast until we know better what's going on. Operating with maneuvering thrusters only."

Gunnar looked up at his chief engineer, who understood the silent order.

"I'll report in as soon as I know," he said, stepping from of the room.

Gunnar took a deep breath, dropping his head back to the console in front of him.

"Please continue, Pip," he said tiredly.

"Are you ok, sir?" the science officer asked concerned.

Gunnar let out a heavy sigh.

"It's been a busy afternoon and I need a cat nap. It's a real mess down here. We're lucky we're not in a dozen pieces right now. I've got Billy working on the main engines. Please...ah, finish your report." Gunnar was having a hard time controlling the shaking in his arms and legs now. He chocked it up to exertion.

"Yes, sir," came a half satisfied reply. "Central computer main frame off line, Weapons and navigation are working on the problem. Com reports General Niker some distance behind us, but no report on his condition yet. Control tie-ins severely damaged due to the structural damage at mid-ship. I don't know how Billy managed to keep us together. By all the reports, we should be in a couple of pieces."

"Yea, he's a real hero," Gunnar groaned. "Have helm and navigation try to plot our position after the computers are back up and then you get down here to aux control and assist Billy in getting things back together," he said sitting up. "I'll be in sickbay." He hit the com control on the console in front of him and just sat for a moment, looking around him at the buckled bulkheads and blackened circuit junction boxes on the inner walls.

"I'd say we lucked out big time," he mumbled. *To still be flying a T-6 Tempest and not having to worry about a crew and holding a ship together.* He then remembered what he was all about and where he needed to be. Strength surged back to him and getting to his feet, he made his way over debris in the hallway to the damaged sickbay door.

Always

"Everything ok in here?" Gunnar asked, trying to push a control hanging from the wall back into its place.

Fuji looked up at the life monitor over Audra's bed, then back at the Mantose twins.

"Stable for now, thank you, Colonel. I didn't think we were gonna make it there for a while."

"You and me both. You on aux power in here?" he asked, moving to Audra's bed side.

"Yes, sir. Whose idea was it to give sickbay its own emergency power cells?"

"That would be Alex 7001. Capital thinking, but don't tell him I said that. So how is she doing?" Gunnar examined the life monitor over Audra's head. For the medically untrained eye, the readings looked normal. "Yamoto," Gunnar asked, looking at the readings a little closer. "What does this mean?"

Fuji glanced up for a moment, but then went back to what she was doing.

"She's heavily medicated to relieve her pain."

"Can she talk?"

"Well of course I can talk," Audra spoke up quietly. "I'm not dead."

Gunnar melted close to his battered wife.

"Of course you're not." He took her hand and smiled. Audra opened her eyes and looked up. Something struck him as odd about the way she moved.

"How are we doing out there?"

"We're still in one piece," he said pulling up a seat.

"I knew you could do it," she sighed carefully.

"Well, it wasn't just me. Without Billy, Frank and Alex, we'd be in a couple of pieces right now. I haven't had a chance to get back up to the bridge yet. Been trying to help clean up the mess down here first. The main thing is that you're all right."

"You look so tired," she said touching his face. "Are you sure you're all right?"

Gunnar tipped his head into her hand, squeezing it carefully between his cheek and shoulder.

"I could use a little nap. I promise I'll lie down after we've gotten a complete damage report." Gunnar noticed something behind him making a funny noise and turned to see Fuji moving a probe around his lower back.

"I'll make that doctor's orders," Fuji said slowly, reading the information on her display. She cracked a smirk and shook her head as she turned back to her other two patients. "One thing is for sure. You're never going to have to worry about gaining too much weight. Your metabolism will never allow it. You understand I'm serious about that nap, Colonel?"

"Yes, doc. You'll get no argument here."

"So what about Rick?" Audra asked, wincing slightly.

"He's still with us." Gunnar looked back up at Audra's monitor. Something didn't seem right.

"Yamoto?" he spoke up, looking over his shoulder.

"Will you leave her alone; she's already got her hands full. I'm just fine."

Gunnar continued to study the life monitor nervously.

"Are you sure you're all right?" he asked looking, searching her tired brown eyes. "You look different somehow."

"What would you expect?" she winced, looking away.

"That's just it," Gunnar continued for an answer. "You were in pretty bad shape and no offense to Fuji, but she's not that good."

"Don't be rude," Audra chastised with a rasp.

"What's rude about that?" Gunnar persisted, perplexed.

"Can we please talk about something else?"

"No," he responded stubbornly.

"What's all the brew-ha-ha over here?" Dr. Yamoto asked in an angry hush.

"Nothing," Audra said, turning her head stiffly away.

Suspicious now, Gunnar followed her restrained movement. Surely she wasn't in that much pain. He looked back up at the indicators, and then turned to Yamoto.

"I'm pretty sure I'm not so incredibly thick not to figure out something is wrong here, Doctor." He pointed back at the monitor and glared threateningly at her. "I want to know what's going on here. She can barely move! Is she paralyzed?"

Fuji glanced up at the monitor, then nervously down at Audra, still turned away from them.

"Her Nociceptors have been nuetranized," she finally blurted out.

"This is good, right?"

"She sustained a lot of internal damage and was in severe pain when you brought her in. She wouldn't have lasted this long if I hadn't done it. This way she can be comfortable before...," she hesitated.

"Before wha...," he stopped mid-sentence, and turned back to the monitor. He suddenly understood what was happening and whirled angrily at the ship's doctor.

"You get back to her and fix whatever it is needs fixing on her or I'll...."

"Gunnar." Audra's touch instantly melted his anger.

He dropped back to her side, reading the sadness spreading across her face.

"I'm sorry," she spoke softly. A look toward Fuji and the doctor motioned to Sindee.

"We'll be in engineering, then up to the bridge if you need anything," Fuji said, turning to the exit.

"Don't be hard on Fuji," Audra rasped. "She's done only what I've told her to do, and against her better judgment."

"I don't understand," he blurted.

"You can't understand," she said, putting her hand on his. "Not unless it's you on this bed. I need to have a talk with you and I couldn't do it in the condition I was in."

"Well, couldn't this wait until you're feeling better?" he asked, still simmering.

Audra smiled, feeling the emotion for her husband. She squeezed his hand, holding it tightly.

"Gunnar, we've had a wonderful life together, you and I, haven't we?"

He remained silent. In the silence, a faint rumbling could be heard along with the occasional burst of crew coms throughout the ship. He slowly began to smile, returning the embrace to her hand.

"We've done so much together," she started again. "More than most couples do in their life-time. We've had so much fun. Remember the time we buzzed through the Deltain star base ground hangars on clean up at Mach-3 in your T-6?"

Gunnar let out a quiet burst of laughter.

"Sergeant Tilly lost his lunch and his temper when we went through number four."

"Of all the crazy things," she grinned carefully.

"A lot of stupid things too," Gunnar added quickly.

"Yea, like the time you and Rick took out the beam antennas under the H section of the Republic building while Commodore Gardner was in conference with the Republic High Command."

"He wasn't very happy about that, was he?" Gunnar asked, chuckling.

"Not happy?" Audra repeated. "That was the longest space probe you and Rick were ever sent out on. Not to mention you could have gotten yourselves killed pulling a dumb stunt like that," she chastised good-naturedly.

Gunnar chuckled to himself, thinking back to more of the things he and Rick had done together. Most of them, he hadn't dared tell Audra about. She worried enough about the things she did know about. But he remembered that Audra wasn't always wearing a halo.

"Ok, what about the time you ordered a foam landing for Gardner's shuttle when there was no emergency?" He pointed an accusing finger at her. "You've pulled your share of dumb tricks as well."

Audra smiled through a cough and a wince of pain. Even nuetranized, her insides were so broken up and failing, pain still managed to find an outlet.

"Yea, well who says you and Rick should be the only ones to get all the fun? Besides, you know Gardner got everything he deserved. The pompous windbag."

"Always my outspoken girl," Gunnar smiled. "It's a wonder we achieved any rank at all."

"When you're young, it seems like you can do anything." Audra let out a quiet sigh. "You feel like nothing can stop you. Like what you're feeling and living will never change or end." Audra looked at her husband's tattered uniform. "You're fairly safe from your own recklessness now," she said, referring to his command of the *Constellation*.

"Come on, I'm not that careless."

"Yes you are! Feel what you're holding, how fragile it is," she grasped his hand tighter. "I'm made out of the same stuff you are, well, a lot of it is anyway. But these bodies we have, they do break, sometimes beyond repair," she said softly. "And yes, even yours."

"What you're saying is, we're not invincible."

"You're not invincible," Audra pointed out. "You might have a different physical structure that makes you tougher, but you can't just go off halfcocked into something without thinking it through first. Promise me you'll never get back into a cockpit again," she whispered, squeezing his hand. Gunnar nodded.

"Some situations don't allow you to think things through beforehand. You just have to do."

"But more often than not, you don't think it through at all," she ended, appearing to fall asleep.

The room fell silent again with only the sound of distant crew coms bursting sporadically throughout the ship. Audra winced again and Gunnar glanced back up at her life monitor.

"You ok?" he asked, returning the squeeze of her hand. She bit her lip and turned her eyes back to her husband.

"Remember the little talk we had the other day? You know, about when one of us is gone?"

"Ssshhh, you need your rest. Lie quiet."

"I don't want you to be alone, Gunnar," she whispered, raising a trembling hand to his chest. "You have to find room in here for someone else. I know there's room, you just need to find it."

"I don't want to be with anyone else," he said quietly.

Audra smiled, looking up into Gunnar's frightened eyes.

"Why are men so stupid? Don't make this any harder than it already is. I have loved you more than anything I have ever known," she rasped. "And that's more than most people recognize in an entire lifespan."

Gunnar closed his eyes and dropped his head to his dying wife's chest. How could he get any closer to her? Trying to clamp off the flood of tears welling in his eyes, he couldn't hold back the heartbreak and began to weep.

"I don't want you to go."

Audra slowly ran her fingers through his thinning hair.

"Yes, I know," she whispered, wincing again, bringing Gunnar back up from his sorrows.

Gazing sadly into her fading brown eyes, he carefully leaned in and gently kissed her. He watched helplessly as life continued to slip from her. A tear slowly made its way from the corner of her eye as she struggled to speak.

"...always," she whispered in final silence.

"No, don't..." he wept as the indicators on the life monitor, sank to zero, activating the alarms.

Alone

The element of existence moves time forward, even when turning time backwards through a worm hole. One may go back in time and regain the space around them and experience the space fabric and the measurement associated with it, but existence is still just that. Traveling back in time doesn't make you any younger, it only changes everything around you. You're just as old as you were before and the aging that besets you during that period remains with you. *Log entry by General Richard Alexander Niker, Commander, Athena, SAC 9.*

Certainly if Gunnar could have gone back in time, he wouldn't have ordered Audra down to engineering. He kept telling himself that, running the scenario repeatedly in his mind. If he had sent someone else down, maybe even Alex. The droid was so much better equipped to have dealt with the Asium chamber than Audra. Yes, she was well versed on Asium chamber operations, but there had to have been someone else that could have gone down instead. Maybe they would have been able to affect the containment needed on the Asium assembly.

Preliminary scans made thus far revealed that while they were indeed back in their own time, they were hopelessly lost. The point at which they had exited the worm hole had been identified, but that was the extent of it. As space is multi-dimensional, the possibilities were nearly endless. But somewhere out there, there had to be a star, a black hole, a pulsar, galaxy cluster or a recognizable nebula cloud that could lead them back home, if only they could find it.

For now, they had more pressing issues to deal with, namely getting their two ships back to some kind of operational status. Even sitting back at space dock, fleet operations would take months to make the needed repairs, and they had all the right tooling. In open space, they had only emergency field repair systems. Hardly designed for the major repairs required now.

Damaged sensor arrays made it difficult to scan the systems directly around them in any detail. But it was vital they find a suitable space port to make any major repairs. Automated composite printers could handle most hull repairs. Most of the internal structural damage could be dealt with using standard field repair equipment supplied onboard, but both were limited and slow. And while repairing advanced composite material and carbon fiber interlacing was a basic element of science, it did take a certain amount of skill, requiring weeks just for small sections. As the *Constellation* had taken the most damage, she would take the longest to finish. Both ships were without main FTL drive propulsion, compounded by damage to their Asium crystal assemblies. Replacing the damaged crystals was vital if they expected to ever achieve light speed and find their way home in any appreciable amount of time.

As time continued its relentless march, Gunnar noticed he became irritated more often at the smallest of things. But somehow he managed to keep his anger in check. Moreover, he found it astounding how draining it was to maintain control. With both ships essentially floating hulks in space, unable to move anywhere fast, he threw himself into helping with his ship's repair. Focusing intently on every task to keep his mind from thoughts of Audra. Idle time only led him back to reliving the accident and having to watch it happen over and over in his mind. Sleep cycles were particularly difficult and he often had to activate one of his Hallavertor programs to escape. One such program, in which he found the most solace, was on the forested planet, Pantos Three, he had once visited, high in its mountains during its autumn season. The trees had been at the height of their seasonal foliage colors. Most of the time, he found relaxation, even sound sleep, by laying beneath a giant tree as it let its leaves fall silently around him. With the sun warming the calm morning air, he would awaken, warm and comfortable, finding himself completely covered by fallen leaves.

"Oh this looks comfortable," Rick commented, stepping around a gently rising and falling lump of brightly colored leaves.

"Not so bad when you let your mind accept what the eye sees," Gunnar responded stirring beneath the blanket of fallen foliage. "Then the body follows suit and you just go with it. You're not part of this program. What are you doing here?" Gunnar popped his head out from under the leaves and looked up at his friend.

"Nice program. What, no fan slaves? Hadn't gotten any reports from you in a day or so. Was wondering if you might have broken something important. Thought I'd come alongside and make an inspection."

"You make an inspection? You know how to do that? Everything is still broke on this bucket. Lana did tell me her coms systems are all working now. Hurray for us. Who ya gonna call?" Gunnar slipped partially back down beneath the leaves and closed his eyes, a vision of Audra instantly filling his mind.

"Composite repair with a field replication unit is frustratingly time consuming, especially when you don't have the factory printers to do it."

"Tell me about it. Billy has barely gotten one of the main structural tears repaired and only a quarter of the crew quarters bulkheads replicated. It's going to take ten months to finish at this rate."

"You've got somewhere better to be?"

"I can think of a couple of places I'd rather be right now."

"Cockpit?"

"Maybe," Gunnar paused a moment. "Wouldn't that be the bomb? Want to steal a couple, maybe practice some interweaves like the good ol' days?"

"You know there's too much to do. My ship is in only marginally better shape than yours." Rick sank to the ground next to his friend.

"At least you can move without your AI having to get out and push," Gunnar responded quietly.

"Without a full set of calibrated Asium crystals in these birds, we're not going much of anywhere very fast. At least our environmental and food replicator systems are working fine."

"Great, we'll all be fat and happy out here in the middle of nowhere. Even if we knew where we were or how to get home." Gunnar seemed to slump a little deeper into depression.

"How have you been feeling?" Rick asked, knowing full well his friend's condition.

"Do you really need an answer?"

"What I mean is, Fuji's worried about what your chemical makeup is doing to your system. It's rough enough for a normal human to drag a road like this. No one can even imagine what it's like for you. You're charting new territory here."

"That certainly is true. It's tough to deal with some of the dumbest things normal people do. I just about slapped Cooper clean across the engine room yesterday for something that wasn't even his fault. By the end of the day, I'm exhausted with trying to maintain control. Sort of ticked off that you woke me up, so I'm barely tolerating you right now."

Rick was stunned at first, but then recalled the lengthy conversations with both ship's doctors about Gunnar's psychological and emotional condition. Were they in a circumstance where they needed to be operational, he might have to relieve his friend and have Jayda assume command of the *Constellation* while Gunnar underwent some intensive therapy. His condition was understandable, but not acceptable for a Starbird commander.

"Sorry, Bud. I am glad you can practice some restraint," Rick said.

"You know I hate it when you call me that."

"I know, just trying to get a feel for what's going on inside you. You're pretty good at hiding what I can only imagine is boiling through those veins of yours."

"Call me "Bud" again and you'll find out real fast."

"Come on," Rick said noticing his friend's eye color change. "Bud is a perfectly good name."

"Fuji advised it best if I was upfront with what was going on inside my head and you're the one that gets to hear all about it. You want to call me Gunnar or Buddy," Gunnar said becoming tight lipped, "I'm fine. But I hate "Bud". How's that for wondering what's going on inside me?"

"I'm not going to pretend I know exactly what you're going through. Truth be told, I haven't got a clue here. I still have Jayda and I haven't lost my parents, yet. You and I have known good friends that have been lost to enemy action and so we both understand the feelings associated with this kind of thing."

"You realize this sounds like a lecture, right?" Gunnar responded quietly. "You know, the talk?" his voice starting to elevate.

"Yeah, I know. I just want to make sure you understand that everyone on both ships is concerned about you. They want to help."

"Goodie for them." Gunnar rolled over and sat up next to Rick. "I don't want to sound ungrateful here, but the way I feel, I don't want any help. I'm sure Fuji will jump all over that, telling me how important it is that I mingle with the crew and interact as much as possible, but there isn't a person between these two ships that has any clue how rough this is on me. I'm not looking for any pity here, but..."

"Exactly what are you hoping then?" Rick asked quietly. "Tell me what you want."

Gunnar remained silent, leading Rick to believe he wasn't going to get an answer. Rick would do anything for Gunnar if it would help. They had become like brothers and the years of being together, saving each other from their own recklessness had mixed an emotional epoxy that bound them together by something unbreakable, even in the worst of times. Rick finally got to his feet and turned to leave.

"Audra." Gunnar's voice had cooled quiet again, his mind wandering back to the image of his wife.

Rick looked over his shoulder at his friend. Were it within his power to do so, Rick would move the galaxy for his friend. For an instant, he thought he could actually feel Gunnar's pain. The stabbing at his insides accompanied by a wave of depression enveloping him felt unbearable. Perhaps it was empathy for a good friend, he wasn't sure, but it was intensely uncomfortable all the same. It took him a minute to regain his composure and as he did so, a thought entered his mind that could possibly be of some help. It would involve a certain measure of risk and of course Fuji would have to sign off on it, but as Gunnar was a different sort of being, not subject to the normal human emotional and physiological rules, it might just be the tonic required to help in this situation.

"See to the comfort of your crew," Rick finally said leaving the scene. Once outside in the main hall of the ship, he was joined by Fuji and Dakota.

"Well, any improvement?" Fuji inquired, peeling herself from the wall while Dakota remained leaning.

"You know, this could have waited until tomorrow when he was scheduled to see you," Rick responded.

"I wanted to get a feel for how he's doing beforehand. You know how people are about opening up to a medical professional, and the Colonel is worse for it than anyone else on this ship." A worried expression dominated Fuji's demeanor.

"Afraid him and I are kind of programmed that way."

"So are the other fighter pilots on this ship," Fuji cast a glance back at Dakota. "Why is that?"

"It's the mentality of the code we live by," Dakota piped up. "We can count on just one person. Just how it is."

"I've got an idea I'd like to discuss with you privately," Rick said, starting down the hall with the ship's doctor.

"I'll take that as a hint," Dakota said, heading in the opposite direction.

"Do you think assigning him to some kind of scouting duty in one of the ship's Interceptors would help him?" Rick asked.

Fuji was trying to think of anything she could apply from her medical training.

"For most humans, throwing yourself into what you love to do is excellent therapy for the mourning process. But the Colonel doesn't quite fit the mold. It's true he's certainly thrown himself into trying to fix this ship. But his physiology is different and normal things just don't apply to his chemical makeup. I'm sure the cocktail running in his blood right now would nearly kill a normal human going through the same thing, at the very least cause insanity. It's a wonder he's not having any psychotic episodes." Fuji stopped just before the sickbay door and turned to Rick. "In this instance, I don't think I would recommend it."

"Why not? It's where he spent most of his professional career. It's where he loved to be the most. It's what he did better than anything else. Heck, I had to run to keep up with the guy."

"I have no doubt," Fuji agreed, pausing. "But I was checking the sickbay log recorders and found out he made her a promise."

"Oh boy," Rick sighed seriously. "What did he promise?" He kind of already had an idea, but was hopeful he was wrong.

"She made him promise never to fly a fighter again."

"Nuts," Rick breathed. "Jayda has tried to get me to take a similar oath as well. I swear those two girls were in cahoots getting Gunnar and I into the command chair. I'll have to have a little chat with Admiral Mandell when we get back."

"Would either of you change your minds about your commands now?"

"No," Rick responded quickly. "But it might shed a little light on how we got here so easily."

"I think you should trust your wife a little more," Fuji chastised gently. Certainly she was right and Rick knew it. While Jayda might have helped to encourage their appointments to a Starbird command, they wouldn't have gotten these assignments if they weren't right for the job. Rick nodded carefully, watching Tiana Mantose through the open engineering room doors working with Billy Moon.

"I am open to any other ideas you might want to suggest," Fuji said turning for her door.

"Well, I do have another suggestion that just came to me while I was in there, but it's pretty far out there."

"Please, have a seat and tell me all about it." She gestured to the chair in front of her desk just inside the medical bay.

*   *   *   *

Gunnar emerged from his quarters at a late hour. Most operations were on automation now and the crew in their sleep cycle. He was sure Billy Moon was still awake working on something and there was a requirement for someone to be on the bridge at all times. Gunnar had no particular direction he wanted to go, nothing he really wanted to see. He just wanted to get out and about, do something besides be where he was. He faced the bridge door, looking at it for a moment. If he entered, certainly the crewman on watch would want to visit and he wasn't in the mood for polite chit chat. In fact, he was feeling rather aggressive. No, better to head the other direction. He thought about looking in on Fuji, just so she'd leave him alone about getting out and about, mingling with people and being social in some other setting besides focused work, but thought better of that. He'd get the standard lecture about getting out when no one was awake, that it didn't count. Besides, it would just bring on more talk about his feelings and he was so weary of that. He looked in through the open teleporter room doors and wandered silently in, but then tried to back away when he detected someone working on the other side of the teleporter control console.

"Good to see you, Colonel," Billy remarked, popping his head up on the far side of the console. Gunnar slowly stepped inside and looked carefully around the room, finally stepping to the teleporter pads.

"What's the good word?" Gunnar asked.

"That I'm not going to be out of a job anytime soon, sir." Billy continued to watch the Colonel step around the teleporter pads, looking at the many things in the room that were in differing states of repair.

Gunnar smiled and looked over at what the engineer was doing. The console was half disassembled and circuits were splayed everywhere.

"Don't you ever sleep?" Gunnar asked, always impressed to see Billy hard at it.

"Sure, doesn't everyone?"

"Some easier than others," came a mumbled reply from Gunnar. "So why aren't you asleep now?"

"Would love to be, but this has been bugging me and I'd like to see some kind of results other than what little the composite replicators are doing on the hull structure. Besides, I caught some zees earlier while Cooper and Tiana were working on the sub-light inverters."

"You've got Tiana working on the sub-light drive?"

"Sure, smart girl. Really knows her stuff. I told her to knock off for the cycle about an hour ago. Practically had to drag her out of engineering."

"Really," Gunnar responded quietly. "You the only one up back here?"

"Should be, sir. As long as there's no action, there isn't much else to do on this ship during the sleep cycles. It's not like she's going anywhere."

"Hopefully she will again, right?"

"As long as there's ship and engines to move her, she will, I promise."

"Good man. I'll hold you to it." Gunnar turned and stepped toward the door.

"Sir?"

"Yeah Billy."

The engineer hesitated a moment, looking for the right words.

"I don't know if I've said this before, but, Cooper and I really miss Commander Atlanta. She was top notch. This crew couldn't have asked for a better exec." Billy felt like he should be saying something else, something he hadn't already said, but awkwardness had invaded the exchange. Gunnar quickly let the engineer off the hook.

"Thanks Billy, she certainly was." Gunnar nodded and moved from the room. He knew Billy felt genuinely bad about Audra, the entire crew did. Audra was indeed one of a kind as officers went and he felt a great sense of pride in her, knowing that while he played only a modest role in shaping her as an officer, she was who she was and that was what made her so great and why so many people naturally loved her.

Examining everything as he went, he slowly made his way through the engineering vestibule, carefully inspecting the work being done on the main structure of the ship. Much of it was still torn apart, with exposed superstructure and composite plating in various states of repair. It would be hard to ever walk through this area again without thinking about what happened here. He finally moved into engineering, stepping right up to the immense engineering consoles. Most of the glass display was dark, with only a few readouts flashing information sporadically. He started for the turret elevator, but then caught sight of the open Interceptor shaft to his left and stepped up to it. He stood trying to decide if he wanted to go to all the bother of climbing up through the Starbird wing and into the fighter. The elevator cradle that sent the pilot into the fighter wasn't working. He finally crawled through the shaft and situated himself in the soft cushion of the pilot's seat.

From here, his gaze was quite broad. He hadn't spent much time in the Interceptor simulators and had never flown it for real, but it certainly felt right. He gripped the control yoke, waiting for the thrill to envelope him. What should be something akin to riding a roller coaster to him, instead there was something else, but he couldn't quite put his finger on it. He activated the master switches, bringing the fighter's systems online. The displays in front of him were dazzling and letting his hands sweep over the other controls, it all felt like old hat to him. It all felt right, it's just that he didn't feel right sitting here. Frustrated, he looked up at the star field all around him. So deep, so vast, so endless, so beautiful, yet now, so empty. He noticed tears welling in his eyes and feelings of confusion. He finally let his hand drop to the engine controls and brought them online, listening to them wind up. As the thruster intermix signaled operational, he gripped the yoke again, feeling the turbo thruster buttons on the back side of the control. He was sure if he just took the fighter for a spin that everything would return to the way it was. As he continued to finger the thruster buttons, Audra's voice seemed to echo through the fighter's sound system.

Promise me you'll never get back into a cockpit again.

"Can I get out before you launch, sir?" came a groggy voice from behind in the shadows. Gunnar instantly relaxed his grip on the yoke, removing his fingers from the thruster buttons.

"Oh, Colonel. I'm sorry, I didn't know it was you. I thought it was Captain Abrams heading out on a patrol," Tiana said sitting up. "Engineer Moon wanted me out of engineering to get some sleep, but I couldn't sleep with Taron snoring so loud. Let me get out of your way and you can do whatever."

Gunnar glanced down at the engine controls, feeling the ship's engines gently humming at the ready. As Tiana started for the entry way, he shut the engines off and worked the controls to secure the fighter.

"Didn't I say something about you not calling me sir?"

Tiana stopped and looked back at the Colonel.

"Excuse me, sir, I mean, Colonel, but what are you doing up here, especially during this cycle?"

"It would be considered nighttime on Commenor right now," he said looking back out into space. "I could ask you the same thing."

"Sleeping."

"Good answer."

"Were you really going to go somewhere?"

Gunnar looked back at the now dark controls of the Interceptor, then out at the stars.

"No, just remembering what it felt like."

"Star pilots must have nerves of steel." Tiana said relaxing a bit. "I get scared just looking out a port window."

"That extra dimension of space can be a bit unnerving."

"Sir, are you all right?"

"Told you not to call me that. Yes, I'm fine."

"Are you sure?"

Gunnar looked over at Tiana for a long moment. He was getting really sick and tired of people trying to psychoanalyze him and the aggression he was feeling before, had only ratcheted up a notch. Maybe he needed to have Fuji give him something to help. Certainly he was frustrated he couldn't shake this all on his own.

"Tiana, just... don't..." He held up his hand and waved it slightly as he tried to move past her to get down the shaft to engineering, but she held onto him.

"Gunnar, please talk to me. Tell me what you're feeling."

"Why should I? Who are you that you need to know or even understand what's going on inside me?" He tried to pull free from her, but she held fast to him, pulling him back.

"I'm someone who cares and wants to help you."

"Everyone on this ship cares. Everyone wants to help. What makes you different from everyone else? You're not even a part of the crew." Gunnar relaxed a little, looking at the shaft bulkhead.

"Mourning the loss of a loved one is tough for anyone."

"Your father isn't dead, remember?"

Tiana let go of Gunnar's shirt and leaned back.

"I keep telling myself that, so I won't have to let him go." Tiana finally admitted. "I keep telling myself he's just on a long trip and he'll return to put my stepmother in her place and take Taron and I away from that whole mess."

"Well," Gunnar finally spoke up quietly. "You two are certainly far away from her now." Tiana smiled and looked over at him.

"You have to know, there isn't a person onboard this ship that wouldn't have done anything to save Audra. Everyone loved her, how could they not? She saved my life at the Oneida. She was one of a kind and I admit I'm jealous of her and not just because she was your sealed mate, but because she was such an extraordinary person."

"Yes, she was certainly all those things." Gunnar stared blankly down the Interceptor access tube, pondering. Tiana could see him struggling. She could feel him hurting.

"You feel like you've lost a part of you." Tiana's voice was quiet, therapeutic.

Gunnar's vision remained locked, looking into nothing, feeling nothing, his mind empty.

"I've lost the better part of me," he finally said, looking back at Tiana. She had her hair pulled back in a ponytail and it was just light enough in the access shaft that he could see her facial features. "How do you ever get that back?"

Tiana could sense a quiver in his voice, something she had never heard before in her time onboard. While she sensed his pain, she wasn't sure what to say that would help.

"I don't think you ever can," she offered. "You change the pain into happiness and fill the emptiness with something wonderful."

Gunnar let the words imprint on him, knowing that he had tried so many different things to help get him through what he was enduring. He knew Tiana was probably the sincerest person on this ship and wanted more than anything to help. He let a smile drift across his lips, hoping Tiana could see it. She was good medicine, but it was a deep wound to heal.

Gunnar finally started back down the shaft with Tiana right behind him and upon entering engineering, he turned to help her out of the tube. As he lifted her carefully to the floor with his hands around her waist, she turned and put her hands on his shoulders. Landing on her feet, she held him where he was, looking up at him.

"If you need to just talk, about anything," Tiana pulled herself closer. "I'm here to listen." Her eyes were clear, calm pools, focused solely on him, not in the way they had been when they had first been introduced on Commenor. Now she was looking past his exterior, deep into his soul.

Gunnar could easily get caught up in something new here, but his thoughts wouldn't allow it. While he found Tiana attractive, his heart was not here, but still solely with Audra. He smiled, gently pulling her hands from his shoulders.

"Thanks Tiana. I might just take you up on that offer. Now you should really try and get some sleep, and no, a cockpit or a turret chair is not the place. Use the isolator hood if your brother is making too much noise." Gunnar turned and started slowly for the engineering consoles, his hands clasped behind him.

Tiana was a little disappointed to say the least, but quickly took him at his word and smiled, heading for the door to the main hall. Certainly she was hoping for a kiss, but if talk was the starting point to get there, then she was good with it. She stopped at the doors and looked back at him standing near the engineering consoles gazing up at the engine bulkheads. She fingered her Chyropaz necklace and smiled again, then turned, heading for her quarters.

Shore Leave

Gliding slowly through an unfamiliar star field, the *Constellation* held herself within scanning range of *Athena*. Able to make only limited scans of the closest systems, Gunnar and Rick had positioned their Corsairs far enough apart to extend their scanning equipment's limited range. A year had elapsed since they had made their escape from the Oneida and thus far, they had been unable to determine where they had sent themselves in the vastness of the universe.

Helping to spread the bridge crew work load, Lieutenant Starman was assisting Ensign Kramer cross-reference several star coordinates Pip was transferring for data storage. Tired of the redundant and mundane, Lynette pushed back from her station, pulled off her headset and leaned back, stretching.

"Six months getting to ya?" Nigel asked, not looking up from his displays.

"Six months of charting?" Starman repeated. "Is that all the longer we've had the arrays back online? And we still have no idea where we are."

"Sure we do; right here."

"Ha, ha. I think it would be faster if we shot a string to the nearest star and plotted from that. There's so many bugs still in these systems I can't imagine the information we're plotting is even remotely accurate. I don't know, I must be starting to get space fever or something. I hate white, I hate metal and I hate florocarb lighting. I don't care much for rectifier lighting either," she grumbled.

"Haven't you been using the Hallavertor in your room?"

"That thing can only do so much," Lynette frowned. "With the limited space in the room, you can only go so far, besides, you know it still isn't quite the same. I'm dying to go to a party, with a whole bunch of people and lots of food. I'd like to go hiking in a rainstorm, or just rock climbing on a cloudy day." She leaned back even further, putting her feet up on one of the consoles.

"Can't you program any of that into your Hallavertor?" Nigel asked, turning to some of his other displays. "I hear the unit in

the Colonel's quarters is off the chart awesome. It's set to
maximum."

"Mine sure isn't. You should have seen what it came up with
for the rainstorm," Lynette responded not noticing a figure
stepping up behind her. "It was raining everywhere but where I
was standing. I need to get wet without standing in a shower."

"That's because the program knows to keep that kind of
interaction low due to our confinement. You get too involved in
the interaction and you might not come back out of it. Where's
your imagination anyway?"

Lynette jumped, recognizing Gunnar's voice. She instantly
turned back to her station, trying to look like she was hard at
work.

"Oh, sorry, sir. I was just draining my feet. You let them
stay on the floor too long and they get full of blood." She
cringed at her response, but Gunnar chuckled anyway. He
understood how it was. Everyone had the freedom to do just
about anything they wanted in the privacy of their own room so
long as it didn't interfere with what their roommates might be
doing.

"Need it up in your head huh? Would you like to do a hand
stand here on the bridge to help that along?" Gunnar stepped
back over to the command chair at the summons of the comlink
on the armrest.

"That's the first time I've heard that man laugh since we
buried Commander Atlanta in space a year ago," Lynette
whispered carefully to Nigel.

"Could be a sign that maybe a shore leave is in the works,"
Nigel whispered back, continuing his work.

"Shore leave to where? Have you been paying attention to
the rocks we've encountered?" Lynette carefully glanced back at
the Starbird commander who was still looking at her.
Embarrassed, she quickly went back to work.

"Conrad here," Gunnar spoke quietly into the comlink.

"Hey, buddy," Rick responded. "I'm pulling alongside. Time
to mix things up again. Is your docking airlock working?"

"Yeah, but if you need to come onboard, why not just use the
teleporters? Mine is online and working fine. You didn't break
something, did you?"

"Funny boy. Trying to conserve power, buddy, you know how
much draw those Klystrons have on a partial set of Asium
crystals. I've got a doctor over here who wants to have a little
conversation with yours and my engineers are itching to run
some ideas with yours. You know engineers. Plus, I think it
might be a good idea to let the crews mingle again for a little bit.
Let the two ships breathe each other's air for a while."

"Probably a good thing for everyone I expect." Gunnar sat slowly in his chair. "You and I need to have a little discussion as well."

"Any particular topic?" Rick was trying to sound carefree. He knew his friend was still struggling with the mourning process and reasoned that trying to do a tap dance around him wasn't going to do him any good.

"Shore leave," Gunnar mumbled. He didn't want to get anyone excited about it. It had been quite some time since any of them had set foot on anything but metal and composite.

Presently, the bridge door opened and Tiana Mantose walked in flanked by Dakota. Tiana stepped up beside the command chair and stood at attention while Dakota just looked around the room holding a small glass screen.

"How's your brother?" Gunnar asked, interrupting his conversation with Rick.

"He's doing just fine," Tiana responded happily.

"I'll meet you in your quarters about a half hour after we dock," Rick announced, bringing Gunnar's attention back to the comlink.

"Understood." Pressing the comlink button, Gunnar turned to Dakota. "You have a report, Captain?"

"Yes, sir," came a slow reply. Most of Dakota's attention was on the information being displayed on the engineering consoles.

Gunnar waited patiently, twiddling his fingers on the armrest of his chair. He glanced up at Tiana momentarily, then back at the Captain.

"Well, do you think you could give it to me before I outrank your cousin?" Dakota didn't respond immediately, so Gunnar added a little more emphasis. "This week sometime?"

The first officer finally looked over at his commander and snapped to attention.

"Oh yes, sorry, sir." He stepped up next to the Colonel amidst the soft muffled chuckling quietly rolling around the bridge.

Gunnar slowly scanned the room, noting that he too was smiling but trying to hide it. He cleared his throat carefully so all could hear and looked back at the Captain. Like Rick, Gunnar ran his command a little more loosely than Kalamar command would like to see, but since they were a long way from anywhere close to home, it seemed pointless to be quite so strict.

"Need some time off do you?"

"Yes, sir," came the quick, quiet response from Captain Abrams. His attention remained straight ahead.

"Suppose you're hoping for shore leave," Gunnar responded just as quick, his voice down low.

"Be a nice change, sir."

"Yes, Dak, it would. I think we all need a break, but until Rick and I can figure out where that'll be...."

"We all need to do what we can to keep things running smoothly."

"Good man. Glad you understand how things are, now can we continue with your report or at least start it?" Gunnar took the glass screen from the Captain and began looking through it. "And do it at ease."

"Yes, sir," Dakota said, relaxing a little as the bridge crew got back to doing their assignments. "Sub-light drive is fully operational. Weapons and shield power up to about forty-five percent, array repairs have been slow. Guidance systems are back online as are all of our Atheon cores, but we're still working on all the tie-in circuits. Mr. Moon reports the FTL drive will be down indefinitely due to insufficient spare parts and a messed up Asium crystal assembly. Complete technical details are on the master-script, including our hull integrity analysis, in your office. I've uploaded a file to your office profile and had a hand viewer delivered to your desk by Alex 7001, as per your orders that no one enter your quarters."

"You let Alex go in my quarters?" Gunnar burst back quietly. "No one is allowed in for any reason. The upload would have been fine. I've got my own hand viewer."

"I thought it better for you to have it right there without having to search for it. Our file systems are still a little scrambled. I instructed Alex to go straight to your desk and nowhere else," Dakota answered quickly. "He's the only ship's personnel I trust not to let their vision wander from anywhere but the assigned task."

Gunnar glanced up at Tiana and instantly calmed himself. Thinking for a moment, he understood the logic of the Captain's thinking.

"Then you acted responsibly of course," Gunnar finally said, letting the Captain quietly off the hook. He hadn't allowed anyone in his quarters since Audra's burial in space a year ago. It had been their place and he meant to keep it that way.

*   *   *   *

As the two ships carefully pulled alongside one another, a long clear ringed, tube extended between the two, connecting mid ship at the main airlock doors. As soon as pressurization stabilized, the environmental, direct comlink and data umbilicals were established to provide better inter-ship circulation and communication. As ship's personnel began to move back and forth between the two ships, Gunnar soon found himself walking among them. They worked well together, but after being in space for a year with only Hallavertor programs to provide any kind of variety to their lifestyles on ship, a chance to interact with other people was a welcome change of pace.

While both ships were identical, there was just something different about the air of the *Athena* as Gunnar walked its main corridor toward Rick's quarters. Upon entering, it was obvious the decor was all Jayda's doing. He knew Rick far too well to think he could, or would, do all this himself. Pictures adorned the walls everywhere; relic ship instruments, battle tools, military citations, and all manner of paraphernalia. Gunnar recognized Rick's fighter pilot certificate immediately. He took great pride knowing that he had been wingman to the galaxy's youngest fighter pilot ace, ever. Gunnar's quarters were essentially the same, with a sloping wall on the opposite side from the entry door and a lavish desk against it, facing a wall viewing screen. A small com station occupied one corner of the desk.

Rick sat at the desk studying several readouts on a small display off to his right as Jayda stepped from a food generator. A former Royal Princess of Kalamar, Jayda Niker was a short woman with an unassuming face and long platinum blonde hair reaching to the small of her back.

"Enjoying the good life eh?" Gunnar asked in jest, reading Rick's concentrated expression.

"Ain't nothin' like a fighter, right?" Rick answered back. He thanked Jayda as she set a drink down next to him.

"Don't tell me she let you go for a ride, and without me?" Gunnar smiled at Jayda and took the glass she had poured for him. Watching her step across the room and sit down next to Rick, he couldn't help but think of Audra.

"You've got to be joking."

"Hope springs eternal, right?" Gunnar sipped his drink, looking around the room. He finally settled on the couch behind him, beneath another wall of artifacts and citations.

"I wouldn't mind it too much right about now." Rick finally pushed the display away and turned in the direction of his friend, his chiseled face and high forehead still drawn up in concentration. "Even if it were a deep space patrol. We've sent ours out how many times so far and they've come back with next to nothing. I'd sure like to know where we are."

"Toby and Pip found a glitch in the calculations we used when we created the Hap void and the time winder. Explains why we're so lost out here. We've got a starting point now, but without long range scanning capabilities, there's no way to know a direction to home. But hey, at least we're back in our own time." Gunnar grinned broadly, holding his glass up.

"I'd love nothing more right now, than to push these young bucks aside, climb into one of those Interceptors and go look at one of these planets myself instead of staring at them from here."

"Speaking of which..." Gunnar leaned forward. "What are we gonna do about that?"

"You want to steal a couple while no one's looking?" Rick passed Jayda a mischievous look, then turned to his desk and touched a control.

"Sounds like a burst of brilliance."

"Will you two stick to business," Jayda finally interjected. "You're just torturing yourselves with all this fighter talk. You both command Starbirds now and it's somebody else's responsibility to fly the fighters, so leave them to their pilots and concentrate on telling them what to do."

"Kill joy." Rick rolled his eyes toward Jayda.

"Can't blame us for wishful thinking," Gunnar smiled.

"Just make sure you two keep it that way," she warned firmly. "Don't make me have to grab you with a hawser and bring you back in here."

"Yes ma'am," Gunnar blurted.

"Took forever to get our long range sensors back online, certainly nowhere close to one hundred percent, not even half." Rick turned to his wall screen. "Clancy has the Nano-mech working on the critical stuff, but there isn't nearly enough to go around for as much damage as we've received. All of the secondary repairs are being handled by the crew. We've had to rob from one place and adapt circuits to do stuff they were never designed for, but at least they're working, sort of."

"Billy reports pretty much the same story on my bucket," Gunnar said. "Note to Kalamar command; outfit Starbirds with more Nano-mech."

"Well, by all rights, we should be chunks of junk spinning forever out here. I think the only thing that saved us is the new composite material."

"You ought to see the designs for the new sensor panels Alex has come up with. Cutting edge stuff, very impressive."

"I heard he designed a new shield array system too," Rick said.

"Yes, no more external antenna arrays to get beat up. It's all integrated into the ship's carbon fiber skin."

"Cool stuff, too bad it'll be a while before we can even think of getting into that kind of an upgrade. So, back to business. From what little we've been able to pick up so far, it looks like we've been between galaxies, hence the reason we've spent the past year looking at a whole lot of nothing."

"So what have you been able to make of the few planets we've encountered?"

"They appear to be in differing states of mass decomposition," Jayda cut in. She leaned toward the scientific, so Rick gave her leave. "They probably came from a system that lost its sun for one reason or another. I suspect they'll eventually break up or freeze solid."

"The great news is," Rick said pointing at his screen, "as we've gotten close to the nearest galaxy boundary, about every place you look has activity in one form or another. Nice to see something out there besides dead planets, asteroids, comets and rubble. From this distance, my sensors are having a difficult time telling exactly what kind of activity it is. But at this point, I think everyone would be thrilled just to step on something besides metal."

"Basically the same thing in our search grids," Gunnar responded, pulling a small device from his pocket and activating it. A holographic image appeared displaying various information.

"Like I said, I think we're all ready to chow down on some dirt about now." Rick gave Gunnar a quick smile and pointed to the sixth planet, in a small outer system on the displayed star chart. "What about this one? It's the only planet showing a sizable Asium signature. The one next to it has a signature, but it's faint, probably associated with its mineral rings."

"Unfortunately our sensors can't provide us with any detail either, but there is definitely Asium somewhere on the surface and it looks like there ought to be something there by way of an outpost of some kind. We tracked what looked like a couple of larger ships patrolling the outer planets of the system, but again, the returns were showing only primary targets, no detail."

"Like to venture a guess as to whether or not they might let us land on their rock, maybe even help with any repairs?" Rick was trying to keep things as they had always been between him and his friend.

"Only way to know is to drive in there and try to make contact; hope for the best. In addition to the primary targets, we were getting some smaller echoes bobbing about, again no detail, but if I had to make a guess, I would say they were fighters."

Rick instantly sat up in his chair, glancing momentarily over at Jayda, then back at Gunnar.

"Making regular patrols?"

Gunnar only shrugged, nipping at his bottom lip.

Jayda watched the two as they continued.

"You couldn't get any readouts or specs on said fighters?" Rick asked, becoming more interested.

"It's all preliminary scans only, but they were fast and highly maneuverable," Gunnar continued in a matter of fact fashion. "Probably a two-seater, large Delta foil, twin fins, heavily armed and light speed capable."

"That's a preliminary scan?" Jayda leaned forward, not believing Gunnar could come up with that much detail. Gunnar grinned from ear to ear.

"Don't get excited, Jayda. They were dots on a screen," Rick said, trying not to sound excited himself.

"I don't like where this conversation is headed," Jayda interrupted. "This is supposed to be a briefing, now push your eyes back in their sockets, wipe the drool from your chin and focus. This sounds like a lot of detail coming from equipment you said was only kind of working."

"I was kidding, Jayda. They were just dots, no detail," Gunnar mumbled.

"I'm not stupid," Jayda grinned. "I know how you two operate."

"Come on, Jayda," Rick complained, "It's been over a year now. We're all starting to get a little crazy."

"Understandable," she agreed. "Anyway, we're agreed to look for Asium on the sixth planet," Jayda said. "But I'm not so sure sending fighters in first would be such a good idea anyway. I recommend looking as unhostile as possible," Jayda offered.

"Probably right," Gunnar agreed. "There could be some kind of action going on in there, so if we can make ourselves look just as plain and inconspicuous as we can, we've got a better chance of making a friendly impression."

"Options then?" Rick asked.

"One of the Orbiters," Jayda spoke up. "It'll look like a scout vessel or a small freighter."

"It'll have to be the *Constellation*," Rick volunteered. "The *Athena's* TI circuits are still in tough shape."

"We'll start getting her ready to leave right away," Gunnar said, getting up and starting for the door. "Anything else?"

"Just be careful buddy. Until we can lay our hands on some Asium, we can't afford to get tangled up in anything. And try not to break anything."

Gunnar only waved a hand on his way out as Jayda got up and stepped back over next to Rick.

"He's getting better at hiding it," she commented, watching the door close. "I can't even imagine what he's going through, and I'm not sure I want to. Do you think he'll ever get over her?"

"I don't know," Rick responded, quietly taking Jayda's hand. "I wish he'd at least try to use the Hallavertor program Fuji and I created. He's got to confront this head on before he can start to fully heal. He and Audra were very close. It would take quite a woman to fill her boots. I don't know, maybe I need to give him another nudge or something."

Rick knew the help Gunnar needed couldn't come from him or Fuji. This was something Gunnar was going to have to confront on his own. Rick had watched his friend trying to deal with Audra's absence in his own way, but Gunnar was still struggling after all this time. Somehow, he had to get on with life and that meant admitting that Audra was gone and wasn't coming back. Rick had hoped the Hallavertor program he had installed on Gunnar's unit would help kick start that process, if he'd just activate it.

The Orbiter

Gunnar walked into engineering completely preoccupied with thoughts of their fast approaching mission. Finally, they were getting back to being an operational ship. Maybe this was the first step to finding their way back home. Walking past the engine assembly, his attention was drawn by Billy Moon's head poking out over the top of the main engine bulkhead, working on something. Starting for the Interceptor turbo shaft, Gunnar tried to figure out just what it was his chief was doing.

It wasn't often a Starbird's engines required any hands on servicing while they were still installed. These ships were designed with a modular engine bulkhead. Being so technologically advanced, it was far easier and faster to just change the engine out with a new or overhauled unit.

"Got a problem up there, Billy?"

The engineer looked up from his work, somewhat startled.

"Huh? Well I hope not. Just checking this damper. It was giving me some trouble this morning. I've run a system four diagnostics on it twice now, but I'm not finding anything wrong," he grumbled.

Gunnar stared at the engine mass for several seconds then nodded, turning for the turbo elevator that spanned out through the rear wing assembly of the ship. While finally working again, the pilot cradle was shut down for fighter launch maintenance, so he climbed in and crawled out to where the fighter docked with the ship. There, he found Logan and Frank, in an access tube working on the fighter's control tie-ins. Gunnar crawled up into the fighter itself and sat back in the pilot's seat. It was the most comfortable seat in a fighter he had ever snuggled into. These fighters were designed for extended range recon with their own FTL drive, so comfort was certainly a big design factor when they were built. The Interceptor was quite large by the standards of a normal fighter. This machine would have dwarfed his T-6, a two seat fighter. The T-6 Tempest was designed for short range and close quarters dog fighting. The Interceptor was designed not only as a long range heavy fighter, but also as an integral part of the Starbird's anatomy. When docked, the Interceptors helped the Starbird design perform at its optimum, especially in a gas atmosphere. Looking at the instruments in front of him, he played with the flight controls a moment, detecting someone working behind him.

"How's it coming there, Dak?"

"I'm all done here now." Dakota put down the fuser he was working with and turned to his commander. "Never thought I'd be pulling engineer work when I got my wings."

"It's good to know your ship inside and out."

"What's the status on shore leave?"

Gunnar looked up at an overhead console, turning on a few of the fighter's com systems and watching the readouts boot up.

"We're taking the Orbiter out on a little sightseeing tour to the sixth planet. It's got a good Asium signature and I'm hoping the outpost there will be willing to help us."

"Halla-freaking-looya!" Dakota paused a moment. "Sir."

"Amen brotha, amen." Gunnar smiled at his exec.

Dakota put his tools in his jacket pockets and started back down the turbo shaft.

"All done here, Cooper, I'm going back down," he called to the assistant engineer in the access tube as he slid past.

Gunnar shut everything off and followed his first officer back down to the engine room. Starting for the door, Gunnar's attention was drawn again to the chief engineer at his consoles.

"You find the trouble, Billy?" Gunnar and Captain Abrams stepped over to have a look.

Troubled about something, Billy remained preoccupied working the immense touch panel in front of him, then looking up at the big monitor overhead. There were a myriad of complex systems currently displayed, some of them overlapping the others. Trying to make sense of what it all meant was nearly impossible to the untrained eye.

"I don't know, Colonel," he finally responded slowly. "Certainly nothing a new AC assembly module couldn't fix. It's working fine now, but I was getting some weird readings earlier this morning." He looked up at the engine bulkhead again. "Excuse me, sir, I want to check something." Without looking at anyone else, Billy started to hoist himself up onto the mountain of engine parts.

"Now there's a guy that loves his job," Dakota said, turning to leave. He took a couple of steps before he realized that Gunnar hadn't moved and turning back around, waited for his commanding officer.

Gunnar felt quite secure knowing he had one of the best engineering teams in the fleet and if anyone could find a problem, it was Billy. The chief could be exceptionally tenacious when troubleshooting. Gunnar understood what it took to get from point *A* to point *B*, so Billy's concerns had his attention. While they weren't taking this portion of the ship, this intermittent trouble could create problems later on.

"We're taking the orbiter out in a little under an hour, are we gonna be good to go?" Gunnar stepped around to the side of the engine bulkhead, watching the engineer examine something up close with a little probe. Receiving no acknowledgment, Gunnar hoisted himself up a little closer to get a better look.

"Billy, does this phantom problem of yours affect us taking the Orbiter out?"

Silence continued to dominate the conversation, greatly frustrating the Starbird commander, but Billy finally answered.

"It could, but unless I can see it happening again or get something from the diagnostic Atheon systems, it would be silly to hold up a mission."

"What are the diagnostic logs showing?"

"I can't seem to replicate the symptoms."

"If the problem comes back, how could it affect the Orbiter?"

"She'll feel like she's gonna puke her guts up. You'll lose power and the intercoolers won't be able to handle the increase in thruster heat. The thrusters will go offline automatically within thirty seconds unless you can figure out how to keep them cool." Billy glanced down at the Colonel and the Captain, reading their puzzled looks. "The Orbiter's sub-light converters operate on stored Asium energy at the sub-light thrusters on the back side of the bridge pod. While the sub-light power couplings are engaged, energy flows forward to the thruster batteries where it's stored until called on by the sub-light drives, sort of like charging an old solar cell. Asium crystal modules are all carefully balanced. Ours and the *Athena's* had cracks in crystal number five and had to be removed. That put both ship's assemblies out of balance. Makes for flow control difficult at best. I'm looking at the fly back regulators controlling the Asium flow from the engines. There doesn't seem to be anything wrong with it here. It all checks out."

"Then the problem must be forward at the sub-light thruster ports, right?" Dakota asked.

"Checked all that out earlier," Billy said shaking his head. "The Advial flux relays were acting kind of glitchy earlier, but that shouldn't have caused the premix converters to act up. She's ready to go, sir, so long as you keep an eye on it and be ready with plan *B* if something happens."

"You've got my confidence level rather low at the moment," Gunnar grumbled. "I don't suppose you could spare either yourself or Frank to come along for the ride, just to keep an eye on things and be ready with a plan *B*?"

Billy gave it some thought, shaking his head slowly.

"I need Frank here if we're to have the rest of this ship ready to go when you get back. You'll have the Captain here," he motioned to Dakota. A name suddenly popped into his head. "The only other option is Tiana." Billy started to climb back down with Gunnar beside him.

"You're serious?" Gunnar was surprised at the recommendation.

"She's actually quite smart and appears to get all this stuff. Said she got several semesters of Fulton sub-light and Massey FTL engineering courses in the Tonks academy on Ferrus Three. She's been dogging me and Frank for some time now and actually knows the sub-light drive system as well as Frank. As an engineering monitor, she'd be fine, besides, you'll have Alex 7001 with you as well. He can fill in the gaps where needed."

"Yeah, I don't think so." The Colonel was hardly convinced. "No training of any kind, especially in combat situations. If this were a standard long range mapping probe, maybe, but this? We could encounter hostiles."

"Well, you'll have to make that call, sir," Billy said, heading back to his consoles. Gunnar dropped to the floor and headed for the door.

Dakota held his arms folded, giving the chief engineer a long look as Gunnar brushed past him. Thinking about what Billy had suggested, Dakota turned to follow. It was no secret Tiana had heavily involved herself in assisting the engineering team. With her background of drive systems, she could be helpful at the bridge engineering console.

"I think you should at least consider Tiana, sir," Dakota finally spoke up.

"You think I'm overlooking something important here?" Gunnar responded, stepping into the main hallway.

"I think it might be a good idea to consider. Even as your ExO, I'm still pulling fighter duty. You need a good executive officer. With her knowledge of sub-light drives, she could bridge gaps I could only dream of. Maybe Tiana could fill that position."

Gunnar stopped in the middle of the hall and faced his first officer. He knew all about Tiana working with engineering. He had even helped on projects where she had been involved. He had a mind to give Dakota a good butt chewing for trying to dictate to him what he should or shouldn't be doing. But Gunnar understood all too well a fighter pilot's mentality. They didn't want to be saddled with anything except flying.

"You may well be right. I'll consider it."

Dakota had expected to get a lecture, but was surprised when Gunnar abruptly turned and continued up the hall.

Approaching the bridge, Gunnar dodged a few of the *Athena's* crew members and veered to his right, ducking into his quarters. The dark Lexan doors opened and closed automatically as he walked into his bed chambers. Stopping next to the couch, he touched a control on the night stand and watched the full sized bed slowly extend. Gunnar lay down with a heavy sigh and looked up through the overhead window at the star field beyond.

Dakota was going to make an excellent first officer. There was no better officer between the two ships to fill the position. However, there was something to the notion of considering Tiana. She had the basic makings for an executive officer, though a couple of things weighed against her. She wasn't military personnel and she had an uncanny ability to read other people's emotional disposition, causing some discomfort among the crew. He was no different. Perhaps more importantly, was her attraction to him. He could not deny he was drawn to her as well, but he wasn't anxious to start something that could get complicated. How could he possibly consider starting a relationship with someone else when he still felt so tightly bonded to Audra?

Like a battle wound or the painful scars from a terrible accident, some things never fully heal and the loss of Audra still ached deep within. In his weekly counseling sessions, the good Doctor Yamoto had indicated he would feel the pangs of the mourning process for some time. Advising him that a good way to counter the defeating effects of depression was to throw himself into his work. He had done well up to this point, now that they were starting to get back to being a couple of starships and not just two floating hulks in space. But Fuji had also indicated that he needed to come to terms with the fact that Audra was gone and wasn't coming back. The only way forward was to let go of her, but that was something he couldn't see as possible. How do you separate, "as one"?

Gazing quietly out at the vastness of white specs, the pain of Audra's absence swelled. He glanced over to his night stand and picked up a small memory chip attached to a chain. Rick had given it to him, encouraging him to use it. Judging from the Hallavertor sequencing specifications governing its operation, he was sure it was some kind of psycho analysis exercise Fuji had devised. He had been so sure that having two hearts was going to be a blessing. He could do so many amazing things, but now something so remarkable had turned out to be something almost unbearable. He had no idea how long he could keep ahead of what his body was putting him through. Every emotional shift was being amplified tenfold. Since drugs didn't have much of an effect on his system, he was certain a self-help psycho exercise wasn't going to help with this either. He gently tapped it against his upper lip while staring out into space. No, this would be a useless waste of his time so he dropped the chip in the refuse container and pulled his glasses off.

Trying to do the same thing repeatedly and expecting different results seems kind of stupid, doesn't it? Rick had asked him earlier. *Try all possibilities before you give up. Oh, by the way, never give up.*

Yeah, easy for him to say. *I've never gone through what you're going through.* But maybe he was right, dang it, he usually was.

Rolling to his night stand, he retrieved the chip and pushed it into the slot next to the Hallavertor control pad, touching a series of controls.

"Begin program," he spoke quietly.

The room instantly brightened and his surroundings shifted to his mountain meadow, in front of his favorite tree. It was different this time. It was late spring and his tree was almost completely foliated in new green and blue leaves. He stepped confidently toward it, happy to lean against its towering trunk and soak up the sun. As he did so, a short figure in a blue casual dress she liked to wear when not on duty, rolled from around the trunk and smiled. The program was flawless.

"I was wondering when you would finally get to this?"

Gunnar stopped a couple of steps from her and trying to control his emotions, forced a smile. Audra stepped up to him and took his hand. Her touch was real enough and felt warm on his hands.

"I don't know what I want to say to you," Gunnar muttered, realizing his eyes were starting to flood. He ached for her and it was all he could do to keep from throwing his arms around her.

"That was never a problem before, what's wrong now?"

"Missing you I guess," he sniffled.

"I suppose that's understandable," Audra replied, reaching up and stroking his hair.

"You left me alone." Gunnar forced a gulp.

"Are you mad at me?"

"Yes."

"Really?"

"No."

"Is that how you want to remember me? You want to be angry with me for the rest of your life?"

"No."

"Then how do you want to remember me? How do you want to feel when you think of me?"

"I don't know." Gunnar wiped the tears from his eyes and took her other hand. "I can only see what I've lost, what I miss, what I want."

"I'm hearing a whole lot of I, I, I and me, me, me. You're sounding very sorry for yourself. I suspect there are plenty of people around you doing that. Why would you need to?"

"Cause I'm the only one who knows what I'm feeling, not them."

"You think you're the only one in the universe that has ever lost someone close to them? You're the only one that's ever felt this way and so no one can possibly have any empathy for you. Whannie woohoo." Audra stepped out from under the tree, into the sunlight.

Gunnar quickly lost himself and stepped out next to her.

"I'm sorry. I'm just not doing well with being alone."

"No one likes to be alone. Do you suppose I'm enjoying being away from you?"

"Well," Gunnar hedged a bit, feeling silly now. "I would hope you're not enjoying it, I mean… I don't know what I mean."

"Let's flip this and see if that helps." Audra turned to him. "Imagine you were the one that got piled on a year ago. Happy birthday by the way."

"Is it my birthday again?"

"Happens every year at this time."

"Are you sure?"

"Tomorrow."

"Seriously?"

Audra gave Gunnar a good natured look. She was like a machine when it came to remembering dates and faces. Couple that with how she was appearing to him now, gave no room for error.

"Yeah ok, my bad," he admitted with a smirk.

"How do you think I would be dealing with all this were it me instead of you standing here? We talked about what would happen if one of us were gone." Audra held her gaze on him, waiting for him to reverse their roles. Gunnar forced himself to think about it, to imagine how she would react were she in his present position.

"You'd be in command, probably wearing my cool jacket" he finally responded.

"Oh, and wouldn't it look so nice on me?" Audra reached up and adjusted the high fold collar of Gunnar's uniform jacket. "I've always liked this uniform, especially on you."

Gunnar watched her carefully, remembering everything about her, especially her eyes. How soft they were, how brown. He wanted to climb into them and wrap them around his aching soul. Being this close to her again, took all the pain away and he felt like his old self again.

"How would I feel standing here looking all fine and snappy without you? What would I be going through?"

Gunnar thought a moment, back to their discussion. At first, he hoped she would be miserable, but deep down, he knew he would want her to be happy. He would never want her to experience even a tiny portion of the torture he was going through.

"If it's anything like what I'm going through, misery."

"And you would want that for me?"

"Of course not."

"Then listen to me now, for I feel no different for you. You have so much to give of yourself. Take the pain of my absence and change it to love for others. You'll find room within that you never knew existed."

"Easier said than done."

"Certainly it is. Whoever said it was easy? Only worth the investment."

"You're suggesting I stop looking inside at what I've lost and look outside for what I can give to someone else."

"How philosophical you've become."

"I'm not sure I know how to do that."

"Sure you do. You did it all the time with me. Well, not all the time..."

"You're different."

"I'm different. How am I different?"

"Just different."

"I'm a person just like the next person and it doesn't matter who it is, you can find room inside for any and every one. You have always had an amazing ability to love and you have such a larger capacity for love than just what you and I shared." Audra turned back to the scene before them. Gunnar turned and stepped behind her, carefully sliding his arms around her.

"What you and I shared is still inside me."

"I hope it will always be there, but I know there is room for so much more."

"I don't want more," Gunnar whispered. "I want you."

Audra turned around in his arms and swung her arms around his neck, pulling close.

"I'm always here with you and someday, this will all be real again."

They came together in a kiss, bringing Gunnar back to the full remembrance of what it was like to hold her, to have her close to him, to be *as one*.

A door summons calling his attention brought him back to reality and he reluctantly pulled from Audra, looking into her eyes. He wanted to stay here with her, but Audra beckoned him to answer.

"I'm waiting here for you when you need me."

Gunnar smiled and stepped back.

"End program," he said softly, Audra's image and their surroundings immediately disappearing. In profound thought, he pulled the chip from the Hallavertor slot and put the chain around his neck, then reached for the comlink.

"Come on in, my house is your house." Since Audra's passing, he had been guardedly private, especially when it came to his personal space. Right now, it didn't feel important anymore.

A few moments later, Tiana Mantose stepped tentatively to the commander's private chamber doors as he put his glasses on. She remained silent, appearing to look right through his glasses at his damp eyes.

"You're missing her, aren't you?" she spoke reverently.

"Come again?" he inquired, trying to hide what he had just experienced. Perhaps it was Tiana's unsurpassed gift of empathy or the Chyropaz around her neck. Whatever *it* was still made Gunnar uncomfortable.

"Would you like to talk about it?"

"Nope."

"Well, if you ever do..."

"Tiana, how can I help you?"

"I heard you were getting ready to take the Orbiter out," she said, shifting gears. "I'd really like to go along."

"Have you been talking to Billy?"

"No, sir, I haven't seen him all morning."

"You don't have to call me sir. You aren't in the military."

"I know, but I think I'd like to be. Serve on a ship like this one."

"What about your brother?"

"No, I think he's more interested in helping Dr. Yamoto."

"Most of the men on this ship think that way. Still, medicine is a noble profession."

"About the Orbiter..."

Gunnar lay down looking up through the window. Closing his eyes, he hoped the tears would somehow evaporate faster.

"I don't think it would be a very good idea, Tiana. You'd just stand around doing nothing. I have no idea what we're gonna find out there. The idea of having you on board this ship is for protection, not to send you out into the thick of the unknown."

"That was to protect us from the Terrellians. Clearly that threat no longer exists. Besides, I'd say we're already in the thick of the unknown. Look, I really want to help. I've been tailing Billy for quite a while now. My field of study was applied Massey Trans-FTL engineering and comprehensive Fulton sub-light drive systems. I could be helpful at the engineering station. Think of me as an independent contractor."

Gunnar was beginning to think everyone was going to start questioning his orders. Was he going to have to corral the entire crew in a room and give them *the talk*? He didn't like being super strict, but at the same time, when you make a decision and a command is given, the discussion is over. He was being a little more patient here because the Mantose twins were not a part of his crew and technically not under his command, only his protection. Remaining silent and composed for a moment, he finally yawned and opened an eye.

"Tiana, I'm trying to power nap here." He settled a little more, feeling like he had made his point while sending her a gentle message. But Tiana was not to be put off so easily. She was ready to make a difference and somehow become a productive member of the crew.

"Gunnar, please," she asked, a little more insistent. Gunnar was caught a little off-guard at her tone, but remained unmoved. Tiana stepped it up a little more. "Come on Gunnar, you know you want me there. You need me there."

Silence continued from the commander's bed, while Tiana became even more impatient. Infuriated and feeling quite defeated, she turned and stormed out.

"Tiana," Gunnar called after her. "The flyback regulator circuits on the bridge need some work done to them and the engineers won't get to them before we leave. You should be able to step over to the *Athena* and get what you need from Clancy. Get back here soon enough and it should only take an experienced independent contractor about an hour and a half to finish the project. Do you know any?"

Tiana remained frozen for a moment, then turned back to the open Lexan doors when she realized where this assignment would take place. She smiled softly, looking back into the room at Gunnar. She liked him, a lot, and the thought of their images in the Chyropaz, gave her hope that somehow they were supposed to be together.

"Thank you, Gunnar," she whispered softly, backing out as the lights dimmed.

*   *   *   *

Sitting in her chair at the helm, Lynette rubbed her tired eyes, letting out a frustrated sigh. She swung her headset mic boom away and popped the ear piece. The chatter between stations aboard the *Constellation* and the *Athena* made it difficult to concentrate. Both ships remained docked to better facilitate system efficiency. After several more frustrating minutes, she finally gave up on what she was trying to do. Shoving her stylus up into her hair, she sat back and hoisted her feet up onto the edge of one of her consoles.

"Wow, Nigel, I'll tell ya, I've had it." She executed a large stretch and yawned. "I can't see anything, neither can the diagnostic Atheons." She sounded quite defeated, rubbing her aching fingers.

"Well, at least your terminal is working," Nigel responded, frustrated with his own situation. "I can't plot diddly with our Navi-computers," he continued, dropping his stylus. "It's got more bugs running through the system than a swarm of litter ants at a picnic." The navigator touched a control on his comlink panel and looked over at Lynette, who was giving him a rather odd look. "On a hot day," he emphasized, raising both eyebrows. He abruptly swiveled his chair toward the rear of the bridge and pushed his mic pickup a little closer. "Hey, Lana, could you set up a Navi-computer tie-in with the *Athena*? I'm having some real trouble up here with ours." Nigel turned back to the Starbird pilot. "I don't see how the Colonel can expect to take the Orbiter out on a recon when half our gear isn't even working right. Flying blind in space is one thing; there isn't much of anything to crash into out here. But if we find this planet they're talking about, mind you that's a big *IF*, with the problems this gear is having now, we're going to have a hard time making any kind of a controlled entry let alone a safe landing."

Lynette looked over at Nigel's readouts, then at her own, then back at the navigator.

"Right," she said slowly, watching Nigel begin to smile. He picked up his stylus and started to work again.

"Thanks, Lana, you're a champ," he finally said, looking over at the Starbird pilot. "Ask and you will receive."

"What is there for me to ask for?" Lynette gave him another look, then turned back to her own station as Captain Abrams and Alex 7001 came into the bridge.

"Stations everyone," Captain Abrams called out, stepping toward helm control. "We'll be launching the Orbiter in about twenty. Have you found anything, Lieutenant?" Dakota leaned down a little closer to Lynette. She reinserted her ear piece and swung her boom back to her mouth.

"Not a thing, sir, and onboard diagnostics can't see anything either. I think it was just a power flux," she vented.

Dakota scanned the vast console to Lynette's right.

"Power fluxes don't show a shutdown on a PM-39 converter assembly. Something is causing a damper to malfunction."

"I'm a pilot, sir, not an engineer," Lynette shrugged, not knowing what else to say.

"Well, there isn't time to run any more diagnostics on it. I'll set up an engineering stage program to monitor it. Get the Orbiter ready to disengage."

Lynette rolled her eyes and started working with her touch screens as Captain Abrams stepped away.

"Yea, like that's going to help," she mumbled. A stage program was nothing more than a logging program and didn't do anything to alert anyone of a developing problem. What they really needed was an actual body sitting at engineering. Alex 7001 could perform the operation himself, but was so over tasked maintaining other ship's functions that adding one more thing, could compromise the droid's ability to maintain critical functions.

Dakota sat down in the command chair, activating the comlink at the same time. There was silence for a moment, then a response.

"Conrad here."

"Abrams, sir, preparations are under way for Orbiter separation."

"I'll be up in ten." The com line went silent and Dakota turned to Lana at communications.

"Lieutenant, make sure Commander Niker understands she will have command of the *Constellation's* aft component while we're gone and she's not to disengage from the *Athena* unless emergency dictates otherwise."

The Lieutenant acknowledged her orders and turned to relay the message, while the Captain turned the command chair forward again, an odd look forming on his face.

"Did I say dictates?" he asked himself. He purposely shivered, pressing the comlink for engineering. "I've got to watch my language. Mr. Moon, we're ready for CTI and main pod separation." Moon acknowledged as Captain Abrams pressed another button.

"Colonel Conrad to the bridge." His voice resonated throughout the ship. Scanning all bridge stations, his attention was drawn to Tiana Mantose working in an access panel behind the engineering console. Seeing that the crew was doing well with their assigned duties, he stepped over to where the woman was working. He was a little surprised to see her on the bridge, considering the Colonel's attitude toward the matter.

"Miss Mantose?" Dakota sat quietly down in the engineering chair and scooted around next to where she was working. "Does the Colonel know you're in here?"

"He's the one that assigned me to this." Tiana held her focus on what she was doing.

"And what exactly did he assign you to do?"

"Independent contracting," she smiled. "Reworking these regulator circuits." She held her focus on a small portable display she had propped up next to the open panel. "This would be a whole lot easier if I had some Nano-mech I could just smear all over it."

Dakota glanced down at the information on the glowing screen in front of her, and then in at the actual components she was working with. He wasn't a technician by any measure, but he had seen the fruits of good work and he was impressed.

"You gonna be done before we depart?" Dakota already knew the answer to the question, but wanted to hear her response.

"No... Dang it!" she answered with controlled glee.

Dakota glanced over his shoulder as Alex 7001 hovered into position, observing her work. It wasn't long before Tiana started to feel a little bit self-conscious and looked up at her audience.

"Should I be selling tickets?"

Dakota cracked a smile, pulling back and stepping over to the command chair to let Alex finish supervising. A minute later, Colonel Conrad walked into the bridge just as the communications officer turned from her consoles.

"Colonel on the bridge. Engineering reports clear for separation and the *Athena* is signaling all clear."

Dakota spun the command chair around and Gunnar moved to sit down.

"Alex, status?" Gunnar inquired.

"Transferring circuits are all functioning. The bridge doors are sealed and all onboard systems showing ready for separation."

Satisfied with Alex's response, he turned to the Starbird pilot.

"Helm, maneuvering thrusters, ready for separation."

Lynette turned back to her controls and touched a number of points on her immense touch panel. Then she reached for several mechanical switches to her left.

Outside, at the neck of the bridge pod, the main holding clamps gently retracted and the bridge pod silently pulled away from its mounts and the rest of the ship. Lynette banked the Orbiter around alongside the rest of the ship and bringing her thrusters to station-keeping, she turned to several other readouts on the console in front of her.

"Ready to go, sir," she announced, confirming Ensign Kramer's course directions.

"Well-done, helm," Gunnar said sitting back. "Ahead full sub-light."

Lynette tapped more commands on the helm control panel, and then started pushing forward on the sub-light throttles. The orbiter began to move faster and faster toward the sixth planet in the second system. At full sub-light speed, it would take them less than a day to reach their target destination.

Colonia

The Empire of Colonia had existed for millennia. But as often happens as a mechanism grows beyond itself, corruption for wealth and power take root and blossoms out of control. As a Duchess of Teleknee, Stephanie Benetar married into the royal family of Pintar and almost overnight, the other members of royalty either mysteriously died off or disappeared. Without definitive answers, disputes among the galactic nations quickly arose. Without a rightful Blood Heir, the strongest of these dynasties would assume the role of ruler in the Hadrian galaxy. As the squabbling escalated into heated warfare, the Albion military assimilated a good portion of the Hadrian directorates, amassing enough assets and manpower to pose a serious threat to the sovereignty of Colonia. Unless the illegitimate royalty of Colonia stepped aside or produced a Blood Heir, the Albion Empire would take power by force.

Carolon is the sixth planet in the Nulark system. A short distance further out is the darker planet, Reako. Twins, Tanis and Maver, are sandwiched between Reako and the furthest planet Boris. During Carolon's week long day its dual suns light the sky, but during the long calm night, tiny glowing Triticalie particles suspended in the airborne moisture, illuminate the sky.

"Now this is what I'd call worthless," Colonel CJ Barker mumbled, looking out across a vast flatland below her. "Benetar has got to be zardocs if she thinks this planet is of any use to the Empire."

CJ sat on a large rock, a gentle wind blowing her bright auburn hair across her faded freckles and crystal blue eyes. Brushing the hair from her face, she tucked her single white lock of hair behind her ear. Tossing several clear stones, she turned her gaze to a new base laying partially sprawled across a vast barren plain, the rest built into the low rising hills. A fair sized base, though it wasn't exactly what she had in mind for a first Command with the Colonian Empire. Being Albion, she had previously served with its military for most of her career, much of it on the *Tarzana*, their flagship battlecruiser. This being her first deployment with the Colonian military, she would have rather been assigned a capital ship, Daliger or a Hesson class destroyer or battlecruiser. Still, an entire Colonian base with five squadrons of F-2 Flightstreaks, servicing capacities for front line battle support and a small flotilla of light and heavy cruisers was a great starting point for the remainder of her military career with Colonia.

Surveying the view of the base for as far as the eye could see, CJ jumped from her perch, stumbling in the soft Carolon soil. It had the consistency of sand littered by myriads of the clear stones she had been throwing earlier. Stepping cautiously, she probed the ground in front of her before taking a step. There were many covered fissures and deep sink holes hidden just beneath the surface. This broad volcanic landscape was barren of vegetation and there were only a few large rocks and boulders strewn across it.

It was getting late and she needed to be back to receive debriefing reports from the incoming scout ships. Moving along the designated path toward the edge of the plateau, she looked up as two F-2 Flightstreaks materialized from the high overcast and circled as they descended, a sonic boom accompanying their appearance in the sky.

She suddenly felt herself teetering sideways into nothing, she put her hand out to break her fall. Looking down into a sink hole that was opening beneath her, she caught something solid and grasped as hard as she could.

"How utterly stupid," she grumbled, hanging one handed. She reached up with her other hand and grasped a piece of the partially buried rock jutting from the side of the hole. Struggling for a bit, she found another one near her foot and secured herself. Spitting dirt, she carefully reached for her communicator and raised it to her mouth.

"Willis," she fumbled, lose dirt still raining on her. "Canella plateau, North ridge, get your butt up here on the double." Trying to replace the device, she fumbled and it dropped. She never heard it hit bottom, she couldn't even see the bottom. The communicator did have lights on it, but there was nothing but blackness below her. Maybe the dirt coming in had buried it as it hit the bottom or it landed upside-down. Or maybe this hole had no bottom. She had no desire to find out. Looking back up at the dull overcast, CJ occasionally caught a glimpse of a fighter streaking across her view. The walls continued to drop more dirt on her, threatening to give way at any moment. She would be kicking herself right now for getting into such a stupid predicament if she weren't afraid of dislodging what hand hold she had. In the dim light from above, she looked up at the rock that was her only life line. It didn't feel firm anymore, but all she could do was hope her aide wasn't far.

*   *   *   *

A dirty white craft launched from the Carolon hangar bays, rocketing nearly straight up into the thick evening air. The Colonian F-2 Flightstreak was a well-seasoned front end fighter used as a long range recon craft and a ground support vehicle. A side by side two seat craft with windows surrounding a wide cockpit and doors at the back and side of the cockpit, it was well suited for just about any of the environments found in the many systems of Hadrian. This early version was due for retirement. Well-worn with plenty of battle scoring marks on its hull and exhaust soot behind its ventilator ports, the main power converter assembly cover had been removed due to the frequency of maintenance on its Isom engines.

Willis Ruston turned her craft sharply toward the Canella plateau, scanning the ground below. Bringing the Flightstreak in low, she slowed to a near crawl, touching her communicator button.

"Colonel Barker, I need your position please."

Only a soft hiss came back through her headsets, giving her cause for worry. There was no sign of life of any kind on the dull, flat landscape below her throttling craft.

"Colonel Barker, your position please," Willis called again.

She banked gently around in a circle for a minute, looking, watching for anything that might indicate the presence of her commander. Colonel Barker's last reported position was somewhat vague, but being her personal aide, Willis knew where her favorite spot was. The Colonel liked to hike the plateau to vent and relax. Something the command staff and the perimeter security weren't comfortable with. It wasn't the prettiest place to be, but it offered solitude and plenty of it.

Willis made a wide sweeping turn over the entire area again and headed for the plateau's safe landing zone. While surveyed as having a solid rock base beneath, it could still be subject to the constantly shifting soils of the plateau. The Delta wings of the F-2 smoothly hinged upward at the fuselage as Willis gently set her craft down on the spot she knew well. Willis climbed out over the back of the fighter and made sure her pistol was secure on her hip. It would be difficult for any indigenous animal life to sneak up on her with this kind of terrain. She paused next to the exposed Isom converter assembly and pulled her communicator.

"Colonel Barker, can you send me a marker beacon, anything?"

She made a full turn-about, scanning the immediate area, then pulled out a set of electronic binoculars, slowly turning a full circle again before she jumped down onto the dark Carolon soil. Cautiously shuffling around the back side of her craft, she surveyed the ground around her resting fighter. She had been briefed by perimeter security of the unstable ground on this side of the base. It had little to no moisture in it and the dirt seemed like it was always in motion. Having the consistency of quick sand at times, it could open up without indication, swallowing animal life, people and machines.

Stepping carefully away from the relative safety of the F-2, her eye caught the glimmer of the dusk light reflecting off something in the dirt some distance away. Willis knew a little more about this planet than most of the others at the outpost, with the exception of the sentries, but then again, they were always out here scouting around. They were supposed to know what was here.

"It's not like there is anywhere to hide out here," Willis mumbled. She liked getting away from the rigors of base life just as much as the next person, but she much preferred the forested areas on the other side of the base. Generally, that's where she kept Colonel Barker's F-2, a small hangar deep in the twisted Fowles forest, just inside the base shield arrays. She didn't understand why CJ thought she needed to be out here in the middle of nothing.

To each their own, was all Willis could come up with. She noted the marked trail over the side of the plateau's edge, put there by the base sentries marking where the pathway was stable and could be counted on to be there longer than the surrounding areas. Walking like she might be trying to avoid stepping on eggs, she moved to the trail and down the side of a low ridge toward where she had seen the reflection.

A large opening came into view on the right, off the marked trail and next to it, she found a blaster lying in the dirt, not good. Willis scanned her surroundings again, and then carefully looked over the edge of the opening.

"Colonel Barker, come in," she called again. "Please tell me you're not down in this big dark hole I'm looking into."

She tried looking further down the hole, but wasn't reassured by the unstable dirt around the immediate area of the opening. She had little choice here, as it seemed the most probable option. Colonel Barker had somehow stepped off the marked trail onto a sinkhole.

Willis pulled a powerful light from her utility belt and gingerly crawled to the edge of the hole, laying as close as she dared and shined her light over the edge. There was something down there, but she had to wait for her eyes to adjust before she recognized Colonel Barker's uniform. Appearing to be mostly buried, the Colonel lay on a large mound of loose dirt, her right arm, shoulder and head still showing above the constantly cascading dirt, lightly covering the unconscious officer. It looked like the hole had opened up a cavern. Willis could see tunnels branching off in several directions.

"Colonel Barker, CJ, can you hear me? Oh come on, don't make me climb down the dark scary hole after you. I'm gonna get all dirty."

Visibly irritated, Willis got back to her feet and started down the plateau's face searching for an alternate entrance. There were plenty of holes, but nothing she felt comfortable trying to crawl into. Using her light, she peered into one of the larger ones.

"Ick, I hate dirt," she complained, pulling at the soil to try and widen the hole. If she could just loosen this one rock, she'd have no trouble climbing through. Grunting and clawing to move the dirt, she was becoming frantic.

"Oh come on! You mean to tell me that you step in the wrong place around here and you fall to the other side of the planet, but I can't get one stupid rock to..."

She let out a muffled yelp as the rock suddenly disappeared ahead of her and she went through the hole, along with what seemed like half the hillside. Coughing and spitting, she pushed off something solid and hitting hard ground, rolled as far as she could. Back on her feet she froze, waiting for the dust to settle and hoping her presence wouldn't disturb the entire plateau. Fumbling in the dark for her light, she switched it on and squinted in the dusty light.

"Hate this," she grumbled, afraid to even breathe. The tunnel was big enough, so she was glad she wasn't going to have to go spelunking. Imagine having to drag someone through a tunnel only large enough to wiggle through.

"How do these even get here?" she whispered perplexed. Every step she took, every move she made appeared to cause her surroundings to crumble. Exploring carefully for several more minutes, she came upon a large chamber, or rather stumbled into it. *There she is!*

Willis sprang onto the large mound to the aid of her commander. Climbing the huge mound of dirt was like trying to run up a sand dune, you took a step up, but then slid backwards an equal distance. Finally, Willis had ahold of CJ and brushed the dirt from her face. Feeling for a pulse and checking for breathing, she began to dig frantically around the Colonel, constantly tossing glances above and around her, watching the dirt cascading in on them at an even greater rate.

"Not liking this scenario, sir! Not one bit, come on, Colonel, wake up!"

Tugging as hard as she could, the Colonian aide pulled her commander from the mound, but the dirt beneath them would not hold them and Willis went over backwards with CJ on top of her. Having to struggle to get out from under her, Willis could feel the ground trembling, material coming loose from the walls. She tried to pick her commander up, but couldn't manage it, so she dragged her from the chamber, constantly dusted with falling dirt. Pulling her for some distance down the passage, Willis finally had to stop, prop her commander against a crumbling wall and tried again to wake her. Now the passage was starting to crumble and it seemed to Willis they would surely be buried.

"Wake up," Willis exclaimed breathlessly, shaking her commander. "Come on, sir," she continued in growing frustration. "This isn't the time for snoozin'!"

Finally, CJ began to come around.

"Oh man," she coughed, putting her hands to her head. "Must you yell? And can't you shut off your converters until I'm in the cockpit? I feel like my head is gonna explode." CJ hacked some more and opened her eyes. Looking around, she realized the walls were moving.

"Gotta go, gotta go!" Willis struggled to help her commander to her feet. Still wobbly from being unconscious, CJ steadied herself, holding onto her aide. "I think this whole plateau is gonna go," Willis hollered as they started back down the passage.

"You wouldn't believe the dream I was having," CJ commented from behind, as the two quickened their pace. "I dreamed I was a giant Ploomear fruit and this big Redips was about to suck all the juice out of me, turning me into a shriveled Tamar."

"Can't you dream about normal things for once? Maybe a man?" Willis complained, catching a glimpse of light to their left. She swung a still disoriented CJ in the direction of the light and pushed her through a small hole that had opened up to the outside. CJ had little trouble diving through. With the walls all around her starting to shift, Willis hoisted herself into the hole and squirmed madly to get her curves through.

"How come you got through so easy?" she yelled frantic, noticing the outside surfaces starting to slide.

"I have smaller hips." CJ grabbed her hands and started to pull.

"But you're a lot older than me!"

"It's a hole, Willis!"

"Sort of messed this one up," Willis gasped. She wiggled harder, trying to get through as more dirt came cascading down nearly burying her.

Kicking frantically, the Colonian aide gritted and squirmed while her commander pulled with all her might. As more of the hillside came loose, Willis suddenly pulled free and slid right out on top of CJ who lost her balance and fell straight back as the ground slid further away. Moments later, a choking cloud of dirt filled air came blasting out after them as the hole collapsed. One catastrophe averted, now it was apparent the whole plateau was starting to sink.

"The ship is back up here," Willis directed, bounding back onto what was left of the marked trail. "I hope." Running for the top of the plateau, Willis finally stopped and looked around for the familiar shape of the fighter.

"Last time I ever come up here for the view," CJ puffed, stumbling up the trail next to Willis.

To their horror, they found the F-2 starting to slide into a yawning crevasse and by the time the two women reached it, the Colonian craft was nearly on its side, half in the gaping crack.

Willis jumped onto the ship, pressing the side door activator and falling rather unfashionably in as the hatch slid to one side. CJ came quickly behind her and hit the release mechanism as soon as she was in. They might have been better off just leaving the fighter for lost, but right now, it seemed like a better option than trying to hike out on foot.

"You always climb aboard that way?" CJ asked, as Willis struggled to get to her controls.

"Not very lady-like, huh?" Willis responded as CJ reached for her seat. The fighter continued to slip further as Willis worked frantically to get her craft started. "When you come to get away from it all, you really go all out," she commented excitedly, hitting the converter generators.

Console displays came alive and a low throb commenced to drone from somewhere behind the cockpit. CJ flipped on a console to her right just as Willis grabbed the yoke and yanked back on the throttles to bring the welcome roar of the Isom engines from behind. She looked up at the dirt cascading down over the side of windshield and pushed forward on a lever, then gave her craft thrusting power. Power indicators rose, as did the whine from behind as the Isom engines labored to pull the ship from its hole.

"She's starting to heat up, Will. Better think of something fast," CJ coughed while trying to help get everything turned on.

"Working on it, sir," Willis responded, wrestling with the controls. Suddenly, the whole ship leapt from the ground, shooting skyward. The pilot eased back on the throttles and banked sharply to the left, giving both women a look at where the plateau had been.

"I bet that seismic ruckus shakes the whole base," Willis commented, banking the ship for home.

"Status on Swenson Shipley and Drax Blair's progress?" CJ asked, shaking dirt from her hair and uniform.

"Don't you ever stop?" Willis complained. "Let's talk about finding you a man." She would have thought CJ would rather decompress from her leisurely little adventure that had nearly gotten them both killed. Willis was certainly ready for a couple of hours in the officer's lounge. The look on her commander's face told her that wasn't going to happen. "He's still milling around just outside the elliptical of Boris," Willis finally answered, as she started her approach.

"Sure wished the Queen would send us more support other than a couple of cruisers. What about Blair?"

"Nothing since yesterday," Willis responded shaking her head.

CJ sat back and thought quietly to herself. The outer planets had little to offer anyone. In fact, this entire system had little to nothing to offer. She was just now starting to question why this base was even here and why the Albions and the Ratronians were showing such an interest in it. It's not like the Empire was practicing squatter's rights.

They'd be on the ground soon, and then she'd have to make her report to Queen Benetar. Normally, CJ would only address the high command with her quarterly reports, but Queen Benetar fancied herself as a military mind and seemed to take an unusual interest in Carolon. Most of the Colonian royal family kept their noses out of military matters, but Benetar was much the exception. With the formation of this Colonian stronghold on Carolon, CJ had been selected because she was an outsider possessing the required experience. But if she failed to hold the planet, she would surely be run out of the military and Colonian society. Not a pleasant thought for CJ as being Albion herself and in the Colonian military, didn't leave her with too many options.

Reporting in

CJ and Willis trudged slowly into the Operations Center of the Carolon base looking quite bedraggled.

"Well, I must say," a voice from across the room called out as the two women plopped down onto a nearby bench. "You two look as though you are ready to attend the Grande Sarst. Anyone I know?"

CJ looked up at Val Fry who leaned over the rail of the command overview deck smiling broadly. The two women tried to brush the dark Carolon dirt from their soiled uniforms as they slowly got up and made their way up to the overview deck. Willis stopped at the top of the stairs and pulled a boot off, emptying the dirt.

"Look at this! The whole south plateau is now a great big sink hole. Couldn't we have at least showered first?"

CJ gave Willis a *not-now* look and turned back to her group commander.

"We saw you coming in. Is there anything to report?" CJ noticed a couple of buttons missing from her navy blue uniform.

"Yeah, you'd better come have a look," Val answered.

CJ motioned for Willis to hurry up as the two made their way around the large floor viewing map and to the command deck. CJ seemed to have found a hidden energy reserve as she bounded up the stairs, stopping behind the main controller.

"What have ya got, Bubbles?"

"I'm picking up a large squadron of Black Tigers taking off from an Albion carrier that just came out of Quadra-light in sector eight on the back side of Boris." Lieutenant Talia "Bubbles" Reese continued to punch in commands to the base central command computer.

CJ studied the objects on the main viewing map below, then turned to Val.

"These will be assembly reinforcements for Blair. Have the ground crews turned your fighters around yet?"

Val shook his head.

"It'll be another hour or so before they're ready to recharge the guns and reload torpedoes."

"I want to make sure these guys know we're not just sitting here sunning ourselves. Have Quarto bring his two squadrons of

A-5s up to join your group as soon as you can get airborne. I'll have Bubs scramble Bonnie's squadron of TL-42s from the *Trinoid* to join you. Just run formation sweeps between here and Reako. The Albions will think we're up to something."

"Getting these squadrons together for formation runs to Reako is going to take some time." Val was on his way before his commander got all her words out. "Quarto hasn't even landed yet."

CJ turned to the Talia as Val trotted from the room.

"Better get Benetar on the line, and tell flight com to get the *Trax* out there, ready or not." She then pointed a finger at Willis. "You, get my F-2 refueled and ready to go. You're coming with me when I'm done here."

Willis seemed quite pleased. As the Colonel's personal aide, she wasn't allowed to fly into a combat zone often and finding her own reserve of energy, she bolted from the room.

CJ watched an odd expression develop on the com officer as she fiddled with several tuning controls, putting a finger to her headset.

"What's up Bubs?"

Talia adjusted a control, listening carefully.

"I'm picking up some subspace transmissions coming from outside the quadrant. Scancom is trying to unscramble it, but it's proving to be in a codec we're not familiar with. I'm listening to it and I've never heard it before."

"Well that's saying something. I can't think of anyone who knows communications better than you."

"I'm sure there are many others," Talia commented still listening. "What I don't get is this codec being used. Most subspace transmissions use an encrypted digital cypher style arrangement in their data codes. This is like nothing I've ever heard before."

CJ drooped her eyelids and sucked in a quiet breath. Her talents were not in the technical jargon of the communications world, but her com officer did sometimes go on a little.

"Have Scancom stay on it and if they do get it deciphered, pass it along to me as soon as they have it ready." With Q.C. Blair and Swenson Shipley muddling around on the outskirts of this system, she didn't need someone else sneaking into her back door and really causing a ruckus.

CJ turned to a large video screen hanging over the viewing map as the screen began to glow slightly and a face materialized. Looking down at Colonel Barker, her Royal Highness, Queen Stephanie Benetar furled her beautiful hair back across her silky smooth shoulders, giving the Colonian officer a slight sneer.

CJ disliked the Queen. Royalty had no place in military circles and were only barely tolerated in politics, but the Colonel understood her position and the need for restraint when dealing with the Queen.

"Well, Colonel Barker, what is it now?"

"QC Blair is making her move on the tenth planet and I haven't got the firepower you promised to send me to hold her back if she throws anything heavy at us." Frustration highlighted her whole statement and the Queen of Colonia didn't much care for her tone.

"I have given you everything I can possibly spare. We are spread out quite thin right now. You are hardly at the top of the list for reinforcements. However, General Monit informs me that two destroyers are in your area and can supply you with any assistance."

Colonel Barker clamped down hard on her teeth. Why did she have to deal directly with the Queen? It seemed her Highness had it in for her. This would have been so much easier, not to mention more appropriate coming from a general. CJ needed much more than two destroyers that were probably on their way to be mothballed, but the added firepower would be welcomed. The accompanying fighter groups that should be aboard each ship would be invaluable. She glanced down at Talia, and then nodded, trying to look humble and sound grateful.

"I appreciate anything you can send me."

"As well you should," Benetar cut in. "You must keep Blair out of that system at all costs, Colonel." The Queen's tone sounded final, blunt. The screen went blank as the transmission ended and all eyes were on the upper command deck. There was no talking, just the soft hum of equipment and space chatter. They all watched to see what Colonel Barker's response would be. CJ fidgeted, glancing back at the dark screen a couple of times. Wanting to give the viewer the elbow and fist gesture, CJ sensed she was being observed and thought better of it. As commander, she needed to be the adult and set the example for those under her command.

Turning from the screen, she faced the com officer.

"Her Royal Highness?" She made a fist and gave her palm a good punch. "Her Royal pain in my hinny."

Talia began to chuckle a little, then finally started to laugh. CJ couldn't help but snicker at Talia's contagious bubbly laughter. It was hard not to be happy when Talia was laughing, the reason for the nick name, Bubbles. Confident she had done the right thing and the tension of the moment defused, CJ started slowly down the command stairs, smiling.

Even from as far away as the personnel lounge, CJ could hear the roar of throttling Isom engines in the hangar bay. Speeding around several corners on her ground transport, she was suddenly in the launch bay. The roar of fighter engines rose in pitch as four of the sleek looking F-2s rocketed from the open bay doors, arcing skyward. As Colonel Barker's driver slowed her transport and came to a halt, she shoved her hands into her gloves, grabbed her helmet and jumped off.

Bounding up the portable stairs to the side entrance of her fighter, CJ stepped into the cockpit and closed the hatch behind her, heading for the copilot's position beside Willis.

"Still wished we could have at least showered," Willis complained still finding bits of dirt and grit. "Look at this…"

"You can clean up on the *Trax*. We're fine, let's go," CJ said, shoving her helmet down into place and buckling herself in. "We rendezvous with the *Trax* in fifteen minutes."

"The *Trax*?" Willis repeated, working several of her controls to get their craft moving. "I thought it was an old derelict. It's only an F class cruiser. A super cruiser from a long time ago, but it's been sitting in the Clandice wrecking yard for twenty years."

"Oh so true," CJ agreed, looking up at an overhead console and reaching for several controls. "Exactly why I choose her for a refit. It didn't cost enough in time and materials for the High command to take notice and I knew Benetar wouldn't have even thought about bringing her back. It's doubtful she even knows it still exists. She only likes new sparkly things. Systems show clear and departure control is signaling us to get out of the way," she said pointing at the last group of fighters soaring out of the bay.

The dusk shaded sky quickly turned into the black void of space as the F-2 powered away from Carolon, and as Willis brought her fighter close up behind one of the others in the squadron, the *Trax* came into view. It did look rather old compared to what the current ships in the fleet looked like. But its redesign specifications had brought it up to operational codes required for Colonian capital ships. You could hardly tell the F class Star cruiser had languished in a wrecking yard for twenty years. As the squadron of Flightstreaks set down in the cruiser's landing bays, CJ touched a com control on her control yoke.

"Captain Leavitt, this is Colonel Barker. We're in; flank speed to Boris."

With that order, the *Trax* turned gracefully behind her three escort ships.

Getting to know you

Colonel Conrad knelt down beside Tiana, watching her work on the computer main frame located on the rear bridge wall. She had already finished her original task on the flyback regulators and was just finishing the repairs to the relay sub circuits interfacing with the onboard Navi-computer circuits. She handled the micro-fuser with the grace of a seasoned engineer. Perhaps he had misjudged Tiana's abilities with things technical. He had sort of thought of her as more of the Yeoman type of girl, an administrative runner. Now, he was glad he hadn't voiced his thoughts.

"You do that very well," he finally commented.

"Nano-mech is better suited for this," she said smiling. "I did have great teachers," hinting at the engineering staff.

Gunnar chuckled quietly, somehow the statement hitting him funny. It was hard for him to visualize Billy or Frank being patient enough to teach her how to use any of their tools. The feeling associated with laughter felt good, if only for a moment. It was something that didn't happen often enough.

"The student is only as good as the teacher," Gunnar finally said.

"Exactly," Tiana agreed, finishing her last circuit. She put the fuser down and replaced the cover. Gunnar looked up at the wall of electronics winking at him.

"So you think you've fixed it?"

The two stood up together and let out a collective sigh.

"Gimmie a sec and I'll tell you. Navigation," she called forward. "Can you run a level two through your NC now?"

Gunnar folded his arms listening to how she was trying to sound just like one of the crew. Alex 7001 floated over next to navigation to supervise while Nigel ran several level two diagnostic checks through the Navi-computer. After everything appeared to be in order, the aux link with the *Athena* was terminated, switching over to the *Constellation's* main Nav-com systems.

"Bet you think you're hot stuff now?" Gunnar smirked, stepping toward the command chair.

"Depends on who's looking at me," Tiana winked playfully. "Certainly more useful." She picked up her tools and turned to the engineering station.

Gunnar smiled slightly, looking after her as she sat down at the engineering consoles and started working with the instruments. *She certainly is a bit playful, isn't she?* He liked it, but memories of Audra's playfulness came to mind, instantly bringing his thoughts back to her.

His eyes came to rest on Pip, who seemed more preoccupied than normal. Gunnar motioned for Dakota to follow him as he got up, stepping quietly to where Pip was closely studying his displays. Not wanting to alert the rest of the crew, he leaned slowly back against the console.

"What is it, Pip?" he asked in a lowered voice, looking around the bridge.

Pip switched several controls and touched a number of points on his touch screen, trying to identify the objects he was scanning.

"It appears to be a cluster of ships moving on the tenth planet in this system. I'm also picking up two more groups moving in from another direction." The science officer glanced up at his commander, and then went back to work.

"Can you give me anything more?"

"Some of the returns look smaller than the others. I would suppose the smaller ones are fighters and the larger ones are probably capitals."

"Tactical readouts?"

"Not at this range, sir. Looks like a battle a brewing."

Gunnar thought a moment, turning to watched the information flash before him. He didn't have the time nor did he want to get tangled up in a war of any sort, especially in an Orbiter in need of repair.

"Possibility of a dimensional readout?"

"Negative, sir. We've left a lot of our sensory capabilities with the rest of the ship. If we were to get a little closer, maybe."

"So many things busted up on this ship, it's hard to remember everything," Dakota complained from behind. "Maybe we should turn back and wait it out?"

"We need those crystals," Gunnar whispered looking at the returns. He wished they had a better view of what was out there. "Better steer clear of all of it for now," he finally said, turning toward helm control. "Helm and navigation, change of course. Slow us down a bit and give the tenth planet a wide birth."

"Can you define, *a bit,* and, *wide birth*, a little better, sir?" Lieutenant Starman asked.

"Pilot's discretion."

"This diversion will add a considerable amount of time to our arrival time," the Starbird pilot replied, somewhat bewildered.

"Understood. Com, let the *Athena* know what we're doing." Gunnar leaned back to Pip.

"I thought you said there wasn't much traffic in this system?" Dakota asked, continuing to study the readouts in front of them.

"There wasn't." Gunnar rubbed his chin, thinking.

"Didn't our scanners indicate this system was empty before we left?" Dakota asked.

"Nay, I say," Gunnar answered, looking over his shoulder at his exec. "They didn't say empty, just not much traffic going through it. This little tussle we're looking at could well be the reason why. Would you want to run through a battle zone on an outing to a Nebula or something?"

"That would be some outing. I still think the Interceptors would have been better suited for this little recon."

"You'll get no argument from me, but we both understand the possible ramifications of sending fighters in to the middle of all this," Gunnar said.

"Besides we couldn't get them out anyway," Dakota said.

"Exactly. The point is, we don't know what's going on anywhere around here or what we'll find."

"Maybe we ought to be trying to raise someone? Tell them we're inbound. See what turns up. Might give us time to turn and run if need be."

"Good idea, but I don't want to draw any attention to ourselves until we absolutely have to. If we make too much noise this far out, we might end up with a whole herd of unfriendlys before we can get close enough to the sixth planet for a good deep scan. Com, continue communications silence and go to yellow alert," Gunnar ordered, stepping over and sitting back down in his chair.

After hours of silent running and a roundabout approach to the sixth planet, an alarm sounded off on the science station's console. Gunnar carefully eyed the information being displayed on the overhead monitors above Pip's workstation.

"What the-," Captain Abrams blurted, stepping over for a closer look.

"Where'd that come from, Pip?" Gunnar demanded.

"I can't understand why my sensors failed to pick this up before. Well, yes, I sort of can actually." The science officer made no apologies. "It would sure be nice to have all our arrays operational. It's not just a small outpost," Pip paused, touching

several points on his glass screens. "It's a large base with a personnel complex the size of the Kalamar's control center back home. It's got a lot of flight decks and hangars, some chuck full of transport-type craft, I even see fighters milling around."

"Chuck full," Dakota repeated, looking down at the science officer.

"Sorry," Pip hedged, returning to his screens.

"Any chance this could be the base for one of the forces fighting over the tenth planet?"

"Very likely, sir," Pip answered, letting his fingers sweep over the immense console before him. "Some of the ships look similar to the ones massing over the tenth planet. Here's the tactical data you were asking for."

As Lynette dropped the Orbiter into the dusk atmosphere, Dakota leaned a little closer to the readouts Gunnar was looking at.

"Looks friendly enough," Dakota commented, studying the readouts in front of them.

"Hold it," Pip paused a moment, readjusting his sensor controls. "Six ships have just launched, heading right at us."

"Dimensional," Gunnar ordered, looking closer. The image of a delta foil fighter with twin fins appeared giving Gunnar cause to wonder if he weren't clairvoyant. "Nice."

"Shields up, full intensity," Dakota ordered turning to the weaponry officer. "Arm the secondary guns and stand by."

"Time to make ourselves known," Gunnar commented, studying the information closer.

"Com, hail on all frequencies. Tell them our intentions are peaceful. Guess I spoke a little too soon," Dakota said turning back to Gunnar.

"A little," Gunnar repeated, staring at the information in front of him.

"Specifications above you," Pip announced.

Both command officers stepped back to get a better view on the overhead monitors as the dimensional readouts and specifications of the fighter were displayed.

"It don't look too good, do-it?" Gunnar said purposely wrong.

"For them, I hope you mean," Dakota responded slowly, studying the information before them. "I guess this means they're not friendly?" They were definitely fighters, and heavily armed.

"Not sure what it means. Could just be friendly's protecting their own," Gunnar said. "Too bad, nice looking fighter." He looked at the planet below, then over at the Starbird pilot. "We need to give Com more time to make contact, otherwise this could get ugly really fast. Helm, ease her back up into orbit and we'll try a couple of rotations until we can establish communications." With that he turned back to his command chair and safety locked himself into place.

As Starman started to pull the Orbiter up into a steep turning climb away from the planet's dusk shaded surface, the fighters overshot the Kalamarion Orbiter as it rocketed right through their formation. The squadron leader had time to turn his head, only to see two of his wingman collide mid-air and disintegrate. Almost instantly, the remaining fighters dispersed, firing at the throttling Orbiter. Lynette turned her ship sharply to avoid a blast only to have the ship's left shields racked by laser blasts. Without the main body, the Orbiter didn't handle well, especially in a gravity atmosphere. Lynette nudged her throttles forward, trying to outrun them as she guided the ship back up toward an outer orbit. If they could get above the outer atmosphere, the Orbiter could leave these fighters far behind. Dodging another round of fire, she could feel something wrong. Pilots become one with their machines as they fly, getting to know them in a personal way. Being no different, Lynette glanced down at her displays for answers, but saw only confusion. She felt a tingle of sickened horror as the Orbiter started to slow and lurch forward again. The ship's power readouts were dropping. She gently leveled off and turned to Alex 7001 for answers.

"Alex, I've got a problem here. Advial flux readouts are bottoming out!"

The droid was scanning the engineering console with Tiana for the reason, but no answers were readily available. The fighters were again closing on them. Sitting down next to Tiana, Dakota leaned over for a closer look while Alex worked with several controls, trying to correct the problem. The ship continued to shudder. Lynette was doing her best to keep her ship flying straight, but it was becoming increasingly obvious she wasn't going to be able to stay airborne, let alone reach an orbit and remain ahead of their adversary.

"Sounds like she's thrown a rod," Dakota commented, thinking of Billy.

"A rod, sir?" Alex asked.

"Stay focused, Alex." Dakota turned to Tiana. "Time to cash in on some of that teaching, Miss Mantose. How about you? See anything?"

Tiana felt all eyes on to her. Even Alex 7001 turned his face plate toward her. She worked the controls in front of her as quickly as her limited experience would allow, while Alex continued to scan the readouts.

"I can see the malfunctioning relays, but I'm not seeing what's causing them to fail." Tiana madly scanned the information in front of her, sweeping her hands across the touch screen, searching. "Intercooler mixes are running off the scale," she continued grimly. "Estimate full thruster shutdown in thirty seconds. We need to reduce power and try to reconfigure these dynamic flux inverters. They'll act as a kind of intercooler regulator."

"A little?" Dakota repeated as the ship lurched again and again.

"Where have we heard this before?" Gunnar threw Alex 7001 a glance for a response, but got nothing. He impatiently snapped his fingers several times, glanced at his first officer, and then turned his chair to Com.

"Anything, Navall?"

The com officer was still busy trying to raise the fighters outside. Starting to shake her head, she stopped and put a finger to her ear piece.

"I've got something," she announced. The signal was badly garbled at first, the words coming from the speakers sounded like gibberish, but as she worked with her controls, the broken transmission started to make sense.

"... Carolon Command ... Colonian Empire, under the rule of Queen ... Benetar." Any deviation... your present course... bring about your immediate destruction. You are ordered to follow the escort fighters down into the approach flight path and await further instructions, acknowledge."

Gunnar looked over at Dakota and Tiana.

"Not exactly the something we were hoping for, is it?" Dakota tried to jest. "Com, did you get a distress signal out to General Niker?"

"I sent one, but I'm not sure it got through, sir. Something in this atmosphere is really screwing things up. I'm trying to reconfigure my gear here, but it will take some time. They're on a really weird frequency. It's like Bob's channel," the com officer smirked.

Gunnar looked out at the fighters now flying alongside the whining Orbiter, then at the Starbird pilot.

"Follow them down," he ordered reluctantly. He had little choice here. If they had tried to make an escape, their engines would have surely failed and they would crash. What a happy site that would have been. No dead bodies, just a large crater in the ground. He turned to Lieutenant Navall, indicating he wanted to speak.

"This is Colonel Conrad of the Royal Kalamarion Starbird *Constellation*, understand your instructions, we'll follow you down."

He leaned slowly back in his chair, letting a heavy sigh go. *Rick isn't going to be happy.* This wasn't what either of them had in mind when he had set out earlier. When operating properly, the Starbird was tough to get at and Gunnar couldn't help but lament the fact that *Constellation* wasn't in better condition. Now Rick was going to have to come in and somehow pull his butt out of a sling, again. That's if they lived long enough for Rick to figure out that something was wrong. He hated having someone come dig him out of a hole.

As the base came into view, Lynette piloted her ship down behind the escort fighters into the landing bays. Dakota stepped over and put his hand on Gunnar's shoulder. He knew what it was like to surrender. As a wet behind the ears flight cadet, he had had to give up his fighter to overwhelming odds. But sometimes it was better to surrender and wait for a better time, when the playing field was a little more level.

Setting the failing Orbiter down in the hangar deck, Lynette watched a garrison of troopers encircle the Kalamarion craft with weapons at the ready. As the crew secured their stations, Gunnar ordered the bridge shut down. For several tense moments, the troops outside waited for the ship's occupants to disembark. Finally, the hatch at the rear popped open and several of the crew stepped out of the Orbiter, then Gunnar and Dakota stepped out. Both were immediately taken away while the rest of the crew disembarked.

The treatment of the suspected command officers was less than nice; in fact, it was down right rough. There was little Dakota could do against the three guards that had him in a head lock and both his arms pinned behind his back. Gunnar was treated in much the same manner, although he could have taken the whole place apart had he chosen to. Using restraint, he exerted only enough pressure against his foes to keep them from hurting him, difficult as it was. Finally, the guards stopped at a holding cell and opened the door. They tried to throw Gunnar to the floor, but all he would allow was a good shove, just to make it look real. Dakota didn't fair quite as well, being thrown headlong into the opposing wall. As Dakota got up, Gunnar had to restrain the enraged Captain kicking at the door.

"Hey calm down, save it for another time, when the odds are a little better. At least they didn't use stunners on us."

"Well, what about the ship?" Dakota asked calming a little. "They'll get in it and tear it apart." He was still quite incensed about the way they were being treated.

"They'd have to be able to get into it first."

"Well, we sort of left the door wide open."

"Alex activated the shield generators right after the crew left the ship. He's also working on the ship with some Nano-mech."

"No he's not, you ordered him shut down in one of the corners. Wait, he's got Nano-mech on him?"

"Emech," Gunnar corrected. "Emergency use only. I gave him orders to turn the shields to P mode right after we left and affect all the repairs he could before he went dark."

"So you can communicate with him now?"

"Not directly." Gunnar checked the window in the door, pulling one of his rank clusters from his collar.

"I'm pretty sure our communicators won't work here," Gunnar mumbled. "Whatever caused the communications difficulties in the Orbiter will likely be having the same effect on any of our hand devices, not that we'll get a chance to test that theory."

Sitting down against a wall, Gunnar fiddled with the cluster for a moment, then pushed it back into place. Dakota's expression turned puzzled.

"Yeah, so what's that all about?"

"Oh just a little something your cousin and I whipped up in the unlikely event something like this should happen."

"So what is it?"

"For now, a little dumbness can go a long way in making the situation work in your favor."

"Whatever you say. Can't feel much dumber than I do right now," Dakota complained, sitting down against the opposite wall to wait.

*　　　*　　　*　　　*

Stepping out of her F-2, CJ studied the curious looking craft in the hangar bay and the odd blue hue surrounding it. A lot of commotion was rolling around the crowded bay and she quickly joined a small pack of medical technicians bunched near the ship. Approaching it, her security chief joined her and gave her a handful of unfamiliar gadgets.

"The ship's shields came on automatically right after the crew disembarked and one of the guards was too close."

Colonel Barker cringed at the sight of the badly burned and mangled body of the Colonian guard.

"Where are they being held?"

"Cells 42-R through V. The Commander and his Exec are in cell R. Sir, they look like Colonian officers."

"Colonian?" CJ stared at the strange ship for a moment. "What were their communications like?" She inquired, heading for the complex hallways on the other end of the hangar bay, Willis trotting to keep up.

"We called repeatedly for some time when we tracked them coming in. They finally hailed peaceful intentions on approach, but when our fighters came up for a sweep, they blew two of them out of the sky and then tried to make a run for it."

"Is that all?"

"No, sir," the officer continued. "The Commander identified himself as Colonel Conrad of a Royal Kalamarion Starbird called the *Constellation*. Like I said, their uniforms look Colonian."

CJ looked back at the Kalamarion ship. Past the strange blue hew, she could see the form of a large colored insignia in the shape of a bird and beneath it, the name, *Constellation*. *Royal?* She wasn't aware of anything like this in the Queen's inventory, and she had certainly never heard of a Kalamarion Starbird before. *Perhaps a spy or secret service vessel? Maybe a Tomplie pirate ship?*

"Any groupings by that name anywhere in Hadrian?" she asked, heading down a hallway toward the detention cell block.

"Nothing."

"Keep trying. I want to know where it came from and whose side they're on. If this is the queen's secret service sticking their nose in my command... Which one is this Colonel Conrad?" She turned the corner down the cell blocks.

"We don't know," the chief shrugged, stopping in front of the locked R cell and motioning for the door to be opened. "No one would say anything and there are no recognizable markings. The way the Tomplie pirates dress, you wouldn't know a Captain, from a Private."

Colonel Barker had to agree. The pirates liked to dress just any way they pleased. Whatever they could buy, borrow or steal on the black market.

When the cell door opened, two security guards stepped inside, followed by the security chief and Willis Ruston, then CJ stepped in and faced the two prisoners just getting to their feet.

Gunnar and Dakota sized up the officers just entering, then relaxed a bit.

"Oh goody, military people," Gunnar mumbled toward his Exec.

"Yeah," Dakota responded looking, or rather gazing over at Willis. "Real military people."

Gunnar got a good look at the Colonian Colonel at the same time CJ got a good look at the Kalamarion Colonel, thinking they had raided each other's closet. Their uniforms were nearly identical. High fold collar with silver leafed embroidery around the outside edge and silver leafed clusters around the sleeve cuffs. Shiny brass buttons all the way down the front center on CJ's and the left side on Gunnar's. Cream military pants tucked inside black knee high military boots. About the only differences were the utility belt he wore and the red stripe running the length of each pant leg on Colonel Conrad's uniform. Colonel Barker had only a sashed belt around her waist.

While the Colonian Colonel seemed to be Gunnar's only focus, there came an odd tingling to his ear. He tried to shake it off, but it was becoming more prevalent as the woman sat down at the table, her attention drawn toward the man wearing the uniform resembling her own.

"Please, sit down," she motioned, spilling their belongings on the table before her. "Take a load off. I'm not going to bite...hard."

Neither of the Kalamarion officers wanted to come to the table. Dakota felt quite naked without his twin blasters in their holsters. Gunnar carefully eyed Audra's memory chip still on its chain amongst their personal affects. His thoughts turned to his ship and crew, not to mention the strange tingling in his ear. What a time to get an ear ache, right when he needed his wits about him the most.

"Please?" Colonel Barker again beckoned, trying to soften demeanor. The two Kalamarion officers finally sat uncomfortably across the table from the Colonian officer.

"There, that's better, isn't it?" she reassured them, remaining polite. "So there are no mistakes, I am Colonel Barker of Carolon Command in the service of Queen Benetar of the Colonian Empire. Now, I'm not one for interrogations and quite frankly, I don't have the stomach for it. I doubt you do either. Normally, I'd just have my security chief here do all that nasty, *pluck the information directly out of your heads using and ice pick*, kind of thing. But I don't have the time to wait, so I'm appealing to your better judgment as officers to answer a few simple questions."

Gunnar and Dakota glanced at each other, Gunnar lifting an eyebrow and Dakota mouthing her choice of words, *ice pick*?

"Which one of you is this, Colonel Conrad?"

"Colonel Gunnar Lee Conrad, Royal Kalamarion Starbird *Constellation*." Gunnar carefully spoke up, taking everyone by surprise. "First officer, Captain Dakota Abrams," he motioned to his exec.

"Now we're getting somewhere." Colonel Barker relaxed a little and smiled, thinking she wasn't going to have to use the *ice pick*. "You've gotten yourself into some hot water here and at a very inopportune time."

"I'd say," Dakota piped up. "Are you aware of what's going on around your system here?"

"Quite," Colonel Barker snapped back seriously. "Hence the urgency for information, Royal Kalamarion Starbird? Where are you from? Are you a branch of the Queen's secret service? Come to check up on me or are you aligned with Drax Blair and the Albion Empire? Your uniforms suggest you are Colonian. Can you explain?"

"Neither." Gunnar let out a deep sigh. "We're new to your neck of the woods, from outside your galaxy," he continued, choosing his words carefully. "Kind of got slung here by way of a sizable black hole. Busted up our ships pretty bad. Our sensors picked up this system and planet. Our hope is that you can help with some repairs. We started having some engine difficulties shortly after we entered your atmosphere and had a little trouble communicating with your approach control. I'm afraid that brought about some unfortunate misunderstandings."

"Why did you fire on the escort patrol?"

"We didn't."

"They were destroyed on your approach."

"Scanners showed the two fighters you're referring to, struck each other mid-air. They must have gotten confused."

CJ cast the Kalamarion Colonel a skeptical look.

"Can you confirm that?" she finally asked.

"Can you disprove it?" Dakota cut in sharply. Gunnar held his hand up a little, signaling his exec to remain calm.

Captain Abram's tone only frustrated Colonel Barker, who shifted in her seat, looking at a device on her wrist.

"How did you activate your shields from the outside?"

Gunnar remained silent, Dakota casually casting his gaze back over at Willis, making her feel a little uncomfortable. CJ smacked the table with her fist, startling everyone in the room. Gunnar jumped a little and Dakota's focus was brought back to the table and the now angry Colonian Colonel.

"Now look you two, I just lost two air crews and a guard to you and your ship. Your ship's shields just came on by themselves and squashed one of my men into liquid!"

"Then he shouldn't have gotten in the way, Colonel!" Gunnar shot back, his eye color shifting. "We have security measures aboard our ships just like you have them here on your base! Now," he said calming down a bit. "I've provided you with plenty of information to chew on."

CJ drew her lips up tight. She'd have done the same thing had she been in his boots, maybe not with as much patience. She took notice of the different color revolving through the

Colonel's eyes. Twiddling her thumbs for a moment, she stood up looking back down at the two officers.

"Your crew is fine, but confined to our assembly quarters for now. There's not much room here at Letoh detention. You two, on the other hand, are to stay put until further notice. If your story checks out, we'll see about access to your crew. We're still going to need to have another little visit very soon, so be prepared. The guards will keep all your little gadgets safe until we give you clearance. This includes your guns," she said, waving a finger at Dakota and his empty holsters.

"What about my ship?" Gunnar asked as she turned to leave. CJ gave him an indignant glance over her shoulder as she headed for the door.

"It has an energy field around it." She left the room without breaking her stride, followed by the other base personnel.

"Well, that went well," Dakota complained. He stepped to the door as it shut.

"Could have been worse."

"Yeah, they could have stunned us on the face or we could be chained up and dangling over a pit of starving Torags."

"Not sure how we're gonna get out of this one," Gunnar mumbled.

*   *   *   *

Working her way through the Operations Center, CJ looked for Talia as she started to ascend the stairs to the command level.

"Bubbles, bring up the flight recorders of the intercept fighters that went up after the Kalamarion ship."

Willis and the security chief had to trot double time to keep up with the fast moving Colonel Barker until she came to a halt behind the com officer. It took only a couple of seconds to get the file up and playing. CJ watched and listened carefully as the scene played out from the four different angles of the fighters. Once it had finished, Talia looked to CJ, who turned to the security chief and Willis.

"He was telling the truth," Willis stated the obvious. The security chief shuffled nervously, a little embarrassed he hadn't gotten the full story by following proper procedures.

Colonel Barker didn't care at this point. She knew how the chief was feeling and that he would take the proper steps to correct the problem. She was more concerned with how to grant general access to these officers without creating a problem for her personnel already ramped up on high alert.

"Give them back their belongings, minus their communicators and the Captain's pistols. Provide level four access to the complex with an armed escort at all times. Make sure they know where their crew is being held."

"Colonel?" the security chief objected.

"Are you sure that's a good idea?" Talia looked up. "You don't know anything about these guys. We've got our hands full of Albs and Rats and you want to grant free access to people who are likely spies from the Queen's Secret Service?"

CJ remained silent, gazing at the Orbiter on one of the hangar bay displays. Colonel Conrad had indicated they needed to make repairs to their ship. Perhaps an arrangement could be reached.

*   *   *   *

Gunnar and Dakota looked suspiciously at the guards as they dumped their belongings on the table in front of them, announced they were free to move escorted about the base and stepped back outside of the cell, leaving the door open.

"What happened?" Dakota asked surprised, holding up his empty holsters. He had expected to be in this cell for a long time.

"Search me," Gunnar answered, grinning at the missing weapons. He checked his own belt to see what was missing. "Maybe we've caught a break here." He snatched up Audra's memory chip and put it back around his neck.

"More likely they're fattening us up."

"I totally expect that. Why don't you do a little snooping around and see if you can get a little info about what's going on here?"

"Got anyone particular in mind?" Dakota asked, thinking of the Colonian aide.

"Just don't get into trouble," Gunnar smiled, stepping out into the hall and coming face to face with two large security guards.

"Oh, yeah. I almost forgot about you guys." He sized up the two guards, and then pointed to one of them. "I guess you can take the ugly one and I'll take the tall one."

"Ah man, I wanted the tall one," Dakota frowned. "You always get the good looking ones. You know how hard it is to attract women with an ugly security guard hovering over your shoulder."

Gunnar snickered and started down the hall with the weapon clad guard right behind him, while Dakota turned to his guard and sighed.

"Ok, Chuckles, let's go see what kind of mischief we can get into."

The guard didn't like the Kalamarion Captain's attitude from the start, his scowl made that abundantly clear.

"Just kidding," Dakota added, hastily holding his hands up with an innocent look. He too started down the hall, but in the opposite direction as Gunnar, hopefully, to find a cute Colonial aide.

*   *   *   *

Under the direction of his armed escort, Colonel Conrad made his way to the crew assembly quarters. He half expected a long dreary corridor of dank cell blocks. It's what he would have been used to. On his home world of Commenor, if you were incarcerated, you were lucky to get a cell. Most of the time you were penned up like animals, and usually treated worse. Instead, what he found was a cheery environment. Wall partitions had been removed to make one large room. Well lite, it was lined with various lounge furniture and large dining tables. There he found most of his crew eating. There appeared to be plenty of heavenly smelling food, so Gunnar picked up a plate and sat down next to Lieutenant Navall and Pip.

"What a way to get a shore leave eh, Lieutenant?" he asked, filling his plate.

Lieutenant Navall looked up from her plate at her commander with a rather odd look. This whole situation had her completely blitzed. Her experiences with being a captive were old training files she had been assigned to study back in her academy days. Nobody ever watched them and this was nothing like she had pictured.

"Ah, yes, sir," she mumbled nervously, trying to enjoy her food. The food tasted good, she just had no idea what it was. It could be a Rhime Sloth for all she knew. Those thoughts could really turn a stomach. Gunnar read the disconcerted look and glanced over at Tiana and Pip.

"Everyone being treated well?" He shifted, a little more serious.

Tiana nodded carefully and Pip spoke up smiling.

"If this is capture, we should have tried it a long time ago, sir. They haven't laid a hand on any of us. They haven't even asked us any questions."

"What about the ship, sir?" Tiana inquired, "How are we going to get out of here?"

"Told you not to call me sir," he mumbled, giving her a quick look. "I'd like to remind all of you that we are likely being watched, so I will leave most of my plans on a need to know basis. For now, at least try to act like you're glad to see me and are enjoying yourself."

"I can do that," Tiana mused with a sparkle in her eye.

Gunnar stuffed his mouth full of food and looked around the room. Noticing a lack of guards, he surmised they were being observed by a sophisticated security system. He was already aware of the visible security cameras all around the room. Boots were probably close by or needed elsewhere.

"This is good stuff. Anyone bother to ask what it is? Navall," he used a low voice while looking and smiling at Tiana. "Please continue with your meal and speak to Mr. Habba only."

"Yes, sir," came an uneasy reply from the com officer.

"Tiana, if you'd please follow suit, only with me."

"Gladly, sir," came a pleased response.

Gunnar gave Tiana a quick glance, and then shoved another wad of food in his mouth.

"I don't see you in a uniform, so nix the whole *sir* thing. Never mind about asking what this is, it'll ruin it for me. Lieutenant, if I wanted to send a message from the ship, how would I go about it?"

Lieutenant Navall froze momentarily, but then remembered her instructions and continued her meal.

"I was able to get the gear reconfigured for these atmospheric conditions before we shut down," Lana started.

"Access is going to be a whole lot of fun," Pip chimed in. The look from his commander brought him back to the seriousness of what the Colonel was asking. "Ah, sir," he finished carefully.

Lieutenant Navall glanced over at Tiana, and then back at the Colonel. They were acting their parts well, completely riveted to each other. Tiana was certainly enjoying the focused attention.

"Just like starting up a fighter when you get right down to it, sir," she finally began again, looking right at Pip. "Only difference here is you don't have to have the whole bridge up and running."

"I don't get it," Pip butted in again. "Why can't you just send a message to Alex 7001? He's still onboard in shutdown mode. Why risk getting shot?"

"I can't reach Alex with anything I have on me."

"Then how are you going to get to the ship and then inside?"

"You let me worry about that. Please keep in mind these people aren't stupid," the Kalamarion commander stated coolly.

"I'm sure they're listening and watching us. Keep your mouths full while you're talking, makes it harder to read lips. Captain Abrams and I have been given limited level four security access, whatever that is. I suppose, *Spanky* there behind me will let me know if I'm in the wrong place," he motioned slightly to the guard in the doorway some distance away. "No doubt they want access to the ship, and they can't while the shields are in P mode, so they'll wait till one of us tries to get in. The trick is to keep them guessing who and when. Lieutenant, you were saying."

"At my station, the mains are located on the rear mainframe, right next to where I sit. Would you like detail, sir?"

"Within reason."

"The mains are four large pressure controls about halfway up from the floor. Can't miss them if you're sitting down, but chances are it will be quite dark."

"Quite."

"As you activate the mains, you'll get several pretty lights coming on the console where I sit. You can activate the work station light if you want, but I wouldn't recommend it as it does tend to put out a bit of light. The console is big. It has to be; lots of stuff goes on there."

"Yes Lieutenant, you're indispensable, I get it, please continue."

"The secondary Nav coms are already set at the *Athena's* frequency, access is not difficult. You will have several displays come online on the console, one marked R Nav, and Loran TS. You can't miss them; they're very pretty in the dark. You'll want to access the Loran TS. When you do, several manual buttons adjacent to the screens will light up. Push four, seven and nine, then key into the terminal, option three, put on my headset and you're in business. I'll thank you to please try not to spit into the mic or get your ear wax in the ear piece."

Gunnar continued looking at Tiana, and for a moment, she was his only focus. She really was quite fetching. His eyes dropped to her lips and thoughts began to form until the image of Audra materialized. Now was not the time for this and as quickly as he had focused on Tiana, his attention shifted back to his com officer. He found it hard to fathom how they would ever manage without Lieutenant Navall. How could anyone remember how to run something so sophisticated?

"I guess this is why you're paid the big bucks, Lieutenant. You're up for promotion, if I live through this."

"Big bucks," Pip repeated sarcastically. "Thanks, I'll keep my job all right."

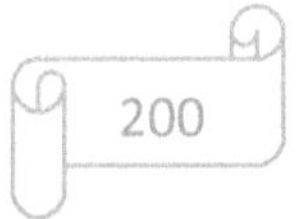

Gunnar gave him a side glare, which gave Pip cause to stop chewing and look over at his commander.

"Uh, sir," he blurted stupidly.

Gunnar smiled slightly indicating all was well, finished his meal and got up, leaving the room with his Colonian guard in tow.

*　　*　　*　　*

Colonel Barker and her security team watched the displays in front of them as Colonel Conrad got up and left the detention quarters. The operators at the monitoring stations switched their controls to the corridors and watched as the security cameras followed him as he made his way through the hallways. CJ watched him carefully as he wandered about the complex, finding his way to the cell block he and his exec had occupied, and then finding the corridors to the hangar bays. His security guard made it unmistakably plain that he could go no further, catching only a glimpse of the fighter bay at the other end of the hall. Looking satisfied that he had explored the limits of his confinement, the Kalamarion Colonel made his way back to his assigned sleeping quarters. Deep in thought, Colonel Barker turned to her command personnel and ordered up the hangar deck cameras. For several passing minutes she studied the Kalamarion Orbiter carefully, clicking her fingernails.

"Reduce the guards around their ship until further notice."

"Then you think one of them will try and gain entry to the ship?" Willis inquired, looking at the ship.

"Isn't it obvious?" CJ answered readily. "He just cleared his perimeter and will be formulating a plan for his best route in when he thinks the time is right. When he does, I want to be ready. Have squad seven and our Hessen engineers ready to board it once it's been secured."

"Wait, do we even know why they're here?" Willis inquired.

"The Queen sent them," Talia spoke up. "They have to be part of her secret service. They're the only branch that could have something like that," she said pointing at the orbiter in the hangar bay.

"I think I'll ask again," CJ said quietly. The command personnel dispersed and went about their assigned tasks, but CJ remained. She turned her attention back to the security monitors and watched Colonel Conrad relax in his quarters. Putting a hand to her cheek, she felt a strange warmth move through her. No doubt her freckles were enunciating. She carefully passed a glance around to see if anyone had noticed anything odd about her normally controlled demeanor.

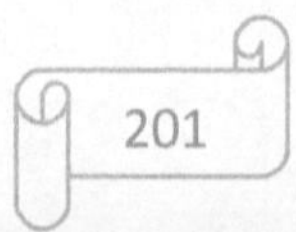

Willis watched her commander from across the command platform. She carefully stepped a little closer and looked down at the display CJ was watching, and then back up at her commander. Colonel Barker finally stepped away from the monitor and exited the control room, Willis eyeing her closely as she went.

*   *   *   *

After a couple of hours of pretending to sleep, Gunnar was out and about again, casing the hallways of the Carolon complex. Knowing why he and Dakota were able to move so freely about the base was going to make his objective even more difficult.

Still casually searching, he rounded a corner and noticed someone leaning against the wall on the other side. The tingling in his ears instantly rematerialized. Keeping his hands clasped behind his back, he slowly approached Colonel Barker, smiling. CJ returned the pleasantness and stood up straight, stepping closer to him.

"How have you enjoyed your freedom here on the base?"

Gunnar glanced back at his escort and chuckled slightly.

"If you call this freedom, it has been all right. I wouldn't mind seeing some real sunlight and some fresh air, maybe a little dirt under my feet."

"The suns are down for a while now." The two turned and walked slowly down the hall together. "The dirt is like sand and the air is a little stale, kind of humid. It grows well enough, but I've found the environment inside more enjoyable to breathe than outside. But it's nice to see a view sometimes, rather than walls."

"You have to understand, my crew and I have been in space for quite some time. We're no more immune to confinement than anyone else, on the job or off."

CJ scanned his attire and smiled slightly.

"I find your uniform curious. It looks Colonian," she pointed out, looking at her own.

"Yes, it's very odd," Gunnar admitted. "As yours looks Kalamarion."

The two only smiled, continuing down the hallway and turning the corner together.

"May I ask how your battle is going? Still fighting the good fight?" Gunnar asked carefully.

CJ thought for a moment then nodded.

"The Albions have retreated, for now. We've had to throw quite a lot of our resources at them, but it seems that for now, they've backed off."

202

"Who are the Albions?"

"A faction of Colonia that have teamed up with another faction called the Ratronians to try and overthrow the Empire. All of a sudden they've taken an unusual interest in this system, specifically this planet."

"Is there anything on any of the other planets in this system?"

"That's the odd thing. This whole system is pretty much a waste. I'm not even sure why Colonia set this base up here. There is nothing here. It is so far out on the outer rim of Hadrian that it just doesn't make sense to have anything here. None of the other planets in this system are inhabited. The next one out is Reako and we haven't found anything of redeeming quality about it. It has lots of fresh water."

"At least you don't have to worry about being thirsty."

"Colonel," she stopped and faced him. "Why are you here? And please don't make up some cockamamie story even a Kilar wouldn't believe."

Gunnar paused, wondering what a Kilar was, then turned to CJ.

"Ok, what I've told you so far is true. We need help. Our ship is broken, in fact, very broken. We need Asium to help make our repairs."

"What is Asium?"

"It's a highly energized crystalline mineral that is the main power source for our ships."

"So how did you get your ship here?"

"The power source is damaged. We can run sub-light engines, but only barely. Our FTL engines are damaged as well, but even if they weren't, they would be inoperative because of the damage to the power source."

"So why choose Carolon?"

"This planet has a very high Asium signature. I was hoping we might come to some kind of an arraignment."

"What does this Asium look like?"

"In its raw form, it would look like clear stone. It's usually found deep in the planet's crust and has to be mined, but on volcanic planets, like this one, I've seen it just lying around."

CJ instantly recognized what he was talking about. She had been tossing them just this morning. They were just rocks, scattered everywhere on the plateau. They both started walking again.

"Ok, so I think this is a pretty good story. I think I might know what you're talking about," she said choosing her words carefully. "Just any of these clear rocks? Is it really that simple?"

"Well, yes actually. In its raw uncut form, it's harmless; just another clear rock. But you cut it a certain way and its energy signature changes and it becomes quite active. The explanation gets a little technical from there, but I think you get the idea."

"Certainly, I would think something with that much energy output would be lethal to even be around."

"Only after it's cut."

"Curious we haven't been able to detect this Asium."

"You have to know what you're looking for, otherwise it's just another rock."

"I have scouts on the outpost perimeter that can have a look around. I'll see what I can do."

"So what now?" Gunnar asked.

"I'm not entirely sure," CJ said. "Normally, you and your crew would be transported directly to Colonia Command on Tintee for processing, but there have been so few flights in and out of here from there, that I think I'm going to deal with this myself and let them gripe about it later."

"So what have you got planned for us?"

"Still trying to work that out." CJ was thinking of his ship. She'd love to have a look inside. Based on the scant technical information he had provided and her own observations, his ship could augment her current inventory nicely.

"For now, I've authorized a small, low keyed celebration for some of our forward crews, mostly as a diversion for them. You and your crew are invited to join in if you'd like."

They stopped again just beyond the corner. Gunnar scratched at the annoying tingling going on in his ears, looking at her carefully. There was a beautiful woman behind that tough military exterior and he felt himself drawn to her, but the visions of Audra crept into his mind, reminding him where his devotions were firmly seated. He nodded in a strange uncertain fashion.

"I think we'd all be glad to be there with you and your people."

"Wonderful! Your guard can direct you to the Scotchline assembly room at the appointed time." CJ paused a moment, smiling broadly now. "It will be good to have you there." She quickly turned, leaving him standing in the middle of the hallway looking after her striding gracefully around a far turn at the end of the hall. As she disappeared, the tingling in his ears abruptly stopped.

Gunnar smiled, shaking his head and turning to his escort.

"Let's see you get a date that easy."

Brief encounter

The Scotchline assembly room was at capacity with Carolon base personnel constantly mixing in and out. The room appeared to be used for a variety of things, probably as a base personnel briefing room. It was certainly large enough for it. Having left their escorts at the door, Gunnar and Dakota wandered about the room freely. If one needed to leave for any reason, they could simply pick their escort back up at one of the exits. The two officers stuck close together, moving about the room, greeting their own crew members and being cordial to the base personnel. With the curious similarities in their uniforms, they were constantly mistaken as Carolon officers. Finally finding the punch bowl, they grabbed a couple of glasses.

"Find any Asium lying around?" Dakota asked, smelling the contents of the glass.

"Working on it, how about you?"

"Ditto. So," Dakota sipped at his drink, scanning the room like a teenager at his first dance. "When do you plan on trying to get to her?"

"The Colonel or the ship?" Gunnar replied. Even he couldn't believe that came out.

"My, my, my," Dakota grinned broadly. "Oh, how the young ones grow up so fast. Our own little Colonel has got himself a crush. Gunnar loves a red head, Gunnar loves a red head," he sang quietly, keeping the glass up in front of his mouth.

"Very funny, Cadet Abrams," Gunnar came back.

"So worth it."

"I need to meet with the Colonel first, let her know I'm here, then if opportunity presents itself, I'll try ducking out. Apparently, with my uniform, that shouldn't be too hard." He took another sip of his drink and grabbed some finger food.

"You realize they're probably expecting one of us to make a move for the ship."

"I'm sort of counting on it."

"Wouldn't want to disappoint them." Dakota finally spotted Willis over next to a wall at an empty table. "How do you plan on sneaking past their security?"

"I have skills," Gunnar replied quietly, touching the rank clusters on his collar. "I can multi-task."

"Well, someone will have to sacrifice and run some interference. It's a tough job, but just doing my part for the war effort. You know, keeping one of them occupied." Dakota shoved off, weaving his way through the crowd toward the Colonian aide.

Gunnar smiled after him, thinking about how much of a player this young pilot was. Then again, he was a handsome man, much like his older cousin had been in his younger years. He remembered the mentality all too well. Fighter pilots were a gift to everyone, especially the women. Chomping down on whatever it was he had picked up, Gunnar felt a tingle return to his ears. He started scanning the room more carefully for the red headed base Colonel, then felt a tap on his shoulder. Turning around, he came face to face with Colonel Barker, smiling back at him. Gussied up considerably more than normal, her curly red hair was down, rolling gently back from her bangs along the sides of her face and meandering down around her shoulders. She didn't wear a lot of makeup; she didn't have to. She figured she was old enough that it just didn't matter anymore. Normally, she wouldn't dress up except for formal occasions, but this time she had felt an odd urgency to do so. Now she felt a little silly.

"Well, hello," he greeted politely, bowing.

CJ was delighted and bowed as well. Reading his gaze, she felt young and attractive.

"Greetings to you, sir. Are you enjoying yourself?"

"Very much, thank you," Gunnar nodded. "This is quite the place you have here and quite a dinner."

CJ smiled and moved closer to him, but only enough for him to notice. Gunnar coolly sipped his drink, looking into her crystal blue eyes. They seemed to turn big and tender as he looked at her. Now he was feeling rather odd, his hearts were beating a little harder and the tingling in his ears was spiking. He wanted to stick his finger in both of them and ream them as hard as he could. How would that have looked?

I find this woman very attractive, he thought. His mind started to wander a bit, thinking of what it might be like to fly left seat with the Colonel, but then thoughts of flying with Audra came to mind and he was again aware of her memory chip around his neck. A beep from CJ's communicator brought them back to reality before the engagement could blossom any further. She reluctantly acknowledged it, pressing a button on her wrist communicator.

"I've got to step out for a couple of minutes. Be here when I get back?"

Gunnar sighed and nodded.

"You really think I'm going anywhere?"

CJ smiled, set her glass down and started for the door, turning around several times before she exited the room. Looking around to see if anyone was watching, Gunnar took one last sip, set his glass down and ducked out. Slipping past the guards, he watched CJ turn a far corner on one end of the hall and he turned in the opposite direction, toward the hangar bays.

*　　*　　*　　*

Entering the Operations Center, CJ bounded up the stairs to the command overview deck. Out of the corner of her eye, she could see several new objects on the main viewing map.

"What have you got, Bubbles?" she asked, approaching Talia.

"Wow, you look great," Talia admired, giving her commander a double take. CJ smiled, a little embarrassed.

"I have to look good for our guests, what's up?"

"I think if you looked like that more often you might have a man on each arm."

"You called me out of the dinner," CJ reminded Talia. She couldn't help but feel attractive after multiple compliments.

"It's Blair and Shipley, sir. Recon reports they're starting to deploy ships just outside our scanner range. It looks much larger this time."

"Better call in squadrons one through eight. They can refuel on the *Trax* and the *Realistic*." The two were interrupted by the security chief.

"Colonel, we're having some difficulty with our security systems through corridors Beta, Omega and Tera."

"Those are the halls to the hangar bays," Talia announced, watching CJ move to the security station.

"I'm assuming you've rebooted your systems in that area," CJ suggested coolly.

"Twice. All the systems are working. Look, Tera hall just came back online."

"Any intruder alerts on the proximity scanners?"

The chief shook his head, frustrated.

"Nothing, although they went off line at the same time the other systems did. Almost like a glitch is rolling through the entire network."

"Which bays do those halls lead to?"

"Hangar bays Green and Orange, where the Kalamarion ship is being held."

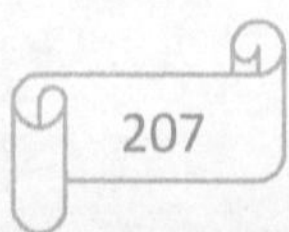

Talia watched CJ's expression as she studied the displays, trying to puzzle out the situation.

"Should I switch on the main lights and alert my squads?"

"No, I'll go down alone," she said turning to leave.

"Colonel, you'll need this." He held out his blaster pistol, but CJ just stared at it. She had expected an objection, stating regulations or something. She passed a glance to Talia, then grabbed the pistol and trotted down the stairs for the exit.

*   *   *   *

Entering the hangar bay, CJ found only the blue gowning lights on, making for good cover, but not for seeing things distinctly. Holding the blaster up, she hugged the corner of the bay doors, looking over at the Orbiter. The bright blue glow was gone and at the rear she could see the open hatch. Moving silently next to the hull, she crept up next to the hatch and peered in, hearing the soft hum of equipment working inside. Stepping carefully, she silently made her way in through the open turbo door. The bridge was almost completely dark, but she could see control station shadows cast from the hangar's gowning lights. Blinking lights on the back wall of the bridge attracted her attention until she became aware of a figure standing over a partially lit up console. Good light wasn't required to know who it was; she just hadn't figured out how he had gotten past all the level five base security.

Gunnar was about to activate the four controls that would allow him to contact Rick, when her heard the generating of a blaster's energy converter behind him.

"Please stop," her voice shaking slightly but still in command. "Bring your lights up and turn around slowly."

She watched cautiously as the figure slowly moved a hand to another console and touched several controls. As the station lighting system in the Orbiter came up, CJ recognized the uniform as Gunnar slowly turned around. The two stared at each other for what felt like an eternity. Gunnar carefully sat down in Lana's chair and leaned back. CJ shut off her blaster and raised her communicator.

"Security teams stand down."

Gunnar let out a relieved sigh while CJ leaned against the back wall.

"I was so hoping that it was your exec and not you," she finally blurted out, still shaking.

"The plan was to confuse you as much as possible," Gunnar replied coolly, feeling the tingle start to return to his ears. "Hard to do when there's just two of us. But to be honest, I doubt he could have gotten this far. He's young and I've had to pull him from fighter pilot status to fill in for my previous exec. He's a little impulsive and his mind is still in a cockpit."

"How'd you get past my security?"

"Do you really expect me to answer that?"

"Who were you trying to contact?" CJ asked, starting to relax a bit. "Benetar? Blair? Shipley?"

"No, none of those." Gunnar smiled slightly, understanding her apprehension. "I was trying to contact General Niker."

CJ's eyes shifted to the console he was sitting at, wondering if he had actually gotten his message off.

"General Niker? He's not one I'm acquainted with. You guys are with the Queen's Secret Service, aren't you?"

"Nope," Gunnar responded instantly. "He's Kalamarion. I told you before; we're with another ship. My friend commands the other Starbird. He's waiting for me to signal him."

"For what?"

"Let him know I'm all right and that it's ok to come in for repairs. You're only looking at part of a ship here," Gunnar said, gesturing to the whole bridge.

"And there are two of these ships?" she asked, looking at the other consoles a little closer.

Gunnar sat up, motioning for her to come over to the communications station. She was hesitant at first, but was just as curious as anyone else when it came to shiny new things. Besides, she had the gun. Cautious, she kept her pistol up in front of her, stepping up next to the Gunnar. He carefully reached over and brought up the lights a little more and turned on a couple of the other systems, then pushed slowly back a little so CJ could have full access to the technology before her. The touch screens and immense flat panel displays in front of her were dazzling. She couldn't read any of it, as the displayed language was foreign.

"Like I said before, my friend and I came here by way of a worm hole some time ago. We've sustained extensive damage and are looking for a place to make repairs. Carolon has the Asium we need and your installation here is the best we could find for making repairs."

"While I appreciate that you thought we were friendly enough to approach for help, I'm not sure we can do you any good. Your technology is far more advanced than ours. What could we possibly offer?" Still holding her pistol in his direction, CJ was becoming more comfortable with the situation and slowly let it drop to her side.

"Helping us get some Asium would be a good start. I think we might be able to help each other out. An exchange of

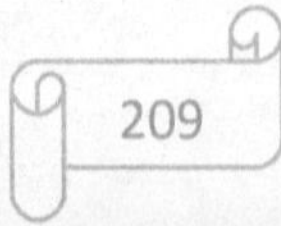

information for access to mining, manufacturing materials and repair facilities?"

CJ continued to study the vast array of colorful technology in front of her. She looked all around at the dark consoles of the bridge. The temptation was far too great to resist. Perhaps they could offer a tactical advantage right now? Something she was in desperate need of.

"I would like to think we could work something out, Colonel." She was cut off by Gunnar's lowered voice.

"Gunnar, please call me Gunnar."

"Gunnar," CJ repeated smiling. "I like that name. It's a good name."

"I know lots of good names," he commented smiling back. She continued looking at him until her wrist communicator sounded off again.

"Yes, what is it?" she asked, kind of in a daze.

"Movement from the two outer planets. Blair and Shipley have engaged the *Trax* and her support ships. Our fighter squadrons are getting hammered by overwhelming BT and TL numbers."

CJ came alive.

"Better alert the base. I think this is it. Red alert Bubs, scramble everyone." She looked back at Gunnar. "This could get messy. I'm sorry, but there's just no way for me to help you right now. The best I can do is release you and your crew. You'd do well to get as far away from here as soon you can."

Gunnar looked at her for a long moment; his thoughts still focused on his objectives. As she turned to leave, he stopped her before she could reach the hatch threshold.

"Could you use a little help?"

"Anything I can get my hands on."

"I'm not sure what we can do, but if you could supply us with some crystals, I think I can convince my friend to help a little. It'll take us almost a day to get back here though. When do you need us?"

Lights were starting to come on in the hangar bay, alerts blaring.

"Just as fast as you can get back here. I'll have your crystals ready when you get here." CJ turned and ducked out as Gunnar turned back to the communications equipment.

Albions

The *Tarzana* was the flag ship of the entire Albion fleet, having her own battle group assigned to her and squadrons of Black Tigers in constant motion. The battlecruiser resembled a large ocean going battleship. Its four massive Isom engine ports glowed a dull purple, pushing the gargantuan warship majestically toward the eighth planet in the Nulark system. She had a mountain of massive gun turrets stacked one on top of the other. The conning towers, above and beneath the ship, along with the command towers, provided an awesome overview that made vision nearly Omni-directional. Above and below the massive thruster ports were the landing and launching bays. Each entry way was guarded by a large number of laser emplacements. In fact, there was virtually no angle unguarded by guns and reinforced armor.

On the command deck of the *Tarzana*, Queen Captain Drax Blair, stood with her hands clasped behind her back watching fighters zip back and forth from the fighting front to the ship's bays to repair and refuel. Watching the *Trax* in the distance, Drax remained unmoved, sensing a figure step up behind her. A young man glanced over his shoulder at the bustling bridge personnel, then back at Drax.

"Reports coming in indicate the *Trax* is taking heavy damage, but we're losing more fighter and bombers than we can replace. We hadn't counted on the Trax being here and their F-2s are far superior to our TB and TLs. Their destroyers have a lot more snuff guns than our intel had previously ascertained. Shipley reports he's taken the seventh planet and is now moving on this one from the other side." There was a hint of excitement in the young man's tone. Drax noted a flare from the *Trax* as it took a hit.

"These outer planets are just a bunch of useless rocks. Any movement from Carolon yet?" She acted quite unconcerned with any of the actions of Swenson Shipley.

BachTL pulled a small device from his belt, looking at its readout.

"Nothing big yet. Several squadrons of F-2s, a few squadrons of T-47 Invaders have launched. We did track a large

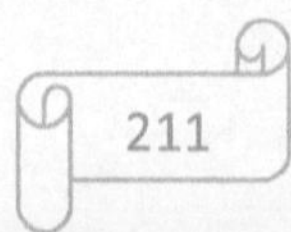

"

scout sized vessel traveling outbound before we could make any identifications on it." He pushed the device back down into position. Drax seemed a little dismayed, biting her lip.

"Come on, what are you up to, CJ? What are you waiting for?" she whispered. Turning, she slowly paced the length of the command deck once, then turned to BachTL.

"Get the Metro-star ready. Have SoKnack take the *Tarzana* to flank speed and pass the *Trax* on her port side, but don't stop. The cannons on that thing will cut us to ribbons if we try to go toe to toe with her. He needs to get this ship to Carolon and set up a perimeter. Carolon is the real prize here and I want to be the first one there. Let Shipley deal with the rest of the fleet out here. He's always going on about how superior his Dreadnaught is. Time for him put up or shut up."

BachTL nodded, moving without a word to carry out his orders. Drax paced the length of the command deck again, taking one last look at the *Trax*, then turned from the main window and exited the bridge.

The *Tarzana* made a wide, graceful swing and headed straight past the reversing *Trax*. As it did, an Albion transport and a group of escort fighters shot from one of the launch bays and banked hard around, quickly blending in with the moltey array of stars, but toward one twinkling speck slightly brighter than the rest. Drax piloted her own Metro-star with BachTL in the copilot's seat. The young aide hurriedly checked several readouts on overhead consoles then reached over to a console between them and flipped several switches. Lights blinked all over, dramatically blending with the red hews in the dark cockpit. He glanced over at the involved Queen Captain.

"The assault transports are already starting their landings beyond their ground shielding. It looks like Carolon has launched all the fighter groups it's going to." BachTL paused a moment and studied another readout, then several live feeds from the battle. "Our ground troops are meeting heavy resistance and will likely take the better part of the day to reach their targets, but we should get there just when they've taken the control center." BachTL sounded overly excited and Drax passed him an emotionless glance, and then looked back at the slowly growing Carolon.

"Better have two escort platoons ready to disembark as soon as we land. We can wait in the secure zones while Colonel Sung's Special Forces work their magic. I want to be in that control room when we take it. Instruct Major Belone that under no circumstances are they to enter unless I am standing right there," she ordered, leaning back. BachTL leaned back at the same time, sighed deeply and looked at an overhead console.

"Shipley isn't going to like you charging in on Carolon without him. He wants to be in on everything you do."

Drax chuckled a bit, as she pulled back her short blonde curls.

"What Swenson needs to understand is that in order for us to best the Empire, we can't be on each other's back wanting to know what the other's every move is. We have to trust each other. Having said that, I wouldn't trust him any further than I could throw him." Drax checked several readouts, and then gave the Metro a little more power. "Have the ROACH's engaged the command base yet?"

BachTL shook his head.

"They're having trouble getting to it. The Carolon base is heavily defended with multiple shielding generators. Even if you take one out, the others pick up the slack. Reports coming in of individual ROACH commanders taking on the generators while the others jump through the holes they create. Then there is the terrain. They're breaking through the surface of the planet into caverns all over the place. The other side of the base is heavily forested in hilly terrain. Not a good place for ROACH driving."

"Clever girl," Drax commented admirably. "Make sure SoKnack holds the fleet around Carolon with as many Tigers as he can push out the launch bays. I want nothing getting off that planet, especially Barker. I want her most of all. She is every bit the prize as the planet itself." The level of determination and inflection in Drax's voice gave BachTL cause to carry out his assigned tasks without another word.

*　　*　　*　　*

The Carolon Operations Center hummed loudly with the sounds of equipment and bustling people working to carry out their assigned duties. With her headset pushed down over her light curly brown hair, Talia "Bubbles" Reese was busy directing intercept squadrons to assist in the defense of the Albion air and ground assaults. The Operations room trembled slightly as CJ Barker stormed up to the command platform, stopping next to the com officer.

"Get Colonia on the line now. Tell them we are under attack and need reinforcements." She drew in a deep breath and turned to the security chief. "Ok, what's going on out there?"

As the security chief switched multi-viewers in front of him, they could see all over the base complex.

"It doesn't look very good, Colonel. Their ground troops and assault vehicles are overwhelming our forces, but for once, the caverns surrounding the base complex have worked in our favor.

Their ROACH's are having a lot of difficulty getting close. A few have pushed past the arrays, but the shields are still deflecting anything the capitals can throw down at us. I'm a little worried about the ROACH's reaching any of the actual array locations. If they take enough of them down, it could severely compromise the efficiency of our shield systems. Our automated airborne anti-aircraft turrets have been able to take out any Tigers or Star hoppers that have gotten through the F-2 perimeter."

CJ tried to gnaw on her fingernails, but they were already gone. Her forces had lasted longer than she had originally anticipated. Brave to be sure, but just not enough numbers or superior tactical equipment to fend off the overwhelming numbers the Albions were throwing at them. She turned to Talia.

"Are all of the escape ships ready for departure?"

"All ships are ready for immediate departure. Preprogrammed waypoints have been downloaded into all transport navigational systems. They'll be able to jump as soon as they can clear our atmosphere, then make a series of decoy jumps to Tintee." Bubbles leaned forward, and cycled through several display feeds showing different craft in different locations around the base in a state of readiness for a hastened departure. The last feed showed CJ's F-2 sitting in a small hangar somewhere off the main base, quietly waiting for its pilot.

"If our troops keep getting pushed back at this rate, it won't be long before your ship is cut off from us."

CJ watched as her troops fought to hold back the overwhelming Albion troops. The onslaught of the ROACH's combined with the overwhelming numbers of Albion troops proved too much for them and they were slowly pushed back within the base grounds. Her only hope of holding Carolon rested with the reinforcements that had to come from Colonia. She was startled to attention by the com officer.

"I've got Queen Benetar on monitor five."

CJ turned and walked back over by com.

"What's wrong with the main view monitor?" she asked, looking up at the dark screen overhead.

"The mains on the com arrays are out. They took a direct hit from a ROACH blaster cannon. Most of the base com systems are completely dead. I have little to no routing capabilities right now. I was able to reach Tintee with one of the older Alpha-band arrays still in operation, but I don't expect it to last very long. The signal will be weak, but talkable."

CJ frowned. She felt like she could have prevented all this if she had been more persistent from the beginning, but she was so enthralled by the acceptance of the new command, that she took anything she could get her hands on. Now she was going to have to deal with the situation as it was, not as it might have been. The small video screen in front of her flashed on and Queen Benetar appeared.

"Well, Colonel," her voice gruff. "Have you secured Carolon once and for all from Blair or should I send someone else to do your job?"

CJ clinched her teeth to hold her tongue.

"Far from it, your Highness! Blair and Shipley have joined forces, as I warned you they would, and are overrunning our battle groups as we speak. They've already landed and as you can see," she said, a tremendous explosion near the base shaking the Operations center. "They're moving to overrun us here. Now it's too late for you to send me the help I could have used two days ago. So, with or without your permission, I'm going to evacuate this precious little rock. If you want it, you'll have to come and get it yourself." CJ paused a moment for dramatic effect, smiling politely. "Colonel Casey Janae Barker, out." CJ motioned for the transmission to be terminated, and then turned to the viewing map below her as it blinked with a stiff tremor. Albion troops and ROACH transports were almost on top of the base hangar bays; the security chief was reporting heavy fighting in the Orange hangar bay. Her attention was drawn again by a summons from Bubbles.

"I've got two more ships approaching from the back side of the planet. They have no Albion or Ratronian identifiers. Give me a sec and I'll see if I can get you a dimensional."

The Operations Center rocked again with another nearby explosion as CJ looked over Talia's shoulder just in time to see the main viewing map go dead. She turned her focus back to what Bubbles was doing. The video screen off to Talia's left flashed on, the dimensional readouts of the Kalamarion Starbird appearing. A spark of hope came to CJ's mind, thinking of Gunnar and his friend. Reflecting on the conversation they had before he left, she glanced over at an unremarkable metal box sitting on a bench next to one of the many consoles, then turned back to her com officer.

"The *Constellation* is here. See if you can open a channel. I need to talk to Colonel Conrad." She looked over the rail at the command personnel running back and forth, working with quickly faltering equipment. It was almost too late for any help.

"Better start the evacuation sequences right now," she directed. The Operations Center shook again and a chunk of concrete ceiling came down, crashing onto the dead viewing map on the main level. As the monitor in front of her flashed on,

Gunnar's face appeared and there came momentary rush of relief knowing he and his friend were somewhere overhead.

"Hey, Colonel, have you seen what's closing in on you up here? You better get out of there while the getting is good."

"Yeah, looks pretty bad," CJ nodded quickly. "We've got ROACH's down here and fighting going on in the outside hangar bays. I've got your Asium stones in a box here. Is there anything you can do for us?"

Gunnar didn't look too reassuring.

"It's like playing tag team up here. There's a lot more enemy hardware flying around up here than I was figuring on. One of them quite large and very angry looking."

"The *Tarzana*," CJ said thinking of the enormous battlecruiser.

"From the looks of it, I'm afraid there's not much we can do. We didn't get as much repaired as I had hoped. The best we can hope for is to provide interference while you make a run for it."

CJ grimaced a bit, realizing there was no way to fight Blair and Shipley off. Without the manpower and equipment to guard against them, her efforts had been all for naught. Gunnar looked away from the screen for a moment.

"We can teleport you up right now if you can assemble your staff."

CJ wasn't sure what that meant, but it sounded like a good way to evacuate her staff. The control room shook again, dust and debris continuing to fall in bits everywhere. She looked back at Gunnar, confusion swirling across her face.

"I need to stay here until I'm sure all my people are away. I've got your package with me and will contact you as soon as I'm ready to leave."

Gunnar nodded slightly.

"Ok, Colonel. I'll have General Niker cover for the escaping ships, but you better make it fast. It's a little hairy up here playing dodge ball with all these ships and from our vantage point, you haven't got much time. My ship will follow you out."

CJ gave a quick nod and the screen went blank, leaving her smiling until the Operations center shook again. She turned to her staff, smacking her hands together.

"Command personnel! Get to your ships, let's go! Evacuate!"

The Operations center shook again as staff workers dropped what they were doing and started hurrying for their assigned exits.

Outside the Carolon base, it was an all-out battle between the depleting Colonian troopers and what appeared to be an infinite swarm of Albion infantry and armor. Several of the

Ratronian or Albion Cargo Haulers, ROACH, had finally crawled past the soft dirt and caverns of the plateau. These ROACH's, looking like giant beetles or cockroaches on six stalky legs, pounced mercilessly closer to the outside hangar bays of the Colonian base. Each vehicle was formidably armed with turnstile guns on its foresides and atop its articulating head. Looking like the antennas of a giant insect, the metallic spikes and protrusions emitted deadly bellows of fire and light.

Each step the ROACH's took sent shock waves rolling through the base complex. The front hangar bays crumbled under the intense fire power the ROACH pilots were laying down. Every so often a Black Tiger would sweep across the dull, dusk ridden sky, looking like a giant Manta-ray, diving gracefully toward the crumbling hangar bays and command base, only to be incinerated by the airborne anti-air attack laser turrets. In the Colonian hangar bays, troops scrambled for cover as chunks of ceiling and walls caved in under the tremendous firepower of the bug-like monster machines. More Albion troopers poured into the Colonian hangar bays as the Carolon ground troops were overwhelmed and pushed back into the adjoining hallways. As the last transport in the hangar gracefully lifted from the bay floor, it roared skyward. The ROACH's lifted their mechanical heads and fired at the fleeing vessel, but the transport soared well out of range, untouched. Now only a few base personnel were left. The quickly depleting Colonian infantry and a few command staff. Short intense fire fights were breaking out in most of the outer halls now, as the retreating troopers fought to retard the Albion onslaught.

CJ Barker frantically tried to get the failing ground monitoring systems working again. Talia watched the hangar bay monitors as Albion troopers disembarked from their ROACH machines and together, began destroying everything in sight. This was apparently going to be a scorched earth policy at play. Nothing was to be left intact. Talia finally pulled her headset off.

"Just lost the mains on the long range coms."

CJ turned, dodging a piece of falling ceiling.

"What's left out there?" she asked, feeling the intensity of their situation growing.

Talia began switching damaged displays, showing intense fighting going on in the main halls now.

"We're being pushed back into the Alpha sections now. They'll be on top of us in minutes. If we're going to get out of here, it's going to have to be soon or our escape routes will be cut off."

"We don't leave until those troops out there are on their way."

*   *   *   *

Heavy fighting continued in the Purple hall of Alpha sector as Colonian troopers took cover at one end of the hall and the Albion troops began firing at them from the other end. As the battle intensified, two figures began to materialize into existence right in the middle of the hallway. Gunnar instantly dropped to the floor, ducking the intense laser fire bouncing along the walls and the floor. He quickly rolled quickly and checked both ends.

"What the blazes?" He looked up at Alex 7001 floating above. "Alex! You tin plated eggplant! You've teleported us into the wrong place! I said the Operations center!" He scrambled through a nearby door, partially blown open.

"Nobody's perfect, Colonel," the little droid commented, dodging several nearby laser blasts and ducking into the doorway. "All this fire play must be scrambling our destination sensors, throwing our positions off target."

Gunnar got to his feet, pulling his blaster and giving the droid a quick, angry look.

"Get us mixed up again and I'll rupture your servo motivator. Now which way?"

Alex floated around Gunnar and started down an adjoining sub-hallway.

"A moment, sir. I have to say, the complexity of determining teleporter coordinates are..."

"Alex! Which way?"

Alex continued forward, scanning the halls ahead of him for a new route and any fire fights that might be in their path.

"This way, sir, but I'm afraid if the Colonian fighting positions are this fluid, we're going to have to rethink this whole operation. I'm not sure I understand the logic here anyway. Wouldn't we be better off giving this system as much distance as we can and find a better place that has Asium?"

"I'm game if you know where to look, Alex, but right now we need those crystals. Logic is not always the driving force behind one's actions. You'll do well to remember that."

Gunnar had to crack a smile. Using plain logic, Alex was correct. This was a hornet's nest, plain and simple. They would be money ahead if he and Rick were to just sail off in the other direction for a couple more months. But what Alex lacked was the human component to his programming which would allow him to respond to humanity in any form. Trying to help here wasn't necessarily the smartest thing to do, but it was the right thing to do.

*   *   *   *

Albion troopers made way in the smoke filled corridors as Queen Captain Drax Blair strode carefully through a secured passage, stretching her long legs over dead troopers. Drax wore her full Albion command uniform. She wanted to look impressive when she walked into the Operations Center to confront its commander and her one-time friend. Caped in a green cloak and her finest dress uniform, she methodically made her way through the sub halls stopping several times to wait for an area to be secured before proceeding.

The Operations Center was nearly dark now, only a few lights and monitors still functioned as the ceilings and walls continuously quaked. In the midst of it all, two officers remained stubbornly on the command platform trying to see to the last of the evacuations on failing equipment. CJ and Talia coughed at the same time as more dust rained from the ceiling. Both officers watched as the last of the transport ships lifted gracefully from their launching pads and soared skyward. There were only two ships left to depart now and they were waiting in small hidden hangar bays on the far side of the base, away from all the fighting. The ground troops were falling back to a larger ship, while CJ and Talia would evacuate in her personal F-2.

The two women could hear heavy fighting going on right outside the locked Operations Center blast doors. CJ dodged another piece of ceiling that fell at the same moment she noticed movement on the far side of one of the lower levels. Pulling a blaster, she pointed it at Gunnar as he came into the failing brain of the Carolon base.

"Hey! Don't shoot! It's me," he yelled, ducking behind a pile of rubble.

CJ instantly disarmed and leaned anxiously over the railing and look and toward the blast door.

"What are you doing here, Colonel?" she asked, glad he was here. Alex 7001 followed Gunnar in as he quickly made his way for the stairs, climbing over broken junk.

"I've been trying to contact you for a while now. You said you'd signal me when you got away."

"Yeah, our communication systems are having problems."

"Problems? Ya think?" Gunnar responded, coming up the stairs.

"I was just getting ready to leave. Your Asium is over there in that box. I have to make sure all my people get out first." She reached for a knob that probably didn't work. "You'd better get back to your ship." She then felt Gunnar's firm grasp on her arm and turned, looking right up into his eyes.

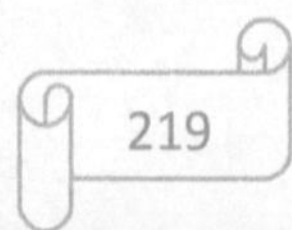

"I leave as soon as I know you're safely away." His voice was firm.

CJ caught a gulp before she could speak. His hazel eyes were full of confidence, but she could also see he wasn't going to take command of her responsibilities and slowly turned to Talia.

"Give the final evacuation code signal."

"Colonel, my sensors are detecting movement outside the main level entry doors," Alex warned.

Gunnar glanced down at the locked blast door below. He could hear troops on the other side banging on it.

"You're out of time. We'll teleport up to my ship." Without another word, he pulled his communicator. "*Constellation*, this is Conrad, come in," his voice turning anxious. He could hear the sounds of blaster bolts exploding against the blast door on the lower level. A moment later, the welcome voice of Captain Abrams crackled over the static obscured transmission.

"Yes, sir. We're ready to bring you back up. Are you standing in an open space?"

Gunnar grabbed Talia and placed her next to CJ, while Alex anxiously took a position next to them. He grabbed the box of crystals and raised his communicator to his mouth.

"Ready down here, Captain!"

Seconds later, Talia began to sparkle, a snapping noise surrounding her and then she disappeared, but only Talia. Alex, CJ and Gunnar were left standing on the quaking command platform. Gunnar raised his communicator back to his mouth, but the blast door below suddenly exploded in a shower of sparks and hot shrapnel. Thick smoke filled the lower decks and he could see the outline of troopers in the doorway.

"Oh boy," he puffed. "Got a back door?" he asked, looking anxiously around. CJ shook her head the same moment Gunnar caught sight of something on the back wall near the floor. Setting the box down, he stepped over to a large steel grating and peered through.

"Where does this go?" He asked, looking up at CJ.

"You're asking me?" CJ dropped to her knees and examined it carefully. "I'm guessing it's an air relief shaft. Probably empties out in the caves on the back side of the base complex, but this is a blast rated-..."

"I guess there is only one way to find out for sure," he grunted, pulling on the edges of the grate. CJ glanced at the thickness of the blast rated shielding, then watched Gunnar.

"What do you think you're doing?"

Gunnar slipped his fingers through the grating and pulled harder. The attaching fasteners suddenly popped and the grill curled back, sending Gunnar tumbling. He passed a glance over the rail as he scrambled back to his feet, turning back to an astonished CJ Barker and the open chute. Albion Troops were beginning to pour into the wrecked Operations Center.

"How'd you do that?" she asked, astonished. Gunnar grabbed her and pushed her down the open hole.

"Vitamins... Alex, you're next."

"Sir, I'm not so sure this is such a good idea. I can't navigate down one of these," the floating droid retorted. Gunnar grabbed the little droid by the antenna, popped his rear panel open and touched the power off.

"You'll navigate down it just fine now." He could hear the droid banging ungainly as it dropped out of sight down the chute.

Gunnar turned and started for the box of Asium crystals, but caught sight of two troopers coming up the stairs. Pulling his blaster, he fired a couple of shots at them and ducked for cover behind a console that began to tremble with blaster strikes. He stuck his pistol around the corner firing blindly, but his hand was peppered with metallic bits as enemy fire bounced off the floor and side of the console. Glancing to his left, he crawled around the other side, poked his head out near the floor and popped off several shots. A lucky hit in the leg brought one trooper down, but the other targeted in on his new position, laying down a barrage that skipped along the floor. Gunnar felt a sting to his ear as he pulled back behind the cabinet and listened carefully as the injured trooper moaned in agony. Something struck the box of crystals above his head, knocking it off the console and sending it rattling away. There came a noticeable clicking noise and a small round object dropped to the floor beside him.

"Not again," he grumbled, batting the grenade over the edge of the command platform. A moment later it exploded and he rolled back around the cabinet and started firing. The trooper that had thrown the grenade was so close that not only did Gunnar blow a large hole in his chest, but the muzzle flash from his blaster set his clothing on fire. The dead trooper fell flat on his back as Gunnar started for the box, but he was suddenly struck by a tremendous force to the left shoulder, strong enough to spin him around. He struck his head on the back side of the console. Ignoring his spinning head, he put a hand to his shoulder, feeling something warm and wet. He could feel blood coming down his neck from his ear as well. Multiple footsteps were clamoring up the stairs as Gunnar looked beyond the consoles to the open vent shaft. The box of Asium crystals were laying close by and he felt sure he could make a dive for it. Peering around the cabinet again, he got up, fired a couple of rounds and ran for the open shaft, scooping up the box as he went. Realizing his target was moving, the injured trooper opened up on him, grazing the outside of his left boot. The hit knocked Gunnar off balance enough that instead of diving through the hole, he slammed into the wall and crashed to the floor, dropping the box. His wits still with him, he turned over and pumped several shots at the trooper. Finally tumbling back with a shot to the head, the trooper fell into his companions coming up the stairs. Gunnar rocked back up onto one knee and started for the box but thought better of it. More troopers were scrambling up the stairs. Exasperated, he popped off two more shots and dove for the hole.

The shaft was cool, smooth, and slippery. Picking up speed, it began to turn in a broad spiral. Gunnar suddenly found himself sailing through the cool air of a cave, finally hitting the ground, and coming to a sliding halt on his stomach. Spitting dirt, he got to his feet and dusted himself off, looking around for CJ. Kneeling next to a motionless Alex 7001, she was trying to figure out why the droid wasn't moving. Gunnar trotted over and flipped open Alex's rear panel.

"The *shut-up* switch for this thing is right here," he said, reactivating the little droid.

"I'll have to remember that," CJ responded. Getting back to her feet, she stepped back as the little white droid rebooted and became airborne, surveying its surroundings.

"Colonel, could you please refrain from doing that? It's kind of embarrassing," the droid complained.

"Embarrassment is for humans Alex, not droids."

"Are you ok?" CJ asked, looking at Gunnar.

"Fine, we best get a move on. Where to?"

"Colonel, where's the box of crystals?" CJ looked all around them in the dim light of the cave.

"Sort of lost track of it I guess, which way?" Gunnar looked around making out the faint light of the Carolon dusk coming from a tunnel. Sounds of sliding coming from the air shaft behind them, CJ pointed to the passage and started running with Alex sailing right behind. As they exited the tunnel, they could hear the distant explosions of heavy combat, but also the strong thumping sound of something mechanized.

The surface of Carolon, where the three had emerged, was covered with rolling hills and thick trees. Dead dry leaves and twisting vines tangled around everything on the ground, making running a hazard. Quickening their pace, they started through the tangled mess of forest with Alex right behind. Gunnar felt the ground beneath them tremble rhythmically and scanned the woods for the source. Crossing a dry stream bed and starting up the side of another vine twisted, gnarled tree covered hill, CJ and Gunnar fell several times, both stopping to help the other. They were about to the top of the hill when CJ's foot became entangled in dead vines.

"How much farther to your ship?" Gunnar puffed anxiously, working to remove the tangle from her feet.

"It's just over this hill, about a three to five-minute run. There's a path, but I suppose the Albions are using it now." CJ noticed something on Gunnar's neck and shoulder.

"Colonel, you're hurt."

Gunnar put a hand to his shoulder as CJ examined his ear.

"Yeah, took a little doing to get out of your Operations center. Afraid I'm not as young as I used to be."

Alex seemed a bit nervous.

"Colonels," the little droid hedged.

"How bad is it?" she asked trying to look at Gunnar's shoulder.

"I think I just got grazed. Doesn't seem to hurt very much. I'm fine, really."

"Colonels," Alex repeated. A noise was rising in volume.

"At least you're not bleeding all over the place," CJ commented, pulling on the vines around her ankle.

"Colonels," Alex's volume increased.

"Quiet Alex, you want the whole planet to know we're here?" Gunnar whispered, but Alex persisted.

"Colonels, might I suggest..."

Gunnar shot the droid a particularly mean look, but noticed CJ looking over his shoulder, a horrified expression etched through wide eyes. He turned to see a monster Albion machine looming almost on top of them at the crest of the hill. Astonished at the awesome size of the ROACH tilting its head at them, Gunnar looked down at his blaster and decided it would do little good in this situation. The machine's pilots were clearly visible, looking right at them from the cockpit, working to rotate their cannons toward them.

"Make yourself comfortable, I'll be right back." He gave the rest of the vines a final yank from her boot and took off.

"Wait, what are...?" CJ tried to ask, but a second later Gunnar was bounding effortlessly over dead logs and small trees, right at the Albion assault vehicle. All the while, the ROACH had opened fire on the charging Starbird officer. Maneuvering closer, he could see the pilot and gunner trying to aim the machine's guns at him. He thought he could see them smiling, even laughing about whether a lone man could do anything to them other than maybe start hitting the ROACH's legs with a big stick. In a second, Gunnar was relatively safe under the belly and turned his head up, examining the underside of the rumbling craft and the joints of the massive legs. Fortunately for Gunnar,

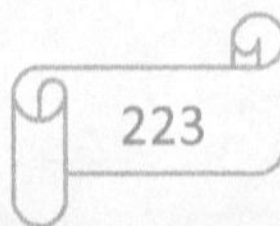

the trooper squads normally carried in the assault vehicle had already disembarked. He hoped there was unstable ordnance still onboard. Laser bolts weren't the only things that could cause extensive damage, just usually easier to handle. What he needed was a thermal grenade or something that could do a little damage, but he had nothing but his blaster, which would be useless against this kind of armor. Somehow, he'd have to improvise. He watched the machine's stalky legs moving up and down, then holding in place, as the ROACH pilots tried to maneuver back to his companions.

The legs appeared to be hydraulically powered with long metal tubes providing pressurized fluid to powerful lifting pistons and half gears. At each joint, armor covered flex hoses bridged the joints from one leg section to another. He didn't have any tools with him to perform any disassembly, but he was sure he didn't have to be so neat about it. As the joints seemed to be constantly moving, trying to blast at the supply hoses wasn't too much of an option. Without further thought, he dodged the constantly stomping feet, and jumped for the nearest joint.

CJ watched wide eyed as Gunnar took ahold of the supply hoses on each side and tore them effortlessly out from under the armor and off from both sides of the fittings. Hydraulic fluid spewed everywhere. He launched himself from the leg, keeping clear of the high pressure jets of thick, hot fluid. Passing the center leg, he moved to the back leg and duplicated the operation achieving similar results. As high pressure hydraulic pumps rapidly emptied their reservoirs of fluid, the legs simply pulled up beneath the belly of the ROACH and froze in place. Jumping to the last joint, he rehearsed the procedure again. By now, the pilots had diverted their attention away from CJ and Alex and tried to maneuver back around to locate and dispose of the Kalamarion officer.

Now the ROACH was off balance and only able to move in a half circle. Gunnar moved to the other side and gave the vehicle a hard shove to the side. With only one leg still extended and no way to lock it in place, the joint folded and the whole machine crashed to the ground. As Gunnar headed back to where he had left CJ and Alex, the assault vehicle exploded, the concussion throwing him for some distance. Shaking his head as he got to his feet, he dusted off his now tattered uniform and looked back at the burning heap. That didn't go off exactly as he had planned, but the result was the same. As he started searching for the others again, Audra's words echoed in his mind.

"Reckless, careless. You don't think things through before you do them. You have to be more careful."

Out of the corner of his eye Gunnar could see troops off to his right and another assault machine moving to intercept from his left. He made his way back to where he had left CJ and Alex, only to find CJ wincing in pain.

"She's been injured, sir. It appears to be shrapnel from the explosion," Alex informed his commander.

"How bad is it?"

"I was enjoying the show a little too much I'm afraid. I'm sure it's just a flesh wound."

"Trying to outdo me or something?" Gunnar snarked.

"Oh, you know, his and hers," she winced trying to get up. "I'll be all right. Come on, we can't stay here."

Gunnar helped her to her feet, then decided it would be faster if he just carried her. Scooping her up, he began to run, but at the crest of another small rise, he stopped and looked down into a large hollow. In the middle, snuggled back partially into the hill was a small building attached to a hangar, its doors closed. Giving CJ a wink, he bolted down the hill, the ground vibrating as the second ROACH spotted them.

Troops behind them reached what was left of the burning ROACH the same moment Gunnar stumbled into the small building adjoining the hangar. At her insistence, he set CJ in a chair in front of a small console. It appeared to be in sleep mode as only a couple lights winked on and off. Several monitors displayed external views of the woods surrounding the hangar complex. CJ reached for a control, but winced trying to work it. Stabbing pain fired through her right side making it impossible for her to get at what she needed. She finally had to use her left hand, keeping her right arm at her side. Lights came on all over the board, even as the approaching ROACH began to fire at the small hangar complex. Gunnar glanced down to see what she was doing as she keyed in several commands into an input terminal and adjusted several controls.

"I was wondering if you could explain to me what you are doing that's more important than us getting out of here?" he asked, a little frustrated they weren't making more of a concerted effort to get to her ship.

The assault vehicle firing at them had more than enough firepower to bring the complex to ground. He glanced out the window to his right, seeing Albion troops pouring over the hill with what looked like their leader, clad in a dark green flowing cloak. The building quaked violently, the roar of heavy machinery shaking the windows from the outside. He hoped that with the troops coming so close that the ROACH would stop pummeling the building. The ceiling above them shook more violently with every passing second. CJ finally set her last control and struggled to her feet, Gunnar noticing a small pool of blood on the floor next to where she had been sitting.

"Colonel, you're bleeding pretty bad there." A vision of Audra being buried beneath debris suddenly flashed through his head. The look on her face as she pulled herself out from under the ship's broken wall frames banged on his mind as he stared at the blood.

"What are you going to do, stitch me up right here and now?" CJ retorted, refusing to be helped as she staggered toward the door. "I've set the base destructors. The whole base has charges buried beneath it and should go off in five minutes," she said, stumbling into the adjoining bay. CJ hit the activators for the main hangar doors and they instantly began to move apart, revealing the dark Carolon sky.

"Five minutes?" Gunnar exclaimed surveying the vessel they were to depart in. "You've got to be joking." Gunnar studied the F-2's condition, a worried look forming across his anxious face. Several parts and cover panels were missing, giving it the illusion of being in the middle of a substantial restoration. "The real ship on the other side, right?" Gunnar started for the side doors of the fighter, but CJ redirected him toward the Delta wing.

"Leave it closed," she winced. "We're going to need its armor for cover."

Following CJ to the front edge of the Delta wing, Gunnar had to help her up as Alex flew into the open back hatch. CJ struggled to get up onto the fighter's back and hold herself steady. Gunnar was certain she was going to fall as she staggered toward the rear hatch. Steadying herself in the doorway, she stopped a moment, wincing through the pain in her side. Gunnar looked back through the open door and a window in the adjoining building, seeing troops closing in. Their escape largely depended on this craft's ability to get air borne.

"Are you sure this thing still flies? Looks like it belongs in a museum." The main engine converter assembly looked to him like useless junk. "Not even sure a scrapyard would take this thing," he added under his breath.

CJ winced, staggering to the copilot's chair and gingerly slipping in behind the dual controls. She was in no condition to be piloting anything.

"She'll do Quadra-light, she may not look like much, but she's never let me down," CJ said, looking out the cockpit window at two troopers that had just entered the adjoining building. She glanced back at Gunnar who was closing the hatch. "Come on, come on! The natives are restless," she winced again, reaching for the mains.

Gunnar sat down in the pilot's seat and strapped himself in, watching more troopers coming into the hangar with weapons raised. The fighter trembled slightly as the troops began to fire their blaster rifles, but they soon found they could do little against the armor plating of the F-2. Gunnar toyed with the controls as the instruments began to light up.

"This thing actually works?"

CJ gave him a weary glance, flipping several switches. She was too preoccupied to be insulted at this point. Lights started blinking and flashing all over the console and she stopped, glaring angrily at the controls in front of her.

"Oh please, not now," her voice elevated. "You're making me look bad ol' girl."

More troopers appeared outside in the bay, some moving to climb onboard the ship, while others worked to set up heavier weapons capable of inflicting significant damage.

"Just a little sweet talk me and her have all the time," she added, knowing Gunnar had just cast a look at her.

"Right...Uhm, who's the lady?" Gunnar asked, looking out the right hand window.

CJ turned as a figure clad in dark green strode into the hangar. Queen Captain Drax Blair and Colonel CJ Barker's eyes locked the instant the F-2's engines kicked over, roaring to life. Gunnar looked back over at CJ and seeing that the two were locked in some kind of a mind tug of war, grabbed the yoke and clicked on the anti grav system. It wasn't hard to figure that one out. The fighter gently rose from the hangar floor as the ground troops continued pounding the ship with small weapons fire trying to stop its hastened departure.

"Gear and shields!" he called. The ship trembled under the barrage of laser bolts bouncing off its heavy armor plating. He wasn't getting any kind of a response from CJ, who was still eye-locked in mental combat with the Albion Queen Captain.

"Colonel, are you going to just walk through those doors?" Alex pointed out, looking at the closing hangar doors.

"What? I thought those got opened when we came in?" Gunnar looked up from the controls to see the main doors sliding shut. "Futs," he grumbled, feeling the gun activators on the back side of the control yoke. He tried touching the activators on the yoke, but was only met with a warning light to his right on the center console. He couldn't read what the light was for, so he just started pushing buttons and pulling on the triggers. The troopers now opened up with the more substantial laser cannons, the ship jolting with every blast and the muffled sounds becoming louder with the heavier firepower being thrown at them.

"Try this one," Alex directed him at another button, but nothing happened.

"We need gear and shields! At least that can buy us some time!"

"Ok, try this one here," the droid directed again, but still nothing. "How about this one?" Alex continued, still producing no results.

"Here's a pretty one," Gunnar shot back sarcastically. "It looks like it makes the most sense."

The ship shuddered, laser blasts flashing on one side of the cockpit as each attempt failed to net any results. A hand appeared in the area of the console they were working with, touching a couple of buttons in sequence. Gunnar felt something beneath them make a noise and a clunking sound. He tried the triggers again and the bay doors suddenly exploded outwards in a shower of fire and debris. The excited exchange between Gunnar and Alex had broken CJ free from her stare down with Drax, but she still seemed preoccupied. Gunnar shoved a set of throttles all the way forward, bracing for acceleration, but nothing happened.

"What are you doing over there?" CJ complained. "Quit messing around. Those are the Quadra-light throttles." CJ reached for the other set. "They're inactive right now. Try these."

She threw the correct set of throttle handles forward and the engines screamed in acknowledgement of the sudden burst of Isom fuel. Everything behind the thruster ports turned liquid, as the fighter leaped from the hangar, through the wrecked doors, and skyward. In its wake, dead troopers littered the torched floor of the small hangar. The Albion Queen Captain watched, frustrated, from the safety of an adjoining hallway as the F-2 quickly disappeared into the dark Carolon sky.

*   *   *   *

Rick turned his command chair and faced his science officer. Toby Mavis adjusted his controls while studying the tracking screens.

"They appear to want us pretty bad, sir," he said, focusing in on their pursuers. "There are about ten squadrons of those Black Tigers, a whole bunch of other ships I haven't been able to get to yet and a large scale Dreadnaught class vessel. I mean it's really big!"

Rick looked up at the rear viewing screen, studying the pursuing armada.

"Can you get me a dimensional readout on the capital and the other fighter?"

"Capital readout coming up now. Take a minute or two more to get to the fighter."

Rick turned to the communications officer.

"Anything from Colonel Conrad?"

Lieutenant Laura Habba turned, shaking her head grimly.

Rick clinched his teeth, looking back outside. If Gunnar didn't hurry, he wasn't going to make it off Carolon. In front of him, he could see the *Constellation* moving into position directly beneath one of the transports while Captain Dayton maneuvered the *Athena* into position under the next one. Because the Kalamarion vessels were unable to accomplish a light speed jump, Colonel Barker had made arrangements with the commanders of two of the Colonian transports to magnetically lock directly to their hulls. The Starbirds would ride with them during light speed operations until they reached Tintee airspace.

He turned to the dimensional readouts of the Capital vessels in pursuit. A moment later, Toby motioned to Rick as the dimensional readouts of the second fighter type came up. He gave it a glance, considering, but made no other indication.

"Turn the ship around," he suddenly ordered coming to his feet.

Everyone on the bridge turned, not believing what the General had just ordered. Rick looked up at the dimensional readout of the pursuing Dreadnaught. It was certainly big. Silence continued on the bridge as the crew remained stunned, until Jayda finally rose to her feet and stepped over to her husband.

"What's this all about?"

"I said turn the ship around," he repeated, directing his attention at the navigator. "Plot a course back to Carolon, the same way we came, shouldn't be too hard."

"Not getting this one, General," Jayda responded. "That place is teeming with unfriendlys and we're only half operational at best."

Normally, no one would question the order, even one this odd, but given what was following them and the fact they were in no imminent danger, time to understand was available. Rick took the questioning looks as a good sign and fully understood that Jayda would be pulling on his ear for an answer anyway.

"We're not leaving Gunnar. Keep the *Constellation* covering the Carolon transports until they reach their destination. Com, alert Captain Abrams and relay my orders. Helm, standby to execute your maneuvers. Looking forward to seeing some fancy flying out of you on this one."

Rick sank back into his seat and Toby returned to his scanning equipment to aid in the oncoming attack on the Dreadnaught, its support ships and squadrons. Jayda let her hand come to rest on Rick's shoulder, preparing to ask a question, but Lieutenant Habba spoke first.

"Captain Abrams is on the line, sir."

"Of course he is," Rick mumbled low enough only Jayda heard it.

"Course information laid in, ready to execute, sir," the navigator announced, transferring the information over to the pilot.

"Execute," Rick ordered, reaching for the winking comlink button. He watched as the *Constellation* and the Carolon transports appeared to tilt away from view as the *Athena* banked sharply up and around in the opposite direction.

"Rick, what in blazes are you doing? What do you mean, stay with the transports and you'll rendezvous with us later? How will you know where to find us? They've almost reached their waypoints now. We're about to jump to light speed!" Dakota's voice was excited to say the least.

"Not sure how hard that is to understand, cousin," Rick stated coldly. Now, he was in no mood to be questioned by another subordinate acting ship commander, cousin or not. "We're heading back to find Gunnar. Figure out how to follow your orders and stay on course."

"Colonel Barker's aide told us their Operations center was overrun when our teleporter malfunctioned trying to bring them up. It's not likely either of them could have escaped that mess. What makes you think you'll find them?"

Rick looked out at the star field ahead of them and the tiny specks of light growing brighter as they closed in on the pursuing fleet.

"I'll find him," he stated, resolute.

Having already given the red alert warning, the *Athena* was now in range of the first swarms of Black tigers, the weapons officer already targeting several of the lead Tigers pounding their forward shields.

"Shield strength down fifteen percent," Jayda reported from the engineering station. "I would advise a speedy shot right down the middle."

Rick reached over and touched a button on the armrest of his chair.

"Launch Interceptors. Zek and Zak, run a close pattern right in front of us, but don't get drawn off on any individual entanglements. Make sure you stay in touch with weapons control so you don't end up as boiler fuel." Moments later, the

Interceptors crossed paths directly in front of the *Athena*, guns blazing.

*   *   *   *

The Ratronian Dreadnaught's main purpose was to outsize anything in the Albion or Colonian inventory. Gun turrets and laser cannons lined the hull of the *Maxell* at every attack angle conceivable. Her launch and landing bays, like her Colonian counterparts, were located at the bottom of the craft. On her sides were multiple rows of missile launchers. Further up the side of the Dreadnaught were more turret towers and lining the top decks. A narrow line of windows accentuated the bridge with various clusters of nose and chin cannons, giving it a sinister look.

The bridge of the *Maxell* was loud with the sounds of combat chatter and higher officers barking out orders to lower personnel. As the Ratronians were more excitable by nature, the noise was far above what the Colonians or the Albions would tolerate. Amid all the noise of combat, was the supreme commander of the Ratronian fleet, Swensen Shipley. Sitting in a large, lavish command chair, he watched the fighting going on outside as the Colonian F-2 escorts constantly harassed the Ratrons, slowing them down and giving the Carolon transports time to reach their waypoints for their jump to Quadra-light. The hope was to slow the Carolon fleet down before they made the jump to Tintee airspace.

Swenson lifted an eyebrow, taking note of a growing white speck coming right at his massive Dreadnaught. He turned his head slightly, listening to the information being shouted from the command personnel to their superiors on the lower decks. One of the Colonian transports had turned and was making a suicide attack headlong into the fleet. Swenson chuckled slightly, knowing there was no way they could get through their fighter escort and even if they did, they would be incinerated by the *Maxell's* myriad of gun emplacements. But the smile slowly melted as he watched his fighters disintegrate before the Colonian ship, fighter parts winging away in the wake of its flightpath. His aide jumped at his summons, as Swenson was quick to anger and wasn't going to let any Colonian ship get past his fleet.

"Dimensional! I want to see a dimensional on that ship right now, Captain! Now!" The aide bolted in response, knowing first hand that his commander's bark was as bad as his bite. Supreme Commander Shipley could be unmerciful, especially when it came to failure, his own or others. The aide trotted over to one of the many control consoles and picked up a portable viewing device, carefully handing it to his commander. Swenson looked at it for a moment, and then handed it back to the aide as he gave his report.

"Their deflector shields are of a different configuration than what our equipment can penetrate. We can't get a fix on any of their binary signatures. It's certainly alien of some kind. No ship of any kind in Hadrian has that kind of deflector shield technology, Colonian or Ratronian."

"What about Albion or the Tomplie?" he suggested angrily.

The aide nervously hedged his eyes to the window, then back to his commander.

"No, sir, Tomplie or Cross have nothing capable of this kind of firepower or shield strength. We're in treaty with Albia, why would they turn to attack us even if they had such a weapon?"

"Exactly my point, Captain," Swenson snapped angrily. "I don't trust Blair. First, she barges in on Carolon without me, then she's off on some wild goose chase after the base commander. I don't trust her. It could all be an elaborate trick to weaken us and take over."

Warning alarms began to sound throughout the bridge, a controller's voice blared over a loudspeaker somewhere.

"Enemy vessel closing in at mark two point four."

Swenson jerked his head back to the window. The alien vessel's features were quite distinct now, moving at a high closure rate toward the mammoth Dreadnaught.

"Are they moving to attack this ship?" Swenson asked, awestruck at the small size of the ship. He turned back to his nervous aide. "Shields up, open fire!" he ordered, turning back to watch. Horror sprang to his face at how close the alien ship and its two escorts had advanced. It appeared a head on collision with the bridge of the *Maxell* was imminent, all three ships pulling up at the last moment, just skimming over the top of the Ratronian capital ship, guns blazing. Turret emplacements pivoted, firing as they went, trying to track the speed of the Starbird as it soared over the back portion of the *Maxell* and into clear space toward Carolon. The maneuver happened so fast there was no time for any Ratronian vessels to pursue. Only a small squad of Black Tigers and Starhoppers had any hope of staying with the alien ship.

*   *   *   *

"Ship status," Rick asked, deactivating his safety locks. He stepped over to engineering, looking over Jayda's shoulder for a closer look at the readouts in front of her.

"Shield power is down to seventy-three percent. Weapons'
batteries limited to secondaries and still no FTL drive. Our Navi-
computers are doing ok, though we've still got bugs slowing
things down."

"Doesn't look very optimistic, eh?"

"Well," Jayda responded, looking up at her husband. "Let's
just say that making strafing runs on fleet ships all day probably
isn't the best course. Now, if we could just get some of this stuff
fixed, then we'd be sitting pretty."

"Sir," Laura beckoned from com. "Lieutenants Zek and Zak
are requesting permission to redock." Rick stepped over to the
science station, shaking his head as he passed the com officer.

"Nope. Have them run cross sweeps behind us, just in case
any of those fighters catch up."

"Toby, any sign of Gunnar or Colonel Barker?"

"Not exactly sure what I'm looking for here. We're still a little
too far out yet and there are all kinds of primary targets out
there."

"Lieutenant Reese indicated they'd be in an F-2, probably
headed in this direction."

"Most of what I can see out there are clusters of medium
destroyers and a few Corvette class ships. Fighters buzzing
around everywhere, but nothing distinguishable."

"Keep scanning. I think you'll know when you see them."

Jayda got up from her post as one of the engineers entered
the bridge, replacing her at the engineering station.

"Keep us at red alert, but shut those indicators off," Rick
ordered, settling back into his chair. Jayda stepped next to him,
seeing the concern etched on his face. "Gotta find him, Jayda,"
he commented in a low voice.

Jayda leaned against his chair.

"I just wished we had a little more detail on his
whereabouts."

"You and me both," Rick agreed taking her hand.

Cat & Mouse

The battered Colonian Flightstreak was but a mere speck in comparison to the awesome size of the Albion Battlecruiser *Tarzana*. It was a wonder the little fighter hadn't been destroyed. The firepower being thrown at it was more than enough to pulverize many other ships daring to go toe to toe with the war ship. It was evident the cruiser was expending an enormous amount of energy in a concerted effort to disable the fleeing Colonian fighter. Perhaps the advantage was given to the small fighter in this instance. There was so much fire being laid down from behind, trajectories were a mass of confusion. The pilot wasn't helping the gunner's plight as the F-2 performed maneuvers that couldn't be anticipated or tracked. The small craft just would not hold still and gave no indication as to where it was going next.

It had been some time since Gunnar had flown a fighter and the Flightstreak's instrumentation and technical controls were completely foreign to him. But one thing remained the same, a fighter goes up, down, slides sideways and turns both directions. Some did it better than others, but in the hands of a skilled pilot, even a sluggish fighter could be a formidable weapon. Keeping one eye out front and the other on the rear tracking screen, Gunnar was finding it increasingly difficult to out maneuver the buffeting flak flying at them and tried to give the F-2 more throttle.

"Dang girlfriend! Who keeps your engines tuned? Time to hire someone who is certified, not certifiable." To his dismay, he found full throttle for this fighter at sub-light wasn't enough to outrun the pursuing battlecruiser. He took note of several other objects appearing from behind, just in front of the *Tarzana*.

"I tune my own engines," CJ grumbled tiredly. "Keep your mind on flying. You're doing just fine." She was busy trying to get ready for the jump to light speed and finding it increasingly difficult to concentrate. Feeling light headed, the pounding they were taking from behind was making her quite ill. A near miss slammed a portion of the rear deflector shield and nearly overrode the ship's small anti-grav system.

Gunnar had no time to feel embarrassed for insulting CJ's mechanic abilities as another near miss kept him focused on his maneuvers. Throwing her a quick glance, she appeared to move sluggishly, her face pale.

"Hey, you ok over there? You don't look so good."

"What about you?"

"Huh?"

"Your shoulder? Remember, you got hit too?"

"I'm fine. It's you I'm worried about."

Gunnar swerved the vessel to the right, and then let it slide back to the left, letting it make a lazy roll, pushing the yoke erratically forward.

"I'd be a whole lot better if you'd hold level flight or at least shut the anti-grav off."

"I need it on to keep my equilibrium heightened. How come this thing won't go any faster?" he asked, impatient with the performance. He had been led to believe that the Flightstreak was a hot machine. This one felt like it was missing something, like, oh maybe an engine?

"Sir, I don't know much about this ship's design," Alex offered from behind, sitting locked to the floor. "But I did detect some problems with the electrical flux conversion controls back here. It could be an indication of bigger problems and why we're not getting the desired speed."

"We must have taken some hits before we left the hangar," CJ grumbled tiredly. "Is there any way you could level us out, even for a few seconds?"

"Not if I want to keep from getting our tails blown off, and from the sound of things, this ship won't take much more. We need a place to duck out of sight long enough to give them the slip, maybe put some distance between us and your friend back there."

The ship was pummeled by several blasts, these coming from the Black Tigers as they closed in on them. Several more direct hits on the rear shield gave cause for great concern as a warning light came on in front of Gunnar.

"Goodie, what does the blinky light mean?"

"Rear deflectors are down below minimums. You need to find a way to let them recharge or divert power from somewhere else," CJ slurred.

"Yeah, like that would be easy for me to figure out. None of this stuff makes any sense," he complained, scanning the instruments in front of him.

Gunnar checked the tracking screen, suddenly pulling back on the throttles and shoving the yoke all the way forward, turning it sharply to one side. The F-2 whined with the

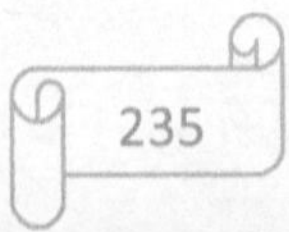

maneuver as it slowed considerably and rolled over 90 degrees from its level course with the Albion battlecruiser. The maneuver worked well in his Tempest, but this ailing F-2 was not a T-6 and it started spinning wildly. He tried frantically to correct the spinning fighter, but none of his basic training maneuvers were working with this craft. He considered himself an expert, practicing recovery maneuvers until he could do them in his sleep, but this ship was not responding to the usual techniques. He felt the yoke jerk free from his grasp and noted the sounds of the engines revving back up. The star field stopped spinning and his instruments returned too normal. He made a quick glance over at CJ who now had control of the Flightstreak. Her face almost white now with waves of green passing across it, but she seemed to be in full control of the fighter now. Once she had finished stabilizing the ship, she released the controls and leaned back.

"Think you can handle it now, hotshot?" She was trying to sound sarcastic, but was barely holding herself above consciousness.

"I hate this thing," he grumbled, taking the controls and banking the ship hard over again, noticing the Tigers regrouping to follow. The *Tarzana* was still firing, but having to remaneuver to pursue. As they spun again, he detected a dark sphere appear in the windshield for a moment. He passed a glance back at Alex, still clamped to the floor.

"Alex, I think I saw a planet out there. See if you can interface with the ships scanners and get a fix on it." Gunnar corrected the spin and then swerved the ship to the left, then to the right, then up, and then down.

"What if I can't interface with it or find what you're looking for?" the droid complained from the floor.

"Get to it, Alex!" Gunnar yelled, rolling the fighter into a spin again. While the maneuver was still effective, the Tiger pilots were catching on to it, figuring out how to recover faster. Also working to the advantage of the F-2 was their close proximity to the Tigers. With the battlecruiser throwing everything it could at them, at times the gunners became confused. Friendly fire had whittled the BT swarm pursuing the F-2 considerably. Only a few of the manta-ray like fighters remained tailing the Flightstreak, but what few remained pushed their attack hard, pounding the rear deflectors on the F-2.

Gunnar glanced over at CJ again. She sat silent now, not moving, her eyes draped half shut and pale faced. She had finished the preparations for light speed, but they were nowhere near the waypoint required to make the jump.

"Alex! Come on!" Gunnar shouted, frantically dodging the Tigers. They were completely on them now.

"I can't find anything that will be safe. None of these readings make any sense."

"Anything is better than getting cut to ribbons out here!" Gunnar responded, twisting the fighter.

"I can't argue with that," the droid commented. "To your left at four point five."

Gunnar immediately banked the fighter tighter around to the new heading, the outline of a dark planet appearing along with several moons and a thick belt of asteroids. He looked down at the scanner to see if he could recognize any of the readouts on the planet. Asteroid flying wasn't his favorite pass time. He was breaking a promise flying the F-2 as it was, but under the circumstances he hoped Audra would forgive him.

"Alex, it's a dead puddle! The suns are so far away from this thing it will be nothing but an ice chunk."

"How can it be a puddle and an ice chunk at the same time, Colonel?"

"Ice puddle? I don't know," Gunnar complained, swerving the fighter back and forth.

"What would you like, Colonel, luxury pools and a swimming suit?" Alex locked himself back into place.

"It's called Reako," a tired voice slurred from the copilot's seat.

Gunnar passed a glance at CJ.

"What?" he asked more concerned about her than the planet ahead.

"It's the planet Reako, and it's quite warm. It's volcanically heated from within. Lots of electromagnetic storms in the atmosphere. They won't follow us through the belt, Tigers have no shields... They can't track us either... A lot of fresh water..." CJ faded off, losing consciousness as the Tigers continued to close the gap.

Gunnar saw no other choice. He had to slow that battlecruiser down and get rid of the Tigers dogging him. Pushing the throttles as far forward as they would go again, he steered the fighter toward the asteroid belt. Once he got past the first couple of slowly floating rocks, the pounding from the fighters behind him nearly stopped. He checked the rear tracking screen and noted they were falling back considerably. He let out a sigh of relief and pulled back on the throttles again.

Maneuvering carefully now, he tried to keep the F-2 in the thickest part of the belt, but as he did so, he noticed a larger signal on the tracking screen. He made a quick glance through the overhead window at the bottom of the *Tarzana* gliding overhead, taking an occasional shot at the F-2 as the fighter weaved between the gently rolling space rocks. Gunnar looked back down at the rear tracking screen, taking note that the Tigers had dropped back far enough that it was difficult to see them. He looked back over his shoulder at Alex, still anchored to the floor.

"Alex, do you have your radion fuser with you?"

"Colonel, I always carry my equipment with me. What do you want it for?"

"I need you up here in my seat."

"What?"

"You're pilot in command," Gunnar announced, getting out of the seat and helping Alex get situated. The fighter seat was not designed for droids, but Alex somehow made it work.

"And just exactly what am I supposed to do?"

"Get us to Reako without hitting any of those rocks out there."

"And what are you going to do?" A door popped open on the droid's side. Gunnar reached in and pulled a little pencil shaped tool from its caddy.

"Colonel Barker has a pretty good bleeder going on here and she's going to be in a world of hurt if I don't do something about it quick."

Carefully pulling his jacket off, Gunnar knelt beside the unconscious CJ and noticing a med-kit beneath her seat, pulled it out. Her uniform was soaked on the right side just above her hip, blood dripping down the side of the chair into a puddle under the seat. He hesitated a moment, looking at the mess. Images of Audra lying broken and dying on the med table flashed through his head. What could he have done to save her? How was he going to save CJ? Trying to shake the images from his mind, he gently lifted her right arm and gritting his teeth, examined the tear in the blood soaked uniform. Thankfully, the shrapnel had fallen out sometime earlier, probably while they were running to the hangar bay in the woods, but the gash and the bleeder it had left would become dangerous if not closed up, even Gunnar could see that. He gently unbuttoned her uniform jacket and pulled it off, then unbuttoned the bottom half of her service blouse about half way up, carefully lifting the fabric away from the wound. Cringing at the bloody mess, he pulled the sash from her waist and cleaned the wound as best he could, then picked up the micro fuser, setting it on high and activating the trigger. Looking at the tip, he waited until it glowed red hot and then started working with it to cauterize the bleeding wound. The smell was horrible, but having done this before, he knew exactly what to expect and what to do. He and Rick had been injured in the field without medical help before, and had to rely on primitive procedures until tended to properly. It was crude, but when he finished, the wound had stopped bleeding. He finished cleaning around it, applying a bio gel that quickly setup and then he rebuttoned her blouse. For now, that would have to do. Taking a moment for himself, he slathered some of the bio gel on his shoulder wound under his shirt and dabbed a little on his ear. Putting his jacket back on, he noticed the shoulder fabric was torn and epaulettes were damaged. He was missing several buttons as well.

The fighter lurched a bit, bringing Gunnar's attention back outside. Great walls of gently undulating rock enveloped them as Alex carefully guided the ailing fighter between the large asteroids. Gunnar looked up, trying to see the *Tarzana,* but could only see an ocean of rock above them. They must be in the thickest part of the asteroid ring. He looked over at the scanner, but saw only a wall of echoes coming back at them.

"Any idea how far from Reako we are?"

"It is difficult for me to calculate distance with this equipment, sir, but at this speed it will take a considerable amount of time to reach the planet surface. I can detect no sign of our pursuers now, but the battlecruiser has moved ahead of us, probably to try and get between us and the planet."

"You're learning battle tactics, Alex, good for you." Gunnar relaxed, feeling a little more secure safely tucked in the thickest region of Reako's asteroid belt. But he knew he couldn't stay in here indefinitely. Gunnar turned to the wall of flashing readouts on the back near the rear hatch.

"Since we have lots of time on our hands now, I wonder if I can get a little more juice out of this crate?"

*   *   *   *

As the *Tarzana* hovered motionless just inside the asteroid ring of Reako, a burly man paced nervously back and forth in front of the main command consoles on the secondary level of the bridge. Short in stature, it took Commander Dalton SoKnack a little longer to make the trek back and forth. A bushy uni-brow crossed above dark piercing eyes. He wasn't a particularly aggressive officer, but he did like to get things done and you didn't achieve rank in the Albion military without having to be a little forceful. His hands clasped tightly behind his back as he paced, he had hoped to have the F-2 disabled and safely tucked away in their landing bays before the Queen Captain had returned from the surface of Carolon. Alas, the runaway Colonian ship had somehow evaded them and the Queen Captain had finally caught up with the flagship and was already headed for the bridge. Dalton felt confident in his decision to position his battlecruiser and supporting ships between the planet and the asteroid belt. He knew this was where the renegade Barker was heading, as they hadn't jumped to light speed for some reason when they had fled Carolon. Perhaps the Queen Captain knew why. Commander SoKnack didn't have long to wait as the elevator on the command bridge opened up and the Queen Captain appeared, BachTL right on her heels. Ascending the short flight of stairs, he could see the unhappy look on her face, but then again, he rarely saw her with a smile. She pulled her cloak from her shoulder, handed it to BachTL and stopped in front of the nervous SoKnack.

"I'm certain you had me chase you to Reako because Barker is here somewhere, right?" Her voice was gushing with sarcasm. "I'm sure I was mistaken that I didn't see Colonel Barker's F-2 in our landing bays. I feel certain you put it in the launch bay, though for the life of me I can't even fathom why. I'm also certain there's a perfectly good reason you've parked this ship at such a moronic angle in orbit around this mud puddle?"

Dalton lowered his eyes just a little as he started his report.

"Colonel Barker is a better pilot than our intel had previously indicated. Even with Tigers on them, she was able to evade us into the asteroids. I have situated the ship here to keep them from leaving the ring and reaching the planet's surface."

"Did it ever occur to you they might shift course and travel along the belt for a distance and then try and make a break for the planet? How about the possibility she could be hiding on or in one of the bigger ones and is waiting for her chance to slip out the other way before anyone notices her?"

Dalton remained silent.

"Where are our support ships stationed?"

"Around the planet QC." Dalton was sure she would approve of that decision.

"Please tell me they're spread out and not all bunched together like a bunch of old women at a card game," the Queen Captain inquired, folding her arms. "How many Tigers did you send out after her?'

"We started with eight."

"And how many are left to run probing sweeps of the belt?"

"Three."

"Three! You sent eight Tigers out and there are only three left?" The Queen Captain's blood pressure elevated. "How did you manage that? Wait!" she held her hand up angrily. "I don't want to know." Drax closed her eyes and gently rubbed her forehead. She kept her hand up as if she was trying to hold the cruiser commander away from her enough to keep from striking him. In all reality, she had killed for far less. Perhaps who they were trying to capture here had her softened just a bit. BachTL folded his arms and silently took a side step behind the Queen Captain.

"If you want something done right, you have to do it yourself," he slurred quietly.

Drax gave her aide a quick nod, keeping her head turned slightly.

"Ain't it the truth? You get those Tigers back in here and send out the AP-10s."

"QC," Dalton edged. "The AP-10 isn't fast enough to keep up with the F-2."

"Speed isn't your problem here, Commander. They're in an asteroid belt. You need to find them. The Tiger doesn't have the detection gear or the shielding needed for the task, the AP-10 does. Deploy Tigers above and below the belt to run detection sweeps and insert the AP-10s inside along their last know trajectory. And have my ship refueled and ready for departure."

Dalton motioned to his Lieutenant and turned to the bridge window with the Queen Commander. Drax thought a moment as they looked out at the asteroid belt.

"Let's give you the benefit of the doubt here, Commander," QC Blair snapped. "Run a vertical S pattern through the belt, we'll see if we can flush them out a little faster."

Dalton developed a worried expression. Even BachTL was a bit taken back at what the Queen Captain was proposing. Dalton hedged forward slowly, thinking carefully about how to present his concerns.

"QC, you want to drive this ship repeatedly through the belt layer in hopes of flushing Colonel Barker out?"

"Yes, that's right. Is there a problem?"

"You understand this will cause considerable damage to this ship as it will be impossible to clear all the asteroids before penetrating the belt, nor will our deflectors be able to protect us completely from that much debris?"

"Understood," the Queen Captain acknowledged.

Dalton lingered for a moment, thinking perhaps the Queen Captain had something to add or would maybe reconsider her intensions, but after a brief pause, he finally turned to carry out his orders.

"You're not going down after her, are you?" BachTL asked.

"Not if I don't have to," she responded unmoving. "She's hurt; you saw the blood in the hangar. She needs my help. I have to find her before something else happens to her."

BachTL looked out at the asteroids as the ship began to maneuver into position to start its run in and out of the belt. He dared not probe any further. The relationship between Drax and CJ was a complicated one.

*   *   *   *

Gunnar slipped back down into the pilot's seat, letting Alex re-anchor himself to the floor.

"You done good, Alex," Gunnar commented, buckling himself back in.

He was starting to get a bad feeling about his plan to get to the surface of Reako. Tucked deep in the asteroid belt gave them plenty of safety, but he knew sooner or later they would have to make a break for the surface and then the Albions would be right back on them. It would be a mad dash to see who got there first. He looked over at CJ, still slumped back, buckled in her seat. The color had returned to her face and she appeared to be resting a little more comfortably, but he knew she still needed proper medical attention. Keeping a wary eye on the tracking screen, he continued carefully navigating his way through the belt. Occasionally, he caught sight of a ship at extreme range, but nothing threatening.

"Don't mind these rocks at all," Gunnar commented, casually maneuvering the F-2 carefully around the gently floating boulders. "They're certainly a lot friendlier than the Oota belt when we were at the Oneida. I don't even see any dust or small rocks to slowly beat this thing to death."

"Without further analysis of the belt's dynamics, it would be impossible to say, but if I were to venture a guess, I would say they're of ancient origin and so stable because of the lack of radiant heat or solar storms in this area."

Gunnar felt a gentle vibration shudder through the ship, not just the yoke, but the entire frame. He scanned the readouts in front of him trying to see if anything had changed, but saw nothing. The vibration continued to grow and a moment later he took particular notice of a flood of strobing light ahead of them. Even with the gentle movement of the space boulders outside, it was apparent something out of the ordinary was happening. He checked the scanner for information, but it was still mostly obscured with the reflections.

"Alex, can you get a read on what's going on in front of us?"

The droid unclamped from the floor and hovered over the center consoles for a look.

"Your scanner shows me the same thing it shows you. Without creditable information I can only venture a guess. I would say there is an ion burst passing through the belt somewhere ahead of us, or perhaps a comet."

Gunnar eyed the glow ahead of them, feeling the vibration starting to fade off. Traveling on for some distance he felt it again, the glow and flashes becoming even more pronounced.

"This is too weird," Gunnar mumbled. His concern was growing with the glow ahead of them. "I'm going to take her up for a look see across the top of the belt. We can always duck back down and do a shift and maze."

"You're the Colonel, Colonel."

Gunnar gently maneuvered the F-2 up and around several giant rocks until they started to thin out, becoming somewhat smaller. Leveling out, he checked the scanner for any signs of the Albion fighters. Seeing nothing, he steered the ship clear of the belt and throttled up a little more, holding a straight course for Reako.

"We ought to make a little better time this way," he commented, keeping a wary eye on both scanner and tracking systems. Still clear, but he wasn't about to hinge all his hopes on the Albions giving up any time soon. As he grew more confident they would make it undetected, he felt the vibration returning and noted a spot in the asteroid ring directly in front of them start to glow sporadically.

"How's this?" Gunnar exclaimed, pulling the throttles back. The area in front of them was vast, taking up nearly his entire field of view. The belt began to bulge slightly directly in front of them, bits of rock and debris starting to spray straight up in a huge, ever growing plume. Brilliant spectrums of colored light fountained up in multiple layers before the fighter. Gunnar had thought about trying to go around, but it was so big and he could see that they were almost to the edge of the belt, it might be better to take the gamble and go straight through whatever this disturbance was. Pressing forward, Gunnar's eyes widen, abruptly finding his vision filled with a sea of stark metal as the bow of the *Tarzana* suddenly breached the belt directly in his flight path.

"Colonel!" Alex bellowed, dropping to the floor in anticipation of the collision.

"Hang on!" Startled at first, Gunnar shoved the throttles all the way forward and twisted the fighter right at the side of the giant war ship slicing up through the belt. Asteroids and debris spewing in every direction, the F-2 passed through a volatile firestorm of turbulence as it reached its top speed. Gunnar rolled the fighter toward the underside of the ship, just skimming along the hull. Looking to his right, the lower conning tower flashed into view, coming right at them. He twisted the yoke hard to the left and flipped the F-2 on its back relative to the ship, trying to avoid the imminent collision.

"This is good! I was rusty on panic!" Gunnar exclaimed, looking up as they swept past the windows of the bottom conning tower. He could see figures standing on the lower bridge, some pressing their faces to the glass watching the fighter streak right past. Gunnar pushed harder on the throttles, but they were already up against the stops. He could see faces clearly now. He had to figure out how he was going to squeak past the final structure of the lower tower without striking it. Being inside their deflector shields meant he wasn't getting pummeled with space rock any longer. But now he was wondering if that wouldn't be better than having a collision with a battlecruiser, especially the one bent on their capture. The only thing he could do now was pull back on the controls and arc the fighter toward the curving edge of the conning tower. As he did so, he felt like he could reach out and shake their hands as he flew by. *Thanks for dinner and the show!* He closed one eye and cringed, waiting for the sickening sound of metal striking metal, but it never came. In an instant, he was once again blasting through the Albion deflector shields and back into the thick of the pulverized asteroid debris.

"I think I saw the whites of their eyes," Alex commented from the floor.

"One of them offered me a fist bump," Gunnar grunted, struggling to maintain control of the F-2 plowing through the turbulence of the asteroid debris. The ship suddenly took a tremendous hit, sending it cartwheeling, end over end. He struggled to keep his wits about him. If not recovered from quickly, this kind of spinning will make anyone sick, incapacitating them. He frantically reached for the anti-grav system and shut it off. At least now the artificial gravity wouldn't hamper his attempts at recovery. An alarm filled his ears as he fought for control. It wouldn't take long for the fighter to appear on the Albion's scanners as the ship was spinning right out of the belt and into the open. He would make an easy target now, as they were wheeling right at the planet. Gunnar pulled the throttles all the way back to idle and worked the controls to counter the spin. Finally, the ship was flying straight and level, but they were clearly visible.

"Can you see what we hit?"

Alex was up in an instant and looking out both side windows, back at the sweep back foil of the Flightstreak.

"Your left fin looks damaged. I would guess you hit an asteroid. Could have been worse."

"Dandy! Just dandy!" Gunnar complained. *As if this ship wasn't having enough problems.* "Well, they're not gonna beat me down there," he growled, shoving the throttles all the way forward again. His rear tracking screen caught his eye as his ship coughed, throttling as fast as it could go. Several signals appeared, including one larger than the others. He could only imagine that the Albion cruiser was executing a hard left dolphin flip out of the belt and heading right at them, launching its fighters to intercept before they could reach the planet. It would take only a few minutes for the Tigers to close within firing range. For now, Gunnar only caught sight of an occasional laser blast streaking past them, but knew the pounding on their shield would commence shortly. Even though it had only recovered to about half strength, it would have to be enough.

The Black Tigers followed the fleeing Flightstreak down into the outer atmosphere of Reako, each firing its six wing mounted guns and dual forward cannons. The rear shields on the Colonian craft again started taking a beating as they closed the gap. Entering the upper troposphere, the F-2 shook violently and Gunnar detected a light glow developing on the nose of his ship as he let it plummet toward the surface. Turning laterally, he began to weave as they continued to be hammered. The F-2 jolted fiercely as another burst pounded the rear shield, its warning alarm sounding again. He reached over and switched the anti-grav back on, adjusting its sensitivity a little. High speed maneuvers could create G-forces the body couldn't deal with. There was a little light outside, making it possible to see the outline of clouds below him, and steering toward a high bank, he hoped to find some cover. Approaching the tops of the clouds, he noticed something odd forming on the outer surface of the fighter. Tiny sparks danced all across the skin of the craft as he entered the cloud bank, one last burst of fire from his pursuers and the rear deflector dropped. As they were engulfed into the turbulent blackness of the clouds, Gunnar noted all the cockpit instruments acting erratic. The displays all fuzzed out and the few basic analog instruments used for atmospheric flight either froze in place or rotated aimlessly.

Completely blind, he turned a careful series of lengthy patterns, heading off in what he hoped was a completely different direction. Finally, he broke through the bottom of the clouds, being met by several blinding strikes of cloud to cloud lightning and their accompanying ear blasting claps of thunder. Sparks continued to dance wildly around the hull as the ship plummeted toward the surface through the last of the clouds. Many of the sparks converged, forming fingers of plasma crawling around, as if looking for a way to get inside the ship.

The dancing plasma was abruptly replaced by an obscuring rain that vanished as suddenly as it had started. Reaching over he flipped on the landing and exterior Nav lights. It was then he realized just how close to the ground he actually was. He could see what looked like a forest and lots of water.

Leveling out, he circled in low, looking for some kind of dry stable landing spot that might provide good cover, but there were mostly small lakes. He turned the F-2 sharply to the left, just skimming the tops of the trees and headed for a large circular open space of water. His thought was to land close to the edge so if the craft decided to sink, they would be able to get out, though he hadn't thought beyond that.

"Hope she floats," he mumbled, throttling back. He carefully brought the ship into a landing hover and gingerly set it on the water. He didn't feel it hitting anything beneath him and as his luck seemed to finally turn in his direction, the Flightstreak did in fact float, sort of. He sat for a moment, letting the engines idle, then finally reached over and shut them down, snapping off the other system's master switches. Finally, the cockpit was dark and quiet with only the light from an occasional burst of cloud to cloud lightning and the little lights on the front panel of Alex 7001.

Gunnar leaned back and let out a heavy sigh. Outside it was calm but far from quiet as rolls of thunder continuously rumbled overhead. He looked out through the overhead window at the dark Reako sky, then carefully around at their surroundings. There was almost no light to see, but he wanted to make sure he hadn't set the fighter down in a clear pool inhabited by some kind of enormous water creature. After surveying just dead twisted forest and water, he pushed his seat back as far as it would go and unbuckled his harness.

"Alex, can you figure out how to bring up the interior lights without turning everything else on? I want to save as much power as we can. I'm going to take a little trip outside to see what I can see."

Alex turned his little motovacs to face the rear wall as Gunnar stepped to the rear hatch and activated the door mechanism. He expected the air to be cold and damp with a dreary feel to it, but it was exactly the opposite. It was warm and pleasant, just as CJ had indicated earlier. He carefully made his way around the back-line cannon and part way down the foil to inspect the damaged fin.

"Nothing a hammer can't fix," he said out loud, checking to make sure it wasn't going to fall off. It was certainly bent and had a sizable ripple running the length of the surface down where it attached to the foil. He then turned his attention to the engines. He had no idea what he was looking for. Somehow, they needed to gain access to the ship's system control computers in order to try and do a diagnostic on the problems plaguing the fighter. He tried to make a quick inspection anyway. It was too dark to see anything clearly. He was about to give up when he became aware of Alex hovering over him with one of his external lights spotting on the assembly. Working together, they looked over the exterior of the Isom converter, finding two or three trouble areas that could possibly cause a problem. Being completely unfamiliar with Isom power plant theory, there was no way to know for sure if they were doing any good. In a couple of instances, it was just a matter of reconnecting harness plugs. In another case, it was obvious a feeder tube to some kind of booster pump was damaged and had been venting Isom fuel. This would require some extensive reconstruction. Alex could probably do it, but as they finished their inspections and repairs of the simple things, Gunnar discovered he was standing in about a foot of water. The ship was in fact sinking. Confident they could always restart the engines and resurface, he stepped back inside and let the ship sink to the bottom of the lake, providing even further cover from the Black Tigers and the *Tarzana* somewhere above them, searching. After securing the hatch, Gunnar examined the rear wall of the fighter and all the control system readouts, displays and widgets Alex was working on.

"Have you figured out a way to interface with this bird yet?"

"No, Colonel, I've been trying to interface with the control system, but I'm detecting multiple command engines and they're all arguing in some odd language I can't make sense of. Its data streams are more like raging rivers. A direct terminal connection would be helpful if I had CORA 500 here to act as a controlling host."

"Do what you can."

"I will do my best," the droid responded, maneuvering toward one of the access ports.

"Can you provide me with some diagnostic power? Want to see if what we did back there did us any good."

"What about the booster pump feed? It's still broken."

"I think we'll wait it out on the bottom of the pond here until the Albions move off. Then we can resurface and try to make those last repairs."

"There is no bottom to this lake," a quiet voice casually remarked from the copilot's seat as the water level began to rise above the windows.

"Hush, Colonel, I'm trying to have a conversation with Alex here and…" Gunnar stopped short, realizing he was talking to a conscious CJ. Both he and Alex were at her side in an instant.

CJ smiled, enjoying the added attentiveness and tried to sit up.

"I really need to get out of this chair," she groaned. Gunnar carefully helped her onto wobbly legs. Once she had stabilized herself, feeling light headed and wincing once or twice from the pain in her side, she looked out the over window as the water engulfed the ship.

"You won't need the engines to maneuver around in water. Just use the maneuvering thrusters. They're not much good for anything but docking and little stuff like this anyway."

"Well, we may not need them for a while, but what do you mean, there's no bottom?" Gunnar wished she would take it a little easier. He watched her stagger a little as she stepped to the rear wall and looked at some of the readouts on the equipment Alex had applied power to.

"Most of these shafts go almost straight down. I'm not sure where they go. The oceans do the same thing. We've tried sending probes in for a look, but have never gotten them back out. We would just lose telemetry after a while. We weren't picking up any volcanic activity, but we're sure that's what's heating the planet. This water is fairly warm and the atmosphere doesn't dissipate the heat into space like other planets do." CJ staggered, holding onto the rear wall. Quite ill, her head was starting to spin.

"What's the shelf life of your batteries in this thing?"

"Indefinite. It has an Isom integrated energy core that will keep the electrical system operating indefinitely, provided the engines don't vent fuel for some reason."

"Uhm, we may have a problem then," Gunnar said, leaning against the center console. He sure wished she would come back and sit down. "We found a broken booster valve tube, along with a couple of other things."

"Metal looking tube shaped like a sideways hook and bolted to a round black barrel looking thing?"

"That would be the one," Gunnar commented, watching her legs start to wobble.

"Hhhmmm, yes that would cause a bit of a problem, but I think as long as you don't try to restart the engines until we can get it fixed, you shouldn't have any problem running the internal systems in here."

"And I think it's time for you to come back and sit down," Gunnar insisted, escorting her back to her chair. "Have you got anything you can drink in here? You've lost a lot of blood and I'm sorry, but I'm fresh out of plasma bags."

"There should be some plasma jell in the med kit." CJ pointed to the medical box.

Gunnar dug around for a moment, then pulled out an odd looking tube and handed it to her.

"You should probably chow down on all of that?"

"What about you? How are you doing?"

Gunnar put a hand to the tear in his uniform.

"No worse for the wear. You got torn up more than I did."

"How bad is it?" she asked, opening the tube and examining the dark spot on her outer uniform.

"Let's have a look see," he said, reaching for the bottom buttons of her service blouse.

"I beg your pardon, but just what do you think you're doing?" she glared, instantly slapped his hands away. An angry look streaked across her face as she started refastening her buttons.

Gunnar paused, reading the situation and started to chuckle lightly.

"Calm yourself. I had to patch you up while you were out and I just want to make sure it hasn't broken itself open again." He could see the embarrassment mixed with anger flushing her freckles. "Don't worry, I didn't see anything, now let me have a look...please."

CJ held the hard glare, then toned down a little and began unfastening the bottom buttons. She got about half way up the long row and Gunnar stopped her.

"That's enough. Geez, you don't have to take it off."

CJ tried to smile, but was still smoldering with embarrassment. Gunnar carefully lifted the bottom edge of her blood stained blouse for a look at her wound. After examining it for some time, he let her button back up.

"You'll live," he stated coolly, purposely being cavalier. He got back to his feet and stepped back over to where Alex was working while CJ re-buttoned her blouse. She painfully got back up on uncertain legs, staggering again. Once she had regained her balance, she made her way to the rear wall next to Gunnar and looked down at what Alex was doing.

"So what do we do now?" she asked, leaning against the side window, her head still in a fog.

"We sink," he said focusing on something inside an open panel.

"We sink," she repeated, not wanting to believe that was all he was going to offer. "Really? We're just going to sink?" she snorted infuriated.

Gunnar turned to her, feeling a bit playful.

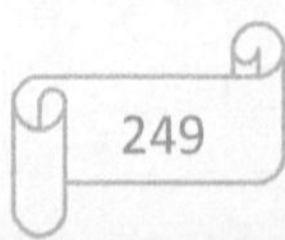

"You need to sit back and rest easy, Colonel. We've got nothing better to do for now," he said, moving back to the pilot's seat.

Fuming, CJ was not pacified in the least. Daggers in her eyes, she carefully folded her arms and leaned back to watch the dark water beyond the window. She glanced down at the little droid below when she detected simulated laughter, but when CJ made a growling noise, the laughter abruptly stopped.

Tintee

From a distance, the planet Tintee is a mostly brown planet with some green and blue regions mixed in. Most of its fresh water bodies are subterranean. While its salt oceans are located at the poles, there are plenty of life-sustaining mineral deposits found all over the planet. The vast, lush forests are found in close proximity to these bodies of water, whether on the surface or subterranean.

The capital city of the arid planet is called Tintee. Built on top of the largest mountain range on the planet, the city is enormous. Great spires rise high above the jagged peaks, some scraping the high, thin cloud layer. The hub of commerce and military traffic alike, ships of all kinds constantly move in and out of infinite lines of hangar bays and docking ports located all around the great city. Those ships too large for the hangar bays, typically military capital ships, either sat silently before the city on the vast plain, or hovered lazily in various places around the city. Some of these ships are able to rumble slowly in and out of one or two hangar bays built specifically with the war giants in mind. The wind storms are quite severe, creating problems for ships waiting long periods for service.

On the dry desert plain, among the many sitting war ships, Colonian ground troops marched back and forth in the midst of assault tank maneuvers. TR-10 & 15 tanks moved swiftly back and forth across the flat terrain, taking up positions in preparations for something big. Within the city an unusual excitement buzzed around all of the military personnel as they gathered at their respective posts for what appeared to be preparations for a battle of some kind.

In the center of the city sat a large round building ringed with short crystal spires. Not the tallest building in the vast city, this round structure was but the cap of an enormous complex. Beneath the city, the largest military installation known in all of Hadrian bustled. In its main control center, a group of high ranking officers hovered around her majesty, Queen Stephanie Benetar, ruler of the Colonian Empire.

Gazing at a viewing screen taking up nearly an entire wall, the queen studied the detailed two and three dimensional depictions of the different types of ships all over the map. Dressed in tight glistening blue pants and a bright red cashmere shirt that appeared to glow softly, she stood with her arms folded. She wore only a Colonian patch on each shoulder. Her long, well-kept brown hair curled beautifully around her shoulders. She listened carefully to the reports of the traffic controllers and the long range scanning officers as they relayed their information back and forth. One of the higher ranking officers behind her was becoming impatient as more images appeared on the viewing map, indicating a large concentration of ships headed in their direction.

"Your highness, we must launch immediately," the officer insisted. "The Albion and Ratronians are gaining on the Carolon fleet too rapidly to delay any longer."

The Queen gracefully shifted her weight, combing her beautiful curls back with spread fingers.

"Instruct Admiral Duncan to position his ships between the Carolon fleet and the Ratronians. I want Colonel Barker brought before me within the hour." The Queen turned to leave but the officer's voice stopped her.

"Your highness? What about the escort assignments?"

The queen turned her head to the side, looking only part way behind her.

"I expect my Generals to do some of the work." She then continued to her chambers.

*   *   *   *

Captain Abrams sat forward in the command chair of the *Constellation*, a tense expression chiseled into his face. They had come out of light speed close to their destination and had detached from the transport that had given them a ride, but were now facing a different problem. Watching the Carolon fleet loom closer to a growing spec of light, his attention was drawn by Pip at the science station.

"Hey Pip, what goes?"

The science officer gave the Captain an odd look. Fighter pilots were certainly a different breed, operating on a completely different level. One would have hoped that filling in as executive officer, would have taught the Captain a little more about how to be a proper command officer.

"It appears our pursuers anticipated where we were going and are just coming out of light speed directly behind us. But that doesn't make any sense. If they knew where we were going, why didn't they just jump directly here and intercept us?"

"Nobody said anything about them being smart, just a whole lot of them."

"It looks like we should be able to reach Tintee before their fighters ever get into firing range. I'm not sure what happens after that."

"Yeah, trying to think about what the Colonian military would think of this ship showing up with the rest of the Carolon fleet. No doubt they've already figured out we're here."

Pip shifted his attention to several other displays in front of him, continuing to work with his instruments.

"Well, sir, you're about to get your answer. Here comes our welcoming committee. There's a large body of fighters coming at the fleet from Tintee."

Dakota sat up, looking at the displays over Pip's head.

"Oh goody," he said slowly. "Lieutenant Navall, have Tiana bring Lieutenant Reese up here please." Good training for a better executive officer than he could ever be. Dakota finally left the command chair for a better look at the incoming fighter squadrons.

"Would you suppose these are escorts?" he asked Pip.

"Difficult to speculate at this point. The Carolon officer will be better able to answer that question."

"Nice to have some operating equipment again," Dakota suggested in a low tone. They continued to study the information being displayed in front of them until the bridge door popped open and Tiana and Talia stepped inside, Tiana stepping directly to the command chair, wearing an Ensign's uniform. Dakota gave it a peculiar look.

"You realize you're impersonating an officer, right?"

Tiana looked at herself smiling and started to speak, but Dakota stopped her.

"Where in the world did you find that? Never mind, I don't care. Lieutenant Reese, please," he motioned for the Colonian officer to join them.

Talia stepped in their direction, but kept her eyes scanning the vast array of technology displayed on the bridge.

"What do you make of this, Lieutenant?" Dakota asked, pointing at the displays in front of them.

Talia finally focused on the question and the information in front of her. At length, she stepped closer to the console, looking for a knob to adjust.

"Wider view please," she requested, searching for the right control. The characters were foreign to her, the information impossible to read.

Pip adjusted the touch control and the image on the screen changed to the requested view. After careful study, she stood up straight and drew in a deep breath.

"It looks like the Queen is sending up a flotilla of quick strike attack squadrons to defend against the pursuing Black Tigers. She'll send up heavier stuff a little later to deal with the capital ships if they pose a problem. Her usual behavior is to order up large numbers to beat them back. She really hates it when they enter her space."

"Sounds great," Dakota responded.

Talia looked forward at the pilot and navigator.

"Not so fast. She's going to be looking for Colonel Barker and her support staff."

"That would be?"

"Her personal aides, security chief, squadron leaders, ground assault leaders and upper command personnel.

"So...Willis Ruston?"

"And me," Talia added.

"That's bad," Dakota scratched his head.

"And since I am with you guys and Colonel Barker isn't, and you're not a part of the Carolon fleet, this ship and its crew will be under arrest."

"That's really bad."

"I don't get it," Tiana finally cut in. "We're one of the good guys. We're helping you. Why are we in trouble?"

"Couple of things at work here," Talia said, arms folded, still watching the traffic outside. "First, you're an alien ship full of alien technology. Some really awesome alien technology I might add," she indicated, looking all around the bridge.

"Never been called an alien before," Dakota mumbled close to Tiana.

"Second, you're harboring me."

"What about Willis?" Dakota was interested to know of her fate.

"She'll be taken into custody as soon as she lands."

"What ship is she on? Is there any way to get to her?"

"Not unless you can magically transport her off."

Dakota, Tiana, Pip and even Lieutenant Navall all looked at each other collectively.

"We'd have to at least have her location on whatever vessel she's on, Captain," Pip finally said.

"I can home in on her exact position if she has an active communicator," Lana offered.

"She'll be onboard the *Rex*, that one over there on the right," Talia said, pulling her blonde hair back and resetting the band holding it in a ponytail. She pointed to one of the ships just

ahead of them. "We can contact her now and give her instructions. The high command will be going over each of these ships with a fine tooth comb looking for Colonel Barker. We are to be charged with treason to the Empire."

"Treason? That's a little harsh for trying to save your butts isn't it?"

"Desperate times call for desperate measures," she responded, turning to face them again. "The Empire is faced with massive defections to the other factions in our struggle to maintain political sovereignty. Passing the law of treason for defection or desertion has drastically reduced those numbers. Technically, we left Carolon without authorization from the Colonian high command, defying a direct order from her majesty, Queen Benetar. There aren't too many places in Hadrian someone can go to get away from the Empire."

"Too late to make a run for it now," Pip informed them, pointing to his displays. While they had spoken, several of the F-2 squadrons had already passed by, engaging the Tiger squadrons. The other squadrons completely encircling the rest of the fleet in a protective swarm. The quick strike vessels moving past the fleet, took up positions ahead of the Ratronians.

"I think I would have rather gone with Rick," Dakota complained. Launching anything or trying to put up any kind of a fight now would be unwise. He couldn't even escape in the Interceptors. There were just too many of them. His only recourse was to remain in position and on course with the rest of the fleet.

"Sir, I'm getting a signal," Lieutenant Navall announced, turning to the exec.

"From?"

"Sounds like a fleet wide transmission from the Colonian High Command." Tiana and Dakota looked over at Talia. "I'll put it on audio."

"Colonel Barker hasn't contacted them," Talia responded grimly. "They're starting their search for her."

"Attention Carolon personnel. Colonel Barker, respond immediately."

The group listened for several minutes as the Colonian com officer repeated the order several times, but was met with silence.

"It could get a little ugly if they don't get some kind of a response," Talia commented wondering if anyone was going to do anything. Tiana nudged Captain Abrams with her elbow and he finally stepped over to Lieutenant Navall.

"Open a channel."

"Open, sir."

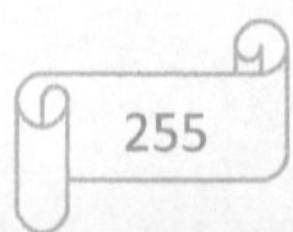

Dakota was hoping it would have taken a little longer to figure out the com line, but Navall was superb at her job. He hesitated a moment, then spoke.

"Colonia Command, this is Captain Abrams of the Royal Kalamarion Starbird *Constellation*. Colonel Barker is not with us. She and our commander became separated from our departure on Carolon while escaping the Albions."

Judicious language wasn't Dakota's strong suit, he only hoped it would be convincing. The transmission was quiet for a couple of minutes, then Pip detected movement on his screens and looked outside.

"Captain, we've got company, perhaps the curious?"

The speaker came alive again as several F-2s pulled in close, alongside the Starbird.

"*Constellation*, you will surrender immediately or be destroyed. Any aggressive action you take will bring about your immediate destruction."

"Or not," Tiana complained.

"Haven't we heard this somewhere before?" Dakota asked, casting a suspicious look over at Talia.

"Standard intimidation response to get you and the escort on the ground in one piece, but I'd say you've got more muscle here than you did back on Carolon," Talia responded in a matter a fact tone. Dakota motioned for Lana to mute the transmission.

"Pip, ship status?"

"Primary weapons batteries at 18%. Shield strength at 23%, sub-light power at 80%, no light speed available. Not enough to effectively out run them, or out gun them in a prolonged firefight."

Dakota looked over at Tiana, who returned the look. While she appreciated that he was trying to include her in this process, technically she wasn't military and he was still the executive officer in command.

"Well?"

"What would Gunnar do?" she responded.

Dakota understood where Tiana was trying to lead him. When in doubt, what would your last line of authority have you do? However, there were other variables to be considered. He finally motioned for Lieutenant Navall to open the channel back up.

"This is Captain Abrams; we'll follow you down. Can I get assurances we'll receive good treatment of our crew?"

"Granted," came the immediate response from the controller.

"Follow them down, helm," Dakota ordered, turning to the pilot.

"You understand there are no guarantees here," Talia informed him, understanding how the whole process worked. Dakota understood, but knew there wasn't any other choice. Talia did offer something of an idea that might prove useful, motioning Tiana and Dakota over to the command chair.

*   *   *   *

The thin Tintee air screamed with the sounds of every engine noise imaginable as the Carolon fleet took turns landing on separate pads on the Gercor flats. The whole mountain side seemed to tremble as the *Trax* moved into position and anchored to an airborne mooring station close by. With the exception of a couple of other cruisers and a lone frigate hovering at airborne moorings, the *Trax* dwarfed everything else there. Several F-2s circled lazily overhead as Lieutenant Starman brought the *Constellation* gently to rest below the floating *Trax* on a marked landing pad, its bridge windows going dark in the bright sunlight. Several assault tanks took up positions around the strange Kalamarion craft as its engines shut down. Queen Benetar watched curiously from inside her hovering armored transport as ground troops quickly surrounded the white vessel, creating a wide perimeter just inside the circle of assault tanks. There was no movement or indication from the ship, but the troops kept their weapons at the ready all the same, waiting for a hatch to open.

After waiting for some time, Queen Benetar became impatient and ordered the hatch removed from the craft. Several higher ranking ground officers examined it closely and ordered in an engineering crew to perform the operation. After several failed attempts and ruined extractor kits, it became obvious it would require something a little more substantial. As they moved away from the hull to make their reports, a few of the troops took notice of a dull hum starting to issue from inside the back of the ship and suddenly its powerful shields came online, making entry impossible now. The Colonian Queen frowned, realizing what had happened.

"It appears our new friends are a little shy. Have you scanned it?"

"Yes, Highness." One of her aides passed her a large hand display. "We can't tell for sure, but it looks like there's no one onboard. Looks like an automated drone or something."

"Is there more detail than this?"

"No, Highness, the shields came on before we could finish our scans. We can't penetrate this shield technology."

"See if the ship can be towed and brought into the Alpha decks where we can do something with it." She then turned to another officer standing close by. "Have you located Colonel Barker or her support staff yet?"

"No, Highness. Her assigned ship is not here. The *Rex* over there," he said, pointing to one of the smaller transports, "shows its manifest had her personal aide onboard, but she has not been located yet. We're starting an extensive search of all the ships as we speak. It was reported that Colonel Barker had been cut off from the rest of the fleet and was being pursued by the Albions."

"Sounds convenient," the Queen responded, still eyeing the glowing Kalamarion Starbird. "She has probably rejoined that treacherous herd of Albions she came from, but she'll not get off that easy." The Queen turned and looked up at the underside of the massive cruiser above them. "Send Admiral Motti's 5th fleet to find her. I don't care if they have to march up to KC Barton's door step. Just bring her to me, and I need Barker's command staff in my throne room within the hour." She motioned for her driver to depart, but kept her gaze on the Starbird until she was out of sight.

*   *   *   *

The Gercor flats are a wide expanse of nothing but flat ancient sea bed. Its hard packed clay surface, almost as hard as rock, is able to withstand the heavy beating of massive ship traffic constantly landing on its surface. These flats stretch out for miles in all directions from the base of the city, finally breaking up into low lying hills and gullies. Here, the climate begins to change as sub-water percolates near the surface, nourishing the vegetation into a hot and humid tropical landscape.

Standing upright, indigenous animals called Kilars are generally contented to graze lazily through fern forests. Having no lips, they just use their straight human-like teeth to grind down their food. Their leathery skin is translucent, allowing some light to pass through, revealing their organs and skeletal structures. Their eye lids slide sideways and their pupils reflect any light entering the retina, creating glowing orbs. Adding to their ghastly appearance, only some thin strings of hair grow from the back of the head and down along the spine.

At the top of the food chain in these hot tropical forests, Kilars didn't mind the heat at all, in fact, the hotter the better. They didn't like precipitation of any kind and went to great lengths to seek shelter wherever available when the rains came.

Most of the time it came in heavy downpours, sometimes lasting for days. This made it harder for them to forage for food, but being almost human-like, they did have upper cognitive functions allowing them to problem solve to a certain extent. Exceptionally playful creatures among their own kind, they become fiercely territorial if an intruder crosses into their boundaries, working in packs to drive the invader from their territory, usually by killing.

Munching quietly near a large clearing at the edge of the forest, a Kilar's acute hearing picked up a disturbance directly behind it. Without moving its shoulders, its head turned completely around. Cautiously peering around its dinner, the humanoid creature zeroed in on sounds coming from the clearing, images of humans materializing out of nowhere. Letting out a short burst of ultra-low pitched burps, the alert was sent out to the others directly around it. In the clearing, more humans appeared, the count reaching over a dozen.

Captain Abrams pulled Talia, Tiana and Willis to one side.

"Uhm, that had weirdness written all over it," Willis commented, looking at her hands to make sure she was all there. This was her first experience with teleportation and the sensation was quite frightening.

"Glad to see you, Miss Ruston," Dakota smiled, scooting a little closer to her.

"So what just happened? How did I get from the *Rex* to here with you guys?" She had a mixed expression of fright and bewilderment. "Am I dreaming?"

"I think they call it, Teleportation?" Talia asked, trying to help her friend comprehend the experience. "I'm certainly glad they know how to do it. And why are we standing in a Kilar forest? This is about the worse place on the planet we could be."

"Time was short," Tiana piped up. "You'd rather be on one of the other ships?"

"Any place is better than here."

"Hey," Dakota cut sharply. "I got us off the ship and the shields are up. Against my better judgment I might add, so now what?" He was busy trying to shove the security control back into his holster belt.

Talia was far more concerned with their surroundings right now than explaining why being off the ship was better than being on it. When she had suggested they find a way off the ship to some kind of a hiding place, she wasn't sure what she had in mind, but this wasn't it. Her cause for concern was quite evident, as a shrill chirping began to issue from the surrounding forest.

"First priority is to get out of here as fast as possible. This is not a very good place to be. Why did you send us here?"

"Excuse me," Dakota retorted in a hush. "I picked the first place that had any cover. Have you seen what surrounds your city out there?" Dakota was pointing in the direction of the vast openness that was the Gercor flats. "I think it would have been a little obvious if we would have teleported out in the middle of that."

Tiana finally stepped in as Talia started to rev up a little more.

"Ok, you two. It sounds like we have a problem and we're not getting anywhere arguing about it. Talia, the Captain picked the closest place he could with the time and information available. Dakota, there is obviously a problem here that we need to deal with. Talia, speak."

"The short version, there are nasty creatures in these forests that would just as soon have us for an afternoon snack if we don't get moving." Talia looked all around their surroundings, detecting movement in the under growth. "Kilars."

"What, is that some kind of a man eating beast or something?" Dakota asked, pulling one of his blasters from its holster.

"Move your crew as quickly and as quietly as you can in that direction, out of the forest, go!"

Dakota didn't quite get what all the fuss was about and was still trying to understand as Tiana and Taron started out with the rest of the crew. Talia and Willis tugged at Dakota's arm, beckoning him to make a hasty retreat, but he seemed more interested in what was out there that could create such a scare. It didn't take long before he figured out that running face forward was the better option.

The Kilars were fast, frighteningly fast. How can something that appears to have no muscle support move with such speed? Dakota went down several times as he ran after the others, tripping on thrown objects. Fruit or improvised spears would entangle his legs and feet. Each time he would fall, he was quick back to his feet and firing his weapon. The weapons discharges seemed to slow the skeletal creatures, but moments later they'd be right back on his heels.

Talia came to a halt at the edge of the forest, ducking behind some large rocks, followed by the rest of the crew. She could tell the Kalamarion Captain was approaching, as there was fruit landing all around them, along with an occasional rock and a few sticks. She could also hear his weapon discharging occasionally. Then he came, his blaster pointed behind him as he ran. Dakota dove over the top of the rocks, landing just beyond Talia and

Willis, but was up with both his pistols pointing over the rock in an instant. There was a peculiar look of frustration, fear and mixed admiration etched on his face. He passed a glance over at Talia and Willis as they both pulled their pistols and started to fire. Keeping the endless stream of Kilars from reaching their stronghold behind the cluster of rocks was starting to prove difficult. Hayden and Logan joined the others with their pistols to bear, leaving Tiana and Taron to keep the rest corralled, but Kilar herds could be enormous and could easily outlast the amount of available power in their blaster cartridges.

"Didn't believe me, did you?" Talia popped off a couple of shots, passing a glance over Willis at Dakota.

"In a word, no!"

"There are plenty of women on your crew," Willis piped up. "Why would you ever doubt any of them?"

"Fighter pilot mentality!"

"Oh yeah," both women responded in unison.

"We know all about that," Willis finished.

"Talia, we need an out!" Dakota called without looking behind him. "Take Mantose and Dalley with you and find it!"

Talia quickly scanned the area behind them, motioning the other two to follow her. The rest of the crew understood what needed to happen here as they crouched down as best they could to keep under cover and watch their flanks. While intelligent, Kilars didn't have a mind for strategy, so it was unlikely they would try and out flank the group, but the possibility did exist. Tiana, Logan and Talia took off, keeping low as they scampered around several piles of rock and low hills making up the edge of the Gercor flats. In the far distance, across the flat, they could make out the enormous shape of the *Trax* still moored. It was a long way back to Tintee and it wasn't possible for them to cross the flat on foot undetected.

Because of the enormous size of the flat, it had great strategic value as you could see any ground assault coming from any direction. Regular Colonian patrols swept the perimeter constantly and the little fire fight playing out had already caught the notice of a patrol of two assault tanks, moving in their direction.

"They must have picked up our little skirmish," Tiana surmised, lying low at the top of a small rise.

"I think that's a pretty good bet, but that'll be our out," Talia announced. "We just have to figure out how to get them out and us in."

"I could step out there, get their attention and when they're taking me into custody, I could create a diversion that would get them outside." Tiana's plan was brave to be sure, but it had little substance and she had no experience.

"What kind of a diversion do you have in mind?" Logan asked skeptical. Tiana was busy unbuttoning her uniform top. Talia grinned broadly, realizing what she was thinking.

"That will certainly get their attention. Chances are they're not bothering with heat sensors to see what's going on out here, too hot. Maybe I better be the one to do it."

Logan reached over and stopped Talia and Tiana before they got too far.

"Uhm, not to be a male chauvinist, but I think this is a dumb plan. I have a better one," Logan interjected.

"You're not going to take your shirt off are you?" Talia asked, snickering. Logan chose not to be insulted.

"How about if I stun them and we get them out that way?"

Both women turned to the Interceptor pilot at the same time.

"You want to stun them..." Talia repeated coldly, positive he couldn't make good on such a claim.

"Beats what you ladies have in mind," he replied, handing Tiana his blaster and fumbling with something else on his holster belt. He finally pulled out what looked like a tuning fork with a wooden handle. Both women looked at it, wondering if this was his great weapon of choice? This was how he was going to "stun" these heavily armored Colonian assault tanks? They watched as he pulled a couple of exhausted blaster power packs from his belt and handed them to Talia.

"What are these for?"

"Incendiary grenades."

"These aren't grenades."

Logan gave her an odd look, hoping she would have figured out his plan.

"I know that and you know that, but do you think the crews in those two tanks are going to know that?"

Ok, it made sense to her now.

"Two sink holes coming up," he said, pointing the device at a spot in front of the approaching tanks.

"What is that thing, some kind of a laser shooter?"

"It's called a Hozan. It's a sonic extender. Projects my brain waves in the form of sonic waves."

Talia passed a look at Tiana who only shrugged. How were sonic waves going to produce his intended results? Whatever it was going to do, they needed to be ready. Talia handed Tiana one of the power packs and waited.

As the approaching tanks rumbled around several rock formations and a small hill of dirt, there was a sudden shudder in the ground and a huge plume of dirt and dust erupted directly in their path, the ground abruptly opening up in front of them. The tanks were moving too fast to stop or avoid the large hole and both armored vehicles dropped completely out of sight. Only the top hatch and their violently swaying whip antennas were visible. Both women were sprinting to the hole the moment the tanks dropped. The top hatches finally came open and the commander of each tank appeared, they were instantly blasted as the two women scrambled onto the turret, dropped their power packs in the opening and reclosing each hatch, then jumped back and waited. It didn't take long before crewman started tumbling out of every hatchway available to escape the perceived explosive devices that would surely have gutted each vehicle. There were a few tense seconds where crew were scrambling for their own weapons, but Talia and Tiana were quick to dispatch them before they had a chance to get off a shot.

"I'm assuming you can use that thing to get these out, right?" Tiana asked, looking at the hole the two tanks were sitting in.

"No problem. You ever drive one of these?" Logan asked, passing Talia a confident look. He framed the tanks with his fingers, sizing up the correct angle to cut an escape ramp from the hole.

"Plenty of times. I'll be glad to give you a crash course in tank operations. Just get me a way out." Talia said, climbing back into one of the idling tanks.

*   *   *   *

Dakota was about to call another retreat when the Kilar attack abruptly ended, a low rumble quaking the ground. The crew ducked for cover as two armored Colonian assault tanks skidded to a stop between the Kilar herd and the defending crew. One turret swung in the direction of the Kilars, while the other spun around and pointed right at the frightened crew. They waited for it to open fire, but the fire came from the first tank as it opened up on the scattering Kilars. Then, a familiar head popped out of an open hatchway, smiling at a relieved Captain Abrams.

"Need a ride mister?" Tiana asked confidently.

"Going my way?" Dakota asked, scrambling out from behind their cover. "We need a little help here. Sindee's been hurt bad."

"What happened?"

"She caught a rock to the head from our friends out there."

Dakota turned back to help Fuji and Hayden carry the mortally wounded nurse into the back of the tank. As the rest of the crew split up and clamored inside the tanks, Talia kept her guns trained on the Kilars still determined to get at their quarry. Finally loaded and hatches secured, the second tank turned its laser turret and started blasting, scattering the rest of the attacking herd.

*   *   *   *

Commander SoKnack had his arms folded, gazing sternly down at the empty tracking screen, his battlecruiser hovering menacingly over the dark sphere of Reako. Brought back to attention by the summons of a communications officer and a nearby scanner technician, he turned and approached the tech at his station.

"Sir, I've got an unidentifiable ship passing through the outer rim of this system," the young officer informed his superior.

Dalton looked down at the tracking screen.

"Unidentifiable? Can you provide any technical data? Does it have a transponder code?"

"No data signature, sir, but I think I can get you some technical data based on our scanning returns." The young technician turned back to his workstation and started working to acquire the information. "It's certainly not Colonian and definitely not one of ours. Perhaps it's Ratronian or Tomplie?"

Dalton turned to the communications officer while the scanning tech continued his work.

"Yes, what is it?" he asked, rubbing tired eyes.

"Report from the *Ranger,* sir. They experienced heavy losses in Tintee airspace. The Colonians got to the Carolon fleet before Commander Shipley could overtake them. There was a report of two alien ships in their numbers. One turned back and fought its way straight through the Ratronian defenses, heading straight back towards this system, presumably to Carolon. Curiously, our ground forces and the support ships in orbit haven't tracked it there yet. Commander Shipley was able to get some partial data on the alien ship."

Dalton looked back at the scanning tech.

"Put them both up." He turned to a larger screen and watched two images appear. Raising an eyebrow, he compared the two. "Have the Hesson engineers run an eval on this yet?"

"No, sir, you're seeing it as it's coming in."

Dalton studied the scans closely. There were no recognizable features, other than what was obvious; guns pods on the front and back, bridge pod and tail section.

"Send it down to them and have them get as much information out of these as they can." Dalton turned for the

264

stairs that would take him to the command deck above. "And keep me informed on that ship."

The Queen Captain slowly turned as Dalton approached.

"Commander SoKnack, is my ship ready?"

"Yes, QC, both of them," the battlecruiser commander acknowledged quickly, coming to a halt in front of her. "All ready to go on A deck. We're also getting reports back from the *Maxell's* support ship, the *Ranger*. The Carolon fleet made it to Colonian airspace before they could be intercepted." Dalton hesitated, reading the displeased look on QC Blair's face, but continued. "Reports coming in of two smaller alien starships guarding their flanks. One of the ships turned on Shipley's Dreadnaught and fought its way through the entire fleet, heading back toward Carolon, but it happened so fast that no ships were able to pursue. We think we've picked up that same vessel passing through this system. The other ship landed on Tintee with the rest of the Carolon fleet."

Drax's displeasure abruptly shifted to interest and she started for the stairs and the control pits below.

"Show me," she barked, descending the circular staircase.

Dalton and BachTL stepped quickly, trying to keep up as they made their way to the sensor array station. The immense console was covered with monitors displaying a dizzying array of information and images. Waiting patiently, BachTL moved beside Drax to get a look at what little information there was available and caught the expression on Drax's face. He knew this look, having seen it several times. It would manifest itself when she wanted something or thought it could be a means to move her further up the ladder of success. There was a certain gleam in her eye now, signaling an obsession. Perhaps this would be just the thing to divert her attention away from CJ Barker as he felt like the energy they were expending to capture one person was a little lopsided.

She had been seeking something that would give her the edge against the Colonian Empire, but thus far, she had been matched, man for man, weapon for weapon and ship for ship. If any of the specs on this ship were accurate, it could shift the tide in her favor. Even if they couldn't take it, if they could just get close enough to it, they could scan it in more detail, and perhaps replicate its design.

Drax wasn't about to give up on the hunt for Colonel Barker, however. She had a vast arsenal of ideas and assets at her command and wasn't afraid to call in any of them on a whim. She thought about just sending the *Tarzana* after the alien ship, but then thought better of the idea. Dalton didn't hold her confidence and would likely bungle the operation, ending up with nothing to show for it. She could take command of the operation herself and give pursuit to the ship, but she knew Dalton couldn't handle giving further chase to Colonel Barker either. Thinking a moment, she noticed BachTL looking at her and returned the look with a glance. It was time to take a gamble and use those around her to bring about her designs. If she were successful, not only would she gain a powerful tactical advantage over the Colonian empire and her rivals, but also make great strides to gain favor with the King Commander. She turned to the opposite side of the control pit, stepping over to a communications officer, leaving Dalton and BachTL still looking at the readouts of the alien craft.

"Contact Albia Command and have them locate Blinda Koss. I want her here as soon as possible."

The entire bridge within ear shot, went silent, even the equipment seemed to tone down. The sound of the Queen Captain's boots echoed loudly as she stepped back over to the sensor control station.

"Drax," BachTL whispered, leaning in her direction. "Why are you sending for her?"

Drax didn't move, but shifted her eyes slightly in the aide's direction. Most of the information available on the alien craft was now being displayed with only minimal detail. They were going to have to get a lot closer to it to get anything more.

"Am I going to have to answer to you for everything I do? Who is in command here?" Her voice sounded just irritated enough for BachTL to get the warning.

"You are, of course. My apologies, QC." BachTL gave a humble sigh.

"I sometimes wonder. However, since you asked the question and I'm in a good mood now, despite the apparent failures I am constantly surrounded with, I'll tell you both what I have in mind." She pointed at the images of the ship on the screen. "Have a look at the available specs on this ship. It's far more advanced than anything we or anyone else has. Makes me wonder what our friends on Cross are up to and why Administrator Diord hasn't offered this design to Albia. Even if a tenth of this is accurate, it will out maneuver and out gun anything comparable in Hadrian. We need to get close enough to it to not only improve our technical readouts, but perhaps board it and take it. Blinda is the only one who can provide that means." Drax directed her last comment over BachTL's shoulder at the commander of the *Tarzana*. Yes, this was a direct slap in the face to Commander SoKnack.

"Now you," she said, toning down and directing her attention solely at her personal aide. "I want you to take MS One to Tintee and retrieve the other ship."

Panic instantly set in as the blood in BachTL's face drained to his sweating feet. Surely there were spies or mercenaries available for this kind of work. He had no stealth or covert training. He felt like he was barely adequate for the job of QC aide. Shuffling people, taking messages and getting her favorite drink was difficult enough, and while he was descent with small craft operations, stealing an entire ship was a little bit above his pay grade.

"You want me to do what?"

"I didn't stutter. What's the problem?"

"You want me to go to Tintee, alone? How am I supposed to take on the entire Colonian military to get to this ship, let alone steal it? Surely there are others more qualified?"

Drax motioned for her aide and the battlecruiser commander to follow her back up to the command platform. Dalton tried to remain in step with the other two, listening to what he thought was the craziest idea ever. He felt relieved he wasn't asked to provide another failure point as these assignments would be squarely on someone else's shoulders. He just wanted to make sure he was getting all the details so when everything came crashing down again, he would be able to remain well clear of the fall out.

"I feel certain you'll think of something. Not once have you ever let me down, not once."

"But getting you something to drink or the right cloak for the day is one thing. I don't have the resume for this?"

"You're Castellian and carry no Albion signatures. You can travel as a diplomatic courier, being well respected on all fronts. You can move nearly unrestricted in most areas that require a high security clearance. You're perfect for the job."

"But I want to be here to help you with CJ," he objected.

"I share your devotion to CJ. You feel indebted to her as you do me. But I don't need your help to retrieve the likes of CJ Barker."

Dalton rolled his eyes. He would have been ejected alive into space if he had even made a hint of this kind of a response to an assignment. Sure, what the Queen Captain was ordering was impossible, but why would you argue with it? Drax stopped and turning, put a hand to the Albion aide's shoulder.

"There are few people I trust to get this job done right. I'm sending Blinda and Commander SoKnack after this ship, I'm going after CJ and I need you to go after that other ship. At the very least, you need to lay your hands on the tactical specs. If you can make this happen, there won't be any more QC aide. I'll make sure you get something a little more fitting. Maybe a battlecruiser," she said, shifting her eyes over her shoulder toward Dalton.

BachTL didn't want a battlecruiser. He was content to be where he was, where he felt the safest. Seeing there was no way he was going to talk his way out of it, BachTL finally accepted the assignment. This isn't what he signed up for at all. He had little to no military training, only political etiquette and protocol. He was a Castellian attaché and knew how to handle people, not steal military secrets, least of all starships.

"Now, off you go, and be careful."

Dalton smirked slightly, watching a humbled BachTL start for the launching bays, but instantly straightened up when the QC turned to him.

"You, listen and learn from Blinda," she said, pointing a threatening finger at him. "And don't piss her off."

With that, she turned and headed for an elevator that would take her to the launching bays and her waiting ship. Accompanied by a couple of AP-10s and four Black Tigers, she launched her Metro Star II as the *Tarzana* made a wide, graceful arc away from the dark surface of Reako, heading off into open space.

Upside-down water

The cockpit of the F-2 remained relatively dark, continuing to sink into the depths of the bottomless pond. The ship's navigational beacons had been turned back on to provide some small measure of outside lighting without drawing attention to themselves from above or the surrounding water. There was no telling if anything living was lurking in these dark waters. One had to think there was.

Only a few internal auxiliary work lights shown down on the consoles and instrumentation of the fighter as it continued to sink in the warm, dark water. Gunnar knelt close to Alex 7001, working on the failed deflector shield circuits.

"Do you really think you can make these rechargers work more efficiently?"

"The chargers I can certainly do something with, sir," Alex replied. "I can even design some new shield arrays that will work far better than what they have now, but not without spare parts to work with."

"Sorry buddy, I'm fresh out. By the way, nice work on the new shield designs for the ship. Integrating the array sensors into the skin instead of external antennas, stroke of genius."

"Thank you, sir. My observations of our difficulties when we came out of space dock sort of pointed that weakness out."

"It's a good design. Can't wait to see it for real." Gunnar passed a glance forward at CJ sitting in the pilot's seat. "How long have we been sinking? I would have thought we would have hit bottom by now."

"My sensors indicate we've been descending for well over eight hours at a little over a hundred meters per minute."

"Do the math," Gunnar commented in jest.

"That would be roughly..."

"It was a joke, Alex, I get the picture."

"Here is something I haven't been able to calculate, sir. At well over twenty-seven thousand feet, the pressure on this hull ought to be causing some serious stress and while this ship appears to be designed to take this kind of stress, there is no more pressure at this depth as there is at the surface."

"Equal pressure?" Gunnar asked wide eyed. "How does that make any sense? What I don't understand is why we didn't just shift into light speed before we even got here?"

"You have to be at a certain calculated position in space in order to make a Quadra-light jump, the Hadrian version of light speed," Alex informed his commander. "Their technology isn't advanced enough to allow them to do light speed maneuvers while in flight like we do. Everything is point to point. A waypoint is a required calculated starting point. You have to reach that waypoint before you can make a jump. You can jump anytime within a certain calculated window after the waypoint is reached."

"Sounds like a whole bunch of math to me."

"It would explain why they have so much space and energy dedicated to their navigational systems on their ships," Alex said.

Gunnar let out a big sigh and turned to the copilot's chair. Sitting down, he looked over at CJ sitting in the pilot's chair staring out into the darkness. He was sure she had noticed him, but could tell she was deep in thought. Probably still a little upset with him.

"Do you think we can reach Tintee in this thing if we can get off this planet?" he asked quietly.

CJ shifted stiffly in her seat, turning to Gunnar.

"Do you really think we'd be any better off on Tintee?"

"That is your home world isn't it?"

"Not even," CJ responded instantly. "I'm from Albia."

Gunnar twisted a surprised look.

"Am I missing something here?" He finally blurted out.

CJ got a chuckle out of the confused look scrambling around his face. She developed a fond look recounting her childhood on Albia, but the expression slowly faded as she remembered her all-girls academy.

"Drax Blair was very kind to me. I would get teased by the other kids all the time about my hair and freckles, but she wouldn't put up with any of it. I later learned after she broke up any encounters I'd have with the others, she would visit with them privately and if she couldn't convince them with words to stop and apologize, she would end up making them wish they had."

"Sounds like a real pal."

"Certainly she was back then. Everyone gets bullied in some form or another."

"Uhm," Gunnar hesitated, thinking of his own childhood and subsequent adolescence. "Not so much for me, in fact, I don't recall it ever happening to me." Smiling lightly, he motioned for her to continue with her story.

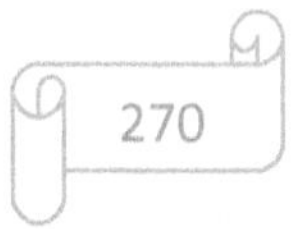

"Drax and I used to get into all kinds of trouble. Well, to be fair, Drax was usually the brain child behind all the mischief we'd get into. That mischief turned into vandalism, which then turned into downright illegal stuff. I'm not very proud of those younger years. They steered me into painful directions."

"What will you tell me?" Gunnar wanted to be understanding.

"Drax ended up getting me into the Albion academy for their military officers. To understand what comes next, you have to understand how this military works. It's more of what others might call a big organized gang or crime syndicate. While Albia has the biggest armies of all the rival governments, it isn't large enough to overcome the Colonian Empire all on its own. To get any rank in the Albion service, you have to make it happen, by any means possible and once you get there, you have to watch your back at all times or have others you trust doing it for you. I can tell you Drax has many who watch hers very closely. She is kind of high up the ranking ladder."

"How high?"

"She is a Queen Captain. A step below a King Commander."

"So she's almost to the top."

"Well, yes and no. There are many Queen Captains and King Captains in the Albion military. The differences are obvious, but any one of them could, if they wanted to, figure out a way to unseat the King Commander and take over the entire military and government."

"So I take it your friend Drax has risen in the ranks the same way?"

CJ nodded slightly thinking about the things that had to be done in order to make that happen.

"The things she did, just to make rank are unspeakable."

"So what about you?" Gunnar asked. "Did you have to do the same things to make rank?"

"It's not something I like to talk about," she finally admitted humbly, bowing her head. "But yes, I did things to gain favor." While it was true that many of her promotions were under the wing of Drax, CJ wasn't innocent of her own destiny.

"What kind of things?"

"You create situations where you know people will be harmed or killed, or you send others to take care of business. I really don't want to talk about this anymore," CJ finally said, trying to end the conversation.

"Ok, so how in the world did you end up in the Colonian military? Are you a plant for the Albions, or this Drax Blair?"

"No, I'm here of my own volition. I ran over a lot of good people rising in the ranks."

"They're that bad?" Gunnar didn't want to believe she could possibly be any kind of a monster.

"Yes, they're that bad," she reinforced. Still not wanting to discuss this any further, CJ cringed, thinking about some of the things she did.

"I was first officer onboard a fleet Corvette. A ship called the *Meade*. Her Captain was actually a decent fellow as Albions go, a Captain Dickerson. He wasn't without his flaws to be sure and he was no different in how he rose in the ranks than any of the rest of us, but to get power, you have to be willing to use it. I arranged to have him get stuck in an Isom venting shaft, working on a couple of plasma inductors."

"Don't you have engineers for that kind of a job?"

"Certainly we do, but that's what I meant by *arrange*. He liked to work on stuff like that anyway." CJ fell silent. "Where was I?"

"The demise of your Captain."

"Oh yes, thank you. Spent Isom overrun, that's burnt fuel that can't be used for anything else, vents directly to the outside of the ship. Normally there are fail safes in place to prevent someone from getting blown out during maintenance, but I ordered the fail safes into bypass mode and then, while no one was looking, I opened the vent and jettisoned a burst of Isom. I'm not even sure his body made it out of the vent before it vaporized."

CJ fell silent again, as did Gunnar. Even with minimal light in the cockpit, he could see she was having difficulty recounting the experience. He passed her a glance as she burst into tears.

"He was a family man," she finally choked out. "He had two boys and a girl, and I felt nothing for his wife and children. Drax swept the investigation under the carpet and promoted me to ship's Captain. I treated a human being like a speed bump and patted myself on the back for my ingenuity."

No amount of consoling on Gunnar's part could quell the guilt permeating CJ's conscience. But something wasn't adding up. If she was indeed this monster, it didn't explain the woman softly sobbing in the seat next to him and certainly didn't explain what she was doing as a high ranking officer in the Colonian military.

"I think of those children and..."

"Ok," he stopped her abruptly. "I get the picture. Stop beating yourself up. You obviously feel bad about it."

"Feel bad?" she instantly turned to him, her face wet with tears. "Feel bad?" she repeated angrily now, the raw nerves inflaming. "How about tormented? Tortured! Every day I see these clusters on my collar and shoulders I'm reminded of what I've done!"

"But that's Colonian hardware, Colonel," Gunnar pointed out defensively.

"In my instance, it doesn't matter," she rasped.

"So how did you end up with the Colonian Empire if the Albions hate them so much?"

"It's not that the Albions hate the Colonians. The Queen isn't a Blood Heir and under intergalactic Hadrian law, she can lay no claim to the throne. Even so, corrupt as they are, Colonian society does have principles and life respecting rules they try to adhere to and I value that over what I had become. Achieving rank of Colonel with the Albions was the last straw for me, so I took my ship and its crew, surrendered it and myself to the Colonian High Command, under condition I remain as I am and be given a post of importance. Now I'm being pursued by both. I go back to Tintee and I'm a dead woman. I left my post without the consent of the High Command. That, under Colonian law, constitutes treason, punishable by death. Drax just wants me back with her so she can continue her rise to power with me at her side, but I would rather rot or be buried in this planet. The way I feel right now, if I never come to the surface again, I'm fine with that."

"Well, I'm not fine with it. I have a ship and crew that don't belong with your Colonian military and in the wrong hands it could be perverted into a dreadful weapon."

CJ had a hard time caring. At the moment, she wished the cockpit would flood.

"They'll be just fine, under arrest, but fine."

"How so?"

"They will probably be associated with me and my staff and so they'll be held as coconspirators until I am put on trial and can convince the Queen you had nothing to do with what happened on Carolon. Your ship, on the other hand, will be of great interest to them."

"Do you think they will try to tear it apart?"

"It's difficult to say for sure. The Queen is becoming increasingly desperate to throw down the Albion insurrection and if the other factions of the Ratrons and the Tomplie have made a pack to join against the Empire, then Colonia stands a good chance of falling if a new weapon cannot be found. Your Starbirds may be just the ticket she's looking for and if she is able to gain access to them, she is liable to hold your crew indefinitely and just take your ships."

"Well, that's not likely," Gunnar responded confidently. "I doubt the Empire could get past our shields."

"Let's just hope they can't figure out a way around them." CJ stopped short and looked around. She could see the outside walls of the shaft.

Gunnar noticed the light growing and looked down through the helo glass at his feet, looking at the source of light beneath them. CJ looked down as well, but only shrugged as she turned to Gunnar for some kind of explanation.

"Well of all the crazy things," he remarked slowly, strapping himself in. "Better fire this thing up," he suggested, reaching for several controls. CJ was about to question him further, but hit the master switches anyway, working to get her ship operational.

"Maneuvering thruster igniters are right there," CJ pointed to three lighted buttons and a colored knob as the instruments came alive.

"You guys really need to update your control systems in these things," Gunnar complained, punching all three buttons. The light outside continued to grow, as if they were on the surface during a sunrise. "You strapped in?" He asked, switching on the scanner in front of him.

"We didn't sink all the way to the other side of the planet did we?"

"I don't think so, it would have taken longer," he replied, looking out to see a rising waterline. Their stomachs suddenly leapt to the ceiling of the cockpit as the fighter began to free fall.

CJ responded, instantly applying full power to the maneuvering thrusters and guiding the fighter into a power glide over what appeared to be a deep canyon. Gunnar reached over and activated the landing gear controls as CJ guided the F-2 toward a level sand bar in the middle of what looked like a dry river bed. As the fighter's wings shifted into their landing mode, the craft set softly down on its landing gear and sank lightly into the loose sand. CJ shut the igniters down, dousing the maneuvering thrusters and the cockpit went quiet again.

Unbuckling, they looked up through the overhead windows at the ceiling of a gargantuan cavern. It was light as daylight outside, but they could see no sun as they were in a cave, or were they? Gunnar gave CJ a quick look, but she only shrugged, having no idea. Her only experience with this planet was sending probes down these holes, but that never produced any results.

"Gotta tell ya girlfriend, this has got to be the weirdest planet I have ever been on, or in, as the case may be." He strained to look all around and then back up at the ceiling of the cavern. "What gets me is, how come all that water doesn't come wailin' down on us? Why does it stay at the ceiling in those holes?"

The question was more to himself than CJ. She noticed Alex hovering about the cockpit, trying to get a lay of the land. As they stepped about inside, they detected movement on both sides of the dry river bank and even a flash of some kind of furry figure dashing across the river bed to the thick foliage on either side.

"Alex, can you tell what we're dealing with out there?" Gunnar asked, growing more concerned. This ship was having enough problems without something tearing it apart.

"Breathable atmosphere, if that's what you're asking. But there's a lot of animal life out there and my sensors indicate they are agitated about something."

"Would we be better off moving this bucket somewhere else?"

"I'm picking up similar life forms all up and down this river bed for as far as my sensors will reach."

"Better think of something fast then," CJ announced, watching several of the wooly creatures appear from the cover of foliage.

"Are they intelligent?"

"Do they look intelligent to you?" CJ asked sarcastic.

"Brain scans indicate a limited, simple mind, but higher than animal life, though certainly not humanoid," Alex responded. Gunnar looked over at CJ.

"I would have thought you might have known what they were all about."

"Never been down here, remember the whole lost probe thing?"

"Well, we've got to figure something out, because we have to get outside long enough for Alex to make repairs to that flow coupling." Gunnar watched the strange animals move around outside. "Do you think some well-placed blaster shots would do the trick?"

"Sudden noises and flashing lights typically startle lower forms," Alex commented.

Gunnar pulled his blaster from his thigh holster and stepped to the back door, CJ right behind him with her blaster at the ready.

"Are you ready to start working on this, Alex?" Gunnar asked, reaching for the hatch activator.

"I think it would be more advisable if I were to wait inside until you have cleared out all the indigenous life forms before I try something so delicate."

Gunnar passed a smile and winked back at CJ.

"What he's really saying is... he's scared."

"Yeah, I sort of got that too," CJ agreed.

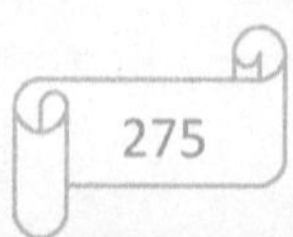

"Just stay put tender foot," he said, looking back at the droid. "The Colonel and I will handle this." Gunnar then gave CJ a quick once over. "Are you sure you're up for this?"

"As long as we don't start doing power aerobics, I should be fine."

"I'll be sure to warn you before it comes to that,"

As he activated the hatch, they stepped cautiously out, the air hitting them like a brick wall. It was warm and heavy with humidity. No wonder the foliage seemed to grow everywhere. What they weren't sure of yet, was where the illumination was coming from, or the oxygen atmosphere. Stepping out, he put his foot up on the barrel of the laser cannon and scanned the edges of the F-2, his finger on the trigger of his pistol. CJ stuck close behind him, nearly knocking him off balance as she pressed her back to his. A sound from under the left wing tip drew their attention and both turned to the source of the noise. A large furry head appeared from under the wing and snarled viciously at the two officers.

"And these guys would be called?" Gunnar asked.

"You're asking me? Call 'em Bud if you want," CJ responded, feeling a chill of fear streak up her back while pointing her weapon at the animal.

Gunnar actually cringed slightly hearing that name he hated so much. *Where in the world did she get that from?* Several more of the animals appeared next to the first and then more crept from under the right wing. These strange animals were small in stature, standing upright might have stretched them to four feet tall. They came in various colors of thick neatly combed fur. Their large ears flipped randomly about the top of their heads, as if swatting at insects. As a couple of them began to cackle, their gleaming fangs became clearly visible. Gunnar and CJ fired into the air once or twice, but the noise only seemed to attract more of the strange animals. Turning their aim down, they fired directly in front of the beasts. This produced only marginal results as the animals continued to advance. CJ finally fired right at two ascending the wing of the Flightstreak, hitting them between the eyes. The creatures let out a miserable wail and slumped backwards, sliding back down the leading edge of the Delta wing and finally to the ground, leaving a trail of yellow brown fluid.

"What do you suppose they eat that they need teeth like that?" Gunnar asked, shuffling carefully backwards.

"Probably anything, especially if it has two legs, talks and flies around in a Flightstreak."

"What a diet, eh? Considering that, they should be half starved."

"More like all starved."

"I doubt there have been too many F-2s down here. They certainly don't seem too afraid of this blaster," Gunnar continued, blindly motioning CJ to move toward the hatch. "Probably best if we get back inside and move your ship to a different location," he spoke slowly. Gunnar fired his blaster at two of the beasts that had gotten too close. Both animals went down immediately, but a third leaped from the leading edge of the Delta wing toward Gunnar. He barely managed to shoot the beast before it landed on him knocking him back into CJ who was trying to back up into the rear hatch. The collision knocked her off balance and she tumbled over the side of the fuselage to the ground. Pushing the dead animal over the side with his foot, Gunnar turned to find CJ surrounded by snarling animals. She looked up at him, stunned at first, then fear gripped her as several of the animals began to paw at her. Gunnar took aim at one of the animals and pulled the trigger. He saw the blast find its mark and took aim at another but never got the shot off. A savage blow struck the side of his head and he felt himself falling. He didn't even feel it as he hit the sandy river bed below. As CJ's screams echoed through his ringing head, he heard the fighter's hatch close. Then his consciousness faded into oblivion.

You call this a weapon?

Rick rubbed his eyes, leaning against one of the science station consoles, listening to his science officer's report.

"I can't be sure if it's a freighter, a tanker or a frigate, sir." Toby continued adjusting his controls trying to get more information on the ship they were tracking. "We took a couple of good hits to our sensor arrays during our little scrimmage with the Ratronians and I haven't been able to get them to work any better since then. Not to mention there's so much interference and sub-space traffic in this system now. At this distance, I can't get a dimensional or anything readable." He tried adjusting his controls, but it was no use, most of what was coming back was unrecognizable.

"No telling what it is in this area now," Rick responded. He straightened up and stretched. "Whatever happened to the term, *clean takeover*?"

"Maybe we ought to steer in their direction, try to get a little closer, see if it looks like a friendly and ask if they've seen the ship we're looking for." Toby started working with his equipment again, but Rick stopped him.

"A friendly in this system? Don't bother. Consider it an unfriendly and move onto the next target profile." Rick let out a yawn and then shook it off. "I want to draw as little attention as possible. We'll hold our course for now." Rick looked back up at one of the displays at the science station, then stepped over to the navigator and gave her consoles a good looking over.

"Anyone know where Jayda is?"

"Engineering, sir." Toby reminded him. "You assigned her to help the engineers with the ball turret circuits and the Fulton drive. They'll be taking it offline shortly for repairs to the induction sequencers. It's in your report. Are you all right, sir?"

His memory jogged, Rick ignored the question.

"Two more planets to go. Are we even in the right system? Which one is Carolon anyway?"

Lisa Dayton pointed to one of the objects on the navigation screens between her and the navigator.

"Behind us, sir, we're traveling outbound of this system along a calculated trajectory based on CORA's recommendations."

"I think I need a nap," Rick said, blinking his eyes. "ETA to the next search grid?"

"Six hours, fifteen minutes," the navigator responded.

Rick's eyes almost stung. He sat down in his chair and closed them, listening to the casual chatter floating around the bridge. As his eyes became more comfortable, he cracked an eyelid, looking around as the bridge crew went about their duties.

"Gunnar," he whispered, resting his head in his hands. "Where are you?"

Letting his eyelid drop closed with the other one, he began to drift. As his mind floated through the nether regions of his subconscious, it wandered in and out of the odd places only the mind visits when asleep. After some travel through the dark regions of space, he found himself in orbit around a green blue colored planet, peering at the surface like a satellite. Taking special notice of a singular building located in a vast forested region on the planet, he zoomed his view closer to the pyramid shaped structure, and then instantly inside. A vast hall with great pillars supporting high, hidden ceilings opened up to him. He changed his view from above, to ground level, looking all around at its interior. A Travertine material lined most places, but dirt and grass, even boulders and some slender trees were spread out across the floor. It looked like they had been purposely landscaped and the floor built around them. Toward the center of the hall he found a smooth elevated space with a small stone bench structure. Sitting on it was a young woman, in her late teens to early twenties. Dressed in white with scarlet striping adorning her otherwise monochromatic clothing, she sat quietly, facing away from him. He stepped carefully around her on approach, taking note of her light, copper colored hair. Circling around to the front, he could see she had pulled her hair to one side of her neck, letting it stretch to her lap. Cradling something in her hands, her head was tipped downward as if in the attitude of prayer or a reverent meditation. Drawing closer, he detected her eyelashes move. She appeared to be looking at the objects in her hands. As he stopped directly in front of her, he could see a glow starting to emanate from the devices. His eyes drew back to her face as she slowly raised her eyes to his and smiled.

"Are you ready to begin?" she asked quietly.

Rick sat up with a start, blinking the blur from his eyes and looking around the bridge. The feeling of exhaustion had left him. The thoughts of his friend came back to mind as he rose and moved to the right of helm control. Watching the stars, his thoughts reached back to the oddness of the dream. He kept rolling it around in his head, trying to keep it fresh in his mind.

That wasn't too difficult, as the experience seemed to be so real. He was drawn to the thought that he needed to seek out this place and this person to find out what she was asking - *Ready to begin what?*

He turned toward Toby at the science station and looked at one of the overhead displays of the Nulark system. The science officer had made considerable headway with the telemetry stream they had acquired from some of the Colonian ships. Additional information about the planets associated with this system were now displayed in detail. The positions of the different ships the scanners were able to pick-up were even displayed in front of him. There were scores of ships in orbit around Carolon and several of the other planets whose orbits took them within close proximity to the recently overrun sphere. The next planet out from Carolon was Reako, a waterlogged quagmire showing little to no signs of life. The thick cloud layer prevented deep scans of its surface regions and the asteroid ring made it difficult to establish any kind of a normal orbit, though it appeared several ships were trying. It looked somewhat suspicious to him, but it was so far off from their current location, it would be easier and faster to just finish their scans of these two closest planets, then make a quick pass by the last one on their way out of the system.

Rick continued to mull over the dream, still replaying in his head. *Am I ready to begin what?* The look on the young woman's face and what she was holding seemed to be the prominent focal point to the entire dream, short as it was.

"Sir," Toby asked. "Is everything all right?"

Rick instantly acknowledged the science officer, but made no explanation. He continued to wrestle with his thoughts, looking out at the planet's surface as they passed close by.

"Toby, how long will it take to complete your scans?" Rick finally asked, watching the Starbird pilot maneuvering the ship into an established orbit.

"Operating with maneuvering thrusters only now. Performing twin axis sweeps on this one, called Tanis, so maybe ten hours."

"What's wrong with the Fulton drive? We ought to be able to cook right through these sweeps."

The science officer developed an odd look.

"Engineering had to take them offline just a couple of minutes ago. You approved it, General. Commander Niker is helping them make repairs to the sub-light induction sequencers. She reported that if all goes well, they hope to have them back up in thirty-six to forty-eight hours. Is everything all right, sir?"

"I'm fine," Rick acknowledged. "Just a little distracted I guess. Hate to be spinning around out here with no way to run. How far is it to the last planet in this system?"

"Boris, with just maneuvering thrusters, it'll take about a day, maybe a little more, provided we finish our scans on schedule, but we still haven't hit Reako yet. It's closer to Carolon but further from us right now. If we had the *Constellation* with us, we'd get this done much faster."

"Certainly," Rick agreed, turning to the overhead screens above the science station. "How about we simulate the *Constellation*?

"Sir?" Toby looked up from his instruments and turned to his commanding officer.

Rick glanced back at the displays, touching one of the comlink buttons on the armrest of the chair.

"Jayda?"

"Yes, Rick."

"How are your repairs going back there?"

"Just peachy-keen. I'll be another couple of hours with this Aquila drive unit before we can even get to these other systems. Thankfully, we've got the parts onboard to repair this. Otherwise this turret would be nothing more than a great place to star gaze."

"I'm taking an Interceptor out to the last planet. Want to see if I can speed the search up a bit."

"How about you come and see me in engineering," Jayda responded in a hushed tone.

Rick knew that tone well. She was being judicious in front of the crew.

"I'll be right down." He looked at Toby as he turned to leave. "Once you've finished your scans here, set your course for Reako and I'll catch up with you."

It didn't take Rick long before he was stepping into engineering. He found his way around the monitoring systems and the engine bulkheads to the turret elevator shaft just as Jayda stepped out. He kind of had an idea of what this was all about and was somewhat prepared. Both he and Jayda were aware of the promise Gunnar had made to Audra. Somehow, that promise had sort of encompassed Rick as well. Being a pragmatist kept Rick from making such an oath, besides, he wasn't confronted with the trauma of losing someone close to him.

"What have you got left to do back here with these boys?"

"IC-9 circuits on the ejection boosters of Interceptor two have failed, but Clancy thinks it's just some intermittent connections on the failsafe's. Don't even get me started on all of the FTL stuff we still need to deal with. We're on maneuvering thrusters only right now. Thomas is working on recalibrating the Asium crystal assemblies while Clancy and Paul work on the Fulton induction sequencers. Probably take a couple of days." Jayda took hold of Rick's arm and pulled him away from the elevator shaft and back around behind the engine bulkhead. "Like to give me a good reason why you aren't sending me or one of the Korack boys out in that bird instead of you?"

He was a General, commander of this ship. He made the rules. Rick had his speech all ready to go and let it come straight out.

"I need my Exec right here. Do you see any seal troops here that can go out on recon? Recon is what I used to do. It was my meat and potatoes for heck sakes."

"Yeah, but you've also got a responsibility to be here for this crew, to keep them alive. We've had this discussion before, remember?"

"That's what my Exec is for, to be here in my absence."

"Why not let Zek or Zak do this? It's what they do, it's their function on this ship, to fly out there and take all the risk so the command officers don't have to. The only thing required for a sensor sweep is a fly by. Once around the planet and you'll know if Gunnar is there or not."

"They're here helping you and Clancy. The more manpower we can put on these repairs, the faster it will go."

"Hogwash!" Jayda retorted. She understood her husband's concern for his friend, but their current predicament was forefront in her mind. "No offence to Zek and Zak, but it doesn't take a genius to fly recon on a planet, and you know these guys are fighter pilots, not engineers. Sometimes they're more of a hindrance than a help down here. You could work circles around those two." Jayda grabbed both his hands and put them on her shoulders, covering up her rank insignias. "Now come on, it's me, Jayda, not your exec, your wife. What's this all about?"

Normally, there would be no discussion here, but Jayda had just played the wife card and all military protocols had just been trumped. Rick wished he had concrete information to go on here, something he could actually show her. He hesitated, carefully thumbing the silvery insignia pins on her shoulders and looking into her searching eyes.

"There is something on Boris that I need to see, I don't know what it is for sure, but I have a strong impression I need to go and have a look."

"An impression?"

"An impression," he repeated. "Maybe even a vision." He didn't like using that term.

"On it or in orbit?"

"On it," Rick affirmed. "There's a structure and someone waiting there to give me something or show me something, I don't know for sure, only that I need to go myself."

Jayda read the determined look on her husband's face and somehow understood how he felt. She had sort of already gotten the feeling that he needed to do this, but she wanted to hear him say it and provide her with reassurance that he should be the one to fly this recon.

"And how long do you think it's going to take you get this something?"

Rick did some quick calculations in his head, rolling his eyes up and side to side like he was doing the math in the air between them.

"Day and a half, maybe two days. If I could use the FTL drive it might be a quarter of the time, but we've got nothing recognizable for the Navi-computers to lock on and coordinate with out there. Mind you, that's just a rough guestimate."

"Ok, sir," she finally nodded, gently moving his hands off her rank insignias. An uncertain smile broke across her lips as she reached up and kissed him. "You'll maintain contact, right?" Military protocol mandated it, asking wasn't required.

"You know I will," Rick responded, a little relieved. When was he ever going to learn that when it came to Jayda, he could tell her anything? He kissed her again and started for the turbo shaft that would take him to the Interceptor.

The cockpit of the Interceptor was dark with the exception of a couple of maintenance lights that came on when he positioned himself into the seat of the big fighter. Buckling himself into the soft, surrounding bucket seat, he reached up and touched several controls and brought the craft's main instruments online. Letting his hands sweep over consoles on both sides of him, he pushed a com piece into one ear and reached for the comlink button on the underside of the control yoke.

"Lieutenant Habba, can you provide me with a direct tie-in with CORA?"

"No problem, sir," the com officer replied instantly.

Only a moment later, CORA's voice came to his ear.

"Almost like old times, eh, Richard?" Her voice was quiet, almost soothing, but there was a hint of playfulness mixed in too.

Rick grinned broadly as he worked to get the Interceptor engines started, more systems lighting up the cockpit as he continued.

"Well girlfriend, if you've got the time, looks like I've got the equipment." He looked out the cockpit windshield at the surface

of Tanis as they worked its orbit. The Interceptor was a far cry
from a T-6 or a Viper. They were much smaller and a little more
agile than this bigger, more advanced fighter. As a fighter pilot,
he wasn't sure which he preferred.

"CORA, I'm ready to launch whenever you are."

"Transferring all launch control circuits to Interceptor one,
launch when ready."

"Oooo cool," Rick swooned with a chuckle. "You sound just
like a traffic controller, so official."

He reached over and touched the launch control and the
fighter ejected from the main wing tip of the *Athena*. Hitting the
turbo thruster button, the Interceptor leapt away from its mother
ship and around the far side of Tanis. Because of the lack of star
coordinates, trying to use the FTL engines in the Interceptor was
out of the question. He'd end up flying into something. As the
V-winged craft throttled away, Rick set his course for Boris and
set the controls to cruise, settled back and gazed out at the star
field. He never got tired of looking at it, even though these
weren't familiar to him, it didn't matter. They were beautiful no
matter what angle you looked at them. At high cruise, the
Interceptor could reach Boris in a couple of hours. Rick was
hoping Clancy and Thomas could get the sub-light engines back
online sooner than the estimates Jayda had given him. The
longer it took to locate his friend, the less likely they were to find
him at all.

Occupying his time in the cockpit while his craft moved
toward Boris, he brought his scanners online and started to study
the system and the traffic moving in and out in as much detail as
his equipment would allow. He concentrated his efforts on
Reako. Though it was the farthest from his current position, if
he didn't find his friend on Boris, it seemed the most logical
place, if he were even still in this system. Rick wasn't looking
forward to traversing his way back to Carolon to look. However,
if he knew his friend, Gunnar would be sitting in a massage
lounge or sunning himself on some distant sandy beach.

Rick continued studying the data the *Athena* was able to
gather on Reako, Tanis and Maver. Reako seemed like a rough
place to try and get to. As he and Toby had determined earlier,
it had a substantial asteroid ring and a heavy atmosphere
sensors couldn't penetrate. Even more curious were the capital
ships working in orbit around the entire planet. Was this just
how the Albions worked to take over territory? There were no
detectable human life forms on either planet and the basic
information indicated they were no more than spheres still in
process of evolving. Rick was banking on the *Athena* being able
to finish its scans of Tanis quickly, and then get a closer look at

Reako. Perhaps a close orbit or even a quick trip down under the interference for a quick scan would produce the needed information.

Once he reached Boris, Rick made a single orbit around each axis, finding only one structure. The planet was certainly capable of supporting life, but he was scanning only sparse animal life. While the surface was lit by distant suns, it had a high luminescent Triticalie count in its atmosphere.

He steered directly for the structure, an ancient looking temple situated on the side of an extinct volcano surrounded by dense forest. Setting the Interceptor down next to it, he secured his craft and stepped out into the thick, humid air. Surprisingly, the temple was not in disrepair, but in excellent condition considering it appeared to be abandoned. After checking in with CORA, he started looking for an entrance. There were a few windows, but they were so high up there was no way to get to them. He wondered if the person assigned to clean them didn't often curse the builder for putting them up so high. The structure was bare of vegetation and after moving to the other side of the building, he found the only entrance. The main entry way was lit by bright torch light, an indication someone was here. Curious none of his scans had picked up anything.

Opening the large bronze colored doors, he stopped and looked around before pulling his blaster from its holster and moving cautiously forward. The doors behind him did not magically close, but remained open, helping to light his way to another open doorway some distance inside. He could see more light beyond and quickened his pace. Passing through the entrance, the decor of the vast room was familiar. He looked all around as he stepped further in, noting several large openings surrounding a high center pillar supporting the highest most portions of the ceiling. Instinctively, he headed toward the center of the spacious hall.

It was no surprise to find a young woman sitting on a white bench, perched on an elevated platform. He recognized the long copper hair combed neatly to her waist. Her gaze was on the objects in her hands. Rick glanced down at his blaster still poised in his hand and lowered it back into its resting place. There would be no need for this weapon here. It would probably be useless anyway as he got a strong impression that any wisdom gained here would be entirely different than what he was accustom to.

He wasn't exactly sure what he was supposed to do now. Where she was sitting and the building she was sitting in, might suggest he should drop to one knee or bow to show some kind of respect. However, before he could, the young woman looked up at him and smiled.

"Are you ready to begin?" she asked quietly.

"I had a dream about this place," Rick responded, stepping a little closer and looking around at the great hall. The woman made no attempt at stopping him, but he felt a little uncomfortable getting too close.

"Was it a dream?" she asked.

Rick looked into her green eyes. He had assumed it was just a dream, but now he wasn't so sure. Most dreams were a bit chaotic and didn't follow a set line in any detail. The dream, or vision he had experienced, had. Everything was in perfect detail, exactly as it was now. It was almost spooky. Now he recognized it wasn't a dream at all, but more like a message. He didn't know and furthermore he wasn't sure he wanted to know. Things of this nature tended to lead into areas of vast responsibility that he didn't have the time or the attention for right now.

"I'm looking for my friend," he finally said, feeling a little silly for saying it.

"Yes, I know. It's rare to find such a friendship."

Rick's spirit leaped.

"But please, don't concern yourself with him. Gunnar can take care of himself...for now." She let a deep sigh go. "He will have need of your help soon enough, so there is no time to be wasted here. We must begin immediately. Are you ready?"

"I really don't have time for whatever you have in mind here," Rick blurted, trying to be polite. "If you know where my friend is, tell me."

"He's fine...for now, but will soon have need of your help. Are you ready to begin?"

Rick nodded and went to sit down next to her but she stood up, handing him a set of tear drop shaped rings.

"I don't even know your name or what this place is called," he commented, taking the odd shaped rings and giving her a half smile.

"Ona," she said quietly. "You may call me Ona. I am quite ancient by your time reckoning. This is an Abura temple. A place of great learning."

Rick was stunned. She looked amazing to be classified as *ancient*. She didn't look a day over twenty. He looked at her demeanor, as she seemed determined to begin immediately.

"Ok, Ona," he responded uncertain. "What are these called?" he asked, looking curiously at the rings. A heat sensor in the grips automatically switched the safeties off as he rotated the rings in both hands.

"Balkrums," Ona replied, pulling another set from under her clothes. "They're an uncommon set of weapons with ancient origins given only to a Thane."

"They look like Razor rings." Rick studied them, carefully pulling the blade guards from the razor edges. He had used them in his younger years: quite dangerous. Rarely did you come away without a few self-inflicted wounds.

"Similar, but so much more."

"So how do these..." he started, squeezing the activators inside the S shaped grips. The weapons instantly activated, startling him to the point that he nearly dropped them. Vibrating gently, they emanated a humming noise at first, but as the anode sensors around the edges charged, they began to crackle, tiny sparkles dancing all along the glowing blades of the rings.

"So why am I holding these?" Rick asked, moving them around and watching the glowing particles gently ripple with the movement. "Aren't I a little old to be learning how to be, a Thane? I don't even know what a Thane is."

Ona installed a set of fighting guards on the razor blades, activated her weapons and slowly took a stance.

"A Thane is a protector, a warrior, but a different kind of warrior. Not one who just fights for any cause, but one who fights to protect specific individuals. Your friend and those he travels with are such individuals."

Rick stood examining the crackling particles dancing along the blades, not quite understanding the enormity of what Ona was purposing. He and Gunnar were just two aging fighter pilots who commanded a couple small fleet Corsairs. Their exploits had never stretched beyond those aspirations.

"Now, let us begin. If this were actual combat, we'd be wearing those gloves." She motioned to an odd looking pair of gloves on the bench. "But for what we're going to be doing, these fighting guards will protect you well enough. I suspect you already have an idea of how to use weapons such as these. But using them is only part of what a Thane can do."

"What's the other part?" Rick installed the fighting guards on his blades as well.

"All in good time." Ona crossed one of her weapons with one of his, letting them touch lightly, each making a hissing and snapping noise.

"They certainly are loud," Rick acknowledged, letting his blades slide along hers.

"Yes, you won't be sneaking up on anyone with them turned on, but you'll learn that you don't need to. They do other things beside just make noise, but first things first."

Ona gently stepped back and then lunged at Rick, letting her Balkrums swing right at the apprehensive General. Rick instantly knocked the swing away and returned one of his own. Having mastered these disciplines in his youth, everything he had learned came back to him in an instant and it was as if he had never stopped.

Old Acquaintances

Gliding lazily along through the vastness of the Nulark system within the vicinity of the planet Reako, the *Tarzana* made wide lazy turns in several directions, as the battlecruiser waited for an approaching Albion transport to land. Dalton SoKnack listened silently to the traffic controllers relaying information and signaling all clear as the craft reported it was secured aboard. Clicking his fingernails nervously behind his back, he knew who had just landed. Having someone else assume command of this operation was a blatant slap in the face. Above all, he didn't want to be on the same ship or in the same system with this Thane coming aboard. Being a Thane was bad enough. They were supposed to be a protector of specific individuals using mind tricks to command or alter the elements. Make any one of them angry and you could end up in big trouble.

Dalton could tell the exact instant Blinda Koss entered the bridge of the *Tarzana*. The noise level instantly dropped to a hush and only the booming echo of her knee high, spike heeled boots slowly stepping toward him rang out across the shiny bridge floor. A chill slithered down his back, picturing her approaching him from behind, but he was determined not to be intimidated and remained focused on the star field before him.

"My dear Dalton SoKnack, what a wonderful surprise to find you in command of a battlecruiser, and the Albion flag ship no less. And don't those commander stripes just make you look so dashing," Blinda teased, sliding up next to him.

Like Dalton, Blinda was somewhat short, but frail looking in comparison to Dalton's stout build. It was a little difficult to imagine this small woman could be so feared and reviled. Her face was stark, large dark eyes contrasted well her bob cut, platinum hair. A nicely shaped woman, she wore a navy blue blouse and a light brown cloak draped over her right shoulder, reaching to just above the knee over dull red pants. Sporting a blaster on her right hip and the weapon of a Thane on her left, her fused Balkrums swayed slightly as Blinda turned to Dalton.

"I have my orders from the QC, now what are yours?" he asked, turning only his head to the Thane.

"I feel certain you have an opinion on this matter," Blinda smiled. "Although I find it somewhat curious that Drax is having me take on this assignment instead of you. What happened? Run into a few, complications, shall we say?"

Dalton turned back to the window.

"Let's just say the intel on Colonel Barker wasn't as accurate as we had anticipated."

Blinda let out a burst of laughter.

"Let me guess, you sent Tigers after her and she ducked into the Reako belt and then to the surface? You'll be hard pressed to find her down in all that mess."

"Her ship is damaged and unable to make the jump to light speed. We'll have her when she comes back out."

Dalton was sure Blinda had been briefed before she ever started her trip to the *Tarzana*. He knew Drax felt he was capable enough, she just didn't like mistakes and would often try teaching lessons by using others to provide an example of what not to do.

"I hope for your sake, you're right. Drax doesn't like repeated failures and chances are, with me onboard, she'll have me do her dirty work. I've grown a little fond of you over the years, Dalton and I would hate to have to exact an order against you."

Dalton's heart was racing now and he had to concentrate hard on maintaining control. He dared not raise a hand against her. He knew better, but he also understood he was a reactionist and making a move that could be construed as provocative, could get him into trouble fast.

"Your orders?" he finally asked again.

Blinda picked up on his lack of patience with the conversation and raised a hand toward him. Dalton could feel the air pressure change in one of his ear drums, but held himself frozen. Blinda's ability to manipulate the elements combined with the use of the Balkrum, made her dangerous for anyone looking to go over the top of her. He wasn't sure who she was a Thane to. He could only assume it was either KC Barton or QC Blair. In either case, she could make things unravel fast for anyone who got in her way.

"Mind your place, Commander, and who you're speaking to. Now, turn this bucket toward Tanis and keep it running slow and unassuming. We'll do a lazy eight around it and Reako. Let that ship come to us. I'll be in the observation lounge." Blinda did a one heel spin and left the bridge. As she disappeared behind the elevator door, the pressure on Dalton's ear drum subsided and he turned, barking out orders to the lower command personnel.

Wild woman

Gunnar sat up with a start and looked around. He was under his favorite tree, its autumn leaves falling all around him. He squinted, looking up into the bright blue sky. There were a few puffy white clouds hanging stationary in the distance of a rolling horizon. He turned his gaze into the limbs of the large tree, feeling a chill in the air. He picked up a flat, colored leaf that fell into his lap. The grass beneath him was still green, but cold to the touch. In his Hallavertor, he had programmed it so he could lie comfortably on the grass and let the leaves cover him as he napped. He didn't feel like napping right now. He felt like he needed to see Fuji about how sore he was. His shoulder and ear were hurting again and he had several spots all around his body that ached. Looking back up at the sun, he realized that now his head was hurting. He rubbed his eyes beneath his glasses and tried to look up again, but this only produced more pain.

"You need something for that headache, mister." He turned as Audra plopped down next to him. She was wearing her blue, casual dress.

"What are you doing here?" Gunnar dropped the leaf and put his hand to his chest. He couldn't feel the memory chip.

"I like to get away from work too you know," she responded taking a deep breath.

"Work?"

"Yeah, you know, that thing we all have to do during our wake cycles? It's how things get done in life? I know, I know, you try to keep that process down to a minimum as much as possible, but the rest of us have to really lean into it."

"Are you saying you work harder than I do?"

"Don't try to start an argument with me, mister."

"What?"

"I don't want to fight with you."

"When have we ever fought?"

"We fight all the time. It's what you do in the service."

"Fight? But you and I never fight."

"Oh, that's right. You're right and I'm always wrong and I have to follow whatever you say." Audra's tone was strange, no inflection at all.

"What? Where is all this coming from?" Gunnar could hardly make sense as to why she was acting like this.

"I suppose you think it's my fault that crystal number five cracked and blew the containment chamber."

"No, I sent you down to help Billy keep that from happening." Gunnar began to fumble with his response. "It... It couldn't be your fault."

"But I was there and didn't act fast enough."

"But that doesn't make it..."

"Why are you blaming me for nearly wrecking the ship and killing the crew?"

Gunnar noticed Audra's demeanor and skin color changing. It was turning pale. Her dress was losing color as well.

"It wasn't your fault." He felt that horrible ache within him instantly rage and he began to weep.

"I'm dead now aren't I?"

"Yes, but that's not your fault," he sputtered, beginning to sob. "None of it was your fault."

"It has to be someone's fault. Whose fault is it that I'm not with you anymore? Who's to blame?" Audra was suddenly standing, looking straight ahead at a now grey, overcast.

"It's not your fault. I tried to save you. I came to save you." Gunnar was in a fit of anguish, his body and emotions were raw. *Curse this body!*

"But you didn't save me. Why didn't you save me?"

"Stop it! Please stop!" Gunnar fell over and curled back up, crying pitifully. "It wasn't your fault, it was mine."

"I can't be here anymore," Audra said. She knelt down next to him and stroked his hair. Gunnar looked up at her through tear filled eyes.

"I don't want you to go," he sniffled.

"I have to go. I'm not here anymore."

"I love you," he whispered.

"I know you do, but I have to go."

Audra got back to her feet and walked away. A moment later, Gunnar sat up and wiped his tears, looking for her.

"Come back, please come back." He didn't want her to leave again. He was sure he could fix it, he was positive. His surroundings turned grey. He looked up into his tree again. It was leafless and scary looking. He shivered as now it was turning cold and snowing.

Gunnar tried to move. He hurt too much. He was suddenly aware that he wasn't lying in grass any more, but dirt and rock.

What? It was a dream. What a horribly vivid dream. Feelings of guilt for Audra's death swarmed over him as he lay motionless. There had to have been something else he could have done to prevent it. As Commander of his ship and as her husband, he was responsible for Audra's death and the resulting guilt was an unrelenting confirmation. His emotions were still running hard and his head throbbing.

At first, he couldn't even open his eyes, but after some concentration, he was able to get one to flicker open, followed by the other. A lot of good it did him. Everything was completely out of focus. Feeling his forehead, he discovered his glasses were gone. He could still see without them, but having them made it easier at his age. For now, he might as well just close his eyes again.

Except for the ringing still blasting in his head, there were no sounds. His right cheek and shoulder hurt horribly and attempts to get up only intensified the pain. He tried his eyes again and after a little work, everything came into focus.

Looking around, he realized he was lying on his back, looking up at the ceiling of a cave. Not like the one they had landed in. The ceiling of that cave seemed so high it had its own climate and pressure gradient, but this was just a cave, nothing more. How the cave was illuminated was a bit of a puzzle, but as he studied its surface, it occurred to him that minerals in the rock or a microscopic fungus growing on its surface produced a luminescent glow. He finally rolled over and sat up. Moving his head carefully, he became aware that he was soaking wet, not from falling in water, but from perspiration. He remembered the humidity outside the F-2 had been abnormally high and realized he could easily dehydrate if he didn't get to some drinking water. Perhaps just as pressing, as he rubbed his shoulder and face where he had been struck, he found his hand covered in blood. Whatever it was that had hit him must have had some sharp claws. Blood oozed from four nasty marks on the right side of his face.

Groaning painfully, he got to his feet and checked himself for further damage. His joints felt nearly paralyzed and it was difficult to draw air into his lungs. His blaster was missing. Too bad, he was probably going to need it. The cave was small and appeared to be void of any other kind of life but his own. Looking down at the dirt floor, he scanned the room for footprints, but there was nothing here to indicate how he might have gotten in. Usually you'd see the drag marks and the prints left by his captors. There was nothing but the marks where he lay. Looking to his right, he could see the ghastly remains of several creatures. They looked similar to the animals that had attacked them at the fighter. *Attacked them! CJ! Where is she?*

He carefully surveyed the room for an exit and finally found the way he must have entered. High above was a hole in the rock, covered with some kind of a make shift trap door. It wasn't likely he'd be able to go out the same way he came in, so he started to make his way to the far end of the cave, looking for another exit. Rounding a stony corner, he came upon two passages blocked by large boulders. Even as stiff as he was, it didn't take much effort for him to roll them away. Both tunnels looked equally dreary and uninviting, but there was a slight rush of air coming from one of the shafts, so he moved in that direction. After some traveling, the tunnel began to descend, giving him a little cause for concern. However, the further he went, the fresher the air felt and the faster it seemed to move.

Hiking for what felt like hours, he had to climb over larger boulders and even slide down a few steep rock faces, but was finally rewarded with cooler air and the sound of running water. Quite tired and sore now, he could barely move as he sat down on a rock at the edge of a running stream. He unbuckled his utility belt and started on the long row of buttons on the front left of his jacket. He pulled his scuffed boots off and dipped his tired feet in the cool, refreshing water. There was an odd, gentle stinging sensation as he swirled them around, relieving the fatigue and stiffness.

Lowering his head to get a drink, he instinctively glanced down his shirt where Audra's memory chip hung. *It was gone!* Panicked, he groped frantically under his jacket and around his waistband for the familiar feel of the chain. Finally calming himself, he closed his eyes, thinking as he dropped both hands into the water. There came a mild stinging sensation to his hands as they came to rest on the sandy bottom.

What happened? He thought with eyes still closed. *Where did I lose it?*

He would have to retrace his steps to find it, even if it took him right back up to where he had started. He felt like he couldn't function without having her with him.

Detecting an odd sound, he opened his eyes and caught the reflection of someone standing on the other side of the running stream, looking curiously at him. Not wanting to scare whoever it was, he lowered himself closer to the water and started gulping the refreshing liquid. It burned mildly as he gulped it down, almost like drinking something alcohol based. Having his fill, he came slowly up, startled by the appearance of a young woman holding something in an outstretched hand. The fact that the only weapon she had was a knife, tucked in the front of her modest animal skin clothing, settled him a little. She wasn't filthy and appeared to have a good handle on her own hygiene. Her hair was tightly braided in one long rope spiraling around one side of her head in a bun. Her face was a bit dirty, but pleasant. Beneath the smudges on her face was a dark complexion with long eyelashes and piercing eyes.

The two stared at each other, waiting to see what the other was going to do. Gunnar finally broke the silence, recognizing what was in her outstretched hand.

"Where did you find that?" He asked, relieved to see the memory chip and chain.

"You drop coming down," she gestured at the great boulders he had just descended from. "Look important."

"Yes, it's important," Gunnar replied holding up his hands to catch it.

"No get wet. Very bad for this I think," she said tossing it to him.

"What about me? Is it bad for me?" He caught the chip and set it next to his other gadgets.

"Very good for you."

He grinned broadly, purposely showing his teeth, and then bent back down to wash his face. As he splashed his face and eyes, he abruptly came back up. Every spot on his skin that had gotten wet felt like it was on fire, his eyes burning. It especially stung in the spots that were bleeding. He let out a yelp toppling backward, trying to shake off the sting and rubbing his eyes. As suddenly as it had started, the stinging stopped and as it did so, he became aware of female laughter. Carefully sitting back up, he looked across at the woman, who was pointing and laughing hysterically at him.

"Sure, it's all funny when it happens to someone else." He gave her a sarcastic thumbs up and reached for his jacket floating in the stream to wring it out. Having already gotten his hands wet, they didn't seem to be bothered by the water. In fact, his battered and bruised body was feeling curiously better, not to mention his eyes seemed to focus just fine now, without his glasses.

"Water sting raw skin, no?" she chuckled, emulating his thumbs up gesture until she saw the claw marks on his face. "You have Binion poison. Must heal you soon. Water help, drink much, wash much. I have Dirum leaves, draw out poison." The woman held up a small pouch tied to her hip, the look on her face quite adamant.

Gunnar gave her a disbelieving side glance and reached for his utility belt.

"You'll forgive me if I have a hard time believing you. I'm sure you think I'm just some old geezer…" he drew out the last word realizing his face was no longer hurting.

"Sting only for short time. Feel better fast," she said, motioning him back toward the water. "You need Dirum leaves."

She reached into the pouch and pulled some odd looking orange colored leaves.

Still not convinced, he got to his feet and reached back down for his boots.

"Thanks, but I better pass."

"Speak truth, it helps. Know power of water. Heal fast, no scar. Pain not last long, jump in."

She urged him into the water with a diving hand gesture. Gunnar wasn't about to repeat getting wet. He wasn't sure he wanted to drink it now either. Better to find a different stream to drink from than this one. He gave her another side glance, shaking his head and stepping carefully along the rocks next to the water.

"Not a chance, I value my comfort too much..." He slipped, his balance teetering, but trying to correct only made it worse and he slipped again making a half spin and falling backwards into the water. It was deep enough that he was fully immersed. The sting covering his whole body was intense, but only for a few moments, and then as he surfaced, the pain gone. Wiping the water from his face, he could again hear the sound of laughter coming from the other side of the bank.

"Ok, so I was wrong. How long do I need to sit in here? Little chilly, but not bad for cave water." He swished his hands through the clear water and took several big drinks.

The woman shuffled down from her rocky perch to the water's edge and dipped her bare feet.

"Look like you need good soak, but no time. Can't stay long, big trouble on top. Binions have big Tomba. Big rain and wind time come, big storm, flood land. Be very bad, worse flood ever I think."

Gunnar doused himself again and then got up, wading back over to the shore where his boots and jacket were.

"What's this big Tomba you're talking about?" he asked, shoving his feet into his boots.

"Tomba big Binion party they have when they make catch. Binions have contest, see who strongest. Who wins, gets prize." She watched him wring the water from his jacket again, the fabric drying quickly.

"Ok, so what's the prize?" He reached for his utility belt and swung it around his waist to buckle it.

"You and fire top girl."

Further explanations were unnecessary. He grabbed Audra's chip and put it around his neck then took a small step back and with an effortless hop, landed firmly next to the woman on the other side of the stream.

"What's your name?"

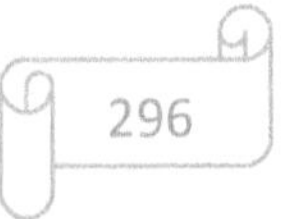

"Janox."

"Pleased to meet you, Janox. I'm Colonel Gunnar Lee Conrad. Commander of the Royal Kalamarion Starbird, *Constellation*."

Janox looked at him, baffled.

"Just call me," Gunnar hesitated, and trying to think of something simple, he blurted out the first name that came to mind. "Bud," he said, cringing and checking his belt. Surely he could have come up with something else. "Plenty of time to get to know you on the way. Do you have tickets to this Tomba?"

Janox looked at him oddly, not quite sure what he had meant, but understood his desire to go with her.

"Move swift and silent, Bud follow fast."

*   *   *   *

Crouching next to Janox, Gunnar peered down toward a large congregation of fuzzy faced creatures. They seem to come in all shapes, fur color and length. Some were racing madly around in a large circle on four legs, while most of the others, Gunnar presumed they were the adult males, stood up on hind legs moving together around the center of the cavern. They constantly cocked their large heads, wagging unusually long tongues through large fangs.

Gunnar felt like it had taken him hours to hike down to the stream, but Janox obviously knew her way around through the labyrinth of tunnels and caves. In the middle of the floor was a make shift trap door over a hole and some distance to the side, in one of the cave walls, there was another hole with a similar barrier blocking the entrance. There were several large rocks near the second door big enough they could easily cover the hole. The animals were all moving excitedly about the open area between the two doors, each one strutting and posturing at any other creature that came close. Carefully surveying the situation, Gunnar surmised that he didn't have enough firepower to deal with a rescue.

"Never got a very good look at these guys before they clocked me at my ship," Gunnar said reaching for his blaster. "Ah nuts," he cursed softly. His thigh holster was empty.

"Why Bud say?"

"I need my blaster. No idea where I lost it."

"What look like?"

Gunnar gave Janox a glance, and then motioned for her knife. Giving the Binions another look, he started drawing the shape of his blaster pistol in the dirt floor with the tip of her knife.

"Bud need this to get fire top girl?" She gave the drawing an odd look, even tilting her head a little, trying to get a mental picture of what it might actually look like.

Gunnar looked back down at the large group of noisy strutting Binions. They appeared to be synchronizing their strut.

"Well, it would sure help even the odds a little."

Janox grabbed her knife and started climbing over the ledge in front of them.

"Whoa, hey, hey, hey," Gunnar reached to pull her back. "Where do you think you're going?"

"I get blaster; Bud get fire top girl. Over in little cave," she pointed a finger at the second door in the wall of the cave. She continued cautiously making her way down the sheer rocky wall.

"I sort of need the blaster first," he whispered after her. Janox only gave him a quick thumbs up and kept going. "I guess that means I need to get ready to do my thing, whatever my thing is," he mumbled, wondering how best to create some kind of diversion.

He looked around at the walls and ceiling. In this cavern there were ledges everywhere, even high cliffs with large openings. Watching the thin young woman make her way along several tight ledges and through a hole in the wall, he started in another direction. Shuffling his way along a ledge, his intent was to position himself high enough above the Binions that he would have plenty of time to lead them on a wild chase through the cavern tunnels. But as he took a step, the ledge gave way and he dropped flat on his back on the outside of the strutting group of Binions.

Stunned, he lay looking straight up at the ceiling of the cavern, little sparkles dancing through his vision. After a couple of silent moments, his lungs started to work again and his vision cleared. Shaking off the shock, he noted several of the Binions had approached, looking down at him. At first, there were just curious stares, but it became apparent things weren't going to end with just a good natured ear scratching. He let out an exasperated chuckle, perceiving his situation as far more complex now. The Binions started snarling at Gunnar. Trying to protect himself from being torn apart from the razor claws hanging over him, he rolled over and tried to get to his feet. Before he could get up, they all started pouncing on him, forming a pile. This almost seemed like playful competition, to see how many of the animals could actually get on the pile. On his hands and knees now, Gunnar held himself perfectly still. As the pile grew in size, he looked at one of the animals next to him at the bottom of the pile.

"Pleased... to meet... you," he grunted, forming a cheesy grin. The Binion responded with bulging eyes and a short string of labored grunts.

Once they were all precariously perched on the pile, Gunnar slowly rose to a kneeling positon and the pile fell apart. When there were only one or two left on his shoulders, he looked around at the animals getting up. They all looked back at him to see his next move. He made a glance over at the covered entrance and decided to try something a little unorthodox.

"Here, catch!" Grunting, he tossed the two Binions at the main group of animals and jumped as far as he could. Not knowing his own abilities in the matter, he sailed right over their heads and into the cavern wall above them. Unprepared to go so far, his arms and legs flailed erratically right before he struck the wall of the cave. Barely able to hang on, he gritted his teeth, enduring the pain of the wall strike.

"Ouch," he finally gasped, looking behind and down.

When Gunnar and CJ had first landed, the Binions seemed determined to tear them to pieces, now they were almost playful. Was it possible he was unwittingly participating in whatever their Tomba ritual was? Not being able to hold his balance on the wall any longer, he turned and dropped back to the cave floor, the entire room of Binions watching him. Once he was standing up straight again, several of the beasts approached him, giving him cause to back up toward the door in the wall. The two Binions he had thrown unexpectedly charged him, snarling viciously, paws raised and claws extended to strike. Startled, he grabbed the first paw that came at him and gave it a quick twist. Bones instantly snapped and the Binion went down, wailing miserably. He grabbed the second and using the animal's weight and momentum, swung it around hard enough to send the creature flying against the cave wall. Gunnar watched the creature crumple up as it dropped to the dirt.

"Ok ladies, step up," he beckoned arrogantly, looking around at the other animals staring at him. He expected them to rush him, but instead, they all returned to their original positions and started moving about the room as they had before, as though nothing had happened. Gunnar was stunned. He had expected an all-out brawl at this point, but now it was as if they had no interest in him. Gunnar remained in what he thought was neutral ground until one of the creatures started pushing him around the room, encouraging the human to join in the ritual. He tried to move toward the door in the wall, but was redirected each time he got close. He found that if he mimicked their motions and grunting noises, they left him alone and he could carefully start to move back toward the door. Making several

circuits around the room, strutting and grunting, he noticed
Janox standing against the cave wall opposite the door. She
held his blaster up in one hand and the other hand balled up in a
fist, resting on her hip.

"Bud, what you do?" she asked giving him an odd look as he
passed by. Gunnar only shrugged and continued the Binion
strut.

"I tried to fight with them, but they're more interested in
doing this."

"It Tomba dance, they get very mean soon. Stop playing
around, get fire top girl, get out fast."

"Don't you think I'm trying?" Gunnar called from the other
side of the room. The next time he passed the door, he got a
good look at what it was going to take to get it open. The wood
was somehow inset in the rock and would not be easily
dislodged. Starting back around to where Janox was standing,
he realized the grunting was getting louder and more excited.

"What's going to happen when they get mean?"

"Big fight, very much noise. Many Binions die, others eat
them. Winner take fire top girl."

"And do what with her?" he asked, knowing the answer. He
veered further out of the circle moving in a wider arc toward the
door.

"Whatever it wants."

"I'm going through that door and when I do, I want you to
fire that blaster at the ceiling," he called out as the grunting
turned to growling.

"Bud, how you work this?"

"Point and shoot, just make sure you're not pointing it at me
when you do," he yelled, bolting toward the door. Several of the
Binions tried redirecting him back toward the center, but Gunnar
would not be diverted. He grabbed ahold of one of the furry
animals, slinging himself back around and crashing right through
the door.

The cavern outside erupted into a fury of wailing and hissing,
as the Binions started for the door, but all of them dropped to
the ground at the sound of a blaster discharge and a cascade of
rock falling to the center of the room. Janox cringed as she let
another blast go, bracing herself against the recoil of the
weapon's discharge. Moments passed and several of the Binions
got to their feet, but instead of heading toward Janox, they all
converged on the door, peering inside. Then, as if following
some kind of silent command, they all worked together to move
one of the nearest boulders in front of the opening in the wall,
pushing it snug against the hole. The strutting started all over
again, only this time the dance appeared far more agitated, and

they were giving Janox threatening looks. Perceiving a bad
situation getting worse, she made her way around to one of the
other tunnels. Circling around toward the large rock as quickly
as she dared, she froze when all the Binions froze in place and
started a loud chatter. Janox recognized she had only moments
to get out and down the escape tunnel before she would be set
upon. Moving to do so, she stepped in front of the boulder
blocking the hole, only to discover it was moving. She spun past
it and to the exit tunnel, turning to watch what was happening
behind her.

The large stone continued to slide across the floor, away from
the opening, finally starting to roll forward and into the gawking
Binions. As the rock rolled away, Gunnar and CJ shuffled out
and seeing Janox motioning wildly for them to follow, ducked
down the exit tunnel.

The whole encounter had been viewed curiously by a figure
clad in green, standing on one of the high ledges near the ceiling
of the cavern. Her four accompanying pilots mumbled to each
other about the strength displayed by one man.

"And how are we feeling?" Gunnar asked, as they made their
way up the passage. Pale faced, CJ was favoring her right side
again.

"Not too well I'm afraid...." she stumbled and fell, but Gunnar
caught her and scooped her up. Janox motioned for him to
follow, running as fast as the tunnel terrain would allow toward a
large opening. Beyond, Gunnar could make out the details of the
outer canyon walls and the foliage growing along the riverbed
they had landed on. A moment later they stood puffing at the
entrance and gazing up at the large pools of water far above in
the ceiling. There was a thick, misty haze forming, looking like
angry rain clouds. Hearing faint cries and a distant clamoring
coming from behind, Gunnar turned to Janox.

"Any ideas?" he asked, the breeze starting to ramp up.

"Rain come soon and so do Binions. We go to safe place
now," she motioned, bolting down the trail through waving
thickets.

Gunnar looked up and down the canyon as he started after
Janox. Nothing looked familiar to him, as he had been knocked
out cold when the Binions had attacked them at the fighter.
They had to get back to it quickly, or become the main course in
a Binion Tomba. Not seeing the Flightstreak or even the riverbed
it sat on, Gunnar reached for CJ's hand and brought her wrist
communicator to his mouth.

"Alex! Can you hear me, come in?"

Only static crackled softly back at him. He looked all around,
smelling fresh moisture starting to filter through the breezy

canyon air. Binions on their heels, a brewing close quarter's
storm and nowhere to go. There came an instant flash of light
right next to them and an accompanying explosion. Another
flash and explosion hit on their other side, then behind them.
Gunnar and Janox turned, looking up. On a high bluff, stood
several figures holding weapons pointed at them. Gunnar
recognized the soldier in green, standing behind the others as
they fired their weapons.

"Colonel, you're lucky I've figured out how to work some of
this equipment." The voice of Alex 7001 came back across CJ's
communicator. Overjoyed to hear the droid, Gunnar continued
running.

"I live on luck, Alex! Can you triangulate our signal and tell
us where you are? And don't worry about being precise."

"I was starting to get concerned."

Several laser blasts landed close to Gunnar's position as they
started through the thickets, hearing the sounds of Binions
behind them.

"Yeah, me too. Which way?"

"The river bed is right in front of you, sir, just keep moving.
Sensors show you have a large group converging on your
position."

"Ya think?"

The clouds grew thick and dark, bolts of lightning starting to
drop in front of a rapidly moving grey wall boiling down the
canyon at them. The path they followed became obscured, as
the foliage grew thicker. The light dimmed and the wind
whipped at them as they pushed through the thickets. Janox let
Gunnar pass, hanging back to cover their escape. He heard
several blaster discharges behind him as he stumbled and fell
onto the soft sand of the river bed. Janox was quick to his aid as
a sheet of driving rain slammed them. Scrambling over to where
CJ lay motionless, he picked her back up.

"Alex! I gotta know which way to go!" He couldn't see the
fighter in either direction. Janox turned and let several more
blasts from the pistol go, trying to keep the Binions back. Claps
of thunder blasted their ears and the drenching rain pelted
harder. They couldn't just stand there and get swarmed.
Several laser blasts hit the ground near them. Through the
driving rain Gunnar could see their pursuers moving down the
side of the canyon after them, firing at the Binions and Gunnar.
He could barely hear the directions Alex was trying to give them
as they turned and bolted to their right, down the river bed.
Gunnar tripped several times as the sand was growing wet with
the deluge of rain and he finally went down, dropping CJ. Janox
stopped to help and glancing back, she strained to see through

the driving rain, hearing something ominous coming from behind. The Binions seemed to have thought better of the chase, or the soldiers had driven them off, as they were nowhere to be found now. Laser fire peppered the ground around them as CJ regained consciousness and they continued down the river bed. Janox repeatedly stopped to return fire as they went. The rising winds and pelting rains had CJ completely awake now as she struggled behind Gunnar along the sandy river bed with Janox hot on their heels.

"I had the weirdest dream," CJ puffed. "I thought you'd never find me."

"Thank that girl behind you. She's a quick study with a blaster and I'd still be lost if it hadn't been for her. You gonna be all right?"

"I'll be fine if we can just get back to the ship. Drax found us, didn't she?" CJ stumbled, but remained mobile.

"Yup," Gunnar responded, listening to an ominous rumbling growing louder. Turning a gentle bend, they could make out the shape of the Colonian F-2, sitting on the sand. As they ran through the torrent, they noticed the water was no longer soaking into the ground, but pooling on the surface. Reaching the back of the Flightstreak, Gunnar stopped to help the other two up. About to climb up himself, he did a double take behind him, seeing a huge wall of water racing down the river bed at them. Not wanting to wait around to calculate how long it would take to reach them, he bounded onto the back and hit the hatch release.

"Alex, get this thing moving!"

Gunnar turned back to help CJ toward the hatch as the fighter's engines started to whine. Reaching for Janox as the first fingers of flood waters started peeling up the rear foils of the F-2, he got a good look at the churning wall bearing down on them. It would easily toss them like a paper toy. The water started to roll up the back of the fighter toward him just as he heard the engines change pitch and rev up. He turned and jumped through the hatch, hitting the release mechanism as the water engulfed the ship.

"Anti-grav!" he yelled, jumping for the pilot's seat, the water roaring over the cockpit. He took only a moment to buckle himself in, noticing his glasses sitting on the center console.

"Wondered where those went," he commented, grabbing the controls and giving the fighter throttle.

"I found them on the ground outside," Alex announced from the rear as the F-2 rose from the water.

Gunnar turned the ship away from the swollen river and the giant wave of water still trying to envelop them. CJ looked out

her side window, back at Drax who stood with her men firing
their weapons, trying to bring the ship back down. Bringing the
gear up, Gunnar turned the ship around, giving it throttle down
the canyon, away from the flood and rains. All the while a
frustrated Drax stood watching.

*   *   *   *

It didn't take long for Gunnar to surmise something was still
very wrong with the fighter. There were new lights blinking
erratically now, along with most of the old ones. There was even
an irritating warning alarm blaring in his ears.

"Alex! I thought you said you figured out how to work this
stuff?"

"I said I figured out how to work it, not how to fix it," the
droid fired back.

"Well, that's something you got right; and do something
about that stupid alarm!" He tried adjusting a few controls and
gave CJ a quick glance. He had hoped she would be a little more
help, but she appeared lethargic, leaning back in her seat letting
Janox look her over as carefully as conditions would permit.
Turning on the scanner and the tracking systems, he worked
with the controls to maneuver away from a dark shape sweeping
past them from the gloom. The Black Tiger was much larger up
close and it nearly scared him right out of his seat. He tried to
bank away as best he could to avoid a collision.

"Futs! Alex, did you do something to the Ion compressors?
I've got next to nothing here." The alarm finally went silent as
Alex turned his little head forward.

"I think they're calling them Isom compressors, Colonel. I
tried to increase their boosting power, but I must have adjusted
the Fadec in the wrong direction. A little hard to do when you
can't understand this fighter's language. I don't even believe our
Nano-mech could do any good with this equipment."

Gunnar throttled up a little more, checking the shield energy.
He had no doubt that it wouldn't be long before they were being
chased by Tigers again. He looked up for an opening in the vast
ceiling, but it was completely obscured by thick angry clouds.

"Janox, any idea which way we can go here?" he asked,
looking down at the two small tracking screens to his right.

She looked up from her examination of CJ.

"That way, look for round tunnel. Careful, Bud, tight squeeze
for us I think."

Gunnar banked the F-2 sharply on its side, turning the ship in
the direction Janox had indicated. The F-2 roared like a bullet

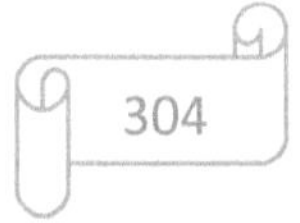

down the stormless passage while Gunnar checked the rear tracking screen, noting several objects appearing behind.

"What's wrong with her?" he asked, trying to keep one eye on flying and the other eye on what was following them. He shot Janox a glance, hoping for good news. He had just gotten CJ patched up and now it appeared she had been reinjured. Janox was looking closely at a good tear in the right shoulder of her blouse.

"Binion claw fire top girl bad on shoulder. Leave part of claw. Claw poison, very dangerous. Bud, must take out soon or she die."

"You best get to it," he said, guiding the ship around a gentle turn in the tunnel. "And watch her hands. I got mine slapped the last time I tried to help."

"She must hold very still."

"Yeah, good luck with that," Gunnar grunted.

"You know, I'm sitting right here," CJ complained, trying to work the buttons on her blouse. "And why does she keep calling you Bud?" Twisting pain defined her expression while trying to work the buttons.

Seeing the condition of her dress blouse, Janox wasted no time in just tearing the sleeve off her shoulder, to the collar. She had her knife out and in an instant, sank the blade tip into the bloody flesh of CJ's shoulder. Gunnar glanced over just as Janox went to work and CJ's eyes rolled back in her head as she passed out. It was quick and clean taking only a couple of seconds.

"Must close wound now, she bleed." Janox held up a sizable claw fragment in her bloody fingers.

Gunnar adjusted a control to his left and glanced back over at Janox, her hand and knife covered in blood.

"Alex, hand her your micro-fuser and see if you can find that Bio-gel in the Med-kit."

"Colonel, my tools are precision and not meant to be used as surgical instruments," the droid objected.

Janox gave the droid an apprehensive look as a little door popped open on its side.

"Little stick looking thing," Gunnar directed without looking back.

Janox carefully pulled the micro fuser out and looked at it. "What do with this?"

"Pull the trigger and use it to burn her wound closed."

Janox activated the fuser, fascinated by the glowing tip. She then went to work, as carefully as she could to cauterize the wound on CJ's shoulder. An explosion to their right rear shook the ship, Gunnar concentrating on keeping the fighter from

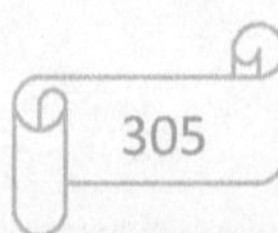

hitting the narrow walls of the shaft. Once Janox had finished, she handed the micro-fuser back to Alex. Another blast from behind struck the floor of the tunnel right beneath them, rocking the fighter violently.

"I sure hope this tunnel goes somewhere instead of just a dead end," Gunnar grumbled, holding his craft as steady as he could. "That would really be the pits. How we doing over there?"

"That cute hot stick. Be good for branding Binion." Janox pulled some of the orange Dirum leaves from a small pocket next to a small flask on her animal hide clothing.

"At the rate we're using that hot stick on her she's going to have brands all over her," he commented. Glancing down at the tracking screen, it unexpectedly winked off.

"Alex... What have you done now?" Gunnar's voice started low and slow, but wound quickly up to a frantic lather. "I've lost the rear tracking system!" He didn't need a vital system to stop working at a critical moment.

The droid made a surprising burst of irregular beeps and chirps that gave Gunnar cause to frown even more as another explosion tested the resolve of the rear deflector shield circuits.

"Just put it back the way you found it and don't mess with it," Gunnar snorted. "I need it now, not later!"

"Try to remain calm, Colonel. I am only making a cross over connection to a different circuit." The droid let another short burst of electronic chirps go.

Janox was a bit taken back by the exchange between the Gunnar and the droid, giving them both an odd look.

"Bud understands what white box says?"

"Not always," Gunnar replied as the rear tracking screen flashed back on. "But we communicate."

Janox crushed the orange leaves she had in her hand and put them down on both CJ's wounds.

"Draw out poison, make heal fast, no scar, like water in cave."

Gunnar let out a laugh.

"Lucky for her she's out cold then."

"Not long, she wakes up," Janox said.

Gunnar couldn't look, his concentration fixed on what he was doing as their rear shields took a hit. He corrected the shift in the flight path, being careful not to overcorrect and slam the F-2 into the opposite wall.

CJ opened her eyes and looked around, bewildered. She felt an intense sense of Deja vu come over her, remembering the dream she was waking up from.

"I've been having the weirdest dreams lately. I feel like I've said that before."

"How you feel?" Janox inquired.

CJ turned her head, touching the orange leaves on her blood stained shoulder.

"I'm fine, I think," she answered slowly, trying to figure out if she was still in some dream scape. She looked forward, seeing that they were traveling through a tunnel. The whole dream idea was about the best explanation right now.

"What's going on? Where are we?"

Gunnar remained focused on continuing to thread the needle.

"Still got your friend with us. I got to admit, that woman has got some real balls and this ship of yours doesn't."

CJ looked over at the tracking screens.

"Let me have it," she reached for the yoke, but a sudden stabbing pain in her shoulder prevented her from doing so. "Ouch," she groaned holding her arm.

"You no move arm until healed. Let Dirum leaves heal wounds," Janox insisted, holding the soothing leaves in place.

CJ looked up at Janox and was about to ask who she was and where she came from, but several laser blasts hitting the walls in front of them kept her attention forward. Debris pummeled the fighter as it passed through a hail of rock bits. A nearby blast forced the fighter to the left and out of the corner of his eye, Gunnar caught a flash of sparks showering away from the wing tip as it made contact with the tunnel wall.

"The walls are getting closer," he complained, continuing to pilot the ship down the narrowing passage. Another explosion blasted the wall on the other side of the ship and the opposite wing tip sent out a shower of sparks. Gunnar jerked the yoke in the other direction when another blast jolted the ship, this time forcing the ship a little harder into the opposite wall. Trying to correct, the fighter began to bounce back and forth as it raced down the tunnel. After several bounces and careful correction, he managed to stabilize the flight path and maintain a safe distance between the walls and wing tips.

"I know what this for and what dots on picture for." Janox pointed at the rear tracking screen. "But what these?" she asked, pointing at the forward tracking screen.

CJ looked down at the screen as another blast struck their rear shields.

"I thought all the asteroids were in orbit?" She looked up and switched on the landing lights.

"There can't be asteroids inside a planet." Gunnar strained to see what was ahead of them. "There's gravity here," he commented, not wanting to believe what they were approaching.

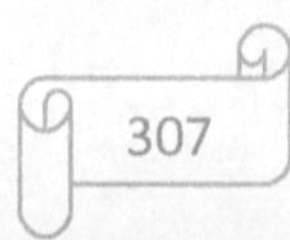

"Can gravity explain why water stays in pools in the ceiling of a canyon?" Alex asked from the floor behind them.

The fighter shook again and Janox's eyes widened.

"No, not floating rocks, not here. Here very dangerous place for us. This Redle cave. It have stringy rock hang from top."

"Stringy rock? That's a new one on me," CJ remarked, looking up at Janox.

"She means stone formations and I think it's exactly what we need right now," Gunnar said giving the F-2 more throttle.

"You're not actually going to try and fly around in there are you?" CJ asked, looking ahead. She drew in a deep breath, a feeling of fear mixed with admiration passing through her as the fighter streaked toward the cave opening.

"We appear to have limited options here people, but I'm open to suggestions. Besides, they'd be insane to follow," he commented coolly.

"Bud be nuts go in first," Janox countered, eyes wide.

Several more explosions rocked the fighter, causing it to graze the walls of the tunnel again. Gunnar did his best to make corrections and push the F-2 a little harder.

"Why does she keep calling you Bud?" CJ asked again.

"Where's the targeting system for this thing?" he asked, the end of the tunnel rapidly approaching.

"You have your fingers on the triggers." CJ struggled to reach over and activate several controls. A small heads-up display with a set of crosshairs appeared directly in Gunnar's field of vision. Several readouts popped up, displaying various information.

"Four buttons on the back side of the yoke."

"Better hang on, kiddies," he announced as they closed on the opening. "This is going to get a little intense."

He pushed two of the four buttons on the yoke, letting the firepower of the F-2 do its work on the dripping limestone obscuring the cavern entrance. The rock shattered, crumbling away, allowing the F-2 to slip effortlessly through the opening and banking sharply to avoid a giant stone pillar. Gunnar pulled the throttles carefully back as he maneuvered the ship between several other obstacles. The enormous cavern echoed with the scream of Isom engines as the Black Tigers, spurred on from behind by their leader, entered the stalactite filled cavern. The first manta-ray shaped craft met its fate almost instantly, slamming into a huge cluster of dissolving rock, exploding and bringing nearby formations down with it. The other two Tigers screamed into the cave after the maneuvering F-2, managing to follow it around the tight maze of limestone pillars. A fourth ship came to a halt at the cave opening and hovered, waiting.

The F-2 banked back and forth sharply, weaving in and out between the pillars as if threading a ribbon pole, many times just missing the huge cone shaped stone chandeliers. Gunnar rolled the fighter completely over once and banked sharply to the right, swerving tightly around another huge pillar, firing his guns at an upcoming pillar of stone. Flying right through the falling debris, he steered his ship back and forth between more pillars as they came at the ship. All this maneuvering was setting Janox off balance so much, she found it quite difficult to stand, even hanging on to CJ's chair.

"Slow turns down," she complained as the fighter tilted on its side again.

The F-2 jolted softly as Gunnar circled a glistening pillar and leveled out, and then banked off in another direction.

"I think we trimmed the vertical fins on that one."

"Very impressive," CJ commented, detecting the whimsy in Gunnar's voice. Watching him handle the controls, he seemed to have finally mastered the F-2. If she didn't know better, she would have thought he was trying to see how close he could come to the rock formations without hitting them. Stone pillars and walls raced by the windows at a blur now and as they banked hard around the formations, she could look up through the overhead window and watch them pass by. Startled at how fast they were maneuvering through the field of pillars, she had to remind herself of his self-proclaimed abilities as a fighter pilot.

"You don't need to show off to impress me," she wheezed.

Gunnar tensed a bit, feeling lucky that so far he had only scraped the paint. He hoped his luck would hold out as he dove beneath another large formation, pulling up and banking hard.

"Wished I had a little more room to maneuver this bucket," he commented, bumping two of the stone pillars as they went. "Sorry, I'll have my guys fix that when we get back."

Gunnar's tone told CJ a different story now. CJ had completely misjudged Gunnar's confidence level. A shiver of fear spanned across her back and neck, tightening her scalp. She noticed his white knuckle grip on the control yoke and the tension twisting his expression.

"You mean you're not trying to impress me?"

Several near misses rocked the F-2 as it banked around another set of crumbling stalagmites. Gunnar took aim at the base of a large cluster directly in front of him. He let a short burst go, ducking directly beneath the cracking rock and out the other side. The massive cluster shuddered a moment, then gave way as one of the Tigers tried to follow. Shrapnel and splintering rock exploded, bringing several other formations down while Gunnar turned his ship back toward the tunnel opening. Even as they did so, the last Tiger became even bolder, pushing harder to catch the Colonian ship and somehow disable it. Weaving in and out behind the F-2, the Tiger got too close and had to bank away to avoid a collision, only to catch a wingtip on a pillar, sending it spinning wildly out of control. Striking a small limestone tower, a section of wing sheared off sending the rest of the ship toppling to the cave floor. Gunnar slowed his craft to an easy glide and sat back to relax.

"Alex, I could sure use those compressors now," he said, letting go of a relieved sigh. "Anyone remember where we parked?" he asked, looking around the cavern as they glided slowly along. Several readouts and indicators lit up on the center panel as Alex worked to replace an access cover on the back wall.

"Try them now, sir."

Gunnar gave the activators a tap and feeling the instant acceleration associated with them, felt a little more confident they would work when needed.

"Good man," he commented, scanning the ceiling of the cavern as they flew. There were many pools of water above them, but none of them were nearly large enough to accommodate the F-2. "I guess we'll just have to find the exit and go back the same way we came." He turned the ship toward a defined cavern wall and followed the contour until he recognized they were close to the tunnel entrance, and then turned straight for it. Leveling the ship out, something appeared on the forward scanner.

"It's Drax!" CJ exclaimed.

Still hovering at the tunnel opening, blocking any exit, was the Albion Metro-star. It opened fire on the approaching F-2. A deadly game of chicken ensued as they closed to point blank range. Something caught Gunnar's eye above them as he opened up with all guns. He pushed the throttles all the way forward and touched the booster control. The cavern walls all around the tunnel opening crumbled as the F-2 continued to fire, abruptly arcing straight up and disappearing into a large pool of water in the ceiling.

"Where go now?" Janox asked, feeling a sense of relief.

"That's a great question," Gunnar agreed, turning to CJ for the answer.

"That is, a good question," CJ agreed thinking about it. "Cross is the only safe place that comes to mind. We should be able to make whatever repairs we need there. I know one of the guys that works the space port. He might be willing to help us."

"And what allegiance does he hail from?"

"Cross is neutral. Because they are the military manufacturing hub of Hadrian, they've managed to stay out of the fray. Having said that, they do have a significant security force and neither the Empire nor the Albions ever take it lightly. Tomplie pirates are Cross's biggest headache."

"Is the waypoint information for the jump to Quadra-light still valid?"

"Provided it hasn't been changed, we should be fine. Once we get clear of the planet, we just need to reach that preprogrammed point and make the shift."

"What about that cruiser and its ships?" Alex asked, becoming airborne to join the conversation. "No doubt they're waiting for us once we break the cloud layer."

"I'm hoping to be clear of the Troposphere and reach the waypoint long before they can lift a finger. But right now, I think we all ought to try and relax and catch a quick nap while this ship finds its way back to the surface."

Gunnar reached up and shut down the targeting system, watching the heads up display disappear, then shut down the landing lights and brought the Nav lights online. CJ checked the autopilot system and turned to ask him a question, but could see he had already begun to relax, settling back with his eyes closed. It could wait. They would reach the surface much faster than they had descended; she could ask her questions then. Now, safely traveling under power up the vertical waterway, she suddenly felt exhausted herself and leaned back, closing her eyes.

*   *   *   *

Gunnar popped up from his napping position feeling like he could take on the combined might of the Colonian and Albion empires all by himself. It was nice not to feel like his hearts were going to burn right out of his chest and lower back. Blinking, he put his hand to Audra's chip still safely tucked under his shirt. A vision of her face smiling back at him came into view in the darkness of the surrounding water as they continued to travel up. He smiled back at her, watching her blow him a kiss and slowly fade back away into the darkness. He turned and looked at CJ. Awake and focused forward, she didn't notice him watching her study the readouts in front of them.

He didn't want to seem like he was watching her, but he couldn't help it. She was a mess to be sure, they all were. Her entire right side was covered in blood and her blouse torn to the collar. Her hair was still damp and matted; they were all still wet. But even in the state they were in, he saw something in

her that seemed, well, she just felt right. Right for what, he had
no clue. She was no Audra, that was for sure. But there was
still something about her. As the cockpit was quiet, he noticed
that same tingling in his ear that had dogged him whenever he
had been around CJ on the Carolon base. How odd, he still had
no idea what it all meant.

"We going to be good for the jump to Quadra-light when the
time comes?" Gunnar finally asked.

"Everything looks just fine," CJ responded slowly. "I think
we're ready just as soon as we can reach the waypoint."

Gunnar looked over his shoulder at Janox who had just
opened her eyes from her nap and was tapping the glass on
Alex's faceplate.

"I wonder how and what she was doing down here?" He kept
his voice low so only CJ could hear.

"Good question and how did she ever survive alone? And
why does she keep calling you Bud?"

"I haven't the faintest idea," he answered, not really paying
attention to the question.

"She just started calling you that?" CJ cast him a funny look.

Gunnar chuckled slightly thinking back to his meeting with
Janox deep in the caves.

"I think I sort of put it into her head when we met."

"Uh-huh," CJ chided him.

"Doesn't make any sense how she got down there though,"
Gunnar maintained.

"Just as mysterious as pulling off blast rated grates with your
bare hands and taking on a ROACH. You still haven't told me
how you did all that," CJ mused playfully, resting her chin on her
hand.

"Alex, how long to the surface?"

"Calculating our speed and depth…"

"How long?" Gunnar repeated, raising his voice.

"About ten minutes, roughly."

Gunnar glanced at CJ, who was still looking at him, waiting
for him to respond. He hesitated, not wanting to say.

"I'm not human," he finally blurted quietly. The comment
didn't appear to faze CJ at all, as she was expecting some kind of
a follow up. "I'm a Dialabron."

"Ok, so what is that supposed to mean? And please don't say
you're some kind of a robot. That would be such a
disappointment."

"Do these claw marks look like I'm an android?" Gunnar
responded, examining the healing marks on his hands and face.
"No, to make a long boring story short, I was born with some
extra internal parts. I guess that means I'm genetically unique.

In my case, I have multiple hearts, but others have super vision, including being able to see in pitch black, something that could be useful right now," he said, glancing outside at the black. "I was friends once with a girl who had two brains. Think that one through."

CJ didn't need to. She imagined his DNA sequences were off the chart in comparison to a normal human.

"My bone and muscle structure is much stronger than a normal human's. I'm told my skin is pretty tough too. It's a random mutation among Dialabrons on my planet, thought to be linked to a certain kind of radiation from our sun."

"Thank you, Colonel..."

"Gunnar, you can call me Gunnar," he insisted.

"Sure it's not, Bud?" she snarked, but got no response. "Ok, Gunnar," she spoke carefully. She didn't want to get too comfortable with the name. She liked it to be sure, but she just didn't want to get too close. The fact that they were stuck in this cockpit for who knew how long, was close enough for now. "Thank you for clearing that up."

Gunnar dropped his hand to CJ's arm.

"Please, let's just keep this between you and me."

CJ's facial expression softened, feeling that he was entrusting her with something personal.

"If that's what you want."

Gunnar leaned back again and looked out into the darkness of the water, then took a deep breath as a warning light came on in front of them.

"Better hang on, we're about to surface." He firmed up his hold of the controls, a sudden blur washing across the windshield followed by multiple instances of lightning streaking across the dark Reako sky. Leveling the F-2 out, they glided over misty shapes of dead trees on the silent watery surface. Trimming the fighter to make a slow comfortable arc toward space, Gunnar leaned back and stretched. He could see nothing on the forward or rear tracking screens. He let go of a sigh, confident they would only have to outrun their pursuers as far as the waypoint.

"So why put an outpost on Carolon? What's it got that's so important to the Empire or the Albions for that matter?"

"I hadn't given it much thought. The decision was above my pay grade," CJ replied, tired. "I suspected it was just a place to stake a claim for territory before anyone else did. It really has nothing. I doubt anyone knows anything about your Asium. I certainly didn't until you described it to me. Carolon seemed like a great place for me to start a new command because it was such a far off place. Spend a while building up administrative command time and then transfer up into a fleet ship."

"Did my time as a ground based squadron commander,"
Gunnar admitted playfully. "But that's a whole other story that
I'm sure would bore you to tears."

"Bet I could match it," CJ smiled giving him a look.

Gunnar gave her a double take. No one had ever challenged
his exploits, but he realized that she had no idea of his career as
a fighter pilot, or he hers.

"You don't think maybe your Albion friend found out about
the Asium, do you?"

"Before you got us out of the Operations Center, Talia and I
were watching them destroy everything. Not that that wasn't
going to happen anyway. The base destructors I set before we
left would have literally turned the place into one big hole in the
ground."

"Scorched earth policy?"

"Can't understand why they were trying so hard," CJ said
studying the navigation readouts in front of her.

"Do you remember how close we were to the waypoint before
we had to duck into your planet here?"

"Not clearly. We can't know for sure until the Nav-computers
can get a coordinates lock on the stars."

"Goodie," Gunnar grumbled. "No time like the present to get
on with this." He carefully checked the tracking screens as the
F-2 broke the cloud layer and throttled slowly away from Reako.
Becoming tense, he tried to nudge the throttles a little farther
forward. They couldn't get to the waypoint fast enough for him.
A nagging feeling slithered up his back as he turned the fighter,
following CJ's directions. All their luck had been bad thus far and
he had no reason to believe it was going to change.

Several specs appeared on the tracking screens, confirming
what he had hoped wouldn't happen.

"Nuts! Looks like our little secret's out."

"It won't take them long to catch us," CJ said glancing at
their speed.

"Got any good ideas?"

"You're the fighter ace," CJ snapped.

"An ace can't make something out of nothing."

"Fibber," CJ came back instantly.

"Fighters gain fast, Bud. Stop talking, get us out of here!"
Janox was tired of the chase.

Several blasts exploded against the fighter's shields as the
pursuing Tigers took turns pounding them.

CJ pointed out the side window, seeing something appear on
the forward tracking screen.

"To your right. We've got two more of them coming at us!
They're going to try to cut us off!"

Gunnar banked the fighter sharply away and gave the Navi-computer readouts a double take. He could see the unit working to calculate where they were and where they needed to be to reach the waypoint. He felt a tug at his uniform from behind.

"I know! I know!" he exclaimed loudly, letting his eyes sweep across the tracking screen forward.

"Know what?" CJ asked without looking up.

"Two Tigers coming straight at us and two of something a lot bigger on our starboard now. Less talk, more do!" He knew he couldn't out maneuver all of them and he could just make out the form of a couple much larger ships moving in their direction from above. They were almost completely surrounded now and he still had no idea where the waypoint was. He reached forward and pulled all five cover caps from the switches. The green display instantly flashed on at the same moment a warning indicator started to flash on the Navi-computer.

"We've got a lock!" CJ announced, watching the numbers flash in front of her.

Gunnar reached up and flipped all five switches into position, watching as the corresponding numbers appeared on the display. He nervously glanced over at CJ, who worked to recheck the numbers to see exactly how close they were to the waypoint. Their shields were being pounded from all sides now and Gunnar was holding the booster control down constantly; something you weren't supposed to do. It was for emergency bursts only and the chambers coil emissions would burnout the feeder jets if left running too long.

"Come on!" Janox slapped the seat back impatiently.

"Remain calm ladies and gentlemen and keep your seat backs and tray tables in their upright positions."

"Are they?" Janox grasped the seat harder and shook it.

"Almost there," CJ focused, watching the display in front of her and reaching for the Quadra-light throttles. Janox tensed her hold on the back of Gunnar's chair as the Flightstreak shook with the Albion pounding. An alarm sounded off and CJ instantly shoved the twin Quadra-light throttles all the way forward. The stars outside instantaneously elongated, flashing into white embers as the F-2 bolted into light speed. Trying to calculate where a ship was going, traveling at Quadra-light and following without a special tracker, was impossible.

Tests

Rick and Ona sparred endlessly in long hard sessions with the Balkrums, the weapons set on low stun to prevent permanently injury when a strike was made. Occasionally, Ona would stop Rick to correct or teach something entirely new about their use. His confidence peaking, he noticed something odd about how Ona was maneuvering. He understood she was a master, but it seemed to him that as she maneuvered around the room, her strides became wider and if she had to jump to avoid him, the distance she traveled appeared unnaturally far.

Though starting to tire somewhat, he pressed his offense hard, utilizing a series of moves he recalled from his youth. As expected, Ona deflected and countered with relative ease, but as he finished his rapid volley of swipes, he spun, throwing in an extra swing. Seemingly unprepared for the move, she abruptly went airborne, somersaulting over the top of his swing and landing just to his left. Rick only caught her move out of the corner of his eye as he turned to face her, but what he did see was graceful and lightning quick. How she was able to accomplish such an acrobatic move in long robes was a mystery she would give him no time to dwell on.

She came at him without hesitation, slinging jabs and swings with increased ferocity. Holding his own, he realized he was able to comfortably battle with her without feeling overwhelmed. In truth, many of the skills he had once known long ago were back in his head, at his command. He constantly nipped at her with the edges of his weapons and kept glancing at her feet, which appeared to just glide across the floor. Sharp stings from his Balkrums continuously snapped at her, giving her cause to retreat, her levitation became even more apparent. At the same time, he detected a pressure developing in his ears. Only an annoyance at first, but becoming increasingly painful.

Doing his best to control the discomfort, he nipped at her arms, even her legs as opportunity presented itself. After several minutes of sparring, there was a sudden rush of air all around the room and she instantly leaped from the floor, sailing directly at one of the huge supporting pillars toward the center of the room. Rick held his weapons still activated, watching astonished as Ona touched the pillar about half way up and hovered there. The air in the room continued to move, but was focused where she hovered. He let his hands relax on the activators of his weapons and the glow around the circular blades disappeared while he watched and waited. Ona looked at him for a long moment, then finally deactivated her weapons and slowly sank to the floor, the air in the room calming. Rick folded his arms and waited for his tutor to approach, but she remained stationary next to the pillar.

"Tests and learning come in many different forms, Richard. The question is how will you respond to each?" Ona waited for an answer.

How was she able to do that? He got the distinct impression her abilities were derived from a method having more to do with science than anything else.

"I'm not too interested in taking any tests right now," Rick chided, still fascinated by her ability. "But my curiosity is piqued. If you'd care to share, I'm open."

"An open mind is the most desirable thing for any one person to have when learning is involved." Ona turned and sat on the bench, setting her weapons beside her and motioning for Rick to join her. "No doubt you've discovered a couple of things as we've sparred. Which by the way, well done. You are well skilled. I sense you've mastered many such weapons as a youth, but there is so much more to a Thane than just being able to use a Balkrum."

"So I've noticed," Rick replied, carefully sitting down.

"Have you ever wondered why you like certain things more than others?"

"We're all individuals, we like different things."

"But why? Why do we like different things? Why do you like a certain color more than another? Why do you like a certain song more than another? Why does that same music turn the skin inside out for someone else? As a male, why do you prefer one female over another?"

Rick considered the question carefully. On his home world, he was considered a gifted scientific thinker, a visionary. Now he wondered just how visionary he really was. Though basic in nature, these questions hadn't even occurred to him before. He had contemplated similar subject matter many times, but ultimately accepted it as how the human machine operated.

"Your molecular harmonic is similar to those things that you favor. Your atoms rotate at a similar frequency."

"I thought it was because the girl looked good. You're telling me it's because we're slinging our beads to a similar beat?"

Ona raised her hand and swung it slowly like a conductor for a choir. The air in the room swirled gently giving Rick cause to sit upright and look around.

"So many things in this plane of existence to learn and to see. So many things we are unaware of, not just in this plane, but all the others. We are all but guests in this existence, allowed to prove ourselves to a higher level. But most of the biological life forms within are too limited and preoccupied, or don't bother to exert themselves enough to experience things unseen. For example..."

Ona twisted her wrist and the air rushed from the chamber. Rick went to take a breath and found himself quite unable. He understood how a vacuum in space worked, so he was sure the room wasn't entirely vacant of air. Ona seemed to be unaffected by the condition of the room and with another twist of her wrist, the air rushed back in followed by a peculiar rumbling and a change of light.

Rick took a relaxed breath, hearing a loud creaking noise, followed by a rustling. The big bronze doors of the temple chamber suddenly burst open and an entire forest grew right into the room. The light continued to change and looking up, he could see why. Not only was the forest growing in through the front door, but also from the openings in the top around the pillars. The room filled at an alarming rate, even encroaching on the platform where the two were sitting. He tried to remain calm and relaxed, as it appeared the foliage had no interest in him, but it was difficult with the incredible movement all around them. As the vines and trees grew thicker, brushing right up against them, Rick pulled his feet up onto the bench.

"Uhm, friends of yours?"

"And yours," Ona responded casually.

"Funny, I don't recall ever having any friends in this neck of the woods."

Ona passed Rick a silly look, holding up her hand signaling a halt to the activity in the temple chamber. The growth instantly stopped, but small white flowers with purple and red highlights popped out of the foliage all around them. Rick noticed Ona twitch her index finger and even the flowers stopped popping. Looking all around at the greenery, he felt entombed now, vines and tree trunks coming down from the ceiling, the rest of the room completely obscured.

"All things are living," Ona started, her hand gliding to the closest flower and touching it gently. "I love the flowers of these plants and their fragrance."

"All things are living?" Rick questioned, eyeing her carefully. "Even these stone pillars?"

Ona pressed her nose to the flowers and let its fragrance fill her.

"Think about it," she instructed. "Right down to its subatomic particles. What do you see?"

"I see stone. It's just a rock."

"Is it?"

Ona plucked the flower from its stem and held it out to him.

"Is this just a flower?"

Rick nodded.

"What is its molecular makeup? How is it constructed?"

Rick started to answer again, but perceived that she wanted him to look at the question a little differently. At the subatomic level, all matter is made of atoms, each atom consisting of a unique set of parts, similar to themselves, but different from the next. Each atom, depending on what the molecule is, has a specific number of electrons, protons and neutrons. Each moving at its own frequency, the electrons rotating in their orbits at a specific speed and angle.

"Most humans can only access less than ten percent of their brain's capacity. Imagine what you could do if you were able to increase that capacity."

"How much can you access?"

"Everyone is different."

"Then how will I know how much I've accessed?"

Ona gave Rick a chastising glance and smiled. She held the flower out to him again.

"Can you see its molecular structure?"

"I see the flower." He looked at it, then at Ona.

She stared back at him for a moment and then gently waved her arm out across the room in front of them. The interior of the temple was instantly changed to something entirely foreign to him. His vision now completely taken up by a wall of undulating, vibrating bands of colored beads. He passed a glance at Ona, who motioned for him to look closer. Stepping to the wall, he could see there were even smaller beads associated with what he perceived already there. These smaller beads were moving and as he got closer he could see they were spinning, or rotating, orbiting the larger spheres. Each set of beads emitted an aura of its own, but combining to make up a specific color. Looking up in other places on the wall, there were other colors. He reached out to touch the vibrating wall, but it vanished in an instant. Blinking, he turned back to Ona, completely baffled. She was still holding the small flower, Rick now recognizing its colors as the same from the wall.

"Did you just..."

"That is from my mind," Ona informed him. "You must see it in yours."

"How? I don't have that kind of brain power."

"All humans have this ability, but it is masked deep within the upper regions of the brain. Few can access it on their own, fewer still ever try. With your permission, I'll enable this region so you can access it."

"Will it hurt?"

"The scientific knowledge you carry is vast for one whose aspirations are to navigate galaxies. Will it hurt?"

Rick thought a moment, knowing the answer to the question. The human brain is an organ used to process information and provide feedback to the rest of the body. There were no nerve endings there to register pain. He took a tentative step forward and Ona raised a finger to his forehead. Gently touching it, she brought her other hand up and closing her eyes, slowly waved it back to her side, then stepped away.

"Just like that?" Rick crossed his eyes and looked up as if he could somehow see his forehead.

"What, did you think your head was going to split open and grow flowers or something?"

"No, but I thought I'd be smarter. Shouldn't I know a bunch of extra stuff now?"

"What you will have need of the most in the near future, I have put there. The rest you must study and learn on your own."

"What do you mean? Need in the near future. What's coming? And what more do I need?"

"Punk kids anyway," Ona grumbled. "That region of your mind is open now. You have to learn how to use it and fill it with understanding and perception. What you put in it, what you teach it will define even more who you are and what you can do. But I caution you, control what goes in and what comes out. Without control both ways, your mind and the power it can access will surely spin out of control and consume you."

"What about..."

"No, there is no what about. Time for you to do. Always remain focused." She held the flower out again. "Tell me what you see."

Looking at the flower in front of him, he imagined he could see the atoms, the electrons in his mind. Bunched together as he zoomed in, he studied them carefully. Much like a great wall, they held steadfast to one another, yet never quite touching, somehow their electrons able to continue their mad spin around each nucleus. Zooming even closer, he noted the wall pulsing and when he drew close to it, reaching out to touch it, it moved

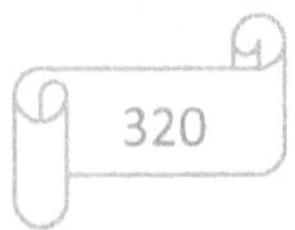

with his movements. He wondered what was behind the wall, what its interior looked like. Did it make sense to just drive a hand into the wall and see? He raised his hand with the thought to do so, but as he did, the wall opened up before him, revealing what he had been thinking. Indeed, the interior was even more vastly complicated than its exterior. Was it possible to rearrange this structure into something else? He wasn't sure what he could rearrange it into, but a quick thought and some maneuvering with his hands, he succeeded in changing how the interior of the wall looked. He then backed away and closing the exterior wall, pulled even further back to look at what he had done. It wasn't until he realized he was again standing back away from the molecular wall, that he could see the entire flower in his vision again and Ona's fingers holding it out in front of him. Giving Ona a puzzled look, he wondered what was so funny. She sat looking at him, grinning ear to ear. Her eyes shifted to the flower, then back up to him. He looked at the beautiful white flower flourishing in her hand, but now instead of purple and red highlights adorning its pedals, they were blue and gold.

"How did you do that?" he asked bewildered.

"I didn't do anything," she replied.

Rick looked at the flower and carefully took it, then looked back at Ona.

"Does it just change on its own?" he asked, examining it closely.

"All living matter has a pattern to its existence. Stone molecules will line up a certain way, as will a tree, a rock, gas, air. It's all in their design. As a Thane, your mind has the power to see their structures and manipulate them."

"What about metal?"

"Yes, but be forewarned." Ona raised a finger of caution. "While metal isn't necessarily a complex structure, its function can be. If you manipulate the structure of a ship's bulkhead, you could introduce unintended side effects resulting in undesirable consequences."

That made sense. If a Thane were to use these powers recklessly, they could cause more harm than good. He looked at her copper hair and cocked a restrained playful smile. Zooming in on her hair strands, he could see the prefect little ringlets layering each strand and zooming in even further, its molecular wall enlarged directly in front of him. He reached for the wall of atoms tightly dancing, but he couldn't touch them. Pressing harder, but still unable to make contact, he felt a buzzing develop at his fingertips. The harder he pressed the more pronounced the buzzing became until it turned to a tingle and finally a bolt of energy blasted him back to reality and he stepped back. Astonished, he looked at his still tingling hands, then at Ona for an explanation. It was only going to be a bit of a prank played on the teacher. Reaching for her hair and pulling a strand from her long flowing mane, Ona gave him a good natured look.

"Only when a symbiont being is no longer in direct control of their molecular structures are you free to manipulate it in any manner you desire. Here," she offered, handing him a strand of her hair. "Try it now."

Rick took the strand of hair and tried again. This time it turned a light yellow color on one end and dark brown on the other. He looked back up at Ona and smiled at his accomplishment.

"You can always tell someone who is not in complete control of molecular manipulation. They will have trouble making things change or keeping them changed. Like if I didn't want to have this lovely shade of bright auburn hair..." Ona shifted her eyes to a lock of her hair and gave it a flick with her finger. Her entire head of hair changed to a pure white, but moments later, it began to change to several different colors until it finally settled back to her beautiful, brilliant auburn.

"Will it be that obvious?" Rick asked.

"Depends on their level of skill." Rick felt the air around him start to move and suddenly found himself airborne. "Remember this," she said raising a hand, "just because you can't manipulate their molecular structure directly, doesn't mean you can't change the conditions of their surroundings. Differing pressures around the different organs of the body can easily rupture blood vessels and create such pain as to render a person helpless."

Rick reveled in the feeling of being lighter than air, but was a little unnerved discovering he had no control over his condition. Sensing his low comfort level, Ona set him back down.

"While all matter is living, a Thane cannot manipulate it if it belongs to another symbiont being without that being's permission to do so. That being said, you do have the ability to distract the mind and control it. But be forewarned, it is a dangerous journey into another person's mind. It is a fragile place and like other complex structures, unintended results could be created by careless manipulation. Certainly you are already aware of the complex Infra-Low Beta waves present in the mind. Carefully focused, you can pierce directly into the mind, repairing or disrupting tissue and neural pathways, offering relief or causing blinding pain. Held just right, a person's mind can be suspended indefinitely or tortured infinitely. You can offer complete comfort and healing, life itself or freakish pain and suffering, even death. This technique of mind penetration, called

ILOB manipulation, is discouraged among Thanes because of their nature and the simplicity in creating them. It takes an extended measure of control to enter the mind without creating unintended problems. You're in just as much danger of their mind as they are of yours. Be forewarned of those who betray all a Thane stands for. You must be able to defend yourself from them in an instant. And you must be willing to do whatever is necessary to subdue in a reasonable and responsible way. So, your first problem," she announced, sitting back and folding her arms, looking all around at her handy work. "I want you to coax our friends here, back to where they belong. Then I want you to bring your ship inside this chamber, without making a mess."

"You gonna help?" Rick was a little nervous. Coaxing the plants back outside might be one thing, but trying to bring a ship inside without wrecking the place might prove a little tricky.

"You won't need my help," she responded casually. "Remember, there are many ways to accomplish a task. Don't over-think it. A Thane is recognized at any level, on any plane. You don't have to blow a gasket trying to make something happen. Just think it through, you'll be fine."

Rick looked at her reassuring expression, then settled back against the pillar and closed his eyes. Trying to clear his mind of all clutter, he once again imagined himself zeroing in on the sub-atomic makeup of his surroundings. He slowly opened his eyes, now seeing the plants and their structures. Each unique framework turned to him, waiting for his command. At first, his only thought was to provide himself more room so he could figure out which way to have everything go. Just the beginnings of the thoughts gave cause for the plants to retreat back to the main floor and partially back up the pillars. Trying to maintain control, he carefully addressed each structure, asking it to adjourn back to where it had come from. As they began to do so, a thought came to him.

"Thank you." Before the thought had finished developing, a warmth enveloped him and the plants retreated on their own, the tree trunks climbing back up the pillars and out the openings at the top.

As the last of the vines retreated through the open bronze doors, Rick stepped out into the middle of the room and turned to one of the walls of the temple. He knew his ship was parked on the other side of the wall, but how do you bring it inside without making a mess? He could always start it up and drive it right through, then clean up the mess afterwards, but that would require a whole lot of work afterwards. One of the instructions given him was not to make a mess in the first place. He thought about dismantling the wall and then reassembling it afterwards, but that too seemed like a lot of work considering his task. His father had taught him as a young lad. *Why expend more energy to accomplish a task than you have to? Work smart.*

Looking at the wall, he became aware he was now looking through it. He could see his ship sitting right there. He thought about just lifting it with the air surrounding it. That would certainly be one way of doing it, but then a better idea came to mind. He zoomed right into the cockpit, activating its systems, then turned on its anti-grav. The ship instantly began to float and using the air around it, he gently twisted it to face the temple. Holding it stationary, he now zoomed in on the wall itself. The ship was far more complex in its structure, so it would be easier to manipulate the wall instead.

Examining the structure closely, he zoomed in at its sub-atomic level. If he added a couple of things and removed a couple, he could change its properties. Once he had it the way he wanted it, he replaced it back in its original position, then waved his hand across the entire wall, asking the rest of the molecules to duplicate his efforts with the first. The entire wall disappeared and his Interceptor appeared, hovering just outside. With the air gently swirling around the ship and a careful twist of his wrist, it slipped inside, coming to rest on the clean white floor. He turned back to the wall and waved his hand carefully across the entire area and the wall changed back to its original structure. Shutting down the systems on his ship, he turned back to Ona who stood with her arms folded watching him. She looked at him closely, stepping toward him with only a slight smile on her face. After circling him once, she stopped in front of him, looking at his ship, then back at him.

"Oh, you're good. You're very good." She held herself carefully, taking a small step backwards. "I like it when everything is already in place. Makes my job so much easier. Just a couple of things I can't emphasize enough before you leave me." Ona turned back to her platform and ascended to the bench. Picking up his weapons, she held them up in front of her, griping them by the blades. Pressing them together like two broken pieces, she touched a control on both sides of both grips. There was an audible pop as the two pieces instantly fused together and she tossed it back to him.

"Your Balkrum will do many things that you'll discover on your own. It's a good weapon when used properly, trust it."

Rick looked at the weapon, once two, now one.

"Always think several steps ahead, but remain in the moment. Make sure you are always focused directly on the task before you act, and above all, remember that in order to accomplish the work of good, sacrifices will always have to be made. Just don't ever let those sacrifices be in vain." She sat down and leaned back. "There is no more to be learned here. Now, go find your friend, he has need of your help. Look for him on Cross."

Rick opened his mouth to ask for something a little more specific, but the look on her face told him any further questions would be pointed to the future. He would have to discover the answers on his own, so he turned to his ship and climbed in. Bringing the ship's systems back online and putting it into a hover, he looked out at Ona. She remained seated, watching him. He gestured toward the wall the ship had entered, but she remained motionless. He realized this would be one of a whole string of on the job training exercises. With careful resolve, he turned his gaze up, zooming in on the ceiling this time, instantly changing it as he had the wall. Bringing his engines online, he bumped the throttles carefully, trying not to disturb the air beneath him. As he cleared the building, the roof reappeared and he gave his ship throttle, streaking away from the temple.

Test one

Ordering full power to the *Athena's* maneuvering thrusters, Toby leaned closer to his displays studying the dimensional readouts on a large ship coming at them.

"What's its speed, CORA?" Several monitors lit up above the science officer.

"Twenty-five thousand and closing fast. They appear to be on a collision course with us. Dimensionals and armor specifications displayed above your head."

The science officer looked up and studied the readouts above him, then looked over his shoulder at the com officer.

"Yellow alert. Call Commander Niker to the bridge." Toby swung his attention forward to the weapons officer. "Shields to maximum."

"Shield strength at thirty percent. Weapons capacity at twenty-five percent," CORA announced.

"Thank you, CORA," Toby responded.

"Yellow alert, Commander Niker to the bridge," the com officer called out over the ship's public address system.

Toby continued to study the technical readouts of the battlecruiser coming at them, as Jayda's voice popped over the comlink.

"Commander Niker here. I'm still in the ball turret, report."

"Commander, is your targeting system up?"

"Yeah, I'm seeing it. They aren't just trolling around looking for space junk, are they?"

"It looks as though they're on a collision course with us."

"It's a good bet they don't want to ask for directions," Jayda responded.

"Their guns are quite large and there are a lot of them, Commander. We have neither the shield power to defend against them, nor the firepower to repel them."

"And we can't outrun them without the Fulton drive back online. Man battle stations and sound red alert. Have CORA call the General back as quick as he can get here.

"I'm sure the General is already on his way. CORA's early warning systems are tied directly into his cockpit."

"The second Interceptor is still stuck where it is and I've got everyone else back here working on getting sub-light power back online so we can throw something besides spit balls at them. I'll stay where I am and see if this turret works." Jayda settled back in the turret gunner's chair, charged its guns and adjusted the controls as the red alert sirens started to sound off.

*   *   *   *

Commander SoKnack fidgeted slightly. Standing next to him on the command deck, Blinda Koss listened to the reports called up from below. An information officer handed her a readout pad, saluted and stomped away.

"That was some lazy eight, Commander," Blinda commented, glancing down at the readouts in her hand. "Blair wants that barge?" she bellowed. "Come on Drax! What could this thing possibly offer? It looks like a glorified Bivovac; a garbage scow."

Dalton glanced over at Blinda as she handed him the display. He was sure she'd be singing a different tune if Drax were actually standing here.

"This glorified Bivovac as you call it, blasted its way right through the Ratronian assault fleet a couple of days ago." Dalton kept his tone monotone and emotionless as he studied the readouts in his hand. He wanted to stay out of any contention that might rear its ugly head if Drax and Blinda got into an argument. All he was doing was following orders. He couldn't possibly get in trouble for that.

Blinda frowned, perceiving his attitude and ploy. Either this man had no backbone or he was playing one against the other. Whichever it was, she wasn't amused.

"Just get me closer to it, Commander," she scowled. "Then I'll decide if it's worth our time." She stepped over to a different window, away from the battlecruiser commander.

Dalton looked carefully after her. He got the impression she didn't like operating under such limiting guidelines. Normally, when given an assignment, she had the autonomy to use whatever methods necessary to make it happen. Those conditions didn't exist here. While she was in command of the assignment, Dalton was still in command of the *Tarzana* and she was supposed to take this alien ship intact, not just wipe it out. *It will be interesting to see how she makes this happen,* he thought, turning to the command pit and the officers below awaiting his orders.

"Stand down the heavy cannons and missile launchers. Bring us broadside and we'll use the Pulse guns on them."

"Just make sure you don't blow it up," Blinda shouted from the other side of the command deck. "Bring their shields down. That's all I require."

"My sole intension, I can assure you," Dalton responded, stepping back over next to the Thane.

"You can assure me of nothing," she spat. Dalton slowly turned back to the command pit.

"Drop your gun intensity back to five. We don't want it destroyed; just bring its shields down." Dalton turned back to the window to watch as the battlecruiser pulled within range and its smaller cannons started firing. "This won't take very long at all. You say when to stop," Dalton smirked confidently. Blinda folded her arms, holding herself steady as the smaller ship began to return fire, the big ship quaking with every strike to its shields.

"I hope so," Blinda commented, trying to hold her balance. The firepower being hurled back at them was surprising. While putting up a good fight, they were trying to run, but the alien ship was curiously slow.

*   *   *   *

Main deck lights winked, as the *Athena* took another hit.

"Helm, get us out of here," the science officer bellowed from his station. His eyes trained on the war ship paralleling them, they weren't going to last long with the amount of fire being thrown at them.

"We can only go so fast," Captain Dayton announced from the helm. "Starbirds weren't designed to go toe to toe with a capital ship of this size. Unless you can get me sub-light power, we're bug squash."

"Weapons officer," Toby called forward. "They have to lower a window of shields in order to fire. Target those smaller guns on her broadside. You can tell they're about to fire because they dip right before they let go."

"Take a course directly below her," Jayda ordered from the com.

"Even with Interceptor Two's engines online I can't get in close enough," Captain Dayton reported, frustrated. "They keep pulling away from my maneuvers, matching my speed. Surprising how nimble something that big can be. What about trying Gunnar and Rick's sling shot maneuver?"

"The tractor hawsers would suck what energy reserves we have down to nothing before we could get under it," Toby said.

"How are we doing with taking out those guns?" Jayda asked, taking aim and plucking off the gun barrels as they dipped.

"There are too many of them," Toby reported, steadying himself and continuing to look for a weakness. "That thing is built to deal with a fighter assault."

"CORA," Jayda called out. "Is there anything you can see, anything we can use?"

"The lower conning tower has minimal defenses. The hull on the bottom is far thicker than on the top or the sides. If you can get in close enough and take out those lower cannons that could provide you with enough cover from their side guns to buy a little time."

"That's a big *IF*," Lisa Dayton responded as the ship took another volley of hits.

"We just need a little more time to get the sub-light drive back online," Jayda announced taking aim again and firing. "Clancy, how you boys coming along down there?"

No answer.

"They're not letting up, maybe communications are down." Toby passed a look back at the com officer as another blast pounded them, overloading several systems between them.

"It's possible nothing is getting out," Laura Habba said turning back to her equipment. "I'm transmitting on all frequencies, but the Archer relays are malfunctioning and the standing wave ratios are through the roof right now. We may not even have connection to our antenna arrays anymore."

"It's not likely they're interested in communicating at this point," Jayda responded, firing again. She gave her power indicators a frown. They were dropping fast and unless they could change their circumstances, they would be in a world of hurt. "How are the shields holding up?" Static burst back at Jayda as they took another hit. She could tell the helmsman was doing all she could to maneuver her ship under the big cruiser, but they were so slow and sluggish, each attempt to turn into them, the cruiser would counter.

"Main shields can only take a couple more direct hits and the gun batteries are nearly exhausted," CORA reported.

"Don't I know it," Jayda mumbled angrily. She fired again and again, trying to knock out the myriad of smaller guns dipping and firing at them. "How are we coming with the sub-light drive?" she shouted frustrated. "Not good, Commander," came the frantic reply from Clancy. "We're doing the best we can."

She sure wished Rick were here.

"CORA, are you still in direct com with the General's Interceptor?"

"No ma'am," came the calm reply. "I lost coms shortly after we came under attack. His telemetry indicates he's on his way, but I am unable to pin-point his position or how long it will take him to reach us."

Jayda bit her lip, letting another volley of blasts go on their pursuers, and then braced herself for another round of incoming. Trying to fire again, nothing happened. Her guns had powered down.

Toby turned to the shield monitor as a warning indicator started making noise. The last of their shields buckled and collapsed.

*   *   *   *

Commander SoKnack and Blinda turned to the command pit noticing they had stopped firing.

"Their shields are down, sir," the pit officer called up. "But they're not stopping."

"Can we grab them with the new tractor beam?"

"Negative, sir," the pit officer shook his head grimly. "It's only good for bringing disabled or auto piloted ships onboard."

Dalton looked up from the pit officer to Blinda, gesturing outside.

"Ok Blinda, their shields are down. We can't bring it in until they're stopped. Get in there and do your stuff."

"Don't you dare try and tell me how to do my job, Commander," Blinda flamed.

Dalton stepped back with his hands up, trying to relax. He already knew he would have no trouble bringing such a small ship to its knees. Now Blinda would have to use her powers of the Thane to bring the crew of the vessel into submission or somehow disable the ship.

The Thane slowly turned back to the window, closed her eyes and zoomed in on the fleeing ship and its crew. Her hope was to go for the ship itself, but after several minutes of feeling for it, finding it and trying to manipulate its complex structures, she pulled back exasperated. She was assigned to take the ship intact and changing things without total control could bring about unintended results she wasn't prepared to take the responsibility for. She tried zooming in on the crew and the air internal to the ship, but the ship's movement made it impossible. Frustrated, she finally turned back to Dalton.

"You'll have to slow them down or stop them, I can't get in," she puffed angrily.

"What are you saying? Is that an order? Drax said she..."
Dalton wanted full disclosure.

"I don't care what Drax said!" Blinda shouted, turning back to
the window. "I said bring it down!"

Commander SoKnack slowly turned to the command pit,
giving the order to fire, and then turned back to the window to
watch.

*   *   *   *

The *Athena* shook, its naked hull pounded mercilessly by the
Albion ship. Frantic to get their sub-light drive back online, the
engineers scrambled to get the last of the repairs in place before
they lost hull integrity. Jayda spun the turret around, nearly
blinded by an incoming volley exploding next to her. The blast
pierced through the upper hull, into the engine room and out the
bottom. Chaos ensued as the engine room erupted. The turret
automatically sealed, protecting Jayda from the massive
radiation flares and heat bursts certain to follow. She noticed
the ship slow and spinning her turret forward, watched the
maneuvering thruster ports sputter and go dark. Horror filled
her as she watched the bodies of the engineers exit the hull
breach in the engineering section, trailing behind the drifting
Starbird.

Trying to blot out the images of death, Jayda spun the turret
back around to the side and tilted up, looking at the massive
bulk dwarfing the *Athena*. Her turret when dark as the ship lost
power and she instinctively reached for the turret's emergency
power controls. Several small interior lights popped on and a
few other emergency systems, but now all she could do was
wait. *They had stopped firing... What were they waiting for
now? There are no boarding ships embarking, no tractor
hawsers. What was to happen now?* Her com systems were
dead. She could see they were starting to list away from the
battlecruiser as it slid a little closer. Then she felt her ears start
to pressure up to the point her ear drums hurt, her sinuses and
chest growing tight. *The ship's environmental systems must
have been damaged or something. But that didn't make any
sense. The turret is sealed off. I've got my own air supply now.
Enough to last for days, even weeks if need be. No, something
else is happening. The pressure hurts! It hurts!* Holding her
hands to her head did nothing as she watched the enemy ship
roll out of sight, the *Athena* tipping on her side. Jayda screamed
as the pain went beyond anything she had ever experienced.
Every nerve ending in her body screamed in anguish,
unconsciousness racing into her mind. She glanced down at the

tracking screen to her left. A signal return appeared at the furthest reaches of its range. She tried to work the controls to get some kind of identification, but her mind was twisting completely out of control. She recognized an indicator on the touch screen in front of her. Interceptor two had just launched. She tried so hard to figure out what that meant, but her reasoning was gone. Her only recognizable thought was for Rick's return.

Blackness shrouding her vision and pain crushing her, she let her hand drop to the emergency panel to her right. Feeling her fingers come in contact with the emergency eject control, Jayda's last thoughts were of Audra Atlanta as she had met her fate a year ago. Now Rick would have to endure the same pain and loneliness Gunnar was dealing with. She heard the sound of the ejection boosters exploding, and then everything went black.

*   *   *   *

Dalton and Blinda looked closely at the large holes in the top and bottom of the aft section of the crippled starship now drifting helplessly next to them. A luminescent grey cloud issued from the hull breaches of the smaller vessel. Dalton studied the life readings and frowned. No life indications onboard and most of the ship's systems appeared to be without power. He turned to the command engineers for more detail on the damage to the ship as Blinda pressed her forehead against the bridge window, looking down at the slowly rolling ship. Flashes were starting to emit from the large hull breach in the top and bottom of the aft section. Dalton studied the readouts spilling from their monitors and listened to the technical chatter rolling from the engineers. There were peculiar readings coming from the aft section of the mortally wounded ship and the command engineers hastily interpreted the information as a buildup to a detonation. Dalton finally turned to the pit commander.

"Can you get any technical data on it?"

"Negative, sir," the lead engineer reported. "Whatever these readings are, they're disrupting all our scans. We're getting nothing but gibberish."

"Get us out of here now! I want as much distance between us and that ship as soon as possible." Stepping back up onto the command platform he folded his arms and came to a halt beside Blinda.

"I hope you're satisfied. Drax is going to blow a gasket. You were sent to bring that ship back, not destroy it and now here we are running from it." Dalton scowled but understood who he was dealing with so he held it back as best he could. They both watched as the *Tarzana* gently tilted, powering away from the scene of destruction. Blinda spun right at him, raising a gloved finger to his chin.

"There was no other choice, SoKnack!" Blinda was hot, but Dalton figured he was somewhat safe for the moment as Blinda wasn't stupid enough to destroy the ship she was sent to capture and murder him in the same five minutes. "Besides, it was your gunners that poked holes in it."

"Oh no you don't, Koss," Dalton fired back becoming incensed. "You were the one that gave the orders to fire both times!"

"I couldn't get to the crew with the ship still moving. It was the only way, Commander! The garbage scow wasn't worth anything anyway. You saw how much fire power and shield power it had. We had no problem cutting through their defenses and outrunning them. Clearly it was a Tomplie piece of junk."

Dalton started past the Thane for the command pit.

"You can explain all that to the Queen Captain when we pick her up from Reako."

"Don't you turn your back on me," Blinda barked fuming. Enraged, she pulled a set of metallic tear drop shaped rings from her hip and activated them. A thin purple ribbon rippled out along the curved outer edge of the Balkrums pointed right at Dalton's back, freezing him in his tracks. The sound of the popping radium streams crackled in his ears as the control room personnel fell silent. All eyes shifted to Commander SoKnack now as he slowly turned and faced Blinda. A wild gleam sparkled in her eyes as she held an attack stance, the glowing Balkrums poised at Dalton's chest. Feeling the air pressure around him starting to close in, Dalton could only imagine what the last moments for the crew of the alien ship had been like. He was aware of the things a Thane could manipulate. If Dalton knew one thing now, it was to do whatever Blinda wanted or get carved up and jettisoned with the refuse. Never, ever enrage a Thane, especially Blinda Koss. Her reputation for a short temper was too widely known and he had pushed his luck a little too far. He was going to have a time of it reeling back his thin thread of life hanging in the balance with his next words. He slowly raised his hands, the pressure on his ear drums nearly unbearable, but he managed a smile all the same.

"I'm merely suggesting that you're going to have some explaining to do," he said deliberately. "And I have every reason to believe that Drax isn't going to be in a very good mood when we pick her up." Now he waited.

"I don't care what kind of mood Drax is going to be in," Blinda growled. "Just keep clear of me." She shut off the

Balkrums, putting them back in their place and turned to a side window, watching the burning alien ship receding to a pinpoint.

Dalton exhaled slowly and grinned shakily, lowering his hands and turning in the opposite direction. He lifted a finger to his mouth to calm his quivering lip. He was sure that she was going to cut him up on that one. Clearly, Blinda had made the blunders here, but wasn't going to own up to them. As he walked carefully from the bridge, he could feel the air pressure returning to normal. Might be a good idea to keep clear of Blinda for the time being, until Drax got back. The facts would speak for themselves.

*   *   *   *

Rick touched the comlink button on the bottom side of the control yoke.

"CORA, come in. CORA?" CORA had sent him an alert, but nothing else. Just an emergency alert and return notification. He gave his scanner a nervous look. There was another ship in the area, but it appeared to be moving away at a high rate. It wasn't until he noticed several spikes on his sensors and a flash of light ahead of him, that his worst fears were realized.

"CORA, do you read? Come in." Only a soft hiss came back over his com system.

"Jayda, come in. Toby, can anyone hear me?"

Nothing.

He maneuvered his ship in such a way as to keep himself in the shadow of the *Athena* on approach so he could not be easily seen by the ship departing the area. Drawing closer, horror gripped him, seeing brilliant flashes coming from the aft section of the *Athena*. He noticed that Interceptor two was missing and the turret was gone. A panicked burble rolled through him as he studied the sensor readouts on the display in front of him. Only sporadic energy readings came back at him and his dimensional readouts showed extensive damage to the slowly rolling craft. *Had they abandoned ship?* Rick adjusted his tracking controls, keeping an eye on the departing ship, making sure it didn't detect him and circle back. He turned back to his sensors, scanning for life readings. His pulse quickened as only faint readings came back at him. He had to get back onboard and assess the situation in real time.

Keeping his Interceptor behind the rolling Starbird on approach, Rick activated the fighter's auto docking computer and prepared to disembark. Sensor readings of the ship's interior indicated the environmental and anti-grav systems were off-line. He would have to go through engineering to get to those system controls. The flashes from the hull breaches on top and bottom of the aft section indicated something violent happening in engineering. The readings indicated the entire compartment was flooded with Asium plasma. As his Interceptor started docking procedures, he donned a G-suit, capable of protecting him from the Asium plasma radiation and sustaining his own life support. Once the fighter was secured, he rode the body cradle down into engineering.

Smoke swirled madly through the entire room and checking his wrist scanner, found no air or life support of any kind. Indeed, the interior temperature had bottomed out. He had to turn his heat compensators up to full. Approaching the engine bulkhead, it was clear why. Stars were visible through a massive hole in the top of the engine compartment and a corresponding hole directly below next to the engine bulkhead. Groping through the thick smoke, he activated the sun shield to protect his eyes from the source of the blinding flares. Looking up at the Asium chamber, Rick could see something wrong with the venting system on the chamber. Not only was the damaged chamber venting directly into the engineering compartment, but several of the crystals had become dislodged from their mounting claws and were contacting each other. Power to the ship could not be restored with the crystals and chamber in this condition. The immense engineering display console was a chaotic scramble of indeterminate shapes and colors dancing wildly all around the glass.

The thick smoke wasn't actually smoke at all, but Asium plasma. Had Rick not been wearing the suit when he entered the ship, he would have been instantly vaporized. The plasma would have disintegrated his cellular structure like a flame to tissue paper. Fumbling in the darkness, his head lamps cutting through the obscuring plasma mist, he found the engineer's equipment. Employing the right tool, he worked to carefully coax the Asium crystals away from each other and back into their mounting claws. Then began the time consuming, delicate work of securing each claw finger at the correct point on each crystal until he was reasonably sure they would remain secure. Rummaging around in one of the engine room storage trestles, he located the chamber containment plate and installed it. Its design was such as to be fitted into place quickly, as a break in containment would require it.

Fighting the urgency to find Jayda, he understood the need to get the engine room habitable first as it had taken most of the ship's critical systems offline, including environmental. Stepping carefully to the engineering turbo doors, he forced them open and struggled through. His bulky suit required his maneuvers to be exaggerated in order to remain clear of debris. Once through the second set of turbo doors to the mid-ship and crew's quarters hallway, he turned and forced the doors closed again, then turned to a control box on the wall. A big manual override handle dropped out and after working a couple of other controls, he pushed the handle up into the locked position and pulled a small valve. An alarm sounded, followed by a blinking light that turned green a moment later. He then opened another control box next to the first and started adjusting several controls. Adjusting the Asium crystals must have allowed the ship's batteries to come back online.

It would take a considerable amount of time to reboot and bring essential systems back up. After checking the indicators here, he turned back to the engineering door manual override and activated the system. There was a loud pop, then a light hissing noise. Rick pulled his shield control from a pouch on his suit and activated it. With power restored to the ship, the shield generators could seal the hull breach. It blinked for several seconds, then the lights went solid, the hissing at the door stopped and several hallway lights winked on. He touched a couple of buttons on a control pad on the sleeve of his suit and studied the heads up display in his helmet. Inside/outside air temperature and quality information flashed up along with various other readings.

Breathable air! After checking it carefully, he depressurized his suit and pulled the helmet off.

The hull breach in engineering had vacated the air from the aft compartment and leached some of the heat from the mid-section. The air was fine, the temperature a little chilly, but warming as the environmental systems started working again. Turning to the teleporter room, he made his way inside and to the ship's auxiliary control console. In the event the bridge became inoperable for any reason, the ship could still be controlled from the teleporter room. Here, he was able to bring the rest of the ship's systems back online, albeit somewhat limited as battery power was at a minimum. He would need to get engine power back online as soon as possible to keep the rest of the ship operational. After working for some time, he touched a control in front of him.

"CORA, are you back online? Come on, wake up." A quiet hiss came back at him as he studied the ship's environmental readouts. With the exception of engineering, everything aboard ship was intact, including air. The bridge was the best place to be right now. It would take some time for engineering's temperature to stabilize. He needed to find out what happened to Jayda and assess the situation with the rest of his crew. It

was a sure bet the engineers and both Interceptor pilots had
perished in engineering, but for now it was impossible to know
the status of the rest of the crew.

"Rick?" CORA's voice rang out. "You made it back!"

Rick stepped back out into the mid-section hallway and
started for the medical complex door.

"Yes, CORA. How are you doing? What's your status?"
There was a moment of silence giving Rick cause to pause before
he tried to open the doors to sickbay.

"Battery power at critical."

"Can you get the doors working ship wide?"

"I'll do what I can."

"Tell me what happened. Where's Jayda?" He stepped
through the partially open door only to find the two medical
officers dead on the floor inside.

"Still retrieving data. Ship scans and com systems are
currently offline, so I can't tell you exactly where anyone is or
their condition. It was a large ship and came at us fast. They
looked like they were going to ram us or something. Then they
opened up on us."

"Who came at you? Who opened fire?" Rick stepped back
out into the hallway and started for the bridge.

"Technical scans show it was an Albion battlecruiser," CORA
responded. "We hailed them on all known frequencies but got
nothing. They didn't even try to board us. They just opened up
until all our gun batteries were down and then our shield power
was gone. Captain Dayton tried to maneuver us under them to
stay out of their range, but we had only maneuvering thrusters
and Interceptor two..."

"Yeah, I know," Rick cut in. "Tough to deal with emergency
maneuvers when all you have are MTs. What happened to
Interceptor two?"

"When our shields failed, they opened up on us again. We
took a direct hit to engineering and after that, I don't know what
happened. Most of the ship's systems either automatically shut
down or crashed. There is no data to indicate what happened
Interceptor two. The launch rails appear to have been fired, so I
can only deduce the craft tried to launch and was destroyed."

Approaching the bridge door, Rick reached to open it, but it
automatically popped open on its own. The bridge was only
partially lit and only a few of the consoles had come back on. A
sinking feeling developed in the pit of his stomach as he took
note of the empty command chair. *Jayda isn't here.* Rick
stepped to the communications console and turned Laura's chair
around. She was still safety locked in, but slumped over.
Checking her for a pulse, he noticed her chest raising and falling

in quick succession. Still holding her wrist, he turned Toby around and found him in the same condition. Both appeared only barely alive. He quickly made his way to the other side of the bridge only to discover the weapons officer and the navigator, still safety locked in their chairs, slumped in death. Stepping toward helm control, he noticed movement on the floor and knelt at Captain Dayton's side. Somehow, she had deactivated her safety locks, ending up on the floor. He held her up in his arms and checked her over, but could see no visible injuries. Her breathing was labored and shallow.

"CORA, do you have your medical diagnostic tie-ins online yet?" Rick scooped up the Starbird pilot and headed for the door.

"My diagnostic functions have been unaffected by the ship's systems crash. Please be advised that the main and auxiliary batteries are at critical. We need to get the Fulton sub-light drive back online within the next two hours or all systems will fail, even the emergency shields."

"Bring your medical diagnostics online in sickbay and have the beds ready when I get there." Rick grunted, trying to hurry through the door and down the hall. Once inside sickbay, he set her on one of the medical tables, looking up at the medical monitor coming on as he set her down. He was no medical expert but even he could see her condition was critical.

"CORA, have the med-assist look her over while I run get the others.

Rick remained only for a moment and then hurried back to the bridge. Deactivating the chair safety locks, he pulled Lieutenant Habba from her chair and carried her to sick bay. He repeated the same process for Toby until he had all three of them on beds in sick bay.

"CORA, what do you make of this?"

"Various internal injuries, Captain Dayton has a collapsed lung and fluid on the brain. Lieutenant Habba and Mr. Mavis have similar injuries. Judging from the extent of the nervous system damage, all three have to be in an incredible amount of pain. Probably best if they remain unconscious."

"What can be done?" he asked looking around for something.

"Medical drawer to you right, there should be several hypos stored there. Administer one full dose of the blue colored one. They all need oxygen. I will see if the medical assist system is working. It can help you get Captain Dayton's lung reinflated."

Rick cringed. This was not his forte by a long shot. He had performed emergency field first aid before, but then promptly threw up afterwards. Hypos he could do. Putting a mask on a face he could do, but he had no idea what it was going to take to reinflate a lung. Pressing the hypo to her arm, he listened to the hiss of the instrument pumping fluid into her, then glanced up at the monitor to see if there were any results. He wasn't sure what he should be looking for, but was hopeful all the same as he repeated the process for the other two.

"Rick, I can help direct what the med assistant does here. After you get them oxygen, please see if you can do something about the Fulton drive." Rick was more than happy to oblige. Working on mechanical stuff made more sense to him than the human body. Seeing that each of the three had oxygen flowing freely into their masks, he turned back to the door as the med assist arm extended from the wall.

Rick cautiously approached the engineering turbo door, studying several of the room readouts before he entered. The temperature had finally stabilized and the radiation readings were within tolerances. Taking a deep breath, he activated the door sensor. Inside, nearly all the lights were still working, except in the vicinity of the hull breaches now sealed by the ship's shields. Their field strength had to be running at minimal. As soon as the battery power was exhausted, the shields would shut down leaving the ship to die in the elements of deep space. Stepping to the engineering control consoles, he couldn't help but glance at the breaches in the ceiling and floor. Refocusing on getting the systems back online, he started going through the engineer's real-time repair logs to see how far they had gotten before the hull breach. His heart sank further after finishing the logs and learning they were only a couple of minutes from reengaging the sub-light drive.

"CORA, how are our patients doing?"

"Still very critical, Rick. We've done just about all we can for the moment."

"Have you scanned these logs yet?"

"I'm just finishing them now. It's unfortunate they were so close to having everything operational. Are you able to complete these repairs?"

"Still trying to access what damage the hull breach caused to the Fulton drive systems, if any. I'm working on these last couple of things right now, but this could take a while." Rick glanced past the engineering consoles to the turret elevator shaft. "Can you bring up the com logs from the last ten minutes before your systems crashed?"

"I will try. There is corruption in the data files containing this information."

Drawing on his expansive knowledge of the Starbird's system designs, Rick worked in silence to affect the repairs the engineering team hadn't completed. In this complicated technical realm, he was at complete ease. He had been working on space craft since he was eight years old. Having natural abilities as a star pilot, he was driven by his talents to not only fly them, but design, maintain and repair them. He had taken an old derelict recon Viper he and his dad had found when he was but a teenager, repaired and modified it with his own upgrades. This was where he had found CORA's main core functions. When the fighter had been badly damaged after passing through a solar storm, he removed her hardware, transferring it to another fighter and ultimately, having it installed into the mainframe of the *Athena*. She integrated well in her new host, even with the advancements of the technology, Rick and Jayda had been able to keep her AI in sync with her surroundings.

"Here's what's available," CORA finally came back on. Rick listened carefully as he worked to finish the last items on the repair list. Stopping several times to focus on the recording, he had CORA replay certain sections to listen closer to the conversations. He wanted to make sure he understood exactly what had happened and why.

"Does the telemetry indicate where Jayda was when engineering was hit?"

"Telemetry does not, but the voice recorders do. She remained in the turret when the attack started. She lost firing battery power moments before the strike and the elevator shaft instantly sealed the turret off. The data corrupts after that, but the evidence would indicate that she was sealed in the turret and it was jettisoned.

"Do you have any information on what was happening to the rest of the crew?"

"Not directly," CORA responded softly. "But I did record some peculiar life support readings before my systems crashed. The atmosphere in the ship began to move and the cabin pressure spiked at levels dangerous for humans. I also picked up some strange wavelengths projecting right at us from the Albion battlecruiser."

Rick stopped and looked up. Not at anything particular, but to clear his mind and allow his Thane training to move forward in his thought processes. *Projected wavelengths?* These conditions sounded like something Ona had warned him about with ILOB manipulation. *Was it possible his crew had experienced a savage ILOB attack in an attempt to gain access to the Athena?* His thoughts turned back to Jayda. *Was she able to jettison the turret pod before succumbing to the effects of air pressure manipulation or worse? Had some of his crew perished as a result of ILOB manipulation?*

"Rick, ship's batteries are down to less than fifteen minutes."
Rick blinked, snapping back to what he had been doing.

"We're good here," he said stepping back to the engineering
consoles and checking his work. "Have you finished running a
ship wide diagnostic?"

"No, I've been holding down most of my functions to
conserve power. You leave a room and I shut it off."

"Well, you should have all the power you need now," Rick
commented touching several controls on the touch screen in
front of him. A low whirling noise gently rose from the engine
bulkhead in front of him as the Fulton drive came back online.
There came a warmth to his soul as the ship appeared to
brighten, feeling more alive now.

"Run your diagnostics now, I'll be in sickbay."

"Their condition remains unchanged, Rick. They are still
unconscious and I have my doubts if they will ever wake up."

"You're forgetting about the effects of the human component
on another human," Rick pointed out, exiting the engine room.

Rick began the grim work of gathering up the ship's dead, he
started with the two medical officers, laying them carefully on
the floor outside the teleporter room. Removing all of their
personal affects and storing them separately in their quarters, he
carefully prepared each crewmen for burial in space. Each burial
preparation would be just as difficult as the next as he not only
knew each one of these men and women as close working crew
associates, but in the last year, they had all become good
friends. As a starship commander, the best relationship tactic
you could take with a crew was to remain aloof, not allowing
yourself to get too close. Being in a ranking position required
that you not have too many friends. It was always lonely at the
top. In his instance, he and Gunnar had found that removing
that barrier afforded them a dynamic with the fluidity of their
crews that few other starship commanders enjoyed. But there
was always a tradeoff, as Rick was now experiencing.

His thoughts turned back to a year ago when he had helped
his best friend bury his wife in this same manner. Now he had
an even better feel for what Gunnar had gone through. He
couldn't help but shed tears for each one as he carefully sealed
their burial shrouds and one at a time, teleported them out into
deep space. Once he had reverently completed the difficult task,
he stepped back into sickbay to check on the others.

Taking turns sitting at each bedside, he quietly spoke to each
one about anything that came to mind. While there was still
some disagreement about whether someone in a coma could
hear what was happening around them, he believed they could
and it was a way to help call them back to health. He considered

trying to peer into them, maybe manipulate damaged structures, but then thought better of it, fearing unintended results. The med assistant had installed a breathing device on their masks to aid their lungs. An arm gauntlet had been installed around each fore arm to provide needed medications and nutritional supplements. Only their spirits could decide if they would pull through.

Rick now had a choice to make. Driving this ship by himself was easy, but it would take him a considerable amount of time to get anywhere. Had he remained in formation with the *Constellation*, he'd be where they were, on Tintee. But he got the feeling that they had problems of their own. It would take him months to reach Tintee at the sub-light speed the *Athena* was capable of and that was if he wasn't intercepted by another ship. There was no point in going back to Boris, as there would be no one there. Taking the *Athena* to Cross to search for Gunnar was out of the question now, as the distance was also too great at sub-light. Contemplating his options, the answer came to him almost immediately. He needed to find Gunnar. Finding him was of paramount importance, above finding Jayda. But was he supposed to just leave Jayda to her own fate? And what about Interceptor two? Had it been destroyed or did the Albions have it? Technology of that kind could be trouble in the wrong hands.

Stepping back into the bridge, he took a seat at the science station and began running scanner sweeps as far as the ship's sensors could reach. A thorough sweep in all directions would take several hours.

"Status, CORA."

"Ship's batteries recharging nominally," CORA announced over the sound system.

Rick glanced outside at the rotating stars. They were still a drift and rolling, but the ship's anti-grav was compensating. He had been so pre-occupied; he hadn't even thought about stabilizing their orientation.

"Bring the maneuvering thrusters back online and orient us to this system's horizontal axis," he ordered, returning to the information in front of him. "Bring the deflector shields up to standard configuration as well."

"What are you looking for?" CORA asked quietly.

Rick remained silent as he worked his controls.

"Interceptor one status?" he asked, preoccupied. The AI circuits within CORA were having a difficult time processing what the Starbird commander was trying to do. Without detailed information she couldn't reach any conclusions based on logic. Her learning protocols helped her understand human feeling, though she was incapable of experiencing it for herself. She was artificial intelligence after all. The fact she had been given a female voice had been Rick's preference. It's what she originally had when he found her in the Recon.

"Interceptor one is fully operational. Rick, what do you have in mind?" Rick remained silent.

"Transfer this sensor data to the onboard database of Interceptor one," he ordered without another word and left the bridge.

"Rick, you're planning to follow the criterion trail from the escape pod to find Jayda."

"Sort of," Rick finally responded as he reentered sickbay to check again on the condition of the surviving crew members.

"What about Interceptor two?"

"Can you fit Captain Dayton, Lieutenant Habba and Mr. Mavis with Cryo tubes?"

"Yes, in fact Cryo tubes would be the better option for them now, until you can get them better medical attention."

"Do it", he said squeezing the Starbird pilot's hand. He looked at all three for a moment longer, and then turned for the door. As he left, he could see the med assistant moving a large tube from a far corner of the room toward the bed Lisa was laying on.

Scooping up the suit he had shed in the hall, he headed back through the engineering turbo door and directly for the elevator shaft to his Interceptor. After stowing the suit, he climbed into the pilot's seat and strapped in, hitting the mains. As the fighter's systems started powering up, CORA's voice came back on again.

"Rick, I don't understand what you're doing. I thought we were going after Jayda?"

"I'm not, you are," he said, instantly setting controls as the navigational systems started coming online. "I've pinpointed her trail and set the navigational coordinates at the science station." Rick brought the Interceptor engines online. "Shut down all nonessential systems and hold to the trail. You are instructed not to deviate for any reason. When you find Jayda, redock with the turret and follow her instructions back to Boris. Either land there at the Abura temple or hold an orbit until I come to get you."

"So where are you going?" CORA's voice elevated.

"I have to find Gunnar."

"Do you even know where he is?"

"I think I have a good idea."

"Well, what happens if..."

"CORA, deal with it," Rick interjected, hitting the turbo boost button on the control yoke. The big Interceptor blasted away from the aft wing of the Starbird, rolled once then thrusted forward, circling the *Athena* twice, then shot off in another direction.

We'll take that!

"This thing drives like my dune ram back home," Dakota commented as the assault tank rolled effortlessly toward the towering city spires of Tintee. With the cruiser *Trax* hovering close by and the destroyers *Realistic* and *Intruder* flanking both sides, it appeared most of the activity on the ground was centered beneath them. Several other support ships were parked on massive landing lifters beneath the three floating mastodons.

"Is that a good thing?" Talia glanced down at one of the small displays directly in front of her and adjusted a couple of controls. Frowning, she tried to keep what she was seeing on the screen to herself. She glanced behind her at her passengers sitting quietly in the back of the armored vehicle. Willis was driving the other tank carrying the other half of the Starbird crew as they sped at high cruise beneath the shadow of the *Trax*. Talia steered her vehicle behind a long column of tanks heading toward a gapping tear in the abrupt side of the mountain base.

"Depends on the day. Not to be a side seat driver here, but any idea where they're going to have the ship parked?" Dakota peered out one of the side window slits in the tank cockpit. He could see several tanks converging alongside them, falling in line with the rest of a column moving toward the mountain.

"Depends on how fast they want to get to it and what else they have going on. I suspect Command has their hands full right now trying to lay their hands on Colonel Barker and the rest of us. But I would expect the techs will be itching to get at your ship."

"Hope they're smart enough to stay away from it while the shields are turned on."

"Like I said, just depends on what they have going on right now. If we're lucky, it will still be sitting in the main hangar bay close to the doors and we can just fly right back out, but I wouldn't put any stock in that hope. It's a pretty ship to be sure."

"We like it. It's kind of our home away from home."

"So wouldn't it have been better to have just stayed onboard and waited until the dust settled a bit?" Tiana had been listening in on their conversation from behind. "Then we could just take off as you two are proposing."

"Combat tactics," Dakota replied. "There's no way we could have gotten through all that Colonian armor. Best to wait for the dust to settle, when the odds are better. This way, the home fleet deploys further away from Tintee. Most of them should be out chasing off them other guys..." He couldn't think of the name.

"The Ratronians," Talia finished.

"Right, that'll give us a better chance at getting our ships out of here."

"But why get off the ship? Why not just stay onboard and wait?"

"The idea is to divert their attention from us and get them to relax," Dakota said. "If they're able to scan the ship, they would've detected us still onboard and hovered around it, waiting for us to come out. This way, they think it's just an automated drone and have full possession and all the time in the world to get at it. Like I said, better odds now."

"And sneaking into their central command base and stealing it back are better odds?"

"Because we drew the Ratronians within close proximity of Tintee airspace," Talia said, "the Queen had to deploy the majority of the base assets to the surrounding areas to keep anything catastrophic from happening. Since it appears the Ratronians are in league with the Albions, she can't take a gamble that they were the only ones attacking. My guess is there will be almost no Colonian armor flying around here."

"What about the *Trax* and all the other Carolon ships? They're still operational and technically Colonian."

"True, but all the command personnel are under suspicion of treason and until Colonia Command can make their investigations, decide on replacements and deploy those replacements, those ships aren't going anywhere."

"Willis, any ideas where they would try and take the Starbird ship?" Talia put her finger to her ear piece, listening carefully, then touched a control in front of her.

"If I were a Hesson engineer, I would want that thing in my shop as soon as I could get it there." Willis's voice was a little quiet coming over the com system.

"And if I were a security chief, I would want it as far inside the complex as I could get it," Talia responded.

"They can't fly it through here without positive control available, even with space tugs. They'll have to drag it. It will take them a while to stage it through all these hangar stacks."

"I'll have a listen to the tug channels, see if I can get anything from the chatter," Talia informed them, going to work. "Here, you drive." She let go of her controls, motioning for Dakota to take his. Unprepared, he grabbed them white knuckled at first, but it took him only a minute to get comfortable.

"How am I supposed to know where to go?"

"Willis is right in front of you," Talia mumbled, working with her com gear.

"Oh, I can do that," Dakota smirked.

After she adjusted her com controls and listened carefully, Talia brought the audio up so everyone could hear as the tank column started inside the gigantic complex.

"I think I've got what we're looking for here," she announced into her mic pickup.

Dakota looked up, trying to find the ceiling of the Colonian facility. The landing and holding bays were enormous and full of ships being built, repaired or staged for something. He listened carefully as Talia did her best to request several different routes that would take them in a roundabout way through many of the bays, looking for the Kalamarion starship. A call from Willis ahead of them brought Talia to attention. Adjusting her com controls, she listened in on several communications from the docking workers.

"What a headache this thing is," one tug operator complained.

"Doesn't command have any idea how tough it is to pull something through these hangar matrixes?"

"They don't care about how hard it is, just that it gets to where it needs to go."

"Well why not just leave it out in the main hangar? They can tear it apart out there just as easily as they can in the SS matrix."

"The Queen's secret service labs want exclusive access to it. It does look impressive. May be a new weapon to use against the Albions or the Ratronians."

"We'll be at this for hours moving this thing around before we can get it into the SS bays. We'll have to turn it this way and that, move it up and down several times. Wait for hours for the other mec bays to clear projects and move doors. Why not just fly it in? We could be done inside an hour."

"The flight tugs can't move it because of the shielding. Something about its composition not allowing their tractor hawsers to lock onto it. I've got the willies just being this close to it. Every hair on my body is standing up wanting to jump off and run."

"Got that right! The harmonics coming off those shields are jarring my teeth and giving me a headache. I've never seen the likes of it before. It's either Tomplie or something completely alien."

"We don't even know whose ship this is."

"Came in with the Carolon fleet."

"Ok, hold up, I'm getting a signal from the yard master of bay twenty-four. They've got some junk to get out of the way."

Listening to the worker's chatter, Dakota formulated a plan. He turned to Tiana, who was already leaning toward him with the same idea.

"How much ground security is there likely to be around the ship?" Dakota asked.

"Next to none," Talia responded. "Look at where we are. Why would there be any?"

"I'd say that's kind of a lack-a-daisical attitude," Tiana responded, leaning a little closer. "Something as important as a ship like that ought to have at least two assault tanks guarding it while they move it."

"Know any tanks available?" Dakota asked smiling.

"Not so fast there, Turbo," Talia cautioned, guessing what they might have in mind. "Just because there isn't any ground security, doesn't mean there isn't any security." She reached over to her left and touched several controls next to a side display screen. "While it's true this is the biggest commercial hub in the system, it's also the biggest military installation in the system." She glanced back up for a quick view out the window then back over at the screen to her left. "Trying to staff ground security in a place like this would be impossible, so they did the next best thing. There are control centers in each bay enclosure, complete with bay traffic controllers, security staffs controlling robotic turbo lasers and small snuff guns mounted all around the upper walls of each bay. There are usually about five to ten roving aerial drones, depending on the size of the hangar bay, and less I forget, the new Vivitar 700 guard droids. A box full of high powered Omni-directional lasers and projectile weapons on high speed tank tracks. Nasty stuff."

Dakota and Tiana studied the duplicate screen to their right as Talia explained. Indeed, the thoughts of treating this like a hold-up might prove to be a little tougher than what had originally come to mind. Aerial security in a hangar bay complex certainly had its advantages over boots on the ground, but whatever they were going to do, they would have to do it quick. It was certain the deeper into the base complex they traveled, the harder it would be to get back out. Each hangar bay had its own set of complex wall doors that could be configured in a multitude of different configurations, depending on how the bay needed to be used. In many instances, entire walls, floors and ceilings could be railed out of the way or reconfigured to link bays together, creating one enormous bay. It would probably be difficult to escape from one bay to the next if they saw you coming and closed the next set of doors before you could get out.

"I suppose we could parallel your ship on both sides, looking like an armed escort, pull in close and let everyone out hot. The tanks will give us a certain measure of cover, then it will be up to your pilot and your ship's firepower to get you out before they close everything up." Talia said.

"Whatever we're going to do, we had better do it fast," Tiana warned. "Once they're alerted to our presence, the outer bays will close up."

"Agreed," Dakota mumbled, paying special attention to the location of several bay systems. "Starman and Moon are in first, followed by Cartwright and Kramer. They can get the ship up and running with weapons online while the rest of us get on."

"If we're going to do this, better get everyone ready, cause we're coming up on it in the next bay." Talia unbuckled her seat harness. "Looks like it's stopped to maneuver stuff out of the way. Willis, we'll take this side, you have the far side."

"Righto," Willis acknowledged.

"Should I go out first and open the hatch?" Tiana volunteered.

"Have you ever worked the security code panel for the entry doors?" Dakota asked.

"No."

"Then not a good idea." Dakota shot back. "I've got the shield control and I know the lock codes. I'll be the first one out and as soon as the doors are open, I'll provide any cover that's needed."

"Just seems like I should be doing something here," Tiana complained.

"You help get your brother and everyone else onboard as fast as you can." Dakota turned back to Talia. "I'm assuming you can set this thing to a slow cruise and use these guns for protection if need be."

"Sure," she responded. "These things come fully loaded, reclining bucket seats, power windows and cruise control." Talia turned her tank in directly behind Willis as they entered another hangar bay and sighted in on the glowing hull of the *Constellation.*

Dakota looked up, seeing the enormous thruster port of the main engine of the *Constellation* directly ahead of them. "Don't stick with this thing too long after we're out."

"Don't worry about me," Talia came back. "I'm just as big a coward as the next person."

"Time to get ready people," Dakota announced getting out of his seat and making his way to the back of the tank. Talia watched him go, and then turned forward again to the summons in her headset. She shut off the external com speaker and started setting controls as they continued to approach.

"Yes, Willis, a little crazy goes very well with dang cute." Talia chuckled softly. She set her autopilot controls and looked back at Captain Abrams again as she steered the tank around one of the aft wings of the *Constellation* and then veered back toward mid-ship. Talia turned in her chair again.

"Honey, if you haven't figured out he has a thing for you by now, then you really have a problem on your hands. Are you ready over there?" Talia nodded at the response in her ear. "We're in position, Captain."

Dakota turned to the rear door mechanism, taking ahold of the release handle.

"Don't be shooting at anything unless I tell you," he said looking directly at Logan and Hayden.

"What's that, sir?" Logan put a hand to one ear. "My coms are down; can you repeat?"

"Very funny," Dakota smiled.

"What if they start on us first?" Hayden asked. He was usually the careful, methodical one, but it was clear he was a little more agitated than normal.

"I just don't want to draw any attention to us any sooner than need be. If we get fired on, find the source and deal with it. Logan, you head for the other door and provide cover." He turned forward. "Let us know when you're ready, Talia," he called as everyone got to their feet.

"Remember to move them out one at a time," Dakota instructed Tiana as he activated the door. "But wait for my signal. I don't want a bunch of people crowding at the door. The faster we go the better chance we have of getting out of here in one piece."

Dakota had to force himself to step causally from the moving tank door and toward the glowing hull of the *Constellation*. As he approached, he glanced back at the tug operator on the back side of the aft wing on his side. He wasn't even looking at him. Scanning the area immediately around them, he could see nothing that indicated he had been detected. Stepping carefully up to the hull, he reached for the security control on his belt and touched the main control on the top, then motioned to Tiana. The blue hue of energy floating across the skin of the ship instantly disappeared and he reached up, poking a finger into a tiny access in the hull. A small door instantly slid to one side revealing a smooth control pad with several displays on it. Punching in several series of commands on the touch panel, he pressed a main control. As crew members started gathering at the open back end of the tank, a feeling of panic streaked through his chest. Nothing was happening. The main side door was supposed to open. He worked the codes again in fast sequence with one hand. Again, the same results. Tiana shuffled next to him, looking back at the open tank door.

"Oh boy," he mumbled, motioning Tiana to wave everyone else off.

"What's wrong?" Tiana asked in a near panic.

"What's it look like? The codes aren't working."

"Not working? You didn't change them before we teleported out did you?"

"No, why in the nip-nard would I do that?" Dakota was struggling to hold his cool. He noticed the tug driver looking over at him, then at the back of the open tank and the men and women huddled in the back. Tiana watched Dakota work the touch pad again and again, his fingers tapping at the glass pad at nearly a blur.

"Slow down!" she raised her voice a bit. An instant later a bolt of light streaked past them both and exploded against the white hull of the ship, several others landing at their feet.

"Get behind me! Get behind me!" Dakota yelled, pulling both blasters and returning fire coming from a small drone moving toward them. They hadn't even seen it there. It must have been attached to the wall in scanning mode or activated by the tug operator. Now it wouldn't be long before the entire hangar bay knew they were there and they would have more than just a drone to deal with. The ship abruptly started to move again. Dakota and Tiana dropped to the floor, quickly swallowed under the belly of the Starbird. It provided good cover, but did nothing for getting the door open. Tiana rolled left, seeing Fuji Yamoto backing into the other tank and closing the door. Everything was going to unravel unless something was done fast. Rolling back next to Dakota, she got to her knees.

"You cover me and I'll input the codes."

Dakota started to object but seeing her resolve, scrambled back out from under the ship and started firing at the drone gliding toward them. As Tiana reached for the touch pad, Dakota noticed the turret on the assault tank swing up in the direction of the drone, several of its guns bellowing bright flashes of light.

The little drone only managed to dodge a few of the light rounds before it disintegrated, others swooping in to take its place. Remote gun emplacements on the near wall high above the moving ship came alive. Tiana methodically began to input the key commands on the control in front of her as Dakota dictated them. He did his best to provide cover, but was quickly being overwhelmed. The tank rolling next to them provided a certain level of cover, but its guns were focused up. The hangar's upper wall gun emplacements rained pounding fire down on the tanks and the side of the ship, where he and Tiana were.

Tiana remained focused as Dakota spouted out numbers and letters in sequence. Despite the commotion all around her, she made sure to touch the right key sequence and only after checking to make sure it was right, did she call for the next sequence of numbers and letters. Finally, the control panel started flashing bright green and a little warning alarm sounded off. Tiana reached for the open control but was suddenly thrown to the side by an explosion landing right next to where she had been walking. Another blast hit her in the right shoulder, spinning her in the opposite direction and throwing her completely off balance. Intense pain fired through her upper body as her legs became entangled and she crashed to the floor. Feeling something wet and warm on her face, Tiana slowly rolled over and looked up at the underside of the *Constellation*. Unable to move her right arm, she had to use her left hand to turn her head, the pain nearly paralyzing. Tiana looked at her hand as she rolled over to get back to her feet. It was covered in a warm reddish colored fluid. The drones must have struck a hydraulic line and spewed fluid all over her. Finally able to look at her shoulder, Tiana could see raw flesh, even bone through her torn uniform. The fire fight developing between the tanks and hangar security was barely audible through the head splitting ringing in her right ear. She had to move. In moments the tugs would have the ship far enough forward that she would be completely exposed.

Her head spinning, Tiana got back to her feet and stumbled forward. Dakota hadn't even noticed that she had gone down, still exchanging laser blasts with the drone security. Talia and Willis continued to spar with the gun locations on the walls, keeping the tanks in sync with the movement of the tugs. Tiana felt sick now as she struggled to make it back to the open security panel, still flashing green. Not even realizing it, she dodged several laser blasts and finally reached the open panel. Her hands slipped on the white hull of the ship, smearing blood next to the open panel. She reached in and pulled a small handle, then lost her footing and fell, but hung onto the handle, letting the ship drag her along as the outer doors hissed open on both sides.

The back of the assault tanks instantly dropped open again and one by one the crew moved toward the open hatches of the starship. Tiana finally got her footing and jumped, pulling herself up inside. She turned back to the crew members sprinting for the open doors as more gun emplacements opened fire on the tanks and starship. Lynette and Billy were the first ones in, not even looking back to see to the welfare of the others as they sprinted to their stations. Dakota ejected an exhausted power pack and slammed another one in its place, taking aim at a drone sweeping in from behind the aft tail section on his side. He passed a quick glance through the open door to the other side, seeing Logan moving alongside with his pistol raised, shooting at anything airborne. Fending off the drones, Dakota looked toward the tank still rolling along side. The last of the crew were just leaving the relative safety of the rolling armored vehicle carrying the body of the fallen ship's nurse, Sindee Conner. His attention was drawn forward to several droids just entering the bay at the far end, right in the direction the tugs were pulling the ship.

Vivitar MD700 killer droids were only a meter wide and meter and a half tall. Square-like in appearance, their heads were dome shaped. A red crescent glowed across the face of each dome, adorned on either side with small antenna-type spikes. The main torso had gun emplacements mounted forward and back, some movable. It was obvious these machines were unmanned, too small to carry anyone inside, but they were lethal enough. The machines rolled rapidly toward them on rubber tank tracks. Calculating they would be there in a matter of moments, Dakota sprinted to the back end of the tank and called up to Talia.

"You're the last one, come on!"

The driver's seat was vacant. Talia was in the gunner's chair firing at anything that moved.

"Come on, Come on! They've got reinforcements coming!"

Talia yelled something into her headset, then dumped out of the chair and started for the back as Dakota turned to check their positioning. Most of the aerial drones had been taken down. Talia and Willis had taken out most of the closest remote gun emplacements. They just needed to make a break for it. Starting out the back of the tank together, Dakota sighted in on the open door of the ship as Tiana was just helping Taron up inside. As he and Talia made a break for it, a hail of gun fire rained down on them, bouncing along the floors and ricocheting off the aft wing of the ship. Talia made a dive for the door as the

Vivitars opened up on them with projectile weapons. Dakota took a hit on the back side of his boot, almost ripping it right off his foot. The blow threw his aim off as he dove for the door. Still at the door, Tiana grabbed his free hand and held on. Dragging now, he nearly pulled Tiana right out with him, but Talia had turned and grabbed ahold of her. Dakota looked forward at the Vivitars coming at him, projectile fire bellowing and laser bolts streaking along the floor at him.

Another aerial drone had picked up the activity and was bearing down on him as well, but before it could reach him, it exploded in a fiery blast. The shots had come from somewhere besides the tanks, as there was no one left in them. He looked around as the Vivitars intensified their fire at the open side of the ship. One of them unexpectedly exploded, veering off into its companions, causing a chaotic collision as the cluster of Vivitars were moving at a high rate of speed. Another volley sent another pair careening out of control and into the hangar bay wall. A second set behind the first started popping off a rapid succession of laser blasts as they drew closer, but again, another set of high powered laser shots tore into the first one sending it crashing. The other turned toward the source and started pumping shots in the direction of a lone man holding a rather large hip mounted rapid fire gun.

The distraction was all Dakota needed to regain his composure enough to climb inside. The man holding the gun turned back in the ship's direction and started running for the door, all the while popping off short bursts with his gun. The mass of confusion seemed to be working as he side stepped past the back of the still moving tank. Another Vivitar sped through the debris of the other wrecks and started laying down more fire, raining a firestorm on the open door. As Dakota pulled himself inside, a hail of laser blasts filled the doorway. There were several loud thumping sounds as projectile slugs struck the inside wall and he suddenly found himself under a pile of people. Dakota heard the sound of the *Constellation's* engines coming to life and the maneuvering thruster pods charging. The figure outside dropped his waist gun and sprinted for the open door. Dakota had no idea who he was, but he was more than willing to help the sprinting man inside. Once they were all safely in, Tiana hit the hatch release and the door slammed shut leaving only the soft noise of occasional laser fire striking the side of the hull. Dakota turned over, pushing Taron off and started to get up.

"Come on people, let's all get to our stations so we can get out of here." He went to help Taron up, but the Mantose twin didn't move. Talia helped Dakota turn him over, only to find several blast holes in his abdomen and chest area.

"Taron!" Tiana screamed coming to her brother's aid. Taron cracked his eyes and smiled at his sister. Blood was coming from everywhere with no apparent way to stop it. Talia and Willis were quick to help carry Taron to sickbay. Dakota turned to the stranger as the door closed on the other side.

"Thanks friend," Dakota said getting a good look at the young man. "You came along at just the right time. Those droids would have had us for sure." Without another word, Dakota turned for the bridge.

"You're welcome..." The young Castellian didn't get a chance to ask another question as Talia and Willis reappeared and instantly pinned him against the bulkhead wall.

"How did you get onboard?" Willis snarled.

"What are you even doing on Tintee?" Talia chimed in with the same enthusiasm.

"Whoa, slow down a little bit here," Dakota said, making an about face. "The guy just saved our bacon and you're about to break his neck?" Dakota detected more laser blasts pounding the hull of the ship, making the urgency to be on the bridge even more pronounced. "Bridge, shields up, let's go." Dakota replaced his communicator and turned to the two Colonian officers.

"Albion Queen Captain personal aide, BachTL," Willis spat holding the Castellian firmly against the wall.

Starman knew how to fly; the bridge would have to wait.

Dakota cast a suspicious look at the aide. *What in the world? How and what was an Albion aide doing in the middle of a Colonian military complex?* He didn't have time for any of this right now. They had to get out of here before the Colonians started throwing bigger stuff at them.

"Shoot him now, Captain," Talia said pulling her blaster. She didn't get a chance to even release the safety, as Dakota was quick to disarm her.

"What is it with you people that you think you have to blast each other to bits first and ask questions later? It might be nice to find out what he's doing here before you blew his brains out, don't you think?"

"Nothing good ever comes from an Albion," Talia hissed, incensed that she had been disarmed.

"Uhm, hello? Colonel Barker? Isn't she Albion?" Dakota pointed out sarcastically. There was a tense moment of silence, then the two Carolon women released the Castellian and backed away. Dakota felt the ship quake gently.

"Have you got a brig?" Willis asked, still holding her blaster up.

"No, and he's not going there." Dakota turned to BachTL. "Do you know anything about field medicine?" The aide nodded nervously as Dakota took him by the arm and led him to the sickbay doors. "See what you can do to help out with the wounded and we'll sort all this out later." The doors hissed open and the aide was pushed inside. "Doctor, a little help for you."

Fuji didn't get a chance to object or even inquire as the doors hissed shut almost as quickly as they had opened.

"You're asking for trouble," Talia warned as Dakota started for the bridge again.

"Maybe, but right now, we have bigger problems." A moment later, the door to the bridge popped open and the three stormed in just in time to see the horizon outside tilt to the left and the hangar walls swinging around behind them. "Anybody in the turret?" Dakota asked, jumping into the command chair.

"Hayden, sir," the weapons officer called back, targeting the wall guns as they approached the open doors.

"Did those tug operators object to you taking off?"

"Didn't ask, sir," Lynette Starman responded, as the other end of the hangar came into view.

"They'll try and close all the doors," Talia warned. "It's a fail-safe in their system. If something goes wrong in a bay, like a fire or something, it will automatically close the doors to shield the other hangars."

"Ship status?" Dakota asked.

"Shield strength at sixty-three percent. All sub-light speeds available. Weapons batteries at seventy-eight percent," Pip informed him.

"Chain the fighter's guns directly to weapons control. If the doors get in the way, blow them off."

"That could cause some serious damage," Willis informed him.

"Exactly. Best way out?"

"The same way we came in," Talia responded, as the weapons officer let several blasts go from the secondary guns of the *Constellation*. "But what are you going to do once you get clear? Didn't you say your Light Speed engines were offline?"

She made a valid point. They could fly off world, but couldn't go anywhere and would likely be set upon before they could find a safe place to hide.

"Since we're making this up as we go along, I'm open to suggestions," Dakota said as several small drones buzzed harmlessly about in front of them.

Talia and Willis looked at each other at the same time, then at Dakota. He held his attention straight ahead, watching Lynette pilot the ship through the open hangar doors. Sirens blared outside and lights flashed everywhere as they moved rapidly from one hangar bay to the next. As doors in front of them would start too close, Lynette turned the ship to another set that had not yet begun to move. She then turned the ship back through another set, putting her back on the right path toward the outer hangar bays.

"General order fifteen," Talia finally spoke up.

"What's that?" Dakota asked, unmoved. "We don't have a General Order Fifteen."

"Neither does Colonia," Willis maintained. "Only the Carolon Command personnel are aware of a G15. In the event of catastrophic events such as capture or special circumstance, if General Order Fifteen is invoked, all command personnel are to take their ships and head directly to the planet Cross as fast as they can and surrender their ships."

"Why didn't you say something about this General Order Fifteen when you first left Carolon instead of heading here and getting into this big mess?" A little frustrated with the unfolding circumstances, Dakota preferred being proactive instead of reacting.

"At the time of our evacuation, we weren't under a capture warrant, so coming home to Tintee was still a part of our directives. G15 holds true now. Without any of Colonia's fleet ships here to stop us, we should all be able to jump to Cross without any trouble. You can hitch back up to the *Rex* or hop a ride in one of the destroyer's landing bays as soon as we're away from Tintee."

"You people and your general orders." Dakota motioned for the two women to head back down the hall to the teleporter room. "I'll have one of the engineers meet you in the teleporter room. I'm assuming you need to be on the *Trax* or the *Rex*."

Both women turned for the door as Lynette Starman brought the ship to a halt in front of a couple of enormous doors that had just closed.

"Blast through them," Dakota ordered.

"Better idea, sir," the ship's pilot grunted, tapping the glass in front of her and hauling back on the yoke. She focused her gaze above the bridge at the opening in the ceiling of this hangar. Part of it was missing, pulled out of the way to allow for larger ships inside. Not only was the hangar matrix configured along a horizontal axis, but up and down a vertical one as well. Lynette guided the starship straight up and into the hangar above them, then started forward again through another set of open doors. At the first opportunity, she dropped the ship back down into the main level and continued toward the outside.

"Well done, Starman. You earned your stripes today," Dakota complimented the Starbird pilot. The weapons officer maintained a barrage of fire not only keeping the hangar security guns immobilized, but also preventing the hangar doors from closing. It didn't take long before they could see the light of day beaming through the enormous opening in the side of the mountain and as they steered directly at it, Dakota's com panel lit up.

"Permission to launch fighters once we clear?" Hunter asked over the com speaker.

"Only if we get a swarm on us. Otherwise I want to be able to catch a ride with one of those bigger ships when they make their jump to light speed."

"What if they don't make the jump?"

"We'll make up that scenario as we go along. Helm, throttle her up." There were no longer any hangar bay doors between them and their escape, only the ground forces and none of their weapons were big enough to do any damage to the shield protected hull of the white starship breezing out into the open atmosphere of Tintee. The outer windshields instantly dimmed the bright glaring light of the planet's close dwarf sun as they rose higher in the thin air past the *Trax* and several other ships.

"Should we hold in a pattern near the *Trax*?" the ship's pilot inquired as they soared over its massive bulk. There appeared to be little to no movement from any of the ships still moored around the Colonian base.

"No," Dakota responded. He reasoned there would be heavy F-2 fighter squadrons patrolling the space directly around Tintee. "But stay in the atmosphere until we can establish communications with Lieutenant Reese. We'll rendezvous with them before they make their jump."

"Captain," Fuji called from the comlink. "I need you down here in sick bay right now." Reluctant, Dakota got to his feet, then remembering the doctor and the Albion aide were working on the Mantose twins, quickened his pace.

*   *   *   *

As Dakota stepped through the sick bay doors, a visibly shaken BachTL turned and faced him. The Castellian's clothing was covered in blood and his dazed look told Dakota most of what he needed to know. Behind him, Dr. Yamoto worked at one of the elevated medical tables on a motionless Taron. Tears streaming down her cheeks, Tiana huddled up in a tight wad with her arms wrapped around her legs in a chair on the other side of the table watching Fuji work. Dakota gave the life monitors above the table a long look as he approached. Staying back, he could see things had not gone well. While Fuji worked in one place on Taron's torn body, the ship's med assistant worked in another.

"He took two direct blasts from a Vivitar pulse gun and four hits from a projectile weapon." BachTL spoke in a low voice from behind Captain Abrams. "It nearly cut him in half."

Dakota continued to watch Fuji work with the med assistant, keeping an eye on the life monitors.

"How did you end up with your gun?" Dakota turned his head to one side. "You're a long way from home my friend and probably in a lot of trouble."

"Certainly that's true," BachTL responded. "Where I got the weapon is of no importance. That I am here aboard your vessel is."

"Captain Abrams," a faint voice called from the medical bed.

Fuji looked over her shoulder at Dakota, who stepped quietly forward. Tiana was instantly to her brother's side, the med arm moving out of the way. Tiana tried to warm Taron's cold pale hands.

"Did we get away all right?"

"Yes."

"Have you found the Colonel yet?"

"He's on Cross," Dakota said quietly. "We're headed there now,"

Taron carefully turned to his sister, Fuji slowly pulling her bloody hands and instruments from Taron's body. A quick shake of the head confirmed what the Captain had already surmised.

"Tiana, it's very dark in here...I'm cold."

"I know," Tiana sputtered. She understood how bad it was when they had brought him in. She had tried to numb herself to be there for her brother in his final moments. "Lay quiet, Dr. Yamoto is trying to concentrate."

"I wonder where I'm going to go?" Taron whispered, looking toward his sister.

"I'm not going to know how to behave without you," Tiana smiled, unable to hold back her grief.

"You didn't know how to behave when we are together," Taron smiled quietly. He turned his head back, looking out into the room. "Tiana," he paused, as if recognizing something. "Mother is here..." Tiana squeezed her brother's hand and leaning down, kissed him gently on the forehead. She let her fingers slip down over his open eyes, carefully helping them close.

Plan B

Metro-star I wobbled clumsily toward the lower landing bay of the *Tarzana* as the battlecruiser hovered in orbit over the dark shadow of Reako. The substantial damage to the transport was quite apparent to the approach controllers as the ship yawed ungainly toward the landing bay opening. Seeing it had minimal control, the docking master ordered emergency landing procedures implemented to prevent a catastrophic collision. Using the cruiser's new tractor beam technology, a pilot would not have to rely on manual or onboard computer control to bring a damage vessel in for a safe landing. The powerful beam would hold the ship within its prescribed approach parameters and deposit it safely in the landing bay. Of course this technology was still new and being tested. It certainly couldn't handle more than one ship at a time and required the pilot to voluntarily relinquish control.

Once deposited on the hangar bay floor, emergency crews surrounded the badly damaged craft to ensure there was no danger of volatile fuels creating a disaster in the landing bay. Several other emergency extraction personnel worked the forward hatch open and helped Drax Blair out. Quite unhurt, she looked all around the landing bay. Even as she boarded an elevator that would take her to the upper landing bay, she continued to scan the spacious landing bay. She was anxious for a closer inspection of the alien craft that showed such great promise for the future of the Albion Empire.

"QC, are you all right?" Commander SoKnack inquired, jumping onto the elevator with the Queen Captain.

"As you can see, I'm standing here quite unharmed," Drax replied, hoping he would come to the point before she had to ask.

"Scans indicated your ship had been heavily damaged. Where are your escorts? We've been very worried. What happened? Were you able to retrieve Colonel Barker?"

"Nice to know I would be missed," Drax responded, her expression remaining stoic. "Did you have any trouble with that ship I assigned you and Blinda to go after? Really anxious to see it in the upper landing bay." Her gaze at the grey walls of the

elevator was stone. Dalton fidgeted slightly, shuffling just a bit.
She let her eyes drop shut, trying to find a happy place, then
opened them again, shifting them to the ship commander who
held his eyes glued to the floor. When he didn't respond right
away, she turned directly to him as the elevator began to slow
and the door opened.

"What happened? You didn't damage it did you?"

Drax stepped out into the upper landing bay, but a quick scan
confirmed her greatest fears. Only Albion marked craft crowded
the hangar floor. She had half expected this, but ultimately
hoped it wouldn't happen, another failure. BachTL may well
have been right. If you want something done right, you have to
do it yourself and while that rang true with most things, she was
reminded of the last day and a half she had just spent chasing CJ
through the subterranean mazes inside the planet below them.

"Would you like to explain your version of events or should I
go to Blinda first?" She was fuming. Never mind her own failure
to retrieve CJ. Catching smaller class vessels shouldn't be a
problem for the experienced Albion military. Dalton stuttered
awkwardly for the explanation, trying to keep the facts straight,
yet keep himself out of the crosshairs of any possible retribution.

"We experienced more than anticipated resistance from the
alien craft in trying to capture them."

"Of course you did..."

"Blinda ordered continued fire to bring down their shields,
even then the ship refused to surrender. She directed us to
open fire again to immobilize them for boarding. We must have
struck their main power source. The ship exploded or was about
to, so I ordered a retreat to protect this ship."

Stepping back into the elevator, Dalton could see Drax's face
turning crimson with controlled anger. He didn't want to get
back on alone with her. He might not ever be seen again, but he
also reasoned that if he weren't present when Drax finally did
find Blinda, he would certainly get the blame for the destruction
of the alien prize.

"Can I assume Blinda is on the bridge?" Drax asked, her
voice quivering.

"Your command lounge, QC," Dalton answered in quick
military fashion. He felt the elevator start, pressing his feet to
the floor as they rose higher in the super structure of the
battlecruiser.

*   *   *   *

Blinda stood looking out the wall window of the command
lounge with one hand on her hip. She leaned slightly to one

side, an elbow resting on the rail, hearing the elevator door hiss open and several sets of footsteps approach from behind.

"Idiots! I'm surrounded by utter and complete idiots," Drax stormed, tossing her cloak on one of the circular couches. "I send the two of you to retrieve one little ship and what do you do? Blow it up!" Awkward silence filled the room, Blinda remaining unmoved.

"Did you do any better, Drax?" Blinda came back unmoved. "Where's CJ Barker?"

Drax toned down a bit, the cold waters of her own failure dampening her fuming anger.

"Again, I was surrounded by incompetence. Barker slipped by us in the atmosphere of Reako and then made the jump to Quadra-light before we could disable her ship. She has nowhere to run though. She's wanted by both Empires now."

"Sucks to be her," Blinda commented, turning around and leaning against the railing.

"So let's hear your version," Drax demanded. Tired, she sank into the soft cushions of the couch and buried her face in her hands.

"I'm sure Dalton here has already given you the detail that will absolve him of any wrong doing." She passed a disgusted glance over at the ship commander. "So I'll cut to the chase. We simply engaged the ship and being unable to convince them to surrender, had Commander SoKnack here bring down their shields so I could be a little more persuasive, but they continued to try and run. I couldn't get a concentrated lock on them, so I ordered their ship disabled. Their systems must have been more sensitive than what we had hoped for. We had to get clear because it was about to explode."

Dalton let out a silent sigh of relief. Blinda's story was convincing and certainly the truth; it absolved him of any wrong doing.

"You're better off without it anyway," Blinda commented, crossing her legs. "The ship was slow. They couldn't out-run or out-maneuver us, even in close quarters. True they were able to throw a good amount of return fire, but nothing we weren't able to deal with. If this is one of Diord's new tactical penetrators, then he goofed."

"We lost about a third of our starboard snuff guns," Dalton reported, making sure the detail was there. "But they didn't have enough sustainable return fire for a prolonged campaign."

Drax felt a headache coming on. Things were not going the direction she had hoped and she leaned back, softly rubbing her forehead.

"Did you at least get a heading?" Blinda stepped over to one of the lounge chairs across from Drax and sat down. "Anything you can use to track CJ's ship?"

"No, there was no time. Not sure where she learned to fly like that but she has become considerably better since she was under my wing."

Dalton couldn't help but let a smile creep across his lips, but held his hand up to hide the expression. Drax slung a quick glance in his direction, but did not hold it there.

"I'm sure she's on Cross by now." Blinda picked at her fingernails. "That viper Diord has always had the hots for her. He'd give her his left arm if she asked him to."

"Well, if she is on Cross, she's out of our direct reach now." Drax brought a finger to her lips to bite on a nail. "Diord's fleet is as big as ours and he knows how to place them in his system, which is why he has been able to remain neutral through all this fighting. Not only would I not want to try and go up against someone so well equipped, but I don't want to ruin any trade relations we have with him. That guy can crank out some serious hardware. That ship had to be something he conjured up. He's the only one with that kind of brain power at his disposal."

"His tractor beam technology got you landed safely," Dalton pointed out. "You can thank him for that."

"Could have used it on that alien ship," Blinda teased in Dalton's direction. Commander SoKnack let a harmless sneer pass back at the Thane sitting across the room. His ears abruptly popped a couple of times. A reminder not to mess with Blinda.

"How about a special task force?" Blinda offered. "I hear your Alpha eight forces are pretty good at stealth."

"Aren't we allowed a small shuttle or transport landing?" Dalton was anxious to have some agreement with Blinda, just to keep her happy. "A well-disguised unit could sneak in and extract her before Vandmire even knew they had landed. She's managed to evade us three times now. Maybe a special unit is the answer? Send them in and either take her there on Cross or flush her out and take her in open space.

"Special Forces won't work on Cross." Drax rubbed her tired eyes and let her hands drop down her face so only her eyes were visible. "No, we'll have to send someone else in. Someone not connected to Albia. Someone Diord wouldn't expect."

"Alvadore is a big place," Commander SoKnack reminded them. "If she is even in that complex, it could take days to find and flush her out, especially if she is with Diord. You're going to need someone who knows that city like the back of their hand."

"I still say Special Forces could..." Blinda started again.

"Enough with the Special Forces crap," Drax bellowed. "I'm done sending in men and assets only to lose them for no good reason. As much as it pains me to admit this, SoKnack is right. We need someone who knows the city well, the whole planet for that matter. No telling where she'll be holdup. It's very likely Diord has her. So we'll send in someone who can get close to him."

"Who do you have in mind?" Blinda asked, trying to follow. "You're not going to hire a bunch of bounty hunters are you?"

"No," Drax muttered. "Too messy, hard to control and they rarely bring anything back alive. Makes containment a real problem."

"So what does that leave you?" Blinda asked.

"Commander SoKnack," Drax directed her comments. "Set a course for the Helios system." Dalton came to attention and clicking his heels together, marched from the room. Drax fiddled with something beneath her cloaks, letting her eyes work their way back up to Blinda, who was looking through the clear observation dome overhead.

"Do you think she'll agree to help?" Blinda asked.

Drax drew in a deep breath and let it out slowly.

"The Albion Empire hasn't the slightest grasp on what Seelix Monroe does." Drax fell silent for a moment. "If she'll agree, it's because it pleases her. She certainly doesn't need the money."

"You'll find no love lost between me and Seelix. I've butted heads with that woman more times than I'd care to admit," Blinda pointed out, thinking of her own rocky history with Seelix. "But she's more of an arms dealer. The woman plays the commodities on the black market. She's an exotic hunter, only hunts for sport. You can't even be sure she'll bring CJ back out alive." Drax slowly got up and starting for the door, but stopped half way, turning back to the Thane.

"Yeah, that's just what I'm afraid of. CJ has other people with her now, helping her. One in particular, a man. A superman."

"Oooo, I like men," Blinda swooned. "Especially supermen. But there are plenty of supermen on Albia."

"Not like this one. If I didn't know any better, I would have thought he was an android or something. He was tossing boulders. You should have seen what he did to a ROACH on Carolon. I don't know where he's from, but if we could get our hands on him..."

"Yeah, yeah," Blinda mussed, acting like she had heard this story before. "Clone him and build an army of super guys with minds of their own. Drax, you've been down this road before. It can't be done. They either end up as mush puddles in the lab or uncontrollable animals that have to be put down. Your answers are Diord's T-90 military grade Bio-mechanical suits."

"That is some powerful hardware," Drax agreed, "but they have their limitations just like a droid army does. The cloning will work this time," she said trying to make her case. "This time we blend the DNA. It works now, it really does." Blinda was not convinced, but Drax continued anyway. "I sent BachTL after the other ship and if he can get his hands..."

"You sent BachTL after the other alien ship, just him, no one else, all by his lonesome?" Blinda was nearly giggling now, but held it back. While they were friends, she and Drax weren't that close and even a Thane can disappear under mysterious conditions.

"Well, I sent two of Albia's finest to get the other one and they blew it up." Drax's piercing stare fired right through Blinda. Seeing that she got her point across, Drax continued. "He's Castellian and even as young as he is, has a better than even chance of getting it out of Colonian hands as anyone else."

"Seems like suicide to me," Blinda murmured.

"I have faith in him," Drax maintained confidently. "I believe this could work. Having CJ and this superman she's running with and the alien ship technology. Albia could go much further, much faster."

"If he's as strong as you say he is, you won't get this ship's new tractor beams to hold him," Blinda pointed out. "Controlling this guy is going to be your biggest problem. He's not just going to sit still sipping juice while you check his pulse and take a tissue sample."

"That's where you come in," Drax said, taking a couple of steps closer to Blinda.

"As we've seen with the crew of that alien ship, some can't be controlled."

"I've thought of that too," Drax responded smiling. "Pump him full of Evco."

"Whoa, that's some strong stuff. Liable to burn his brain."

"Not if administered properly. It should make him quite cooperative."

"Sounds like you've got this all figured out," Blinda sighed. Drax's look of confidence wobbled a little bit, thinking of the past couple of days and how well those went. Yes, she had secured the Nulark system, but had paid a heavy price chasing CJ and the alien ship. She understood that in order to get things of great worth, you had to be willing to give up much. Her hope now was to minimize that as much as possible. That hope hinged in large part on the planet Moyle.

Lonely Together

Cruising at Quadra-light for hours, the interior of CJ's Flightstreak was quiet, its exhausted occupants resting. Janox had fallen fast asleep on the floor by the rear hatch while Alex 7001 sat motionless, anchored to the floor with a power cord attached to his torso. Up front, Gunnar had the pilot's seat pulled all the way back from the controls and in a full reclining position. CJ was sitting on the floor, leaning against the center console facing the rear wall. Resting her head on the back of the center console, she dozed silently. She had been feeling progressively worse as time dragged on. Their plan was to reach Cross, see a physician and get her ship repaired while they took time for some rest.

Gunnar lazily gazed at an overhead console thinking of the differences in technology he had experienced so far in his adventures with the Colonians and the Albion. Even with this fighter's problems, he had come to like its flight characteristics. You just had to get to know the ol' girl.

He carefully turned on his side and faced CJ, thinking about the last couple of days together. There hadn't been much time for real chit-chat to be sure. Certainly it had not been boring. Still, it would be nice if he could get to know her in more comfortable circumstances. Looking at her now, brought back thoughts of Audra. While he and Audra hadn't been chased across a galaxy or through a planet, they had experienced enough adventure together to forge an unbreakable bond.

Gunnar fingered the memory chip just inside his shirt, remembering Audra's short dark hair. As he did so, he realized he was looking at CJ's auburn rolls, or what was left of them. Everyone was a mess. He was sure he was no prince, but he remembered the Colonel all gussied up when they had met for the short lived victory celebration on Carolon. He followed the contours of her profile, down her nose, across her lips and chin. He wasn't even fazed when she slowly opened her eyes and turned in his direction.

"Whatcha thinking so hard about?" she asked, smiling softly. Gunnar remained silent, still fingering the chip. He finally let out a deep sigh.

"The first time I saw you," he responded in a hushed voice.

"Funny we should be thinking of the same thing," she replied.

"Two days ago and look where we've been since then. When you take a guy out on the town, you really take him out."

CJ's smile broadened, resting her arms carefully on her knees.

"Sorry, this isn't what I would term, *a good time*, either. I don't make the situations, but I do try and make the best of them."

"So what would be a good time for you?"

"Oh goodness," she sighed, thinking. "It's been so long since I've been in a position to even consider it; I would have no idea anymore."

"Lonely at the top, eh?"

"Yeah, you could say that. Rank doesn't afford you much personal time. Everyone wants a piece of you in one form or another."

"I'm right in there sluggin' with ya sister," Gunnar responded, taking a deep breath.

"But you appear to get along with your crew much better than other commanders I've observed."

"And how would you know how well I get along with my crew?" Gunnar asked after thinking about it. CJ cracked a smile realizing she had just tipped her hand about surveillance on Carolon. Not that it was any secret.

"Wouldn't you have put me and Willis under surveillance had the roles been reversed?"

"Colonel, I can assure you without a shadow of a doubt that your aide was under close surveillance from the moment you two walked into that cell."

CJ pulled a questioning expression lasting only a second when she realized what he was talking about.

"Yes, I suppose you're right about that. Your exec was having a difficult time focusing on anything else."

"Pretty obvious huh?"

"Uhm, yeah." Both chuckled softly, then fell silent again.

"Gunnar, call me Casey."

"Ok, Casey. What does the "J" stand for?"

"Janae, I don't mind CJ at all if you'd rather."

"CJ it is, but I think you'll know when I mean business."

"As will you."

Again they let out soft chuckles, looking at nothing in particular, but wondering which direction to take the conversation to keep it going.

CJ glanced back over at Gunnar, who was focused away. She noticed the chip in his fingers and wondered about it, but didn't ask. She hoped it wasn't some kind of military security file or key, what a waste. She guessed it contained a keepsake of some kind. Watching him carefully, she realized she was running out of time to do so. Any moment he would look back at her and she would feel silly for gawking at him.

"What's her name?" She felt awkward asking such a presumptuous question.

Gunnar immediately came back to CJ. At first he considered not even acknowledging the question. He had kept his visions and thoughts of Audra to himself and on the chip in his fingers where he could hold her close. No one could intrude or change anything. She would remain forever with him. But now, something softened in him and he felt it might be a good thing to tell someone a little of what he was feeling.

"She must be quite a woman," CJ continued, "to hold a man such as yourself so enchanted with just the mere thought of her." CJ was trying to remain a bit aloof, but reverent at the same time. She didn't mean to pry and she kind of wished she hadn't brought it up now. She stiffly turned around, carefully kneeling forward, resting her hands and chin on the center console.

"Is it that obvious?" he asked quietly, trying to remain emotionless. "Yes...she is."

"Is she pretty?" Silly question and she wished she could take it back the instant she let it go. *Of course she would be pretty. Of all the dumb things to ask, is she pretty?* CJ cringed in her head, almost visibly.

"Yes, very pretty." Gunnar chuckled softly. "Her brown eyes are something to behold and she knows how to use them."

CJ didn't have brown eyes, feeling plain and unattractive now. Her hair was matted and tangled, her makeup a mess, and she was sure her embarrassment was giving cause for her freckles to accentuate. Her light blue, crystal eyes couldn't compete with sultry dark brown eyes, especially if they were big. Willis had eyes like that and CJ often wished hers were that soft, that brown.

Gunnar detected an odd tingle tickle his ears again. He wondered if it was brought on by a lack of oxygen, similar to when fingertips begin tingling and the like. He didn't feel light headed. This was the same silly tingling he had felt back on the Carolon base. Sitting up carefully, he looked the instruments over. He had no idea where the readouts were that indicated the environmental parameters inside the F-2, not that he could read them anyway. CJ watched him, wondering what he was up to.

"What's wrong?" she finally asked. Gunnar gave up looking and lay back in his seat, looking back at her.

"Nothing, just thought I felt something. So, what about you?
Pretty girl like you can't go unnoticed." He thought about telling
her more about Audra, but now realized CJ had wandered away
in her thoughts.

"Yes, there was someone, a long time ago. I can hardly even
remember now. But it's in the past and should stay there.
Seems like when you achieve rank, your social life takes a nose
dive."

"Duties and responsibilities," Gunnar affirmed.

"Exactly," CJ agreed quickly. "You don't get much attention
as a person, only as an officer. It's difficult and generally unwise
to get to know anyone because you have no idea, well..." CJ fell
silent, Gunnar seeing her wrestling with years of loneliness. He
knew exactly how she was feeling, the loneliness part anyway.

"No idea what could happen to them or yourself?"

"Yes." CJ responded entranced, staring straight ahead. "It's
easier to just remain invisible. I don't notice them and they
don't notice me." Her trance was broken by a sleepy snort
bursting from behind, but she shifted her view back to Gunnar.

"Tell me about her?" she asked carefully. She had kind of
gotten the impression that he didn't want to talk about it, as he
hadn't given her name yet. But at the same time, she was
curious as to what kind of a woman could hold this man a
prisoner to such strong feelings.

Gunnar still felt a little hesitant, but the look on CJ's face
softened the feeling. He remained guarded, choosing his
description carefully.

"She was one of the best traffic control officers I have ever
known, like your Lieutenant Reese.

CJ settled in for what she hoped would be a long detailed
description.

"We met at a concert on Kalamar."

"What's a concert?"

"Large gathering of people where a famous group plays
musical instruments and sings?"

"Oh, yes," CJ recognized it. "We call it a recital festival. That
makes it sound sort of blasé, but some of them can get a little
rowdy. I like your word for it better."

"Turns out she had been handling most of my traffic control
for almost a year before we actually met." A pleasant look
wisped across his face as he thought of that first meeting.
"There was a way about her that could defuse just about any
situation."

"How?"

"Just a word, a look or a touch." Gunnar wandered in and out of his memories, nearly losing himself in the thoughts and emotions of Audra.

"Is she tall?" CJ could see he had drawn deep within himself, in a place only he could go. She was trying to keep things basic in nature, realizing she was treading in personal space here.

Gunnar came back out of his memories of Audra, feeling the pangs of emotional pain because of their separation.

"No, not even close to it," he tried to chuckle to hold his composure. "Maybe a little shorter than you. Dark brown hair, above the shoulder. You're a little skinnier."

CJ suddenly became self-conscious about her bright auburn hair and freckles. The fact that she was a mess only added to her self-consciousness. She did like the fact he thought she was skinny. What woman doesn't want to hear that?

"What's her name?" She asked again, hopefully.

Gunnar thought a moment, hesitating... He carefully fingered her memory chip again.

"Audra, Audra Atlanta."

"Is she waiting for you?"

"Yes, you could say that, but I think it will be a long time before we're reunited."

CJ recalled him mentioning their travel through a worm hole to get to Hadrian. Black Hole and Worm Hole theory was a required study course at the Albion academy, but all cadets were instructed to avoid them at all costs. Nothing good ever came of an encounter with a Black Hole, so she had no understanding how Gunnar and his friend had successfully encountered one. Worm Hole travel was the stuff of fantasy in the space travel world, though the engineers of Hadrian believed it possible. Thus far, Quadra light travel was the best their scientists had come up with. His ship must be quite impressive to handle the stress loads imposed by such astrological phenomenon. Space and time were inexplicably connected and she perceived his chances of getting back to his home world and Audra, rather remote.

Janox let out another loud snort, drawing CJ's attention.

"So what's her story?" CJ asked watching her sleep. Gunnar stretched a little more to see Alex directly behind him.

"No idea," he grunted. "I was sort of hoping you'd be able to help out with that one. I found her, or rather she found me in the caves. Seemed perfectly happy to help out and follow along."

"She didn't say anything about where she came from or how she got down there? Was she with anyone?"

"Not a word, but then again, it wasn't like we had a whole lot of time for chit-chat. We were pretty much running most of the time."

"Well, maybe when we get to Cross we can find out a little more about her. And you really ought to set her straight about calling you Bud."

"Leads right into my next question," Gunnar smiled, lying back again. "Do you suppose your friend on Cross will have anything he would loan us to help get my ship and crew back?"

"I'm afraid trying to mount some kind of an assault on Tintee for such an endeavor wouldn't get you very far. There has got to be a different solution we could come up with."

"What about those, what did you and Willis call them, Tomplie pirates? What about those guys? Do you think they could be recruited to help?"

CJ let out a forced burst of laughter.

"Not even. They're interested in one thing, what they can lay their hands on."

"Everybody has to have to a price," Gunnar commented. "We just need to find out what their price is."

"Oh, price they've got; money we haven't got. My friend is pretty good at thinking things like this through. I'm sure he would be willing to offer us plenty of suggestions."

"I hope so. We can't just leave it or my crew there. I would think the same thing about your people as well."

CJ understood Gunnar's feelings. She just didn't see how there was anything they could do about it. They were only two people, a wild girl, a tiny droid and a beat up fighter. The odds were certainly *not* in their favor.

Bring her back

The *Tarzana* was undergoing the same torture in orbit around Moyle as it had experienced shark tailing through the rings of Reako several days ago. A deep shroud of meteoroid layers protected Moyle's atmosphere from the neutrino emissions of its twin suns. These meteoroids were small particles, no larger than a grain of rice, but the layers were as thick as flying through a sand storm. Not only was the battlecruiser subject to the constant bombardment, but these particles reacted violently to the ship's shield energy, exploding on contact, causing the ship's hull to glow a brilliant gold.

Blinda Koss watched fascinated from a small window in a dimly lit room as the lumbering giant cut through the lower layers and out into a wider orbit to avoid the punishing effects of the particles. It had been necessary to dip into the lower orbit in order to bring a small landing craft in to deposit personnel on the surface. Anything smaller than a Corvette sized vessel would not survive the reentry through such layers.

The Thane shivered slightly, feeling a chill in the room she had been ordered to wait in. She refused to wear warmer clothing unless it was absolutely necessary as it inhibited her ability to react quickly and fight without restriction. The room was somewhat small, but lavishly decorated. Heads of animals, even some ghastly looking humanoids, lined the walls below a shiny wood ceiling.

A burst of laughter drew her attention to a closed, heavy wooden door. Listening for a moment, she finally turned to a large chair and carefully sat down, rubbing her arms. She looked around the room again. There was a fire place, but it didn't look like it had been used in a long time. Not seeing any other means of heat, she finally closed her eyes and carefully waved her hand in front of her. The room instantly brightened and the temperature rose to something a little more comfortable.

Another burst of laughter from the next room gave Blinda cause to wonder what was so funny. She was sure Drax was spinning all kinds of yarns about the last couple of days chasing Colonel Barker and the idiot alien ship that turned out not to live up to all the hype Drax had built. The laughter wasn't that of

Drax however, this was different, whimsical. Blinda finally couldn't take it any longer and waved her hand, opening the big door and stepping out to face Drax and another woman sitting across from her. It wasn't often the Queen Captain was able to just relax with good friends. In her position, she had so few. The smile on Drax's face instantly dropped, the woman sitting across from her continuing to chuckle softly.

"I told you to remain in that room until called for." Drax's tone was quite condescending.

"If there is going to be jokes made at my expense, I want to be a part of it," Blinda bristled.

"Do you really believe I came here to exchange petty gossip?" Drax countered irritably. Seelix was still smiling. Blinda fidgeted, now wishing she hadn't entered the room. Her hair color changed several shades and she became aware her fingernails had grown nearly two inches, starting to curl on the ends. She hap-hazardly compressed the air, drawing an immediate response from Seelix.

"Don't try using your Thane tricks on us," Seelix fired. Blinda dropped her eyes to Seelix's lap and the muzzle of a blaster pistol pointed right at her. She hadn't noticed the power generator whistling up, as she had been too focused on herself.

"My good friend Drax and I were just catching up on old times, but if you have something you'd like to share with us, then by all means, I'm always keen for a good laugh."

Blinda carefully relaxed, realizing she had escalated this whole situation needlessly. For now, she needed to be a team player and upsetting the hired help wasn't playing nice in the sand box. She sheepishly tried to cover her fingernails as they shrank back to their normal length and her hair turned platinum again.

"Now," Drax asserted, remaining seated with her legs crossed, "return to your room until I call for you."

"With your permission," Seelix drew in a deep breath. "If Blinda is a part of what you came to see me about, then let's get down to it. I do have business appointments scheduled elsewhere." Seelix moved her thumb, shutting off the blaster. Drax appeared to grumble a bit, motioning for Blinda to sit.

"So what brings QC Blair and the mighty Blinda Koss to my humble abode?"

Blinda looked around. This dwelling was hardly humble. It would almost be considered a palace. It was spacious, lavishly decorated, each room having its own distinction.

"I would like your help with a little project," Drax started carefully. Seelix was exceptionally selective about the jobs she accepted.

"Little project and Drax Blair don't go together," Seelix responded setting her blaster on the table next to her. "What's this all about?"

"CJ Barker."

"Ah, I heard you ran her off Carolon. Congratulations on conquering the biggest waste of a rock in the galaxy. If you have the place, what do you need my help for?"

"She's on the run and badly wounded."

"So have your girlfriend here pick her up," she countered, motioning to Blinda.

"I sent her and Commander SoKnack after a new tactical ship Diord has been secretly developing, but they ended up blowing it up."

Blinda clamped down on her teeth, trying not to move anything.

"And you don't want the same for CJ..." Seelix started putting the puzzle together, passing a glance at the Thane.

"She's headed to Cross and I want you to go and pick her up," Drax came right to the point. "While you're at it, do a little poking around. Find out where Diord is manufacturing this tactical penetrator."

Seelix burst into laughter.

"Drax! You want me to invade Cross, infer the wrath of Diord to snoop around his top secret R & D facility and pick up CJ while I'm there? Come on! You know me better than that. I have a good working relationship with Diord and I don't want to piss him off. I do things because they're a challenge. I'm not a taxi service and certainly not a spy. Besides, if she's hurt, you know Diord will more than take good care of her."

"She's not alone, Seelix. She has a man with her."

"Well good for her. It's about time she got over Neil and got on with life. So who is this mystery man she has?"

Drax fell silent, thinking of what she had witnessed on Carolon and Reako.

"I don't know who he is, but I do know he isn't any ordinary man."

"CJ isn't any ordinary woman, Drax. Get to the point here, I'm losing interest."

"He's some kind of a superman or something. I witnessed him doing things ordinary people just can't do."

"And you think you can have Blinda here, ILOB control his mind while your medical ghouls clone him or something? Come on, have you lost your mind, or have you made a new medical break-through I don't already know about? Just pour more effort into the T-90 program."

Drax sat forward, a fire developing in her eye that made even Seelix lean in a bit.

"It's clear to me that Benetar has no intensions of producing a Blood Heir, so I mean to break the back of Colonia, bring the Ratronians to their knees and make Albia the new leadership in this galaxy once and for all."

"With you as the new Queen?"

"I wouldn't refuse the position."

"Wonder what the King Commander would have to say about that."

"He doesn't have to know until it happens."

"So what if Benetar did produce a Blood Heir? What if all of a sudden one showed up, and Albia confirmed its authenticity, what then?"

"I'm afraid the political situation has grown beyond just producing a Blood Heir."

"But if they did, would you back off? Would you defend the rights of the Blood Heir?"

Drax just stared at nothing, thinking.

"I don't see that happening," she said quietly.

"So you think this superman is the answer?"

"Along with Diord's new ship design and CJ Barker."

"But why all this fuss over CJ? She has no strategic purpose, no secrets. She's just an officer, and a wanted one at that."

Drax drew in a deep breath, passing a glance over at Blinda, then turned back to Seelix who had leaned in even closer looking for more of a reason to offer her services.

"Casey Janae is my friend. She was once like a sister to me. She was one of the few officers I ever trusted and in our military you have to have people you trust watching your back all the time. I need Diord's new penetrator; at the very least its designs and I need this new superman. I must have CJ with me to make all that happen. Most of all, if I'm to achieve a new order in this galaxy, I need her with me."

"And you mean to achieve all this at any cost?" Seelix was still looking for something more. She gave Blinda another quick look, and then returned to Drax.

"At any cost," Drax reiterated.

Seelix understood all too well the brutality in the Albion military. She wasn't military, though she had served a short stint herself. This attempt to bring CJ back to Albia and this superman running with her seemed like silliness as military strategies go. Still, there was a certain element of intrigue in all this.

"Ok, Drax," she finally relented. "But I have several conditions that if not met and kept, I'm out. I have far better things to do than chasing off after someone with other people and equipment getting in my way."

"Name them," Drax responded instantly.

"First, I go in alone and bring them out alone. I don't want any of your troops down there tripping and falling all over the place mussing things up. Besides, I'm sure Diord wouldn't like it either."

"Done," Drax agreed without objection.

"Second, I need eight Vivitar 700s."

"700s?" Blinda chimed in. "That's Colonian hardware. Where are we supposed to come up with those?"

"Done."

"Programmed to my specs and voice command, and..." she paused making sure both Drax and Blinda clearly understood her terms. "I keep them after the mission is over."

"Agreed." Drax seemed unaffected by the Moylian's demands, but had some demands of her own. "Just remember, Seelix. I want them both alive and in good condition."

"You don't need the man in good condition," Seelix countered. "Just a piece of him. What's it going to matter?"

"In good condition," Drax repeated firmly. "No garbage sack deliveries or excuses," she grumbled pointing a threatening finger at Seelix. "I've seen enough failures in the last couple of days. Afraid I've picked up a bit of a headache."

Seelix cast a suspicious look over at Blinda, who had dipped her head slightly, settling back in her seat.

"I want one of your transports," Seelix continued, getting to her feet and stepping over to a set of metallic doors, pressing a button.

"Done, you can use one of my Metro-Stars. It's been damaged and needs some repair. It'll make a good cover."

"How bad?"

"Bad enough. I'll have its ident codes setup as a diplomatic courier. That will get you on a landing platform. After that, you cut your own throat."

As the doors slid to one side, Seelix reached in and pulled out a rather mean looking blaster rifle with an attached scoping monitor, along with several long energy clips.

"Whoa, pull back on the throttles a second," Blinda objected, impressed at the size of the arsenal opened to them. "You're not going to need that kind of muscle."

"I'm always prepared," Seelix countered, pulling out a large shoulder bag and placing a large utility belt inside.

"You'll use this," Drax said holding something up. Seelix only glanced at the small vial of milky grey liquid. Seemingly unconcerned with what was in the vile, she reached for another weapon among many in the large storage compartment. Pulling an odd looking pistol from its resting place, she checked its parts, making sure everything was in order. Loading it into the empty holster on the belt, she grabbed several long energy clips and dropped them into the bag.

"Let's have it," she said holding out a hand. Drax tossed it to her and she carefully loaded it into one of the pockets of the utility belt.

"It's Evco," Drax informed her watching her pull several other gadgets from the storage area. "It helps dampen the energy waves in the brain."

"Please," Seelix shot indignantly. "I know what it does. I mix my own cocktails right here at home. You don't want me to hit CJ with this do you? If she's in a weakened state at all, this stuff will kill her."

Drax tossed Seelix another vile.

"Gonesh."

Seelix caught it and placed it into a different location on the belt.

"Even this stuff is a little strong for CJ, isn't it?"

"If there is one thing I know about CJ is she won't go down without a fight and is liable to hurt herself even more in the attempt. I don't want there to be any doubt that she's down. Hit her and her superman with the Gonesh first, then hit him again with the Evco.

"Crud," Blinda complained, looking at all the weaponry Seelix had loaded in the bag. "You're gonna fill him so full of drugs, he's not going to be able to think straight."

"That's the whole idea," Drax said getting to her feet. "Once we have him calmed down and that Evco in him, you should have no trouble convincing him to join us for a little trip to the lab."

Seelix checked all her gear again, making sure she hadn't left anything out. Working the fasteners on the bag, she picked it up and checked to see that everything was secure.

"Shall we dance?" she suggested playfully, turning for the door. Blinda was the first outside, turning toward the hangar bay complex where Seelix kept all her transports, but Drax stopped Seelix at the door.

"Thanks for doing this," she said, giving her a good shove on the shoulder. Seelix returned the shove and smiled.

"Hey, what are friends for? CJ's a good kid. Maybe a little mixed up, but a good kid." Seelix pushed past Drax after Blinda.

"Kid? At our age, we're hardly kids," Drax called after her.

*   *   *   *

Once inside the hangar bay, Seelix moved ahead of Blinda, who stood dumbfounded at the vast array of ships stored inside.

"These are all yours?" Blinda asked amazed. Drax stopped next to the Thane scanning the hangar. Not only were there ships of various sizes settled neatly together on the floor, but there were an equal number anchored to moorings just below the ceiling.

"Most of them. The others I'm storing for friends who either don't have room or want to keep them out of sight." Seelix turned every which way, admiring the vast assortment of ships anchored inside. Drax couldn't help but be amazed as well. Some of these ships she recognized as general purpose ships, some for transport, others for specific tasks.

"How did you get all these down here?" Drax asked, moving to follow Blinda and Seelix.

"Brought here the same way you got here. Larger ship brought them through the layers and then launched."

"How do we get back out then?" Blinda asked as they moved toward one of the larger ships.

"In this," Seelix gestured toward a light blue colored cylindrical craft. "It's the only ship that has shield generators strong enough to hold up against the Oort layers."

"So why did you ask me for a ship?" Drax asked as they started up the boarding ramp.

"Don't want to take a chance of losing this one on Cross. Better to bust up your gear than mine. Remember Diord hasn't kept what he has by just renting a couple of converted garbage scows to protect his assets. You know as well as anyone that Cross is the number one manufacturer of military grade hardware in the galaxy. I bet 90% of your battlecruiser was either made on Cross or taken from factories subcontracted by Diord."

Once inside, Seelix went to work on the ship's controls, carefully maneuvering it out the automatic doors and skyward, toward the explosive Oort layers of Moyle. She adjusted her shield controls as they entered the first set of layers and sat back, passing a look over at Drax, trying to relax. She had a silly look waving about her expression.

"Being Queen Captain isn't all it's cracked up to be?"

"It's not that bad. I suppose if I were mentally geared toward other things, it might be drudgery. But I'm not, I'm programmed for what I do and I enjoy it for the most part."

"What's the part you don't enjoy?"

Drax thought a moment, watching the windshields darken as the explosive particles outside began to strike the ship's shield energy.

"Failures."

"Most successful people have more failures than successes."

"Maybe, but I feel like I'm having to work too hard to get CJ back with me. It shouldn't have to be this difficult."

"You think she should just come to you with open arms."

"Certainly," Drax agreed. "If she would just slow down and talk to me."

"And how have you tried to communicate with her?" Seelix asked checking her instruments. "Did you call her on your private bestie's com-line and ask to meet for tea?"

Drax remained silent.

"Maybe she doesn't belong with you on Albia anymore."

"She was born of Albion parents, in Zepplin, Albia. We went to school together, attended the Albion academy together. She was the first one in our squadron to achieve ace status in Tusken fighters. She helped me nurse BachTL back to health after we found him abandoned on Lent Nine. We raised him together and taught him the ways of the Albions. She is Albion."

"Just because you raised BachTL as an Albion certainly doesn't make him one. He's still Castellian. Has CJ always thought the way the Albions do? Do you think the way they do?" You are what you believe in and maybe she doesn't believe in what the Albions profess to be. Just because people are one race or another doesn't make them automatically against each other."

Drax fell silent again, as if trying to figure out the sense of the conversation, maybe analyzing the questions Seelix was asking.

"You know where my allegiance lies."

"Do I? Do you?" Seelix maintained. "Suppose the King Commander were in your place. Would he drive half the Albion and Ratronian military across the galaxy to take a useless chunk of rock and bring back one officer?"

Drax's hackles started to elevate, but the more she thought about it, the more she was able to step back and look at the larger picture.

"I've been a military officer all my life." Drax watched another layer of volatile meteoroids begin to explode against the ship's shields as they continued to breach the atmosphere of Moyle. "It's all I have ever known. The same can be said for CJ. We are Albions. It's the root and soul of our existence. Without the Albion uniform, I would be just another human who watches others make change in their own way."

"Maybe it's time for you to stand by and watch for a while." Seelix checked her instruments as they exited the last of the rings of Moyle and turned her ship toward the orbiting *Tarzana* some distance away. "You're so stuck on being an efficient military officer, maybe you've lost sight of what really matters in the galaxy."

"I thought that's why I'm expending so much energy to find CJ?"

"Just consider that maybe CJ is turning to something other than Colonia or Albia." Seelix brought up her landing approach controls and pointed to a panel in front of Drax. "Transmit your approach codes right there," she instructed the Queen Captain.

Drax worked the instruments in front of her and a moment later the verification codes were approved.

"I have to know for sure, hear it directly from her. Right or wrong, I need to know for myself that this is what she really wants."

"And when she tells you no, you'll shake hands and part quietly?"

Drax seemed finished with the conversation. She knew Seelix was a woman of her word and would see her agreements through. It didn't do her business any good if she reneged on a job. As the Moylian ship gently touched down in the *Tarzana's* landing bay, Drax reached up and touch a com control.

"Commander SoKnack, Quadra light to the Jurass system boundary as soon as possible." Drax turned in her seat as Seelix and Blinda were preparing to exit the ship. "I have a modification to make to our bargain." Both Blinda and Seelix stopped what they were doing and turned back to the Queen Captain.

"On what point?" Seelix asked.

"Blinda will be going with you."

Seelix started to object. The last thing she wanted was Blinda getting in the way and messing things up. Seelix might as well have a garrison of real troopers with her.

"Pumping Evco into CJ's friend isn't going to do any good if you don't have anyone there to control him. CJ has had something up her sleeve at every turn and I want to make sure nothing gets in your way. Blinda is the best candidate for that." Seelix wasn't happy, but nodded and grabbed her stuff, turning to leave.

"Fine," she scowled. "Just see that she doesn't get in my way."

Blinda pulled an insulted look, watching after Seelix. She turned back to Drax with an angry look as the Queen Captain got

to her feet. She was about to say something, but Drax beat her
to it, waving a threatening finger at her as she passed by.
    "Like I told Dalton about you, don't piss her off."

Good Friends

Situated in the Jurass system, a tidal locked moon cluster orbits the planet Cross. While small in comparison to standard moons in other systems, their gravitational pull on Cross is substantial. Constantly pushed and pulled, Cross's oceans are forever moving with the enormous tidal forces exerted on them. As the tides move out, the oceans are forced into enormous subterranean cavities beneath the planet's crust. This cycle typically takes several solar weeks.

The moons, Titus and Avalon, are uninhabitable and fragmented. Neither have breathable atmospheres, nor discernable magnetic poles. Important to not only the activities of Cross, but most of the Hadrian galaxy, some of the rarest, heavily sought after mineral and gas combinations are found on these two crumbling spheres and in a seemingly endless supply. A mixture of robot and manned machines worked the surfaces, moving precious ores and gases from the moons to Cross for processing.

Command and control of these operations are handled by two central control centers located on opposite sides of the planet to facilitate the orbital cycles. Called Alvadore and Beltrax, these complexes are nearly cities themselves, managing all moon mining and surface manufacturing plants all around Cross. Located planet wide, capital shipyards and sub-assembly manufacturing plants work nonstop, handling every aspect of ship construction on the surface. Additionally, old decommissioned vessels purchased from scrap yards are brought in for processing, stripped down for parts that could be reused elsewhere and the rest melted down and refabricated into new parts.

Not just a manufacturing juggernaut, Cross is considered one of the finest resort destinations in Hadrian. While the rich felt catered in lavish Letohs and resorts, the surface of Cross has much to offer even the budget conscious traveler. Keeping close rein on how manufacturing pollution is handled and processed help to keep the resort areas of Cross clean and pristine for guests to enjoy. The entire planet has something to offer everyone with just about any kind of taste in scenery.

Administrator Diord Vandmire walked quietly into Alvadore's enormous control center, observing operations, but trying not to be obtrusive. He employed the best and he loved to watch good people do good work. Everything operated at the peak of efficiency, but sometimes he needed to come down from the ivory tower. He had to get away from the mind numbing administration of corporate business. He used to work as a controller in a variety of different roles: air traffic, digger control, loading supervisor, just to name a few.

Consisting of several stories, Alvadore is the main control center, with Beltrax being the secondary sister site. There were many control centers just in this building alone, each handling a variety of functions. This particular control center handled the Letoh resort complex located nearby and the air traffic associated with it.

Carefully meandering about well behind the controllers and technicians hard at work, he turned his gaze up to one of the many giant displays on the wall.

Multiple screens within screens and banks of smaller video windows tiled the entire display before him. Everything could be monitored from this location; the resort areas and associated recreational areas they served, landing operations, people traffic and cargo shipments in and out of the city areas.

He was about to move onto another location when he noticed several of the video windows displaying a rather large ship. Recognizing it instantly, he moved casually to the rotating platform of the control section dealing with orbital traffic. Not wanting to barge right in, he did his best to hold back. Approaching from behind, he could see the lead supervisor working with one of the main controllers. Both operators sported concerned looks as they communicated back and forth on their private com systems. The suave administrator carefully slid in behind them, only getting close enough to hear the conversations.

Diord ran a hand through his jet black hair, listening as the two controllers continued trying to give specific instructions. They seemed to be having trouble with whomever they were conversing. From the sounds of the audible side, he had a good idea who they were talking to. Knowing they weren't going to get anywhere, he finally stepped forward.

"What's the *Executioner* doing in orbit?" he asked, trying not to make a big deal out of the presence of the Tomplie flag ship.

"It's Commander Aura," the controller responded, a little flustered by the Cross administrator's presence. It wasn't often Diord intruded into the goings on of the control center. Yes, he was observed many times strolling about the operations areas, watching and listening to what was going on, but he almost never intruded on what was actually happening.

"Well, so I assumed," Diord said quietly. "Nothing but trouble follows in his wake. What's he asking for?"

The control supervisor turned back to the controls below him and began conversing with the Tomplie ship again. As Diord waited, his attention was drawn by another controller a few stations down. Headsets were not being used there allowing Diord to hear who she was talking to. He thought he recognized the voice coming from the transmission. Touching the supervisor on the shoulder, he motioned that he was going to move. The supervisor acknowledged as the administrator stepped down the line a little bit, passing glances up at the wall screen.

"Control pass seven eight two four, approach clearance one nine five seven three, pattern four, this is Colonel CJ Barker of Carolon Command requesting clearance to landing platform two three six."

Diord smiled, bending down next to the young controller, who pushed back from her station to allow him to speak.

"It's been a long time, Casey Janae." He looked up at the image of an F-2 Flightstreak moving past one the orbiting sentry stations. Diord looked back down at the tracking screen in front of him as the dimensional picture drew out the form of the Colonian fighter. There was a pause in the transmission, giving Diord cause to wonder, and then the glint in his eye brightened as the Colonian Colonel finally responded.

"Hi Diord. What are you doing at a control station? Haven't you got better things to do?"

"Certainly I do, but I need to make sure silly redhead girls who think they can fly don't be coming down here busting up my landing pads." Diord let out a muffled chuckle. "So what brings you to my fair city?"

"Long story short, Drax wanted Carolon."

"So you've come here hoping I'd hide your sorry behind until the smoke blows over." Diord could hear something different in her voice, giving him cause for concern. CJ sounded exhausted, almost sick.

"I know you don't want any trouble. I was hoping to spend a couple of days, repair my ship, and then be out of your gorgeous hair."

Diord's grin broadened.

"You know I can't resist a redhead and them cute freckles. Two three six is yours, follow the controller's instructions down and I'll meet you out there. It'll be so good to see you."

"Looking forward to it," CJ responded.

Diord glanced back at the young controller and thanked her, then stepped back to the supervisor for a report on the Tomplie ship. The supervisor appeared a little embarrassed as he removed his ear piece and handed it to the Cross administrator. Irritated, Diord shoved it into place and touched a control on the panel in front of them.

"Ok, Aura, what do you want?"

"Diord, my good man," came a foreign accent from the ear piece. "What do I usually want when I come to your humble operations?"

"To rob me blind," Diord cut sharply.

"Ouch, you cut me to the heart," Lou Aura responded overly dramatic. "Please, just the contracted amounts of Senok and Clonadine," Lou replied coolly.

Diord studied the information on the screens below him and then passed a glance up at the main screen, watching the ship in orbit. He hated doing business with the Tomplie, especially Lou. Somehow, this pirate always managed to get the best of a deal, lawful or not.

"Aura, tell me why I'm doing business with you?"

"The Tomplie are a faction of Hadrian just like Colonia, Albia or Ratron."

"Smoke screen, Lou. You're boring me."

"Have I ever not paid you for any shipment?"

Diord paused, rolling his eyes.

"I've got a file so big on you…"

"Have I ever not paid your price for our shipments?"

"I do business with you only because you can somehow manage to pay top price, but even then, somehow I always get the shaft, one way or the other."

"Just doing business my friend, just business."

"I don't want to see your prune face down here, is that understood?"

"How am I supposed to do a pickup?"

"Send someone else down." Diord pulled the ear piece and handed it back to the supervisor. "Allow them two escorts and one cargo hauler at a time. Three loads and that's it. No more than three men aboard the hauler."

"That will take a couple of days to load," the controller objected.

"It will, won't it?"

Diord turned to leave, but stopped as the supervisor was about to give instructions to the controller. "Oh, and make sure he returns those containers he used on his last run." Then Diord was gone, moving quickly out of the control center toward platform two three six.

*   *   *   *

CJ coughed hoarsely, lying back on the med table and looking up at the med droids working over her. They had removed most of her torn clothing, allowing the droids to work on her wounds. Janox and Alex 7001 watched curiously from behind the multiple glass panes of the surgical observation lounge while Diord and Gunnar stood at the far side of the glass staring at several large screens. Gunnar constantly threw looks over at the monitors Diord was hovering over while still trying to see what was happening to CJ down on the med table.

"How bad is it?" Gunnar inquired impatiently, trying to see the images on the displays.

"Bad enough," Diord responded coldly. "She's lucky to still be alive."

"Yeah, she took some pretty good hits," Gunnar agreed. "Do you know how hard it is to knock this girl down?"

"You should have done more to protect her," Diord snapped, his voice elevating.

Gunnar gave the administrator a double take, realizing that he was being blamed for CJ's condition.

"You make it sound like I just left her out there on her own."

"Well the evidence here is a little overwhelming," Diord countered.

And just who does this guy think he is? He hadn't been there! He hadn't even gotten the details!

"I pulled her out of her Operations Center at the last second and carried her to her ship, dodging her friend Drax the entire time, hid with her down inside Reako and pulled her out of a Binion ritual..."

"Tomba," Janox added, being drawn by the exchange.

"Yeah," Gunnar fumbled, his anger instantly boiling. "What she said," he tossed a thumb in Janox's direction. "Not to mention carrying her back to the ship, dodging Drax the whole time. Then we got to outrun the Albion fleet to get here. So you tell me what more I could have done?"

By the time Gunnar had finished, it appeared to Diord that he had grown significantly in stature, backing the administrator up against the medical monitors. A little taken back by this man's quickness to anger, Diord backed down.

"Take it easy," he hedged nervously, looking him straight in the eye. "I'm sorry." Diord held his hands up to signal his defenselessness.

"Gunnar," Janox spoke softly from behind, laying a hand on his shoulder. "All are worried for Casey Janae. Now is time for calm. Focus on her. Explain and learn later."

Gunnar looked back at Janox. She projected a certain fearlessness associated with the innocence of the interaction between humans. Something clicked within him and he instantly melted back, stepping carefully backwards. He was out of control and hadn't even recognized it. Suddenly acutely aware of what could have happened, he felt embarrassed by his lack of control.

"No," Gunnar offered humbly. "I'm sorry. I guess we've been running so long and hard we're a bit frazzled."

Diord straightened his clothing and pulled a communicator from his belt as it went off.

"Sir, this is Control Supervisor Delta. We have a cluster of Colonian ships coming out of Quadra light in sector seven."

"Nothing wrong with that," Diord replied, turning away as Gunnar and Janox looked back through the observation window. "That's still quite a distance from here and still within their boundaries."

"Yes administrator. But they're signaling us, requesting permission to enter our space. It sounds like they'd like to have an audience with you."

Diord raised an eyebrow, scratching his forehead and looking back over at Gunnar and Janox. Likely they were here for CJ. But here in the Jurass system, Diord held all the cards and the most the Colonians could hope for was to make a formal request for her extradition.

"Have you been able to make any ship identifications or registries? Who are they carrying?"

"No, sir, still too far out. They're holding their position just outside our boundaries. We're scanning only a couple of war ships, most of the rest are transports. We should have complete scans shortly."

"Tell them to proceed in at sub-light. Have General Tanner bring his cruisers in a little closer, setting his support ships in close so our friends can see we're not just sitting here sunning ourselves. Let me know of any other changes as they get closer." The controller acknowledged and Diord turned back to the medical monitors.

Most of the damage to CJ was on her right side, and the med droids were quick to make the needed repairs. They were already dressing her wounds and administering badly needed medication to help her body fight off any further infections and repair itself. They had had to inject her with Micronites, tiny electronic microbials programmed to specifically seek out the Binion poison and eradicate it.

With his face pressed against the glass, Gunnar was hoping to see some kind of an indication from her that she was all right, but she was heavily medicated, needing rest. Diord turned away from the medical monitors and stepped back over to Janox and Gunnar.

"Well, it looks like she's going to pull through. That Binion poison should have finished her off long before you got her here. The Micronites they've injected her with should seek out what's left in her system and make short work of it. If you hadn't gotten most of it out before hand, it wouldn't have mattered."

"That would be thanks to Janox here," Gunnar commented, watching as the med table moved CJ into a clear tube and transporting her through a wall. A labyrinth of these tubes serviced the entire medical complex, moving patients and medical equipment efficiently under a tight climate control. Janox looked after CJ as her tube moved to somewhere a little more private, but turned and smiled as Diord nearly bumped into a floating Alex 7001.

"She should make a fairly fast recovery," Diord said looking after the droid. "Whatever that stuff is you used on her, saved her life. How did you learn to use medicine like that?" Janox looked back down at CJ as her med table disappeared, then back at Diord.

"My Au Par, Tonnie," she answered matter-of-factly. Diord's expression developed into mild confusion. Gunnar suddenly realized that Janox had not been alone when she found him. But she so willingly came with him, as if she had nowhere else to go. Both Gunnar and Diord looked at each other as Janox stepped from the room to find CJ's private room, followed by Alex.

"I don't know what an Au Par is, but..."

"A royal nanny," Diord cut in. "You said you found her..."

"She found me."

"Found her in Reako?"

"Deep down. Can we see CJ?"

Diord slowly nodded, heading for the door, deep in thought with Gunnar right behind him. Before they could reach her room, Diord's communicator sounded off again and stopping short of the door, pulled it from his hip.

"Now what?" He asked sounding bothered.

"As you indicated, sir. They're asking for a Colonel Barker and a Colonel Conrad." Diord looked up at a surprised Gunnar. "Any registry transmissions yet?"

"Yes, sir, all of the ships have sent ident registries."

"All of them?" Diord was getting all kinds of surprises today. Not what he was thinking of when he woke up this morning. Gunnar gave Diord a perplexed look and seeing the questions rolling across his face, the administrator paused for an explanation.

"Generally, fleet ships will only transmit one registry to ident the entire flotilla. These guys are flooding our system with all their idents. Almost like they're throwing up a white flag of surrender or something." Diord brought the communicator back to his lips, looking into the room to see CJ opening her eyes and greeting Janox tiredly. "What's the registry on the capitals? Who's in command?"

"A Lieutenant Talia Reese and a Captain Dakota Abrams. Colonian ident registries on the capitals are the *Trax*, *Realistic* and the *Intruder*. Assigned to Colonel Barker of Carolon Command. The Captain says he's from a ship called the *Constellation*. Part of the Royal Kalamarion Starbird fleet." Diord looked at a relieved Gunnar.

"Friends of yours?"

"You could say that. Captain Abrams is my exec. The *Constellation* is my ship. This sounds like CJ's fleet. Things must not have worked out too well on Tintee. I don't remember who CJ's execs are. Only her personal aide, Willis Ruston. It could be this Lieutenant Reese is one of her execs."

Diord eyed Gunnar carefully. There hadn't been any time for them to get to know each other. Just the hasty introductions when they landed and CJ nearly collapsed in Diord's arms. But he had no evidence to suggest Gunnar wasn't telling the truth. The facts were he brought her here, or she him and her fleet was asking for permission to approach Cross. He looked back inside the room at CJ, then back at Gunnar. No, there was no reason not to believe him.

"Have General Tanner sweep his ships in behind and escort them all in."

"All of them?

"All of them," Diord repeated clearly. "Stage them on the far side of Cross, beyond Titus. No orbits, keep them on the far side." Diord dropped the communicator back to his belt and motioned Gunnar into the room.

*   *   *   *

The Cross security forces inspecting all landing ships carefully made their way around the enormous Tomplie cargo hauler, *Langley*. Based from its mother ship the *Executioner*, the ship barely fit on the landing platform adjacent to the main Alvadore

Letoh complex. Any larger and it would have had to remain in a manual orbit above Cross and smaller cargo transports would have to shuttle its loads up.

After what seemed like an eternity of careful searching, the Cross security squads were satisfied the Tomplie hauler was clean, meeting all the preconditions Administrator Vandmire had laid out before a landing could take place. Once the ship had been cleared, the hauler's entire body opened up like a split half shell. Inside the middle of its now wide open cargo bay, was a large stack of cargo containers. Not only were the Tomplie returning the containers they had used previously, but Lou Aura had added one of his own for every one he had borrowed. A couple of large overhead I-beam cranes immediately moved into position and started lifting the larger containers off the stack, while manned mechanical Eckto lifts worked the smaller containers out of the ship's inner platform. Tromping off to the facility container storage areas close to the landing bay, the Eckto lifts moved the different sized containers with relative ease. It would take a considerable amount of time to stage this order, partly because it hadn't been preprocessed, but also because of the instructions Diord had given that it take longer to fill the order. Retribution for all the crooked dealings Lou had perpetrated against Cross. This would give the crew of the cargo hauler plenty of time to stretch out and rest while they waited.

After the Eckto lifts had departed the storage area, one of the containers opened up. Several occupants carefully crept from their concealment, making sure they were not being observed. Lou Aura carefully stepped over to a small lifting vehicle and moved it toward an even smaller container. As the other three men climbed inside, he picked it up and started for the main doors. Each man was dressed the same way, looking like they were outfitted for mountaineering or cave exploring. Lou seemed to know exactly where he was going, turning the craft quickly around one of the corners, heading for the main Letoh complexes. After navigating the immense maze of maintenance sub halls, Lou brought his ground transport to a halt next to a large cluster of elevators in the bowels of the Letohs. Once they were out and ready to move, Lou checked again to make sure they weren't being observed. Satisfied, he stepped into one of the elevators with one of the other men and disappeared behind closing doors while the others went a different direction.

*   *   *   *

After several hours in the recovery room, Diord had CJ moved to one of his penthouse apartments in one of the largest

Letohs of the resort complex. Here she would be quite comfortable during her several days of recuperation. Additionally, there was plenty of room for the others without making her feel trapped or crowded. The Letoh penthouse was one of many Diord kept active for himself. He could entertain important interstellar VIPs, friends and associates in relative comfort. For CJ, nothing but the best. He made sure she had every comfort available, including a view of platform two three six, where her Flightstreak sat. For a couple of days, they watched as the craft was surrounded by several human technicians directing the work of an army of mech-droids.

"Casey," Diord insisted. "It's a piece of junk." He stepped to the outside rail with CJ and looked down at the F-2 on the platform far below. "You've beat the living daylights out of it. The poor thing owes you nothing."

"Yes, it's seen its fair share of action, but it's still got lots of life left in it."

"The F-4 is far superior. More guns and more power to them. It has the new advanced targeting system and I've been able to get the Navi-computer down to half the size. I even added the gen three AI system. It's the bomb!"

"Now there's something," Gunnar piped up. "Half the F-2 cockpit is electronics."

"The F-4 is sleeker, more maneuverable, and the price is just right. I'll take your old one in trade. You won't owe me a thing."

CJ carefully rubbed her sore shoulder, slowly stepping back into the room to sit down. The past couple of days of recuperation had helped a lot and she wanted to keep it that way, though getting up and walking around did give her a sense of strength.

"I appreciate everything you've done for us," CJ sighed tiredly, picking up a drink. "But I'm afraid our presence here is only going to be a headache for you. It's only a matter of time before Drax figures out where I am and the Queen isn't going to be sleeping on my whereabouts either."

"Let 'em come," Diord responded defiantly. "They can holler and scream all they want, but unless they're willing to come in here and take you over my dead, twisted body, it ain't going to happen. They wouldn't dare. I supply both war machines with a lot of hardware, and not just military. Without me here, they'd be in a world of hurt."

"Even so, we can't stay here indefinitely. We need another place to be."

Diord's communicator beeped again and he stepped back out onto the patio to answer the call.

"We can't run forever," Gunnar pointed out carefully, sitting down next to her.

"I don't mean to," CJ responded. "As soon as we can get our execs here, we can have a good look at some star charts to try and make a game plan as to where we can take the Carolon fleet. Try and make a fresh start somewhere else. Somewhere out of the reach of all this mess I got you into."

"You don't see me kicking and squirming to get away, do you?"

CJ smiled, letting her hand drop down onto his, squeezing it gently.

"Thank you for staying with me, but you and your friends have your own problems to deal with."

"Well that was a strange request," Diord reported reentering the room. CJ and Gunnar turned to him as he replaced the communicator. "Something about your execs coming here. Don't know how, we've been keeping them all out of sight on the other side of Titus and Avalon. No one has asked for any clearance delivery from approach control either. They just said they'd be coming directly here."

"When?" CJ inquired, sitting forward. A strange snapping sound starting to form in the room directly in front of them.

"Right now," Gunnar announced smiling, watching several forms materializing right in front of them. A moment later Dakota, Tiana, Willis and Talia appeared, facing the other direction. There were several seconds of silence, followed by bewilderment, except for Gunnar. Dakota and the others, wondering if they were in the wrong place, Diord for witnessing teleportation. Talia was the first to turn around, then Willis and Tiana.

Tiana's expression instantly changed when she recognized Gunnar stepping toward them. A feeling of complete relief swept through her and her emotional demeanor immediately shifted. The stress she had endured these last couple of days now seemed a distant memory. Sporting an arm sling and nearly in tears, she nearly knocked Gunnar over, throwing her good arm around him and pressing herself close to him. Letting her pain dissipate, she felt safe in his presence, in his arms.

"I've been so worried. We all have."

Unprepared, Gunnar gave Dakota an odd look. Holding Tiana, he became aware that someone else had moved a little closer to him and he pulled free of the embrace. CJ cast a curious look at the pair. Gunnar suddenly felt like he was betraying someone here.

"This must be Audra." CJ stepped forward to take Tiana's hand in a greeting.

Gunnar's hearts skipped around each other, then realizing the perceived mistake, stepped back a little and smiled.

"No, this is Tiana Mantose, budding executive officer and all around self-taught engineer. And this would be my exec, Captain Dakota Abrams." Gunnar motioned to Dakota, who gladly shook CJ's hand.

"Yes, we've met," CJ started to smile, still eyeing Tiana suspiciously.

"Sure am glad to see you, Colonel," Dakota finally said, breaking up the moment. "Way to leave us sitting out in space while you're resting here in the lap of luxury." Dakota looked around at the penthouse.

"How is everyone?" Gunnar asked, shifting the focus away from him.

"Two casualties," Dakota reported. "We lost Sindee and Taron getting away from Tintee."

"Tiana, I am so sorry. What happened?" Gunnar asked, looking into her tear-filled eyes. Now he understood and enveloped her in his arms, trying to pull as much pain from her as he could.

"It's a long story that's best kept for another time," Talia butted in. "We've got to figure out where we're going to hide Carolon command and fast."

"What's the urgency, Bubs?" CJ inquired stepping up. Dakota produced a black box, handing it to the Colonian Colonel. She recognized it immediately.

"A Colonian tracking device."

"It's a good bet the queen knows where we are."

CJ threw Diord a quick glance, then a look back over to Gunnar, who stepped up and took the box from her.

"Did you see action when you left Tintee?" CJ asked.

"Almost nothing," Talia responded.

"Take a direct route?"

"No, but does it matter?"

Diord's communicator went off again and he stepped away from the group.

"Ship's status?" Gunnar inquired of Dakota who was more than happy to report and relinquish command back to the Colonel. Gunnar handed the box back to CJ who turned to Willis and Talia for a report on her command as Dakota started his.

"Right now, she's anchored in one of the landing bays aboard the *Trax*. Big ship that *Trax*, but kind of old. They're still using what looks like Oculla drive units and their navigational systems, don't even get me started."

"Captain..." Gunnar sighed exasperated.

Dakota caught himself.

"Uhm, sorry, sir. Just really glad to see you. We thought you had been taken by the Albions. Rick must have found you."

Gunnar flopped a blank stare at his exec.

"No, no Rick. What do you mean Rick? Where's Rick?"

"He blasted his way back to Carolon to find you. Said he wasn't going to leave you behind."

"And you let him go?" Gunnar asked, not realizing what he was saying.

"Like I could stop him; he pulled rank on me. Last time we saw him, he was executing a barrel roll over the Ratronian Dreadnaught with Zek and Zak flying point." A gleam came to Dakota's eyes when he thought about what the scene must have looked like. "That Ratronian commander must have pissed his pants when the *Athena* ..."

"Crap!" Gunnar cursed lowly trying not draw attention from the others.

"What?"

"We never saw him!" Gunnar whispered worried now. "And he has no idea we're here. Carolon space was completely overrun by the Albions. Unless they remained on the fringes, you couldn't spit in that space without hitting one."

"Well, none of it landed on me," a familiar voice called from the far side of the room.

Gunnar jumped to Rick before anyone had a chance to even move, wrapping his arms around him in an embrace equaled only by Rick's relief that his friend was ok. Gunnar pulled back and held Rick by the forearms, shaking them firmly.

"You have no idea how good it is to see you," Gunnar grinned.

"I think I have a bit of a clue," Rick responded, thinking of the last couple of days. "How are you feeling?"

"Haven't had any time to stop and think about it much. Ok, I think," Gunnar answered. "I see you have some new toys," he said looking at the rings on Rick's belt.

"Yeah, tell you all about them later." Noticing Audra's memory chip tucked in Gunnar's shirt, he looked past his friend at CJ, who was stepping up beside him.

"And you must be, Colonel CJ Barker. You two sure have covered a lot of distance in the last couple of days. Kind of a pain trying to catch up."

"You don't know the half of it," CJ replied smiling as Rick carefully took her hand. She wasn't feeling well, still wobbly. "Pleased to finally meet you, General."

Rick gently kissed her hand. CJ smiled bashfully, enjoying the heightened chivalry. Gunnar finally took her hand and walked her back to the couch.

"All right, all right," he said giving his friend the eye. "Where's Jayda? Have to leave someone with real authority on the *Athena*?"

Rick didn't get a chance to answer.

"Well, things just keep getting better and better all the time," Diord complained stepping back into the room. He stopped short when he saw Rick. "Can I help you?" Diord continued, stepping forward.

"No, I'm good," Rick responded. The Cross administrator was postured like he might try to throw Rick out or something.

Diord noticed the blaster on Rick's hip and the Balkrums hanging from his belt. Catching sight of several patches on his uniform, Diord turned to CJ and Gunnar for some kind of an explanation.

"Meet, General Richard Alexander Niker," Gunnar announced, sitting down next to CJ. "My best friend and the commander of our other ship, the *Athena*.

"General?" Diord asked, looking a little closer at the insignias.

"We try to ignore the whole General thing," Rick hinted good-naturedly.

"Yeah," Dakota piped up. "He won those stars on a bet."

A chuckle rolled through the room as Diord diverted his focus back to the news he had just received, but still trying to figure out how the Kalamarion officer had breached his security.

"A large flotilla of Colonian ships are assembling in the Teleknee system a couple of doors down from us. I'm not too concerned about them as the Empire routinely performs maneuvers there, though I have to say they picked a curious time to do so. There is also an Albion Metro-star on approach, due to land on platform two three eight within the hour."

"But you expected this, right?" CJ inquired, feeling an intense desire to get away from Cross as soon as possible.

"Certainly," Diord relaxed a bit. "But I can't refuse them. Bad business practices. I'm sure the Metro-star is just a courier requesting your extradition. I have no doubt they have a flotilla of their own parked somewhere off a little more discretely than what the Colonians do. Probably waiting behind the moons of Locke in the Eldora system. They can't afford any kind of entanglements here in this system, not with my ships buzzing around."

"So what are our options right now?" Gunnar asked, noticing Janox and Alex 7001 coming in from one of the back rooms.

"We need to get you folks up to the Bristol mapping room to see if we can find a couple of suitable options." Diord motioned for the group to head for the door. "And in my back yard isn't one of them," he added, helping Gunnar get CJ to her feet. "No offense."

CJ only grinned broadly, starting after her two executive aides. Diord held Gunnar back, Rick hanging back as well, as Janox and Alex 7001 went past.

"I've gotten a little more information on your mystery girl there," he indicated looking after Janox. He passed Gunnar a small device, having a screen displaying information. Gunnar glued his eyes to it as the three walked after the others. He tried to make out what it was saying, but as with all the rest of the Hadrian alphabet, he couldn't make heads or tails of any of it.

"Gonna need a translator for this," Gunnar admitted handing it back to the administrator. Diord gave him an odd look, then motioned the device over to Rick, who gave the same response.

"Sorry, I can't read it either."

"Wished we had the time to sit down and get the full skinny on you guys," Diord complained. "I'll pass this on to CJ when I get a chance and she can give you a run down on your friend. I think you'll find it interesting. Needless to say, you need to keep her safe and secure." With that, the Cross administrator moved ahead of the others, directing them to an elevator that took them even higher up the enormous Letoh building.

*   *   *   *

The Bristol map room was able to seat large crowds in a round theatre setting with a large, odd looking flat device in the center on the floor and one just like it in the dark ceiling. As Diord had several options in his head as to where the Carolon group could find refuge from the warring empires in Hadrian, he had already downloaded the information to the map room computer and had only to turn the system on, grab the control and bring up the holographic images. As they all sat down, Alex 7001 remained aloft, floating slowly about the room, recording everything.

Diord stepped quickly to the middle of the images projected in multi-dimensional format, touching several controls on the device pad he had in his hand. The images of a multitude of galaxies materialized and moving in several different directions, he finally zoomed in close on a bright one.

"The galaxy Hadrian, where we are right now. It's divided up into four sections. As a race of space travelers, we're still fairly young. With the conflicts that have arisen, we haven't been able to do the space exploration we should. Too much time spent squabbling." Diord touched another control and several grid lines appeared through the galaxy depicted. "This section right here is where we are. The planet Cross, Carolon is over here, Albia is here, Tintee is way over here and Krull, where the Ratronians like to call home, is over here." Diord turned to Gunnar and Rick. "So where is, what did you call your home world?"

"Well, mine is Commenor, Rick's is Kalamar," Gunnar offered. "But it's not likely you'll find them on any of your charts."

"Why not?"

"It's kind of far away," CJ cut in grinning. Diord held a questioning look, hoping someone would offer further explanation.

"They're in the Mandell system, in a quad of galaxies called Della-Montrose," Gunnar finally offered. He looked at the map carefully, hoping to see something familiar. Something that might point toward home.

Both Kalamarion officers could have acted out Diord's reaction, as he had no idea what they were talking about. The administrator lifted an eye brow trying to come up with something, but finally turned back to his presentation.

"Our quadrant here, the Mila quadrant, the Teshana quadrant here, Theta Tallus over here, and finally this one next to us, Altanis. These two, Teshana and Altanis, we know next to nothing about, other than they're there and a few rumors and stories that have come out of them. We have nothing on Teshana. Altanis has the dubious honor of being entered only once or twice that I am aware of. My exploration groups swung through once and my pirate buddies got themselves chased out there some time ago. More to get away from me and the Colonian Empire. If you look right here," he said pointing to a tiny spec among millions. He touched his control again and the image zoomed in even further. "There is a tiny planet located in what the Tomplie call the Arista system."

"Why would we go somewhere the pirates know about?" Talia asked, voicing the same question they were all thinking.

"Certainly there are other alternatives, but they're known by both empires and you could be located after some time. Aster isn't in any system. It's a rogue planet. It has no sun, no sisters, no moons, nothing. We haven't spent a whole lot of time trying to figure out where exactly it came from or where it's going, but near as we can guess a dwarf star got too close to its parent system, shifting its orbit and spinning the planet off into deep space. Its characteristics are a lot like Cross, except for no sun, but the good news is that it has retained its geomagnetic core, still producing the magnetosphere required to keep the solar winds from striping away its atmosphere and tearing it apart as it travels. High geothermal and volcanic activity keeps the place warm, and with the right air scrubbers, it'll be quite sustainable. It might be easier to find it if you weren't looking for it. My guys found it quite by accident. The Tomplie only stumbled onto it trying to hide after making a raid on one of my transport fleets. Believe me, you're quite safe from them trying to come in and raid the place. They're after only what's easy to get to. Aster is about as far as they've ever gone and as its path appears to be outbound, it's not likely they will ever find it again. They just don't have the resources available to go there on purpose. And it's never in the same place twice."

Everyone seemed to be satisfied with the idea of Aster becoming their new home. The fact that it lay in an uncharted region of the galaxy, yet still relatively close to the Jurass system, made it a good place to stage a base for those who had no love for either empire. Perhaps on Aster, a new start could be made. Looking at each other, they nodded in agreement as Diord's communicator went off, yet again.

"Well, for the love of Hadrian," he grumbled, tossing a tiny device with Aster's information to Dakota and raising his communicator.

"Sorry for the intrusion, Administrator," a nervous voice responded to the short sounding Diord. "The repairs on Colonel Barker's F-2 are complete. We are also picking up Albion activity in sector 12. Too far out to know for sure of any details. Also, you might want to have a look at that Metro-star landing on two three eight. Scans show two life forms, but the hold registers military grade droids, MD-700s."

"Nuts," he mumbled frowning. "Have Admiral Titus deploy the fleet and General Lankish prepare his squadrons in case we get unwelcome visitors." Diord touched a control on his device and stepped to a nearby wall display. It wasn't long before he was joined by Gunnar and Rick.

"Hey, I recognize that ship," Gunnar said in a low voice. The image of facing off with Drax in the tunnels of Reako were still quite vivid in his mind, but surly it couldn't have survived the ensuing cave-in as they blasted their way up and out.

"There are a lot of Metro-stars out there," Diord commented, still keeping his voice low. "I produce them all right here and sell them on the open market to anyone. They're pretty good at filling a variety of roles. But, to be fair, this one is Albion. It's the courier I was telling you about. Looks like it's had the crap beat out of it. This one is carrying military grade hardware though. Not uncommon, but given the circumstances, a little spooky."

"So what did that document you were showing us earlier say?" Gunnar and Diord looked back at Janox.

"It's a little drawn out, but long story short, you're looking at the rightful Blood Heiress to the Colonian Empire." Gunnar and Rick stared blankly at the administrator.

"Isn't there already a Queen?" Gunnar asked. "A Queen Benetar?"

"Stephanie Benetar is not a Blood Heir. Technically, she's only a Duchess."

"Well, then how...?"

"She's a Duchess of Teleknee. She married into the royal family and by a series of suspicious incidents, became the only one in line for the throne."

"She bumped off the entire royal family?" Rick asked.

"No one can prove it for sure, but everything was a little too convenient."

"Then how did Janox get overlooked?" Gunnar asked.

Diord adjusted several controls on the panel in front of him, keeping an eye on the screen.

"Apparently the Queen didn't want to get her hands dirty with the murder of a young royal daughter, so she arranged to have her smuggled to the Nulark system and exiled on the inside of Reako. Janox couldn't have been more than three or four at the time. Years later, after war broke out between the Albions and the Colonians, the Queen got nervous that the girl might be discovered, so to keep the Colonians or the Albions from inadvertently finding her, she had a base setup on Carolon, just to keep eyes off Reako. No one would think to look inside a planet next to a Colonian base commanded by a former Albion defector. It was nearly perfect..."

"Until the Albions decided Carolon was strategically important for whatever reason and ran CJ off, then chased us down into Reako." Gunnar finished seeing the logic. "Of all the dumb luck. Amazing we found her. Does she even know she's the heir?"

"Not likely," Diord commented glancing over at the young woman. "Seems logical she was put down there with provisions to live with her royal nanny, her Au Par."

"Didn't see her," Gunnar said carefully. "I assume she was killed down there. It's kind of a rough place."

"I can only imagine." Diord pulled his communicator back out as it beeped again, this time just a text flashing across its display. "Never ending story," he complained pushing it back into place. "Gentlemen, never become rich and famous. You become an instant target for every dreg and scumbag in the universe."

"Trouble in paradise?" Gunnar asked smiling at Diord's distain.

"The price you sometimes pay for being nice," the administrator responded. "A series of thefts reported through this entire Letoh complex. I don't get it, I have the best security money can buy and still I get robbed blind by the little guy."

"My apologies," Rick shuffled a little uncomfortably.

Diord gave Rick a double take, then turned back to his displays. "I was referring to the thugs currently fleecing..." Diord dropped off, his attention drawn again by the ship on the screen in front of them. The boarding ramp was coming down and a figure strode confidently down onto the platform.

"Oh photons," Diord exclaimed in a hush. He glanced over his shoulder, then back at the screen. "This time it looks like she's on a hunt."

"What? Who's on a hunt?" Rick asked, getting a bad feeling crawling up his leg toward the bottom of his spine.

"Seelix Monroe." Diord's frustration continued to build. It was clear he hadn't counted on all this attention to CJ. He was all about helping his friends, especially good ones, and he would do anything for CJ Barker, but things seemed to be getting a little out of hand. "She's a good client of mine. A buyer and seller of just about anything you'd like to get your hands on. I've even hosted her in this very penthouse many times. But I can tell you, from the looks of her, she's not here to buy a ship or any military hardware. She will hunt anything or anyone as long as the challenge is to her liking. Call her an exotic hunter. I admit I've had her do some work for me. Never thought she'd come here hunting something."

"That's some serious hardware," Rick commented, studying the weaponry draped all over her.

"Can't you just deny her access?" Gunnar inquired, watching Seelix step carefully all around the platform.

"That's a restricted platform already. Exactly the reason I put them there in the first place. She'll have security forces all over her shortly. She can't get beyond the gate now without my say so."

"Whoa! That's an Albion courier? Wonder what she's couriering?" Gunnar asked.

Rick and Diord looked at the Kalamarion Colonel at the same time.

"Really? You think she's here on a vaca?" Rick shot sarcastically. Diord drooled out a short chuckle.

"Yeah, didn't think that one through very well," Gunnar admitted a little embarrassed. By now, they had an audience, CJ pressing close to Gunnar on one side and Tiana on the other.

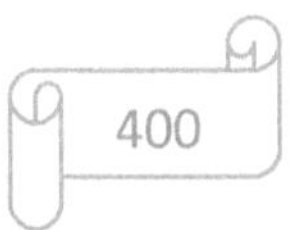

"Seelix," CJ whispered barely audible, then gasped at another figure coming down the gang plank.

"Uht-oh," Talia groaned.

"Blinda Koss," CJ finished, lowering her eyes.

"I take it this isn't just an Albion courier," Gunnar stated, looking at Diord for confirmation.

Diord shook his head, touching a control on the screen, instantly changing the image view to a wider angle. A couple of small observation droids flew in for a closer inspection of the ship and it's two occupants, only to be blasted by two quick shots from one of Seelix's pistols.

"So what's so fearsome about these two?" Dakota asked, not understanding the gravity of the situation.

"Blinda Koss is a Thane," CJ growled.

Rick instantly came to attention, instinctively running a quick scan through his mind and the elements around him. He didn't want to probe too far and alert the Albion Thane to his presence.

"She's a protector," CJ continued. "But has taken her gifts and powers to a whole new level, using them to control minds and kill. She's one tough cookie and we would all do well to steer as far clear of her as we can."

"Not the sort of woman to go around holding a glass of Tarilain milk and a cookie, eh?" Gunnar asked, trying to lighten the mood. It would take a lot more than that.

"It's best we get you guys out of here as soon as possible," Diord indicated pushing through the group for the door. "Any chance you guys could do your little teleporting thing right now?" Diord asked, whisking through the door and toward one of the elevators. "Best thing you could do right now is get back on your ships and jump to the Taree cluster then jump again to a couple of other different places before you head toward Aster, just to make sure you aren't being followed." His communicator went off again, but he ignored it.

"The teleporter can only handle four people at a time," Dakota informed them as they filed toward the elevator. "We need to be in an open area and standing still."

"What about your teleporter, Rick?" Gunnar spoke up, piling into the elevator. Rick didn't even hesitate.

"No, mine isn't functional. Having some trouble with it."

"Nothing to worry too much about," Diord tried to reassure them as they started back down toward the penthouse. "My security won't even let them off the platform."

Starting out of the elevator as the door opened, Rick shuffled next to Gunnar.

"Get your people out of here as soon as you can and I'll cover your back."

"Yeah, like you did the last time?" Dakota jumped in, overhearing his cousin's comment. Rick shot him a quick look, then motioned for the others to move past them.

"I know how to deal with this Thane," Rick asserted.

Gunnar gave his friend a worried look and started to object, but Rick's expression was one of confident determination and something told Gunnar that Rick had a higher purpose to follow and that his friend would be just fine.

"See you on Aster," Rick said, turning in a different direction and trotting off.

"What the heck?" Diord exclaimed, watching Rick disappear around a far corner.

"He can take care of himself," Gunnar reassured the administrator, turning back for the penthouse.

"I can't just have random strangers running around my facility," Diord objected. "I've got security all over the place that will nail him to the wall before he can reach, uhm, well, wherever it is he's trying to get to."

"He got in here without you knowing it, didn't he?" Dakota had paused long enough to hear Diord's complaints about his cousin, but continued on back through the penthouse doors as soon as he let the question go. Diord was still a little unnerved. He had the finest detection and defensive systems, paying the best men to be here backing them up. It just didn't seem plausible for someone to get through such sophisticated security.

Gunnar positioned Tiana, Janox and Talia for transport.

"Don't worry, Janox, you'll love this experience, I promise," he said reading the confused look. "I haven't had a communicator since Reako, so either Alex will have to do the honors or one of you two," he finished directing his attention at Tiana and Dakota.

Tiana already had a communicator out as Dakota was a little preoccupied with getting Willis in just the right position. The only precision required was getting them into the right configuration, they didn't have to be in an exact spot for transport, but Dakota appeared to be overly concerned about making sure he had Willis perfectly positioned. After watching him for several seconds, CJ finally voiced what everybody else was wondering.

"Would you two like a moment alone?"

Dakota froze, moving his eyes around the room, while Willis turned a couple of shades of red.

"You do realize we're all standing here watching you, right?" Gunnar teased. Dakota looked up at an embarrassed, but admiring Willis and finally backed away.

"I...I think you're in position...now," Dakota stuttered, grinning at her and the others.

"*Constellation*," Tiana snickered into her communicator. "Four to bring aboard." Lieutenant Navall acknowledged and a moment later, the air directly around the four women began to snap softly as they dematerialized in a haze of greenish blue color.

CJ turned to Diord and grinned.

"I'll be back for my ship."

"I wouldn't advise it," Diord responded giving her a careful hug. "I'll make arraignments to get it to you when you guys are all settled. Still think you ought to trade her in. Free ninety free."

"Thank you, no. You've done so much already," she muttered holding onto her friend.

Dakota took his position next to Alex 7001 and waited for CJ and Gunnar to get situated for transport. Gunnar stepped forward as CJ let go of her friend and extended his hand to Diord.

"It's good to know she has friends when she needs them."

Diord eyed Gunnar carefully, taking his hand and squeezing it firmly.

"Yes, yes it is," he spoke slowly at first, but then could see the genuine look in the eyes of this unlikely friend from Commenor. Diord had feelings for CJ that he held deep down, derived from a past relationship he may never have fully recovered from. Now he wondered if this Colonel Conrad had some of those same feelings toward Casey Janae. Perhaps the next time they met, he would know.

"You make sure you take better care of her," he insisted, squeezing his hand a little harder to get his point across.

Gunnar smiled confidently, squeezing Diord back just enough more to let him know he could outdo him if challenged. It wasn't mean in nature, just a good show of male confidence. Diord smiled back, sure he had made his point and confident Gunnar would continue to have CJ's back. He finally let go and Gunnar stepped over next to CJ, in position for transport. They both looked back at Diord for a moment, and then Gunnar motioned for Dakota to make contact.

Give that back!

Nearly flying down the stairs toward the mid-level of the Letoh, Rick constantly probed the air around him. He didn't have a set plan, only that he needed to stop, or slow Seelix and her Thane. He ran CJ's words over and over in his head.

"She has taken her gifts and powers to a whole new level, using them to control minds and kill."

Ona had warned him about probing into the mind. It was such a complex and sensitive mechanism. Tampering with it could be deadly or create unintended side effects. Fighting off the effects of such an encounter would take an enormous amount of strength and concentration. Now, he felt both fear for the unknown and confidence in his ability to take on such a foe.

Touching the mid-level floor, he observed people milling about their business. Several folks passed him with wary looks, wondering why he was dressed as he was. Armaments weren't allowed in the Letoh complexes. They had to be checked-in at the security center before you could enter. Nothing appeared amiss here as he scanned the entire floor. This was an observation floor about mid-way up the Letoh tower. All the elevators, with the exception of a private one, came only to this level. From here, guests had to get on a completely different set of elevators to ascend to the upper floors. There were several large open areas inside with long observation patios circling the exterior. Several locations along the outside walls were restaurant eating booths with tables situated next to the large bay windows, allowing guests to enjoy their dining experience high up with open views.

Rick felt the air moving around him as he stepped around toward the elevators on the backside of the stairwell he had just come from. No sooner had he breached the corner than he was dodging a volley of laser blasts, the air around him compressing hard. He quickly reset himself, instinctively fending off the compression and took the offensive, pulling a large swath of air from around the corner and creating a vacuum right where his attackers were located. A rush of wind blasted at the entire floor as he stepped out and confronted Seelix and Blinda, both grabbing at their throats. Blinda had been taken completely off guard, not realizing she was going up against one of her own. Rick reached out and waved a hand, stripping Seelix of some of her weapons. As he did so, he observed the elevator door behind them close. He was sure he recognized something mechanized just inside.

In an instant, he found himself sailing across the floor, rolling into several guest couches and chairs. He quickly popped back to his feet and pulled his blaster, pumping shots at the two. Seelix dropped to one knee with her rifle up, but Blinda started directly for him. She seemed unaffected by his laser blasts. In fact, they appeared to be bouncing right off her, as she continued right at him. Rick felt her trying to compress the air inside him. Still throwing laser shots at Seelix to hold her down, he twitched one of his fingers on the handle of his blaster and the furniture behind him slid around and right at Blinda. Recognizing a perceived rookie move, Blinda merely waved them around her, but was then bowled over by several others she hadn't detected coming in from both sides and the rear. Twisting her wrist as she went down in a crash, she sent a wall of compressed air right at Rick, flinging him across the floor and slamming him into an outer wall. Blinda was thrown back toward Seelix, who dodged the debris flying at them. Somewhat stunned by the encounter, Blinda slowly sat up next to Seelix who was pulling something round from her belt. Activating the lunar grenade, Seelix was preparing to toss it, but Blinda stopped her.

"You'll kill us both if you toss it," she said reaching for her Balkrum gloves.

"Blast pattern is only a couple of meters," Seelix objected.

"Yeah and he'll toss it right back before it even hits the ground. Nothing you have there is going to do any good against him." Blinda carefully got to her feet, pulling her gloves on and watching her opponent lying stunned on the floor against one of the windows.

"Keep your Vivitars out of my way," she continued, throwing off her cloak and pulling her Balkrums from her hip. "I'll be with you at the ship when you're ready to leave."

Seelix got to her feet, replacing the grenade and looking across at the form on the floor.

"Who is he?" She asked crossly, edging toward the elevator.

"A Thane. He's protecting someone, now go," Blinda ordered in a hush. Seelix started pressing the elevator control multiple times, keeping her eyes glued on the Thane on the other side of the room. The door finally hissed open and she nearly fell inside. Getting to her feet as the door hissed closed, Seelix could see Blinda activating her Balkrums, squaring off against the Thane getting to his feet. Blinda took a couple of careful steps closer to the Thane, watching him pull his gloves on.

"You're meddling in affairs that do not concern you," she hissed, stepping closer, probing the air. Her opponent did not speak, but narrowed his eyes at her as he pulled his weapons from his belt. Blinda reached toward his mind with prying mental fingers, digging and clawing at him. To her dismay, she found an impenetrable wall. She couldn't even read his intentions. She fidgeted slightly, wondering, puzzling. "You have chosen the wrong opponent," she growled threateningly. "My mind is a hurricane compared to yours."

Silence continued to expand at her, giving her cause for some distress. The only sound on the floor now was her crackling Balkrums. All of the guests had thought better than to hang around when the ruckus began.

"A hurricane is a confused mass of wind and rain that has no set course known to itself, but others can plot its path," the Thane finally spoke in a clear confident voice.

Blinda scowled, frustrated, unable to breach into his mind. This Thane was inferior to her. She was the best in Hadrian. There were no others on her par.

"Why are you here?" She asked, seeing the activator lights come on around the blades of his Balkrums.

"Come, come, Blinda," Rick countered, readjusting his grip. "Let's not play games, protection is what we do."

"I will have your name then," she demanded, taking another couple of steps closer, raising her weapons into position.

"Get used to disappointment," Rick countered, squeezing his grips and lunging at her. Blinda instantly parried and returned the jabs, only to have her rings met with his, their power sources laboring to overload the circuits of the other. Rick forced his circular blades down along Blinda's until both combatants pushed away and spun, the maneuver nearly throwing her off balance. She quickly backed up and checked herself. She was sporting several tiny cuts to her forearms and thighs, the fabric of her skin tight pants neatly sliced diagonally. A little irritated, she charged again, battling furiously back, her particle blades clashing angrily against his. She continued to probe into his mind, scratching at anything she could find to get in.

"You are superb," she complimented him as they continued to exchange jabs. "So few of us Thanes left and those chosen to walk the path of protector are not as well-disciplined as you and I."

"Indeed," Rick responded quietly, his eyes steely and focused. "They're only weapons Blinda. The true measure of a person is what comes from within."

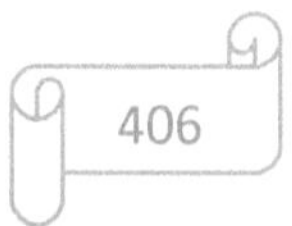

"Spoken like a true philosopher. Where have you come from?" She backed up to rest, panting. Rick continued forward giving her cause to retreat. He threw a diagonal swipe at her, just missing her face, the crackling radium particles searing her skin as the Balkrum blade passed close.

"Is it important?" Rick responded, pulling back to let her rest. He checked himself, noticing several nicks on his gloves and then his shirt and pants.

"You're protecting CJ Barker," Blinda growled frustrated, touching the scorched skin below one eye. "Did she make the request or were you assigned by someone else? Tell me, if you're down here fighting me and my friend is upstairs fetching her, who are you really protecting?"

Rick hesitated, looking up from his wounds. If Seelix came for CJ, then she would have to contend with Gunnar as well. Rick could hold Blinda here indefinitely if need be, but he couldn't be in two places at once. Now something awful clawed into his mind, invading him. His ability to protect his friend was a complete sham with no hope for success. What was he even doing here? He wasn't protecting his friend. He had just acquired the title of Thane and everything that came with it. It took years to master such a discipline such as molecular control. Blinda was obviously a Master Thane and knew things he could only speculate at. He was in the wrong place! Rick glanced around for an exit. He had to get to an elevator and head back up to the penthouse before Seelix got there.

She could see into him now and toying within his mind, she nudged a low roll of torture waves into him, just to see the result. Grinning sinisterly, Blinda pushed more negative thoughts through the breach in his concentration along with a roll of ILOB waves. Snickering quietly, she watched him wincing with the prick of pain.

Disoriented and uncertain of himself now, Rick shuffled backwards, looking for a way out, but Blinda had him up against one of the glass windows. She edged closer to the uncertain Thane with a renewed confidence. Shifting slightly from side to side, Blinda sized him up like a spider to its prey. She would enjoy this. She wanted him or perhaps worse, his now fragile soul.

*   *   *   *

Dakota raised his communicator to his mouth, but never got the words out. The doors to the penthouse unexpectedly exploded in a bellow of fire and a shower of debris, the

concussion throwing everyone back. Even Alex 7001 was
knocked back, slamming into the cooking area wall. His circuits
scrambling, his front panel lights flashed erratically as he
dropped to the floor.

Gunnar opened his eyes and blinked several times, looking
left. Someone lay a couple of feet away. Still feeling somewhat
stunned, he realized he was lying on top of CJ, having shielded
her from the blast and associated debris. They were both
covered with what was left of the front doors, plus parts of the
front walls and some furniture. His ears ringing and head
throbbing, he checked CJ to make sure she was ok. She started
to stir, but a quick finger to his lips kept her quiet. Hearing
movement at the wrecked doors, Gunnar looked to his left again.
It was Diord lying motionless next to them. He turned his head
carefully to the right, but could see only a pile of rubble. Sounds
of machines were moving around in the room somewhere in the
direction of the blast. Perhaps there had been a utility explosion
or something and these were the rescue droids.

Gunnar heard a muffled groan and turned his head back to
his right, looking beyond the pile of debris. As the pile moved,
Dakota's face appeared, covered in pulverized wall dust. Gunnar
moved to quiet him, but felt wall parts suddenly lift away,
exposing him to their rescuers. He turned back, looking up at a
boxlike droid covered in guns, its mechanical arms reaching for
his legs. Its single crescent shaped eye glowed in its dome
shaped head. These didn't look like rescue droids to him.
Quickly rolling over, he carefully pushed CJ back toward the
kitchen bar, away from the softly humming machine. The droid
did not move, but continued to extend its arms, reaching for
him. Gunnar noticed a pair of human legs stepping through the
blown out doors of the penthouse and gave an anxious look
around the mechanical box on tank tracks.

Whoever it was sported a set of pistols, poised and ready to
fire. Dakota moved to get up, but a second droid turned in his
direction, extending its arms and taking ahold of him. Seelix
stepped past Diord's motionless form, aiming one of her pistols
right at Gunnar.

"You must be our super hero," she smiled. Without another
word, she pulled the trigger; letting several darts go in rapid
succession into Gunnar's legs, thigh, and abdomen. He and CJ
continued to scoot back against the kitchen bar.

"There, that's much better. Just give that a second or two to
circulate and you'll be right as rain for a little trip we need to
take. CJ, you're next."

Seelix pointed the other pistol around Gunnar to shoot, but
before she could fire, Gunnar stretched his leg out and kicked

the pistol from her hand. The force of the strike knocked the gun apart, sending its pieces sailing across the room. Exasperated, Seelix watched the gun pieces fall to the floor, spilling its contents.

"Futs! Now what did you have to go and do that for? That was one of my favorite guns. It's easy on the wrist, no recoil, no muzzle flash and almost no sound. If only all my weapons could have those features. But what's a good blaster if it doesn't make noise and give you a sore shoulder after you've fired it?"

Seelix held the first pistol back to make sure Gunnar didn't get the best of her again. She had made a bargain they'd be in good condition and she meant to deliver. Gunnar held a defiant look, still keeping himself between Seelix and CJ.

"Oh, I'm sorry, we haven't been properly introduced. Seelix Monroe, your host for your ride to Albia. CJ I know, and you are?"

Gunnar pressed back against CJ, feeling strange. He pulled one of the darts from his thigh. The tiny vial attached to the dart apparatus was empty, as were the other darts still in his legs. He felt no compulsion to withhold any information and looking around, surmised the hopelessness of their situation. Rick must have failed.

"Gunnar," he answered trying to remain defiant. Relaxation flooding him, he felt soft and warm, as though Audra had wrapped her arms around him. Defiance slipping from his mind, his thoughts took him to another place, when things were simpler and there wasn't the constant stress of finding safety.

"Ah, yes, that's much better." Seelix smiled delighted. "I like the name. Something I can pronounce." She watched CJ wrap her arms around Gunnar to hold him up as the injected cocktail took command. "Oh don't worry my dear. He'll be fine. It's just something to relax him while we travel." Seelix squatted down in front of the two. "It really is good to see you, Casey. I just wished it wasn't like this. But you have a couple of people who are very concerned about you and I promised I'd help you get back to them so they can see that you are properly cared for. How are you feeling, unhurt?"

"I'm ok, Seelix. My ears are still ringing and my shoulder and side are sore. You know, you could have just knocked."

"Would you have let me in?"

"Probably not."

"And as Diord would probably have been the one who answered the door in the first place, he would have given me an even colder welcome. I'm sure he's going to be quite pissed off when he wakes up. I know how proud he is of his security. Nah, I think my entrance was the most appropriate for the occasion."

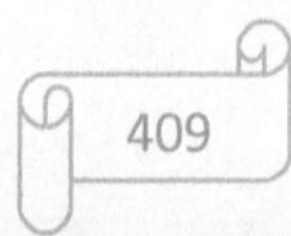

"So are you going to pump me full of what you gave Gunnar?" CJ looked at the pistol still in Seelix's hand.

Seelix gave the gun a glance, then reached out and checked Gunnar's pulse. He lay motionless, lethargic.

"No," she answered, looking over at the pistol parts against the wall. "What I gave him would kill you. Should kill him, but I understand he's not human, so we've improvised a little." Seelix paused, trying to figure out Gunnar's pulse returns. "I don't have any of my med gear with me, traveling light you know, but should I be worried here? His heart is doing some really funky things." Rather than firing two separate darts into him, she had combined the two drugs Drax had given her.

"Leave him alone!" an angry voice called from the far side of a pile of rubble. "He's done nothing to you." Dakota struggled against the Vivitar holding him down. He was sure if he could just get loose and get his hands on a weapon he could turn the tables on their situation. But the Vivitars were well armed and while not designed for manual labor, their mechanical arms were more than enough to hold the normal human immobile. Seelix turned just her head toward the struggling Kalamarion officer.

"You're right, he hasn't. And that's the only reason he's still alive. He and Casey are to be guests of Drax Blair. No more chasing around hiding. Nothing personal, just business that doesn't concern you."

Seelix turned back to CJ.

"So, here's how we're going to play this out. Since Mr. Man here busted up my medication delivery system meant for you, I'm going to have you guys stay right here with a couple of my really cool Vivitars while I take your boyfriend here down to my ship. Once I have him all tucked away nice and comfy, I'll come back for you."

"What about me?" Dakota piped up, still struggling.

"You're kind of hung up on yourself aren't you? You've got nothing to do with this. I have no use or quarrel with you personally, so I'll just let you go after I'm away."

"Why not just take us both at the same time?" CJ asked.

"Some complications down on the Mid-level. And no offense, Casey, but you've already proven to be a hand full all on your own."

"Not offended at all," CJ smiled. "In fact, I'd call that a compliment. Is Drax waiting in your ship?" Seelix motioned for one of the Vivitars to come forward and help Gunnar to his feet.

"Come, Casey, you know better than that. Drax get her hands dirty? She's waiting for us just a little way from here."

"I would have thought it was obvious I wasn't interested in seeing her or her way of life anymore."

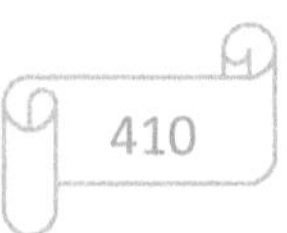

"Well, you'll have to explain that to her face. I'm only here to deliver you two." Seelix stood up and took a step back toward where Diord lay. "Oh dear," she commented, bending down and checking him. "I hope he's all right and this doesn't affect our business relationship."

Dakota continued to struggle against the droid holding him down, drawing Seelix to him.

"Please stop. I haven't had to kill anyone on this trip so far." She stopped and thought a moment. "Wow, I really haven't. Blinda wiped out all the platform and gate security. I'm usually the one doing all the dirty work, so wouldn't it be a shame if you were my only casualty, just because you wouldn't hold still?"

"You have no idea who you're dealing with," Dakota snarled gesturing to Gunnar.

"Oh no, I think it's the other way around," Seelix maintained, motioning for the droid to hold the exec in a nearby chair. "My Vivitars have a lot of neato guns all over them, but if you sit still, they won't hurt you," Seelix instructed.

"Yes, I am well acquainted with these pieces of hucky puck."

Seelix gave the Kalamarion officer a quick look of distain.

"Be nice. You'll hurt their feelings and then I can't be held responsible for what they might do in a fit of anger. I'll be back in just a bit."

With that, she turned and led the way out of the broken penthouse with two of the Vivitars right behind, carrying Gunnar. The other two Vivitars sat motionless, one in front of Dakota, the other at the end of the kitchen counter. CJ carefully got to her feet and stepped over to render aide to Diord. She glanced out into the hall as the elevator doors hissed closed behind Seelix.

Helping him to sit up as Diord finally started coming to, something caught CJ's eye in one of the back hallways of the Letoh penthouse. She gave the hallway a double take, but looking again, saw nothing but darkness. Diord rubbed his eyes, blinking several times trying to clear his vision, his head throbbing from the blast.

"Ok, so that wasn't very much fun at all," he groaned holding his hand to his forehead.

"We're all pretty lucky," she commented checking him over carefully.

"What happened?" he asked looking around, finally looking up at the two Vivitars. "Oh, let me guess, Seelix?"

"Seelix," CJ confirmed, trying to help him up. Pulling his arm over her shoulder, they stumbled over wreckage to the kitchen bar and sat down. Making sure he wasn't going to fall, CJ heard something back in the hallways of the penthouse, but when she looked, she caught only a glimpse of something shadowy, then

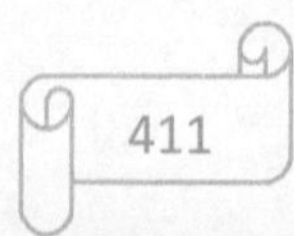

nothing. Turning back around, she bumped into the Vivitar parked in front of the kitchen hallway.

"Where's Gunnar?" Diord asked. He caught sight of Dakota sitting uncomfortably in a chair on the other side of the room, a Vivitar right in front of him.

"Seelix has him," CJ answered letting a cough go. "She's headed down to the platform, then coming back for me." Diord rubbed the back of his neck and carefully wiped the dust from his eyes.

"Remind me to upgrade my security when this is over with." He reached for his communicator, but the Vivitar sitting next to them rose up on its tracks and readied its weapons on him. Diord carefully moved his hand away from his device and the droid instantly relaxed.

"I'm not sure what else you could have done," CJ spoke carefully, watching the droid. She wondered if her friend didn't have a concussion or something.

"Let's review," Diord started, coughing and holding the back of his head to mitigate the painful throbbing. "Your friend gets through approach control, lands on this Letoh and finds his way into this penthouse undetected. Seelix and Blinda get through platform security and then up here with Vivitars. Where is Blinda anyway? Did she go with Seelix?"

"Never saw her. I don't know, maybe Rick got to her first." CJ glanced again at something in the hallway. Her eyes suddenly dilated, seeing the muzzles of several large blaster rifles pointed in her direction. Brilliant bellows of laser fire erupted from the shadows, slamming against the hull of the Vivitar right next to them. The Vivitar instantly rolled back from the countertop and started pumping shots into the darkness.

Diord and CJ dropped to the floor as the droid guarding Dakota spun in their direction, raising up on a heightened torso, its head assembly twisting in the direction of the kitchen hallway. A monstrous hail of gun fire lit up the entire room, including the hallway. Diord pulled CJ out of the way of falling droid parts as the Vivitars took a massive assault on their armor plating. Dakota rolled from the chair and crawled around the corner from the kitchen, followed closely by CJ and Diord. No sooner had they taken cover, than both droids froze, fire and smoke belching from their joints and seams, then everything went quiet.

All three remained motionless, waiting to see if anything else was going to explode. It wasn't until they could hear deliberate footsteps stop near their feet, did they look up. CJ and Dakota had no idea who they were looking at. A tall wiry man with lots of pock marks from years of facial acne. Diord knew Lou Aura well, turning explosive and instantly coming to his feet, completely forgetting about his still ringing ears and throbbing head ache.

"Lou," Diord snarled. "If I had a gun right now, I'd..."

Lou flipped his smoking pistol in his hand and held it out to the Cross administrator. Diord grabbed it, pointing it right in Lou's face, the hot barrel almost touching his forehead. Lou's men instantly responded with rifles up, but Lou motioned them off.

Diord had every right to be angry. A quick scan of their garb revealed bulging camo pockets and packs, full of precious things, no doubt looted from many of the penthouses located in this and the adjoining Letoh. Problem was Lou had just saved their lives. Exasperated, Diord lowered the weapon, but held it ready.

"Gonna give you some options here," he pushed the words out between clinched teeth. "They all involve you dropping everything, and I mean EVERYTHING, and being aboard your ship and airborne in fifteen minutes."

"Fifteen minutes?" Lou objected. "We couldn't possibly reach the loading platform..."

"Fifteen minutes," Diord reaffirmed, letting a shot from the blaster go into the floor in front of them.

Lou instantly motioned for his men to do as directed, dropping their packs and emptying their pockets.

"Leave the weapons too," Diord directed. Lou hesitated.

"Hey, what if we run into more of those droids?"

"You got up here without them seeing you didn't you? I think you can manage getting back down. Now hand them over and git!" Diord waved the pistol in all directions now, ready to let a couple more shots go at random if need be. Hesitating at first, Lou finally motioned for them to drop their weapons where they stood and start moving.

"And, Lou," Diord called after the pirate leader as they turned toward what was left of the front door. Diord melted just a bit, tossing Lou's pistol back to him. "Thanks."

Lou caught the pistol and gave the Cross administrator an uncertain look, then saluted and disappeared down the hall toward a stairway.

"I hate that guy." Diord turned back to CJ and Dakota as Alex 7001 reappeared from behind the kitchen counter. Sporting a number of dents, scrapes, and scratches, his photoceptor faceplate was now cracked in several places.

"You ok, Alex?" CJ asked the little white droid coming to a halt in front of her.

"Still clearing scrambled circuits, Colonel, but I should be fine in a few more minutes. I'm afraid my recent memory storage has been compromised. The Aster information has been corrupted, my apologies."

"It's ok, Alex, as long as you're ok."

"Where is Colonel Conrad?"

Dakota stepped over and picked up the large rifles Lou's men had surrendered and handed one to CJ, but held onto two of them.

"These aren't as fun as my blaster pistols, but I think I can do a little damage with them anyhow."

CJ checked her rifle's power pack as Diord picked up the other one.

"Fastest way to the platforms from here," she demanded, giving Diord a determined look. He would much rather her take it easy. Maybe let Dakota take the lead here. Let his security forces try and redeem themselves. But he sensed that CJ had just shifted her mindset and wasn't about to be detoured.

"We can take my private elevator all the way to the bottom. It'll save time."

*   *   *   *

Rick frantically dodged another savage attack from Blinda, fighting to keep the pounding ILOB waves from overwhelming him. It was all he could do to keep from getting sliced into confetti by Blinda's Balkrums. He was already favoring several deep cuts from her weapons, feeling blood working its way down his sleeves and one of his pant legs. Somehow, he needed to regain his concentration, but there was no time to do so. Blinda continued to push him back, staying as close as she dared to an open restaurant. His defenses were slow and sluggish, Blinda pressing her attack, knowing she had him on the ropes. A quick swing close up spun him around, slamming him hard against the wall with the aid of compressed air. Laughing, she pressed her weapon against one of his gloved hands, forcing him to drop one of his Balkrums and holding his other hand pinned above his head against the wall.

"You pathetic old geezer," she hissed, delighted with her advantage. "Your feeble skills are no match to mine."

Rick heard one of the elevators hiss open nearby and edged his attention to a figure exiting and stepping toward another set of elevators followed by two rather large boxlike droids. Blinda brought his eyes back to hers with her glowing blade pushed up close to his neck, the radium particles cooking his skin.

"You know, these blades work just as well without the particle generators running," she cackled, relaxing her grip on the Balkrum at his neck. The glow vanished as she gently pressed the razor sharp blade against his skin. "You've presented me with a singular, but complex problem." Blood began to seep from under the blade as she pressed harder.

"And what's that?" Rick gasped, feeling the heat from her other Balkrum burning into the glove of his pinned hand.

"So many ways to kill you, and make you suffer before you beg me to die."

"Let nothing but fear stop you," he breathed feeling the pressure build against his neck. Straining, he let go of his other Balkrum ring, letting it fall onto Blinda's already injured forearm. Reeling back in agony as the weapon bounced to the floor, Blinda grabbed her arm and spun around, furious. Both Rick's weapons instantly appeared directly in front of him and pressing them together, he instantly fused them. Blinda brought both her rings across his single ring, a sheet of sparks flashing as the weapons came into contact. Dropping a hand, Rick twisted his fingers as he swung the ring at Blinda, swiping across her left shoulder and cauterizing the searing gash. She fell at the same instant, slipping on a layer of ice that had formed beneath her feet. Receiving a powerful blast of air at the same time, she was sent sliding a short distance, but jumped back to her feet, her platinum hair streaking different colors. The ice beneath her instantly flashed to water and became airborne. Twisting sideways, Rick held his Balkrum out to his side, parting the blast of water, deflecting the brunt of its impact. Slammed against the wall and soundly doused, he twisted his wrist, changed the water into a grey white mist and waved it up at the ceiling. Bringing his Balkrum back down, Rick flicked his little fingers and several of the large panes of glass behind him instantly vaporized into a swirl of blinding sand that he sent roaring from several different angles toward a startled Blinda. Waving her arms wildly, she tried to fend off the pelting storm, but the angles were too much and she dropped to the floor in a crouch to keep her flesh from being blasted away by the abrasive grit.

Lifting her head, she instantly ducked again, narrowly avoiding Rick's flying Balkrum. Tuffs of her hair dropped around her shoulders as she came back up, flicking her fingers as he came at her. Rick nearly toppled forward as his clothes felt like they had turned rigid. Using his toes to turn sideways, he straightened all his fingers at the Albion Thane as she came at him, her clothes suddenly vanishing. She instantly stopped, her expression changing from shock, to embarrassment as she tried to cover herself. A quick flinch of her eyebrows and her clothes reappeared, a smile developing into a grin. She waved an index finger at him while grinning broadly. Rick caught his flying Balkrum and reactivated it as his clothes changed back to normal. The entire scene instantly went pitch black, the only light sources being the radium particles on their Balkrums. Rick separated his weapons and waved them up in front of him, the blackness instantly filled with blinding white. Both warriors squinted as their pupils constricted.

A lightning swing snarled through Rick's uniform, pain streaking through his entire left side and leaving a long seared slash in his left shoulder. Wheeling backwards and aided by a push of compressed air rushing in from behind Blinda, Rick was sent flying through an entire set of dining furniture, slamming against an outer wall. His head spinning and in pain, Rick rolled over and looked back at the elevators. He blinked several times to clear his vision, catching a glimpse of his friend as a set of doors started to close. *They had Gunnar!* Horrified, his only thoughts now were to get to him, but he would have to go through Blinda to do it. A wall of compressed air blasted at him, clearing all the up ended furniture around him as he got up on unsteady legs.

Favoring his shoulder now, he watched Seelix peer back at them as the doors hissed closed. His mind clouding, he couldn't think straight as Blinda came at him.

"Let me show you what I did to the entire crew of a ship I destroyed a short time ago," Blinda growled, arrogantly fusing her Balkrums. She stopped where she was, dropping a hand to a slim hip and lowering her crackling Balkrum to her side.

Rick's mind was slammed with a blinding wall of searing pain, feeling like ice picks were being driven directly through both temples. He had no choice but to drop his weapons, grabbing at his head trying to mitigate the pain. He turned and coiled over putting a hand to the back of his neck, feeling his skull caught in an invisible vise of hot spikes. A blast of pain fired through his being, torturing his entire nervous system. There could be no thoughts, only pain and blackness abruptly driving everything from his mind. *What a horrible way for his crew to have met their fate.* His mind clouding into blackness, thoughts of what it must have been like for Jayda in her final moments, twisted through his consciousness and disappeared. He had but one last thought, holding to it long enough to act. He reached out with all the strength he could muster, twisting his hand and pulling his fist right back close to him. A rush of super compressed air blasted at him, picking him up and twirling him mid-air, sending him crashing through a window and over the side of the outer Letoh deck. His consciousness drifting, he felt nothing but wind.

Blinda shut off her Balkrum, clipped it back into place and let both hands come to rest on her hips. She stood unmoved, a smirk streaking across her face. *He's finished!* Having never been defeated, she often tortured her opponents into begging to die and while certainly the victor here, the smirk slowly melted, feeling cheated out of the thrill of ultimate torture. Indeed, she hadn't compressed the air that hurled the Thane out the Letoh window and over the side, and if she hadn't, only one person could have. Letting her vision drop to the floor ahead of her, she eyed the Balkrums lying in the debris next to the blown out windows.

Blinda abruptly felt the air around her compressing. But not just compression, the humidity instantly spiked and every hair on her body stood straight up. The room went dark, the light blotted out directly around the entire mid-floor. Thick misting clouds engulfed the Letoh floor, the air swirling though the broken windows. Bolts of plasma energy leapt from the floors and ceiling directly around the opening where the Thane had fallen. Blinda took a couple of uncertain steps back, her eyes wide, looking all around. Her hair began to grow erratically and change color as she fought for control of her concentration. She could feel him everywhere now. Her thoughts in disarray, she pulled her weapons, activating the Balkrum and powering up her blaster. She swirled about in the howling wind trying to feel for the source, finally turning back to the broken windows. In an instant, the Balkrums on the floor in front of her abruptly became airborne, sailing through the open window just as a form flew back through.

Rick and Blinda's eyes met the instant he touched the floor, her eyes changing several colors. Holding her prisoner with his gaze, he thrust a hand directly at her, sending a rapid series of plasma balls sailing at her. As there was no time for a defense, she was thrown across the floor and sent crashing through an outer window on the other side. Rick held the weather disturbance he had created in motion for a few moments, watching Blinda disappear over the edge, then instantly waved it all off. The air quickly returned to normal, light debris settling as he walked carefully across the floor toward the other side. At the center of the room, he stopped and picked up Blinda's Balkrum and blaster. Tossing the blaster, he moved toward the window again and stopped some distance away, closed his eyes and waited. Several seconds passed, then without warning he pitched Blinda's ring right at the open window and ignited both his. No sooner had the ring exited, than it was caught and activated, Blinda landing directly in front of Rick with her weapon swinging. He could sense she was spitting mad now, but her concentration had been broken and he felt no ILOB waves coming at him, only a disoriented attempt at compressing air in various locations. Stepping back, he allowed her to rest and recoup, noticing her hair and eye color returning to normal. There was a gaping hole in the abdomen area of her black, body-hugging suit, right below her chest. Her stomach area and lower ribs were severely lacerated, blood running from open wounds.

"So you're protecting the superman," Blinda puffed in agony.

"Gunnar and CJ," Rick corrected confidently. He was in full control again. He couldn't help his friends if he let himself get distracted from seeing only his battle and not the entire war. This encounter was only a piece of what was happening around them. He perceived Blinda incapable of seeing it, thinking only of herself and her abilities. During his fall, he was able to see far more of what was happening around him. Ona had warned him that any fight for good would require sacrifices, a testament of what had happened to his crew and what was yet to come.

"Ah, his name is Gunnar." Blinda gasped painfully for breath. "I like it; maybe he will be my new slave. Imagine blending my DNA with his." Blinda felt somewhat sickly now, but kept her focus on trying to pry back into Rick's mind, hoping to regain her advantage. She unfused her Balkrums and reaffirmed her grip on them.

"Not going to happen and you're about to have a failure on your hands," Rick said.

Blinda's expression instantly changed to confusion. *What was he talking about? Failure? With what? She had only to distract this Thane while Seelix did her job retrieving CJ and Gunnar from the Letoh penthouse. She was doing that now. Was there something she had missed?*

Reading the confusion on her face, Rick's smile turned acid and moving toward her, he compressed the air sharply in front of him. Pushing her back toward the broken window behind her, he swung his Balkrums at her, igniting them at the same time. Hers instantly came up to parry his maneuver. Both sets of weapons hissed and crackled, trying to overload the circuits of the other. Becoming frustrated with her failure to dispatch Rick, Blinda shoved him back and held her Balkrums out, suddenly slapping them together with them pointed right at Rick. A brilliant shaft of blue flame instantly lanced at him. Caught off guard, he felt the heat singeing his exposed hair and searing the skin on his arm. Turning his back to the flame, he ducked down, slamming his Balkrums between his legs. They abruptly bounced back through the blue flames, ricocheting off the ceiling and slamming down on Blinda's weapons, knocking them from her hands. Feeling the heat from his burning jacket, Rick threw it off and caught his Balkrums as they bounced back to him. He flung them at her again, just missing her as she rolled away and came up on one knee, tossing out a quick volley of tiny plasma balls.

Rick instantly fired off matching shots, the balls meeting between them and disintegrating into each other.

While Rick was fatigued, he felt like he could eventually do away with her, but something held him back. Certainly, he would be justified in dispatching her. He perceived that she had been the composer of his crew's demise. Perhaps there was a lesson to be learned here, for both himself and the Albion Thane.

A mess now, Blinda was exhausted. Having regained much of her composure, she surmised a stale-mate. It was all she could do to keep Rick from getting past her defenses. She tried any technique she could think of to get at Rick, even bringing water from the walls and forcing electricity from power sockets, but nothing seemed to faze the older Thane. She had tried several times to duplicate what Rick had accomplished with the severe weather system he had churned up.

Sensing she had completed her objective, she maneuvered near an open door to a patio and passing a final swipe at the Thane, turned and jumped, compressing the air as she fell. Rick carefully stepped to the patio rail and watched her sail off on a cushion of air. He raised his weapon to throw after her, but stopped. *Would a proper Thane act in this manner?* No, he understood he had a much bigger role to play in all this, so he turned and headed for one of the elevators.

*   *   *   *

Seelix carefully scanned the long hallway leading to the landing platform where the Metro-star sat waiting. It was only a short walk from the Letoh concourse, with only dead security guards and wrecked drones littering the floor ahead of her. She glanced back at Gunnar's near lifeless form, still securely held in the mechanical arms of the Vivitar guard droids. Smiling confidently, she felt like everything was going as planned. Ok, so the Thane on the Mid-floor was unplanned, but Blinda had that problem well in hand, making it a leisurely stroll for Seelix to just walk in and take Gunnar and CJ. A quick dash aboard the Metro-star to secure Gunnar and she'd be back up to the Letoh penthouse to fetch CJ. She could have just ordered the droids to bring her down, but with the other Thane in the building and CJ being so troublesome, she wanted to leave nothing to chance.

Turning to one of the large doors that opened onto the landing platform, she activated it and waited for her two Vivitars to exit. Feeling like she had all the time in the world, she turned back to secure the doors. A gleam caught her eye and doing a double take, she noticed an open platform security craft hovering behind the Metro-star. Brilliant bellows of fire erupted in front of her droids. Instantly dropping Gunnar, the droids rotated their guns at the approaching craft. Seelix brought her weapons up in each arm, seeing CJ and Dakota training their high powered blaster rifles on her Vivitars. Piloting the small transport and popping off random shots in Seelix's direction, Diord kept it in constant motion to avoid the fire coming from the box-like machines. Seelix frantically returned gunfire as the hovering craft settled between the Metro-star and the droids.

Dakota held the firing control down on his rifle, concentrating on the armed appendages of one of the Vivitars. Several shots exploded against the heavily armored plating on one of the droids, its weaponry winging back toward a scurrying Seelix.

Dodging incoming rounds, Seelix continued to pump a volley of shots at the craft. Ducking behind the platform blast wall, she checked her power packs and shoved a new one in both rifles. Before she reappeared to shoot, she pulled a box from her belt and raised it to her lips, watching as parts started dropping from one of her droids taking heavy fire.

"Beta squad, activate. Assist Alpha squad outside." Moments later four more MD 700s came rolling down the Metro-star's boarding ramp.

CJ pulled something from behind her and jumped from the little shuttle craft. Rolling next to one of the engine pods of the Metro-star, she slapped a black metallic box against the surface and touched several controls on it. Hearing the MD machines rolling down the gangplank, she swung her weapon around and began popping shots off in rapid succession, concentrating on the tracks of the MDs. The first droid abruptly veered off the side and upended, its broken track spinning wildly back into the unit right behind it. Trying to avoid the possible tangle, the second droid's logic circuits commanded it in the other direction. As it was already traveling at an accelerated speed, it tipped hard on one track, bouncing off the other side of the gangplank and careening over the edge of the platform. The third Vivitar plowed through the debris on the boarding ramp and turned right at the tiny transport, firing.

As the fire fight intensified, Dakota dove for Gunnar's motionless form. Not until the small security craft started taking heavy damage did Diord spin, turning the craft's blaster plating broadside where it could better handle the fire coming from the two droids. Even here, it wouldn't last long. He ducked down as low as he could to keep from getting hit from either side and still provide some kind of protection as Dakota started pulling Gunnar toward them. Diord gently moved his craft closer while CJ popped up and squeezed out a volley of shots in both directions, keeping the mechanized weapons from advancing on them any further.

Checking how close he was to Dakota's position, Diord caught sight of Seelix coming out from behind the blast shield. Both her rifles were up and blazing as she ran toward the single Vivitar left on her side. The droid in front of her was quickly becoming disabled, as most of its weaponry had been destroyed in the fire fight. In the furious struggle and hail of gun fire, no one noticed a figure clad in black, settle to the edge of the platform. No one paid any heed to the wind starting to rise around them. It wasn't until the tiny transport was sliding sideways toward the platform edge did CJ catch sight of Blinda Koss, standing with arms swirling at them. Dakota and CJ frantically grabbed for something to hang on to as they slid. As Dakota was blown over the side, he grabbed for several utility cables attached to the outer edge and fell out of sight. CJ suddenly found herself airborne, spinning until she came to an abrupt halt in mid-air, dropping her weapon. Blinda had her arms raised toward CJ, holding her immobile. As the air swirled around her, Blinda stepped carefully forward, turning CJ around and lowering her back to the platform.

"I never fail a mission," Blinda growled with eyes blazing.

"I have no interest in anything Drax has to say to me," CJ gasped, fighting her invisible bonds.

"Nonetheless, we came for you. Now be a good girl and come quietly."

"You know me better than that."

CJ struggled helplessly as Blinda stood directly in front of her. The Thane grabbed CJ by the hair, but suddenly jerked to one side, releasing CJ and falling to the ground. CJ turned to see the muzzle of Dakota's rifle protruding from over the side of the platform, his eyes were barely visible. Dakota fired another round at Seelix who ducked behind a burning Vivitar. Blinda frantically pulled herself along the platform toward the Metro star as Seelix returned fire. CJ dove over the side of the platform, grabbing the same utility cables Dakota was holding onto.

The fire fight was suddenly over and Seelix ran to a still motionless Gunnar. Moving past the two disabled Vivitars, she gestured for the last two to come and carry him up into the ship, stopping to help a bedraggled Blinda to her feet. The Thane looked back at the edge of the platform, holding her wounded abdomen and bleeding shoulder. Somehow, CJ had slipped from their hands again. Surely there would be hell to pay when they got back to the *Tarzana*. Seelix warily backed herself up into the ship, holding her guns to bear until the boarding ramp had closed. It took only a couple of moments to power up the Metro-star and in an instant they had lifted away.

Diord fought for control of the badly damaged transport, somehow holding it beneath Dakota and CJ long enough for them to drop onto it. Trying to keep the transport airborne wasn't going to last, so he set it down on the platform, its power units failing. CJ turned an anxious look skyward as the Metro-star powered away. She turned to Diord with a hopeful cast, but he wasn't too reassuring.

"I've got nothing in the immediate vicinity that can stop them and nothing in orbit either. I have sentries up there, but that ship will be able to make its jump before they can intercept."

CJ's expression changed to dismay looking around at the other platforms, finally recognizing the form of her F-2 some distance away. She reached into her pocket and handed Dakota Aster's coordinates chip as Alex 7001 floated out onto the platform from the doorway.

"Get this to Talia and you guys get the fleet out of here. I'll catch up after I have Gunnar back."

"There is no chance I'm going to let you go after him alone," Dakota objected.

"That's an order, Captain."

"You're not my commanding officer."

"Listen to me, you have to get the fleet out of here before the Colonian and Albion fleets have them boxed in. Talia and Willis have to know where to go and this is their only road map. You have to get it to them, download it to all ships and go as fast as you can. I'll catch up." CJ had softened her tone a little holding both her hands over the device chip in the Captain's hand. "You're their only hope. You can teleport out. I'll bring Gunnar back, now go!" she urged with a little more conviction.

Dakota glanced at Diord who was a little taken aback realizing what CJ might have in mind. But he knew better than to try and stop her, not with that look on her face. Dakota finally pulled his communicator, raising it as Alex positioned himself next to the Starbird executive officer.

"Dakota to *Constellation*, two to teleport out now." He kept his eyes on CJ as she stepped back watching them dematerialize. Once they were gone, she turned to Diord and stepped back onto the smoking shuttle.

"You think this thing can make it to two three six?"

"Does it matter?" Diord responded, working the controls of the fitting craft.

"No," CJ said. She looked skyward again, still able to see the Metro-star gaining altitude, receding to a pinpoint. Diord raised his communicator and started talking into it as they staggered intrepidly over the edge and toward platform two three six, some distance away. Thankfully, her platform was at a lower level. The way the little shuttle was operating, it would never have been able to gain any height, let alone level flight. As they neared CJ's fighter, she could hear its engines already turning up and saw the pilot's hatch open. She passed Diord a quick glance as the fitting transport bounced onto the landing platform and the ailing power units died.

"The new AI system I had installed," Diord called over the noise of the Isom converters powering up. "It'll keep you company." He smiled after her as she jumped from the transport and headed toward the cockpit of the big fighter, but stopped and turned back to her friend. Mixing her expressions of deep appreciation with stone focus on what she was about to do, she put her arms around the tall Cross administrator.

"Thank you so much," she spoke in his ear so he could hear her over the noise. They let the embrace melt them a bit; enjoying something they had once known of the other.

"You know I can never refuse you anything," he spoke back to her. CJ gently pressed her lips to his cheek, then pulled away, back toward her ship.

She climbed in the side door and closed the hatch behind her. Diord stepped over behind the platform blast shield, watching the F-2 rising, its landing gear folding up into their compartments and the delta wing swinging down into position. He watched CJ at the controls as she let the ship pivot, then a howl of its engines and the fighter shrank to a pinprick in the sky as it ascended nearly vertical.

Watching her go, he wondered if he would ever see her again. He remembered telling Gunnar that he needed to take better care of Casey. Now it was the other way around. It was obvious that they had developed feelings for each other, but neither had acknowledged it. In any case, those feelings would either bring them together, or they would end up dead trying to save each other.

Victory

CJ sat focused on her instruments as she powered away from Cross. Her shoulder ached uncomfortably, but not enough to hinder her ability to pilot. She had every intension of forcing the Metro-star back to Cross or disabling it and calling Diord's people in to haul it back. She had gotten a good look at Blinda Koss before the Thane had boarded the Metro-star. Looking beaten and exhausted, Blinda had probably only just managed to brush them from the platform. If confronted, she would be too weak to offer any resistance. It was a wonder she hadn't required help getting onboard. Seelix, on the other hand, could pose a significant threat and she was just the kind of woman who, when cornered, would just as soon blow herself up rather than be taken alive. That being the case, another contingency would have to be considered. Something even more dangerous than disabling the Metro-star. Something that no one, not even Drax would expect.

Edging her throttles a little more and feeling this ol' girl running better than she had in a long time, CJ activated her targeting controls, letting her hands sweep across the tracking screen controls. She steered her craft after the Metro-star just now becoming visible on her displays. Reaching for the Quadra-light controls, CJ was startled by a pleasing, almost sultry female voice.

"Quadra-Light drive activated. Please input your destination, Colonel Barker."

CJ let a chuckle go, not for the new technology at her fingertips, but the choice of voice for the AI.

"Leave it to Diord to put a female voice in this thing."

"Would you prefer a different voice protocol, Colonel?"

"Why, do you have more?"

"I'm programmed with five different voice protocols, with memory space available for ten thousand."

"Not sure where I'd find that many protocols. Oh, and let me guess, Diord put his in as one of the default protocols."

"Administrator Vandmire's voice replication is contained in my file structure. Would you like me to make the change?"

"I knew it," CJ continued to chuckle. "He just couldn't resist. The man is so full of himself," she finished under her breath. CJ dropped a glance at the scanner.

"No change, do you have a name?"

"Those parameters have not been defined yet, Colonel."

An idea suddenly popped into her head that brought a big grin to her face.

"I think, Bud sounds just right."

"You may refer to me as Bud," the AI responded.

"Gunnar is gonna love this," she grinned. "Run a scan of the area within a parsec from our current location and display all the current Albion and Ratronian traffic."

Almost instantly, the tracking screen changed, impressing CJ to no end. She was used to having to wait a while for that to happen and she would have to make all the control changes herself. She could get used to having Bud in the cockpit.

"Only one target fits current parameters. Directly ahead."

CJ studied the screen to her left, glancing out at the star field a couple of times. There was nothing out here but the Metro-star somewhere ahead of her.

"Lock tracking data to the Quadra-light controls and stand-by."

"Quadra-light tracking telemetry locked to tracking controls. Albion craft within firing range parameters."

CJ charged her gun pods and started firing. While she was certainly within range, she was still far enough away that any hit would be a lucky one and probably not do much damage to the Metro-Star's rear deflector shields. She looked back at the tracking screen again, noting the Albion craft's position.

"Track delta core ninety-three."

"Core ninety-three locked."

CJ continued to fire, noting that she was landing hits as she got closer. A minute or so longer and she would overtake them. They were close enough now that she could clearly make out the outline of the ship in front of her. She passed a look at her rear tracking screens, noticing another target appearing directly behind her, but it was far enough away that it was of little consequence. Continuing to pound the rear deflector shield, she took notice of the Metro-Star's engine pods abruptly brighten and the ship bolted away in a flash of crimson light. Seelix had just jumped to Quadra-light. CJ switched off the targeting system, then settled back in her seat and turned to the Quadra-Light panel. Reaching forward, she flipped up the five red cover caps on the front control panel and pushed the switches to the on position. The readout in front of her began to flash as she waited.

"Whenever you're ready, Bud," she said quietly.

"Stand-by," the AI answered. "Waypoint arrival in 10 seconds."

"I expect this to be a quick trip, so be ready to pop out as soon as your telemetry indicates. By the way, let's make a change to your voice protocols after all, shall we?"

"Yes, Colonel," Bud responded. Several seconds later, a warning light went off on the Quadra-light panel and CJ pushed the Quadra-light throttles all the way forward. The fighter seemed to tilt sharply and bolt into four times the speed of light.

*   *   *   *

Queen Captain Drax Blair watched with profound satisfaction as the Metro-Star set carefully down on its landing pods. Victory had finally come, or part of it anyway. She had not gotten any reports from Seelix as the Albion transport had sent an automated message indicating it had been damaged and unable to converse live. She supposed it was all well and good anyway. Going into Cross and penetrating Alvadore without a scratch would have been a little improbable.

Approaching the Queen Captain, Commander SoKnack could sense an air of triumph and based on the expression dancing across Drax's face when she turned to hear his report, he could rest a little easier. Adjusting his earpiece, he pulled up next to her.

"Tactical scans of the ship as it was landing show its communications arrays are completely destroyed. It's no wonder they couldn't communicate. The automated message was sent through the ELT system. Looks like they took a pretty good pounding before they got away."

"Of course, Diord wasn't going to let them go without a fight." Drax almost giggled. "All that matters is they made it. I want to see Colonel Barker just as soon as she can be brought to the command lounge. That's where I'll be waiting." Finally, it was good to see some results. Turning to leave, Commander SoKnack stopped her with a finger to his ear. His expression turned to puzzlement followed by something akin to worry.

"You need to hear this," he insisted, pulling the earpiece and handing it to her.

Drax gave him an odd look, then examined the earpiece a little, brushing the ear wax off before she stuck it under her blonde hair. She listened for a moment, changing her look, then handed the device back to Dalton.

"Com," she commanded, moving quickly down into the command pits. "Put it on speakers down here," she ordered, stopping in front of the immense console. The technician was quick to respond and a second later the voice of Diord Vandmire boomed out over the sound system.

"Albion approach clearance seven nine five two six. Cross Diplomatic courier requesting permission to board *Tarzana*."

"Incoming F-2 fighter," another controller announced from his station down the row.

"Tactical," Dalton ordered, instantly bolting to the tracking station for a look. Almost before he got the words out, the tactical systems drew out the form of a Colonian F-2 Flightstreak. Motioning for several controls to be activated, he studied the readouts of the incoming fighter.

"No active weaponry and its transponders are broadcasting the correct ambassador codes."

Drax gestured for the controller in front of her to open a channel, and then motioned for Dalton to pass her his earpiece again.

"QC Drax here, Diord. What do you think you're doing?" There was silence for a moment, giving Drax cause to wonder if she was even being heard.

"I'd like to have a private chat with you, Drax. Seems I've had a visit from a couple of your people that didn't end well and I'd like to try to sort this all out."

Drax narrowed her eyes, passing a glance at Dalton and motioning for him to get her an update on Seelix and Blinda. Commander SoKnack was quick to move to the security station for the requested information, but there was nothing available. Drax turned back to her conversation with the Cross administrator. His fighter didn't have its guns charged for battle and the ambassador courier codes all checked out, she saw no problem with granting his request. Sometimes, the best place to hide something was right out in the open anyway and she was under no obligation to tell him anything.

"Sure, Diord," Drax agreed carefully. "I'd be glad to host you for a bit. You won't mind if I keep my ship moving. I'm sort of on a schedule here. Let's put you in the lower landing bay. Do you require landing assist?"

"You can do that now?"

"You ought to know, you sold it to us."

"Well then, let's see how well it works. Bring me in and I'll follow your instructions from there."

Drax tossed Dalton his earpiece and started for the elevator, the *Tarzana* commander stepping lively to catch up.

"Where would you like to host the administrator, QC?" He stopped short of the elevator doors as Drax stepped in and turned to face him.

"Land him in the cargo bays and let him sit for a bit."

"The cargo bays? There's no security in the cargo bay. Why not the VIP landing bay?"

"Can't have him looking right at what he came to get back, can we? Hold him in the cargo bay and I'll call you when I'm ready to receive him."

Dalton let out a worried sigh as the doors closed, then turned back to carry out his instructions.

Reaching the top of the elevator emptying directly into the command lounge, Drax strode in excited to see Seelix nestled on one of the couches. It wasn't until she fully entered the room and caught sight of Blinda that the smile melted.

"What happened to you?" she asked, looking at the battle weary Thane.

Blinda was a mess. A dark stain dropped down her left shoulder from a big hole in her suit. Blood appeared to be still flowing from the wound. Tangled and singed in places, her hair was matted with dried blood; she would eventually have a black eye. She had dried blood on the right side of her face and blood spatter from her shoulder wound on the left side. Her hands were riddled with cuts and abrasions. Her clothes were torn, especially directly below her bust-line, bare skin clearly visible. Several shades of red and dark purple painted the entire surface of her abdomen. An injury like this would certainly involve something broken.

"She had one crazy fight with a Thane protecting CJ and Gunnar," Seelix spoke up on behalf of the battle weary Thane.

"Gunnar? Who's this Gunnar? He had a Thane?"

"Gunnar is the name of your superman," Seelix continued. Blinda was perfectly content to let her have all the conversation. She should be in the infirmary where they had left Gunnar under heavy guard.

"Oh, we're on a first name basis with him are we?" Drax asked sternly, sitting down in one of the chairs across from Blinda. Seelix only formed a smirk and shrugged a little. Drax curved her gaze back to Blinda, who appeared only half conscious.

"Where's CJ?" she asked, realizing she wasn't present. "Is she with...Gunnar?"

"No," Seelix responded, suddenly a little uncomfortable. "We lost her at the platform."

Drax instantly rolled up to a boil, but before she could explode, Seelix tried to calm her.

"With Blinda dealing with the Thane, I had my hands full with your superman. Diord somehow managed to get her loose after I had her secured and they tried to intercept us at the platform.

Blinda had CJ at the platform, but was hit and she escaped. This is one hunt I'm glad Blinda was along for the ride. Lost nearly all my MDs."

"Seems like you've got your mouth open a lot more than Blinda does," Drax growled menacingly at Seelix. "Where is CJ? I want CJ Barker!" Drax was incensed. How was it no one could carry out a simple operation? Yes, they had interference from the Thane. It was clear that Blinda had nearly gotten herself killed, but Gunnar was the secondary target. CJ was the prize! "BachTL was right," Drax grumbled, trying to come back down. "If you want something done right, you have to do it yourself. One can only hope she'll do something insane and come after him, but I doubt it. She's not that stupid." Drax crossed her legs and leaned forward a bit, burrowing her eyes into Blinda for a response. "What happened?"

"He was waiting for us before we ever reached the penthouse." Blinda spoke slowly and with careful effort, her abdomen clearly causing her significant pain. "Seelix barely got past, even with me running interference."

"Where did *he* come from?"

"He wouldn't say, but he knew how to control himself and the elements. I did not feel any ILOBs from him, but I feel certain that if he had wanted to, he could have produced them."

"Do you think he'll be a problem?"

"I don't know." Blinda was too blasted to think clearly and just wanted to get to the infirmary and then get some rest. In her sleep, she could find solitude in her dreams, helping her body repair itself.

"How many Thanes are there anyway?" Seelix asked, trying to understand the whole protector dynamic.

"I am not aware of a set number."

"What about you?" Seelix asked. "How were you chosen?"

"Must we go into this right now?" Blinda complained.

"Very well," Drax agreed still in an angry mood. "Let's all go down and meet with this Gunnar. Perhaps we can still salvage something here."

The Queen Captain got to her feet and started for the door while Seelix lagged behind to make sure Blinda could get up. The Thane seemed determined to rise and go for medical attention all on her own. As the group began their descent in the elevator, Blinda became aware of something external, something probing, something feeling its way throughout the whole of the ship. As they continued down, she again grew unsteady on her feet and wobbled. Seelix tried to help steady her, putting her hand to her shoulder. Feeling something warm and wet, Seelix examined her hand; it was covered in blood.

"You took more of a beating than I thought," Seelix commented, pulling the Thane's arm over her shoulder. The lights in the elevator unexpectedly flickered and went out as the elevator ground to a halt.

Drax examined the control panel, but it was void of any life. Pulling her communicator from her belt, she turned back to the other two as the emergency lights came up. Before she could make an inquiry, Commander SoKnack was already calling her.

"Pardon the interruption, QC," the ship's commander hedged. "We've got some real problems happening here."

"Report, Commander." Drax observed an odd expression develop on Blinda's face as she looked all around the interior of the elevator, as if trying to see something that wasn't there.

"Bridge is almost completely offline, but our main engines are still operating. We have no directional control right now. We've lost main power all over the ship. I have engineering working on the problem, but the cause is unknown. Right before we lost control, sensors picked up a small scout class vessel coming out of light speed right on the edge of our range, heading directly at us."

"You can't get any readouts on it?"

"Not while the bridge is offline, QC. I've launched Tiger squad six to investigate."

"Were you able to get any kind of a directional fix on where it came from?"

"Wasn't possible as it just appeared, probably dropped out of light speed somewhere beyond our sensor range. I hope to have more detail for you as soon as we can get back online in a couple of minutes."

"Stay on it, Commander. We're stuck in the conning elevator. Get someone over here on the double."

"I'll have maintenance to your location immediately."

Drax continued to eye Blinda carefully. The Thane was acting nearly schizophrenic, jerking glances all around the interior of the elevator. Seelix noticed her behavior and tried to calm the Thane, thinking she had become claustrophobic.

"We'll get you out of this, Blinda. The maintenance guys will be here in a moment," Seelix said trying to calm her.

"No," Drax asserted, holding the Thane's head up, looking directly into her eyes. "It's not that, is it?" The look in Blinda's eyes was that of astonishment mixed with fear.

"It's him," she gasped unbelieving. "He's here."

"Who's here?" Seelix puzzled. "Gunnar? He's locked up in the infirmary."

"No, not Gunnar," Blinda whispered, staring at one spot somewhere in the upper darkness of the elevator. "His Thane."

Drax gave Blinda a hard look, slowly raising her communicator back to her mouth. She too, could feel something odd. Perhaps it was just the absence of fresh air flowing into the elevator compartment or the low emergency lighting. Whatever it was, it had to be an external influence and the only thing external was the scout ship coming right at them.

"Commander SoKnack," Drax said. "Instruct BT six to destroy that scout ship as soon as they can engage it, and send out squad five and seven to run swarm patrols around this ship." There was no objection from Commander SoKnack, just an instant acknowledgment and the communication was ended.

Drax turned back to Blinda and shook her slightly, getting her attention.

"Blinda, concentrate. You need to focus." Blinda slowly looked to her commander, still dazed. Drax could see her coming back to full awareness, nodding tiredly. "Can you get us out of here?"

"Yes, I think I can do something," she answered, closing her eyes and concentrating. A moment later she raised her hand, gently twisting it and slowly closing her fist part way. The other two could feel the elevator moving again and then stop, the door slowly coming open.

Drax immediately moved out into the dark hallway, trying to figure out exactly where she was. Emergency lights were working all over the ship, but the lighting was dim and disorienting. Finally relying on signage for directions instead of her knowledge of the ship, they made their way further down several dark sub-halls and stair wells toward the infirmary. The closer they got, the more lights there were, as the medical section of the ship was outfitted with better emergency lighting. Drax came to a halt at a desk just inside the medical complex.

"A prisoner was brought in from the landing bays a short time ago. Where's he being held?" Drax inquired of a tech at the desk. Seelix helped Blinda into a med room close by and a Med-Tec instantly went to work on the Albion Thane.

The young medical technician's face went from blank pale to white. He looked up and down the inner hallways for his supervisor or someone else that could deal with this and get it right, but he appeared to be alone.

"I'm sorry, QC Blair, but that prisoner was moved to the detention cell block shortly after he arrived."

Drax's blood ran cold, a sick sinking feeling rolling over in her stomach. She gave no such order. Only the security chief or Commander SoKnack could give such an order and they knew better than to do so without notifying her first. It might be possible that Gunnar had become violent, and being as strong as he was, had been ordered down to a more secure location by the infirmary supervisor.

"Who signed the order to move him?" Drax asked, trying to remain calm. Her heart was pounding as the tech checked the readouts on the terminal in front of him.

"The prisoner was transferred right after he received the new micro-taut injection. That was about ten to fifteen minutes ago, by a Colonel Conrad, Security chief. Kind of odd," he continued. "The Medtecs were still trying to finish their examinations when he was taken."

"Colonel Conrad?" Drax turned to Seelix. She had never heard of a Security chief named Conrad. It should have been a Major Vought. Seelix only shrugged, glancing in at Blinda, who continued to probe the area around the *Tarzana*. Drax's nervousness continued to spike, turning back to the tech at the desk.

"I've never heard of him before," she said, almost shaking now. "Can you verify the prisoner's delivery to the detention center cell block?"

"Excuse me, Queen Captain, but the officer wasn't a man. This was a female officer, red hair with a white lock on the left side," he said motioning to the left side of his face. "She was very insistent and had all the correct clearances."

Drax's legs nearly came out from under her. Seelix could see her gripping the counter just to remain standing. The Queen Captain abruptly stood up straight.

"CJ," she uttered turning to Seelix.

"It couldn't be..." Seelix gasped.

"Detention...center...delivery...confirmation," Drax breathed in a raspy whisper.

While power was limited ship wide, the tech was able to access the detention center records. After a moment of fiddling with the controls in front of him, the tech turned the display around.

"No, no, no, no, no..." Drax turned pomegranate red, clinching her fists and closing her eyes. Seelix backed away, fearing Drax would literally explode. The Queen Captain spread her arms out across the counter top, bowing her head and taking several deep breathes trying to control her rage. Seelix sneaked a peek around the enraged Queen Captain at the display the tech was cowering behind. She could see no confirmation of any prisoner delivery to the cell block.

"Do you have security access to the cargo bays?" she asked the tech, who only responded with a blank look. Exasperated, Drax stormed from the room, hauling down the hallway at a sprint. Seelix glanced in at Blinda and seeing she was in good hands, took off after Drax.

Holding her shoulder strap firmly in place, Seelix held her rifle back behind her as she ran to catch the speeding Drax. The further away from the medical area, the darker the passages became. Down several levels they flew, jumping several steps at a time and using the hand rails to carry their weight as they went. Drax finally stumbled through a door into a dimly lit breezeway lined with windows on both sides. Below them were the cargo hangar bays. She scanned the length of the bays on one side, seeing only cargo containers and a few odd Black Tiger fighter parts in storage. Moving quickly down the hallway, she looked on the other side, seeing a white fighter at the far end, near the open launch bay doors.

Two figures scurried toward the Colonian vessel, one of them a redhead. Frantic, Drax motioned for Seelix to start shooting. Seelix opened a window and started pumping shots at the fighter as the *Tarzana's* interior lighting came back on. Drax dove for an emergency alert control on the wall and pulled the handle, sirens and warning lights immediately activated. She stumbled back to an open window, looking down at the fighter as the occupants moved to get onboard.

CJ ducked under the safety of the raised delta wing, looking up at Drax. Having served on the *Tarzana*, CJ knew the battlecruiser as well as any fleet officer. Seelix continued to hold them pinned down, pumping shot after shot at them. Gunnar disappeared under the belly of the craft and reappeared inside the cockpit on the other side. Moments later, the Isom converters started coming to life. Seelix continued her rapid volley of fire bouncing all around the converter cover and the wing, holding CJ pinned down. The fighter engines revved louder as Drax watched the side cockpit hatch open up. She pushed her head out the window as the fighter rose from the bay floor, its landing gear folding up into their compartments and its wings lowering into place.

"Casey Janae," Drax called as CJ dove for the open side door, tumbling inside. As the F-2 pivoted in place and started moving for the open launch portal, Drax could see CJ looking up at her. The Queen Captain motioned for her to stop, but CJ slowly shook her head and disappeared as the hatch closed between them.

"Commander SoKnack, close the launch doors! Close them now!" Drax screamed into her communicator, watching the F-2 move toward the launch portal.

Seelix came to a screeching halt next to Drax, as the noise from the fighter rose and the thruster ports brightened. The portal doors were almost half closed when the fighter bolted through and into open space.

Incensed, Queen Captain turned to Seelix.

"Get Blinda back up on the bridge, now!"

Seelix understood that Drax's plans were hemorrhaging and didn't stick around to discuss the matter. As Drax disappeared into an open elevator, Seelix turned on one heel and trotted off in the opposite direction.

*　　*　　*　　*

No sooner had the Flightstreak blasted from the launching portal of the *Tarzana* than they were set on by four Black Tigers and a myriad of snuff turret guns. Inside, CJ started working to get all the navigational equipment online with Bud's help. But even the AI computer had to have time to come online properly.

"Nice party you have going on here," Gunnar commented, twisting the fighter into a tight spiral beneath the belly of the massive battlecruiser. Laser cannon fire from their pursuers pounded their rear deflector shield. "Hot Dang!" he exclaimed.

"A little more get up and go, eh?" CJ jested with a tight grin, trying to ignore what was going on around her.

"Quadra-light navigation online," Bud announced. Gunnar passed a glance over at CJ, wondering if she had changed her voice or something. That certainly didn't sound like CJ, but in the mood they were in, anything was possible. Noticing his quick glance, CJ smiled, trying to hold in her glee.

"Sorry, you two haven't been properly introduced. Gunnar ...Bud, Bud ...Gunnar."

"Hello, Gunnar," the AI answered back.

"Did you say, 'Bud'?" Gunnar asked with raised eyebrows. "Really? You called your AI, 'Bud'?" Gunnar grunted, maneuvering the F-2 around the bottom conning tower of the *Tarzana*. "Oh, this looks familiar!"

He glanced at his tracking screen, taking note of not only what was behind them, but all around them. They might have been better off remaining hidden onboard the battlecruiser and sneaking away at a better time. It looked as though the *Tarzana* had launched all of her squadrons. Most of them were just buzzing around in groups of four, away from the chase. He gave the screen a little harder look, seeing a larger number of returns following a secondary object a little farther out, but closing on the battlecruiser at a high rate. He rolled the fighter around the bulbous bow, seeing several levels of windows and people in them. The long string of Black Tigers tailing them were struggling to keep up with the F-2.

"Too bad there's no tail gun on this thing," he commented, giving the yoke a hard twist and skimming back along the under belly of the war ship. CJ activated several controls to her right and a targeting screen lit up in front of her. Gunnar passed it a glance seeing a set of cross hairs flash on, overlaying a view of the fighters tailing them. Directly behind the cockpit, the top laser cannon instantly rose and rotated into position, aiming directly at the lead Tiger firing at them. CJ touched a control on a small secondary yoke and the cannon began belching deadly bolts of light. It took only a few shots for her to get a bead on the first Tiger and an instant later, one of its wings peeled back and then the cockpit disintegrated in a hail of fire.

"You mean like this?" CJ commented casually as she took aim at the next Tiger and fired.

"This thing had that all this time and you're just now telling me about it?"

"You didn't ask. Besides, I wasn't in any condition to use it before," CJ shot back.

Gunnar glanced up at the *Tarzana*. Under the belly of this enormous beast they didn't have all the upper guns to deal with. Perhaps a weakness of the large battlecruiser's design. The fighter shook as several blasts in succession from the *Tarzana* pummeled them.

"I think it's time you changed your tactics up a little bit," CJ suggested, taking aim at another fighter closing in on them. She glanced over at the Navi-computer screen.

"Better to get blown up out here together than who knows what inside," he responded coolly, turning the fighter on its back and pulling up. Just skimming along the hull of the giant ship, he steered up the side and directly over the top of the ship's massive gun emplacements and then back down over the other side, staying just as close to the *Tarzana* as possible. Sliding back down the other side, he noticed several brilliant flashes to his left and gave the tracking screen another look. The other vessel was now circling to a parallel course, angling closer. Gunnar suddenly recognized the familiar V winged shape of a Kalamarion Interceptor and the insignia on its wings.

"My group's bigger than yours," Rick boasted over the communicator. Gunnar was overjoyed, pulling his fighter in a little closer to the V-winged craft as both ships screamed along the bottom of the *Tarzana*'s hull toward the bow.

"Bet I picked mine up sooner than you did," Gunnar taunted back. "And I have a tail gunner." They were in the zone now; wingmen together again. He glanced out at the wonderful shape of the big Kalamarion fighter as they came out from under the Albion ship.

"Show off. Throw a cross path at them and see how many can follow up and back?" Rick suggested, prepping for a maneuver.

"We should do this more often," Gunnar responded with glee. "Beat you past the conning tower."

"In that old bucket? Ha!"

"I think you'll find this ol' bird has a little more in the tank than you give it credit for." Gunnar banked the F-2 hard into Rick's flight path at the same instant Rick banked behind Gunnar's, his fighter crossing just behind the Flightstreak. Tigers pursuing both ships tried to follow the path, but several collided. Even from behind them, the concussion was intense as pieces of debris were slung in every direction. Both fighters then weaved and dipped their way up the front part of the *Tarzana*, dodging energy blasts and laser cannons as they went.

*　　*　　*　　*

The bridge of the *Tarzana* bustled with the commotion of controlled chaos. Commander SoKnack could barely keep ahead of the incoming requests and reports. While excited, he was still confident in what he was doing until Drax Blair stormed in. The look of frustration the Queen Captain held told the whole story of the last several days.

The Queen Captain watched with agitated frenzy as the F-2 and Interceptor weaved effortlessly between the massive gun barrels of the forward gun turrets, a stream of Black Tigers close on their heels, firing. The ship's snuff guns spun around, spraying a steady stream of ordinance at the two fighters constantly crossing paths between gun emplacements. Manta ray shaped fighters continued to erupt, either running into something trying to remain behind the fleeing fighters or being struck by friendly fire.

A security officer stepped carefully to the Queen Captain and handed her a small black device. Drax studied it, looking back at the officer a couple of times. She finally nodded and handed the charred box to Dalton, who looked at it surprised. He recognized it as a Colonian tracker; it was still functioning. He looked up at Drax, who had turned back to the window, continuing to watch the two fighters crisscross paths toward the main conning tower. Hearing the elevator on the command deck hiss open, Drax turned a glaring eye at Blinda Koss as she stepped toward them with Seelix right beside her. A brilliant flash from the bow of the ship nearly blinded everyone on the command platform.

"Whoa!" Seelix staggered, holding onto the rail. "What was that?"

"The flash of incompetence," Drax growled. The Queen Captain's rage glowed as she turned to the Thane, who appeared to have regained some of her strength, now sporting bandages across her abdomen and shoulder.

"You get those two back here now or I'll have you looking under every grain of sand in Hadrian. SoKnack!" she yelled, turning to the ship's commander. "Turn the ship to port, fourteen Mark two-ten and bring her to flank speed."

"Flank speed?" He questioned, not following her logic. There was nothing out here. Why waste the effort to turn the ship if all they were chasing were two fighters, which could hardly be called a chase? They were buzzing harmlessly around the ship. The fire they were laying down was negligible. It was only a matter of time before both fighters were disabled and dragged back into the ship's hangar bays. Did she know something he didn't? He looked at the black box again, finally understanding what it all meant.

"That's an order, Commander!"

The ship's commander handed the box back to the security officer, moving to carry out his orders while Drax turned back to Blinda, nearly in a panicked rage.

"You do whatever you have to, Blinda, but get them back here now."

Blinda looked out at the string of fighters now moving directly toward the bridge tower, flashes and explosions following in their wake.

"The Thane is in the other ship."

"I don't care if Gunnar's mother is in the other ship! Take them both out!"

Seelix watched with awed admiration as both fighters swung around another massive turret as if performing a careful ballet specifically choreographed to dance all along the top of the Albion battlecruiser.

"Jatoni! I've never seen flying like that before," she gasped, as Blinda crossed her arms and closed her eyes. Seelix glanced over at the Thane, her fists tightening and wrists twitching. A moment later, everyone but Blinda dropped to the floor as both the F-2 and the Interceptor blitzed right across the entire length of the bridge window, a long line of Tigers trailing in their wake. Blinda clinched harder, starting to tremble, expending all her Thane know-how to disrupt either pilot's concentration.

"Come on, come on," Drax hissed impatiently, as everyone got back to their feet. Turning to the rear windows of the bridge tower, she watched the line of fighters zig-zagging back toward the stern. When the Queen Captain turned back to Blinda, the

Thane was slowly shaking her head, her breathing accelerating. Her eyes suddenly popped wide open and her arms dropped.

"NO!" she screamed, grabbing her head and pitching back against Seelix, toppling both of them. Drax stepped to their aid, only to find Blinda writhing on the floor next to Seelix. In a fit of pain, Blinda rolled and kicked frantically, trying to mitigate the torture washing through her with the power of an enormous ocean tsunami.

"What is it?" Drax asked frantically, grabbing Blinda by the wrists and holding her still.

Blinda looked up at Drax, pain rippling through her being. Blinda only barely had control of her own faculties.

"His protector," she gasped, consciousness fading from her mind. "ILOBs..."

Drax let the Thane go, coming up and looking out at the thread of fighters just disappearing behind the stern of the ship.

"Bring all the fighters back in and standby Quadra-light drive," she barked. "Commander SoKnack, get us back to Albia as fast as this ship will take us." The battlecruiser commander acknowledged and went to work. It would take a couple of minutes to program the ship's Navi-computers for the jump, giving them time to get to a pre-determined waypoint. Seelix was a little puzzled as she got to her knees seeing to Blinda as the Thane lost consciousness.

"What are you doing?" she asked.

Drax turned forward again, calmly looking out at nothing.

"Returning to fight another day."

*   *   *   *

"If you two are finished showing off," CJ remarked, switching off the tail gunner controls. She casually leaned forward, lifting the five cover caps from the Quadra-light activation controls and set all the switches. All the Quadra-light readouts winked on displaying the coordinates information.

"Quadra-light drive online," Bud announced.

"Is that thing ready to go?" Gunnar asked, tucking the F-2 in tight on Rick's right wing as they streaked past the structure line of the *Tarzana.*

"Bud?" CJ inquired.

"Quadra-light destination coordinates are verified and locked in. Awaiting arrival at pre-programmed waypoint."

"Can't even believe you named it, Bud," Gunnar said shaking his head.

"What's wrong with, Bud? It's a perfectly good name," CJ responded with a teasing grin.

"Wait, I thought we were calling you Bud? I'm confused?" Rick called out.

"Don't push your luck," Gunnar called as they executed a graceful barrel roll over the top of the battlecruiser as the big ship started making its turn. "We need to get to three one four mark two ninety-one."

"I suppose these boys have had enough," Rick responded.

"I'm surprised Blinda didn't try to interfere," Gunnar replied as he pushed the throttles forward.

"Who says she didn't?" Rick responded, both fighters throttling away from their pursuers. Nearing their waypoint, CJ noticed something appear on the scanner in front of her. She looked up just in time to see a fleet of ships streak out of nowhere, dropping out of light speed directly ahead of them.

"Oh," Rick commented calmly, holding their course. "This is nice."

CJ's eyes widened, as more ships materialized directly behind the first, both fighters driving right into the heart of the massive armada, all with Colonian markings.

"Admiral Motti's 5th fleet," she breathed, her heart racing. "No doubt they're looking for us, for me."

"I'd say they've found us," Gunnar responded, holding his course and giving the Navi-computer a look.

"Nowhere to run," Rick commented, defeat waving through his tone. He looked all around them. There was no way they could possibly out fight what this many ships were capable of throwing at them. Stubbornly, they held their course straight toward their waypoint. There was no sense in trying to run off in another direction. Surrounded, they expected fighters to launch at any moment and the capital ships to maneuver around them. Strangely, nothing happened. The Colonian fleet continued straight toward the fleeing Albion battlecruiser, now outgunned nearly ten to one.

"Ten seconds to Quadra-light waypoint," Bud stated. "Standby Quadra-light drive."

CJ let her hand drop to the chrome plated twin handles of the Quadra-light throttles. Another hand dropped down on to hers. She looked over at Gunnar who had a suspicious look on his face.

"They won't find us here, will they?" his expression turning to a smile.

"No," CJ responded as the alarm went off.

"Waypoint destination achieved. Quadra-light drive at your command," Bud announced.

"They're looking for a Colonian tracker," CJ said, pushing the throttles all the way forward.

Gunnar burst into laughter as the F-2 abruptly bolted into Quadra-light and away from the Colonian fleet now in pursuit of the *Tarzana*. Rick watched the fighter disappear into a brilliant flash of light, leaving behind it a light contrail of expended Isom exhaust.

"Hey, wait for me," he called after them. Activating his FTL drive, the Interceptor sprang forward after his friends. No one would be tracking either of them, now.

Aster

At one time, the planet Aster supported lush forests and beautiful blue oceans. It may have even had a moon or two, but it had been torn from its solar path long ago by another terrestrial body. The shift in orbit sent Aster out into space, away from its planetary system. Having a strong magnetic core, the wandering planet maintained its atmosphere, protecting it from rouge solar winds. Its rotation remained as well, but without a sun to provide for the vegetation, most of the animal and plant life on the surface had died off, leaving barren waste lands. The oceans and lakes went dark, many of them fouled, but still they remained, held there by the planet's own atmosphere and gravity. While it certainly had its cold cycles, it had not become a frozen sphere in the confines of deep space. It was heated internally, its outer crust quite thin, floating on a swirling, rotating mass of molten material. Heat transferring through a myriad of seismic phishers and vents in the outer crust, warmed the atmosphere.

Even in the deepest regions of space, it wasn't alone. The luminescent glow of the infinite stars bore testimony that it had not been forgotten. Though in a sunless state, the glow of the cosmos was enough to softly illuminate it.

In one of Aster's deep, long canyons, a small army of men and women worked nonstop to construct a new base of operations. A fortress stronghold in the uncharted regions of the Altanis quadrant. Even though they had chosen a wandering planet, they still wanted to make sure they could hide in plain sight in the unlikely event someone should happen by and take a closer look. The Tomplie had found it once, it could happen again. An abbreviated survey of the planet had come up with several suitable places. Beneath the vast buttes rising above the canyon they had chosen, an enormous cavern system had been discovered, large enough to house all three capital ships. The trick was to disguise the opening on the surface. With careful blasting, the engineering teams opened up several natural fissures large enough even the *Trax* could hide along with their other ships.

The *Trax*, *Realistic* and *Intruder* patrolled the immediate area around Aster, charting their exact location relative to the closest known system, then passing on the information to the *Constellation* in a close orbit. Colonels Barker and Conrad studied the information in detail as Alex 7001 ran the complex calculations of Aster's path through the Arista system.

Gunnar rubbed his eyes as math always gave him a headache. Thank goodness Alex was here. CJ was still trying to learn Gunnar's alphabet and numerics and how they translated into hers. She in turn, was trying to teach him her system. While CJ shared some of Gunnar's attitudes toward complex calculations and the math used to solve them, she did recognize their need and usefulness. But, she too was grateful for Alex and his many abilities. A light began to blink on the desk next to where Gunnar was resting his elbows, while looking at the big wall display in front of him. He let his hand slide to the com station.

"Speak, oh great, Lieutenant Navall," he yawned. "Keeper of all things communicationable." There was a hesitation, and then the com officer came on. Gunnar and CJ could tell she was smiling.

"General Niker on the line, sir."

"Put the ol' boy through," Gunnar stretched back in his seat. A moment later, Rick's voice came through.

"They're almost ready for the *Trax* down there. Nice big place. You should have no trouble at all housing everything and I think the floor can be smoothed out enough that you won't even have to pave it."

"Have they started hooking anything up for the control center?" CJ inquired, stepping over and sitting on the desk next to Gunnar.

"They just picked up delivery of most of that gear. Took an entire transport. Your friend from Cross can really deliver."

"When do you think they'll have the Voltaic guns operational?"

"They moved the main guns into their housings last night, at least the ones directly around the fissure. You ought to have a good look at them if you can find them. Very clever with the camouflage. They look just like the landscape. The ones located inside are already operational. This is one impressive group."

"Doesn't hurt that they're well supplied," Gunnar interjected, pulling his tinted glasses from his face.

"Thanks to your friend Diord," Rick replied. There was a long silence in the transmission and CJ finally looked at Gunnar with questioning eyes.

"Guys, I need to head out," Rick finally spoke up, breaking the silence.

"Back to Boris?" Gunnar inquired, his voice turning somber.

"Those are the instructions I gave CORA when she found Jayda. Find her and wait for me at Boris."

"It's been quite a long time and you haven't heard anything," CJ pointed out. "Are you sure she's even still alive?"

"Oh, she's alive all right. I can feel it."

"Any idea how long you'll be gone?" CJ asked.

"Well, I'm hoping for a quick trip in and back out again. Seems like I can't leave you two alone for very long without you getting into trouble."

"I really don't know what you're talking about," Gunnar lied, straight faced. "Why would you speak in such terms?"

CJ grinned broadly.

"Shall we begin with the long, long list?" Rick asked with a chuckle.

"Funny man," Gunnar stopped him. "Be safe my friend and hurry back."

"I will, probably about the time I need to swoop in and save your sorry butt, yet again and that goes for you too, Colonel Barker."

"Didn't it take two of us to save this guy last time?" she asked still grinning broadly.

"Later you two," Rick finished, the comlink going silent. CJ and Gunnar watched Rick's Interceptor sweep past the window and blast away into light speed.

"He's a good man," CJ commented, standing up and watching Rick's fading contrail. Gunnar nodded, getting to his feet, deep in thoughts of his longtime friendship with Richard Alexander.

"Yeah, we go back a long way. We're like brothers. I think we're the only family each other has now. We've been through a lot together."

CJ smiled, watching a fond expression drift across Gunnar's face as he fingered the memory chip beneath his shirt. He didn't have to say it; she could see it. She looked at his uniform, the high cuffed collar and the Colonel clusters on both sides. She still found it odd they had such similar dress uniforms. She continued looking at him, not caring if he noticed her gaze or not. She was trying to decide how she felt about him, even after all this time with him. She couldn't help but wonder how he felt about her and watching him watching the stars, she smiled.

Yes, of course there's more...

Robert James Schultz

Robert is a graduate of Ricks College, now called BYU-Idaho. He currently works for BYU-Idaho AV Broadcast Productions as the Chief Video Engineer. Robert holds a private pilot's certificate and works on light general and experimental aircraft avionics at the Rexburg Airport in his spare time. Water sports, RV camping and riding motorcycles are some of his favorite hobbies. He is a 2013 and 2015 Ironman Coeur d'Alene Triathlon finisher. Robert has loved writing stories since his early teens, most dealing with the science fiction genre. Married to Lola Hazel VanLeishout in 1983, they are the parents of five children and reside in Sugar City, Idaho.

If you liked this story, please take a moment and write a short review and post it on Amazon and Barnes and Noble. Just input the title into the website search bar.